A FRACTURED FAIRY TALE

BOOKS 1–10

By

J.E. Taylor

A Fractured Fairy Tale: Books 1-10 ©
January 2023 J.E. Taylor

TABLE OF CONTENTS

What happens when a werewolf hunter falls for her prey?

Red Locklear regularly hunts all manner of woodland prey, but her favorite kill is the beast that tore her parents apart when she was a little girl.

The werewolf.

Now that Red is all grown up, these horrid creatures are terrorizing Dakota Territory once again. As a member of the elite Dakota Guard, Red has a duty to extinguish the life of every last wolf she sees. Failing to do so is a death sentence.

When her grandmother doesn't come back from a foraging run, Red dons her quiver of silver arrows and breaks town law, heading into the forest after sunset to search for her.

The dark woods test her hunting skills as well as her loyalty to the Dakota Guard, and she's left wondering if there is any way out of this alive.

Fans of *Once Upon a Time* and *Grimm* will devour RED.

RED Chapter 1

"WE HAVEN'T HEARD FROM her in months," Pa said, unaware I was just outside my parents' bedroom door.

"You have told me a thousand times how dangerous those mountain passes can be," my mother said in her exasperated voice. "What if we get caught in a storm?"

"The almanac said we have at least another six weeks before the winter rolls in. So now is the perfect time to visit. Besides, my mother hasn't even met Ruby yet. Don't you think it's time?"

A sigh followed.

I coughed, covering my mouth a second too late, and silence settled on the bedroom. The creak of springs sounded, and the soft swish of fabric against the floorboards crossed closer to the door. I darted my eyes around the darkened hallway for a place to hide, my nightmare that brought me to their room forgotten in my panic of being caught listening to their private conversation.

My father opened the door before I could escape into the shadows. "Ruby, what are you doing out of bed?"

"I had a nightmare," I whispered and studied the shadows in the wood grain on the floor.

"You need as much rest as you can get before we head to your grandmother's house in the morning. We need you sharp on this trip. Otherwise, we might not be eating for the next few days," he said.

I narrowed my eyes at him and glanced at my mother on the bed. The dim lantern illuminated her face and made her deep auburn hair blend into the wood frame of their bed.

"I can hit a squirrel at fifty yards while sleepwalking," I said when I brought my gaze back to Pa. Sleep had nothing to do with the quality of my hunting skills.

Pa put his hand on my back with a chuckle and led me back to my bedroom. "I still want you to rest. Dakota is a long ride, and if you are too tired to aim straight, we will be a very hungry family when we get to your grandmother's house."

"Pa?" I asked as he tucked me tightly under the covers. "My teacher, Mrs. Kettle, said there are monsters in the woods surrounding Dakota."

His smile faded and he blinked like he had an eyelash in his eye. "Why would your teacher tell you that?"

I shrugged. "We were studying the territories bordering Weber, and she explained the trails to get to the towns in each territory. She went clockwise, starting with Alberta to the northeast and ended with Dakota to the northwest. She said the road to Dakota is swallowed by a forest full of monsters."

He let out another chuckle, but this time it wasn't amused. "It's bear country, sweetie."

He leaned over and gave me a kiss on the cheek, leaving me without an actual answer. Weber was bear country, too. No one said Weber was full of monsters. The teacher had said the road wound over the mountains and through a river before it disappeared into woods as dark as night. I remember the flash in her eyes and the whisper she likely hadn't intended for anyone to hear.

I didn't think she was talking about bears. My heart clanged at the thought of traveling through a monster-filled forest.

I tried to push the thoughts away and rest like my father asked, but the images that kept running past my eyelids were worse than the original nightmare that had woken me.

⁂

I RODE IN FRONT of my mother on the edge of Bessy's saddle. While the old mare made for a smooth ride, I still ended the day stiff from the journey. My brother, Roy, got the better end of the deal. He got to ride with Pa on Midnight, the fastest steed in all of Weber territory.

Pa never let me ride that horse. He always said I wasn't old enough or big enough to stay on his back, especially when he went into a full gallop.

Figures. My brother had all the luck. At least he didn't have my skills with a bow and arrow. I could shoot rings around him and proved it with a plump rabbit for dinner on the first night and three squirrels the second night.

The third night, we slept in sight of the Dakota border where the road faded into the trees. I was thankful we stopped outside of those woods. On the plateau where we camped, wild life was scarce, so all we ended up with for dinner was a rattlesnake that Pa killed earlier in the day.

The fire crackled, and my gaze kept drifting to the forest in the distance. Neither the height of the mountains nor the icy chill of the river we had crossed brought forth the same level of trepidation as that dense wall of trees. I shivered, wrapping my arms tighter around my chest. I snuggled into the blankets and turned to face the fire, dismissing the thought of monsters.

"CAN I RIDE MIDNIGHT today?" I asked.

"I don't think so, Ruby."

My stomach clenched and so did my teeth. My father attached the travel sack to Midnight's saddle and glanced at me. He must have seen my aggravation because he offered me the same old story.

"You're not big enough to handle Midnight, sweetheart."

"Roy got to ride him when he was eight," I said.

"Roy was bigger than you are at eight. Go help your mother pack the rest of our things."

I stomped away loud enough to make my dissatisfaction known, but not enough to get a swat on my butt for my behavior. I didn't talk, even as we approached the thick forest. The path seemed to disappear, and I shivered.

"We only have two more days before we can bask in the warmth of your grandmother's fireplace," Pa said, and locked his gaze with mine before he coaxed Midnight into the lead.

Roy turned and gave me a smile. Like going into monster-filled woods was a cool thing. I knew with a cold certainty that I wasn't getting a lick of sleep tonight.

Every branch snap jerked my form, and I struggled to see what was beyond the narrow channel. I constantly scanned the deep green brush like I was hunting for small game, but in reality, I was searching for creatures with a more violent nature.

When we finally trotted into a small clearing and dismounted, Roy took the horses and tied them to the nearest branch. My father handed me the bow and arrow. With the weapon in my hand, all the deep fear tightening my muscles gave way to a calmness I welcomed. I crept around the perimeter of our little circle while my parents set up camp.

I caught movement on my right. Before my brain registered the animal, my arrow had pinned the rabbit to the earth. A clean head shot. I grinned, picking it up and bringing it back to the family with a real sense of accomplishment.

Clouds rolled in before the last light bled from the sky, and the full moon seemed to play hide-and-seek in the foggy cover. We ate in silence, savoring the tender meat and licking the juices from our fingers.

With full bellies, we settled into our makeshift beds and gave in to the exhaustion. I stared at what I could see of the man on the moon until my eyes could no longer stay open.

The horses whinnying pulled me from sleep. I darted my gaze at the shadows made by the fire, and I shivered in the chilly night air despite the heavy blanket draped over me. The hairs on my arms prickled as the horses grew more restless. Something had them spooked.

I patted my father's leg. "Pa," I whispered on the still air. My heart picked up the pace.

"Get some more sleep, Ruby," he muttered.

"Something is spooking the horses."

My father rolled over and glanced at me and then the horses beyond me. A crease appeared between his eyes, but he gave me a reassuring smile before he gently shook my mother awake.

"I think we've had enough rest," he whispered.

My mother looked at him, blinked, and then her eyes widened. It was as if a lightning bolt shot out of the sky and catapulted her to her feet. The instant she was standing, she started gathering our things as if the woods were burning down around us.

"Roy, go get the horses." My father swatted my brother's back. "Ruby, you go stay by your mother."

My brother got to his unsteady feet. He yawned and shuffled to the tree where we had Midnight and Bessy tied up.

I stepped towards my mother, close enough to the dying fire to feel the heat radiating from the coals. Her arms wrapped around me tighter than usual while my brother pulled the horses closer. Their hoofs stomped the ground in nervous beats.

My father hoisted me onto the back of Midnight, and my heart jumped into my throat. Alarms sounded in my head when Pa told Roy to hop on Midnight with me. Roy handed Bessy's reins to my mother and stepped towards where Pa held onto Midnight's bridle.

Roy only made it halfway across the clearing when the monsters attacked. A clawed paw severed my brother's throat. A plume of blood shot from the wound, dousing the fire. He didn't have time to scream. I would never forget my mother's cry. The pitch started as one of loss, but soon morphed to a sharp pain-filled wail.

My father smacked Midnight's flank just before a wall of gray fur took him down. The stallion flew forward. I grabbed for the horse's mane to catch my balance.

Midnight's speed was no match for the massive wolves that pursued me. Their radiant blue eyes pierced the darkness as the gap widened until I couldn't hear their snarls over the throbbing beat of my heart in my own ears. My harsh sobs filled the woods along with the steady pounding of Midnight's hoofs. He didn't slow until we arrived at Dakota's darkened town center.

Monsters did exist, and I would never forget their murderous eyes or their equally heinous growls.

RED Chapter 2

"I AM PERFECTLY CAPABLE of going foraging on my own. Besides, aren't you supposed to be going on that hunting trip with the rest of the archers?" Grandmother asked me as she tidied up the breakfast nook. She turned, her silver corkscrew curls falling over her shoulders, and leveled her gray-eyed stare in my direction. One silver eyebrow rose.

My grandmother was the epitome of strength and grace, even though she was nearing her eighties. The woman was feisty and brave, everything I hoped I would be if I was blessed enough to reach her age.

I shifted my stance and crossed to the table with the breakfast plates. "I know you're capable, Gram. But it's really not safe out there. Not with the werewolves terrorizing Dakota."

"Pft." She waved me off and took the seat across from me.

"I'm serious. We lost Mickey last week, and those bastards are getting bolder by the minute."

She waggled her finger at me. "Watch your language, girl." She dug into the eggs in the center serving bowl.

I sighed and studied Gram's coveted curls. I envied her hair. Mine fell straight as the arrows in my quiver, and the color was the cause of my nickname.

Red.

And not the beautiful auburn red my mother had had. No, it was more akin to a forest fire. I had a hell of a time blending in the forest for most seasons, but now that fall was upon us, my hair resembled the burned orange of the leaves.

"You really should go with someone else, Gram," I said and focused on the food instead of her perfect hair.

"They need you on the hunt. You know you are more skilled than anyone else in this town," she said and took a bite of her breakfast.

Gram didn't know how deep on the side of trouble I was with the Dakota Guard. If I missed another hunt, the head of the Guard, Remy Steele, warned that I would have to turn in my archer's bow. It was the one thing I was good at, and losing that would be like losing my family all over again.

But with the audacity of this pack, the idea of having my grandmother out in the berry patch alone didn't settle well. If I stayed and protected her instead of doing my job, I would lose the only status I had in this town. If I let her go alone, I could lose the only family I had left.

My chest tightened, and I sent her a strained smile, waving her off with a sheepish nod. I had a job to do, and the town was counting on me.

Dakota didn't have any outside help. We were too secluded in the deep northwestern forest. Mountains blocked us to the east, and ravines blocked us to the west. The nearest settlement was a good three-day ride at a full gallop through treacherous mountain terrain.

And Dakota was under siege for the first time since my parents died.

Sure, we had had rogue werewolves in the area over the years, but since that horrible night when I was eight, there hadn't been a pack in the vicinity.

Until now. And they were a nasty bunch.

With the fading of the summer heat, people started disappearing. The ones we found were mauled beyond what the local bears usually did. It wasn't until we heard the howls in the distance that we knew what was killing the town's people.

Thirteen years of training had led me to this moment, and my grandmother would not let me babysit her when I could be out there taking down the monsters. One glance from her told me I was right.

"You need to go." She didn't leave me any choice.

"Fine," I mumbled, despite the discomfort scraping my skin. I ignored the warning bells and dug into my food.

We ate the rest of the meal in silence, each of us lost in our own thoughts. Mine tumbled between what I had to do today and the fall harvest. I wasn't sure if Travis was going to ask me to the town dance or not. I secretly hoped he would move on. While he was the closest friend I had, there just were no sparks in it for me. He, on the other hand, had hinted endlessly to me about a future. I wasn't ready to settle down. At least not with anyone from Dakota.

Gram cleared her throat. "You were about a million miles away, weren't you?"

Heat filled my cheeks, and I let out a laugh. "Yes, sorry."

"Thinking about your parents?" she asked.

I flinched at the mention of my family. "No. Travis." I didn't expand any further, but my tone said it all.

Gram cocked her head like one of the neighborhood puppies. "What's wrong with Travis?"

"Nothing. He just isn't... you know..." I said and shrugged as I picked at the food on my plate.

"He has become such a sweet man," she said.

I rolled my eyes.

Gram was a fan of Travis's and had been for as long as I could remember. Too bad it didn't change the way I felt. I took another bite of breakfast.

Gram opened her mouth to ask me another question, and I raised my hand, stopping her.

"I don't want to talk about Travis, okay?"

Gram inhaled enough to expand her chest in that manner that announced her disappointment. "Okay," she whispered, and we both focused on the plates in front of us.

After we finished, I cleaned the dishes in the basin and dried and stored them back in the pantry before dumping the dishwater out the window.

I crossed to the chair and pulled on my vest, hoping it would be enough to keep me warm in the cool fall air. I hated hunting with my thick wool coat that hung on the rack in the corner. With my quiver over my shoulder, I headed for the door.

"Ruby?"

I glanced back at Gram.

"Be careful," she said and gave me a small smile of support. The worry lines at the corners of her eyes belied the smile.

"I always am. You be careful, too, Gram."

She patted the sheath on her belt with a nod and finished gathering her basket for foraging berries in the grove. As I walked away from our cabin, a lump formed in the back of my throat. The same lump that always accompanied me on my way to the Guard, as if this could be the last time we saw each other.

I swiped at the mist in my eyes and continued down the path leading through the woods directly into the center of Dakota. I steadied the bow in my hand, lining an arrow in place, keeping vigilant for any breaking branch, leaf rustle, or wicked growl.

⎯⎯⎯⎯⎯⎯ ❧ ⎯⎯⎯⎯⎯⎯

TALK OF MY PARENTS had me jumpy as I traversed the winding wooded path into Dakota. The cloudy sky obscured the morning sun, reminding me of the night I lost my family to the wolves.

I picked up my pace. While I knew I was running a little behind, I wasn't sure just how late I would be, and getting out of these woods as fast as I could was a priority at the moment.

The last time I was late, I got paired with the worst archer on the Guard, and the day had been an exercise in dodging his arrows instead of werewolves. Not that any of our daily hunts had been fruitful in flushing out the pack. They were well hidden, and it was frustrating.

Hunting at night was not allowed, even though that seemed to be the time the pack was most active. Just the thought of being out with the darkness surrounding me made me shiver.

I tried to focus on the impending hunt, but memories of my family's dying screams kept interrupting my train of thought.

I shook the bloody visions from my head as I stepped out of the woods and onto the gravel road that led into the center of town. With the tree canopy behind me, I stowed the arrow back in my quiver. I kept scanning the area, but I didn't have the same urgency to be vigilant as I did under the tree cover.

The sense of ever-present danger the woods instilled in me kept me alive all these years, but once I was in the town center, that edge faded. Nothing messed with my mind as much as the woods.

"Boo!"

I yelped and spun toward the voice, reaching for one of my arrows.

Travis McGee burst out laughing from his vantage point next to the town hall. He stepped from the shadows, and his blond hair swirled in the breeze. His dark eyes crinkled with amusement, and his smile dimpled his cheeks.

"Damn it, Travis!" I held the arrow against my bow and glared at him. "I should shoot you for giving me a heart attack!"

Travis strolled up next to me with that ridiculous grin still plastered on his face. "You wouldn't dare," he said in a deep timbre.

I supposed I could see why some of the local girls swooned when he went by, but he just annoyed me like only a best friend could.

Instead of agreeing, I smacked his arm with the shaft of the arrow. "You're such a jerk," I muttered as we rounded the bend into the open courtyard where the rest of the Guard stood.

"You're late," a harsh voice rang out over the quiet assembly.

I glanced to my left, right into the annoyed eyes of Remy Steele. His face was lined with ancient wrinkles and his lips formed an unhappy sneer. He was perhaps the meanest guardsman I had ever met. Most of the Guard were afraid of him, but not me. I just thought he was an ass who liked to exude authority.

He sauntered over and glared down at me with sharp green eyes. "This is the third time this week," he growled.

I could have uttered a litany of excuses and groveled for his forgiveness like I had seen countless others do, but we both knew I was the best shot in the lot, so he'd just have to deal with my tardiness. I gave him an offhanded shrug and continued past him.

"One of these days, I'm going to take you over my knee," he hissed.

I spun on him. Threats, whether empty or not, riled me up. "You want to take care in what you say, Remy."

His eyes narrowed, and then he looked away.

I took that as a sign of retreat on his part and returned my attention to the rest of the horde. I was the lone woman among men, but they knew my past. They knew the talent in my steady hands. They knew I had their backs. And they knew my need for vengeance ran deep in my veins.

They had my back out there, too. Even Remy, who was as close to the definition of my nemesis as anyone in this town. He and Gram had a falling out years before I came along and he has held it against me ever since I entered the Guard.

It was Gram's insistence that allowed me to train with the Guard. She saw my raw talent with a bow and arrow after she and I had gone hunting for food. Remy had always treated me as if I stepped in the middle of the boy's club.

However, in moments of danger, Remy had always chosen to protect other members of the Guard instead of letting any of us fall prey to wolves. I lost count of the number of times he saved me from an attacking wolf. He could say the same for me, as well.

"Red, since you and Travis were late, you two will pair up with me today on the hunt," Remy announced.

The relief of the other guardsmen hung on the air. No one enjoyed pairing with Remy. Not only was he less than desirable company, he was a slave driver. Travis groaned under his breath while Remy paired up the rest of the hunters into parties of three.

"I don't have to tell you what's at stake here," Remy said, his sharp gaze landing on me before it moved on. "We need to flush these bastards out, because the longer they remain alive and in our territory, the more of our people die. If you run into a single wolf, kill it. If you run across the pack..." He took a deep breath, meeting every eye. "Take as many of them out as you can."

It was what he didn't say that sent a shiver up my spine. Three men, even three armed men, were no match against a full pack. Taking them on was suicide.

Every one of us accepted the responsibility of keeping the town safe. The possibility of death was part of being a Dakota Guard. We all nodded our understanding.

After everyone dispersed in their assigned direction, Remy turned to me. "Ready to get your ass whooped?" He didn't wait for an answer. Instead, he stomped off into the woods.

Travis and I followed, and dread wrapped a tight fist around my heart.

RED Chapter 3

AFTER HALF THE DAY had passed, I reached into the pack Gram put together for me and stole a bite of one of her oatmeal cookies while I followed Remy. Travis had my back, and I handed him half of the cookie as we rounded a bend, shoveling the rest in my mouth before Remy could turn and catch me eating on the job. Remy didn't like us doing anything that would occupy our hands, even if it only took a second.

His tirades about what could happen in that split second weren't without merit, but we had been going flat out since this morning and hadn't encountered a thing. Hunger could cause just as much trouble with wavering attention as our hands being occupied for a moment, so I chanced his wrath in favor of shutting off the grumbling in my stomach.

I never remembered Remy being amicable. Not even that first day that Gram dragged me into town and made me give the Guard a demonstration. He didn't even show the slightest interest, but the rest of the trainees were in awe that I could slice an apple in half, especially since it was thrown in the air. I did it a half dozen times to prove it wasn't a fluke.

<hr>

"I CAN'T HAVE A child in the Guard," Remy said to my grandmother.

Gram looked around at the cluster of boys that were my age, and she waved her hand at them. "You already have children in the Guard. You mean you can't have a girl in your Guard," she argued with her hands on her hips.

"May," he started, but Gram wouldn't have any of it.

"She can run faster than any of them. And she's a better shot than even you ever were!"

Remy's face reddened brighter than any of the apples in Gram's basket. He grabbed one and pitched it with all his might towards the woods.

I didn't think. I just reacted and when two neat, halved slices fell to the ground and my arrow embedded in the tree that would have blocked the apple's progress, both my Gram and Remy stared at the apple and then turned towards me.

I just smiled and shrugged my shoulders at their matching slack jaws.

Remy's lips pressed together, and he glanced back at the decimated apple before studying the ground.

"Well?" Gram asked.

"Fine, but she isn't getting any special treatment. If she can't keep up with the boys, she's out."

Gram nodded and left me in Remy's care.

REMY SLOWED NEAR THE northern cliffs that lead to the ravine and leveled that same hostile look from all those years ago at both Travis and I.

"Did you bring any of your grandmother's treats?" he asked in a gruff, out-of-breath tone.

I reached into my bag and pulled another cookie out, debating on whether I would just eat it in front of him or not. But I knew better than to aggravate him even more than my simple presence did. Instead, I offered it to him.

He gave me a smile of appreciation, which was rare, and slightly frightening to view. His grin looked more like a toothy grimace than anything resembling genuine happiness, and it never quite reached his eyes. The only time I ever saw glee in his eyes was when he was killing a werewolf.

"What about me?" Travis asked.

I pulled the last cookie out and split it in half, handing him the smaller half this time.

Remy chuckled. He thought he was special getting a whole cookie. He didn't know I shared one already with Travis. Neither of us corrected his silent gloating, either.

"I don't think there's anything in this direction," I said as I scanned the wooded area behind us. This would be the perfect place to launch an assault. We had nowhere to run, and jumping from the cliff was just as much of an automatic death sentence as facing a pack.

We had been stopped long enough to make the hairs on my neck prickle. I didn't want to just stand around waiting for the beasts to corner us, but Remy didn't seem to be in any rush. Pushing him would only make him linger longer.

"One of you needs to climb that tree and do a scan before we head back, and since Red was kind enough to give me a whole cookie, I think it's Travis's turn to do something useful."

I raised an eyebrow. It was the first time I wasn't given the grunt task. I'd have to remember that in the future. Remy had a soft spot for Gram's cookies, and if I saved a whole one for him instead of just offering half, I might get the lighter duty.

Travis didn't grumble or say anything snide like I would have been tempted to do. He just gave a nod and jumped in the air, catching the nearest limb with the inside of his elbow. His feet dangled above the ground, and he hoisted himself onto the branch.

It creaked under his weight. I bit my lip and scanned the woods for any movement. A snap brought my gaze back to Travis. His outstretched hand missed the next tree limb, and he dropped the ten feet to the ground, landing on his outstretched arm. A sharp crack was immediately followed by his yelp of pain.

Both Remy and I bolted to where Travis lay on the ground, holding his arm to his chest. His lips were pressed together, but his red and scrunched face broadcasted his pain more than a scream would have. His forearm was bent at an unnatural angle, and a red stain spread on his sleeve.

"Damn it, boy," Remy growled and raked a hand through his hair. He took a deep breath and closed his eyes for a moment before his gaze turned to mine. "Make yourself useful and grab a couple of arrows."

I glanced at the half dozen arrows strewn on the ground and gathered them up as Remy squatted next to Travis. My heart drummed in my chest. The beasts could smell blood for miles. If they got Travis's scent either in human or wolf form, we would have a hell of a fight on our hands.

The tear of fabric pulled my gaze back to them, and the view of Travis's bone sticking out of his forearm made me regret eating Gram's cookie. I turned away and busied myself with picking up the fallen arrows. Normally, I wasn't a squeamish person, but because it was Travis, empathy crashed through me like a wild storm, making my stomach clench.

Travis's guttural whine made me spin towards him again. Remy had already done whatever it took to get the bone back inside Travis's arm, but my friend's face had gone ashen as a result.

"Get over here with those arrows," Remy barked.

I stepped to his side, handing the arrows to him.

He glared up at me. "Splint his arm." He ripped the sleeves off his own shirt. "One arrow on the inside, one along the side and one on the outside, please," he directed as I fiddled with the arrows.

When I had the right formation, Remy tied one of the sleeves around Travis's wrist and the other just shy of his elbow, making a solid splint. Travis's arm still oozed blood from the bone hole, but some of the color had returned to his face.

Remy helped him to a sitting position and Travis winced, holding his injured arm to his chest.

"I don't think I can run with my arm like this."

"We can't leave you out here," I said and immediately disliked the higher pitch of my voice. I knew that sound—it was my verge-of-panic tone.

"Travis needs a sling to stabilize his arm," Remy said, eyeing me like I had a sling up my sleeve. "Give me your shirt."

I blinked at him before the words sank in. While I was wearing a vest, just the thought of undressing in front of Travis and Remy left me cold. Travis wasn't expecting the directive, either. His jaw hung open from the order.

"Why *my* shirt?"

"Because mine doesn't have sleeves anymore," Remy snapped. "The sooner you hand it over, the sooner we can start back.

It's going to take us longer, which means you and I have to be sharp."

I glanced at Travis and turned my back, dropping my bow and quiver on the ground. As much as I didn't enjoy obeying his command, I understood the rationale. My hands shook as I unbuttoned my vest. I put it between my knees and went to work on the shirt buttons. With a deep breath, I stripped the shirt and reached my arm behind me. A moment later, it was yanked from my hand. The vest wasn't nearly as warm as the combination with the shirt, and I shivered as I finished buttoning the rough fabric over my torso.

By the time I turned around, Remy had Travis on his feet and my shirt formed into a manageable sling with the sleeves tied at the back of his neck.

"Thanks, Red," Travis said.

His gaze remained on the ground, and I couldn't tell if he was just embarrassed by his accident or whether me stripping my shirt pushed him beyond discomfort.

"Think you can do this?" I asked.

"That's a stupid question," Remy growled. "He has no choice. Make sure you watch our backs." He took the lead, leaving me staring after them as they entered the forest.

I threaded an arrow into my bow and followed Remy and Travis into the canopy, gulping down the fear that threatened to close my throat.

In the deep thicket, sounds echoed in my ears. Sweat soaked my forehead despite the chill in the air, occasionally dripping into my eyes. Each time, the sting nearly closed my eyes, but I just gritted my teeth and dealt with it until the sting passed because taking either of my hands off my bow and arrow was not an option. My back was slick as well, and my wool vest clung to me like a scratchy sack.

A branch cracked to my right, and I spun, letting my arrow fly. It whistled through the air, catching nothing. Both Remy and Travis stared at me.

"What in tarnation?" Remy growled.

Travis said nothing. He was bathed in sweat as much as I was, and circles had formed under his eyes.

"I heard something," I mumbled and focused on where my arrow had disappeared. I knew how few silver arrows we had amongst the three of us, and my wasted shot embarrassed me more than stripping my shirt had.

Thankfully, neither of them commented further. Instead, they turned back towards town and continued our slow jog. Remy swept his bow in an arc in front of him as he went. I followed, turning so my back faced both of them and mimicked Remy's sweep of the terrain.

RED Chapter 4

BY THE TIME WE entered the town square, the sun touched the horizon and my muscles were stiff from the intense vigilance. However, my discomfort wasn't even on the same plane as Travis's. His pasty features were marred by random blotches of red, and the dark circles under his eyes aged him by ten years or more.

"We need to get you to Doc Wilton," I said as Travis veered toward home. I grabbed his good arm and led him the opposite way. "I'll stop at your folks' house on my way home."

"I'll catch up to you after I get a head count," Remy said.

With Travis in my care, I navigated him between the row of stores to the smaller homes where the shop owners and other professionals lived. Doc Wilton lived four houses down on the right, and I turned Travis in that direction, adjusting my pace to his.

"Thank you," Travis whispered when we were far enough for Remy not to overhear.

I glanced at him and shrugged. "What was I going to do, leave your sorry butt out there on that bluff? I don't think so."

His smile wasn't his usual bright grin. Instead, it seemed like forced bravery as he trudged towards the doctor's house. His pale features set off my internal alarms, but I couldn't force him to move any faster.

I had him lean against the wall next to the door while I knocked. The kindly gentleman opened the door, and his smile faded when his gaze landed on Travis. His gray eyes sharpened, and his hospitable mannerisms changed to all business, as he pushed open the screen door and waved us inside.

Doc Wilton's black salt and pepper hair belied his true age. He was young compared to Remy and Gram, but despite his youth, he was the best doctor in the region.

I remember seeing him for the first time the morning after I arrived in town. Gram wanted me to be checked out even though she couldn't find anything but stick scratches on me. Doc Wilton had just gotten out of medical school at some fancy faraway place, and had come back home to practice so his father could hang up his stethoscope.

I had been terrified and unable to stop shaking, and Gram was worried. She marched me across town to this very door. Doc Wilton's office smelled like rubbing alcohol and lemons and to this day, any time

I smell a lemon, I drift back to his kind smile and calm demeanor.

As Travis and I crossed the threshold into his corner office, that scent assaulted my nose once again, creating a sense of calmness it always triggered. Like everything was going to be all right, despite Travis's current condition.

"You better get going before night falls," Doc Wilton said as he sat Travis on the exam table.

I traded a glance with Travis, and he gave me a nod. My grandmother's place was one of the few homes still surrounded by woodlands. She refused to pick up and leave, so while most Dakota residents were within the town proper limits, we were still in the woods. The law of the land stated no one was to be wandering the woods after dark.

One look at the gloomy sky and my heart quickened. The light had dimmed enough to set off those damn alarms in my head, and I still had to stop at Travis's home to give his parents the news that he was at the doctor's.

I started back in the direction we had come in, briskly walking with purpose. When I turned into the alley Travis and I had come down, I bumped smack into Remy and nearly fell on my ass. If he hadn't grabbed me by the upper arms, I would have hit the dirt.

"You have to get home," he growled as he steadied me. His green eyes flashed with warning.

"I promised Travis I'd stop at his house and let his folks know where he is."

Remy's gaze rose to the sky, and he shook his head. "I'll take care of that. You need to get home before the sunlight fades. None of the parties encountered wolves today, so be vigilant."

He didn't need to say more. A howl came out of the south, echoing over the valley as if to punctuate his point. A shiver ran up my spine, and I gave him a nod.

He stepped around me, heading towards Travis's home. "Get moving," he barked.

I obeyed his authoritative tone and turned on my heel. I sprinted towards home despite the protest in my already exhausted muscles. Swinging my bow off my shoulder, I approached the woods surrounding the town. The dark canopy swallowed me as I stepped into the forest with an arrow tightly set against my bow.

Twilight was the favored time of attack. The shadows along the path didn't help my pounding chest. I picked up my pace, ignoring the cramping in my calves and arms as I ran and kept my bow and arrow at the ready.

By the time I reached the cabin, dusk had settled in tight and my lungs burned from exertion.

I burst into the house expecting my grandmother to be standing over the stove cooking some delectable meal, but all that met me was the empty and silent cabin.

"Gram?" I called out as my heart thundered in my ears.

No answer.

I ran to her bedroom, hoping she would be in bed, but she was not in the cabin, and no increase in volume of calling her name was going to produce her from thin air. Heat engulfed me, and my breath caught in my lungs, forcing a wheeze. I stood back in the living room as my gaze darted around, looking for signs of what could have happened.

When my gaze landed on the empty spot where she usually kept her foraging basket and gloves, the lump in my throat plummeted. All the heat bled from my skin, and my teeth chattered.

She was still out there. I glanced at the dark woods, and a shiver grabbed hold of every cell. The last time I was in the forest at night, my family was slaughtered.

RED Chapter 5

THE WOODS ENVELOPED ME as I broke the town law. If I was caught, I faced time in jail for this. But that wasn't what shook my muscles taut while my vision adjusted to the near blackness. I knew the path to the berry patch and the fruit orchard beyond like the back of my hand, but the shadows formed by the trees left my mouth dry and tinny.

I tried telling myself that my fear was keeping me vigilant, but I knew I was just fooling myself. The fright was making me jump at every noise to the point I was turning in frantic circles. I forced myself to stop and squat, taking each shaky breath until the quakes stopped.

Wolves can smell terror and if I didn't get myself back to center, my scent would surely drag their beastly asses in my direction. And wolves weren't the only threat in the forest. Wild cats and bears also ran in this neck of the wilderness, so I had to get my head together. Besides, I was already halfway to the berry patch and hadn't run across any signs of danger.

With a deep resolved breath, I climbed to my feet and continued my journey with as soft steps as I could take, making my focus the one-hundred-eighty-degree area in front of me. Stepping into the berry patch didn't bring me any comfort. I was nowhere near as good a tracker as Travis, but even in my sub-expert's eyes, the berry patch wasn't disturbed in a way that would indicate a struggle or even someone collapsing. Still, I navigated each row just in case.

At the far side of the berry patch, I turned, glancing at the woods surrounding the lush berries, looking for any sign that I was followed. Turning back to the orchards, I paused and closed my eyes, pulling whatever bravery I could from that well deep inside me.

I stepped towards the orchards with my bow at the ready. Traversing the orchard was a bit more difficult. My heart pumped pure adrenaline as I stepped out from tree to tree, ready to let my arrow fly. It wasn't until the last row of trees that I found some spilled berries on the ground, along with a snapped branch with an apple hanging on just by the barest of stems.

I tried to swallow as I stepped up to scan the steep slope under the moonlight, but the darkness at the bottom was impenetrable. Even under a high noon sun, the bottom of the hill is shadowed and dangerous to climb down.

I needed to backtrack around the side of the ledge to get to any point where I had solid footing right down to the valley floor. The candle I carried in my pocket wouldn't do any good in the gusty wind that had picked up with nightfall. I trotted to the middle of the berry patch and crossed into the narrow path that cut to the valley floor.

Concern braised my skin, overshadowing the fear tightening my core. I didn't bother with my bow and arrow until I was at the foot of the hill shrouded in night. The moonlight barely lit the valley floor. I glanced up, using the orchard tree line as a guide with my bow grasped tight.

I scanned the dark and sighed. I couldn't see, and I couldn't hold a lit candle while having my bow at the ready. If Gram fell, she would likely be hurt or worse. I slung the bow over my shoulder, digging the candle out along with the box of matches. I struck the match on the side of my pants. It caught the seam and flared to life.

With a candle leading the way, I held it low enough to avoid any sudden surge of air. The light illuminated a few feet at a time. I carefully planted my foot forward and turned, shielding the candle with my body as the light flickered.

I skirted around a boulder and froze at the sight of Gram's basket spilling bruised fruit on the ground. My gaze traveled farther beyond the basket.

The candle slipped from my fingers. I had an arrow threaded into my bow before the rush of air doused the flame. Dipped into sudden darkness, my chest felt like it would explode from the frantic beat of my heart. Sweat peppered my forehead, and hot beads dribbled down one of my temples.

Nothing moved. I squatted slowly, doubting myself. With one hand holding the arrow in place against the bow, I searched the ground for my light source. My fingers brushed the smooth wax, and I grasped it tightly, working the blunt end into the dirt until it stood on its own. Then I struck another match and lit the wick.

I jumped to my feet, pulling the arrow taut. Wrapped around my grandmother was a massive gray wolf. The only shot I had was right between the beast's eyes. I lined up the shot, taking a slow breath before blowing a stream of air out between my lips.

The wolf opened his eyes, but didn't move. Those bright, crystal pearlescent blue eyes I remembered from my nightmares stared back at me. The beast's tongue flicked out, swiping my grandmother's cheek.

Gram moaned and I almost let the arrow sail, but I stalled when her soft voice whispered, "Ruby, stop."

The wolf's gaze was neither afraid nor angry. If read the creature right, it would have been compassion I saw, but I dismissed that as insane.

"Gram, move," I said through clenched teeth.

"No. Even if I could, I wouldn't. If this wolf hadn't come along, I would be dead now. He fought off another wolf and has kept me warm and safe since," she said.

My brain couldn't wrap around her words. All I saw was a monster, and what she said didn't make any sense. Every werewolf I had encountered had operated on bloodlust. I shook my head, calculating the odds of being able to kill the beast, when part of her comment broke through the barrier in my mind.

"What do you mean by if you could move?"

"I'm hurt, dear," she said.

I lowered my bow but kept the arrow strung tight.

"Were you bitten?" The question squeezed from my throat.

Her eyes weren't luminescent like the wolf's, but that meant nothing. I had no idea how long the werewolf change took place if bitten. We always sacrificed the poor soul before they turned. I didn't know if I could kill my grandmother, even if she was poisoned by the beast.

"No," she said, and her eyes closed. "No, I wasn't bitten. But I'm sure I broke a few things."

I glanced at the rocky terrain going up the hillside. I wouldn't have been surprised if she broke multiple things. If Travis shattered his arm from a ten-foot fall, it's a wonder my grandmother could speak.

"Put the bow and arrow away," Gram said. "And help me to my feet."

My gaze locked with the wolf's. If I put my weapon away, that would leave both of us vulnerable.

"Gram..."

"For heaven's sake, Ruby!"

Gram's angry hiss set me in motion. I stepped over the candle, creating enough of a breeze to blow the candle out. I muttered under my breath as my eyes took their sweet time adjusting to the blackness. The wolf's blue eyes became the only beacon I had, and they remained steady. Every cell in my body screamed danger as whatever remaining logic argued that the wolf could have killed both of us already.

His eyes flickered to my right and widened. I spun and let the arrow fly. A thud sounded. I flicked a match against the seam of my pants to see what the hell I hit. Another wolf lay a few feet behind me with my arrow embedded between its fading eyes.

I turned back to my grandmother and the beast that gave me enough of a warning to react. His eyes were locked back on me, but while his form had been relaxed before, it was now tense and broadcasting the same urgent message as that flashing under my skin.

We needed to get out of there. I dropped the match and closed the distance. Getting Gram to her feet wasn't easy, and her cry of pain when she applied pressure to her right leg sent a fiery streak of panic through me. I glanced back the way I came at the dead carcass and then turned my gaze to the wolf now standing on the other side of my grandmother.

I took a step toward home, and Gram made a muffled noise, gripping me tighter.

"I can't make it back in the dark," she whispered in a voice strained by pain. "We need to find someplace safe to hide until the sun rises."

I couldn't disagree, but the valley didn't have anywhere to hide. The wolf moved forward and stopped, looking back over his shoulder, his eyes bright orbs in the dark. When I didn't move, he came back and nudged me.

"I don't think so," I said, glaring at the massive wolf.

Holding on to my grandmother gave this beast the upper hand, and he could have gotten the jump on me. Instead, he nudged me again and trotted a few steps forward.

"I think he wants us to follow."

I knew the bastard wanted us to follow, but I couldn't figure out why. But being out here was just as dangerous, so I listened to my intuition and helped Gram hop on her good leg through the winding path.

The wolf kept looking back to make sure we were following, and he didn't wander ahead too far. But when he entered a thick canopy, I paused and my heart rate picked up. My grandmother's eyes were at half mast, and she looked much worse than Travis had earlier.

The wolf came back and peered out of the canopy at us. Instead of turning and leading, he came over to the other side of my grandmother, stepping close enough for her to cast her arm around his back for more support.

He swung his massive head in my direction and met my gaze. There was no malice evident in those blue eyes, but I still shivered with indecision.

"I think it's safe," Gram whispered.

I stepped into the dark woods, wondering if this would be the last thing I ever did.

RED Chapter 6

BEARING GRAM'S WEIGHT ON my already taxed muscles wasn't easy. I had to stop several times and shift her, and after trying to navigate the tight path, I knew there would have been no way I would have gotten her up the hill of the ravine and out of danger alone. The wolf bore an equal amount of Gram's weight, and there were several times that I thought about hauling her onto his back, but I didn't know whether that would be better or worse than walking. When we finally stepped into a large clearing, the moon had crossed the heavens and the constellations had shifted to a pattern I didn't recognize.

A small cottage sat in the center of the clearing. The wolf led us onto the porch and then pawed at the mat in front of the door until the corner folded back, revealing a key. I let Gram lean on the doorjamb and retrieved the key.

"Only my grandmother and I are going inside," I said and slid the key into the lock.

With a twist of my wrist, the knob unlatched, and I helped Gram inside, closing the door on the wolf with no reservation.

I struck a match and found a lantern within reach. Lighting the wick produced a warm glow, and I blew the match out, setting it in the ceramic bowl next to the lantern. Nails clicked on the porch outside the door, and then a huff came as the wolf settled down to keep guard. I traded a glance with Gram and picked up the lantern as we headed across what looked like a family room into a hallway to find a bedroom and washroom at the end of the hall.

I got Gram situated in the bed and collapsed in the bedside chair, setting my bow and quiver within reach, just in case.

"Ruby," Gram started. "I'm not sure I'm going to make it."

A reprimand remained at the tip of my tongue. I closed my eyes, and taking a deep breath, I stood and pulled the covers back to make sure she didn't have the same type of fracture as Travis. I ignored Gram's gasps as I ran my hands down her side and leg, feeling my way in the low light. No bone stuck out of her skin, but I felt the displacement in her hip and the weird angle in her thigh.

"You'll be fine," I said. "We just need to get you to Doc Wilton in the morning.

"I can't walk that far, honey."

"I know. I'll go get Midnight after sunrise."

"I can't ride in this condition," Gram muttered.

"I need to figure out what I'm going to do with that wolf," I said, trying to get Gram's mind off her injuries. My thoughts jumbled where the wolf was concerned. I knew my duty was to put the beast down, but he helped us, so my heart and my mind were now at odds.

"You can't be thinking what I think you're thinking," Gram said, her stern stare making me look away. "After all he did for us?"

"He's a werewolf." The statement hung on the air between us.

She crossed her arms and pursed her lips in anger. Red flared in her cheeks, giving the rest of Gram's pale skin a more ghostly quality. I just shrugged.

"He isn't like the others," she whispered.

"I don't care." But I did, and it burned under the surface of my skin. My entire life I had seen those things as monsters to be destroyed, and then this beast showed compassion, kindness, and patience like he was human. It didn't settle well. "It's my job."

"It is not your job to become a monster," she hissed. "If you kill him, you will be no better than the rest of the beasts taking innocent lives."

I leaned back in the chair. Her words were as effective as a slap across the face, and they stung just as deeply. I didn't want to believe that any of the werewolves were capable of good, but I couldn't deny what this one had done for us. It was a paradox.

"How do you know he's innocent?"

Her crossed arms loosened, and she sighed. "I don't know if he is innocent or not. But I know he could have torn me to pieces or let the other wolf that came along right before he did. He chased it off and came back, offering me his warmth despite my condition. He also tensed and then relaxed after you killed that other wolf, which may have been the same one he chased off earlier."

"Maybe he was just protecting his meal," I said, but it didn't ring true in my ears.

Gram scoffed and waved her hand at me. The movement caused her to grimace.

"Get some rest," I said and blew out the lantern, dousing us in darkness.

The waxing moon shone through the side window. In less than a week it would be full. I closed my eyes, trying to get some rest, but my mind kept racing, kept turning over what I needed to do when the night was through.

I had already broken the curfew, and for that, I'd be facing jail time if anyone found out. Letting a werewolf live had an entirely different punishment, one that would have me facing a jury of my peers and a potential death sentence.

RED Chapter 7

I JERKED AWAKE AND wiped the drool from my cheek. Another clang from the outer room had me on my feet with the bow threaded with an arrow. Gram still slept, her pale face visible above the comforter. I crept towards the door, padding as silently as I could while every nerve ending pulsed. I opened the bedroom door and glanced down the hall into the brightly lit family room area. The front door was still closed, but the distinct sound of someone inside the cabin filtered to my ears.

I crossed the distance and pointed my bow toward the kitchen. Heat danced on my skin as I stared at the chiseled back of a man standing over the stove. His hair was jet black, matching the color of the pants he wore, and every movement he made rippled through the muscles in his back. When he glanced over his shoulder with the same piercing blue eyes the wolf had last night, heat engulfing me moved lower into my belly.

"Shoot if you have to," he said and turned back to the stove. "But it would be a shame to ruin breakfast."

Even his voice tickled the triggers inside me. It was deep and musical and almost hypnotic. I had never heard a werewolf's voice, only the howls and growls from the beasts.

The man turned with a pan in his hands and dumped scrambled eggs on the two plates sitting on the small table.

"How did you get in?" I asked and cursed the breathless quality of my voice. I still held the arrow tight on the bow.

He smiled, and I nearly fell to my knees at the small dimples in his cheeks and the playful shine in his eyes. "There's more than one way to get into this house." He turned his back and put the pan into a wash basin before taking a seat at the table. "Eat. Then you can kill me."

I lowered the bow and stared at him as he began eating the eggs in front of him. I knew I should put him down, but there was something disarming about the man, and I could not bring myself to shoot him. Frustration gathered inside me, along with something more primal, and I gave in to the civility of the moment.

I sat, but kept the bow and arrow within reach in case the wolf attacked.

"Where did you get the eggs?" I asked, assuming he had stolen them.

"My henhouse out back." He hooked his thumb over his shoulder. "And the milk came from the cows." He pointed to the glass in front of me.

My fork stalled on the way to my mouth, and I just stared at the man. There was no precedence for a werewolf having a farm. At least not one where animals lived long enough to produce food.

He smiled. "Eat up before your eggs get cold, then we can check on your grandmother."

My muscles remembered what they were doing, and I took my first bite. The scrambled eggs were good. Not runny or rubbery, but just right. I focused on feeding my growling stomach. I hadn't realized how hungry I was, but then again, adrenaline kept me moving last night, so my lack of a meal didn't hit until now.

I finished every kernel on the plate and gave him an awkward smile of gratitude.

He stood, cleared the plates, and washed the dishes while I sat dumbfounded.

"Who are you?" I finally asked.

He turned towards me while wiping his hands on a dishtowel. "Lucas Bayo," he said and stepped towards me.

I reacted and strung the arrow in the bow, jumping to my feet as shock and panic filled my muscles. My gaze dropped to his extended hand, and a hot flush filled my cheeks. He was just being polite and offering a handshake. I closed my eyes and sighed.

"I'm sorry, but I don't trust you enough to let my guard down," I said and stepped backwards. "My parents were killed by your kind and..."

He pulled his hand back and slid it into his pocket. "My kind." His voice filled with bitterness, and he nodded like he understood my reaction. "Well, then, you do what you need to do." He leaned against the sink, his expression resolved but not fearful.

I pointed the arrow at him and pulled it back. The tip centered on his chest, but my gaze locked with his. That primal urge to drop the bow and arrow and jump into his arms filled my form. I wanted those full lips on mine, those powerful hands cupping my...

"Damn it," I muttered, shaking the inappropriate thoughts from my head. The fabric of my vest rubbed against my breasts in a way that was both uncomfortable and just as arousing as looking into Lucas's eyes. I lowered my bow. "How many humans have you killed?"

"None."

I stared at him and relaxed my grip on the bow and arrow, but didn't put it away. Not just yet.

"You expect me to believe that?"

"I really don't care what you believe. It's the truth, and you can take it or leave it."

His arms crossed, making the muscles in his chest flex in a way that made me shift to quell the heat pooling between my legs. I didn't know what the hell had gotten into me, but I couldn't bring myself to kill him. Not with my grandmother's words still ringing in my head. I unthreaded my arrow and dropped it back in my quiver.

"If you so much as twitch the wrong way, I'll kill you."

He gave me a huff of a laugh and dropped his arms. "Can we go see how your grandmother is doing?"

"Fine." I waved for him to lead the way.

Lucas rolled his eyes and headed towards the bedroom, his gait that of someone who wasn't at all happy with the situation. It amused me, but my amusement died as soon as the door opened.

Gram's pale features set my heart in overdrive. The bow fell from my fingers, hitting the floor as I skidded to a stop by her side. Her eyes opened at the sound, and she blinked at Lucas standing a few feet away. Her gaze moved to mine, and she formed a smile.

"I guess I've made it through the night." Gram's weak voice came out in a whisper.

"Yes." Lucas stepped around me and put his wrist to her forehead. He glanced at me with sadness in his eyes. "She needs a doctor. Today."

I nodded. "I need to get my horse."

"I've got one that we can use," he said.

"I can get my horse," I said, straightening my back.

"Look, there is no time for you to travel to Dakota and back. She needs to be transported now, not tomorrow."

"I won't bring anyone back with me if that is what you're worried about," I snapped.

He raised his eyebrows. "I'm not worried about a hunting party. I'm worried about whether your grandmother will make it back alive. And I am not taking her through the woods at night. That's a death wish waiting to happen, no matter how good you are with that bow and arrow."

The growl in his voice caught me as off guard as his words.

"I don't think I can ride," Gram said, her voice frail.

"It's okay. You can ride on my lap so you don't get jostled as much." Lucas turned to me. "My mare is out in the barn. I'm assuming you know how to put a saddle on."

I cocked my head and narrowed my eyes. "I'll stay with my grandmother while you go prepare the horse."

"Do you know how to splint a leg?" he asked.

I shifted and nodded, but that wasn't true.

"For heaven's sake, Ruby, go get the horse ready," Gram scolded.

I glanced at her and then at Lucas. Pointing my finger, I opened my mouth.

"I know. If I harm her in any way, I'm a dead man," he cut in.

I swiped my bow off the ground and stormed out of the room while my grandmother apologized for my rash behavior. The last thing I heard before I stepped out the door was Lucas saying I was entitled to my feelings. As unsettled as I was about leaving Gram with him, I was also curious to see what his land truly held.

I made my way to the side of the house and gawked at the barn and the surrounding farmlands. Wooden fences gated the animals and the gardens starting at the back of the house. Just beyond the perimeter fence was the forest. I couldn't imagine keeping the farm safe from the dangers in the woods. Not only were there werewolves, but there were plenty of other predators looking for an easy meal.

Lucas Bayo was one big mystery, and as I unhooked the gate and passed through to the pasture, I realized I wanted to unravel the layers and get to the core of the man. A heat burned deep inside me, one that had never been lit before, and I cursed under my breath.

Lucas was a werewolf.

The thought pounded my brain with each step. I couldn't let this weird attraction take over and cloud my mind. When Gram was back home under the care of the doctor, I would honor my oath and do my duty, even if it killed me.

One bite and he could create an army to overrun Dakota.

I opened the barn door and scanned the interior. Chickens pecked their way across the ground and the hen house lined the wall to my left while stalls filled the right side of the barn. Most of the stalls were empty, but two had occupants. One held a milking cow and the other a horse.

"Focus," I mumbled and approached the old mare that reminded me of a bowl of cinnamon sugar. White and brown speckled her coat, and she whinnied as I approached.

"It's okay, girl," I said softly and reached for the reins on the wall.

I stepped to the stall door and gently ran my hand down her nose and to the side of her jaw. She sniffed my hand, looking for a treat, and then met my gaze. For a minute there, I saw a shadow of our old mare who carried me to that fateful clearing all those years ago, but the vision passed just as quick.

The horse allowed me to fit her bit and strap on the reins without any fuss, and I led her out of the stall. She patiently stood while I threw her saddle blanket in place and fit the saddle on tight. I led her to the post just outside the back of the house and descended a stairwell to a door.

The knob turned easily to Lucas's root cellar. This must have been how he got inside the house this morning. The stairs led up to the door across from the bedroom. I closed the door and glanced at the knob. I engaged the lock and strode towards the bedroom.

My grandmother moaned.

It was as if lightning shot through my veins. I had the bow and arrow in my grasp before my brain caught up to what I was seeing. Lucas was wrapping my grandmother's thigh in gauze. Along her outer thigh and hip, he had placed a piece of sturdy lumber that went from her hip to her knee. Smaller pieces framed her upper and inner thigh, and from the way he was moving her, I would guess there was another piece of wood framing the back of her leg.

Sweat poured from her face. Each time Lucas rolled the gauze under her leg, she whined. He kept apologizing each time he had to move her, and finally he tied the bandage off just above the knee and turned towards me.

"This is going to be a rough ride," he said, his eyes relaying a world of concern.

"I can take care of her," I said, ignoring the pang that went through me.

"I'm going with you two," he said.

I laughed at him. There was no hiding his pearlescent eyes. The town would string him up with silver and slowly torture him to death. I shook my head. "No. They will kill you on sight."

"*You* didn't."

I opened my mouth to speak, but I couldn't find the words. Alarms were already ringing in my head. "You can't come," I finally squeaked out.

"She's right. They won't understand," Gram said.

Lucas ran his hand through his thick hair and crossed to his bureau. He pulled on a shirt, much to my dismay, and then offered me one. "It's colder today than it was yesterday."

I glanced down at my vest, and heat filled my cheeks. I had totally forgotten I lent my shirt to Travis. I had been so preoccupied with my surroundings that I didn't notice how cold it was. I almost declined, but

Gram's raised brow made me take the shirt and retreat as quickly as possible from the room.

In the washroom, I slid the shirt over my head. The material was soft and hung over my slight form. I tucked the hem into my pants and slid my vest back on. I had to roll up the sleeves to almost my elbows in order to not impede my bow and arrow if the need arose.

I stepped back in the room a few minutes later, and Gram gave me that same raised brow.

"Travis fell from a tree and needed a sling. Remy had already used his shirt sleeves for a splint, so I was the last one left with a shirt." Heat engulfed my entire face, and I glanced at the floor. This wasn't a conversation I wanted to have in front of a stranger. A sexy stranger at that. A sexy werewolf, my mind corrected. He pulled on his boots, and my gaze fell to the open *V* of his shirt and the firm, smooth skin peeking out of his tunic.

"So you gave the shirt off your back to help a friend?" His bright blue eyes met mine.

"I guess," I answered.

The dimples in his cheeks toyed with my insides. He stood and crossed to the spot in front of me, his gaze never leaving mine. "I can't let you try to make this trip with just your grandmother. That wolf you killed last night, that wasn't the only one in the area."

"Your horse can't hold all three of us."

"Yes, she can."

I knew there were more wolves out there. A whole pack, but I didn't want to be responsible for this creature's death. "Lucas, they will kill you," I said slowly, enunciating every word to make my point.

His calm smile burned through me. "Then you won't have to make that call." He slid into his coat, pulling the hood over his head, scooped Gram up in his arms, and headed out the front door.

I followed and brought the mare around front, where Lucas hopped on with Gram in his arms, shifting her until she was as comfortable as possible. He offered me his hand, and I swatted it away. Using the porch, I climbed onto the back half of the saddle and wrapped my right arm around his waist.

"I'll do what I can to keep you comfortable, but you and I both know time isn't on our side right now," Lucas said to my grandmother.

She nodded.

He glanced back at me. "Hold on," he said and then kicked his heels into the horse.

The mare took off like a bolt that belied her calm demeanor. She reminded me of Midnight as she traversed through the woods. I clung to Lucas and my bow, wondering if Gram felt every hoof beat or not. Her pale, stressed features worried me.

Her eyes met mine. She offered me a grimace instead of a smile, but just the effort alone was endearing.

"Werewolf coming fast on the right." Lucas's purr reached my ears.

I tightened my thighs and swung the bow in that direction, threading it with an arrow as we rode through the thick woods. The mare never slowed down or veered from her path. I caught the flash of the wolf's iridescent eyes just as it launched into the air.

My arrow pierced right through its head. Lucas sent a punch in its direction so the dead beast wouldn't knock us off the horse. His strength and calmness astounded me, and for a moment, I allowed myself to be in awe of the man, regardless of the beast inside.

I repositioned myself and wrapped my right arm around his waist again, hugging him tight as we continued at breakneck speed.

RED Chapter 8

THE MID-AFTERNOON SUN DIDN'T offer much warmth, and I shivered as I slid off the horse in front of Doc Wilton's. I knocked on the door, and when it swung open, Doc Wilton's kind smile disappeared. He opened the door, waving us inside.

We hurried through the house to Doc Wilton's office, where Lucas laid Gram on the exam table.

"I did my best to keep her broken bones stable on the ride..." he said and stepped back. "I think she may be bleeding internally."

The doctor snapped his gaze to Lucas, as if seeing him for the first time. His eyes narrowed before he grabbed a pair of scissors and started cutting through the gauze.

"You did fine," Gram whispered to Lucas and stretched her hand out for me.

I stepped to her side and took it.

"Get him somewhere safe," she whispered.

Doc Wilton looked up from his task. "Why would you let that monster near your grandmother?"

"He saved me, Jacob," Gram said. "I was stupid and tried to use the berm to grab an apple off a high limb and lost my balance. I fell all the way into the valley gorge. He came around just when another wolf found me. He protected me, running that varmint off, and then curled around me to keep me warm. When Ruby found us, he kept both of us safe through the night. He didn't have to help us at all. And he certainly didn't need to risk his life by coming here, so you just hush up and leave him be."

Doc Wilton looked down as pink bloomed in his cheeks. "Yes, Mrs. Locklear." He slowly removed the outer splint, and Gram groaned through clenched teeth. He glanced up at us. "Go home. I'll come get you when she is stable."

Gram squeezed my hand and then let go, giving me a reassuring smile. When I didn't move, she turned her gaze to Lucas. "Have her take you to our cottage. You should be safe there until nightfall."

Lucas nodded. "Yes, ma'am."

"Ruby, don't let anything happen to him, okay?"

I rolled my eyes and nodded. "Fine." I took a second to give her a hug. "I love you, Gram," I whispered.

"I love you, too, child. Now go, before the Guard gets back." She met my gaze with a clear warning in her eyes.

I knew I'd have to face Remy later today when the Guard got home, but if he intercepted us on the way home, Lucas would not get out of Dakota alive. I gave her a nod and stepped outside with Lucas.

Without a word, he lifted me onto the mare and hopped on behind me. He handed me the reins.

"Lead the way," he said, and gently banged his heels against the mare's sides.

She started trotting as I led her through the back side of the village and into the woods.

"You don't live in town?" he asked as we went deeper down the secondary path that I rarely traveled.

"No. Gram has always lived outside the town proper." I turned the mare to our left, doubling back to the stables behind our cottage. Our clearing was tiny compared to Lucas's land, but it was all we had.

We didn't have issues with predators either, but that was due to the wolf carcasses hanging on every post. Lucas tensed as I stopped at the gate. I slid off the horse and took the reins, leading the horse through to the inside of the corral with Lucas still on her back. The gate closed behind us, and he twitched in the seat. His gaze passed over each pelt before dropping to mine.

His teeth peeled back in horror at the vulgar display of death.

"It keeps Midnight safe." I nodded to the black stallion drinking from the trough. "I don't know what you did around yours, but this works like a charm." I waved at the perimeter.

Lucas huffed and climbed off the horse. "I marked the territory. You've announced death to all who enter." He nodded at the posts. "No werewolf in their right mind would breach that line."

"And yet you are standing inside my perimeter." I cocked an eyebrow.

"I never professed to be of the right mind," he said and took the reins of the horse, leading her towards the water trough.

Midnight reacted as he got closer. My stallion's nose flared, and he neighed, shaking his head before he reared on his hind legs.

"Cool your hide," Lucas said to Midnight. "My girl needs some water." He led the mare to the water and stood between his horse and Midnight.

Midnight stomped his hoof and backed away. He didn't like the presence of a werewolf in his domain, and he trotted over to me, nudging me away from Lucas until I captured his head between my hands.

"Middy, it's okay. He will not hurt us. I promise." My calm voice seemed to do the trick, but my horse wanted nothing to do with either the mare or Lucas.

Lucas took the saddle and blanket off and placed them in the shed with my other riding equipment. He took off the mare's bridle and bit and hung that up beside Midnight's before he stepped out and nodded towards the cabin.

"Do you mind if we go inside? This is kind of unsettling." He twirled his finger around to indicate my safeguards.

His discomfort amused me. So did the fact that he could just throw me over his shoulder and take me inside instead of being so polite. I gave him a nod and headed towards the back door.

He followed and once inside, his entire body seemed to melt with relief. He leaned against the door.

"You're that girl, aren't you?" he asked while looking at the ceiling.

He said *that girl* in the same tone I used when I said *his kind* this morning. When his gaze dropped to mine, I shivered.

"You're the legendary wolf killer that I keep hearing about."

I smiled and shrugged. "I guess."

His eyes closed again, and he took a deep breath that expanded his chest. "There is a price on your head." He straightened and walked past me directly to the icebox in the kitchen.

"What are you doing?" I asked when I rounded the corner.

"I'm hungry, and I was looking at what you had available."

"That's our food," I said.

He shot a glare in my direction. "I shared my breakfast with you." He pulled out a slice of venison from under the ice and held it up. "Do you mind if I cook this up?"

I bit my lip for a second, feeling selfish. I thought about what Gram would want me to do. She would want me to be the perfect host to our guest, but I wasn't willing to go that far. If he wanted to cook, by all means, he could cook.

"Go ahead. I'm going to clean up." I turned, hanging my bow and quiver on the hooks in the hallway as a sign of trust. I still had my silver blade if he decided I was worth the bounty, but I didn't think he'd go through all this trouble in the name of collecting on my head.

I filled the tub with lukewarm water and stripped my clothing. I stepped into the water and sat, sucking my breath in at the coolness of the bath. If I had been a little more patient, the water would have been hot enough to not shiver as I scrubbed the dirt from my skin. When I finished with my body, I dunked my head under the water and shook it, hoping that would be enough to clean the dirt from my braid.

The scent of food drifted under the door, and my stomach responded with a growl. I climbed out and toweled off before dumping the dirty water out the window. I'd have to fill the warmer with wood chips and the pot with water later, but right now, I was hungry.

I wrapped the towel around me and gathered my clothes. I'd have to do the wash in another day, but for now, I'd put on something comfortable instead of my hunting pants and vest. I pulled open the door, and Lucas stood right outside with his hand poised to knock.

His eyes flickered as his gaze dropped from my face to the towel hiding my endowments. His cheeks flared red as his eyes found mine again. "Um, dinner is ready." He backed away, giving me just enough room to scoot by him.

Just being near him turned my skin into an inferno, and I hurried into my bedroom, shutting the door on his curious gaze. I leaned against the wood and stared up at the ceiling, asking for strength. As a member of the Guard, I could not fall for a wolf, no matter how attractive he was.

With a deep breath and a slow exhale, my skin cooled. I pulled on undergarments, stockings, my hunting dress, and boots. It was much less comfortable than my nightshirt, but I would not make myself vulnerable with a stranger in the house.

I stepped out into the living area, and Lucas was sitting at the table waiting for me. Both our plates were brimming with venison, and a half loaf of bread sat sliced between them.

"Thank you," I said and took the seat opposite him.

"You're welcome." He focused on the food in front of him.

For a lone werewolf, he seemed to have impeccable manners. When he finally looked up, his cheeks flared red.

"What?" he asked.

"I'm just surprised you have manners," I mumbled, and cut another piece of perfectly cooked venison. I also did not want to admit to him he was a better cook than I was. My venison usually came out like rawhide, but this came out as good as Gram made it.

"I was brought up by my mother. My human mother," he said. "She taught me how to act with other people, and despite my father's barbaric ways, her teachings stuck with me. I am not like the other beasts out there." He nodded towards the window. "I was born this way."

I stared at him with a raised eyebrow. "What do you mean?"

"I am the only werewolf that I know of that was birthed by a human. Even the original was changed by an ancient rite and not by birth. I also don't have the same bloodlust as my kind. It's the reason I'm on their bounty list, too."

I didn't realize I had stopped with my fork halfway to my mouth until he cocked his head at me. Heat flushed my face, and I dropped my gaze to my plate. "So, you're an outlaw?"

He laughed. "Certainly to humans, but that's because they don't stop to question whether killing me is just or not. They assume my heritage makes me a killer, which is incorrect. I am half human and half wolf and have always refused to attack people. I have never bitten anyone either, because I have no idea what kind of curse I would pass on. Because I refused to kill humans or attempt to turn them, I lost my family."

My eyes softened.

His lips tightened. "I have killed, though. The day they killed my mother, I tore the pack to pieces. So, I've committed the ultimate sin in the eyes of the werewolf clan." He shrugged and went back to eating his meal.

A lump formed in the back of my mouth as a deep sadness filled me. Lucas had no one. Humans didn't trust him, and his own kind hunted him. I cleared my throat and focused on my food. Before I finished, a knock on the front door interrupted us.

Adrenaline rushed through me as I stared at Lucas. His back was towards the door, but if anyone saw a stranger eating in my grandmother's home, there would be hell to pay. I pointed to the kitchen, and he picked up his plate and moved to the corner near the sink, which was a blind spot to the front door.

I waited a second and then cracked the door. Annie Wilton stood on the threshold, with Doc Wilton's horse tied to the front porch post. My heart thundered in my chest at the stricken look on her face.

"There were complications. Come quickly," she said and grabbed my hand, pulling me out the door.

I took one glance at Lucas, and he nodded before the door closed on his worried gaze. My stomach dropped because I was certain I would come home to an empty house, but my grandmother's situation was more pressing than Lucas's. I hopped onto the back of Doc's horse without prompting, and Annie kicked its sides. We were galloping at top speed within a few breaths.

When the horse skidded to a stop a few minutes later at Doc Wilton's house, I hopped off and ran into the house without a glance back at Annie.

Gram was strapped onto the same exam table I had left her on. However, she looked much worse now. Her skin had turned to gray and her lips were almost blue. My gaze dropped to the floor. To the mess of red towels and rags.

Gram moved her hand, and I stepped close to take it. She tried to speak, but all that came out was a harsh rasp. I leaned close.

"Love you, Ruby," she whispered.

I pulled away. "I love you, too, Gram," I said, and it was as if my words pulled the last of the air from her lungs.

Her raspy breath stopped on an exhale. I waited for her to inhale again.

"Gram?" I squeezed her hand. "Gram?" The pounding in my ears drowned out all sound. I shook her arm. "Gram!"

Doc Wilton moved behind me and clasped my shoulders, trying to pull me away from my grandmother.

I spun around to face him. "You have to help her!"

"I can't. That's why I sent Annie to get you. Your grandmother lost too much blood. Her hip shattered and punctured an artery in several places. It was a miracle she remained as lucid as she did for so long. There was nothing I could do." He ran his hand through his hair. "There was just too much damage."

"You can't help her?" I asked with a voice I didn't recognize. "You can't save her?"

"No, honey. She's already gone. She held on to say her goodbye to you."

Tears blurred my vision, and my throat closed against the wail of sorrow filling my soul. The last of my family lay on that table, and my heart broke with the loss. My knees wobbled, but I wouldn't allow them to buckle.

Not here.

Not in front of her spirit.

Gram would expect me to be strong, to carry on without her, but all I wanted to do was curl up in a ball and forget the world around me. I pressed my lips together and turned, taking one last glance at the woman who raised me to be strong and independent.

"Bye, Gram," I whispered and turned towards the door.

"I'll make the arrangements," Doc Wilton said.

I nodded and left his house as fog filtered through my brain. Memories of Gram's laughter and her gumption flashed in front of my eyes. I didn't remember the walk to the cabin, but I found myself staring at the door with arms that were too heavy to lift.

After a moment, the door cracked open, and Lucas's bright blue eyes peered out at me. A wave of relief hit, and my chin quivered. He opened the door wider and closed it as I crossed the threshold. Gratitude that I wasn't alone in Gram's house layered on the sorrow. Without permission, tears flowed hot from my eyes, streaking my cheeks.

My knees buckled, and I dropped, hitting the floor with a dull thud. Lucas's shadow crossed over mine, and his hand cupped my shoulder as he crouched down next to me. His kind eyes triggered the gates, and a sob slipped from my lips. I covered my face to quiet the horrible sounds.

Lucas pulled me onto his lap. His arms wrapped around me, offering warmth and comfort. He didn't bother with meaningless words. He let me purge the pain onto his shoulder in a wealth of tears until his shirt was as wet as my face. When I finally quieted down, he stood with me in his arms and brought me to my bedroom. After he laid me on the bed and slid my boots off, he covered me with a blanket and glanced at the window.

"The sun is setting," he said, and hooked his thumb over his shoulder.

"Stay," I whispered. My request was more for his safety, but I also didn't want to be alone.

"People are going to come by," he said.

I huffed. "Not at night. No one is allowed outside after dark." They would be here first thing in the morning, but while the darkness blanketed the woods, no one in their right mind wandered.

He blinked at me and gave me a half smile. "So you defied town ordinances by searching for your grandmother last night?"

"Yes. That comes with jail time. But having you here..." I shrugged. There was no use telling him I was facing a death sentence if anyone found out I allowed him to live.

Reality slammed home. I put Doc Wilton in the same position as I now sat in. I closed my eyes and buried my face in the pillow because I didn't want to entertain what Doc would do now that Gram had died.

Lucas lit the lamp on my nightstand and then started for the door.

"Where are you going?"

He stopped and shifted from foot to foot as he looked out the window. "I need to go."

I glanced at the darkened window and then back at him.

"Damn it," he muttered and doubled over before falling to his knees.

All my sorrow and every narration in my head halted as his gaze locked on mine. His eyes flared bright. I blinked as the fabric encasing him tore, the sound of it sending a shiver up my spine. His hands clenched into tight fists as the cords on his neck stood out. His muscles trembled hard enough for me to feel it in the springs of the bed.

The transformation from man to massive wolf did not look pleasant in the least. It wasn't done in a snap, where one moment he was a man and the next he was a wolf, like I always assumed. Bones cracked and stuck out at odd angles while he silently endured the pain. There was a final snap, and then the wolf looked at me amidst the ruined clothing.

He glanced at the mess surrounding him and sighed before using his snout and front paw to bundle up the scraps into a small pile that he picked up and brought over to the trashcan in the corner.

Questions surfaced, but I wouldn't get any answers until morning. Lucas curled up in the corner and put his massive head on his paws. I stared at him in silence until my eyelids dropped closed, and I let the exhaustion claim me.

RED Chapter 9

KNOCKING INTERRUPTED MY BROKEN dreams. I rolled away from the noise, curling into a tighter ball and shivering against the morning chill.

"Ruby?"

The strange voice penetrated my sleep-addled brain. My eyes flew open, landing on a bare chest on the opposite side of the bed. I sat up and glanced down at my attire, and then everything fell into place. This wasn't a nightmare, after all.

I stared at Lucas. He stood wrapped from the waist down in the comforter, and what was visible was a sculpted torso like I had never seen before. I wanted to reach out and touch the relief map of his chest and feel the muscles under my fingertips. Another shiver captured me, and I wrapped my arms around my stocking-clad legs.

"Someone is here," he said and nodded towards the bedroom door.

The knocking continued, and I climbed out of the bed.

"Just stay in here," I said before I left the room.

"If you get the chance to grab the saddle bag I slung over the fence out back, I have an extra pair of clothes in there," he said.

"I'll do my best." I closed the bedroom door and crossed to the front door.

Outside stood the entire squad, led by Remy. His solemn features and reddened eyes told me more than I wanted to know about how he felt about Gram. He gave me a nod and went to step inside.

I blocked his path. The last thing I needed was the Guard milling about while I had a naked werewolf in my bedroom.

"Remy, I really don't want any company right now. I'm sorry, but I need some time to let this all sink in," I said and glanced at the twenty men standing outside.

His face hardened, and his eyes narrowed. "You went looking for her after dark, didn't you?" His voice turned as fiery as his glare.

There was no sense in denying it, so I nodded. "It was Gram." My chin trembled and my eyes filled with hot tears, but I blinked them back and closed the door on the group.

"Doc said you had help."

I stared at him. "Yes. A farmer from outside Dakota territory found us and helped me get Gram to Doc's office."

Remy gave a slow nod.

"Gram would have died out in the woods otherwise." My voice cracked. "Lot of good it did, anyway." I shut the door before the tears came in earnest.

"You know where to find us if you need anything." Remy patted the door a couple of times.

"Thank you," I called out.

Footsteps shuffled away. When I no longer heard noise, I opened the door just to check. No one was in sight. I shut the door and hurried out the back and into the corral. Lucas's saddle bag hung by the stable, and I ran across the field and grabbed it.

Back in the house, I tossed the bag into my bedroom and closed the door, leaning my back on it for a moment to get my racing heart under control. I closed my eyes and concentrated on my breathing, slowing it down until I almost felt normal. When I opened my eyes, my gaze landed on my grandmother's room. A lump returned to my throat.

I would not be able to escape her within the confines of these walls.

The bedroom door opened, and I jumped and spun around, right into Lucas's bare chest. His skin was warm and soft, and I pushed off with my hands, taking a step back. His eyes were as wide as mine as we stared at each other.

Another knock at the door broke whatever spell had captivated us. I glanced at the front of the house and then at Lucas.

"You need a shirt," I mumbled under my breath.

A smile toyed on his lips. "I don't have one," he whispered.

My gaze dropped to the rocking chair where my pile of clothes from yesterday sat, and I pointed. "Yes, you do."

He turned, and I swore his shoulders dropped a fraction as if he were as disappointed as I was for him to cover up. I crossed to quell the knocking at the front door.

Travis stood on the other side of the threshold, his face still on the pale side. His arm was set in a plaster cast and held in a much more stable sling than my shirt. He gave me a tired smile and handed me my soiled shirt.

"I'm sorry to hear about your grandmother," he said.

I pressed my lips together and nodded, blinking away the mist that blurred my vision. He stepped towards me, but I put my hand out, stopping him.

"I'm okay," I said, but my shaky voice belied my words. I silently cursed at my inability to stabilize my emotions.

"You're about as okay as I am," he said and raised an eyebrow.

It never occurred to me that anyone else would have a big empty space in the middle of their chest like I had, but on closer inspection, Travis's eyes were more bloodshot than normal. It wasn't cold enough outside to warrant the redness on the end of his nose that matched the lines traversing his eyes.

Anyone just glancing at him would have surmised he had been tossing whiskey back all night at the local pub. But I knew better. I knew what those signs meant in my best friend. He hadn't been able to curb his sorrow, either.

He pointed his chin at the inside of the cabin. "Are you going to just stand there, or are you going to let me in?"

"I'm not up for company," I said and felt about as good as a piece of horse dung about that.

"That's what Remy said when I passed the group." He stepped closer as if he was going to pass my body blockade.

I put my arm up against the doorjamb, stopping him dead.

Travis sent a sideways glance at me. The crease between his eyes was deep enough to broadcast his irritation.

"Are you serious?" He straightened his back and glared. "Do you think you're the only one grieving?"

I opened my mouth to reply, but I didn't have any comeback that wouldn't hurt him more than he looked. It wasn't like him to get angry with me, either. I shook my head and stepped aside so he could enter.

"I'm sorry. I'm just not in the mood for anyone to be here," I said and closed the door.

Travis took a seat on the couch. "I'm not just anyone."

He was my best friend, after all, and even though he had delusions of a future with me,

I couldn't deny he had always been there when I needed him. If Lucas hadn't been in the next room, I probably would have had a house full of people offering condolences and casseroles, and he would have been at my side fending people off so I could have some peace.

"I know." I turned away and headed into the kitchen to keep myself preoccupied. I couldn't pass off the thundering of my heart or the heated flush now filling my form as mourning. If I stayed by the hearth, Travis would soon figure out something else was digging at my nerves more than my grandmother's passing.

I stared at the jar of Gram's cookies.

A hand on my arm pulled a yelp from me and I spun, staring at Travis with wide eyes. I hadn't heard him cross the room.

"You haven't heard a word I said."

I shook my head.

"Have you picked out your grandmother's final resting clothing?"

I recoiled at his words, stepping back like he had produced a rotten tomato. It was as if he'd yanked the hurt right back to the surface where it burned. I didn't want to pick out the clothes she would be buried in. I wanted her burned and her ashes spread on the four winds like we had always talked about.

"Gram didn't want to be buried," I said. "Neither one of us wants to be put in a pine box in the ground."

He arched his brow. "You still need to provide the doctor with clothing, and then they will bring your grandmother to the church for viewing."

I stared at him, my brain unable to comprehend what he was saying. "I thought they'd bring Gram back here?" At least that was the custom I was used to in this town. Calling hours happened at the home of the deceased. As far back as I can remember, Gram and I would walk into town to pay our respects and then come back home until the burial. But in this case, I had promised Gram I would burn her remains after the calling hours and just have a headstone which held up the pretense of her being buried. Now, I'd never get the chance to do what she expected me to. The only bodies that were cremated were those that were riddled with disease. Burning a non-diseased body was frowned upon and thought of as blasphemous.

"You live all the way out here," he mumbled and stared at his feet. "I can take whatever you'd like back to the doctor so he can get your grandmother ready."

"Wrap her in cheese cloth and douse her in kerosene. She wants to ride the winds to wherever God chooses to plant her ashes. She never wanted to be stuck in a box in the cold, hard ground."

"You know that isn't right," he started.

My glare shut him up. "Have them bring Gram here. I'll take care of her."

"Red, they will not do that. Both the doctor and the priest insisted on having the services in town. Your grandmother was loved by every single person in this village, and they want to honor her."

"No, they don't. They don't want to honor her wishes. They want to do what they feel is proper. And so do you. Just go tell them to bring her body back here!" I yelled and pointed at the door.

Travis turned and headed down the hallway into uncharted territory. Before I could stop him, he pushed open the first door on the right. My bedroom. Where Lucas was hiding.

Travis froze in place with his mouth ajar and his good hand still flat on the wood. The creak of springs followed.

"Who the hell..." he started and then took a quick step backwards into the far wall, his eyes even wider than before. "What the..." His gaze landed on my quiver a few feet away.

Before I could move, he had an arrow in his hand and charged into my room, holding the thing like a dagger. I was on his heels in a flash, but not before he struck out at Lucas.

Lucas parried, knocking Travis's good arm away, but the sizzle of silver on skin and a burning stench filled the room.

"Travis, stop!"

He was nearly feral with his lips peeled back and a snarling growl coming from his throat. I would have thought the beast in the room was my best friend, not the man trying to defend himself against a silver arrow.

Travis got a few licks in before Lucas grabbed the shaft and snapped the wood, tossing the silver part aside, but the damage was already done. The black burns where the silver met his skin were proof enough that he wasn't human.

Travis launched at him, digging the broken wood into Lucas's shoulder. Lucas bellowed and pushed him backwards, putting enough distance between the two of them for me to step in.

I turned my back on Lucas and faced Travis with my hands out. "He tried to help Gram," I said. "He kept her safe until I found her."

"Bull! Why the hell is he still breathing? You took a damn oath when you were sworn into the Guard, Red. Your only purpose is to kill those things!" He pointed at Lucas.

"No. My oath is to protect the people of Dakota from harm. To take down our enemies, and to preserve our way of life. It isn't to kill just because someone is different."

"I bet he is the reason your grandmother is dead," he snarled.

"He's the reason she made it back to this town alive," I countered.

"Traitor. You're just as damned as he is," he snapped and closed his fist around the hilt of his silver blade.

"You're the tracker. Go see for yourself. You know how to read the land. If you see something other than what Gram told me, then by all means, I will do my job," I said. "But my job is not to kill an innocent man who tried to help a hurt woman just because of his heritage. He protected her from the more savage beasts that would have torn her to pieces." I took a breath and lowered my arms. "My job is not to commit an act of murder."

His gaze hardened and fixed on me.

The blade shot out of its sheath, and hot fire engulfed my forearm. I pulled my arm to my body and stared down at the tear in the fabric.

"Did you just cut me?" I yelled as blood discolored my sleeve.

Travis stared at my bloody arm and pressed his lips together. A mixture of disgust and fury filled his face, and he turned, marching right out of the house without another word.

"Damn it." I crossed into the bathroom and rolled back the sleeve. The cut was deep, but not deep enough to have hit any major veins. I pulled out the gauze from the cabinet along with some disinfectant. Before I attempted to patch myself up, Lucas took the bottle from my hand.

"It's the least I can do for you," he said quietly and poured some liquid over my cut.

I drew a sharp inhale through my teeth, but didn't make any other noise at the sting sizzling over my wound. He dabbed a cloth to dry the area and then wrapped my forearm in gauze until the damage was covered enough for the blood to be a light pink through the layers. It was a good war wound patch. I glanced up at him after he stowed the disinfectant and gauze away in the cabinet.

"What about yours?" I nodded to the singed tears in his shirt.

"I'm fine," he said and gave me a crooked smile.

"I think I'll be the judge of that," I said.

Lucas rolled his eyes and pulled his sleeve back. The black welt on his arm was nothing like the cut I had. It looked as if he had been branded instead of sliced, and there was no blood to clean up. I reached out and ran my fingers over the rough patch. He pulled his arm away with a grimace.

"What about your shoulder?" His shirt showed red patches where he had pulled out the wooden shaft Travis had stabbed him with.

Lucas pulled the shirt aside so I could see the perfect skin of his shoulder. I lifted my eyebrows.

"We heal pretty quickly when we are hurt with something other than silver."

"Oh." My gaze dropped to the blackened marks on his arm. "Gram has an aloe plant in her bedroom. It might help."

He cocked his head.

"It's for burns."

"I've never heard of it," he said.

I took him by the elbow and led him into Gram's room. On the top of the bookshelf sat a green plant with thick tapered stems sat. I stopped in front of it and pushed his sleeve away from the burns. Reaching up, I grabbed a stem and snapped it. Clear salve oozed from the broken limb, and I quickly drew it across the burn, covering it in the clear goop.

"That actually feels... pleasant," he said, his voice carrying a surprised lilt. He reached beyond me and broke another piece off, covering another welt. When he reached again, I stopped him.

"There is plenty in the piece you have. Just squeeze from the tip, and more aloe will come out."

He did as I instructed, and a smile formed. He looked like a child who had discovered a golden pebble in the brook. It was the kind of smile that made me forget my sorrow.

I glanced around the room, and reality settled in. Travis was mad enough to do something rash like mouth off to the Guard, and if he did that, my life was over. I wasn't going to be able to honor Gram's wishes as far as a funeral was concerned, but I could follow through on her last request. I could make sure nothing else happened to Lucas.

I glanced up at him, and an urgency gripped me. How long had it been since Travis stormed out? Damn it. I turned and left Gram's room. My heart squeezed against the thought of leaving everything I knew, but I had to if I was going to live to see another full moon.

I diverted my focus away from the crippling loss and onto the things that truly mattered to me. If I could just lasso the cottage and drag it with me, this would be so much easier. I hoisted the bow and quiver over my shoulders and grabbed the cookie jar off the counter in the kitchen. In my room, I tossed what little clothing I had into a knapsack along with the cookies.

I glanced at Lucas standing in the doorway, watching me with a perplexed ridge between his eyes.

"We have to leave. Now," I said and grabbed the last item that meant more to me than everything in my backpack combined. The comforter my grandmother quilted for me.

When I turned back to the door, Lucas stood holding the potted aloe plant and wearing a sheepish smile, along with his saddlebag slung over his shoulder.

It was my turn to roll my eyes. However, it was a useful plant to have around, so I didn't give him any grief. With my pack full and the blanket slung over my shoulder, I headed for the back door and an unknown future as a fugitive.

RED Chapter 10

I MADE IT THREE STEPS into the open when every last one of the guardsmen stepped to the fence with their bows drawn.

My heart leaped into my throat. I didn't dare turn to see if Lucas was behind me or not. If he had stepped out of the house, he was just as exposed as I was.

"Please don't shoot him. He tried to save Gram," I said, lifting my hands so they could see I wasn't armed.

"I don't care. He needs to be put down." Remy's growl came from my right.

I turned, taking a step back, so I was closer to Lucas, along with providing us a little protection from the arrows by using the wall to the bathroom as a buffer for our backs.

I knew these men. They were trained to kill werewolves without hesitation. The only reason Lucas was still standing was because I was blocking his front and the house blocked his back.

"Gram asked me to keep him safe," I argued. "It's what she wanted!"

"Move, Red." Remy stared down the shaft of his arrow, lining up the shot.

"Have I ever lied to you?" I glared at Remy and then glanced around at the rest of the Guard until my gaze landed on Travis standing next to Remy. "To any of you?"

"He has you under some sort of spell," Travis said. "One where you'll say anything to keep him alive."

I took a breath because I needed to weigh the words that parked at the tip of my tongue. Another life besides ours was in the balance, but if I didn't offer an objective viewpoint, one that would collaborate with what I was saying, there was no way Lucas would make it out of this corral alive. If I moved, Lucas was dead. If I didn't, I had no idea what the Guard would do, especially if they truly thought I was compromised.

"If you don't believe me, ask Doc Wilton. He was there. He heard Gram tell me to make sure nothing happened to Lucas."

Remy's arrow wavered, and he stood taller, measuring my words.

"The doc knew about him?" He pointed his chin towards us.

"Yes." I said. "Besides, when the hell have you ever seen a wolf put a spell on a human?"

"When a human has been bitten." Remy's eyes narrowed in Lucas's direction.

"I have not been bitten," I spat out the words like bitter medicine.

"Prove it," he replied.

The hair on the back of my neck bristled, and I balked at the head of the Guard. I had seen Remy do this before. When the guard came back from a hunt alone. I knew what command was coming, and I wasn't in a complying mood.

"How would you like me to prove my innocence?" The growl in my voice was evident. I was sure my glare matched the warning.

The corner of Remy's mouth twitched into a smirk. "Strip."

"I will do no such thing!"

Remy's arrow returned to the taut bow. "Last chance."

I pressed my lips together as heat flared in my face. The last thing I wanted to do was remove my clothing in front of the Guard, but that was the only way we would be able to walk out of here. I handed the blanket tossed over my shoulders to Lucas. Unfortunately, that uncovered the bow and arrows slung over my arm.

"Drop your bow slowly," Remy warned, his face as tense as his bow.

I clenched my hands into fists and closed my eyes, pushing the aggravation crawling over my skin away. I held my hands out to the sides with my fingers splayed as I lowered my shoulder. The bow and quiver slid down to my elbow, and I straightened my arm, letting it drop to the ground.

Remy's bow relaxed, and his hard gaze met mine. He knew I could have taken out a handful of guardsmen before any of them got a shot off, and I thought maybe that action alone would let us off the hook.

"Strip," Remy said when I didn't move.

Grinding my teeth together so I didn't tell him exactly what I thought of his order, I slid my boots off and then my socks, showing him the top and underside of each foot before I continued. My knickers came next, and I slowly turned so everyone could see that I had no bite marks on my lower legs. I hesitated at peeling off my drawers, debating on whether it was better to take off my top first. I was hoping Remy would back off, but I knew better.

The heat in my face spread into my neck and chest, and my fingers fumbled with the buttons on my shirt.

"Is this truly necessary?" Lucas said from behind me.

"Yes," I said at the same time as Remy and some of the other guardsmen. I glanced back at Lucas. "As mortifying as this is, it is necessary. So just shut up," I snapped.

I got to the last button and closed my eyes as I dropped the shirt to the ground, exposing my bare chest. I fought the instinct to cover my breasts and kept my hands busy by dropping my drawers. I stepped out of the fabric towards Remy, put my arms out perpendicular to the ground, and did the slow turn so he could see all my exposed skin.

"Lift your braid," Remy said.

I did as he asked. When I completed my revolution, I lowered my arms and waited for the next set of instructions.

"Get dressed," Remy growled.

I did, but I remained blocking Lucas just in case anyone took matters into their own hands and kill the wolf. Once I was fully clothed, I glanced at Remy. A chill rolled across my skin, manifesting my shock. Remy's bow and arrow weren't at the ready. In fact, they were by his side. Only a couple of arrows were pointing in our direction. I missed something significant.

When he stepped into the corral, Remy held his hand out. Travis placed silver shackles into his palm, and Remy approached me with an unreadable expression.

"You were always good at those potato sack races," he said and offered me the shackles. "Wrists and ankles."

"Really?" I snatched the silver from his hands and held it up between us. "You could have just handed me this." I shook it for good measure, again proving to the Guard that I hadn't been bitten.

One side of his lips curved, and he shrugged. "You betrayed the Guard. I think a long look at the goods was warranted." The hint of humor faded at the low growl that came from behind me. "Cuff him, Red. One on each of you."

"No," I said and shoved the shackles back at him. I saw what silver did to Lucas. I would not do that to him.

"Then he dies." Both Remy's tone and his hard stare told me he meant business.

"It's okay, Ruby," Lucas said from behind me. "It won't kill me."

I glanced over my shoulder. "That's not the point," I said and turned back to Remy. "He isn't a criminal."

"But he is a werewolf," he said. "And do I have to remind you of how many laws *you've* broken? Put those things on now."

I gritted my teeth. "I'll do it on one condition."

"You have no bartering power here, little girl," Remy said.

"Honor Gram's wishes." I stared him down.

"Do you see me trying to kill him at the moment?" He waved towards Lucas.

"I'm talking about Gram's final resting wishes. You, of all people, should know what she wanted."

He blinked and took a small step backwards. "We are burying her," he said, like that was the only choice.

I shook my head. "That's not what she wanted."

"She still talked about being turned to dust?" he asked.

"Yes. It's called cremation, and that's what she wanted," I said. "I'll shackle us together if you promise me you will make sure Gram's wishes are honored."

His lips pressed together, and he glared at me. "Put the cuffs on."

I stood taller. "Promise me," I said with the same feral intensity.

He stepped close enough for me to smell the faded scent of a cigar on his clothing, and he grabbed the shackles from my hand. After slapping one on my wrist, he snapped the other cuff around Lucas's.

Lucas hissed in pain as the silver burned his skin. Remy crouched down and clasped my right ankle and Lucas's left ankle together. At least the ankle shackle had the fabric of his pants as a buffer. When Remy stood, he grabbed the chain between our wrists and yanked us forward.

"Depending upon what the judge renders, you may be in the plot next to your grandmother," he snarled as he marched us out of the corral.

RED Chapter 11

THE MOON SHONE THROUGH the window of the cell I sat in. Lucas was still tethered to the silver cuff, and his harried breathing and occasional stifled groans echoed in the dark chamber of the jail. The binds holding him also prohibited him from shifting, and based on the sounds he made, it must have hurt something fierce.

Remy had left us here so he could attend my grandmother's funeral. The entire town would pay their respects, but I wasn't allowed to be there for either the service or the gathering that always followed a funeral here in Dakota. My heart ached. I wouldn't be able to say a proper goodbye.

I wondered if Remy would honor Gram's wishes. I wondered what the town would do to me, and I feared what they would do to Lucas.

I glanced through the bars at him and sighed. As if sensing my gaze, he looked up, his bright blue eyes glowing in the dim light of the moon.

"I'm sorry. I should have left last night," he said in a weak voice.

"This isn't your fault. I asked you to stay," I said. If I had let him go, neither of us would be rotting in jail waiting for our trial.

He closed his eyes and turned away from me. "I should have known better."

He leaned his head against the adjoining bars, close enough for me to touch him. His thick hair beckoned me, and I reached out, running my fingers through the lush strands. Lucas jerked away and glanced over his shoulder. A crease formed between his eyes.

"What are you doing?"

"I, um. I just. I don't know." I stumbled on the words, wondering the same thing. His hair was just so... touchable. I shook my head and clasped my hands in my lap. I had no idea what the hell had come over me.

He slowly turned back around with a sigh. "Why didn't you kill me?"

I remained quiet, and when he glanced back, I just raised my eyebrows.

"Your grandmother," he said with a disappointed lilt. He relaxed into the bars again and let out a soft laugh. "She wasn't the least bit afraid when I approached her. She got ornery, though, especially when she thought I was in league with the other wolf and toying with her." He sighed. "She was quite a lady," he added after a few minutes of silence.

"Yes, she was." I lay back on the thin mattress, distancing myself from the need to run my fingers through his thick hair, and ignored the lump that formed in my throat and the sting in my eyes.

"You're a lot like her, you know," Lucas said.

I wasn't anything like my grandmother. She had been so strong and so independent and so loved by the townspeople.

Lucas turned towards the hall just as a shuffle reached my ears.

"Why?" a gruff voice said from the shadows.

Travis stepped into the light, his eyes rimmed red and his cheeks flushed. He reeked of alcohol, even from this distance. Just the fact he was here after dark said volumes as to his state of mind.

"Why what?"

"Why did you allow that thing in your house? In your bedroom?"

"First of all, *that thing* has a name. And second, he saved Gram from dying alone."

"Then you say thank you, and go on your way. You don't invite the enemy into your bed!"

"Go home, Travis. You are drunk," I said. I wasn't going to have this conversation with him, especially with Lucas in the adjoining cell.

"I did not sleep with Ruby," Lucas said.

My heart twisted. I didn't need Lucas's help with this argument. It would only make things worse.

"I'm not talking to you, so shut up," Travis growled through the bars, his glare murderous.

Lucas raised his untethered hand in a sign of withdrawal from the conversation and stretched out on his cot as best he could, with his wrist and ankle shackled to the bed. "You know what? You're right. I should have left after she came home devastated by her grandmother's death. I should have left her alone to deal with her grief and just thought of myself."

"Shut up," Travis yelled.

"You're not helping," I said to Lucas.

"I see the way you look at him," Travis said. "He has you under some sort of spell."

I stared at Travis and took a deep breath. "How long have we known each other?"

"Too long," he muttered under his breath.

"Have I ever lied to you?"

He shuffled outside the bars and kicked the dirt. "No."

"Then why don't you believe me?"

"Because the girl I know wouldn't have let a werewolf live."

He had a point. Prior to the encounter with my grandmother, I would have put an arrow between the wolf's eyes without question, but it was my grandmother's plea that kept me from killing Lucas.

"What if they are not all bad? What if there are some good ones out there? Ones that don't kill humans?"

Travis stepped back into the shadows.

"What if all our assumptions are wrong?" The fact that I voiced the core issue eating at me since I stowed my bow and arrow away that night was a step in the right direction. But it was also one that made me question my job, my duty to kill without thought, and made me wonder who the actual monsters were.

"They killed your parents, Red. They kill. That's what they are created for. To kill." His words had enough venom to tingle across my skin.

"That's what we are trained to do, too." I couldn't stop the words from tumbling out. "We were trained to think they are evil creatures. That their only purpose is to kill humans." I got to my feet and crossed to where he stood. "We were taught to be just as much of a monster as they are."

Travis glared at me through the bars.

"We were taught wrong," I added softly.

"No. You weren't," Lucas said, and I spun towards his cage. "Not entirely. Most werewolves don't know how to control their primal urges. A wolf in the wild hunts for food. They don't discern between humans and animals in that facet. A human turned werewolf is a different story. The venom does something to their minds almost in the same way rabies turns a docile dog into a monster."

Travis's gaze narrowed.

"Very few can contain the need to destroy. At least that's what I've found in my limited travels," Lucas added.

"So why should I believe you are any different?" Travis asked with little hostility.

Lucas sat up. "If I was one of those things," he started with a voice filled with disdain, "Ruby and her grandmother would have died on the floor of that ravine."

I stared at him and then turned back to Travis. "I know you don't believe him, or me, for that matter. But you are the best tracker in this region. Go find the truth yourself. It's all out there, at the base of that ravine."

His lips pressed together, and he shook his head. "Do you understand what is going to happen to you? No one in this town will believe your story. No one," he whispered, and his eyes filled up with tears. He reached for me through the bars.

I stepped out of his range. "Then you better go find the truth for yourself."

He stared at me and gave a slow nod before turning and disappearing into the shadows. I walked to the cot and lay down again, staring at the ceiling as I processed the conversation.

"Are you okay?" Lucas said after a while.

"So, all converted werewolves are monsters?" I glanced over at him.

"Not all, but most. Especially if they have an alpha that thrives on chaos and murder. It goes without saying that the pack will follow suit."

I chewed on a hangnail and studied the ceiling. "And if they don't?"

"They are usually exiled or killed if they don't comply." Bitterness crept into his voice.

"That's what happened to my father. He still had all his faculties and did not wish to harm humans. If he had, I would have never been born."

"Are there others like your father?"

"I don't know," he said softly and met my gaze. "I don't even know if there are any like me out there. I'm the only one in these parts. At least that's the impression I've gotten, but who knows? Somewhere, there could be a community where humans and werewolves live in harmony, but I have yet to hear of such a thing."

"Farmer and dreamer," I said.

He gave me a soft smile and a shrug. His eyes still held deep pain, but at least he had gotten control over his audible reaction to the silver.

Then his smile faded. "What will happen to you?"

I huffed a laugh and returned my gaze to the ceiling. "If the town finds me guilty, I'll be put in front of an archery squad before nightfall."

Lucas's eyes slowly widened.

"Just because they loved my grandmother doesn't mean they will spare me from a traitor's fate."

"Traitor?" His voice cracked.

"Yes. Violating curfew comes with jail time. But allowing a werewolf to live..." I shrugged. "That comes with a death sentence."

"That is just as barbaric as pack mentality," he said.

The silence between us was stifling, but I didn't disagree with him.

"Have you ever..." He turned away before he finished asking, like he didn't want to know the answer.

"Have I ever been on the firing line?" I finished it for him, and when he wouldn't look at me, I sighed. "No. I wasn't old enough to be in the firing line. But I was old enough to bear witness. It haunts me to this day." I looked out at the moon. "I question just about everything, which has put me in hot water more than a time or two, but I've never questioned the purpose of the Guard. We are here to keep Dakota safe. For the record, I still agree with that purpose. It's a noble pursuit, but I don't always agree with the manner in which we follow through on it. We can act without mercy." I shrugged. "We can be barbaric."

He nodded slowly.

"But the wolves we have put down operate under the same umbrella. Without mercy. Without regard to age. Without exception. So mercy has never been warranted." I closed my eyes. "Until you wandered into that ravine, mercy wasn't a thing I ever entertained before. I never thought I could actually carry on a conversation with a wolf, never mind find myself..." I bit my tongue. There was no use telling him I was attracted to him in a way I had never experienced.

He sat up and turned towards me. When he reached through the bars and took my hand in his, my heart started a skipping beat that encompassed my entire chest. His touch was gentle and his fingers smooth, much like his chest had felt under my hand. The skin-to-skin contact dulled my mind and turned my body into a raging inferno of heat. I pulled from his grip, but a small smile toyed on his lips and he glanced at the bars separating us.

He opened his mouth and then closed it. "Please finish what you were going to say," he finally said, as his gaze locked on mine.

"Locked in a cell because of a wolf," I said, avoiding the truth biting every inch of my skin.

His eyes narrowed and then he lay down on the mattress and closed his eyes, dousing the blue glow lighting the small space. An uncomfortable silence blanketed the cells, and all I could think about was how disappointed my grandmother would have been.

RED Chapter 12

A RUCKUS IN THE hallway pulled me out of the doze I had fallen into. I sat up to see the constable shoving a very intoxicated version of Remy into the adjoining cell. Belligerent was an understatement as the head of the Guard spewed slurred vulgarities.

"What happened?" I asked as Remy fell onto the mattress and immediately began snoring.

Constable Murphy looked at me and turned to leave.

"What did Remy do?" I asked again before he disappeared.

"He desecrated a grave," the constable said over his shoulder. "And had a bonfire in his backyard."

Remy's fingers were covered in dirt, and soot streaked his cheeks. He must have followed through on Gram's wishes despite the consequences. I could no longer contain the grief bubbling just below the surface. My throat tightened, and I stretched out on the bed, letting tears escape the corners of my eyes.

Lucas's fingers clasped mine. His tired blue eyes shined in the dim light as he gave my hand a squeeze.

Tears flowed, and my breath hitched. In the morning light, the reality of our situation settled into every fiber of my body, and with it came an ungodly fear.

I didn't want to die, and I certainly didn't want Lucas to be killed. I wanted to explore whatever had sparked between us, but it was a useless dream. A luxury we would have to forgo because I was fool enough to have asked him to stay.

"I'm sorry," Lucas whispered.

I wiped my face with my free hand and glanced at him through the bars. I couldn't find the words to tell him this was my fault, that the death he waited for with such grace was my doing. I should have killed him on the spot. It would have been more humane. Instead, I shook my head and stared back at the ceiling through blurred vision.

The cell brightened as the morning progressed, and my dread manifested in uncontrollable bouts of shivers despite the warmth bathing the cell. It wouldn't be long before we were paraded through the town to stand in front of the court. Deep in my bones, I knew it was only for show. The sentence wouldn't alter from those before me. A selfish part of me hoped I would face the firing line first so I wouldn't have to witness Lucas's death, but I knew better. They would want me to reflect on my mistakes before they ended my life. They wanted me to taste the bitterness of my choices.

I closed my eyes and shuddered. Mercy wasn't in Dakota's vocabulary where werewolves were concerned. And I couldn't blame them. I carried that exact mindset the day I went out with Remy and Travis. But that mindset changed during the night in Lucas's house with Gram.

Silence blanketed the cells, and then Remy's scruffy voice filled the space.

"Red?"

I looked over at him, and his bloodshot gaze met mine.

"Why didn't you tell me?" he whispered.

"Tell you what?"

He reached into his pocket and dropped a folded piece of paper through the bars. I crossed and picked it up, unfolding it in the light. Gram's neat handwriting scrawled across the paper. I stared at the words and stepped backwards, dropping the note, like distancing myself would change what Gram had told Remy.

I stared at the paper as it fluttered to the floor and then locked my gaze with Remy.

He chuckled. "I gather from your reaction you didn't know, either."

My high-pitched laugh confirmed his assessment.

"It actually explains why you're the best shot I've ever seen. Even so, finding out you're my blood just as you're facing the firing line?" He rubbed his face and glanced away. "Your grandmother had a sick sense of humor."

He swung his legs over the side of the cot and groaned. I turned to Lucas, and his blue eyes sent a shiver through me, adding to the clanging of my heart and the pounding in my temples. My mouth went dry.

Before I had a chance to truly digest the confession laid out in the note, the constable came down the stairs with a dozen guards, none of which I had ever partnered with on any of our wolf runs.

Four of them waited at my door while the constable unlocked the cell, and the other eight waited outside Lucas's cell with their silver daggers drawn. The hatred in their expressions tightened the muscles of my throat.

"Don't hurt him," I said with as much force in my voice as I could muster.

The only one that acknowledged my order was Seth, one of the older guards, but the look he gave me didn't settle my nerves. His smile promised pain.

Lucas got to his feet and braced himself, taking the links of the chain between the silver wristband and the bars. The muscles in his jaw tightened and the stench of burning flesh wafted through the cell.

"No!" I shouted.

Four guards grabbed hold of my arms, dragging me out of the cell. Lucas's door was thrown wide, and the guards filtered in.

"Remy, do something!" I screamed, then the door at the bottom of the stairs cut off my view of the attack on Lucas.

I stopped fighting my captors and let them lead me to the town square. I scanned the crowd. The entire town came out for this trial. Outside of Remy and the guards taking justice into their own hands in Lucas's cell, there was only one person missing. I scanned again to make sure.

Travis wasn't there.

Tears burned my eyes, but I blinked them back. I refused to cry in front of this ungrateful town. Anger finally burned through all the emotions accosting me. My skin heated from it, but I straightened my spine in defiance.

Judge Murphy cleared his throat and looked at the paper in front of him before looking up at me like he had swallowed a bug. Disgust formed in the lines around his mouth, and I glared at him.

"Ruby Locklear, you have been found guilty of high treason." He nodded at the guards holding me.

This wasn't like any of the other court proceedings I had witnessed. "I don't get to say anything in my defense?" I yelled out over the crowd.

"Did you allow that wolf to live?" he snarled at me.

"Yes, but he..."

"Silence!" He stood and pointed towards the post in the center of the courtyard.

"I will not be silent. If trying to save my grandmother is considered a crime, then we are guilty." I scanned the crowd as the guards dragged me to one of two posts and strapped my arms around the back. "The wolf saved her. Killing him would have been murder for the sake of bloodlust, just like the monsters out there!" I nodded towards the northern woods.

A murmur blanketed the bystanders, and some shifted their weight, glancing at their neighbors before looking at the ground.

"Gram said she fell, and that wolf who is being brutalized right now kept her warm and protected her from another wolf attack!"

Judge Murphy glanced at the guards. "Silence her," he ordered.

One turned and shoved a handkerchief into my mouth, muffling my argument. I struggled against the binds, and my gaze jumped from face to face until it landed on Doc Wilton. The moment we made eye contact, he looked away.

I needed him to speak up.

A commotion from the jail erupted. The crowd parted as the guards dragged a beaten and bruised Lucas to the post next to me. He didn't even get the pretense of a trial. They just strung his half-conscious body up by his wrists. He sagged from the binds, and his head lolled to the side.

I shook my head, trying to spit out the fabric in my mouth.

The Guard took their places in the firing line.

Finally, I coughed out the rag. "Please, Doc. Please tell them he didn't hurt Gram!" I cried.

Silence settled as all eyes turned toward the town doctor.

He shifted his weight and stared at the ground before he finally looked up and nodded. "The wolf displayed kindness and civility, and Gram Locklear requested my silence under doctor-patient confidentiality. She confirmed what Red said earlier. He provided her warmth, shelter, and protection when he could have easily ripped her to shreds."

"See?" I said.

"The law states you both must die." Judge Murphy held up the town law book.

The sound of hoofs hitting dirt pulled our attention away, and Travis rode in on Midnight, stopping the horse between us and the firing line. Both my horse and Travis were out of breath.

"Move, boy," Judge Murphy said.

"I have some information that may sway judgment," Travis said from his perch on the horse. He turned to the Guard lined up with their silver arrows. "He isn't normal." He nodded towards Lucas. "He may be a werewolf, but I'll be goddamned if Red wasn't telling the truth. He has a healthy farm filled with healthy living animals. He has a garden. And it looks like the only thing stored in his icebox is venison."

"He is a wolf," the judge emphasized.

Travis shrugged. "I haven't seen him turn. Have you?"

"But his eyes," Seth said from the firing line beyond Travis.

"You all know what kind of tracking skills I have," Travis said and glanced at me. "Red reminded me of that last night, so I went at first light and tracked down what happened. There was no sign of foul play in the orchard. Gram fell. But the patterns along with the dead wolf at the base of the hill confirm Red's version of the story. So does the farm and the conversation I had with Doc Wilton after Gram's funeral yesterday. Hell, the wolf is more of a gentleman than any of us." He glanced at the Guard. "Not one of us averted our eyes when she stripped down to show she hadn't been bitten. None of us looked away. But the wolf didn't look at her."

"Maybe he just isn't interested," Seth said with his bow at the ready, likely waiting for Travis to move Midnight out of his line of sight.

Travis sucked air in through his lips. "He's interested. I've seen the way he looks at her when she isn't looking, and believe me, it's a look that can't be mistaken. But when she undressed, he did not look. He stared out at his mare, at the sky, at us. But not at her." His cheeks reddened. "And be honest. None of us were inspecting her for wolf bites."

Faces reddened enough to rival my hair. Heat filled my own cheeks, and I glanced at Lucas. His gaze met mine.

"I couldn't stop staring at her until I noticed his behavior, and then all I felt was shame. Shame because I knew what I was doing wasn't for the good of this town. It was purely selfish. But this...this..." Travis looked back at Lucas. "This beast showed more restraint than any of us."

"Wolves don't show restraint no matter what form they take," I said. "And they certainly don't raise chickens, or cattle, or have a mare that would walk through fire for him."

"Are you a werewolf?" the judge asked Lucas.

"If you're asking if I'm one of those heinous beasts out there attacking the innocent? No. But if you're asking if I shift into wolf form when the sun sets? The answer to that is yes."

"You don't shift at will?"

My head turned at Remy's gruff voice. He stood in front of the judge's chair, waiting for his own sentence to be rendered.

"No. My change is subjected to the rise and setting of the sun."

"Lucas is different," I stressed. "He had so many opportunities to kill both Gram and me, but he didn't. That has to mean something?"

"He is a wolf. There are laws."

"Yes, there are laws, but isn't there also mercy? Are we to persecute him just because he was born into this life? It was not a choice for him, just like it wasn't a choice for me to have red hair. It was part of my heritage. Are we that cruel and heinous? Are we more like the pack we hunt, or more like the humans we serve to protect?"

My words didn't appear to sway the mob, so I turned my appeal to my grandfather and the Guard.

"I have had your back all these years." I moved my gaze to each of them. "I still do. And out of everyone in this town, you know me best. You know the hell I endured. The pain I suppressed and tapped every time I went on a hunt. You know mercy isn't a part of my makeup."

I turned my gaze to Remy. "The oath we took to protect Dakota is to protect life. This, what you are doing now, this is taking life for no other reason than fear of the unknown. If you do this, you will be no better than the cold-blooded killers we hunt."

Travis turned toward Lucas. "Have you ever killed a human?"

"No." Lucas's answer blanketed the crowd.

Travis glanced at the judge and shrugged his good arm.

Before the judge could speak, I asked Lucas, "Have you ever killed a werewolf?"

"Yes. I slaughtered the pack that killed my parents, and I have been on my own ever since."

A hush fell on the square.

"I've got a bounty on my head, just like Ruby does."

Both Travis's and Remy's gazes snapped towards Lucas.

"Red has a bounty on her?" they asked in unison.

I glanced at Lucas. He just gave them a reason to kill him, but apparently that hadn't crossed his mind before he blew the one chance we had of getting out of here alive.

"So, you figured what? You'd snatch Red and get back into the good graces of the pack?" Judge Murphy asked. "Pull the wool over her eyes and get her thinking you are not like the rest of those beasts out there?"

Lucas blinked and shook his head. "No. I didn't even know who she was until she led me and my horse into her grandmother's corral." He shivered. "Those wolves draped over her fence posts were kind of a dead giveaway." A twitch of a smile formed on his lips. "Pun intended."

Remy chuckled, and so did Travis. Travis's gaze met mine from on top of my horse. He offered me his best "I tried" smile, and I acknowledged it with a nod.

"My mother was human. I want nothing to do with a pack that has its sights on killing people," Lucas added. "And from what I've been able to gather, the pack that's here now wants to wipe out this settlement."

"How would you know that?" I asked.

Lucas huffed. "The wolf who was going to kill your grandmother gave me an ultimatum. Join the pack and slaughter the citizens of Dakota, or die with them. Since you are still breathing, you can figure out the choice I made." He glanced out at the crowd. "When I chased him away, he said I better enjoy the next few days because on the night of the full moon, rivers of blood will flow through this town."

A panicked murmur started amongst the townspeople and they huddled closer together. Tonight was the full moon.

"So, you go ahead. You kill your only shot at taking out this pack," he added as the whispers rose. "Without Ruby, you do not have a prayer."

"And without Lucas, you do not have me," I said, leveraging the gauntlet Lucas so brilliantly wielded.

The entire town fell silent for five beats of my heart.

"How many of them are there?" Remy asked.

Lucas looked past me at my newly revealed grandfather. "I don't know. So far, I've caught somewhere between five and six dozen unique scent signatures, but I can't be sure. Those wolf carcasses around her corral messed up my sense of smell, and because of the silver cuffs, I wasn't able to shift last night. When I'm in wolf form, everything is much... keener."

"You are saying the pack is sixty wolves at minimum?" Remy asked in a gob-smacked tone I had never heard from him.

"I think it's more in the realm of seventy."

The crowd erupted, and I smelled fear in the air.

How in the hell could seventy werewolves hide from our hunting jaunts? The blood in my veins turned cold. Either these were cunning creatures or Lucas was feeding a load of bull to the crowd. Either way, it was working.

I met Remy's gaze, and he just shook his head slowly, still trying to digest the last couple of minutes. The Guard was only composed of twenty members between the age of ten and seventy. Half of them couldn't hit a still wolf with a brick at two paces, never mind multiple wolves on the attack. We'd even had our losses with groups of three trolling the woods.

Remy turned to the judge. "We need her." His statement was absolute.

The judge's lips compressed together until they were nonexistent. The bloom in his red cheeks burned brighter, and his nostrils flared. His gaze jumped from Remy to mine.

"You have just earned yourself a stay of execution while we discuss this matter. Put them back in a holding cell," he ordered.

I looked up at Travis and mouthed the words 'thank you' as guards unclasped me from the post and led me away.

RED Chapter 13

LUCAS LAY ON HIS side on the cot, facing me as I paced in the same cell. Heated murmurs of the townspeople drifted into the window, and I strained to hear what their arguments were or who was taking each side.

"Ruby?" Lucas's soft voice broke through my concentration.

His eyes had dulled considerably from this morning.

I stopped pacing as my heart went into overdrive. "Are you okay?" I asked, which brought forth a tight smile.

Lucas pushed himself up on the cot with a wince and climbed to his feet. "You shouldn't have laid your life on the line for me."

"Are there really that many wolves out there?" I asked.

Lucas gave me a slow nod as he steadied himself on his feet.

"And are you one of them?" I asked, because I couldn't quite silence the nagging distrust inside me. Despite all he had done, and despite the underlying attraction vibrating through every cell, I still couldn't quite trust him with my whole heart.

He was still a werewolf.

He shook his head. "No." He bit his lip and glanced out the window. He crossed the space between us, wincing with every other step until he loomed over me.

I took in his wounds. Besides the ugly black rings around his wrists, his shirt and pants had been slashed in several places. He had over a dozen silver burns based on the holes in his clothes.

"Did they..." I waved at him and gulped. "I can see they cut you, but did they... did they stab you?" The words squeaked out, and the discomfort under my skin increased at the thought of a blade puncturing his skin.

"It doesn't matter."

My gaze jumped up to his. It did matter. It mattered a great deal, and I pressed my lips against letting those words tumble out.

"I can feel the pull of the alpha," he whispered. His hands clenched and unclenched and his jaw tightened. "He wants this town painted with the blood of the dead. Everyone except for the archer with the fiery hair."

I stepped away. "Why didn't you tell me this?"

"I'm telling you now." His eyes flared bright in the tight space. "I went out that night because I heard the call. The alpha is calling every werewolf in the region to join him in this massacre." He glanced up at the ceiling and shook his head. "Your grandmother... I don't know how, but she was able to break the spell that bastard had over me."

My heart jumped in my chest, and I stepped back into the wall of bars on the other side of the cell, distancing myself from him.

Lucas locked his gaze on me. "I'd like to believe I wouldn't have hurt her if that other wolf wasn't already tormenting her," he said, and his gaze dropped. "What I'm trying to tell you is you should have let them kill me, because the alpha..." He stepped closer. "I don't know if I can resist his command."

His hands came up and cupped my chin. Just his touch, in such an intimate manner, doused my skin with heat so strong I nearly melted into him. His thumb trailed over my bottom lip, and he stared at it before his hungry gaze found mine again.

When he leaned forward and pressed his warm lips against mine, my mind spun with the sweetness of his kiss. When his tongue traced my lips, I opened my mouth, letting our tongues intertwine in a dance so slow and seductive that I forgot we were in a jail cell.

His hands slid lower, molding over my breasts with such a light touch, I moaned into his mouth. God help me. Molten lava formed low in my belly, and I gasped at the heat enveloping me. His lips moved to my cheek, to my neck, and I closed my eyes at the silkiness of his touch.

"Lucas." His name escaped in a sultry whisper that felt like home on my tongue.

"You taste like honey," he whispered against my neck. His lips followed the line from my shoulder to my ear. He took my earlobe between his teeth, applying pressure.

I squealed at the sensation.

Lucas gasped and stepped away abruptly, his eyes wide and his breathing ragged.

Hurt flared in the center of my chest at his horrified look, and I wrapped my arms around my torso to shield myself.

"I almost bit you." He ran his hand through his hair and took another step back. "I don't know which is worse, having that alpha bastard in my head or having you in my heart."

I swallowed and wished I could flee from this cell. I wished I hadn't felt his hands on my body or his lips on mine because now... now a fresh fear tingled in my bones. If anything happened to Lucas, I was afraid I'd never feel that all-consuming spark again.

The door creaked above, and six guardsmen came down before either of us could speak. Seth stood outside the cell with an unreadable expression. None of them hinted at the verdict.

"The court is ready for you," Seth said and swung the door open.

I crossed and noted neither guard who flanked me took hold of me. But the other guards grabbed Lucas's arms as they led us out of the cell. My heart plummeted. Whether or not these men realized it, their actions clued me in to the judgment.

Lucas would not be spared, regardless of my ultimatum. I wouldn't defend a town that insisted on murdering an innocent man. Donning my inner rebel, I prepared myself for a different battle.

I positioned myself as close to Lucas as possible without touching him to show the town where my loyalties stood. Remy stepped forward in front of the judge. I glanced at his stoic face and then at the guardsmen, who filled in the space around him.

"Red, we need you," he said. "We've been your family since your parents died. And as much as I resented your grandmother for insisting I bring you into the fold, I can't say I ever regretted you fighting alongside us. I think it was your grandmother's way of letting me share a part of your life without giving up her ghosts."

A lump formed in my throat at the mention of my grandmother, and I blinked the stinging mist from my eyes.

"Unfortunately, there are laws we must abide," he added, and his gaze traveled to Lucas. "We cannot..." He clenched his fists, staring at the ground.

The judge cleared his throat.

"We cannot just let you go," Remy said through clenched teeth. "But we also cannot be the ones to murder you, as Red put it earlier." He waved towards me and pressed his lips together. The disdain etched into his face was usually reserved for my antics, but this time, I got the impression he didn't agree with the sentence about to be delivered.

"If he is wanted by the werewolves, we will leave him to their justice." He nodded towards the poles, and the guard dragged him to stand between the two posts.

They clasped one wrist in a silver cuff that hung from one post and then took off the shackles before securing his other wrist. The positioning gave him minimal leeway.

"He's as good as dead shackled like that," I said, appalled.

"He has a chance. If he survives the night, we will let him go," Remy said.

"What if none of us survive?" I asked.

"Then he dies of starvation, instead."

Lucas lifted his nose like he was trying to catch a scent. He glanced over his shoulder at me, his eyes full of regret, but it was nothing compared to the hurt racking my insides. I'd asked him to stay. He would have left if I hadn't uttered that fateful plea.

"No." I turned back towards Remy.

"We are going to hide the entire town in the church, and the Guard will set up a perimeter, so nothing gets through."

"I told you, if Lucas isn't spared, I'm not fighting."

Remy's face reddened. "We aren't putting a dozen arrows into his chest," he growled. "He is being spared from our justice."

I swallowed and dropped my gaze to the ground, understanding the mentality of the town. They saw this as mercy, and I knew this was the best they were going to offer, but I didn't have to like it. I finally gave a nod.

"Then my perimeter is between Lucas and the woods." I could stop whatever came out of those woods as long as I was armed with enough arrows.

"We wanted you guarding the doors to the church," the judge said from behind Remy.

I glanced over my shoulder at the church, which stood a little farther than fifty yards from where Lucas was strung up. "If I'm set up at the steps of the church, Lucas will block my line of sight. So will these damn posts. If you want to doom the entire town, be my guest." If they could play games, so could I.

"Red," Travis whispered, holding Midnight's reins. "Be reasonable."

I let out a laugh. "Reasonable? You want me to be reasonable? You're the one that put me in this position," I snapped, the anger bursting through with a vengeance. "You are asking me to walk away from the man who tried to save my grandmother. Does that sound reasonable to you?"

I glared at the crowd and then met Remy's gaze. "As long as Lucas is here within the town limits, we have as much of an obligation to protect him as we have to protect every man, woman, and child that lives here. My perimeter is right here." I walked ten paces in front of Lucas and dug my heel into the ground, creating an arc in the dirt. I stepped to the center of my line and glanced out at the woods again. I had enough space between the trees and where I would be crouched to take on whatever those woods dished out.

"You need to listen to them," Lucas said, pulling my defiant gaze away from the woods. "If you are this close to the woods..." He shook his head.

My lips turned up at the corners. Lucas may have heard the rumors about me, but he really only had a cursory look at what I could do with a bow and arrow. He needed to know why I was on a werewolf's most wanted list, and I was going to give him a front-row seat to the show.

Remy's gaze traveled over the vantage point I had chosen, and then he glanced back at the church. His bottom lip sucked in between his teeth as he silently considered my plan.

"Red is right. That is the best spot to defend the church," he said to the judge. "Forcing her to defend from right in front of the church will put us at a disadvantage. There are too many blind spots from the steps, even without the werewolf chained to the posts."

"How many arrows do we have?" I asked.

"We only have forty silver-tipped arrows left."

Goosebumps broke out over my arms and I spun, staring at Remy. If Lucas's numbers were right, and we all hit our marks, that still left at minimum twenty wolves that we would have to kill with our daggers. Even one-on-one, that was a stretch, but four-on-one, that was suicide.

My heart thundered in my chest, and my gaze jumped to Lucas and the shackles holding him in place. We had silver, but it wasn't in the right form to kill a werewolf.

"Do we have time to melt down the remaining silver and coat the regular arrows?" I asked as I looked at the sky.

Remy turned towards the judge. "We need more arrows in order to win this battle. No one has made a silver run in the last few weeks, and right now, the only silver left is the shackles we took off the prisoner and the ones holding him to the pole. We need it, otherwise..."

"We cannot let the werewolf go," the judge said.

"Then lock him up in the jail, and we can figure this out tomorrow," Remy said. "Because without that silver... There. Will. Be. No. Tomorrow."

I had heard Remy aggravated and forceful, but it did not compare to the doom he painted with those five words.

When the judge didn't respond, he added, "And we are not using any of the arrows we currently have on him. We need double what we have, and I'm not sacrificing this entire town on this single wolf, especially since I don't agree with the verdict. Lock him up."

Another shock skipped through my heart, almost jerking me in place. I didn't think I'd ever hear Remy Steele stand up for a werewolf, and from the open-mouthed expression of most of the crowd, I thought they were all in the same place I was. We were witnessing a miracle.

I glanced out at the woods. I just hoped it wasn't the only miracle today.

RED Chapter 14

I STOOD WITH JOHN, the blacksmith, as he melted down the chains. He hunched over the extreme heat, painstakingly turning the bowl of silver until it was liquid. I handed him each arrow, and he dunked the tip. We had enough to coat twenty more arrows, which left a bunch of ifs.

John wasn't much of a talker, so he wandered around the shop, doing what I imagine he usually did on a normal day. When he thought the arrows were dry enough, he put them in my quiver.

"You really think you can save this town?" he asked.

I glanced at our meager bounty and sighed. "You might want to start praying now," I said and slung the quiver over my shoulder.

"Are you any good with a sword?" he asked after I turned to leave.

I had some instruction, but I wasn't as good as Travis. "Is it made of silver?" If it wasn't, it wouldn't help a lick.

"The finest. It's the strongest steel coated with pure Alberta silver." He reached behind the counter and pulled out a long thin sheath with a thick black handle sticking out. He offered it to me. "For when you run out of arrows."

"Thank you, John," I said and took the sword, pulling the blade out far enough to inspect the fine craftsmanship. The blade had intricate designs carved into the silver. "It is beautiful." I tested the blade on the pad of my thumb. "And sharp," I said, offering him a smile of appreciation.

He gave me a nod. "Stay safe, Red."

"Do you have any more silver swords?"

He nodded and stepped towards the back.

"You might need some of those in the church, just in case," I said, stopping him.

He turned and gave me a haunted nod.

"Thank you for this." I held up the sword and left without another word. I had to go give Remy the bad news.

I crossed to the green where Remy was discussing strategy with the other guards and dropped my full quiver at his feet next to the rest of the arrows.

"How many?" he asked.

"Twenty."

A slow whistle came from between his teeth, and he closed his eyes. His shoulders dropped, and my heart plummeted with them. Seeing defeat in Remy's demeanor was more unsettling than the knowledge we didn't have nearly enough firepower.

Remy raked his hand over his face. "We don't even know what direction they'll be coming from."

I chewed my bottom lip and stepped toward where they had Lucas locked up.

"Where do you think you're going?" he asked.

"I'm going to find out if we can narrow that down," I said over my shoulder and headed towards the jail. It was worth a shot, especially since he was the one who gave us a heads-up and the head count of the pack.

I glanced at Travis as I crossed to the door separating the constable's workspace with the jail. He wanted to be out with the Guard, even with his arm immobile, but he would probably be the first to be killed out in the open, with little to defend himself beyond a broadsword his father gave him. He couldn't shoot an arrow with one arm. His scowl broadcasted just how unhappy he was with his current assignment—babysitting the werewolf.

I descended the short stairwell and stepped into the dank holding cell, crossing to the bars. Lucas lay with his back to the door. He didn't budge when I walked in.

"Lucas?" I asked from outside his cell.

He turned slowly, his jaw tightened, and he sat up. He tried to hide the wince, but it didn't fool me. He pushed up from the cot, crossed slowly to where I stood, and went to wrap his hand around the bar, but pulled it away before he touched the iron.

I reached through the bars and grabbed his hand so I could look at it.

"Don't," he said, his voice scratchy.

I peeled his fingers open and stared at the black marks burned into his skin. Without thinking, I brought his palm to my lips and gently kissed the scar.

"Ruby," he whispered. His voice held a deep longing, one that echoed in my heart. His gaze lingered on my lips before it rose to mine. "Stay with me."

I raised my eyebrows. "We can talk about that tomorrow."

He pulled his hand away. "You cannot fathom what is coming," he snarled and closed his eyes, leaning his head against the bars. "Five of you cannot possibly fight that many werewolves on your own."

"We have no choice. You said they were coming to kill all of us. What would you have us do?"

His head snapped up and his eyes flared. "Run," he said, with no hesitation. "Hide."

"You, of all people, can't possibly think there is anywhere to hide from those beasts?"

His face scrunched up in pain as he gripped the bars. "You could hide at your grandmother's house. The stench of death makes all animals avoid your property."

"So they wouldn't come in from that direction?"

Lucas laughed. "No. They will steer clear of that direction."

"Where will they come from?" I asked softly.

"Every other direction, like a tidal wave. I can feel their presence. I can feel their malice in the air." He shivered.

"So the east will be clear, but they will come from the north, south, and west?"

He nodded.

"Where is the greatest concentration?"

Lucas shrugged. "I don't know."

I hung my head and took a deep breath, letting it out slowly before I looked back at him. "I will survive this," I said with a voice much stronger than I felt. I wasn't sure if it was for his benefit or mine.

He reached out and ran his hands into my hair, pulling me as close as the bars would allow. His bright blue eyes blazed. He ran his thumb across my cheekbone. "That is what I am terrified of."

I pressed my cheek into his palm, trying to read what was behind those beautiful eyes. "Why?"

"Because I can still feel the alpha trying to weasel his way into my head," he said. "He knows."

"He knows what?"

Lucas's fingers moved to my lips, tracing them tenderly before meeting my gaze. "He doesn't have control over me anymore."

"What changed?"

The corners of his lips tilted into a smile. "I kissed you."

Heat filled my cheeks, and I glanced over his shoulder out the window at the far side of the cell. The memory lingered, and the heat from my cheeks spread through me.

"I wish I could kiss you now," he whispered.

I moved my gaze back to his. I wanted that, too. I wanted more than a kiss. I wanted a lifetime of his kisses. The realization made every muscle in my body ache for him. I stepped away because I needed that type of want in my soul. I needed something to fight for, something to survive for. Lucas was enough motivation to make me into the warrior I needed to be.

I licked my lips and stared into his eyes. "Tomorrow you can kiss me all you want."

Lucas smiled and cocked his head. "Promise?"

"Promise." I walked out of the holding area with my stomach down by my feet.

I wasn't sure I'd be able to keep my word, but I was going to fight like hell to get back to Lucas. I just didn't know if it would be in one piece or not.

RED Chapter 15

MRS. WILTON BROUGHT EACH of us a chicken sandwich and mumbled something about praying for all of us. It was appropriate that the town pray. We were going to need all the help we could get, and if God landed on our side, we might actually survive.

Remy stared at the ground as he slowly ate. As if sensing my gaze, he glanced up at me with bright green eyes that mirrored my own. Remy's hard features softened for a moment, and he took his last bite. He stood and crossed the distance.

"We never got to finish the conversation this morning." Remy took the seat next to me and remained quiet for a few minutes as he scanned the town green and the remaining three guards.

The five of us were the best shots in the unit. The rest of the Guard was stationed inside the church in case we failed. Except for Travis. He was told to secure the jail and make sure Lucas didn't get out.

"The fact you are my granddaughter doesn't change how things in the Guard work. I'm still your superior. You still have to follow orders," he said and leveled a hard stare at me.

I nodded. "I wish I had one of Gram's cookies," I said softly, changing the subject. I didn't want to be berated by Remy right now. I needed to focus on the things closest to my heart.

He let out a chuckle. "Me too."

"Did you love her?" I blurted. I didn't know why it mattered, but it did.

Remy studied the ground and then looked away. "Yes. But it wasn't enough. I didn't want to stay here locked in this town. I wanted adventure, and your grandmother was happy here." He shook his head and shuffled a foot in the dirt. "I left without saying goodbye. I was foolish enough to think that she'd wait for me, even though every single man in the area would have given away everything they owned just to be with that woman. She was a lot like you."

"Oh," I mumbled, not knowing what to do with the compliment.

"It took me a little over a year to figure out everything I cared about was back in Dakota. I went to see her bearing gifts, hoping she would forgive me." He sighed. "She was already married and had a son." He stood. "I never forgave her for moving on." He glanced at me. "And I'm angry that she never told me

I had a family." Remy stuffed his hands into his pockets and rocked on his heels. "I'm not sure I would have allowed you to join the Guard had I known, even though you are the best shot I have ever seen in all my travels. That would have been a damn shame, too."

"If you were so angry, why did you honor her wishes?" I asked before I lost my nerve.

He smiled a sad smile. "I did that for you. Doc Wilton gave me the letter, and after I read it, I destroyed everything within reach in my cabin. But I came to terms with the truth. And despite being a hard ass with you in particular, I've come to care about what happens to you, and it wasn't because you are my most skilled archer. It was deeper than that." He glanced out at the woods. "That was the hardest truth to face. I thought you were going to be executed today. I wanted you to have a little peace before you met your maker."

A lump formed in my throat, and I looked at the sky before he saw the tears gathering in my eyes. "We might want to get to our posts."

Remy followed my gaze and nodded. His hand landed on my shoulder, and he gave it a squeeze. "Shoot true."

I nodded, and we held each other's gazes for a longer beat. He gave my shoulder one last squeeze and crossed to the pile of arrows and quivers. He split the sixty silver-tipped arrows evenly and handed each of us our quivers. Then he split the remaining arrows, which wouldn't kill the beasts, but it might slow them down so we could use our silver-coated knives. He passed out smaller weapons to each of us.

"I am good," I said when he went to hand a small stash of silver daggers to me. "I have a sword that the blacksmith gave me."

"At least take a couple and stash them in your boots. You are as accurate at throwing as you are with your arrow," he growled at me.

I took them, but did not stash them in my boots. Instead, I took my arrows and knives and lined them up in the dirt in a semicircle around me with the silver-tipped ones closest and the wooden arrows on the outside. I placed the strap to the sword holder over my head and adjusted it so the blade lay horizontally from my shoulder to my hip, where it wouldn't interfere with my bow and arrow. I reached over with my right hand to make sure I could pull it free easily when the time came.

I glanced back at the church as the townspeople gathered with their casseroles and their plates like it was a town picnic instead of a vigil to see if we survived the night or not. I shook my head in disgust and caught Remy's same expression I was sure mine held as he looked on. I turned to the woods, focusing on the growing shadows. The sound of those gathered in the church silenced as the doors closed, capturing everyone within the steepled building.

Silence. I closed my eyes and focused on centering all my energy into one thing. The kill. The thrill of the hunt took over my form, rippling a chill from the tips of my fingers all the way to my core. I opened my eyes and focused on the fading light. Shadows elongated, and the darkness behind them shifted. I couldn't tell what was shadow and what wasn't.

Twilight was upon us. My heart roared into overdrive as I threaded my first arrow. I kneeled on one knee and held the bow steady, waiting for something to fix on. I had a clear view from between the posts and blocked the path into the center of the town.

I slowed my breathing, straining to hear movement, straining to see anything but shadows, willing my body and mind to embrace the calm surety that I would stop whatever came out of those woods.

With my arrow trained, I blinked at the shadows, daring the vermin to come into the fading light. As if I willed it, a shimmering glow filled the space. Rows of them, like an army formation as opposed to a solid line. My heart thundered, blasting through any sort of calm I had attained.

"Oh, Jesus." I pushed the fear clawing at my skin away. I lined up my first shot.

Before the beast stepped onto the grassy knoll, it dropped dead from an arrow between its eyes. I threaded my next arrow and let another missile fly. It hit, like every other silver-plated arrow, until I found no more in my arsenal.

I had a handful of knives, but they wouldn't hit the mark at this distance, so I strung up a wooden arrow. One after the other, they flew until I had nothing but the silver knives and the sword. A dozen wolves lay howling in pain alongside another dozen dead wolves. As soon as the arrows were gone, I grabbed the knives and stood.

It was as if they knew I was out of ammunition. With a loud snarl, they launched. I waited until I knew they were in range, and then the first four wolves went down with knives embedded between their eyes. I missed one, and the last one nearly took me down, but I parried and buried the knife in his neck.

With one sweeping twirl, I drew the sword and landed blows that normally would have been mortal wounds, but these beasts were fast and I only pissed them off more. They surrounded me, wary of the blade in my hands. None of them tried to bite me, which I thought was strange. If even one got a hold of me with their mouth, they could easily tear a limb off.

A long, drawn-out howl came from the jail. My already pounding heart leaped into my throat. I couldn't take my eyes off my enemy to give Lucas any type of signal.

I swallowed and blew out a stream of air to get my focus. I moved into the ready stance that Remy had taught me, ignoring the snarling coming from the jail across the green. I stared down at the rows of wolves surrounding me. I caught movement to my right and spun low to the ground.

The blade whistled through the air, slicing right through the beast's mouth, removing the top part of his head in one clean cut. The sword vibrated in my hands, but it had sheared right through muscle and bone as easily as cutting through warm butter.

The spray of blood doused my left side, the warmth sliding over me, taking the chill from my bones and replacing it with an icy revulsion.

The pack hesitated, eyes widening at the death of one of their own by my hand and not by an arrow. Their wariness amplified my confidence.

I repositioned myself. I think I may have smiled, because the pack snarled as one unified unit. They circled, and I stayed in place at the ready.

"Who's next?" I said, my voice a low, menacing growl that I hardly recognized.

I could have sworn I saw fear in a couple of the wolves facing me. When their gaze jumped to my right, I shoved the blade backwards, putting my palm on the end to hold it steady when I felt resistance.

Just as quickly, I drew it back. The thump behind me told me I hit the mark. I brought the blade back to the ready. Two down, too many to go. I took a breath, taking a second to open my ears to the battles in the distance. Panicked screams filtered in, but I couldn't acknowledge them.

Not with another dozen wolves surrounding me. I caught movement in the back, near the woods. I chanced a look, and the massive black wolf that appeared filled me with dread. His eyes narrowed at me, and he licked his chops.

I forced myself to pay attention to the beasts surrounding me. Had they moved closer while I was distracted? I swallowed the fear and reset my focus.

"Only two of you have the balls to try to take me down?" I said with a laugh, goading them.

It worked. Four rushed me, and I spun, keeping my cool as blood spurted over me. Pain laced my hip as one wolf dug their claws into me before my blade took him out. I ducked and raised the blade. In one swipe, I disemboweled the bastard, blood and guts splattering all around me. I stood and shook myself. My hair clung to my cheeks in wet slaps. Then I spun, swinging the sword again. My arms burned from exertion.

A roar filled the air and caught me off guard. I spun toward the jail. The walls crashed down, and the beautiful gray wolf that had saved my grandmother came barreling out of the debris. Lucas wasn't the calm, docile wolf I'd first met. His bared teeth and horrific growl showed a predator of such power and wrath that I nearly collapsed from the shock.

A growl behind me put me back into fight mode and I turned, swinging the blade, decapitating a wolf that had gotten too close. Before I could reset myself, paws hit my back with such force that I flew onto my stomach.

The sword knocked from my grip, sliding out of reach.

I expected the sharp teeth in the back of my neck, but the wolf stood over me, growling. I rolled onto my back to face my last wolf and stared up at the underside of Lucas's head instead. His body blocked me from any of the other surrounding wolves. His growl sent tendrils of fear through me, but his protective stance warmed my heart. A mix of emotions ripped through me, leaving my entire form trembling. I rolled back onto my stomach and scanned the ground for my sword.

The black wolf crept forward. His ears were back, and his muzzle wrinkled from his ferocious growl. His eyes held a murderous stare. The blade was closer to the black mass than to Lucas.

The rest of the pack widened their circle, letting the lead wolf into the center. Lucas lowered, the soft fur of his stomach tickling my exposed skin, but the blanket he provided didn't last. He launched at the black wolf.

"No!" I cried and scrambled for the blade. I climbed to my feet with the sword in my grip. My heart slammed the walls of my chest so hard, I thought it would rip right through my skin.

Lucas and the black wolf rolled away into the shadows, their growls and yelps filling the night. The eight remaining wolves surrounded me with their teeth bared.

I could no longer hear the screams of the other guardsmen. My body numbed at the thought that the wolves in those directions won. The circle attacked as one unit this time. I think I screamed, but all I remember is fur and blood and the whistle of the blade.

An arrow whizzed by my face. I heard the wet sound behind me. Toward town, Remy had his last arrow drawn. Another wolf went down, leaving five to contend with, while Lucas and the black wolf continued to battle in the darkness.

He dropped his bow, still running at full speed towards the massacre. Drawing his broadsword, he took the same battle form as I had been using. Two of the wolves that had been surrounding me peeled off to attack Remy.

My swings slowed to the point I missed one wolf. I glanced down and caught the reflection of a knife. In a twirl meant to maim, I swung the sword and dipped low enough to scrape the knife off the ground.

Remy cried out. My heart lurched. I spun in his direction and froze. Blood spurted from where his arm should have been. The beast who tore it off dropped the appendage and launches at Remy.

The knife sailed from my grip. It embedded in the wolf's eye before it could finish my grandfather off.

A yelp cut off behind me and I turned, forgetting about the three wolves still surrounding me. When the black wolf stepped out of the shadows with blood dripping from his teeth, I almost fell to my knees.

My ragged breath caught in my throat when the black beast transitioned into a man. He looked over my shoulder at the other wolves.

"Burn it down," he said with a gravelly voice that scared the living daylights out of me.

I spun, and two of the wolves had changed back into human form. They nodded and turned towards the church. A flash of silver flew and buried to the hilt, right through the spine of one of the men. He collapsed, dead, before he hit the ground.

Only one person besides me had that kind of accuracy or strength in throwing knives. I turned to Remy. His gaze met mine, and then the only werewolf left in wolf form attacked him, tearing his throat out before I could get to him.

I swung the blade, but the wolf jumped out of the way. I went to swing around again, but a firm hand caught my wrist and bent it back. I cried out. The sword tumbled from my grip. The leader of the werewolf pack wrapped his hand around my throat and carried me to the post, slamming me into it.

Stars filled my vision. The grip on my throat loosened. I blinked my eyes until the blurring stopped and I stared into the cold, hard eyes of the alpha wolf. He flipped me around and pressed me into the post so my head was turned towards the town.

"Watch them burn," he whispered in my ear.

"No!" I screamed and struggled.

His grip on me was too strong for me to do anything but smash my bones against the hard wooden pole. He grabbed a handful of my hair and put his nose to my neck, taking a long, slow inhale.

"I have been waiting to take you down ever since you rode away from me on that black stallion."

I screamed my frustration despite the pain my thrashing caused. The anger ignited in the center of my being and spun outward until my entire body felt like it had been dropped in a kiln.

He kept a grip on my hair and forced me into the road facing the church. The other wolf had slid a piece of wood between the door handles.

I twisted in the alpha's grip.

His hand snaked around my throat again, and he slammed me against his hard chest. I kicked at his shins. His hardness pressed into the small of my back, and he just chuckled.

The chuckle nearly seized my muscles, sending a different fear through me. I wasn't afraid of dying, but that laugh chilled me into tremors.

He inhaled and sighed. "I love the smell of fear in the air."

The other wolf tossed a lit torch onto the front steps of the church, where it rolled against the large wooden doors. Doors that were locked from the inside, but also barricaded from the outside.

"No! Please, please don't do this!" I struggled again, raking my nails down the length of his arms.

A sharp claw drew from the collar of my shirt down my shoulder, splitting both the fabric and the skin underneath. I screamed. Everyone I loved was lost to these beasts, and I was next.

The other two werewolves stepped in front of me, tearing my clothing while the leader's hand slid under the fabric of my ripped shirt, squeezing my breast, digging his fingers into my skin. I slammed my elbow into his stomach and kicked out at the other men, still fighting to get loose. To survive.

The alpha laughed in my ear.

"Your people will burn while they watch their red-headed savior become my bitch."

I shivered in his grip, aware that most of my clothing lay in tatters around us. His mouth covered my shoulder. It took a second for the pain to register as his teeth tore into my skin.

My scream tore at my throat, nearly bursting my vocal cords. The poison churned, working its way into my bloodstream. My scream wasn't the only one filling the air. I swore I would kill this beast if it was the last thing I did.

His hand moved from my breast down my body as I writhed from both his intent and the poison searing through my veins. His other hand released my throat to explore. I slammed the back of my head into his face.

He stumbled back a step, just enough for me to twist from his grip. I turned in time to see a bloody blur launch at him. Teeth nearly tore the alpha's head clean off. I pivoted back to the other two werewolves, the men who killed Remy and set the church on fire.

Behind me, Lucas's visceral growls and the snap of bone echoed in my ears. The other two were staring with open mouths at the carnage behind me.

A high-pitched whistle caught my attention, and a silver-coated ax pierced the side of the closest wolf-man. The other one snapped out of whatever trance he was in and snarled at me as he transformed.

I spun towards where the blacksmith's sword lay in the dirt and sprinted. The wolf landed on me and I fell, scrunching my shoulders so he couldn't get a grip on my throat. That didn't stop him from raking my back with his claws.

Lucas attacked, and they rolled off me. I sat up and turned towards the owner of the ax, relieved to see Travis pulling the weapon out of the dead man's head. I pointed towards the church and he nodded, holding up the ax as he ran towards the rising flames.

Travis slammed the ax against the wooden plank, shattering through it in one swing. He stumbled back and raised his plastered arm before using the blade to push the doors open. He had seconds to jump out of the way of the frantic townspeople as they flooded the street. It wasn't until they were far enough from the flames before the surrounding massacre registered.

"Wolf!" someone screamed.

I turned in time to see Lucas's wobbly step as he made his way to me, collapsing next to me. His massive tongue swept over the bite on my shoulder several times while his pained gaze met mine.

"It's Lucas," I said with a hoarse voice, and put my arm around him to protect him from the frantic mob.

Travis maneuvered around in front of us, separating us from the townspeople. "Go home and lock your doors," he said, still holding the ax on his shoulder. His back remained facing us until the townspeople dispersed.

The adrenaline faded, and shakes gripped me. My teeth chattered, and my skin felt like I was on fire. My insides twisted, and I curled into a ball, unable to voice my pain. Bright lights bloomed in front of my eyes. My lungs seized. Lucas's whine sounded so far away.

Blinding agony gripped me, ripping through every muscle in my frame. I welcomed the blackness when it claimed me.

RED Chapter 16

SOMETHING HEAVY DRAPED ACROSS my waist. My pillow felt more like pebbles and dirt than the soft down I was used to. My brain remained foggy even as I cracked an eye. An old wool blanket covered me.

My eyes flew wide. I jerked into a sitting position on the town green. The shirt that had been draped over me slid and I gasped, pulling the shirt and blanket up to cover my bare chest. A deep ache in my shoulder and back registered, and I groaned.

My gaze fell to the man who had saved my life. Lucas looked up at me from the ground. His gaze fell to my shoulder, and he covered his face with his hands, rolling onto his back.

"I wasn't fast enough," he muttered.

I looked beyond Lucas at the green, and my hand flew to my mouth at the devastation. Dead wolves lay scattered, and the church was in blackened ruins.

"Tell me they got out," I said to Lucas.

He nodded, and my chest squeezed. Tears sprouted, and I cried. I didn't know why I was crying, but it seemed like the relief was too much to hold inside. I slid the shirt on and glanced at the cut short sleeve and the long sleeve.

"Travis?"

"Yes. He thought you might appreciate something to cover you up besides my bloody fur. He brought the blanket, too." Lucas stretched and winced.

His torso was patched with black and blue, and I reached out, running my fingers over the bruises.

"I'll heal," he said and stood.

Lucas didn't have a stitch of clothing on, and I blinked at his finely chiseled body. The thoughts parading through my head were totally inappropriate in a death field, so I turned away and situated the oversized shirt before handing him the blanket.

I climbed to my feet and took an unsteady step. Everything hurt. I winced and attempted to pass it off as just sleep-induced stiffness by waving him off when he went to give me a hand. But when I took a step and my knees buckled, I couldn't pretend I was okay.

Lucas caught me, and his groan clued me in as to his equally injured condition. The town stirred, and I glanced at Lucas, at his bare skin.

"You need clothes."

He took the blanket and searched the ground until he found a knife. He sliced a hole in the center of the blanket and stuck his head through. As odd as he looked, it was better than walking around naked so anyone could see his fine form.

My gaze turned to the dead. My heart squeezed as I stumbled towards Remy. I dropped to my knees by his head, unfazed by the puddle of tacky blood surrounding him. I fluttered my hand to what was left of his face. One lone eye stared at the sky. The sorrow squeezing my chest let loose.

A howl came from deep in my throat. It was haunting and full of anguish, and I let it fully form as I sang my goodbye to my grandfather. I shivered when the sound died. Tears blurred my eyes, and I covered my face.

I had become what I abhorred.

"Come on, I think we need to get out of here while we can," Lucas said and helped me to my feet.

We limped away from the core of Dakota and into the woods leading to my grandmother's house.

Lucas pumped water into the bathroom basin and set it on the warmer.

"Get in," he said and pointed at the tub.

I blinked at him and then looked down at my bare arm. I was covered in dried blood. My hand shook as I reached for the edge of the tub. I stepped into the cast iron and looked up at him. I wasn't the only one streaked with blood and gore.

"I can't clean you while you are wearing a shirt," he said.

Normally, a request like that would have gotten the man decked in the jaw with all the fury my fist could carry, but this was not a normal situation. I stared at him as he lit the fire under the warming pot, debating on whether or not I should follow his request. I glanced down at my bare legs and shivered.

"I think we're going to need a lot more than just a pot or two." My voice shook.

Lucas smiled, but it looked more like a grimace. That was when I noticed his hands weren't steady. At all.

"Are you okay?" I asked.

A high-pitched laugh escaped from him as he stood with his back to me. "I wasn't fast enough," he whispered. His voice sounded haunted by his perceived failure.

"Lucas?"

He turned, his jaw tight and his lips pressed together. His eyes sparkled with unshed tears. I pushed myself to a standing position, but he shook his head. I wasn't sure if it was to rid himself of the tears or if it was to tell me to sit back down. When he didn't speak, I reached my hand out.

He stared at my dirty fingers.

I almost pulled my hand back, but Lucas finally took it in his. I drew him to where I stood and wrapped my arms around his neck, hugging him with all my might. Silence settled like a comfortable blanket wrapping around both of us. The hug lingered until he finally moved out of my grip.

"Soap?" he asked, his voice hoarse, but at least his hands weren't shaking anymore.

I pointed to the cupboard above the heating basin.

"Please sit," he said in a soft but firm manner.

I sank into the tub. He worked the bands holding my braid out and then poured the water over me. I gasped at the coolness. Lucas cranked the water pump, filling the basin again, and then he kneeled next to the tub, cupping a handful of water. He drizzled it on my hair.

I stared at the red-stained water rolling off my skin and clenched my teeth against the unwanted shiver. Lucas grabbed a washcloth off the shelf and dipped it in the water before lathering it with the soap. His gaze met mine, and then he focused on wherever the cloth wiped. The gentleness in which he cleaned me magnified the horrors of the last few days, and tears escaped from the corners of my eyes in a silent deluge, mixing with the soap.

Lucas handed me the cloth. "Stand up."

I followed directions, and he pulled the stopper in the base of the tub. The water filtered into an empty pot beneath. After the last of the water drained, he placed the plug back in.

"Sit," he said, and as soon as I sat, another bucket of water doused me. This time, the tinge in the liquid was pink and not the vile red from the prior washing.

I ran the cloth over my body while Lucas pumped more water into the warming basin. He rinsed my hair and worked the soap in from my scalp to the tips of my red locks. His fingers worked in gentle circles, cleansing every inch of my head.

Instead of using the pink-tinted water to rinse the soap from my hair, Lucas opted to drain the water and start all over again. He continued the process until my tears dried up and the water ran clear.

All remnants of the battle washed away, but deep scars remained both on my back and in my heart.

He stood and extended a clean towel to me, and I climbed out of the tub, wrapping the soft cloth around my body. Just the feel of the fabric brought some normalcy back into my mind.

Lucas's hand cupped my cheek as he studied my face. "Go get some rest while I clean up, and then we'll figure out what we are going to do."

I nodded and turned before he stripped off the fashioned poncho. Another basin of dirty water went out the window, and I had a moment to wonder if I should reciprocate his kindness.

I paused at the door, and Lucas gave me a warm smile.

"It's okay. You need some rest," he said.

I couldn't argue with him. My body felt like it had been through a meat grinder. My eyelids drooped from the emotional drain.

In my bedroom, I glanced around the neat space and sighed, crossing to the dresser to retrieve undergarments and my nightshirt. Just as I sat down on the edge of the bed, a knock at the front door interrupted my stupor.

The knocking persisted, so I shuffled to the door, cracking it. Travis stood on the other side with Doc Wilton. His eyes widened, and he recoiled with an open mouth.

His reaction shot heat to my cheeks, and I reached up, thinking I must be horribly disfigured, which would also explain Lucas's strange behavior.

"Your face is fine," Doc Wilton said and slid by Travis with his medical bag in hand.

"Then what is wrong with him?" I waved at Travis, still staring at me like I had grown a second head.

"Nothing," Doc Wilton muttered, and his gaze dropped to the floor.

"What is it?" I insisted.

Travis fidgeted and stepped inside, closing the door behind him.

"Your eyes..."

"What about them?"

"They're green."

"They've always been green."

He laughed and glanced at the doctor.

Doc Wilton cleared his throat and set his bag on the table. "She clearly was the one who scared the town this morning," he said to Travis, and then turned to me. "I'm here to examine you. Travis said you sustained some nasty wounds last night?"

"She's fine," Lucas said from the hallway.

I turned and any chance of concentrating on what either Travis or the doctor was saying ended. I stared at Lucas's towel-clad form. His wrists still carried the blackened burns from the silver. His bare torso had black welts from the silver knives that the Guard used to torture him before they dragged him to the posts. But even with all the scars, he was one fine man to look at.

A fire started in my toes and swirled through my body to the top of my head like a cyclone ripping over the plains. Hunger ached, and I blinked at the visceral reaction gripping me. His lips twitched, and he pressed them together, suppressing a knowing smile.

"I've never seen eyes like that," Travis was muttering.

Lucas pulled his gaze away from mine. "Ruby is fine. The cuts on her back have already started to heal."

"Eyes like what?" I asked as Travis's words sank in.

"They are glowing green, not blue like his." Travis pointed to Lucas.

I raised my eyebrows. I had seen my fair share of werewolves, and every one of them carried the same unique trait. Radiant blue eyes. I glanced at Lucas. He shrugged.

"Why don't you look at him instead?" I nodded towards Lucas. "He's still got burns from the silver shackles you put him in."

Doc Wilton glanced at Lucas. "I don't have medicine that will help that."

I knew what would help. I turned, trudging down the hall to the back door where all the things Lucas and I had been carrying when the Guard arrested us still sat neatly piled on the steps. On top of my grandmother's blanket sat the aloe plant. I opened the door, and the stench hit me. I stumbled back a step and covered my nose.

"Smells like death, doesn't it?" Lucas said from down the hall.

I held my breath, opening the door to grab the aloe plant as quickly as possible. I slammed the door on the offensive smell, letting out a cough and a shiver.

He wasn't kidding. Now I knew why neither my grandmother nor I ever got attacked by werewolves. I wouldn't come within a hundred miles of that stench if I didn't have to. I crossed to him and handed him the plant.

"I'm fine," I said, echoing what Lucas had said earlier. "I just need some rest," I added, and yawned.

Travis shifted his weight. A tangy scent filled my nostrils, and it was coming from him. I tilted my head.

"You're... nervous?"

Travis chuckled and scratched the inside of his cast. "Well, um..." He glanced at the doctor.

Doc Wilton picked up his bag. "I wish you the best, Ruby," he said and stepped out of the cottage, leaving us with Travis.

Travis let out a high-pitched laugh and stared at the floor. When he swallowed hard, I knew it was more than just nerves I was smelling.

"I'm not going to attack you," I said.

He met my gaze. "You sure?"

"You're my best friend. Why would I hurt you?"

"Um... because you were bitten by a werewolf last night." He shoved his good hand into his pocket.

I shrugged, holding my hands out palms up to show him his logic was ridiculous. "I'm still me. I haven't gone all crazy... yet. But if you don't spill what's on your mind, that may change."

"Doc was sent with me to examine you to confirm your condition." He stared at the floor.

"Okay..." I rolled my hand in a circle, prompting him to continue.

"They want you to leave." His gaze snapped up to mine, and he chewed on his lip.

It took a few moments of silence, along with his steady gaze for what he was saying to sink in.

"After everything that I've done?" I waved toward town. "Do you know how many werewolves I killed last night?"

"Yes. I do. And that is the only reason the Guard isn't here taking care of this mess," he snapped and then closed his eyes. His good hand curled in a fist of frustration. "I told them you insisted I go open the church instead of helping you. And that was *after* you were bitten. You still fought for them, and I wouldn't allow them to take your life." His gaze pierced mine.

I bit my lip. This was my home. I didn't want to leave. I glanced at Lucas for help, but he was no longer standing in the hallway.

"Where am I supposed to go?" I asked Travis.

"Your wolf-boy has a pretty nice place," Travis said and glanced around. "Where did he go?"

"To find something to wear," I said. The sounds of drawers opening and closing in my bedroom reached my ears. I wasn't sure Lucas would find anything at all that would fit him.

"I don't like this, Red, but it was the only way I could ensure they wouldn't put the two of you in front of a firing line. Remy isn't around to fight for you, either. At least a few of the townspeople took my side this time. Otherwise..." He pressed his lips together. When I opened my mouth, he put his hand up, palm facing me. "I already argued that your grandmother's house was far enough away from the town."

It was uncanny how he knew what I was going to say. I sighed and dropped onto the bench by the fireplace.

He crossed and took the space next to me. He took my hand, and we sat in silence, staring at our point of contact. Travis finally sighed and pulled his hand away.

"I have loved you since that first day your grandmother marched you out on the green and insisted Remy train you."

"Did you know Remy was my grandfather?" I said, trying to move this conversation in a different direction. I wasn't in the mood for one of Travis's undying love speeches.

He leaned away from me with his eyebrows arched. "Is that what you were howling over this morning?"

I nodded. "As much as I bitched about him, I had a soft spot for him, even before we were told the news. He challenged me. Pushed me to be better. If it wasn't for him, I would be dead a dozen times over."

"I'm sorry," he said and slung his arm over my shoulder.

I winced, and he pulled it back quickly, his eyes widening at my reaction.

"I'm healing. Not healed."

"Oh." He picked at his cast. "You really never felt the same about me, did you?"

There it was. The point-blank question I had dreaded for the past couple of years. I looked down at my hands. "You've always been my closest friend, and I love you for that. But that's where it ends for me. There's never been..." I trailed off because I didn't want to bruise his ego.

"A spark." His shoulders slumped.

I nodded and kept my gaze averted.

"But there is one with him, isn't there?" he asked with a low voice filled with bitterness.

I turned to him, a flare of anger on the surface. "Is that what you think? That Lucas is the reason for my not wanting to be romantically involved with you?" I stood and stepped away, distancing myself before the growl in my voice became something more.

He opened his mouth to answer, but his lips closed on whatever was lurking in his head.

"It wasn't Lucas. It was the fact I am not attracted to you that way."

He tried to hide the wince, but I caught it. He stood, his eyes hard, and he stepped close, looking down at me with those fawn-colored eyes. He moved fast, grabbing the back of my head and crushing his lips to mine.

I blinked at the pressure on my lips, and my heart jolted in surprise, but there was nothing else behind the physical contact. Travis slowly pulled away, his eyes wide, like he had just had the world's biggest epiphany. He let out a giggle and covered his mouth as his cheeks flushed red. It was the oddest reaction to kissing me, and it turned my insides into a defensive mode.

"No spark." His eyes searched mine, but not that begging look that I had seen for years.

If I had known a kiss would have stopped him from pining for me, I would have allowed it the first time he attempted it. He ran his hand through his hair and laughed.

"Why are you laughing?" I asked, a little put off by his reaction.

"Because he just realized he has been chasing a fantasy all these years," Lucas said from the hall.

We both spun towards his voice. Lucas leaned against the wall with his arms crossed. The tension in his shoulders and arms wasn't lost on me. He had seen the interaction, and I was sure he heard every word. Tan dungarees hung on his hips that he must have found in the back of my grandmother's closet, and they looked like they were painted on. The length fell short of his ankles, but at least he found something.

Travis gave me a shrug.

"And we have to leave Dakota," I said.

"So I heard. Is Ruby allowed to pack up, or are you going to run her out-of-town like she's a common criminal?" he asked.

I caught the warning in his eyes, even though his tone was conversational.

"She can take whatever she wants," Travis said. "Midnight is out front, along with your bow and the sword you had last night."

"The sword belongs to the blacksmith."

"He's the one that insisted you take it. He was one of the people that stood by me, along with Doc Wilton and a few others."

I didn't know what to say. That weapon was gorgeous. I wondered if I would need it now that I had tainted blood pumping through my veins.

"How much time do I have to pack?"

"You need to be out of Dakota by dark."

A lump formed in my throat, and I swallowed it. I didn't want to succumb to the wild pendulum of emotions mixing in my blood. I nodded and started towards my room, but stopped before going down the hallway.

"Can you do me a favor?" I asked Travis.

He nodded.

"Do you think you could saddle up the mare in the corral for us and bring her around front for me?"

"Sure." He turned to leave. "Do you mind if I visit you sometime?" he asked with his back to me.

"I'd like that," I said. Travis left via the front door, and I turned to Lucas. "You're right. The corral smells like death."

RED Chapter 17

I STEPPED OUT FRONT TO load my saddle bags on Midnight, and my horse whinnied, stomping his hoofs. His eyes went wild, just like they had when Lucas approached him in the stable the other day. I grabbed the reins to keep him from rearing.

"It's me, Middy," I said and placed my hand on his jaw.

He whinnied again, but stilled at my touch, searching my eyes. Then he nudged me like he was afraid of me.

"It's okay. I know I smell different. So do you," I whispered and ran my hand down his neck. My stomach growled, and I licked my lips, trying to staunch the growing hunger in my belly.

I turned as Lucas came out with another set of saddlebags and my grandmother's folded quilt. His mare was tied up next to Midnight, courtesy of Travis.

"You good?" Travis asked from the doorway.

"Almost," I said and handed the saddle bag to Lucas. "I want to do a last walk-through."

"Take your time," he said in a soft voice that assured me we had all the time in the world.

But I knew the clock was ticking. My hunger was biting into my focus, and I didn't know what would happen when I gave in to the craving for something hot and bloody.

Travis stepped to the side as I crossed the threshold of my grandmother's house for the last time. I pulled the key off the wall and held it in my palm. The weight of it didn't match that of the sorrow in the pit of my stomach. I crossed to my room. There wasn't anything in the bedroom that I had any emotional attachment to, but when I stepped into my grandmother's bedroom, her warm scent filled my soul.

I hadn't gone in here to pillage her things. But now that I stood in her bedroom surrounded by the warmth of her, I wanted to pack everything into a box and keep it with me at all times. I crossed to her bureau and ran my finger along the fine wood grain.

I pressed the back of my hand to my lips. I caught my reflection in the mirror on her desk and reached for it, mesmerized by the glowing green eyes looking back. The minute my hand touched the handle, I yelped. Fiery pain singed my fingertips, and I stared at the mirror with wide eyes. The handle was silver.

I turned on my heels and nearly ran out of the room, but paused at her bed and grabbed the pillow. This held her scent, and I prayed it would hold it through a long ride through the valley to Lucas's place. I needed my grandmother with me, or otherwise I might give in to the growing need accosting me.

I gave Travis a quick hug and slid the cabin key into his hand. "The house is yours if you want it," I said and turned to Midnight, mounting him with one quick step into the stirrup.

"Red?" Travis said as Lucas coaxed his mare next to Midnight.

I met his gaze and gave him a pained smile. There was nothing more to say, so I nodded and tapped my heels on Midnight, moving him forward.

"Take care," Travis called as the woods swallowed us up.

Lucas took the lead and when he gave a hee-ya, his gray mare became a lightning bolt. I tightened my grip on the reins and kicked Midnight, and he took off at a full gallop until he caught up to the mare.

Lucas glanced back at me with a teasing grin. It was the most playful look I had seen on him since we met. My heart burst into a wild rhythm as we passed the Dakota line into the badlands where no one had traveled until the night my grandmother fell down into the ravine.

The woods on the other side of the plains were as thick and lush as they had been the other day, but this time, there wasn't a threat in the area, so I had a chance to appreciate the scent of pine and brush of the leaves as they passed over my exposed arms.

I pushed Midnight forward until Lucas and I were side by side. His smile was infections, and his eyes sparkled. I just wanted to hop onto his horse and hold him tightly against me. Actually, I wanted to stop the horses and ride him instead.

Heat filled my cheeks at the thought. While there was never chemistry with Travis, the opposite could be said about Lucas. Even his glance set me alight with the dirtiest of thoughts.

We breached the woods moments later, riding across the expanse of saw grass towards his cottage and the farm beyond. The thought of beef and chickens set off the saliva glands in my mouth and the growl in my stomach.

Lucas slowed his horse, and I followed until we were outside his home. He piled our stock onto the porch and set the aloe plant on a wooden table in the shade before he took Midnight's reins from my hands.

"I'll let you figure out where all that needs to go while I get these two set. I'll cook us up something to eat when I get inside, okay?"

My stomach made a glorious noise.

Lucas smiled. "I'll hurry," he said and led the horses away.

I tested the door. It opened freely, and I took his advice, carting the saddle bags packed with my clothing inside. On my last trip, I grabbed the aloe plant. Now that my adrenaline had faded, the burn on my hand raised its ugly head. I sat amidst my pile of everything I owned and cracked a spine off the plant, squeezing the ooze onto my hand. I gently worked it into the black welt across my palm.

It stung at first, but then the soothing coolness seeped in and I closed my eyes. Lucas shuffled into the house, but didn't say a thing. I kept my eyes closed, focusing on the acuteness of my hearing and smell. Lucas reminded me of a fresh breeze mixed with a sexy musk. I just wanted to lick every inch of him.

The closer he got, the more my heart thundered in my chest, and when his lips captured mine, my eyes flew open at the instant fire that engulfed me. He was on his hands and knees in front of me, his gaze intense.

He licked his lips, and I nearly moaned. How could a man have this much command over my body?

"You said I could kiss you all I want today."

A soft groan escaped from my lips. The slow smile that formed dimples in his cheeks made me forget about the pains in my stomach. Hunger gripped another part of my body, but I wasn't ready for this intensity. I scrambled to my feet. When I took a step back, I tripped on the saddlebag.

Lucas was fast. He caught me in his muscular arms before my head connected with the wall. He spun me so I faced the wooden logs and pressed against my back.

His warmth engulfed me. His fingers tickled my neck as he moved my hair away so his tongue could trace the line of my throat. A low growl of contentment flowed from him as he nibbled my earlobe.

His hands traveled from my sides to the buttons of my shirt, nimbly releasing each one until it hung on my frame. His fingers scraped my skin as he peeled the fabric off my shoulders. The pressure on my body released, and my shirt drifted to the ground. I looked over my shoulder, and his eyes were locked on my back. He gently traced my scars, his touch creating a tingle in my skin.

The slide of his hands from my back around my sides to my breasts created a shiver. My arms broke out in gooseflesh as his mouth found the back of my neck again. He rolled my nipples between his fingers until they were hard nubs before his hands traveled down the length of my stomach in a soft caress.

He fumbled with the buttons on my pants as he sucked and nipped at my neck and ear. With a growl of frustration, he gave up on trying to be civilized and yanked each side of my pants, sending buttons pinging into the wall. My hands pressed against the wall, pushing my body into his, feeling his excitement against the small of my back. When his hand dipped inside my undergarments and traced the sensitive bud between my legs, I moaned.

"This is going to hurt," he whispered.

My heart stopped at his words, and then his teeth severed my skin in the same place that the alpha bit me.

I bucked in his arms, pushing him away and turning.

"What the hell do you think you're doing?" I snapped.

All the heat that had been pooling in my belly evaporated. Anger replaced it, along with the sensation of whatever poison he possessed filtering in through the bite.

"Replacing the alpha's mark," he said and wiped my blood off his chin.

I crossed my arms over my exposed chest and glared at him. "Why?"

"So every wolf we encounter knows you're mine."

"I'm nobody's bitch," I said and reached down, swiping my shirt off the floor. I slipped it on and growled at his audacity.

His intense, questioning stare pierced through my anger. A crease appeared between his eyes, and his head cocked.

"That is what that bastard called me. His bitch. If you think this means you own me, you are sorely mistaken." I waved at the bloody welts on my shoulder and went to step away.

Lucas stepped close, blocking my retreat. He threaded his hands into my hair on either side of my face and crushed my lips under his. I opened my mouth to protest. The sweet tang of blood followed his tongue, and I nearly dropped to my knees. Time stilled and an icy heat spun from the wound in my shoulder. His saliva mixed with my blood, creating a whole new fascination for the man kissing me.

I gasped as he broke the kiss, wanting more, but still aggravated with him for the possessive mark. I broke away from his powerful grip and grabbed his shoulder. Before I knew what I was doing, my teeth sank through his skin. He tasted delicious, and I forced myself to step away when his wince registered.

"Why did you do that?" he asked, grabbing his bleeding shoulder.

"Because if you can be all possessive, so can I." I propped my hands on my waist and stared at him. I licked the remnants of blood still left on my lips, and my stomach cramped again. "I'm hungry."

Lucas's eyes blazed, and he turned towards the kitchen, stomping across the house like I had just broke his favorite toy. The slamming of pots and pans announced his aggravation.

I turned my attention to the mess I made of his living room. It took me a couple of trips to move all the bags into one of the two bedrooms in his cottage, and then I stepped back into the kitchen. A plate of scrambled eggs sat on the table along with a fork. He slammed his plate down opposite mine and dug into his food without a word.

I had no idea what I did to deserve this treatment, but my stomach decided that it needed attention before Lucas. I scooped up a forkful of eggs, and they were just as good as they had been the other morning. When I took my last bite, he ripped my empty plate from under me. Anger oozed from him while he cleaned the dishes.

When he finished, he leaned against the sink with his head bowed. It was time to address this head on.

He turned when I stood from the table, and I crossed the distance and put my hands on his chest. His heart pounded against my palms. I took a moment to tune in to my senses. His musky scent remained the same, thrilling me with each inhalation.

"What's wrong?"

Lucas laughed and glanced at the ceiling before he met my gaze. "You're the alpha," he whispered.

I cocked an eyebrow. "What?"

"In this little pack..." He pointed between the two of us. "You are the alpha."

"Just because the alpha..."

"That's not how it works. If the alpha of that pack had survived..." Lucas snorted a laugh and maneuvered around me, putting a little distance between us. "If he had lived, he would have had to challenge you or obey you. The only time you would have been his bitch would have been that evening before you fully absorbed the venom."

I narrowed my eyes at him. I didn't understand.

"Do you hear my commands in your head?"

"No." I laughed, thinking he must be insane.

"If I was your alpha, you would."

I stared at him. *Come here*, I demanded in my head, testing out his theory.

Lucas pressed his lips together tightly and stepped forward.

"Whoa. Wait a minute..." I put my hands up, trying to ignore that nagging sense of power. I didn't know how this was even possible. I didn't want this.

"No. You bit me. You put your claim on me. Now I'm subject to whatever you command of me."

"This is what you expected when you bit me?" My voice rose to a high pitch. The thought of being at anyone's beck and call turned my stomach.

He closed his eyes and hung his head. His cheeks flared red. "Yes."

The fact he admitted it blanketed me in a cold sweat. "How do I undo it?"

This time he crossed to stand in front of me. "There is no undoing it. At least your heart is pure, not like that shit who bit you. I guess things could be worse. I could be his bitch." Dimples appeared in his cheeks.

I pressed my lips together at his lame attempt at humor. "Why am I alpha?"

He shrugged. "Spirit of the warrior. You have it. I don't."

He reached out and tucked my hair behind my ear. His touch ignited the heat inside me, and I suppressed the urge to wish his arms around me. I needed to know if what was here between us was real, or if I was in the same fantasy world as Travis had been.

"Lucas, why did you kiss me in the jail cell?"

He cupped my cheek. "Because you stole my heart. You are everything I am not. Brave. Fierce. Beautiful." His thumb traced my cheekbone. "And I just wanted to taste you before I died." He leaned forward and pressed his lips to mine again. "Why did you kiss me back?" he whispered against my mouth and pulled back, waiting for me to answer.

Just being in this proximity increased my heart rate. "I couldn't help myself, especially since there was something in the air between us. I couldn't tell if you felt it or not."

"The spark?" he asked, and dimples appeared in his cheeks as a smile danced on his lips. "Yes. It hit me like a lightning bolt the moment you rounded that rock in the ravine."

Heat flushed my cheeks, and I smiled. "I didn't feel it until I was standing in this room with my arrow trained on your back, and you turned to greet me." I tilted my head. "You knew I was there, didn't you?"

"I knew the minute the bedroom door opened. You smelled like sweet honey and a summer's day and all I wanted to do was devour every inch of you." He smiled. "I still want to devour you."

"And this has nothing to do with *my* desires?"

He pulled me against him. "No."

His mouth was on mine, and every inch of my body ached for him. Our tongues tangled in an intense kiss that yanked the air from my lungs. When he pulled away from my lips, I whined.

"But it will have to wait until morning," he said and glanced at the window.

The setting sun painted the room in a red blaze that matched the fire burning inside me. I didn't want to wait.

He looked back at me. "*I* want to take my time, so you, my sweet alpha girl, will just have to have a little patience."

A pout formed on my lips, but a nagging itch tingled along my spine. I blinked at the sensation and flexed my shoulder blades together to staunch it.

"Clothes," he said with urgency as the light faded. He nearly ripped my shirt off, and I thought maybe my influence actually jump-started him into action. It wasn't until he stepped away that I understood.

He yanked his shirt over his head and kicked his boots off, stripping his pants a second before he fell to his knees. I stepped back, watching in fascination.

A yelp yanked from my mouth, and the itch in my spine turned into a torrent of rippling agony. I dropped to my knees the moment Lucas became a full-fledged wolf. Tearing fabric combined with popping joints, and I gasped as I looked down at my hands. They were covered in red, gray, and white fur spread over massive paws that matched Lucas's. My transition was much faster than his had been, but not quite the easy shift that the werewolf pack exhibited last night.

I wondered if I could transition at will or if I was at the mercy of the night, like Lucas. I swept my tongue over my teeth, dragging my attention away from my thoughts. The sharpness of my fangs held marvel, as did the sweep of my tail. The power of my new form pulsed in my veins.

Lucas closed the distance in two strides and ran a wet tongue over the side of my face. I rubbed my nose to his and stepped closer, wrapping my head over his back in a canine hug.

I wanted to run, to play, to hunt. I wanted to learn my speed, my strength, my agility, and Lucas seemed to understand. He crossed to the front door and paused, glancing back at me.

His musings in the jail flooded to the forefront of my mind, and I trotted next to him, sensing his unease. I licked his face to ease his fears. My stomach rumbled in concert with his. The transformation used every bit of energy the eggs he had cooked provided. I needed more food.

Doubt shaded his blue eyes.

He didn't realize the rules of the Dakota Guard still reigned true in this foreign body. Even though the urge to hunt overwhelmed me, *what* I hunted still mattered.

Humans were not on that list. Neither were the livestock in the fields behind us, even though they did smell divine.

The hesitation in Lucas evaporated, and his tension eased. With his paws, he unlatched the front door, and it opened on the night. I stepped out onto the porch and scanned the woods before I glanced at Lucas.

Try to keep up, I thought and then exploded from my haunches. I flew through the air, landing on my front paws before my hind legs hit the ground and pushed off. I ran so fast, the wind pulled tears from my eyes and my lungs burned. Lucas matched my pace, and his tongue lolled out of the side of his mouth as he panted.

I slowed and came to a stop on a small grassy knoll stretching my limbs. Lucas nipped my haunches, and I whirled on him, jumping up and putting my teeth on the back of his neck. He rolled under me, and before I knew it, I lay on my back under him as he stared down at me with his big wolf smile.

I climbed to my feet and froze with my nose in the air. Venison filled my senses. A deer was downwind, and I turned in that direction. Lucas turned with me. My mouth watered at the thought of the deer, but without a bow and arrow, I had no sense in how to take it down with wolf teeth.

I glanced at Lucas. *Teach me.*

He led the way with steps so light that even I had to strain to hear him. The doe came into view, and Lucas nodded his muzzle to the right. Crouching, he moved to the left. I followed his lead, veering to the right of the deer. Her ears straightened, and her head rose just as we came even with her front shoulders.

Lucas launched and his mouth clamped down on the underside of the deer's neck. I followed, but I landed on the top of the deer, clamping down on the back of its neck. I jumped off, twisting the deer's head enough to snap its spine.

Warm blood flowed into my mouth, and I swallowed, cherishing the sweet taste. We tore at the carcass, both eating greedily until our bellies were full and only bone and sinew were left.

We licked each other clean before Lucas led me back to the cottage. He led me to a soft mat in the corner of the porch that I hadn't noticed before. When he curled around me, I let out a soft sigh of contentment. I breathed in the night, thankful to be alive and at Lucas's side. My future revolved around the werewolf next to me, and I knew it would be filled with unending adventure.

A pair of white doves landed on the railing near us and fluttered their wings. I stared at the birds, so out of place in the northern Pacific woods. I blinked my eyes to make sure I wasn't seeing things, but the birds remained in place. The doves almost glowed in the darkness.

I shifted, cocking my head at their intense stares. In concert with each other, their wings spread, and they took flight. On the breeze created by their wings, I could have sworn I heard my grandmother whisper how proud she was of me.

The End

175

Elle must escape a life of despair to find magic in a Prince's arms.

Elle Seeley's world turns upside down when her mother passes unexpectedly. Her father brings her into his business, teaching her the art of negotiation in the marketplace and how to defend herself against attack.

All his training and grooming comes to a halt when he brings home a new wife and the woman's daughter. Elle's father makes her promise to listen and obey.

The minute her father leaves, her new stepmother transforms into a monster with one goal—to humiliate Elle into submission.

When news of a ball is announced, Elle wants to escape her mentally unstable captor, but she is forbidden to go.

Will Elle find a way to escape a life meant only for despair?

CINDER Chapter 1

THE SOFT KISS ON my forehead should have brought forth a warning.

Instead, it was the usual, mundane good night routine I had had with my mother for the last seventeen years. She tucked me into bed and placed that sweet, comforting kiss in the center of my forehead before she took leave to meet up with my father at the latest social event. She was dressed in a golden gown that would put the rest of the city's women to shame.

I wish I had known that would be the last time I saw her.

Had I known, I would have asked for more.

More hugs, even though it would have wrinkled that beautiful dress.

More stories, even though another one of her tall tales would make her woefully late for the party.

More time for her to stay with me instead of leaving me alone with my grieving father.

Three days after she died, I stared out the window at the fields drenched in the morning sunlight, wishing for my mother once again.

"Elle!" My father's voice echoed up the marble staircase.

I turned, pressing the fabric of my mourning dress into place. My eyes stung from the unrelenting cascade of tears. No matter how many times my father told me to stop crying, I could not staunch the fountain. At least I was silent now, without the accompaniment of the wailing loss that had gripped me when I was first given the news.

I climbed down the stairs into the grand entry, avoiding eye contact, but my sniffling caught my father's attention.

"Girl, you need to get yourself together. The entire city is coming out to extend their condolences, and I cannot have you sniffling like some small child."

I nodded and sniffed.

"Oh, for heaven's sake," he muttered and handed me a handkerchief.

I dabbed my nose and folded the fabric in the palm of my hand. I would need it for the funeral and the procession to the pyre, where they would honor my mother by reducing her beautiful form to dust.

Such was the way of the elite. Only royalty had their bodies bound and stored in crypts under the castles. I never understood the fascination of being put in a marble casket with my likeness carved in the elaborate stone, and my essence trapped in the same dark space.

The funeral pyre cleansed and reduced the human body to ash, which traveled on the wind, partnering with nature once again.

My thoughts kept turning these two disparate forms of internments over until I stood in the front row of the great chapel next to my father. He remained stoic, and I continued my silent sobbing throughout the service.

I was unsure how my legs held my weight from the church to the pyre built on the hill in our backyard overlooking the king's valley. As the flames engulfed my mother, my knees weakened, but my father caught me, steadying me. I glanced sideways with a nod of thanks.

He clenched his jaw and remained standing tall despite the stench of burning wood mingled with charred flesh that hung on the air. A single tear crested and slid down his cheek like a drop of molasses first tapped from a tree trunk.

The king's emissaries rode up the hill, stopping a distance away to pay their respects. My father crossed his left arm across his chest and bowed, showing his allegiance to the crown even in this difficult time.

I wasn't as diplomatic as my father and couldn't have given a rat's ass that the king's people were here. All I wanted was my mother.

My father cleared his throat. I curtsied as best as my shaking knees would allow, given the circumstances. They didn't seem to mind my obvious lack of attention, but I knew I would get a stern talking to later that evening from my father.

<hr>

"ELLE, YOU MUST REMEMBER your manners, especially at such trying times as these. It is what differentiates us from the beasts."

I stared at Father. I knew he was right. I also knew my mother would have been sadly disappointed with my behavior, but my father had the decency not to bring my mother's expectations into his berating.

"The prince was with the king's guard," he said.

I blinked and shrugged. "What would you have had me do? It was my mother's funeral, and honestly, I wouldn't have cared if the king himself had shown up."

My father's lips pressed together, and his cheeks flushed. He turned and walked out of the room without another word.

<hr>

OVER THE NEXT FEW months, Father and I found a comfortable rhythm. Between my daily chores, he showed me how to maintain the property books and where all our finances were held. He taught me how to barter with the local shop owners and how to defend myself if I ever found the need.

All his attention helped fill the emptiness in my chest every time I picked up one of Mother's knickknacks. When her loss overwhelmed me, I wandered into her closet to touch her silk dresses. The soft fabric brought back more happy memories, and I felt closer to her when I shared the quiet of her dressing room.

When the holiday season started, I climbed up into our attic and started going through the trunks, looking for the decorations Mother used to hang. I had already pillaged through a half dozen chests filled with linens and other mundane household items without luck.

I crossed to the opposite side of the attic. The third trunk had what I was looking for, but as I gathered the decorations, a breeze tickled my ankles. I turned. In the far corner sat a dust-laden trunk. Drawn to the ancient sigils on the side, I placed my armful of ornaments down on the holiday trunk and traversed threw the boxes to the old one hidden away in the corner.

Standing over the ornately carved wood, vibrations filled me. I reached for the lock.

"Do not touch that trunk!"

I jumped at my father's stern voice, spinning towards him with my heart thumping in my throat like I had done something terribly wrong.

His wide eyes gave me more of a start than his reprimanding tone. They were eyes of a man filled with fear.

I blinked and stepped away from the trunk, even though every fiber in my body craved to open it. It called to me in a way nothing ever had, but I obeyed my father.

"I was just looking for the holiday decorations." I pointed to the pile I had put down before I got sidetracked with the ancient chest behind me.

"Well, get what you came up here for and come back downstairs." His features smoothed out, but his tone remained clipped.

I grabbed the pile and headed back downstairs with him following close behind. The moment I put the decorations on the table, he turned me around, placing his hands on my shoulders.

"I want you to promise me you will never go near that trunk."

The seriousness in both his tone and his expression wiped out any plan I had to sneak up there and open that chest. However, curiosity tickled my skin.

"Why?" It wasn't uncommon for me to ask questions, especially given the training my father had given me over these last few months.

His lips pressed into a frown. "Because I am ordering you to stay away from it."

I cocked my head and studied his blue-green eyes. There was no leeway there, so I nodded assent. "Can you tell me what is inside that has you so scared?"

He let out a laugh and stepped back, putting distance between us. "Why would you say such a thing?"

I got the distinct impression he was avoiding my question, but I remained quiet, waiting for him to answer.

He sighed. "It's just some old things from before I met your mother. Things unsuitable for a young lady."

I raised an eyebrow, my curiosity piqued. However, both Father and I knew I would not go against his word, no matter how interested I was in seeing what could possibly be hidden away in that box.

CINDER Chapter 2

THE FOLLOWING JUNE, I was sparring with Nathan, the neighbor's squire, while my father watched from the balcony. I bested him for the first time since I had started training, and with my sword to his throat, and my heart pumping with the glory of the win, I glanced up at my father.

He stared down at us with a scowl, dampening my mood.

I bowed to Nathan before handing him the training sword. When I stepped out of the courtyard, I wasn't in the frame of mind to confront my father, so I went for a walk on our lands, heading towards the winding brook.

I sat on the rock near the long, straight portion of the stream, skipping pebbles across the surface. I had been so pleased to win the sword match with Nathan, but my father looked as though I had killed the squire instead of besting him.

The next rock skipped five times before it plunged beneath the surface.

"Impressive."

The voice startled me, and I was on my feet before my brain registered who was on the other side of the brook. Prince William's dark eyes sparkled in the bright spring sunlight, and his lips turned up in a whisper of a smile.

"My lord, forgive my manners." I stumbled over the words and attempted a curtsy, which almost made me tumble off the boulder. I caught myself and glanced at him. Heat filled my cheeks.

Deep dimples appeared, and he looked away as a smile captured his lips. I had never seen the prince this close. I had to agree with the gossip that he was quite the looker. Prince William was handsome enough to make my heart flutter, especially when he was trying to hold back laughter.

"My lady, I wager I can skip a rock farther than you can," he said.

I cocked my head. "And what exactly are we wagering?"

He blinked, and his eyebrows rose. Prince William glanced at the waterway with an open mouth, like he didn't quite know what to request. He licked his lips and looked back at me. "How about a kiss?" he asked, his voice hushed enough so I barely heard him over the rushing water. His cheeks reddened, and he grinned.

I bit the side of my lip and reached down to pick up a pebble I had saved for last. "And if I win?" I palmed the smooth rock, waiting.

"Anything the lady desires," he said and bowed. The mischievous glint in his eyes made me smile.

"Anything?"

He nodded.

"I desire a true swordsman to spar with." I let my rock fly before he could speak. When it skipped eight times before plunking in the water, I turned towards him with a satisfied cock of my head.

He stared at me with his jaw hanging ajar.

"Well, my lord, it is your turn." I waved towards the water.

He picked up a pebble at his feet and swiveled, flinging the rock close to the surface. My heart pounded in my chest as I silently counted each skip.

One. Two. Three. Four. Five. Six. Seven. Eight.

And then the rock disappeared under the surface.

He stared in the direction of the rock as his smile slowly melted away, and then he turned to me. I swear he looked disappointed.

"It looks as though we are at a stalemate," he said.

The sound of hoofs beat in the distance.

He sighed. "I would love to continue playing this game until I won, but I have to get back before the king's guard finds me and drags me back to the castle." He bowed and turned into the thick grass.

I hopped down and started back towards home. Just before I stepped into the woods, I glanced back. The prince had disappeared into the wheat field. The chaotic beat of my heart settled.

The interaction with the prince made me forget my melancholy, and I walked back home, still feeling as if I were floating on clouds. My euphoria ended when I saw the servants carrying my mother's fine china out of the dining room and up the stairs.

I rushed into the dining hall and stopped, staring at the nearly empty hutch. I spun on my heels and marched into my father's den. "Why are the servants moving Mother's china?"

Father looked up from his books and leaned back in the chair. "It is about time I cleared out her things. The constant reminder of her everywhere I look still makes my heart ache for her."

"Having her things near gives me peace," I said, trying not to let my voice rise, but the thought of her things disappearing left me hollow.

"I am not throwing them out. I am putting them in the attic, so when you finally agree to a betrothal, you will have a nice dowry to go with you."

My eyebrows rose. He had never once talked to me about marriage. I knew my parents had spoken to several of the families in the village, but my mother knew I believed in love and I didn't want to be saddled into an arranged marriage. Since my mother passed, there hadn't been any talk of betrothals or dowries in any of my conversations with my father.

"What makes you think I'll agree to any betrothal?" I put my hands on my hips, challenging him.

His eyes narrowed at my tone. "When I find you the right man, I expect you to obey my wishes. I don't want you to become an old maid."

I bit my lip on my response. I would rather be an old maid than marry a man I didn't know. "I want what you and mother had. Your marriage wasn't arranged."

His expression softened, and he sighed. "No. It wasn't. But it also wasn't without sacrifice. I want to spare you hardship."

"I don't have an issue with hardship, Father. I have an issue with moving Mother's things into the attic." I crossed my arms.

All the softness in my father's expression vanished, and he slowly stood, his face reddening. "I am still the lord of this manor, and you would do well to remember your place. Your mother would be very disappointed in you right now."

For nearly a year, my father had never brought up how my mother would feel about my behavior. I had never pushed him that far. My stomach plummeted at the dig. I dropped my gaze as shame heated my cheeks. Humbled, I nodded, waiting for him to say more.

"Days like this, I regret giving you the knowledge and means to stand on your own, but I never expected it would give you the audacity to question my authority." His hard gaze blazed at a spot on my forehead and was just as damning as his words.

"I'm not questioning your authority," I whispered. A part of me bristled at the meek tone, but he was right. I pushed him too far and deserved his stern demeanor.

"Be thankful I am not giving everything away," he muttered and pointed at the door.

My chest tightened, and I gave him a nod before taking my leave. I went to my room, so I didn't have to see the exile of my mother's things.

CINDER Chapter 3

THE NEXT FEW DAYS were quiet. I wandered from room to room, surrounded by emptiness. My mother's things were relegated to the attic, including all her silk gowns, shoved into trunks like they were old linens, or hung haphazardly to wrinkle and collect dust. My father didn't acknowledge my sadness. Instead, he went about things as if nothing had happened, with one exception. He was absent for hours every late afternoon, coming home long after dark.

He had been out late several times before he moved Mother's things from all the rooms, but I never questioned it. Now, I noticed a pattern. By mid-afternoon, he kept looking at the candle and out the window at where the sun was in the sky. When he left, I had nothing to dote on; I noticed his absence.

On the last day of the week, I woke to him still gone. The servants said he hadn't come home the prior night, and no one had information where he might be. The same panic that had filled me after my mother died constricted my chest. As my breath wheezed and my head spun, one servant informed me that our carriage had just arrived.

I ran towards the front door and came to a halt halfway down the hallway. My father escorted a dark-haired woman into our home. His attention was solely on this woman, and the way his gaze lingered tightened my stomach. I had only ever seen that sparkle in his eyes when he looked at my mother.

Everything snapped into place in my head. The late nights, the moving of all Mother's things. He was courting this woman.

He glanced up and smiled at me. "Elle, I would like you to meet Lady Githa, my new bride, and her daughter Lily," he said, and stepped aside, revealing a girl a few years younger than me.

My brain stalled at the phrase 'my new bride'. I stared at the woman and her taunting smile as she gave me the once-over. Her daughter blushed, dropping her gaze.

My mouth couldn't form words, not even a hello. My body remained stock-still when I should have given the new lady of the house a curtsy as formality dictated. But none of the manners both my mother and father taught me came to the surface. I was too stunned.

"Elle?"

My father's question contained a warning, which snapped me out of my shocked paralysis. I bent into a weak curtsy and forced a smile.

"Welcome," I croaked out.

My father left his new bride's arm and crossed to me to take hold of my elbow. "I know this is a shock, but I didn't know how else to tell you. I fell in love, and I didn't want to spend another night alone. As for you, I expect you to obey her as you would have obeyed your mother, understand?"

I nodded because I had no other choice. I was still thunderstruck.

"Be a dear and collect our things?" Lady Githa asked, as if I were one of the servants.

I glanced at my father, and he raised an eyebrow, nodding his head towards the carriage.

"Yes, my lady," I said, although I was not thrilled playing the role of her housemaid.

Lily smiled weakly, but it wasn't malicious. She turned to follow me outside.

"Not you, dear. Let Elle get our things while Lord Seeley shows us to our rooms."

Lily glanced at me and pressed her lips together in a frown. She shrugged and followed her mother's instruction, leaving me to collect their things by myself. Normally, I did not mind helping around the house, but the dismissive nature of Lady Githa nipped at my nerves.

I lugged her bags up the stairs and stood in the hallway, unable to bring this woman's bags over the threshold of the bedroom my parents shared for seventeen years of my life. I could hear the woman gushing over the tapestries and the view from the window. I dropped her bag at the entrance and turned to continue unpacking the carriage.

Lily's things were less bountiful, and as I crossed the hall to deposit her bags in the guest room, Lady Githa stepped out into the hall.

"This room will do for Lily," she said, waving towards my room.

"I'm sorry, but that is my room," I said.

My father stood behind her, his eyes wide like a deer who had caught the scent of a predator.

"Githa," he said softly.

She turned on him. "You said we had the choice of rooms for Lily. Well, I choose this one."

"But..." My father seemed to be at a loss for words, looking between his new bride and me.

"It's okay, Mother," Lily whispered.

"You said you liked the room. Do you?" Lady Githa snapped.

"Of course. It is a beautiful room, Mother. But..." Lily stared down at the floor.

"Lily gets this room," Lady Githa said.

I started towards the room and Lady Githa stepped in my path.

"I would like to get my things." I met my step-mother's glare, trying not to send back as searing a look of my own. I wasn't sure I kept the fire from my eyes because her lips pressed tighter together and her nostrils flared.

"It is no longer your room," she said.

There was such a dark undercurrent radiating from her I moved back, distancing myself from the wrath rolling from her skin. My father idly stood by while this woman brushed me aside, and I wondered if this was some sort of retribution for my questioning him about Mother's things the other day.

Instead of arguing, I turned and took my leave. I would figure out what room to occupy as soon as I cooled down. I wandered to the courtyard and headed straight towards the sword rack. The wooden training blade felt good in my hands. I started doing the forms the squire had taught me, concentrating on my steps and the presentation of the weapon.

After doing four different forms, I started over again. In the middle of my next set, a gasp sounded behind me. I turned to see a wide-eyed Lily with one hand over her mouth and the other over her heart.

Sweat pasted the edges of my hair to my cheeks. I lowered the sword.

"What are you doing?" she whispered and glanced furtively over her shoulder.

"Practicing." Based on the fear etched into her features, I put my training weapon in the rack. I brushed my hair back and turned in time to see Lady Githa step into the courtyard.

She stared down her sharp nose at me, and her face seemed to pinch, like she had smelled something bad.

"You're not preparing dinner?" she said.

I shook my head. "The cook prepares dinner."

"There is no cook. I asked your father to let the staff go because there really is no need to keep paying wages to an idle staff, especially since this place isn't big enough to warrant having butlers, maids, cooks, and footmen," she said.

I glanced up at the two-story building before bringing my gaze back to hers. From her expression, I could guess who she thought would do all the work.

"I am not sure my meals are fit for eating," I said. While I knew how to bake cookies, I didn't know the first thing about cooking a meal.

"Well, come child, it is time you learn how to prepare meals for a family." She waved me over with a smile.

I reluctantly stepped closer, mystified at how her smile made all the difference in appearances. I glimpsed why my father could have fallen for this woman. But that ended the minute I got to her side.

She reached out and grabbed my wrist in a viper hold, nearly dragging me out of the courtyard, down the narrow hall, and to the kitchen. She rambled on about how creating scrumptious meals was an important household task, as was keeping the place clean and orderly. Not once did she talk about being properly educated in the ways of the world.

In great detail, she instructed me on how to construct a meat pie big enough to feed the four of us. I boiled a chunk of beef that the cook had left in a pot of clean water. Then I chopped dates and nuts into fine pieces. Luckily, all my fingers remained intact when I was through.

Next, I peeled potatoes at Githa's direction and boiled those after I lit the stove warmers. With all the ingredients cooking, she then walked me through making a pie crust. That was work in and of itself. Once I had the dough rolled out, I fit it into a pie pan and collected the wine and spices Githa spouted off.

Then we waited until she deemed the meat suitable for cutting. I sliced it, added the dates, nuts, and a little wine before mixing it together. The mound in the pie tin warranted a little more rolling of the dough in order to cover it.

When I finished prepping the pie to her specifications, I slid it into the open oven. Wiping my forehead, I leaned back against the counter, dripping with sweat and soot from the fire under the stove.

"Keep that fire hot, and in three hours, the pie should be ready."

Lady Githa turned on her heel and left me to tend the stove. Lily followed her out and gave me a meek smile as she left the room. My feet hurt and all I wanted was a bath to wash away the sweat, but I had to make sure the fire and temperature remained steady.

Instead of just being idle while the dinner cooked, I made myself useful and baked my mother's favorite pastry. Honey cakes. I hummed the same tune my mother did whenever she overtook the kitchen to make her sweet treats.

Birds fluttered to the window and joined in the melody, making my task seem much lighter than moments before. I finished my baking preparations and added more wood to the stove before I slid the honey cakes into the oven beside the meat pie.

Now it was just a waiting game. I swept up the floor and neatened up the kitchen while both dinner and dessert cooked. When all was clean, I gathered the plates and utensils for the dining table. I had set the table before when the cook was busy, and the servants were indisposed, so at least I had been schooled in such matters, and would not receive the evil eye from the new lady of the manor.

When I stepped back into the kitchen, my father was waiting for me by the preparation table. He stared in contemplation at the oven. The deep creases around his mouth gave me a start. It was almost the same expression he had the day I won the sparring contest with the squire.

I knew he didn't have good news.

He gave the slightest shake of his head before he broke out in a smile. "Elle, it smells divine." He waved towards the oven.

"It wasn't as hard to make as I imagined." I wiped my hands on a dishtowel and leaned against the table. "But you aren't here to compliment my cooking skills, are you?"

He chuckled under his breath and gave me a sideways glance. "No. I have to go to Dover in the morning."

I had forgotten all about the Dover trip and the cattle market. He had spoken to me about this annual event shortly after mother died and had said we would go together so I could get a sense of a large marketplace. My skin tingled with excitement and I grinned.

My father's heavy sigh made the smile on my face fade, and the happy tingle turned into a rock that dropped into my stomach. I swallowed and stared at him.

"I know. I know you're disappointed. But you need to stay here and help Lady Githa get settled. Can you do that for me?" he asked.

His eyes were filled with a dread I had never seen before, as if he thought I would make a mess of his life. It tore me up from the inside, creating a hot pain that nearly doubled me over. I did not want to cause my father such angst.

"Yes, Father." I dropped my gaze.

"And you'll follow her rules?" he added, his eyebrows arching and his voice lilting higher with the question.

I nodded.

"No matter how ridiculous you may think they are?"

I rolled my eyes. "Yes. I will not question her authority as you feel I have questioned yours."

The apprehension melted from his face, and a genuine smile formed in its stead. He grabbed my hands and squeezed gently. "Thank you. I know this must be hard, but we will work out all the kinks when I return. I promise."

DINNER WENT SMOOTHLY, AND I had another glimpse of why my father fell under this woman's spell. She charmed as if it came naturally. However, I caught the edge in her in a simple sideways glare. I didn't want to cause my father anymore dread than I already had, so I played along despite the unease settling in my bones.

"I made dessert," I said after everyone finished their fill of the meat pie.

The corners of Lady Githa's lips turned downward, and her eyes narrowed.

Before she opened her mouth to spew whatever thoughts caused dark clouds in her eyes, I stood and hustled into the kitchen to retrieve the honey cakes. I turned with the bite-size pieces displayed proudly on a platter and nearly ran into Lady Githa.

"You did not clear this with me," she spat out like I was delivering spoiled meat instead of dessert.

My eyebrows shot up. I glanced at my tray and back to her lips pressed together until her anger bloomed in her cheeks. I didn't know how to respond.

"I- I'm sorry," I muttered and dropped my gaze.

"Before you use precious resources on such frivolous things, you will check with me first. Understand?"

I nodded.

She turned, swinging the door open and adopting that glowing smile as she waved me into the dining room. "Elle has made some lovely pastries for us."

The switch in personas had me blinking in confusion, but I stepped into the dining room with my meager offerings and set them on the table. My appetite vanished, and I just picked at my serving. No matter how hard I tried to eat the honey cake, I couldn't. From what the others stated, it was divine, but I couldn't get past the venom that had been in my step-mother's voice.

After dinner, I was left to clean up by order of the new lady of the house. My father wouldn't even look at me as she issued the request. I stood in the kitchen, staring at the stack of dirty dishware. All I wanted to do was soak in a tub to scrub off the smoke and sweat that had accumulated on my skin. Instead, I had to search for the cleaning bin and start scrubbing the dishes, silverware, and pots until they all gleamed like the rest of the utensils and pans.

By the time I crawled into the guest room bed, my muscles ached worse than I could ever remember, even more than the first time I sparred with a sword. While my eyelids remained heavy, sleep evaded me. Every time I rolled, I clenched my teeth against a moan of discomfort.

I finally drifted off when the night was at its darkest, but my sleep was riddled with nightmare after horrid nightmare.

CINDER Chapter 4

MY FATHER RODE OFF at morning light with half a dozen of our cows tied to the back of the cart. I stood in the road until I could no longer see him and then turned back to the house. Dark clouds rolled across the sky, bringing forth uneasiness.

Lily crossed the distance between the door and stopped next to me, staring at the road as well. She reeked of nervous energy, like the absence of my father meant dark times. When she finally glanced at me, her lips twitched into a smile before it disappeared.

"Momma wants to speak to you," she said with a soft voice.

I took one last look down the road and a glance at the storm clouds before I stepped inside our home. The minute I closed the door, Lady Githa marched into the hallway with her arms crossed and a sneer that sent a shiver through me.

Father's words echoed in my mind as I stared my stepmother down. I took a breath, calming the bristling inside me before I tried on a smile. "What can I do for you, my lady?"

"The house needs cleaning, and I expect breakfast in the next hour." She turned and strutted off.

I bit my tongue and headed into the kitchen. What I really wanted to do was go down to the stream and just sit quietly in the sun while I digested this massive change in our lives. Instead, I was Lady Githa's servant, and while I wanted to tell her to sod off, I couldn't. Not with the promise I made to my father yesterday.

I gathered grains and almond milk and attempted to make porridge, sweetening it with a little honey. When it was bubbling hot and thick, I poured it into three bowls, carrying it into the dining room where both Lily and Lady Githa sat expectantly. I passed out the bowls and took a seat on the opposite side of the table from Lily with my bowl.

Lady Githa cleared her throat just as I reached for my bowl.

"What are you doing?" she asked.

"Eating." The answer came automatically. The edge in my voice didn't go unnoticed.

Lady Githa's eyes narrowed and her lips thinned. "Not in here with us."

My eyebrows rose and my mouth popped open. I stared at her, dumbfounded. Where exactly did she expect me to eat?

She pointed towards the kitchen. "You eat in there while your father is gone."

Any doubts of where I landed in the family vanished with her statement. I was no better than a hired hand, and it rubbed me wrong. But instead of creating any more animosity by speaking my mind, I stood and picked up my bowl, retreating into the kitchen while my hands shook enough to slosh the porridge in the dish. I staunched the urge to throw my breakfast across the room. Instead, I brought the bowl to my lips and slurped my meal. My body needed food, and I was sure if I went without it, my day would be much more grueling.

As soon as I finished my food, I dropped the bowl near the washing pot and turned, heading out the back door into the field and the brook. I climbed up on the rock and hugged my knees as I stared at the running water. The chill in the air penetrated all the way through my clothing, and I clenched my jaw against my chattering teeth.

The sun penetrated the dark clouds for a moment, sending slivers of light over the land like a beacon of hope. But it left as quickly as it came. Darkness covered the land, and lightning painted the sky just before the clouds opened up, letting rain fall in buckets. I stood, tilting my face into the beating drops, relishing the clean feeling of water running through my hair.

When lightning spiked through the sky, striking a boulder on the other side of the brook, I jumped off my perch and headed back home.

I slid through the back of the kitchen and closed the door gently. My clothing dripped on the floor, leaving a puddle wherever I stepped. I crossed to the doorway leading to the dining area and pushed open the door. The room was empty, and I crossed to the stairwell. I needed to get out of these wet clothes before I caught a death of a cold.

I made it halfway up the staircase.

"Where have you been?"

The harsh voice froze me in my tracks. I glanced over my shoulder at Lady Githa's red face. I swore fire spit from her eyes, and she peeled her lips back in a sneer.

"I went for a walk," I answered, keeping my voice steady.

"You are not entitled to a walk. Not while your chores are still outstanding." She marched up the steps and grabbed my arm, dragging me into the guest room, where she released me and pulled a bamboo rod as long as my forearm from her pocket. She gripped the end of it so hard, her knuckles went white.

I had seen less patient riders use a similar tool to smack their horses to get them to move faster. What I saw in Lady Githa's eyes matched the intensity of those crazed riders.

I took a step back, splaying my hands out in front of me. "What are you doing?"

"Knees. Now," she barked.

"I don't think so," I said, taking another step. Neither my mother nor my father ever raised a hand to me, but I had seen enough of it in the town market to understand what this woman had in mind.

She swung the stick. I parried and lifted my arms as if I had a sword to deflect the blow. Instead of my backside, the wood connected with my arm. I spun away, clasping my stinging limb to my chest.

The next blow hit the small of my back and I yelped, dropping to my hands and knees.

"You will not disobey me again," she bellowed.

I covered my head, and she belted me at least six more times. Each hit stung like a nest of bees attacked me instead of a wooden stick.

When Lady Githa finished, the stick disappeared in her pocket, and she ran her hands through her hair, putting it back into a neat coif. She cleared her throat. "Now, you will change out of that wet garment and clean this house. I expect the floors to shine when you are finished, or we will have another session with the rod."

CINDER Chapter 5

I SCRUBBED FLOORS, COOKED meals, and scrubbed some more for almost two days straight without so much as a nap. Every time I stopped, Lady Githa was there with her rod. My back sported black and blue strips where the stick connected with my skin.

I prayed for my father to return soon. I knew when he came home, the beatings would stop, and perhaps that would be the end of Lady Githa's reign in this household.

The fifth day after my father left, knocking interrupted my daily scrubbing of the entry. I rose to my feet and stumbled to the door, nearly blind from exhaustion. I swung the door open to a familiar face. Nathan stared at me, and his gaze traveled the length of me before it snapped back to my eyes. He blinked and brushed his dark bangs away from his face.

"Elle," he started and shifted his weight, glancing over his shoulder for a moment. He licked his lips and met my gaze again. "Your father..." He glanced down at the ground and closed his eyes.

My heart hammered in my chest. "What about my father?" I gripped the door tight to keep steady. My exhaustion vanished, and a boiling panic filled my muscles.

"He was attacked on the way to Dover. The thieves ran off with the cattle."

I glanced behind him at the cart in the street and started towards it. Nathan grabbed me by the arms, trying to hold me back.

"Elle, he's dead."

Nathan's voice echoed in my head the way it does in a nightmare. I broke free from him and ran towards the cart and the covered lump on the wooden planks.

As fast as I ran, Nathan beat me to the platform, blocking me from seeing the bulk of what was under the ratty blanket. However, a bare foot stuck out of one corner. My chest tightened, and I reached around Nathan. The moment my fingers touched the cold gray foot, my body stiffened from the spark that passed between me and my dead father.

Visions flashed before my eyes. I could not stop the channeling of thoughts and images accosting me. It was as if he waited to share his last breath with me. Sorrow draped over my soul as completely as the blanket covering my father. I pulled my hand away, and whatever connection had been spawned by my touch severed. I covered my mouth, shutting off the keening I'd had no idea I was making.

Nathan wrapped his arm around my shoulder and led me back inside the house, supporting me despite my trembling legs. His kindness touched me. I patted his hand in a show of thanks. He gave me a squeeze of sympathy back.

"What is all this noise about?" Lady Githa bellowed from the top of the stairs.

Both of us stopped in place, startled by the venom in her tone.

"Elle's father was killed on the way to Dover," Nathan said with a flat voice, like he had no feelings on the matter himself.

I kept Lady Githa's gaze through a veil of tears. What I saw in her face turned a piece of my heart black. There was no sorrow present—just a nod of acknowledgement—but at least that look of eternal irritation had been replaced with a mask of neutrality.

"Prepare the body for burial," she said and turned.

"No." I glared up at her. "Prepare a proper pyre for my father," I said to Nathan. "My father's ashes will join my mother's."

Lady Githa matched my glare. "Lord Seeley will be buried at the church burial grounds."

"Lord Seeley will be cremated on our lands," I growled.

"He was my husband. I have the final say in how and where his funeral will take place. And I have the final say on who attends," she snarled back. With a dismissive gesture, she moved her gaze to Nathan. "Prepare my husband's body for burial."

"Yes, my lady," Nathan said and bowed.

I stared after her as she marched out of sight. I didn't know if her ultimatum was a veiled threat or not, but there was no way I was missing my father's funeral, whether by pyre or burial.

I turned just as Nathan stepped out the door.

"What are you going to do?" I asked him.

He leveled his green eyes at me. "I'm going to do as the lady of the house demands." He waved towards the stairs and turned on his heel.

The cart pulled away at Nathan's direction and headed towards the town church. Fire filled my veins as hot as the tears tracking down my cheeks. My mother deserved a companion in death, and the vile woman of the house denied that. I slammed the door and turned to head up the stairs.

Lady Githa stood a few paces behind me with the rod in her hand. Her face scrunched. She roared as she approached me with the rod at the ready.

Hot pain flared in my cheek. Before I could raise my arm to stop the next swing, my ears began ringing. My vision narrowed as blackness filled the edges. The third strike hit my temple. Pain flared through my head, and then nothingness yanked me under.

⋘•❖•⋙

MY HEAVY LIDS WOULDN'T cooperate. Darkness surrounded me, dulling all sound. I cleared my throat, and while I felt the rumbling in my chest, the sound was muffled, bordering on non-existent. My chest constricted, and I tried to raise my hands. They only moved a fraction before being restrained.

My wrist stung like it had been bitten. Fabric moved, and hollow sounds became full again.

"You never talk back to me in front of others, understand?"

Her cold and stern voice sent shockwaves up my back. It took a matter of moments to realize my situation. My arms were straight out to either side and my wrists were tied down. My cheek rested on a cold, flat surface and my ankles were bound and anchored. The reason I couldn't hear before must have had to do with the fabric binding my eyes. A chill bit at my skin, so I was either bound in the courtyard or more likely in one of the rooms far enough away from the hearth where warmth did not penetrate.

The sting of the rod on my back made me gasp.

"Do you understand?"

I pressed my lips together as tears stung my eyes. The fighter inside me reared up, forbidding me from acknowledging Lady Githa's ultimatum. And then my father's face drifted into my memory. His sad and desperate eyes begging me to follow her orders bloomed forth.

"Yes," I shouted as the rod connected with my shoulder.

"You will make this place shine and prepare a feast for the funeral guests. Understand?"

"But..."

The rod snapped against my lower back, hard enough to lock my breath in my chest. Burning pain flared. I forced myself to nod while tears stung my eyes.

"If I see your face at the funeral, this will seem like a walk in the countryside compared to the next beating. Do you understand?"

Hollowness filled my chest, and I choked on my words.

She mistook my silence for disobedience and gave me a preview of what she was referencing. The rod didn't spare any part of my body from the bottoms of my feet all the way to the back of my shoulders. By the time she was done, she huffed with exertion and I whimpered my assent.

"You are my servant girl, understand?"

Before I could respond, she wacked my buttocks.

"Yes," I whispered, accepting my station in her home. I had nowhere else to go, and I had a feeling if I ran, she would hunt me down and do worse things to me than she did today.

Lady Githa untied me and pulled the blindfold from my head. She threw my dress at me. "Get dressed and start cleaning."

I pushed myself onto my hands and knees, clamping my lips against a groan. Every muscle in my back screamed in agony. My head pulsed with the pain. I reached for my clothing and dragged my dress over my head. The fabric might as well have been hot pokers against my skin. I arched, trying to get the fabric off, but it was no use. I climbed up on legs that felt like wet clay, ready to crumble at any moment.

I used the table for support as I crossed the room towards the door.

"You have twenty-four hours to get this place clean and prepare a meal for fifty people. Do not disappoint me." She walked out, leaving me alone.

The minute the door closed on her, my legs stopped supporting me and I crumpled to the floor. Silent sobs wracked my bruised body, sending tendrils of both physical and mental anguish through every cell.

A hush fell over the room, and I swore I felt my mother's arms surround me and her soft coo telling me everything would work out.

It filled me with warmth and comfort, even though I knew it couldn't be real. Just the same, it gave me enough strength to climb to my feet and do the tasks doled out by the wicked witch.

CINDER Chapter 6

FUNERAL DAY. I STOOD stirring a pot of stew instead of mourning my father in the front pew of the church. Before she left for the service, Lady Githa had walked through the house to inspect its cleanliness. I didn't get another rod whipping, so I thought she found the condition of our home satisfactory.

I set the pot aside and checked on the bread. Twenty golden loaves sat in the opening. I pulled them out one by one and carefully cut them so there was enough for fifty people to have at least two slices with their stew.

I moved the bread tray to the center of the banquet table and then set up bowls around it, leaving a space for the stew serving bowl. The vat was heavy, and when I tried to haul it up onto the table, I nearly dropped it. My heart jumped in my chest. If anything marred the floor, it would mean scrubbing until it shined again. Luckily, not a drop spilled. I let my breath out as I centered the pot on the table and rearranged the bowls for easy serving.

With the meal ready to serve, and the quiet of the house pressing down on me, I retired into the kitchen with a piece of bread and a bowl of stew. Eating it before anyone arrived for the after-funeral activities was probably not a good thing to do, but I was hungry, and a part of me didn't care about the impending punishment for stepping out of line yet again.

What she didn't know wouldn't hurt either of us. However, if she found out that I had thrown my manners out the window, I was sure my back would have new black and blue welts on it before the sun set.

I finished the meal, cleaned the bowl, and returned it to the table. As I grabbed a second piece of bread and headed back towards the kitchen, an explosion of noise filled the banquet room. People I had never laid eyes on filtered in around Lady Githa.

I scanned the crowd, looking for a familiar face. None of our neighbors or my father's friends were present. I turned and escaped into the kitchen before I let the sudden onslaught of anger out in front of anyone. The price for that sort of insubordination would likely turn me into a cripple. I stood with my hands pressed firmly on the cutting counter to keep them from shaking, slowly counting down from one hundred to get control over the beast rearing inside me.

I glance up when the door squeaked open. Lily slid into the kitchen and averted her eyes from me.

"I'm sorry about your father," she said in no more than a whisper.

Tears clouded my vision, and I nodded, acknowledging her.

She crossed to the counter with a tentative glance over her shoulder. The fear etched into her features was all too familiar. When she reached out and squeezed my hand, I didn't move, but the gesture gave me a new strength to persevere, if only to protect this meek child.

She skittered back into the dining room while my heart pounded in my throat. I couldn't stomach the noise bleeding through the door, so I retired to my room, collapsing on the hard bed. Sleep had been scarce this past week, and despite my internal warnings, the moment my eyes closed, I dropped into the black.

DARKNESS SURROUNDED ME, AND my skin heated in panic. When I lifted my hand, it came to my face with no restraints. I blinked, trying to let my eyes adjust to the night. There was still noise coming from the lower floor. I exhaled as my clenched muscles relaxed.

I snuck down the back stairs, into the kitchen and stared at the pile of dirty bowls and the stew pot, wondering who brought this into the kitchen. On the heels of that silent question, tension filled my skin again.

If Lady Githa noticed it wasn't me who cleared out the dining room, a reprimand would be carried out once her company left.

I focused on cleaning, which had become both my punishment and my temporary salvation when I met Lady Githa's expectations.

By the time I finished putting the bowls away, the noise level had diminished to a quiet whisper. I wiped my hands on my apron and hung it up by the door before I ventured into the banquet hall.

Those who were left in the room were lounging in their chairs with their heads back and eyes closed. I hurried across the room as silently as possible, scanning the remaining faces. Lady Githa wasn't among the drunkards.

I slipped into the short hall leading to the grand entry of the house. Just beyond the staircase was the sitting room, where low voices conspired. I crept closer, trying to identify the voices, but none of them sounded familiar. I stood just beyond the entryway, debating on whether to stick my head inside or not.

The rustling of fabric startled me. I jumped and turned towards the stairs. My eyes widened at the sight of Lady Githa. Her normally neat, coiffed hair was messy and unkept like she had just woken after a restless night in bed. Her steps were sluggish, and she grinned at me like I was her best friend.

When a young man came out of the upstairs hall buttoning his britches, my eyebrows rose and my mouth popped open.

Lady Githa's pleasant smile turned mean. Her eyes narrowed, and she pointed a hooked finger in my direction. "Go to your room. Now."

I didn't hesitate. I moved up the stairwell, giving her a wide berth. By the time I got to my room, my jaw ached from clenching it so tightly. If I had access to a real sword...

I shook the thought out of my head. No matter how much I despised the woman, I would never resort to killing. Life was too precious.

I stood in the center of my room. Emptiness wrapped around me and I shivered. I needed to be near my parents. I glanced at the ceiling. I hadn't been in the attic since my father cleared out my mother's things.

I needed something that anchored hope into my soul, because if Lady Githa remembered anything in the morning, I would have another session with the rod. Before I was even aware of moving, I found myself at the foot of the attic stairwell with a small lantern in my hand.

I climbed the steps and set the lamp on a closed trunk, far enough away from my mother's gowns to ensure nothing would catch fire. As I walked past the garments, I let my fingers run over the silky fabrics.

My throat constricted, and tears blurred my eyes. I missed my parents. I missed their warm laughter, their proud gazes, and, most of all, their soft words. Since Father brought Lady Githa into our home, kindness had disappeared.

Perhaps I had been a nobleman's spoiled brat like Lady Githa had said on multiple occasions, but I would rather be raised with parents of pure hearts and kindness than one so full of hatred and jealousy. I did not want to become bitter, but the sour taste of abuse had already worked its way into my bones.

My gaze dropped to the ornate trunk hidden in the shadows. I stepped closer, pulled by an invisible rope. The moment I laid my palm on the wood, warmth encompassed me.

If I closed my eyes, I could almost feel my mother and her soft coo in my ear telling me everything would be okay. The nightmare was over, and the morning sunshine was just over the horizon. I almost laughed aloud at the sentiment.

I pulled my hand away from the wood and turned, cocking my head at the shuffling below. I jogged across the room and doused the lantern, holding my breath and feeling my way to the stairs. Halfway down, I took a seat and strained to hear anything outside the door.

A mischievous chuckle came through the wood, and it sent an eerie chill through me.

"What have we here?" a deep voice purred.

"Leave me alone!"

My heart skipped a beat. The anxiety and fear in Lily's voice brought me to my feet. A fierce protectiveness blazed through my veins, and I charged into the hallway.

One of the men from the funeral gala had her pinned to the wall and was trying to kiss her even as Lily pushed against his chest, turning her head away.

I slammed the door, making them both jump.

"I suggest you leave my sister alone." I gripped the lantern tight enough for the brass handle to dig into my palm.

The man turned his bloodshot eyes in my direction. The minute they landed on me, he let Lily go. Interest reflected in his gaze. I swallowed as Lily fled towards her room.

I squared my feet. The lamp in my hand was my only weapon, but it would do nicely if this charlatan thought I would be easy prey. While I accepted punishment from the lady of the house, I would not allow the same from a drunken stranger.

"You'll do nicely," he slurred and started towards me.

I cocked my head and narrowed my gaze. "I think you should take your leave now before your blood stains these floors." My heart hammered in my chest, belying the calm sureness of my voice.

He pulled to a stop and blinked a few times. Interest transformed, widening his eyes into saucers of fear.

I didn't flinch. I held my ground and stared him down. He backed away slowly and then turned, stumbling down the stairwell like a frightened child. I took a deep breath and glanced over my shoulder. The dark and very empty hallway met my gaze.

My grip on the lantern loosened, and the sting in my palm subsided. Instead of worrying about what might have frightened a grown man, I set my sights on making sure Lily was okay. I hurried down the hall to my old bedroom and knocked gently on the door.

"Lily?" I opened the door and peeked inside. She lay on her bed sobbing. I slipped inside, closing the door behind me before I set the lantern down on the table near the door.

Lily startled at the scrape of metal against wood. Her wide eyes shot around the darkened room like I was the man who had accosted her in the hallway, coming to finish whatever he had started. She relaxed when I stepped out of the shadows.

I crossed to her side and perched on the edge of the bed. "Are you all right?"

She reached for me, shaking her head. I took her in my arms in the same way my mother used to console me. My hand ran over her back as she silently cried on my shoulder. I didn't tell her it was going to be okay. I couldn't bring myself to lie to appease her anguish.

Finally, she pulled away and wiped her face. "You are so brave."

I giggled and shook my head. "I'm not brave."

"What did you do to him?" She jutted her chin towards the door.

"I just told him he best be on his way." I shrugged. "Maybe he just didn't want to be picking any glass out of his scalp." I hooked my thumb over my shoulder at where I had placed my lantern.

She grinned. "Too bad you didn't get to clock him."

I raised my eyebrows and looked down my nose at her. A blush bloomed in her cheeks, and she looked down at her hands. She got my silent berating and shifted.

"I'm sorry."

"You never *want* to spill blood. You only strike out of necessity," I said, recanting the lessons I learned while Nathan taught me to sword fight.

"You are very wise," she whispered.

"No. I just listen and learn and hold life dear." I took a deep breath and gave her a sad smile. "My mother was wise and brave and loving. I want to be like her."

Lily took my hands in hers and squeezed. "You are."

CINDER Chapter 7

THE FOLLOWING MORNING, SOME stragglers remained. Lady Githa strutted into the dining room like she hadn't drunk a barrel of wine all by herself the night before. I had porridge made and ready for both her and Lily, and a forced smile on my lips as I waited to clear her dishes.

"Where is breakfast for my guests?" she snapped and waved at the still passed out collection of half a dozen men and women.

I glanced around the room and then back to her. "They aren't even awake."

Storm clouds filled Lady Githa's eyes. She stood, reaching into her pocket just as Lily stepped in the room. Lily's smile faded at the tension between her mother and me, and she quickly scuttled to the table.

"Hello, Mother," she said, drawing Lady Githa's gaze away from me. "Did you sleep well?"

I exhaled and slipped from the room, escaping into the kitchen before Lady Githa's rage returned. I focused on making another six bowls of porridge. With a tray loaded with the newly made breakfast bowls, I kicked the door open, crossed to the table, and set the tray down in front of Lady Githa.

"Breakfast for your guests, my lady," I said as I placed the bowls on the table and turned to leave.

"Who told you to waste our food on these people?" The challenge in her voice turned my blood to ice.

I slowly pivoted to face her. I licked my lips and glanced around the room, formulating my words carefully. My nerve endings screamed to flee, but I knew if Lady Githa was on one of her rampages, I would only make the beating worse by running.

"I thought that was what you wanted," I said and chewed the inside of my cheek, waiting for her judgement.

The redness that bloomed in her cheeks gave me my answer, as did the progressive thinning of her lips as she pressed them together. She pushed her chair back and stood, reaching for the rod in her pocket.

"Elle saved me from one of the drunken men last night," Lily said. She delivered the information in a conversational tone right before she scooped a spoonful of porridge into her mouth.

Lady Githa blinked as her hand froze halfway out of her pocket. Her gaze darted to Lily.

"He threw me against the wall and was trying to hurt me. Elle made him stop." She continued to eat and act as if a beating hadn't been on the morning docket.

Lady Githa slid the rod back into her pocket, and she lowered herself back into her chair. "That will be all," she said to me.

Lily's gaze remained on her food. I headed into the kitchen and leaned against the wall, exhaling. Relief flooded into my tense muscles, making them rubbery. I had to lean on the counter to make sure my knees wouldn't buckle under the sudden evaporation of stress.

When I got to the washing pot, I leaned on the counter and closed my eyes. Hope wiggled its way into my heart, banishing the blackness that had infiltrated. With Lily on my side, if I remained patient, I could almost see the end of this difficult journey at the hands of that mad woman.

HOPE DIED THAT AFTERNOON when I was moving a large vase of flowers. It dropped in the entryway and shattered on the tiled floor. Lady Githa was close enough to hit me square behind the knees. I fell, catching shards of glass in both my hands and my legs.

The sight of my blood mixed with the water on her beloved tile floors sent her over the edge. The rod must have connected with my back and legs over a dozen times. I cradled my head in my arms despite the blood flowing into my hair from my sliced hands.

When she finished her tirade, she snarled, "Clean this mess up!"

I climbed to my feet, wincing at the agony wracking my body. With shaking hands, I plucked the glass from my wounds in my palms and legs, pressing my lips against crying out. Before I addressed the floor, I needed to stop the flow of blood from my wounds. Otherwise, another beating was imminent.

I tore fabric strips from my skirt and bandaged the wounds. Once the bleeding stopped, I swept the glass into a bucket and brought it to the garbage ditch in the back field. The ditch was nearly overflowing with waste, which meant it was almost time for another burning ritual to clean the dump.

I sighed. The last burn included my mother's funeral pyre. It stayed lit for three days before the flames finally died. My throat tightened, and I turned, trudging back to the house to resume cleaning the mess I'd made. I needed to finish and then clean my wounds properly. The rags I used were not in the best condition, and the longer they pressed against the open sores, the higher the likelihood of an infection.

I was sure Lady Githa would rejoice if I fell ill and died. It would mean one less mouth to feed. But it would also mean Lily would have to take up the housework and most likely be the recipient of Lady Githa's fickle rage.

CINDER Chapter 8

IN THE WEEKS FOLLOWING my breaking of the vase, my hands and knees healed and things around the homestead calmed. I worked daily from before the sun kissed the horizon until late enough in the evenings to watch the progress of the stars. My cooking skills became more well-rounded with Lily's secret help.

Lady Githa seemed more frustrated with me the better I did, and while my sessions with the rod became less frequent, I could tell she was waiting for the moment I failed with the same barely contained glee a child has while waiting to open their Christmas presents.

With the snowy season now in full swing, Lady Githa insisted I move out of the main house and into the servants' quarters. The chill in this section of the house was maddening and made my muscles ache almost all the time. The main portion of the house was warmed by the large fireplace, which was another duty I was tasked.

I had found a cadence to my schedule that began with hauling wood inside, and once the main fireplace and kitchen ovens were lit, I would clean the entry and then make breakfast for Lady Githa and Lily. Clean breakfast dishes before getting a second haul of wood, which required a second cleaning of the entry and halls, to both the main fireplace and the kitchen. Then lunch and dinner preparation, more cleaning, serving, and stoking the fires before I hit my mattress at night. The sameness in my schedule grew comforting, although I never knew when Lady Githa would snap.

It was after the second wood run that a knock interrupted my schedule. I climbed to my feet and hung the rag on the edge of the bucket before I crossed to answer the door. Lady Githa appeared at the top of the stairs as I swung the front door open.

The king's footman stood with his hands behind his back.

I immediately bowed and waved him inside out of the biting wind. The minute he set foot in the house, I closed the door.

Lily came around the corner and joined her mother on the landing.

The footman pulled out a scroll of paper from behind his back. Unfurling it, he cleared his throat. "The king is hosting a ball this coming Saeterndag. Every available woman in Canterbury, no matter her station"—he looked at me before returning his gaze to

Lady Githa—"is required to attend. No exceptions." His gaze landed on me again.

"And what is the purpose of this ball?" Lady Githa asked.

The footman smiled. "Since the prince has not agreed to any of the matches the king has set forth, he is required to choose one of the women at the ball as his wife."

Interest sparked in Lady Githa's eyes.

My mind drifted to that day by the stream and the way the prince had looked at me. I couldn't help the smile that formed.

"We will be there," Lady Githa said and slung her arm around Lily.

The footman glanced at me and nodded, bowing before he turned and left. I closed the door and turned with the smile still plastered on my face. I met Lily's gaze, but she wasn't smiling. Instead, she was looking at her mother.

"Why are you smiling?" Lady Githa said to me.

"I have never been to a ball at the palace," I said.

"And you never will."

I blinked and pressed my back against the front door. "But..."

"You have nothing proper to wear to a ball, and I will not have you embarrassing this house by going in rags."

I thought of all my mother's gowns in the attic. "So, if I had a proper dress, I could go?"

She crossed her arms and raised a critical eyebrow. "If I approve of the gown, perhaps."

I grinned and jogged upstairs, bypassing Lady Githa in the hall without so much as a glance. As soon as I was around the corner, I disappeared up the attic stairs. I walked through the selection of gowns and stopped in front of a powder blue dress of the finest silk. I pulled it off the hanger and folded it over my arm. When I turned, both Lady Githa and Lily were on the landing, staring at the abundance of formal dresses.

"Where did these come from?" Lily asked. Her voice held awe that matched her wide-eyed expression.

"My mother." I glanced around. "Would you like one for the ball?"

Lily's eyes lit up. "Really?"

"You should have a new gown, not some hand-me-down from the dead," Lady Githa said and glared at me. With a nod, she turned on her heel and escorted Lily back down the stairs.

I followed and retreated to my room to hang up the dress before I returned to finish my chores. The floors sparkled when I finished, and not a speck of dust clung to the furniture. I put away my cleaning supplies and headed to the kitchen to whip up dinner. I nearly skipped down the halls with the excitement budding in my bones. A ball was just the divine intervention I needed.

Lady Githa remained stoic as I served her and Lily's dinner. As soon as I cleaned up the dishes, I was ready for a good night's rest and hopefully a dream or two about the prince with his devilish smile.

My light step halted as I entered my room. Bits of shredded fabric covered the floor. I squatted down, holding the light closer. I recognized the blue fabric. My gaze jumped to where the dress should have been hanging, but no dark outline showed. I crossed and stared at the empty hanger. My breath caught in my throat at the horrific deed.

Someone shredded my ball gown.

A lump formed in my throat, and my gaze moved to the ceiling. My heartbeat sped. I whirled on my heel, flying up the attic stairs, praying the iron ball in my stomach wasn't right. Praying that the lady of the house hadn't destroyed *all* my mother's gowns.

I stood at the top of the stairs on shaking legs as I surveyed the damage. Every single garment my mother owned was in shreds. But that wasn't the only thing ruined. It was as if a storm had rolled into the space and destroyed anything that had been my mother's. Her knickknacks were in shards alongside the fabric. Her china was in pieces. Even her books were torn apart.

Nothing remained. My breath departed from my chest, painfully, like someone had punched a hole through my midsection. I couldn't draw air into my lungs. I dropped to my knees on the cold wooden planks. The light from my lantern danced across the space, illuminating the few crates and trunks remaining. The ornate one that my father forbade me to open sat unharmed.

The sight of it loosened my lungs, and I drew a great inhalation. I covered my face, hiding my hot tears from the rest of the surrounding disaster. There was only one person under this roof that had the level of hatred and spite to carry out such a heinous act.

"I expect you to clean this up tonight," Lady Githa said from behind me.

I tensed and turned slowly. Lady Githa stood halfway up the stairwell with her hands on her hips and a smug smile on her face.

"You did this." I waved at the ruins in front of me.

"This is my house now. I can do with it as I please." She glanced around the room. "It looks as if you have nothing to wear to the ball."

The chill in her voice was as icy as the wind whipping through the cracks in the attic.

"You did this?" I was on my feet with my hands clenched into tight fists. A blaze of fury encompassed me, and I was sure the feral snarl in my voice matched that of my expression.

Lady Githa narrowed her eyes and pressed the smirk on her lips into a tight line. Within a blink, she roared up the remaining stairs, pulling the rod free from her dress.

As upset as I was, instinct took over. I moved backwards, wary of the stick in her hand. Several thoughts occurred at once—the first was just as horrifying as the mess surrounding me. I thought about pushing Lady Githa down the stairs. The second thought was the need to defend myself, but there was nothing within reach to stop the beating rod from connecting with my skin. The last thought was one of survival. I raised my arm just in time to interfere with the rod hitting my skull.

I blocked as many strikes as I could. Each time her rod connected with my arm, it stung bone deep, but I refused to cry out. I refused to cower this time. Not with what she had done. Murder flashed in her eyes as I fell to my knees, and I wondered if I would live through this beating.

"Mother! Stop!" Lily's voice pierced the near blackness.

The blows halted. Lady Githa turned with her hair in a state of disarray. Her wild look calmed, but not enough for me to swallow the lump of fear in my throat.

I prayed Lily wouldn't be the next recipient of Lady Githa's temper.

"Clean this place up," Lady Githa snapped and marched down the stairs, slamming the attic door closed.

My vision faded as I clung to stay awake. If I passed out in the attic, I would freeze to death, although that didn't seem like a bad way to go, considering what kind of future awaited me downstairs.

An old broom sat in the corner, along with a bucket. I limped over, wincing with every step. Each movement, each scrape of broken ceramic, lit a flame in my soul.

I needed to survive, and the only way to do that was to escape Lady Githa's wrath.

CINDER Chapter 9

MY BODY STILL HURT from the attic beating on the morning of the ball. Lady Githa had gotten Lily a dress that was sure to turn heads, but it paled to that of Lady Githa's. I'd avoided eye contact with the woman for the entire week. If I looked at her, I might actually spit at her vile audacity. The woman was delusional. The prince wouldn't even look twice at the old hag.

I entertained pilfering her closet for a gown after they left, but I was in no condition for a ball. Not with black and blue marks so prevalent on my arms and my face. Besides, tonight was my perfect opportunity to escape this hellhole.

Lady Githa was so occupied with the thought of charming Prince William into her bed that all my preparations had gone unnoticed. I had enough food to last a week on the road. I had warmer boots tucked away and a couple of saddlebags hidden inside the pantry, so I could pack whatever was in my father's trunk upstairs.

My mother's horse, Misty, still remained in our barn, along with three other horses. If I couldn't sneak her saddle out without alerting one of Lady Githa's stableboys, I would ride that mare bareback. Technically, Lady Githa could say I was a horse thief, but everyone knew my mother's horse. They wouldn't arrest me for taking something that rightfully belonged to me. At least I hoped so.

"Elle," Lady Githa said, interrupting my scheming thoughts.

"Yes, my lady," I said, keeping my gaze lowered.

"I have guards posted at the doors to make sure you don't attempt to come to the ball, despite my wishes."

I glanced at her, cursing under my breath.

"Or..." She pulled out a bag and dumped the contents on the entry floor. The food I had stored tumbled out. "Just in case you thought you would try to run away. I own you now." The bag dropped from her fingertips, and she trudged up the stairs. "Clean that up."

I stared at the mess she'd made. Hope fled from my body. I grabbed the broom and cleaned up my food stash. My mind couldn't wrap around how she found it, but then again, the woman seemed to sneak up on me whenever she wanted. Other times, I could hear her coming from any corner of the house.

I was still scrubbing the floor when Lady Githa and Lily descended the stairs. Lady Githa wore a form-fitting ruby red dress with gold accents. Lily wore a powder blue dress similar to the color of the one I had chosen from my mother's garments. It wasn't as form-fitting as her mother's, but it showed off her curves. She looked about as terrified as a deer surrounded by wolves.

I tried to give her a smile to calm her nerves, but her sad eyes bore into me, almost as if she wished I were going alongside her instead of her mother. As soon as the carriage pulled away from our home, two guards stepped in place, flanking the front door.

The back door held the same type of sentries, and I closed the door on their stark stares. I would figure out a way to get to the stables tonight if it was the last thing I did.

I grabbed the saddlebags from their hiding spot, marveling that Lady Githa hadn't found them. I paused before I climbed the stairs and turned each one of the bags upside down, just in case she hid something deadly inside. Nothing came out, even when I shook them. I brought one bag close enough to the lantern to see there was no surprise inside. With an exhale, I hauled them upstairs into the attic. My lantern lit the way through the array of boxes to the back corner where my father's ornate trunk sat.

I dropped the bags as the familiar vibration filled me. When I laid my hands on the top of the wood, the sigils on the outside glowed. I crouched to look at the lock, energy filling my form.

"This would be much easier if this thing wasn't locked," I muttered. My body jolted as the lock clicked open. Pure adrenaline filled me, along with a healthy dose of fear that made my mouth twinge like I had bitten on a piece of steel.

I stood, afraid to open the box, but just as afraid to take my hands off it. The glow illuminated my body. I stared as it flowed up my arms, erasing the bruises that riddled my skin. The light cleansed as well as healed. The dirt etched into my knuckles faded, and all the deep aches in my bones disappeared. I lifted my hands away from the wood, testing what my eyes derived as fact.

As the unnatural light faded, I shined my lamp where the worst of the bruises were clustered. All that remained was unblemished skin. I stared at the trunk for a few heartbeats, and then my body started responding to the urgency of opening the trunk. I flipped the lock off and heaved the heavy lid up. It creaked as it opened, and I shivered, pushing it until it fell wide.

I blinked and shifted back. An ornate wooden stick tipped with gold glowed, illuminating a white ball gown laced with gold trim. I reached to move the stick, and the minute my fingers wrapped around the wood, it was as if I stepped into the only thread of sunlight on an otherwise stormy day. Warmth spread from the point of contact, wrapping itself around me in a bright glow.

I clenched my hand and fell to my knees with a thousand images flashing before my eyes. The lives and legacies of all the mages that held this wand before me absorbed into my bloodstream, including the most famous sorcerer of all history, Merlin, pumping my heart with vigor and strength. When the last to hold the wand appeared before my eyes, I gasped at my mother's kind smile.

I blinked as knowledge seeped into every cell. I was a descendant of Merlin and the lone heir to the house of Cinder.

My gaze landed on the bodice of the gown where the crest of my ancestors was threaded in gold. It reminded me of an ornate phoenix rising from the ashes.

I touched the soft fabric, and more memories flowed through me. This was the gown my mother wore the night she fell in love. The night that changed the course of her future and made me possible. That night after dancing until almost dawn, my mother traded her heritage for a future with my father. Magic and marriage rarely coexisted peacefully, so my mother made her choice and put her wand in safekeeping until the day her daughter turned eighteen and fulfilled the Cinder destiny by bringing glory to the family crest.

A chill climbed my spine. I glanced at the barren attic as my thoughts turned to Lady Githa and what I could do to her with this new-found magic. My lips drew into a smile as I imagined all sorts of justified tortures.

Before I could shake the visions from my head, the air clouded around me.

My heart leaped into my throat as my gaze frantically moved from one side of the attic to the other. A few feet in front of me, the fog shifted, and my mother stepped into view. My eyes widened at the sight of her ethereal skin.

"Elle, you must never use the magic you now hold to harm another soul. That will turn it into dark magic, and you will tumble down a rabbit hole forevermore. Any action you take will come back upon you thrice. Remember that any time you think about casting a spell born of vicious intent."

I nodded and averted my eyes as my cheeks heated with shame.

"Heed the warning. You will be lost to my consultation if you give in to the darker human traits."

I wanted to ask where she had been the past year while I endured beatings and insults as if I were a common slave girl, but I quelled the urge. It was petty and foolish to let the bitterness get the best of me. I curtseyed deep as a sign of respect. When I looked back up, my mother, along with the fog, was gone.

I tore the rags off my shoulders and slipped the beautiful gown over my head. It fit as if it was made for me. Under the gown sat a pair of crystal slippers. Again, the fit was perfect, and I stared at the dozen manuals strewn over the bottom of the trunk. I slid the wand into a pocket in the silky fabric I wore and grabbed the books, feeding them into the saddlebags until none remained in the trunk.

I closed the lid and reengaged the lock before heading down to the back door. I closed my hand around the hilt of the wand in my pocket.

"I just need to be invisible until I make it into the stables." My whisper filled the surrounding air until it shimmered. I kept a grip on my wand and reached for the doorknob. Dragging the door open, I envisioned a breeze strong enough to push an unlatched door open. The moment the guards turned towards the creaking wood, I bolted, running right between them while they argued about what had happened.

I made it into the stables unnoticed, but the stable hands were still milling about, cleaning stalls and talking about the ball. Only noblemen had been invited even though every single female in all of Canterbury, regardless of being noble born or not, was invited. I grabbed Misty's saddle and reins and made quick work of getting her ready. With the saddlebags in place, I stepped into the stirrup, hauled myself into the saddle, and grabbed the reins.

As I trotted out the door, it was as if whatever cloak I had donned fell off.

"Stop her!" someone yelled.

I kicked Misty's sides, willing her to gallop. She flew past the front guards before they could react. I didn't look back.

It was time I met my destiny head-on. And this time, I would not let Lady Githa cheat me out of it.

241

CINDER Chapter 10

MISTY WAS BARELY WINDED when we pulled up in front of the castle. I tied her in a free spot at a water trough between two stallions that were draped in their owners' crests. I ran my hands through my hair to free the knots that had formed and climbed the stairs.

A guard stood watch at the door, and he looked down his nose at me. "You are late."

I nodded as heat filled my cheeks, and I gave him my best curtsy. "I'm sorry, sir, but I had some difficulty escaping from my home to come this evening."

His eyebrows rose. "Escaping?"

"Yes. My step-mother forbade me to come tonight."

His features hardened. "The king's message was not clear?"

"No. The message was clear. She does not know I am here, sir, and she is likely to cause a scene when she sees me."

His lips twitched before he set them into a rigid line. "Your name?"

"Elle Seeley."

The guard pulled a small scroll out of his pocket, glanced at it, and nodded. He opened the door, waving to the footman inside. "Charles will escort you to the ballroom, my lady."

The footman led me through a maze of halls and finally opened the doors to the ballroom. I stood at the top of a grand staircase, scanning the massive crowds of finely dressed maidens. Prince William stood to the side of his father in a receiving line. He smiled politely and kissed every hand that was offered, but I saw the dullness in his eyes, even at this distance.

A murmur ran through the crowd, and the prince looked up. He dropped the hand he was kissing the moment our eyes met. He cocked an eyebrow, and his polite smile morphed into the genuine grin I had seen the day he challenged me to a rock-skipping contest.

The woman in front of him turned towards the stairwell. The movement pulled my gaze from Prince William's, and I shivered as Lady Githa's glare met mine. When the prince stepped out of the receiving line, Lady Githa turned and marched towards me at a pace that was twice as fast as William's. She reached me first and grabbed my upper arm, trying to drag me back up the stairs.

I yanked my arm from her grip and raised an eyebrow. "Do you really want to be caught defying the king's orders?"

Lady Githa paled.

We both turned as the prince approached. Lily was a few paces behind him, but she wasn't looking at the prince. She was looking at me with wide, wonder-filled eyes and a broad smile, which only infuriated Lady Githa more than she already was.

Lady Githa turned the same shade as her red dress.

I stepped down to the first landing and met Prince William halfway. He smiled and took my hand, formally kissing it like he had done to the procession of women in the receiving line. However, his lips lingered on my skin, creating a pleasant web of anticipation inside me. I wondered how his lips would feel on mine instead of the back of my hand.

I curtseyed, but didn't look away from his captivating gaze.

The silence of the ballroom finally tore my eyes from his, only to find that the crowd was staring at us.

"My lady, you look stunning tonight," he said, his voice low and every bit as charming as it had been by the river.

I licked my lips and smiled at him.

Lady Githa stepped to my side and cleared her throat. "This is my servant," she said, waving towards me. "And this is my daughter, Lily." She yanked Lily to her side, almost tripping her on the steps.

The prince cocked his head and glanced at me. "Elle was never a servant," he said, surprising me. I didn't realize he knew my name. "She is Lord Seeley's daughter, and, from what I understand, can wield a sword like a seasoned knight."

Lady Githa's face turned crimson. "When Lord Seeley married me, she became my servant." She turned to me. "Did you steal that dress?"

"No. This was the dress my mother wore the day she fell in love with my father. It was in my father's trunk in the attic."

"Anything of your father's became mine when he died," Lady Githa snarled.

"Is this truly the time and place for your antics, my lady?" I asked, embarrassed to be the center of this kind of attention. I turned to Prince William. "I may be Lord Seeley's daughter, but I am also the rightful heir to the house of Cinder."

His eyes widened, but before he could speak, Lady Githa's face scrunched in anger.

"You are not the heir to Lord Seeley's fortune. I am, and you are my servant. I have provided for you since I stepped into that house. It is mine!"

Lily covered her face with her hand.

"I couldn't care less about my father's fortune. All I ask for is my father's trunk in the attic. And as far as being your servant, I am not indebted to you for anything. The only reason I obeyed your insane orders was because of a promise I made to my father. A promise that should have died alongside him." I straightened my back and scanned the crowd. "My father was not the heir to the House of Cinder." I glared at Lady Githa. "My mother was, and now it has been passed to me."

I pulled the wand from my pocket and waved it in a circle over my head, wishing for the heavens to twinkle through the ceiling. A stream of sparkling stars illuminated the dark ceiling, shining their heavenly lights down on the shocked faces of the crowd.

The king himself took a knee, bowing in respect to the House of Cinder. The entire ballroom followed suit. In a matter of seconds, the only two people who remained on their feet were me and Lady Githa. She spun on her heels, grabbed Lily's arm, and marched up the stairs.

Prince William looked up at me as I tucked the wand back into the folds of my skirt. Heat filled my cheeks at the awe filling his eyes. His lips formed that devilish grin, and he stood, taking both my hands. He leaned in close. "May I have this dance?"

"I thought you'd never ask." I smiled and let him lead me to the center of the dance floor.

The crowd parted, and I stepped into his arms. The music began, and he led me around the dance floor with practiced ease.

"I'm sorry about all that." I nodded towards the stairs.

He smiled at me. "Honestly, I didn't know if you were still alive. You never came back to the river, and I did not see you at your father's funeral." He sighed and glanced around the ballroom. "This was for you. I haven't thought of anyone else since that day at the river. When I didn't see you among the guests, I thought the worst." His dark eyes stared deeply into mine. His waltz was graceful compared to my two left feet. He smiled in such an intimate and tender way that my insides melted.

His smile faded as he studied me. "You didn't put a spell on me that day, did you?"

I shook my head. "I didn't even know about the house of Cinder until tonight. I disobeyed my father's wishes and opened his trunk in the attic. The minute I touched the wand, my family's magic flowed into me along with all the knowledge of all the mages before me."

"Even Merlin?"

"Yes. Even Merlin." I glanced around. "And I thought my new knowledge was intimidating," I whispered in his ear. "But having everyone's eyes on me is more so."

"You are doing just fine. You are the envy of every woman in the palace right now."

I wish he hadn't said that. Heat filled my every pore. I tucked my forehead under his chin so I wouldn't have to take in the stares of everyone around us. Some were clearly perplexed, and others were outright hostile, like I had stolen their only future.

The song transitioned to a slower beat, and the floor was filled with dancing patrons. We danced through a half dozen more songs before the prince swept me out of the center of attention. He led me to the balcony overlooking the city, where it was quiet and private. He closed the door, shutting out the music before turning to me. His gaze held interest, and as he approached, I couldn't help but shiver, even though the chill in the air felt good against my overheated skin.

The closer he came, the more my heart pounded. What had started as a simple hot flash turned into an inferno of anticipation. He cornered me against the railing, smiling down at me with that same wicked grin he sported by the river. The one that made my knees weak.

Prince William leaned in and brushed his soft lips against my cheek. "You are as intoxicating as I imagined," he whispered.

Intoxicating was an understatement for the current that flowed between us. When his breath caressed my cheek like a soft feather and his hands found the curve of my waist, I couldn't help but sigh. My skin tingled under his touch, and I leaned into him.

He pulled away, his eyes widening at something in the distance. I turned, following his gaze, and my heart jumped another notch. Flames engulfed a section of town. The section where my home stood.

I pulled out of his grip and flew through the doors and across the ballroom, dodging people as I went. I didn't slow, not even when I heard my name being called. I nearly tumbled down the castle steps, losing a shoe in the process, but I would not stop. By the time I got to Misty, I was out of breath. I unwrapped her bridle from the post and hopped on her back, ignoring William as he ran down the steps after me.

Misty was already galloping towards home by the time Prince William reached the road. The icy wind drew tears from my eyes and pelted my skin like a wave of sharp pine needles. My father had impressed upon me the hazards of fire with houses so close together. He had taught me how to start and douse a fire safely.

I pulled Misty to a stop a half block away from the blaze, leaving my horse in the middle of the road, I ran the rest of the way, choking on the billowing smoke until I skidded to a stop in front of my burning home. The sound of laughter pulled my attention to the road heading out of town. My father's ornate trunk winked in and out through the smoke, along with Lady Githa's laugher.

Fury encompassed me, and I stuck my hand in my pocket and wrapped my fingers around the wooden wand. I had the power to strike down that awful woman. I gritted my teeth as a litany of horrible curses swirled in my mind, but my mother's soft voice of reason cut through the building rage.

Once I stepped into the darkness, there would be no escape.

The smoke burned my nostrils and teared my eyes. I clasped my wand, fighting the urge to do harm. Instead, I channeled the intense magic elsewhere, where it would do the most good.

The town needed help. Otherwise, more homes would be engulfed. I pulled the wand from my pocket, took a big breath, and closed my eyes.

We needed buckets and buckets of water to douse the flames. What better to drive the fire out of existence than a rainstorm?

Lightning cracked through the sky, and the heavens opened, dropping sheets of rain fast enough to put out the fire. White steam rose from the rubble as I stood drenched in the street, staring at the remains of the only home I had ever known.

The houses on either side held blackened shutters and minimal charring from the heat, but they stood solid despite the surface damage. The barn in the back smoldered like the house. I gasped, thinking of the animals that had been inside.

Now that there was no longer a wall of smoke, Misty trotted over to me and nudged my shoulder. I took her bridle and ran my fingernails lightly up her snout. Neither of us had a home with a roof to go to.

I leaned my head against Misty's cheek, devastated.

CINDER Chapter 11

HOOF BEATS IN THE mud turned me toward the castle. Prince William stood out against the dark smoke that had settled over the town. His white horse trotted like it was in a damn horse show instead of trampling through the mud in front of the remains of my home. I looked back at the smoldering ashes, unsure of the emotional storm brewing inside me.

"Elle!" Prince William dismounted and crossed to stand by my side and stare at the rubble with me.

His soft touch pulled my gaze away from the last of the smoke. His hand slid down my arm until his fingers threaded with mine. The simple gesture brought burning tears to the surface, but I blinked them back.

"You are welcome to stay at the palace," he said.

He had no idea how grateful I was for that offer. My jaw trembled with a shiver, but I clamped my mouth closed, shutting the tremor down before my teeth joined in the chatter.

I nodded and allowed him to lead me and my horse away from the mess. As I walked, my uneven gait became more prevalent, so I reached down, plucking the solitary muddy shoe from my foot. With no shoes, the cold mud sifted between my toes, sending a chill up my back. I shivered, wrapping my arms around my midsection to conserve body heat.

"What do you have in the saddlebags?" he asked as he glanced at Misty.

"Spell books," I answered. "They were in my father's trunk." I shrugged. "It seemed important not to leave them behind, especially since I intended on leaving town after the ball."

Prince William chuckled and wrapped his arm around my shoulder, bringing me closer. "We can ride instead of walk, if you'd be more comfortable."

I entertained the thought, but my feet had a healthy layer of mud, which helped with the cold. "While riding back to the castle would be quicker, it would also be unbearably cold in my wet clothes." My teeth chattered between words.

"You could always ride with me," he said. "It would be a little warmer," he added when I raised my eyebrows at him.

"I'm soaked, Your Highness."

"I don't mind. And please call me William. Your Highness is a bit formal for my betrothed, don't you think?"

His words hit me like a lightning bolt out of a clear sky. I stopped and turned, looking up into his dark eyes.

He brushed a few strands of my wet hair off my cheek and smiled. "I made my choice the moment I saw you skipping rocks on the river."

"Oh. *You* made your choice..." I started walking again, leaving him staring after me. I hid the smile that had formed on my lips. I had plenty of dreams about that day, and some were more risqué than others, but in almost every dream, I lost the bet.

He caught up with me and swept me up into his arms before depositing me on his horse. He climbed up behind me with Misty's reins still in one hand. "Yes. I made the choice," he whispered in my ear and wrapped his arm around me to grab his stallion's reins before he pulled me flush against him.

His warmth seeped through my dress. While my back was toasty, the front of my body felt as if ice shards were pelting my skin. He tied Misty's reins to the horn of the saddle and wrapped his arms around me as we cantered back to the palace.

I wasn't the only one shivering, either, but he never once complained. In no time, we were back at the palace. He helped me dismount and handed over both sets of reins to the stable hand.

"Please bring Miss Seeley's saddlebags to the guest chambers and have a lady-in-waiting run a hot bath for Miss Seeley." He glanced at me, measuring me with his eyes.

"I'm sure the queen has something suitable for Miss Seeley to wear. Please see that some clothes are delivered to the room as well."

"Thank you, my lord," I said and went to bow.

William caught my arms and shook his head. "You do not need to bow to me, nor do you need to be so formal. I thought I made that clear."

His hand moved to the middle of my back, and he guided me inside the castle to a great room with a roaring fire. The music from the ball seeped through the walls, reminding me of all that had transpired this evening.

I stood as close to the flames as possible without jumping into the fireplace, and I glanced at him over my shoulder. He stood behind me to my right. Not nearly as adventurous as I was with the fire. But he wasn't wearing a soaking gown. His hands splayed out like mine, soaking in the heat, and he smiled.

I shifted to stand next to him so I wouldn't block the warmth. The silence stretched out.

"I'm sorry," I finally said.

His eyebrows rose, and the smile on his face faded. "Why are you sorry?"

I hooked my thumb towards the music. "I ruined your evening."

His laugh filled the room, and he gently turned me towards him. He leaned in and captured my lips in a kiss that transcended all my dreams. Sweet and sincere soon turned more erotic as he pulled me against him. His tongue explored my mouth in a seductive dance that made me want to peel my wet garments off and see what else his endearing mouth could do.

He pulled away. "You did not ruin my evening. You made it perfect."

Now it was my turn to laugh. "Really? My stepmother caused a scene and set my house on fire, and then you froze your ass off riding back with me on your horse. And it looks like I ruined your fine clothes." I waved at his wet clothes and the mud streaks on his pants. "And you call this a perfect night?"

The grin that spread on his lips sent a sweet tingle through my body. "Well, it hasn't gotten this exciting around here in a while. And I believe my ass is still intact. But you can check if the spirit moves you. So, yes, this has been a perfect night."

My cheeks burned from more than the proximity to the fire.

Prince William looked up and stepped back. "I believe your lady-in-waiting is here to bring you to your room and a hot bath." He bowed to me and turned, heading out of the door on the other side of the room.

I turned and beheld a young girl with fire-red hair and freckles who smiled at me and crossed the room.

"Hello, my lady, I am Miranda," she said and took my hand. "Let's get you out of those wet clothes and into a hot bath."

I looked down at the dress that had once been the most stunning of my mother's gowns. The mud-caked hem dragged on the floor with the weight of the wet fabric. "I hope

I can get all the mud off both my dress and my shoes."

"I'll take care of it for you, my lady," Miranda said and pulled me along through the halls and up a back stairwell opposite where the ballroom had been.

"How old are you?" I asked.

"I'm almost eleven." She smiled back at me. "And I've always wanted to take care of a princess."

I laughed. "Princess?"

"Oh, yes, my lady. Rumor has it the royal wedding will occur before the week's end."

Before I could respond, she pulled me into a room with a large tub filled with steaming water that smelled like lavender and sage. I crossed, peeling the soiled dress from my skin without an ounce of modesty. All I could think of was that hot water taking the chill right out of my bones.

The minute my muddy foot breached the surface, I winced at the temperature, but it didn't deter me. I sat down, and the burn of the water mixed with my cold skin created tingling pain from my neck down to my toes.

"My lady, what shall I do with this?" Miranda said.

I turned, remembering the girl was in the room. She held my wand between her thumb and forefinger like it would bite her if she held it wrong.

"You can put it on the table over here." I patted the table next to me.

"I heard you put out the fire," she said as she laid it down and handed me some scented soap and a cloth for me to clean the filth off my body.

I nodded.

"Thank you. My family lives out that way. If the fire had spread, they would have lost everything."

I knew precisely how that felt. I had lost everything I owned. The only thing of my family's that remained was the soiled dress and shoes, along with the magic wand and spell books.

"You're welcome," I said.

She stepped behind me, started cupping water in her hands, and ran it through my hair.

I pulled away from her. "What are you doing?"

"Trying to get the ash and soot out of your hair before I wash it, my lady."

I blinked at her. I knew my feet were muddy, but I had no idea the state of what the rest of me looked like. "Do you have a mirror?"

She crossed to a small dressing table and picked up a handheld looking glass.

The minute I saw my reflection, I covered my mouth. My wide eyes stared back from a streaked face surrounded by soaking hair that didn't resemble my normal fair color at all.

Prince William had kissed me looking like this. Mortification crept through me. I handed the mirror back, dunking myself under the surface of the water to speed up the effort to get clean.

When I resurfaced, Miranda was there with her gentle touch. She shampooed my hair while I scrubbed my skin with the soap she had given me. I dreaded rinsing in the gray water surrounding me, but the hot temperature did its magic. By the time I stood and stepped out, the water was murky with the dirt that had clung to my skin.

Miranda had a warm towel for me to wrap myself in, along with a pair of cloth slippers for my feet. I grabbed my wand and stared at the soiled dress piled on the floor. My gaze dropped to the source of magic in my hand.

I smiled and glanced at Miranda before I wished my gown back to its original, stunning state. The air swirled, picking the dress up off the ground and spinning it like a tornado. Dirt and grime stripped from the dress, cascading to the floor and created a circle of soot. When the dress was restored to its prior glory, I wished it away from the dirt and grime left on the floor. I held out my free arm, and it floated down and gently landed there.

"Wow," Miranda said. Awe filled her voice, and then she shook her head, scurrying to the far corner where a broom sat.

"You don't need to clean up my mess," I said and willed the dirt into a bucket in the corner.

Each time I used the magic, the power in my soul increased, as did the clarity of my knowledge of my heritage. It overwhelmed me, and my knees shook.

Miranda was at my side in a flash. Her eyes were sincere as she reached to steady me. "My lady, are you okay?"

I smiled despite my light-headedness. My stomach rumbled.

Her face transformed. "Let's get you to your room, and then I'll fetch you something to eat."

"That would be wonderful." With all the excitement, I hadn't had a bite to eat this evening, and the expenditure of magical energy was having an effect.

I let Miranda lead me to an ornate bedroom with an adjoining sitting room, and she brought me to a dressing table, forcing me to sit while she stripped the dress from my arms and laid it beside the saddlebags on the lounge chair. She returned and started brushing the knots out of my hair.

It was strange having someone pamper me. My mother used to brush my hair, and having this young girl taking care of me both left me uncomfortable and missing my mother more than I had since she'd died. Miranda braided my hair, and when she was done, she brought a simple dress of yellow silk over to me and helped slip it over my head.

"The queen said this was her favorite when she was your age."

I smoothed the silk over my body. The dress was sleek and unlike anything I had ever seen in public. The neckline plunged in a V that revealed more of my breasts than I was comfortable with, and the skirt ended just past my knees. I could not see returning to the ball in this.

"I have never seen a gown like this," I said as my fingers ran across the form-fitting fabric.

"It's a nightgown, my lady, not a formal gown," Miranda said and smiled. "The queen's clothing from her younger days fill these closets. She said you are welcome to anything you fancy that fits."

My nightgown was floor-length and made of rough cotton. This strange fabric caressed my skin. I shifted as gooseflesh peppered my arms. Miranda noticed and handed me a robe made of the same silk fabric, but this covered my arms and my legs to the ankles.

"Thank you."

"Before I go get you something to eat, would you like me to turn down your bed?"

I glanced at the gigantic bed. It had been a long time since I slept on soft bedding. "I can do that if you don't mind."

"Yes, my lady." She left the room.

I sighed, crossed to the bed, and folded the linens down. My hands ran across the soft fabric, almost as lush as the clothing I wore.

The door swung open, and the prince walked in with a tray of strawberries, grapes, bread, and pastries that smelled divine. He had a simple tunic that showed the definition of his muscular arms and chest and matching slacks. His dark hair was slicked back and wet, and any evidence of the soot from the fire was gone.

He stopped inside the door. Hunger flared in his eyes as he took me in. That devilish smile appeared. "I intercepted Miranda and promised her I would deliver your dinner, my lady."

"Thank you," I said, aware that all I had on was a simple silk layer between the prince and my skin.

He placed the tray on the table in the sitting room and waved to the couch in a silent invitation.

I padded across the floor and curled up on the corner of the couch within reach of the food. However, my appetite had vanished the moment he stepped in, replaced by a more carnal hunger. He stepped to the spot in front of me, dropped to his knee, and opened his hand, presenting a solitaire diamond ring to me.

"Marry me, Elle. Be my queen," he said.

I stared at the diamond in his hand and then into his deep, sincere eyes. Doubt filled my mind, and my heart fluttered in my chest. I reached down and pinched the back of my hand, wincing at the sharp pain. I let out a nervous laugh and met his gaze. Dimples etched into his cheeks.

"This is real," he said and slipped the ring on my finger. "As real as you want it to be."

With him holding my hand in his and his proposal still hanging in the air between us, my entire body flushed. The sweetness in this moment sent a bolt of heat right between my legs as all the decadent dreams I had flashed before my eyes.

He finally lifted an eyebrow, and I realized I hadn't answered him. I let out a soft laugh. "Yes, I would love to be your wife."

His lips covered mine with the same seductive kiss he had given me in front of the fire while I was a soot-covered mess. But this time, he didn't pull away. Instead, the kiss deepened, and his hands dropped from mine, fumbling with the sash of my robe. He pulled me to my feet and stripped the robe off.

"Intoxicating," he whispered and pulled me against him, kissing my lips, my shoulder, my neck before he dropped to his knees, running his hands up my bare legs, pushing the hem of the nightdress higher.

My heart raced, and I licked my lips, unable to form a coherent thought as his touch ignited me. When his fingers ran up the inside of my thighs and brushed my center, I tilted my head back and threaded my hands into his wet hair. He grinned up at me and touched the same spot again.

"William." His name escaped my lips in a breathless whisper.

"Is this what you want?" He moved his fingers against me again, teasing me.

"I just..."

He teased the spot again, stopping the words in my throat. He climbed to his feet, leaving his hand in place, slowly circling his fingers on a spot that left me speechless. This time, his kiss was possessive and thrilling. His tongue demanding even as his hand kept that slow, leisurely pace.

Heat built up, pooling in my belly, our breaths labored. He took my hand and placed it on the front of his pants. His manhood strained against the fabric, and he guided my hand up and down his long shaft.

A thrilling fear ran through me at his intentions, but I was under his spell and unwilling to let this desire end. After months of pain and torture at the hands of Lady Githa, this bodily pleasure was foreign and ever so welcomed. When his finger slid inside my folds, I moaned in his mouth.

My knees weakened at the yearning filling me. He lowered me onto the couch, falling to his knees between my legs. He pulled me to the edge and dropped his head so his tongue could play with the magic spot his fingers had plucked before.

The sins in my dream didn't compare to this heaven. I moaned his name softly. Each lick brought me closer to the edge, and my hands fisted in his hair as the wave overtook me. I cried his name as wetness rushed from my core. He didn't stop with my first orgasm. He continued until my body responded with each swipe of his tongue like an exquisite torture.

He kissed his way up my body through the silky nightshirt until his lips claimed my mouth. His hips pressed against me, grinding into the same spot his fingers and tongue had turned into an ultrasensitive bud. The cloth between us created a friction that was nearly enough to ignite.

His teeth nibbled my earlobe, and I squealed. William's soft chuckle filled my world. "I don't want to wait until our wedding night," he whispered. "I want you now."

My heart pounded in my chest with want, but my mind clouded with fear. When William caught my glance, he paused, and the intense passion in his features softened. His hips slowed.

"I've never..." I couldn't finish the sentence.

"I never presumed otherwise. If you want to wait..."

I sucked my lower lip between my teeth and studied his steady gaze. My body screamed for him. I wanted him as much as he appeared to want me, and yet I still hesitated. He pulled away from me, and every cell reacted, pulling him back to my lips.

He groaned in my mouth and wrapped his arms around my waist. He stood, still kissing me, carried me to the bed, and threw the covers aside. Before he lay me down, he stripped the silk fabric from my body. His tunic and pants followed, and he crawled on the bed towards me, the look in his eyes far from the sweet and gentle man I'd glimpsed before.

It thrilled me to the core. He entered me, filling me in a single, painful thrust. I gasped and my eyes widened in response as my body stiffened under him.

"Sweet lord, you are so damn tight," he said with a smile and stared down into my eyes.

His hips circled slowly, easing the pain and replacing it with a delicious pleasure. My body relaxed, and I moved my hips with his. His pupils dilated, turning his eyes darker with each thrust of his hips.

He whispered my name and gave me a searing kiss, intertwining our souls into a single union.

CINDER Chapter 12

MY EYES OPENED TO a bright streak of sunshine cutting through the room. My stomach rumbled, and the arms holding me tightened. I glanced over my shoulder at Prince William's sleepy smile. His eyes fluttered closed after briefly meeting my gaze. He squeezed tighter and planted a kiss on the back of my neck.

I wrapped my arms around his, mystified at how my life had changed in the last twenty-four hours. I went from Lady Githa's punching bag to the prince's fiancée. I pinched my hand again just to make sure this wasn't a dream. The stark pain told me otherwise. I snuggled closer, despite the hardness pressing against my back.

William groaned and rolled onto his back, stretching. My stomach rumbled louder, and he chuckled.

"We never got you any food last night." He swung his legs over the side of the bed and disappeared into the other room. A few minutes later, he came back with the tray.

He climbed into the bed next to me and sat against the headboard, offering me a grape. I took it between my teeth and propped myself up on my arm, admiring his chiseled chest.

"We have a busy day today," he said after I devoured the rest of the food.

"Mmm?" I mumbled, my mouth still relishing the taste of fruit and bread.

"Wedding plans. We are getting married this week."

I grinned. "You really want to marry me?"

"I wouldn't have shared a bed with you if I didn't," he said and put the tray aside. He swiped his clothes off the floor, and to my disappointment, covered his sweet backside from view.

I sat up and pulled the sheet over my breasts. "I'm not sure what to wear today." I glanced at the gown I wore last night. "I think that is a bit too formal, and the nightgown isn't appropriate."

"The closets are full of things my mother outgrew after she had me. Find something comfortable and suitable for meetings with bakers and dressmakers." He bowed. "Until this evening," he said with a smile, and left the room.

The minute he exited, Miranda stepped in. "My lady, the queen has asked for your company this morning to go over the plans for your wedding." She went to the closet and pulled out a couple of simple, yet elegant, dresses for me to choose from. They were nowhere near as ornate as the ball gown, but they were eons more formal than the dress I wore to clean the house under Lady Githa. I chose the simple blue dress.

Miranda neatened my hair and handed me my wand before she took my hand, leading me through the grand hallways into a sitting room with walls filled with knickknacks.

"The queen will be here shortly. If you need anything, just ring."

Miranda handed me a small bell. I set it down on the table and crossed to the shelves. I didn't dare touch anything, but I studied each of the figurines and statues until I came to a painting. I stopped and stared at my likeness standing on a countryside hill with a group of people dressed in finery with both the stars peppering half the sky while bright streaks of sunlight bathed the other.

My brain seemed to reset to the eyes of the girl in the painting. To my ancestral grandmother and the hills rolling all around them. Magic filled the air like a string quartet. It thrummed through my veins along with a distant tribal drum beat.

A door creaked. I turned away from the photo, and my eyes widened. I dipped in a curtsy as the queen herself entered the study. Queen Samantha commanded any room she entered. In some ways, her stunning beauty reminded me of my mother, but there were obvious differences. The queen's hair was raven black and her eyes were dark like Prince William's, versus my mother's fair hair and blue eyes I inherited. As the queen drew closer, I caught glimmers of green flecks in her dark irises. It was an interesting combination. She smiled at me and glanced at the painting.

"You certainly look like your ancestors," she commented with a voice as smooth and sweet as honey. "I had no idea what to think when my son said he met the woman he was going to marry and then to see his disappointment when you never returned to the brook." She shook her head and sighed before her gaze switched from the painting to me. "Did you not find my son desirable?"

Heat filled my cheeks. "No, My Queen. I found him very charming."

"Then why did you not return to see if he sought you out?" she asked, studying me.

"My father remarried, and his new wife was...strict." I chose my words carefully.

The queen chuckled. "Would that be the same woman who attempted to drag you out of here after making a fool of herself in front of my son?"

I dropped my gaze and nodded. She went to put her hand on my shoulder and I flinched. I didn't mean to, but it was a learned reaction from being Lady Githa's punching bag.

The queen hesitated, her eyes widening. "What did that woman do to you, child?"

I had no visible bruises or deformities from her beatings because of the healing properties of the magic. If I were still broken and bruised like I was yesterday, I would have had proof of her behavior, but with my skin as clear and beautiful as it was the day she walked in the house, I had no prayer of being believed.

I clasped the wand in my pocket and wished I could show her how hard things had been since my father died.

The queen gasped, and I met her horrified stare.

I pulled my hand away from the wand.

Her hand fluttered to the cheek that had at one time been as swollen as the rest of my face. If I hadn't disobeyed my father's wishes and opened that trunk, I would have likely been dead or halfway across England by now.

Whatever vision I projected, the queen's features hardened. Anger flamed in her eyes and she shook her head. "Why?"

I wasn't sure what to tell her. I thought about showing her, but using magic exhausted me. "She broke every knickknack that had been my mother's and shredded all my mother's dresses so I couldn't go to the ball. I yelled at her, and she nearly beat me to death."

"How are you..." She waved at me.

I pulled the wand out of my pocket. "The magic. It healed me the moment I picked this up. I am just learning how it all really works."

She stared at the wooden stick and put her hand out. I gave it to her to inspect. She closed her eyes, and when nothing happened, she handed it to me.

"Wish me a bouquet of roses," she said.

I closed my eyes and imagined a beautiful bouquet of multicolored roses. When my eyes opened, the queen grinned. I handed her the dozen cut roses that had materialized in my hand.

She put them on the table and turned to me with narrowed eyes. "So, if you were to see that woman again..."

My smile faded. "I saw her last night. Riding away from the fire she set, laughing as everything I ever knew went up in flames."

A crease appeared between her eyes, and her head tilted. "And what did you do?"

"I put out the fire."

She took a seat on the couch, studying me.

"Every wizard has a choice, My Queen. Cultivate life, or cultivate death. In that moment, I chose the path of light, and I put out the fire to save the town."

Her soft smile put me at ease, and I took the seat adjacent to her.

"I'm not sure I would have been so forgiving."

I laughed. "My Queen, you would have done the same thing had you been in my shoes." She had always been just and charitable with her subjects. I couldn't envision her being spiteful, but from the sardonic smile on her lips, perhaps I was wrong.

"I have a very vengeful heart, Elle," she said. "And I am very protective of my only son."

"Yes, my Queen." I bowed my head.

"Did you put a spell on him that day at the brook?"

My gaze snapped to hers, and I shook my head. "No. I did not know magic truly existed until yesterday evening."

"Did you wish for him?"

Heat filled my cheeks. "I think every available girl in the kingdom wishes for Prince William," I said. "But no, I didn't. The magic doesn't work without the wand. At least I don't think it does. I have some studying to do to really grasp all the knowledge it infused in me, but nothing I ever wished for before I opened that trunk came true. And believe me, over the last couple of years, I have wished for a lot of things, and every one of them went unanswered. If this wand hadn't been on top of the gown, I'm not sure I would have bothered touching it. It was almost as if the fates knew where to place it so I would pick it up." I shrugged. "And now I seem to have been endowed with the knowledge of my ancestors. Disobeying my father's wishes and opening that trunk saved my life," I admitted.

Sadness filled the queen's eyes, and she reached out and took my hands in hers. "I think I understand why my son is so enamored with you."

"Truth be told, he has been on my mind since that day as well," I whispered.

She squeezed my hands and smiled. "He tells me you wagered for sword-fighting lessons?"

I laughed and nodded. "Yes, My Queen, I did. I was taught by the neighboring squire. I wanted to spar with a proper knight."

"Soft and fierce. You are every bit the enigma he described."

I glanced at my fidgeting hands, uncomfortable with the compliment.

"I am sorry we missed you at your father's funeral. I found it odd that you didn't have him cremated like your mother, though."

I raised my gaze to hers. "Lady Githa and I disagreed on how my father should be put to rest and she forbade me from attending his funeral."

The color bled from the queen's cheeks, and her lips pressed together. "And you did not put an end to this woman when you saw her?" she asked through clenched teeth.

I shook my head. "I wanted to. I really did, but she is not worth losing my soul over."

She leaned back in the seat. "If she crosses my path, she will not be so lucky." The queen rearranged her skirt, pressing it smooth with her hands before she looked up. "Would you like your father cremated?"

I blinked at the question and stared at her. After I regained my senses, I cleared my tight throat. "I would like that very much. My mother is waiting for him to join her, and with him locked in a box in the ground, I don't know that he can find her."

Her smile softened again as she leaned over and rang the bell sitting on the table. Miranda stepped into the room.

"Child, will you go get me the head of the King's Guard?"

Miranda ran off down the hall, and a few minutes later, the largest man I had ever seen stepped into the room dressed in full guard armor. His deep eyes stared at me for a moment before they moved to the queen.

"You called, Your Highness," he said with a bow.

"Yes. I want you to dig up Lord Seeley's grave, bring the casket to the courtyard here, and set up a funeral pyre, please."

My eyebrows rose, but the guard didn't blink at the request. He just turned and marched away.

I couldn't speak. I just stared at that space where the guard had stood while my brain caught up to what had just happened. That empty ache at not being able to say a proper goodbye to my father bloomed into something I had not felt in ages.

Gratitude.

I bit my bottom lip, glancing at the queen. She patiently waited for me to speak. I tried to smile, but I couldn't quite manage it. I blinked back the mist that sprang up, forcing it away.

"We will go have a private ceremony for you after we finalize some of the wedding details," she said, as if having your father's corpse dug up was a common occurrence.

I nodded, still numb from being blindsided by her kindness.

AFTER DINNER HAD BEEN eaten and the plates cleared, the king and queen escorted William and me into the courtyard, where a large pyre sat with my father's freshly wrapped figure atop the pile. I recognized his dress shoes that Lady Githa had insisted he wear in his eternal slumber, grateful that the King's Guard understood the proper formality of a funeral pyre and did not include the casket.

The care that the guard took tightened my throat with hot tears I refused to shed in front of the king. When the guard handed me the torch and bowed deep, I pressed my lips together against a tremble.

With shaking hands, I lit the wood and hay, tossing the torch into the lower opening underneath the body. I stepped back far enough to not get singed by the fire, but close enough for the heat to sting. I stood there for as long as I dared before I moved a safer distance away.

William stepped beside me and clasped my hand, threading his fingers through mine. I didn't look his way as hot tears crested and slid down my cheeks. I stared as the fire reduced what was left of my father to ashes. They swirled in the air like a dust devil, and just for a moment, I glimpsed the forms of both my parents in an eternal embrace before the ash shifted and fell to the ground.

I squeezed William's hand to let him know I appreciated his silent support and then turned to the king and queen, who stood stoically together with sadness in their eyes.

"Thank you, Your Highness," I said, curtsying in a way my father would have been proud of.

When I straightened, she reached out and cupped my chin in such a gentle manner that my chin trembled and a fresh wave of tears flowed. She pulled me into a gentle hug that reminded me so much of my mother that my heart ached in my chest.

All the grief I had not been allowed to release came forth in a wave of shakes and tears. The queen held me and cooed in my ear, stroking my back as I purged my pent-up anguish.

When the last of my tears dried up, I pulled away from Queen Samantha and wiped my face. "Thank you," I said and wasn't sure how else to express my gratefulness for everything she had done for me in such a short time.

William wrapped his arm around my shoulder and escorted me to my room. Bleary-eyed and exhausted from the day's emotional drain, I headed straight for the bed. Without words, he helped me undress, and instead of taking advantage of my vulnerable state, he pulled me into his arms, snuggling as if he knew I needed to be held more than another bedroom adventure.

Quiet blanketed us, and his soft breath caressed my neck in a gentle cadence that matched my own. Being in his arms was like coming home after being lost in a deadly storm. The knowledge that I had found my true soulmate overwhelmed me, mending the pain from the last few years and weaving hope into my soul again.

My muscles relaxed, and I traced the back of his hand, finally lacing my fingers through his. He kissed my cheek gently, igniting the flame low in my belly, but I was too bone-weary to follow through with any of the delicious thoughts that drifted to mind. When his breathing turned deeper and more even, and his arms became heavy, I smiled at the ease with which we fell into this relationship and could finally see a happy future ahead.

As the night deepened, I finally succumbed to sleep.

CINDER Chapter 13

THE NEXT FEW DAYS flew by in a flurry of activity. Planning a royal wedding usually took months, sometimes years, but we did it in less than a week. By the time I made it back to my bedroom with the prince, I was exhausted, and my head spun from all the details still yet to tackle.

Prince William made up for those long days of wedding planning with evenings of lovemaking that exceeded our first night together, leaving us both exhausted and panting in each other's arms. In those moments, I forgot everything. His gentle touch transcended reality, lifting me into the clouds where all my prior strife was meaningless. He made me forget my sorrow and pain, replacing it with a joy I had never experienced.

On the eve before our wedding, Prince William led me down the hall towards my bed chambers, whispering his intentions in my ear. My muscles tingled with anticipation, and I couldn't wait to get inside my room so the Prince could make good on his hushed promises. He kissed me and pushed open my door.

A throat cleared, and our lips parted.

Miranda stood in the center of the room with her arms crossed. "It's the night before your wedding. You are to sleep in separate quarters."

We both balked.

"Queen's orders," she said.

I exchanged a glance with William and shrugged. I wasn't about to stomp on an order from the queen, no matter how much my body wanted the prince's naughty suggestions. She had been too good to me to defy her wishes.

"Good night, William," I whispered in his ear. I loved the way his eyes closed whenever I whispered his name. It was as if he were tasting the most delicious delicacy known to man.

He glanced sideways at me as a grin toyed with his lips. "Good night, Elle," he said and planted a searing kiss despite Miranda being in the room.

My breath quickened in response. When he released me, my knees wobbled, but held my weight. My gaze stayed with him until he closed the door and then I turned and dropped onto the couch, aware that every nerve ending in my body was calling for him. I glanced at Miranda.

"I'm sorry, my lady, but the queen..."

I waved her off. "I understand. It's just when he does that, I lose my mind."

Miranda giggled.

Heat filled my cheeks. "I hope someday you find someone who makes you lose your mind in the best ways possible." I smiled at her.

A yawn caught me off guard, and I stood, heading into the bedroom. Now that the promise of a sexual romp had been removed, utter exhaustion sank in, and it took all I had to keep my eyes open as I peeled my clothing off and crawled under the covers.

"Good night, Miranda," I said.

"Good night, my lady," Miranda replied, dousing the candles before she retired to the couch with a blanket.

THE ENTIRE CASTLE HUMMED with excitement as I stood in the vestibule of the castle chapel. The bodice of the wedding dress I wore fit my form like a second skin. The satin was soft and lined with gold. The detailed beauty reminded me of my mother's dress that I wore to the ball, but this was more beautiful and made just for me. Roland, the head of the King's Guard, stood at the door waiting for the signal from the court. He had agreed to walk me down the aisle in my father's place. Miranda doted on me, straightening my train and making sure my veil was just right.

"It's okay," I said to her on her fifth check.

She was worse and more endearing than any little sister could ever be. I adored this child, and I hoped she realized her job was not done the minute I said 'I do'. I would need a lady-in-waiting to help me with my day-to-day duties as a princess.

She blushed and curtseyed before taking her place behind me.

Roland turned. "Are you ready, my lady?"

My stomach fluttered, and I closed my eyes, taking a deep breath before I nodded. He hooked his arm in mine as the musicians started to play. We walked through the doors of the chapel, and I nearly stopped at the amount of people filling the seats. Even the balcony was occupied. I recognized faces of our neighbors and some of the craftsmen we used to barter with at the market.

My nervousness disappeared with one look down the aisle. Prince William stood in his full formal dress, including the king's crest. The man I approached was stunningly handsome. He flashed that smile that made my knees weak, but I continued until Roland placed my hand in his. Miranda fixed my train and stepped to the side.

The priest looked just as ancient as the chapel. His white hair stuck out in tufts on the side of his head, and his wrinkled face split into a grin.

"Dearly beloved, we are gathered together here in the sight of God to join together Prince William and Lady Elle in holy matrimony; which is an honorable estate, instituted of God in paradise, and into which holy estate these two persons come to be joined. Therefore, if any man can show just cause why they may not lawfully be joined together by God's Law, or the Laws of the Realm, let him now speak, or else hereafter forever hold his peace."

Silence blanketed the church for a fraction of a second.

"I object to this union!"

The voice sent an unpleasant shock down my spine. I stared at Prince William before turning my gaze down the aisle. Lady Githa stood in her finest dress, glaring at me from the opposite side of the church. She had Lily's wrist clasped in a grip that left her knuckles white enough for me to see at this distance. Lily's face was hidden behind a wave of hair, but I recognized the stance. I recognized the defeat in her shoulders.

"She stole my husband's body from the grave. No prince in his right mind would marry a grave robber!"

The queen stood and stepped into the aisle. "I had her father exhumed and brought to the castle to cremate him in a proper funeral pyre."

"The servant girl has cast a spell over the royal family!" Lady Githa cried, eliciting a wave of murmurs through the church.

"I did no such thing," I said.

The queen splayed her fingers at me to quiet my argument. "What proof do you have of this?" she said, her voice icier that I had ever heard.

Lady Githa pushed Lily in front of her. "Tell them, girl," Lady Githa ordered.

Lily looked up through her hair. My heart plummeted at the shade of black and blue, outlining her right eye. Her gaze met mine, pleading silently.

"Tell them!"

Lily closed her eyes and pressed her lips together, straightening her back. She ripped her wrist from her mother's grip. Gasps filled the chapel when she brushed her hair out of her face, revealing the bruise for all to see. My chest tightened because Lady Githa could be so coercive with her fists and I had an idea of what falsehoods she would plant in her daughter's brain.

Lily cleared her throat and took a step away from her mother towards the queen. "My step-sister…" She stopped and clenched her fists. The struggle in her was visible, and it broke my heart.

"I promise…" I started, but the queen gave me a glare that silenced me.

William squeezed my hand in a silent show of support.

Lily gave a small shake of her head and looked straight at me. "My step sister protected me, even though my mother continually beat and humiliated her on a daily basis."

"Why you ungrateful…" Lady Githa launched at Lily.

"Stop!" I yelled before Lady Githa doled out her vile form of punishment.

I reached towards the two of them. Power shot from my fingertips. Flashing across the distance, my power pushed Lady Githa onto her ass, far enough away from Lily that her swing wouldn't connect.

Lily continued, "My mother set fire to our house hoping it would burn the whole town to the ground, and then she planned to blame it on Elle." She glanced over her shoulder at her mother. "My mother is not right in the head. To have so much hatred for someone as sweet as Elle is wrong. I cannot stand by and take part in a plan to destroy the only person who ever truly protected me from harm."

A blanket of utter silence fell over the chapel.

After three fast heartbeats, the queen issued an order. "Take her to the dungeon."

The guards descended upon Lady Githa and dragged her out of the chapel.

As soon as the doors closed, I pointed to the front row. "Lily, the front row is reserved for family. Please, come sit up here."

Lily brightened like a flower opening to the morning sunshine. I would make certain that she would never be touched by her mother again. Lily sat next to the king and queen, and she smiled at me with a nod of gratitude.

William turned to the priest. "I think you can continue now," he whispered and winked at me.

The priest cleared his throat and looked to the king and queen for approval. They both nodded their assent.

"William, wilt thou have this woman to be thy wedded wife, to live together after God's ordinance in the holy estate of matrimony?

Wilt thou love her, comfort her, honor, and keep her, in sickness and in health, and forsaking all others, keep thee only unto her, so long as ye both shall live?"

William grinned. "I will." His voice rang out, echoing against the stone walls.

The priest looked at me.

"Elle, wilt thou have this man to be thy wedded husband, to live together under God's ordinance in the holy estate of matrimony? Wilt thou obey him, and serve him, love, honor, and keep him in sickness and in health, and forsaking all others, keep thee only unto him, so long as ye both shall live?"

"I will."

William reached into his pocket and pulled out a wedding band adorned with diamonds, rubies, and sapphires. It was the most beautiful ring I had ever seen. The wedding band even outshined the diamond on my finger. He laid it upon the priest's bible.

"Bless this ring, O merciful Lord, that those who wear them, that give and receive them, may be ever faithful to one another, remain in your peace, and live and grow old together in your love, under their own vine and fig tree, and seeing their children's children. Amen." He made the sign of the cross over the ring and held it out to William.

William took my left hand and slid the ring onto my ring finger. It fit as if it was made for me. My eyes misted. "With this ring, I thee wed, and with my body I thee honor, and with all my worldly goods, I thee endow. In the name of the Father, and of the Son, and of the Holy Spirit. Amen."

He released my hand, and we turned to the priest, lowering to our knees in front of the cherub-like man.

"Let us pray. O Eternal God, creator and preserver of all mankind, giver of all spiritual grace, the author of everlasting life, send thy blessings upon these thy servants, the man and this woman, whom we bless in thy name, that as Isaac and Rebecca lived faithfully together, so these persons may surely perform and keep the vow and covenant betwixt them made, whereof this ring given and received is a token and pledge, and may ever hereafter remain in perfect love and peace together, and live according to thy laws, through Jesus Christ our Lord. Amen."

The entire congregation said, "Amen!" and then recited the Lord's Prayer in unison.

I closed my eyes with William's hand still covering mine, reciting the words as well. I had never felt so close to God as I did in that moment, and the joy of faith renewed in my heart.

We stood, and the priest joined our right hands together.

"Those whom God hath joined together, let no man put asunder." He smiled at the two of us and then looked out over the congregation. "For as much as William and Elle have consented together in holy wedlock, and have witnessed the same before God and this company, and thereto have given and pledged their troth, each to the other, and have declared the same by giving and receiving of a ring, and by joining hands, I pronounce therefore that they be man and wife together, in the name of the Father, and of the Son, and of the Holy Spirit. Amen."

His gaze returned to us. "May God the Father, God the Son, God the Holy Spirit bless, preserve, and keep you, and look upon you with his favor, and so fill you with all spiritual benediction and grace, that ye may live together in this life, that in the world to come ye may have life everlasting. Amen."

The congregation echoed the "Amen."

"Son, you may kiss your bride."

William leaned in and pressed his lips gently upon mine, and the clapping in the congregation disappeared. His kiss deepened, and he pulled me to him. It wasn't until the kiss broke that I heard the cheers.

Heat filled my face as I grinned at William. Light danced in his eyes, promising me a life filled with passion. My body responded to him, stirring a need so great in my core that I wished we were not in this chapel in front of hundreds of people.

William took my arm and walked me out of the chapel towards the reception hall. "We could just go get the bedding ceremony over with now if you'd like," he whispered in my ear. "That way, I can spoil you tonight."

My eyes widened, and I glanced at him. "That's really a thing?"

It was a stupid question on my part as I had been schooled in the ritual by my mother in the event I was ever to marry a nobleman, but the idea of someone in the room while we made love sent chills up my back and cooled whatever anticipation had been fueled by his kiss on the altar.

"You know they don't actually watch, right?" he asked.

"Yes, but still. We aren't exactly…quiet," I whispered as we walked into the royal hall. The wedding feast was laid out across the dining table. My stomach growled at the sight.

William chuckled. "True, so they will get an earful," he said and shrugged. "Do you have a preference for who you want as your witness?"

I chewed the inside of my lip. There were only two people I would allow in the room to bear witness, but Miranda was much too young to be subjected to our passion first-hand. "Lily," I said.

"Roland will bear witness for me."

I smiled. Roland was a fine man, and I had caught him looking at Lily with interest when she took a seat in the front row at the chapel. Perhaps the archaic ceremony would spark something between them.

"What will your parents do with Lady Githa?" I asked.

His smile faded. "Exile or execute, depending upon how benevolent they feel when they pass judgement."

I swallowed my horror at the second option. While I loathed the woman, I did not wish her dead. "Please impress upon your mother and father that the woman's crimes do not add up to a death sentence."

He stopped and stared down at me, and his head cocked to the side. "You amaze me. If someone treated me the way you were treated, I would gladly chop off their head with my sword."

I sighed and glanced around at the people still filtering into the room, distracted by all the festivities around me.

Everyone was dressed in their finery, and it reminded me of the night of the ball, except the women's gowns were more reserved. Most of them were on the arm of a nobleman or a knight instead of alone.

Lily and Miranda stood near each other, partaking in the fine spread at the table. I was happy to see them getting along. Roland was nearby, lurking. To see such a formidable man shy in the shadows pulled an amused smile to my lips. I wondered how they would fare tonight in the shadows as William and I made love.

I turned back to my husband. "I'm not a saint. I have had those same dark thoughts before, but giving into that train of thought would have drawn me down to her level. It lets the darkness in. I prefer hope to despair, even though I have intimately flirted with both. I also prefer to think people are capable of change, given the right motivation."

"This is why you have captured my heart forevermore." He kissed my lips and took my hand, leading me to the dance floor as the music started up.

As he pulled me into his arms for our first dance as husband and wife, I gazed up at him with a heart so full of love and joy that I thought my chest would burst. I thanked the stars above that I'd found someone who would put a smile on my face and a fire in my soul for the rest of my life.

The End

An ultimatum. A curse. A forbidden love.

May Stewart's father, King James VII, demands she choose a husband within a fortnight. The list of approved suitors leaves her uninspired at the courtship festivities until fate intervenes, and an uninvited stranger sparks her interest.

Unfortunately, even uttering handsome Aiden MacMahon's surname is a capital offense, for it whispers of a dark curse that dictates the daylight belongs to the beast on their family crest.

The MacMahon name is *not* a choice the king will allow for May, but she cannot deny the connection she has with Aiden.

When May discovers her own secret lineage holds the key to reversing the MacMahon curse, her choice of suitor becomes so much more than just a marriage match.

But choosing Aiden MacMahon could lead them both into death's icy embrace.

292

BRAVE Chapter 1

BEING BRANDED WITH A hot iron would be a more pleasant experience than this fresh hell.

My gaze rose to the ornate architecture surrounding the throne room as the last in the long line of suitors bumbled through his offer for my hand. My father, King James Stewart VII, sat on the throne with my mother next to him. He played with his white-speckled beard while his gaze remained stoic. It was one of his more identifiable tells. He was just as bored with these simpering fools as I was. My mother, on the other hand, seemed to be enthralled with each suitor. She smiled endlessly and every so often she wound a stray wisp of her auburn hair around her finger as she listened.

She was trying, which was more than I could say for me. My father called these men noble, but while they may have been from a family with high political or social ties, they certainly did not represent what noble meant to me. This entire ordeal was a farce, and what made things worse was my father expected me to pick a husband from this sad lot.

It wasn't as if they were the bane of human existence—a couple of them were lookers—but none of them truly had what I was looking for. Spark. Fire. Passion. These things were missing, replaced with a cockiness that I abhorred. Their demeanor suggested I should be the one bowing down to them, as if God had granted me a unique viewing of perfection incarnate. Others offered the brawn without the brains, and I really needed someone intellectually stimulating.

I glanced at my father after the last had stated his lineage and what he offered. Every one of them only offered goods in exchange for my hand, like I was something to barter for instead of an equal to build a lasting connection with.

If one had said he offered a promise of a lifetime of adventure, love, and happiness, that would have been the man I chose in a heartbeat. I wanted someone who saw me as their partner, not a possession.

Not one of these men would do. I met my father's gaze and shook my head.

He gave a wave, and the room cleared. Both my parents waited until the audience was gone and the doors to the throne room closed before turning to me.

"May, what was wrong with these men?" my father asked.

My mother let out a chuckle and exchanged a glance with me. "They think of her as a prize, sweetheart. Not a heart to be won."

"That's poppycock and you know it," he said as he stood.

"Did you hear a one offering her a future like no other?" she asked.

My father's lips thinned. "This isn't negotiable. You are going to choose a suitor, one whom I approve of, within the next fortnight. Understand?"

"Do you not want your only daughter to be as happy as we are?" my mother chided.

"My dear, Katherine," he said, taking my mother's hands, "our marriage was arranged as well."

"Aye, but I did not know that when you went about wooing me. You had long weaseled your way into my heart before my parents told me we were already betrothed. Had you come before me in this setting, in the way these boys did, I would have scoffed just as much as May."

I could see the wheels in my father's head plotting against me with his choice of a proper husband. "I will choose when I am good and ready," I said.

"You have a fortnight. If not, I will choose for you." He gave me a final nod before he spun and stalked out of the throne room.

My mother sighed and turned her gaze to me. "You're going to have to stop being so fussy, my dear." She glanced at the window as the last of the light faded from the sky. "It's time to gather in the great hall."

I sighed and brushed my flame-red hair out of my face. "Do I have to?"

"Aye. Mingle, see if anyone grows on you."

"Fine." I followed her to the great hall where the families of the line of men volleying for my attentions all gathered.

The tension in the room was as thick as the scent of the feast. The boys posturing with each other was like watching dueling roosters. The minute they noticed I was in the room, they made a mad dash to my side, doting on me in the most annoying of ways.

While most girls would love a group of men getting her drinks, and food, and dessert, nearly falling all over themselves to do so, it grated on my nerves.

"I can feed myself," I snapped as spoons and forks were shoved in my face. "Now, please, give me some space!"

As if they were one single unit, they all stepped back, letting me breathe a little before they all tried to engage in further conversation.

That was when *he* caught my eye.

A man stood in the shadows, leaning against the wall in a manner that was both relaxed and possibly the sexiest damn thing I had ever seen. He had not been amongst the suitors in the throne room. I would have remembered that intense stare and sense of aloofness.

He stood taller than most men in the room with a build that was one hundred percent muscle filling out his shirt and his tight knickers. His dark hair curled at the ends, matching the lashes on his bedroom eyes, the blue of his irises as distinctly bright as the daytime sky.

He kept my gaze, and a hint of a dimple appeared in his cheek before he gave me a slow nod of acknowledgement.

I wondered if he had the mind to go with all that eye candy. Curiosity won out, and I crossed the room. All talk ceased when I stopped a few feet from the interesting stranger, studying him. Up close, he was even more stunning than from a distance, especially when he flashed a smile revealing a set of the whitest teeth I had seen all day.

"Princess May," he said in a deep baritone voice that dried all the saliva in my mouth. He bowed with the formality of common folk, but his clothes indicated he came from the highborn class.

"I am at a disadvantage. You know my name, but I have yet to make your acquaintance." I couldn't help continuing my study of the man. I had to staunch the urge to reach out and touch his chest to settle the silent argument in my head that he was just a figment of my imagination.

"Aidan MacMahon," he said.

"Aidan." The name played on my tongue in the most delicious manner.

He cleared his throat and grinned as his eyes panned the audience behind me. "I apologize for missing the formalities in the throne room." An interesting hue of pink bloomed in his cheeks, and his gaze dropped to mine again. "But I could not make it in time."

A litany of questions came to mind, but I didn't know which one to ask first, so instead, I bit my bottom lip and just stared into the depth of his eyes. Being tongue-tied wasn't my usual affliction, but Aidan seemed to have that effect on me. He didn't seem to mind the silence between us. In fact, it almost suited him.

I blinked, broke eye contact, and licked my lips. "May I inquire as to why you missed the formalities?"

He laughed lightly. "I had a bear of a time getting here." He winked at me, and then his gaze moved over my head. He dropped to his knee. "Your Highness," he said and bowed his head.

My father stepped by my side with narrowed eyes. "You were not among the nobles in the throne room," he said with a sharpness that made me want to cower.

"No, Your Highness. My duties required my attention. Therefore, I was unable to make it in time." Aidan stood, but kept his eyes averted.

My father crossed his arms, unimpressed by Aidan's response. "Are you of noble blood, boy?"

Aidan's gaze jumped to my father's and then mine. He shifted his weight and nodded. "Aye, but it is an ancient line that has all but been forgotten."

"And what line might that be?"

Aidan sighed and cleared his throat. "The House of MacMahon." His voice was so soft it was almost a whisper that only my father and I could pick up in the din.

My father tilted his head and narrowed his eyes. "Didn't they die off nearly a hundred years ago?"

Aidan shrugged. "Almost, but not all of us were put down."

The way he described his family's demise piqued my interest. The phrase "put down" was usually reserved for animals, not human beings. His gaze moved from my father's to mine, and it set a fire in my soul.

"I suggest you find your way out. Now." My father gripped my arm and turned, leading me away from Aidan.

I glanced over my shoulder and caught Aidan's frown. His shoulders sagged, and he turned, disappearing into the dark hallway.

My heart dropped into my stomach. I sent a glare at my father. "Why did you do that?"

"Because the MacMahons are cursed."

I stopped walking. "Explain," I demanded.

"No. You have a fortnight. I suggest you find a proper suitor among the men who are here."

"And if I said I choose Aiden MacMahon?" The words slipped out of my mouth before I could catch them. Being obstinate was a part of my charm, but my father did not take it well.

He paled and pressed his lips together. "That is not an option." He let go of my arm and sauntered away.

The moment he left my side, the vultures attacked as adamantly as they had before. Each boy vied for my attention, but my mind was elsewhere. I half listened to their stories, nodding occasionally until I finally excused myself.

I could not take their leering any longer.

As I walked away, a fight broke out between a few of the boys. I did not stop to see what the outcome was. I had no interest in any of them. The only man tonight who sparked my curiosity was forbidden.

BRAVE Chapter 2

THE CASTLE CLEARED OUT by the middle of the next day. I made my way to the grand hall to get some food, happy with the quiet now permeating the building. It gave me a chance to really focus on all that had transpired the prior evening.

In the wee hours of the night, I had made up my mind. Aiden MacMahon was at the top of my list. Curse be damned. If my father wouldn't agree to the arrangement, then I would refuse to marry any suitor he chose. I knew my position would incite the full fury of my father, but he'd clearly stated I needed to make a choice, and soon.

My parents looked up as I entered the dining hall. My father sat back in the chair and crossed his arms. "I have narrowed the field down to the House of Cameron, House of Dundas, and House of Fergusson." His tone was magnanimous, as if the men who had those affiliations were the only ones on Earth.

They were the ones who had offered the most for my hand. I ground my teeth together. My hands clenched, and I shook my head. "No."

His eyebrows shot up in surprise, and my mother looked up from her stitchery.

"MacMahon," I said.

My mother gasped as if I'd said a forbidden word. She covered her mouth, and her eyes widened like a frightened child's. "You cannot utter that name, ever!"

"Why not?"

"Because it is a capital offence to bear that name," my father said, glaring at me. "That is what I meant by the family is cursed. The fact that the young man stated his house in the confines of my castle means he is daft, or actively looking for death." He pulled out a parchment from his pocket and handed it to me.

I unrolled the thin paper and read the words of a king who had ruled the lands in the early years. He denounced the surname MacMahon and promised death to all who still claimed the name. I stared at the law and shivered before I threw the roll back at my father.

"You are the king, and you can withdraw this ludicrous decree."

His face reddened.

I turned on my heel and left the room before either of them could say a word. My stomach rumbled, but it was nothing compared to the rage pumping heat through my veins.

Why on God's green earth would a king wipe out an entire house and set forth such a vile order?

My stomach growled as the lessons I was taught of our history came flooding back. The name and all its gory history came forth. Their clan had attacked the king, along with the noble class, in a futile effort to overtake the throne. Thus, the law. My belly churned, demanding food, so I grabbed my bow and a full quiver of arrows and headed out of the castle. On foot, I stormed into the woods, hellbent on finding my own sustenance.

Muttering under my breath and walking with a heavy foot paid a warning to all woodland animals. I took a deep breath, closing my eyes and calming the burn in my chest. With my anger under control, I opened my eyes and readied my bow.

I walked with a lighter step, near silent in my quest. Deeper into the forest, I went until the sunlight faded in the thick canopy above. I had no sense in how far I had traveled from home, but I was intent on catching a rabbit or a squirrel.

I approached a grove of thick trees and dense brush. There didn't seem to be an obvious way through. My arms dropped to my sides as I searched for a reasonable way around the obstruction. A rumble built behind me, like a roll of thunder. I spun, bringing my arrow back to my bow.

A large brown bear stood behind me, but his eyes were not normal brown. No, they were as blue as the late afternoon sky peeking through the leaves above. His feral growl ceased the moment I faced him, and he dropped to all fours with a huff that disturbed the strands of my hair.

My heart slammed in my chest. My hands shook as I stared at the beast down the shaft of my arrow. He was just as frozen to the spot as I was, our eyes locked in some strange death dare. And then he turned and lumbered through the woods at a speed that I never would have imagined a beast that big could attain.

Instead of firing my arrow, I ran after the bear, pulled along by something stronger than my curiosity. It was then I realized the darkness falling on the woods had nothing to do with the canopy above. My senses cleared as I stepped into a field. The bear galloped across the open space as the last of the sun's rays faded.

I followed. Before the bear reached the woods on the far side, he reared up on his legs. I slid to a stop as light surrounded the animal. It roared as the glow transformed it. When the glare died down, the beast was now a man.

My eyes widened at the naked male a hundred yards away. He stretched, making every muscle glisten as it flexed. When he turned in my direction, I gasped at the familiar profile. His eyes widened as well.

We stood frozen in time, our gazes locked together in a mesmerizing dance of shock and recognition. He looked away, breaking whatever hold he had over me. When he turned and headed for the woods, my feet moved from the spot I stood.

"Aiden, wait!" I called as I sprinted towards him.

He stopped, keeping his back towards me.

I slowed as I approached. My eyes kept wandering down to his muscular ass. I had to stifle the urge to reach out and cup it just to see if it was as firm as it looked under the moonlight.

"What are you doing out this far from the castle, Princess?"

His gruff tone made all the hairs on my neck stand on end. "I was looking for some food, and I didn't realize it had gotten so late."

"Don't they have enough food in the castle?" He glared over his shoulder at me.

I sucked in my bottom lip and nodded. "I just didn't want to share a meal with my father."

He nodded and stepped towards the woods.

"Where are you going?"

"To get a pair of pants on, if you don't mind," he said without looking over his shoulder. "Just wait here. I'll be back in a moment, and then I will make sure you get back to the castle safely."

He disappeared into the woods and came back a few minutes later dressed in pants, boots, and a half-buttoned shirt. As disappointed as I was that he had covered his nakedness, I had to admit how good he looked in his rugged clothes.

"My father thinks you are either daft or have a death wish," I said as he approached.

A dimple appeared in his cheek. "What say you on the matter?"

"I haven't the foggiest idea. I am still trying to reconcile the bear with the man." I waved the arrow in his direction and then slid it back into my quiver. I shouldered my bow and cocked my head at him. "My father also said you come from a cursed clan."

Aiden laughed, and the rich sound of it tickled my fancy. "Did your father also tell you who cursed our family?"

I shook my head and followed him as he stepped onto a beaten path in the woods.

"His ancestors had a witch at their disposal and not only did they mark the MacMahon name forevermore, they had that witch curse the entire lineage. I have yet to see the sun rise or set. I am cursed to bear the symbol of our name during the daylight and wander as a man while the moon crosses the sky. This is why I did not make it to the throne room in time, and I suspect it is why the king never has evening viewings, so I cannot challenge his authority."

Venom filled his voice, and his glare caused shivers across my skin. I slowed, putting a little distance between us.

He stopped and turned towards me. "You are afraid?"

My heartbeat thrummed in my ears, but I wasn't willing to admit I was afraid. I shook my head.

He stepped closer and leaned in, inhaling through flared nostrils. "Your scent says otherwise."

I pressed my lips together against the nervous energy in my stomach. "Well, can you blame me?" I had seen a lot of strange, unexplained things in my twenty years on this earth, but seeing a bear turn into a man, sexy or otherwise, had me a little scatterbrained. Especially one who blamed my family for his dire circumstances. "How do I know you are not leading me deep into the woods where you plan on eating me?"

He stared down at me with a wicked grin. The light dancing in his eyes matched the salaciousness of his smile. "There's an idea," he whispered with a sexy growl, and pulled me against his hard body. "But I'm sure if I did something so sinful, you would have my head on a platter."

I blinked at him as his words sank in. He wasn't talking about having me for dinner. Heat filled my entire form, exploding in my cheeks as I pushed him away.

"If you had stood in front of my father yesterday, what is it you would have said?" I asked, changing the subject. I walked on the path, letting him follow me this time.

He didn't answer me right away. Instead, he walked at my side with his thumbs latched on the edge of his pockets. A crease appeared between his eyes as if in deep thought.

"Whatever I had the mind to say changed the minute I laid eyes on you." He sighed and glanced sideways at me.

"How so?"

"One does not challenge the king to a duel for the right to keep his name on the eve where the king's only daughter is to claim her life partner. Especially when the sight of her melts all one's resolve, replacing it with a need so strong that namesake or curses no longer matter."

I digested his words. "So, you do have a death wish," I said, meeting his intense gaze.

He stopped and cocked his head, narrowing his eyes at me. The flare of red in his cheeks preceded his swagger down the path in front of me.

A smirk toyed on my lips, and any fear that had been at the edges of my mind dispersed. Aiden had felt the connection as acutely as I had the prior evening. And he did not refer to my dilemma as having to choose a prince or a betrothal. He'd said the magic word. Partner.

I slammed into his back.

"What..."

He partially turned with his finger on his lips, telling me to shush.

I didn't move. He smelled of honey and the deep woods. I closed my eyes, getting lost in his unique scent.

"Hand me your bow and an arrow, quietly," he whispered.

I placed the bow in his waiting hand, pulled an arrow out of my quiver, and handed it to him over his shoulder. The woods were too dark to see what had him spooked.

"Please have another arrow ready once this one flies," he said and pulled the bow back.

A low rumbling growl came from the blackness in front of us, and it took me a moment to place that sound. Aiden exhaled, and the twang of the bow as he let the arrow go drowned out the growls. Before he ripped the next arrow from my hand, a howl of pain filled the darkness.

He let the second arrow fly. "Another!"

The urgency in his voice sparked me into action. The moment I slammed the arrow into the palm of his hand, another pain-filled howl sounded. Moments after the third arrow took flight, that same high-pitched whine shocked my ears.

"They are getting much bolder these days," Aiden muttered under his breath as he handed me the bow and sauntered off into the darkness.

By the time I caught up to him, he had three scrawny wolves hauled over his shoulder and a small pup held by the scruff of its neck in front of him.

"Don't hurt it," I said, hurrying to his side. I reached for the wolf pup.

Aiden hesitantly handed it over. The little thing mewed in my arms, crying for a mother that was now just a wolf pelt over Aiden's shoulder.

"If they had stayed in the shadows and left us alone, that pup might still have a mother."

He started walking again and glanced over his shoulder. "What are you going to do with that thing?"

"I'm going to keep him and name him...Shadow."

"Are you sure that is going to fly with mommy and daddy?" he asked, mocking my exuberance over the small life I held in my arms.

"Well, considering I haven't planted an arrow in your heart like the law states I should, I wouldn't worry too much about what my parents think about a wolf pup. I would worry more about what they will do to you if you show your face in the castle again."

He slowed and kept pace next to me.

I glanced at him. "What would you have offered my father for my hand?"

He chuckled. "I have nothing of monetary value to offer, Princess. Besides, bartering for a lady's hand is an archaic practice. A heart should be won, not traded for goods."

It was as if this man had been inside my head.

We walked in silence, the wolf pup cradled in my arms, sleeping peacefully. Aiden held the bow loosely in one hand and had his other wrapped around the three wolves hanging over his shoulder. Carrying three adult wolves did not seem to be a burden to Aiden. My heart fluttered as I watched his easy stride.

There had to be a way to convince my father that Aiden MacMahon was the right man for me.

BRAVE Chapter 3

"WHO GOES THERE?" A guard at the gate asked as we approached.

"Tis I, Princess May," I answered, taking the position in front of Aiden. "Stay close," I whispered over my shoulder.

"The king has been looking for you." He raised the gate for us to enter and gave Aiden a sideways glance.

"This nice gentleman found me in the woods and helped me find my way back." I kept going as if all was normal.

It was a gamble bringing Aiden into the castle, especially with all that had transpired in the last twenty-four hours, but I needed to show my father that the law was ludicrous. Only he had the power to change it.

As for the curse, I would have to look into that further once things settled down. My mind was made up. I would do whatever it took to make sure Aiden was pardoned for the sins of his ancestors and reverse the damn curse that turned him into a beast by day.

"Stop that man!"

I jumped at the sound of my father's voice. We were halfway across the courtyard, and guards came out of the woodwork, all brandishing swords.

Aiden handed me my bow and laid the wolves on the ground before him. He raised his hands, showing he would not fight. The guardsmen, however, approached as if he were fully armed for battle.

I stepped close to Aiden out of a need to protect him. "He saved me from these wolves." I pointed to the pile on the ground. "And spared the pup in my arms. He is not a danger."

"He is a MacMahon," my father growled, stepping into the moonlight. "And as such, is sentenced to death."

"Is there no mercy for the man who saved your daughter's life? A man who insisted on accompanying me to safety without so much as a thought for his own?"

My father's lips pressed together, and his hands clenched into fists. The way his face pinched, I knew my words were puncturing his resolve.

"The law of the land..." he started.

"*Can* be changed," I interjected. "He is not his ancestors. He is not the ones who terrorized the nobles and stormed the castle over a hundred years ago. Why should he be crucified for his ancestor's sins?" I stood my ground, challenging my father in front of his guardsmen. My palms sweat under the heat of the puppy still in my arms. My stomach clenched at my audacity, and nerves bit at the surface of my skin. My heart pounded as I prayed I had not just taken away any chance for Aidan's survival.

"May, this is my battle, not yours," Aiden said softly.

I glanced at him and swallowed the lump in my throat.

"Take him to the dungeon," my father growled, glaring at me in a way that promised an epic lecture about his dignity in front of his men.

The order was a concession, but it didn't mean Aiden was out of danger.

"Don't hurt him," I said as the guards grabbed Aiden and shoved him forward. They were not known for their patience or their gentleness with prisoners, and while I knew Aiden would live until my father saw fit to pass his sentence, I didn't know if it would be without bruises or broken bones.

As soon as Aiden was out of sight, my father stormed over to where I stood. He glanced down at the dead wolves and then the puppy in my arms. His jaw clenched tight and his glare was as deadly as I had ever seen it.

"I should lock you up in your room until your wedding day."

"You are the one who dictated I make a choice." I glared back at him. My voice was low and full of the same venom his words held. "And if you see fit to execute Aiden, I will never agree to marry anyone you decide is worthy. If you try to force it on me, you will not like my reaction."

"Do not threaten me, girl." He stepped closer, towering over me.

"It's not a threat, Father. It is a promise."

A small growl came from my arms. The little wolf pup was about as pleased with my father as I was. I scratched behind the wolf's ear and the growl faded, but its sharp little eyes never left my father.

"I should have beaten this obstinance out of you the first time you showed it."

"Mother wouldn't have allowed that."

He pressed his lips together. "Go to your room. Now."

Instead of instigating him further, I turned and trudged inside with Shadow still in my arms. My father ordered someone to bring him the pelts of the wolves once they were cleaned, and I shuddered, clasping my wolf pup a little tighter.

"Sheri, can you please get me a bowl of milk?" I asked my lady-in-waiting as I entered my room.

"Right away, my lady." She scuttled out of the room and returned with a bowl of milk a few minutes later.

I took the milk and put it under Shadow's nose. The pup nearly dove into the bowl. Both paws and his snout dipped into the white liquid as if it were made of gold. His tongue lapped the liquid as fast as possible, splattering it all over the front of his fine gray coat. I smiled at my little treasure.

But my smile disappeared as my mother stormed into my bedroom, her face as red as her hair.

She stopped halfway across the room, planting her hands on her hips as she stared down at me. "What have you done?"

My eyebrows rose in response and the little ball of fur in my lap started that low growl. The hair on the back of Shadow's neck bristled. I slowly ran my fingers down behind his ears, scratching to distract him. My mother wasn't one to take being challenged lightly, and the sternness in her expression matched that of her demanding tone.

She turned and started pacing the length of the room. Red bloomed in her cheeks, and she chewed on her lower lip.

"Why are you so upset?" I finally asked when the pacing didn't cease.

She stopped and turned, facing me. "Bringing him here was not wise," she finally said, with eyes so full of fear that I gulped whatever words had been waiting to come out.

"Shadow?" I asked, holding my wolf a little tighter.

My mother rolled her eyes. "No. MacMahon."

"He wasn't willing to let me cross the fields alone. Not after the wolves attacked us in the woods."

"You should have insisted!"

I leaned back away from the panic pulsing out of my mother. "Why?"

"Because..." She clamped her lips closed and shut her eyes. When she opened them, I swore there were unshed tears before she blinked them away. "Because he wants your blood."

I cocked my head. "If he wanted my blood, why in the world wouldn't he have taken it in the forest?" Her logic did not sit right with him protecting me the way he'd done. "He had plenty of opportunity to kill me, Mother. And he did just the opposite. He protected me."

"Of course he protected you. If you die, the curse becomes permanent."

I stared at her, trying to comprehend what exactly she was telling me. "What?" The word came out in barely a whisper.

"You are his key to reversing the curse, but if you die before the ritual is complete, he will become the bear for all time."

"How am I the key?"

She bit her lower lip again. "You are the only female descendent of the witch who placed the curse on the MacMahons. That is why that heathen came to the palace."

"I still don't understand how I am the key." I ignored the fact I was a descendent of a witch. I would deal with that once I understood how I factored into Aiden's cure.

"In order to reverse the curse, the last descendant of the MacMahon clan must drink a qist of fresh blood from the last descendant of the witch Marigold within the confines of the great stones when the mid-day hour becomes as dark as night. If

Marigold's descendant lives despite the loss of blood, it will cure the curse. But if Marigold's descendant dies before the sun takes over the sky once again, then the last MacMahon will die with her, and only the beast will remain."

My mind raced just as fast as my heart. "So, my blood and being at Stonehenge during an eclipse will cure Aiden?"

My mother paled and reached for the bedside table to steady herself. Her slow nod of acknowledgement created a pressure inside my chest.

"What if the last descendant of Marigold and MacMahon were to wed?"

"It is forbidden." She looked at the pup in my lap. "Just as it is forbidden to have wolves as pets."

I cocked an eyebrow at her. "Shadow isn't going anywhere." I bit my tongue before I added anything about Aiden. I had to have a conversation with the man before I stuck my neck out for him again.

Had his attentions all been a ruse?

LONG AFTER THE CASTLE quieted, I slipped out of my room and down to the dungeons, sneaking by the dozing watch guard. I snatched the keys off the table next to him. As stealthily as possible, I tried each key in the door to the vault until the click of the lock echoed. I stiffened.

The guard mumbled and shifted, but didn't wake. Finally, I exhaled the breath I had been holding and slipped through the door, closing it behind me. I lit the lantern and kept it on low as I tiptoed down the hall, glancing into each cell.

I stopped when the light shone on Aiden.

"Why have you come?" Aiden asked from his prone position on the bare cot. He didn't even lift his head to look at me.

"I was going to ask you the same thing." I turned up the lantern and glanced at the door to the castle proper. If the guard woke, I would be in a great deal of trouble. I inspected the keys in my hand until I found one that looked like the lock on the door, slid the metal inside, and turned it. At first it didn't budge, but a moment later, a satisfying click sounded. I opened the door and stood at the entrance to the cell.

His eyes opened, and he sat up, meeting my gaze. A dimple appeared quick before it disappeared. "I have a dilemma," he said and sighed, glancing down at the floor. "I want a whole life." He stood and crossed to the bars. Fire burned in his eyes, and the next few words came out between clenched teeth. "I wanted it bad enough to believe the sacrifice was worth it."

His intense stare froze me in place. When his hand snaked out and tangled in my hair, his touch zapped me with enough sizzle to create steam between us. He pulled me closer. The metal of the lamp handle bit into my hand as I gripped it tighter, and my breath caught in my throat.

"And then I saw you." He leaned his head against mine. His dark bangs tickled my forehead as his thumb caressed my cheek. "That was as bad as a kick in the balls."

"Why?" My voice barely registered.

He met my gaze, and it was as if the room had ignited. His lips covered mine as he swung me around and pressed me against the bars. I gasped. His tongue slipped into my mouth in a delicious dance, exploring, twirling, teasing. One of his hands caressed my breast through my nightshirt before he pulled away.

"What I wouldn't do to hear you calling my name in ecstasy..." His lips touched mine, and then he was gone.

The cell clanged shut, leaving me in the grungy accommodations as he slipped out the door.

He glanced over his shoulder before he disappeared into the dark, like a soldier looking at his loved ones just before he was shipped off to battle.

"Damn you," I muttered under my breath and pushed on the gate. It didn't budge. I hadn't even noticed him taking the lamp or the keys out of my grasp. I was too lost in the sweetness of his mouth and the gentleness of his hand cupping my breast.

I pressed my lips together against a scream of frustration. Alerting the guards would be an immediate death sentence for Aiden. I was angry with him, but not enough to put his life at risk.

I sat down on the cot, letting out a huff. A waft of Aiden's sweet honey scent drifted from the thin fabric, and I closed my eyes, allowing myself a moment to relish his smell. It dissipated as quickly as Aiden had. I ground my teeth together, lying back on the lumpy fabric while I waited for someone to uncover my duplicity.

BRAVE Chapter 4

SHADOW'S DISTANT HOWL PULLED me from a restless sleep. I sat up on the cot and rubbed my eyes, letting them adjust to the dank cell. The morning sunrise lit up the space.

I certainly hoped Aiden made it out of the castle, because no one inside these walls would spare the life of a wild bear.

The howling ended. My heart jumped into my throat. Had someone cut my wolf down? Tears stung my eyes.

The door at the end of the hall opened and light from a lamp illuminated the hall outside my cell. The sleek form of Shadow stopped in front of the cell and whined. When my father stepped next to him, the stoic expression on his face made me gulp.

His gaze traveled over the entire cell before it landed back on me. His lips pressed into a thin line, and the red hue filling his cheeks and nose announced his aggravation as loud as a crack of thunder in a stormy sky.

"Where is he?" he asked in a menacing growl that made me glad a row of bars stood between us.

I shrugged. "Probably halfway across the country by now."

He closed his eyes and his nostrils flared.

I bit my lip, waiting for my punishment to be delivered. But my father just turned and sauntered down the hallway, leaving Shadow and me alone in the dungeon.

My wolf pup stretched out on the floor outside the cell and put his head on his paws. His sigh filled the stale air. I flopped down on the cot again and stared at the ceiling as the morning light shined brighter through the window.

I didn't know how much time passed, but the room was at its brightest when Sheri snuck into the dungeon with a plate of food for me and a bowl of milk for Shadow. I nearly attacked the food through the bars. It had been over twenty-four hours since I'd had a proper meal.

"I had to sneak by the old guard to bring this to you. Your father ordered that no one was to come in here," she whispered.

"Thank you," I said after I stuffed the last morsel into my mouth.

Sheri smiled, reached down, and picked up Shadow's empty bowl.

Her words sank in. "Old guard?" The only time father put elderly guards to work was when he and the rest of his army were out of the castle.

Sheri nodded. "Aye. The king called his army together to go bear hunting."

My heart nearly stopped in my chest, and I gripped the bars. "Get me out of here."

She stepped away from the bars, her eyes wide with fear. "I can't. Your father threatened me. Told me that if I helped you, he would have my head on the post outside the castle." Sheri hurried out of the dungeon.

I banged my forehead against the bars and let out a yell of frustration. The echo in the empty dungeon ran a cold shiver up my spine. I gritted my teeth and closed my eyes, holding on to the bars until my knuckles ached. Fury and fear played in my bloodstream, making every fiber hum.

I released my grip on the cold iron and stepped back. I tilted my head to the ceiling and bellowed every ounce of anger in an ethereal cry.

The guard rushed into the cell and slid to a stop in front of my cage. His chest rose and fell in frantic gasps as he stared at me with wide eyes.

"Let me out," I growled, sounding as feral as those wolves had last night.

He fumbled with the keys and dropped them on the floor before reclaiming them with shaking hands. He slid the key in the lock and threw the door open, then plastered himself against the wall on the far side of the hallway.

I stepped out of the cage and put my hand out. "Your sword," I demanded.

He blinked and then undid his belt, handing it over to me with the sword still in its scabbard. I clasped the leather around my waist and stormed out of the dungeon with Shadow on my heels. Instead of exiting the castle through the courtyard where I would surely have been caught and detained, I went out the secret path that led to the woods on the far side of the castle.

I had no idea where I was headed, but an internal guide pulled me along until I stood just outside the forest, staring at Stonehenge. My chest constricted at the sight of my father's army closing in on the stones from all sides. I ran, unsheathing my sword. Shadow kept pace with me as we raced across the field. I weaved through the line, sliding under the arms that reached to grab me and broke free of the group, rounding the entry until I stood alone in the center of the great stones.

I turned in a circle as the rumble of footsteps outside the walls pounded up my legs. I stopped my inspection at the sight of the bear in the far corner, cowering away from the sound. His back and sides were protected by the rocks.

Shadow and I approached, bent on blocking the only way to get to him. His gaze moved in my direction now that I'd shifted position into a downwind draft. His eyes widened, and he backed into the rocks more.

I turned, thinking the guards had breached the rocks. No one had entered. With my heart beating so hard that the whoosh of blood in my ears drowned out the sound, I turned back to the bear. Forcing my breathing to slow, I sheathed the sword and put my hands out to show him I was unarmed.

The beast's reaction didn't change. I glanced down at Shadow and he was looking up at me with his head cocked, like he was waiting for his next instructions. His gaze jumped behind me, and I turned, pulling the sword out, putting myself between my father's army and the bear.

I held the sword at the ready, lightly bouncing on the balls of my feet. The guards parted, and my father stepped through the line.

A deep crease appeared between his eyes. "May?" His gaze traveled down my body and then back to my face.

I looked down at my thin nightshirt. The belt held my bodice tight against my breasts, and my legs were bare from just above the knee.

The men surrounding him shifted uncomfortably as they attempted to avert their eyes from so much bare flesh.

None of them were in battle-ready stances, but that did not sway me from keeping vigilant.

"Move out of the way," my father said, recovering from his prior shock.

"I'm sorry, Father. I cannot let you or any of your men pass." My voice was calm, despite my racing heart and dry mouth. There were too many of them. If they all charged at once, I wouldn't stand a chance.

But I was the king's daughter and rightful heir to the throne.

His hands clenched, and his sharp glare sent a shiver over my bare skin.

"Leave us. Go back to the castle," he commanded.

The army filtered out, leaving only my father and me with Shadow and the bear in the clearing.

The moment we were alone, he unsheathed his sword and pointed it at me. "You really want to play this out?"

I took the stance he'd taught me. "When I win, you will pardon Aiden." I had never bested my father in a sword fight. Hell, we'd never fought with real steel before, and I wasn't as sure of myself as I projected.

He stepped forward, and so did I. Shadow moved between us, growling in an effort to protect me.

"Oh, for Heaven's sake," my father said and lowered his sword as he stared at Shadow.

I used the diversion to my advantage and swung my sword. It was met with steel; the impact vibrating all the way up my arms. My father sneered.

The bear behind us roared. We both turned to see the thing rear up on its hind legs. It was then that its dark eyes struck me. Aiden's eyes were blue, not brown like this beast.

I gasped and pushed backwards into my father's chest. "That's not Aiden."

"How do you know?" my father asked, moving, so he was at my side.

"Because Aiden's eyes are blue, even when he is in bear form."

We both readied our swords, moving away from each other, strategically splitting the bear's focus. How I wished my father hadn't sent the army away. We could use a little back up right now.

Shadow continued to growl, but this time his attentions were on the bear and not my father and me.

"Shadow, come here!" I snapped, and the wolf pup obediently took up residence at my side.

The bear thundered at us, its head swinging from side to side, trying to keep both of us in view as he stepped closer. His massive paw swatted in my direction. I dropped to the ground, grasping my sword with all my strength. The tip caught its paw, and the power of his swing knocked the handle right out of my grip. I rolled in the opposite direction from my sword, trying to put distance between me and the furious animal.

"Hey!" my father yelled, calling the bear's attention away from me.

Blood dripped from the paw I'd sliced, and the beast swung it at my father. My father wasn't as quick as I had been, and the bear's claws caught his breastplate, flinging him against the rocks.

My father slumped to the ground.

The bear went after him.

"No!" I yelled.

It spun toward me.

Shadow growled. All the hair on the back of his neck stood on end. My little wolf pup was no match for an adult bear, and neither was I.

I scooped Shadow up in my arms and backed away, trying to draw the bear away from my father. My heart slammed against the walls of my chest as I calculated my dwindling odds.

My sword was too far away, and my father was just coming to in the far corner. Blood flowed down his face, and he rose on shaking legs.

The bear lumbered towards Shadow's fearless growl. I backed into a rock, staring down the snarling bear. He cocked his giant paw back, ready to swipe his sharp claws from my crown to my toes.

A brown blur flew through the air and hit the grizzly before he could strike his death blow. The ball of fur rolled away in a pile of roars and howls of pain.

Blue eyes amidst brown fur flashed before another blow knocked him back. The fight raged, leaving me shaking and cowering behind my little rock fort.

My father hid behind a boulder as well, and I caught his eye. He tilted his head towards the fighting bears. I nodded. He needed to know it was Aiden who had saved me yet again from a horrible fate.

The slam of bone meeting rock echoed. One bear went down hard. The remaining bear fell onto all fours and turned towards me, snarling, his brown eyes full of fury.

"No!" I dropped Shadow to the ground, sprinting to where my sword lay. Hot anguish and rage fueled every cell, and I slid, swiping my blade from the ground and bouncing to my feet. I spun towards the beast, holding the blade like a javelin.

The grizzly reared up with a roar. My scream matched his.

I launched the blade at the same moment my father appeared in the air behind the bear with his blade clasped in two hands over his head. The bear was not fast enough to knock my sword off target. It buried in his chest all the way to the hilt. My father's blade sank into the base of the beast's neck. Bone was no match for the metal and the snap of it resounded.

The bear took a shaky step towards me and then collapsed. I spun out of the way and when he hit the ground; it shook like a mighty earthquake.

My father stood behind the dead bear, looking more formidable than I had ever seen him. He gave me a nod of approval, even though his chest heaved from exertion.

My gaze fell to my blue-eyed bear, and I ran to where he lay. Shadow followed, whining as he sniffed the prone animal. He lay on his side with his face away from me. The rock his head lay against was stained red. My heart tripped in my chest, and my hand fluttered to cover my mouth.

I kneeled next to the massive bear and touched the soft fur on his arm. Warmth still radiated. I leaned my ear against his back, and after moving a few times, I picked up his heartbeat.

I let out the breath I had been holding and glanced at my father. "He's alive." I climbed to my feet and circled around to his other side. Gently, I lifted his head, inspecting the ugly gash on his brow that still oozed blood. The ground underneath his abdomen was sticky with it, and when I lifted his paw to see the damage, I winced at the jagged slices running across his stomach. They were deep enough to provide days of discomfort, but at least he had not been disemboweled.

"He needs help," I said, looking up at my father. My gaze turned to the pink and orange brushstrokes in the sky. When the sun set, Aiden would transform. I did not know the extent of the damage or if it would transform with him.

My father said nothing, but the corner of his lower lip sucked between his teeth.

A burn started in my blood at his quiet study of the situation, as if he were contemplating making me leave Aiden.

"He saved my life." My harsh whisper brought my father's gaze to mine. "He deserves amnesty."

"How do you expect us to get a five hundredweight, unconscious bear back to the castle?

I glanced at the darkening sky again. "In a few minutes, he will be a man, and I'm sure between the two of us, we can drag him back to the castle before daybreak."

His jaw tensed, and he glanced at the dead grizzly bear. "Fine," he conceded in a tone that was anything but peachy. "But he is going to the dungeon. I don't want an angry bear terrorizing the castle tomorrow."

"The dungeon is no place for an injured man. He can stay in my room where it is clean, and I can dress his wounds."

"And when the sun rises?" he snapped and crossed his arms.

"I'll give him honey and berries and make sure he doesn't break out to terrorize the castle."

The last rays of the sun faded from the sky, and Aiden's transformation took the form of a low glow. It wasn't the spectacle of the other night. This time, he shrank in place without the magnificent stretch or flexing of muscles.

He was just as unconscious as he was a moment ago.

My father's eyebrows rose and he balked. "Ye didn't tell me he'd be naked."

"Does it matter right now?" I asked, exasperated. I didn't want to argue with my father. All I wanted to do was get Aiden back to the castle and clean out his wounds. The longer we stayed here, the more likely he would come down with an infection. "Help me get him to his feet."

I slung his arm around my shoulder and pulled him into an awkward sitting position.

The dead weight was almost too much to hold, and I nearly toppled over.

"Jesus, Mary, and Joseph, what are you doing, child?" my father muttered and reached down, yanking Aiden's other arm over his shoulder.

Together, we stood, both of us clasping our free arms around Aiden's blood-streaked waist. We skirted around the dead bear and started the long trek back to the castle, with Shadow at our heels.

BRAVE Chapter 5

"WHAT IS THAT MAN doing in May's bed?" My mother didn't even try to keep her voice down in the hallway. "You know how dangerous having him near her is."

"You don't have to keep reminding me of my family's curse, woman." My father's low growl came through the door. "I am well aware of what a MacMahon could do to Marigold's descendant."

I washed the last of Aiden's wounds, and carefully covered it with a clean cloth as best I could. The pile of rags at my feet told more of the story than I cared to digest. I pulled the sheets over him, picked up the blood-and-grit filled cloths, and marched to the door with the evidence.

I flung it open and nearly threw the rags at my mother. "Father had no choice. Aiden saved my life, and I would not leave him to die out there. If Father hadn't helped me carry him, I would have dragged him here myself."

"What exactly do you think will happen when the sun comes up?"

I narrowed my eyes at my mother. "He is going to turn back into a bear."

"How will you contain him from terrorizing the castle?" My mother's voice rose to a near hysterical pitch.

"Honey and berries," I replied. We had had a long walk home supporting Aiden's weight, and I took that time to figure out what I would do in the morning. An injured animal of any kind was unpredictable, and while there was danger in having him in a confined space, I was confident I had this under control. "I already sent Sheri to get as much of both as she can find before the sun rises."

"We can have the guards bring him to the dungeon," my mother said.

"No. I'm not having them put him in that filth. Not when my bed is available and clean."

She opened her mouth.

"No." I turned and retreated into the room, closing the door on any further conversation.

Aiden looked peaceful as he slept. The gentle cadence of his breathing brought a sigh to my lips. I glanced down at my bloody hands and crossed to the basin.

After my hands were scrubbed clean, I changed out of the dirty night dress into something clean and warmer than the night shirt. I moved my vanity chair to the spot next to the bed and reached for Aiden's hand. My fingers traced his fingers, and the contact lit a fire deep within me. I turned his hand over and followed the intricate lines in his palm with my index finger. Each path led to his wrist, and there was an intimacy to my actions that left my breath shallow and my heart pumping.

The door opened, and I dropped his hand, pushing back in the chair while heat filled my cheeks.

Sheri stood in the doorway with a full tray of fruits and berries, along with a large stack of honeycombs.

"Thank you." I smiled and pointed to my dressing table. "You can put it there and then take your leave."

"You don't want me to stay, my lady?" Sheri asked as she put the tray down.

"No. While he isn't any danger now, I'm afraid that will not be the case in the morning." I met her wide-eyed stare. "But you can take Shadow with you for a while. I don't think it is prudent to have a wolf and a bear sharing the room, either." I smiled.

She curtseyed and gathered Shadow up in her arms before she left the room.

I turned back to Aiden and stared at his palm, just waiting for me to continue my exploration of the patterns. Tentatively, I started tracing the lines again, memorizing each curve and intersection.

The overriding sense of someone watching me settled in, and I glanced up at his face. His eyes were open, revealing that blue that captured my heart. His lips formed the slightest curve of a smile. Heat filled my face and soon flushed through my entire body.

When I went to pull away, his hand grasped mine.

He winced at the movement and his eyes squeezed closed. "Jesus," he whispered, and his free hand reached towards the bandages on his head.

I grabbed his arm before he could disrupt them. "Don't."

He stopped and pried one eye open. "What happened?"

"You didn't win the fight with that bear, but at least he didn't kill you."

Aiden pulled his arm from my grip and tried to sit up.

"Please, just lay back before you start bleeding again." I stood and gently pressed his shoulders back down on my bed.

"Where am I?"

"In my bedroom," I said.

His eyes widened.

"My father and I dragged you back here. And I patched you up the best I could." I adjusted the sheet and met his questioning gaze. "It's okay. They aren't going to lock you up in the dungeon."

He glanced towards the window and the lightening sky. "I can't stay here." He attempted to rise again, wincing as he moved.

"Aye. You can." This time, I pushed him down with more force. "You are in no condition to be wandering the forest today. Besides, I have honey and berries. I think I can handle the bear."

He let out a high-pitched laugh. "You are insane."

"You were the one who saved me. You aren't going to hurt me."

Aiden pressed his lips together and stared at the canopy of my bed. "Why would you even chance it?" His gaze traveled to mine, the question in his eyes just as clear as his underlying pain.

Fueled by the memory of his searing kiss, I leaned in and pressed my lips to his. His soft groan sent liquid fire to the spot between my legs as our mouths opened, allowing the slow exploration of our tongues. I clamped my thighs together against the sudden wetness. His hand threaded in my hair, holding me in place as the kiss transformed into something irresistible.

When his other hand skimmed over the flesh of my thigh, I pulled away with a gasp. He had navigated the fabric of my dress while we were kissing, and now his fingers found that sweet spot between my legs that erased logical thought from my head.

I stood in place as he rubbed my folds in slow circles. His blue eyes locked with mine as he plucked my body like a master minstrel. I let him bring me to the brink, and I pressed the back of my wrist to my mouth to stop the moan that wanted to escape as every muscle tightened and a warm rush coated his hand.

His fingers slid inside me, adding to my heat. My hips ground into his hand, demanding more. Aiden's eyes closed. His mouth parted, and a soft sigh slipped out. The sheet tented with the stiffness of his manhood and all I could imagine was that thick length filling me instead of his hand.

When his eyes opened, a raw need filled them, but he turned away, glancing at the window again. He pulled his hand from between my legs, and I let out a squeak of protest.

He drew his fingers into his mouth, sucking my juices from his flesh as he groaned. "You need to leave unless you want to be taken by a bear."

I stepped back. The warmth filling me turned frigid, and I blinked as his words sank through the lingering euphoria he had created.

"Go," he whispered. His voice filled with as much urgency as his eyes. When the nails on his finger grew into sharp claws, he rolled out of the bed, landing on the floor on the far side with a grunt.

I took a step towards the bed and a roar filled the room. Nails scraped wood. The arch of a brown-furred back appeared over the side of the mattress. The metallic taste of fear filled my mouth, but my feet still refused to leave the spot where I stood.

When the grizzly grew to his full height, the last of the bandages I had used fell to the ground. His sharp, blue-eyed gaze locked on me, reflecting that same intense want.

My feet finally listened to my brain, and I turned, running to the door. Before I could get the knob turned, his enormous paw slammed on the wood, blocking my escape. His warm body pressed against mine, and his snout tickled my neck. His low, suggestive growl was beyond what I could take. I jabbed my elbow into his hurt side.

His teeth pressed down on the back of my neck.

The pressure froze me in place. "No. Aiden," I said. My voice was steady despite the tremors filling me from my toes all the way to where his sharp teeth dug into my soft flesh. "Let go."

To my surprise, the bear followed my demand and let me go. He backed up a few paces, and I turned to face him. He shook his head like he was shaking water off and roared at me.

I pointed my finger at him. "You are going to behave. Understand?"

He growled low, remaining on all fours, and huffed before he turned and assessed his surroundings. He circled and then settled on the floor to stare at me.

The howl outside my door made me jump, and as soon as my heart started up again, I rolled my eyes. I had to let my wolf in before he woke the entire castle. Without taking my eyes off Aiden, I cracked the door, and Shadow darted inside. I shut the door once he'd cleared.

Shadow slowed his gait, stopping a few steps in front of me. The hair on his neck rose, as did a vicious snarl from the back of his throat. He bared his teeth at the bear.

"It's okay, boy," I said and squatted, pulling the wolf to my side.

He calmed immediately and glanced back at me as if to make sure I was okay with the gigantic beast in the room. I stroked his back to make my point, and he turned to me, swathing my face with his tongue.

I sighed, pushing my wolf's snout away from my face. Now that I'd assured him there was no danger, Shadow turned and bounded in Aiden's direction with his tail up like he had found a new playmate.

Aiden climbed into a sitting position to where Shadow couldn't nip at his face. His gaze moved from the little thing weaving between his legs to mine, and he cocked his head as if to say, "Really?"

I smiled just as Shadow jumped onto Aiden's haunches. Aiden swatted Shadow, sending him rolling across the floor. But that only fueled the playfulness in my wolf pup. He ran straight at Aiden.

"He's just a puppy," I said before Aiden could snarl.

He glared at me and lay back down, resigned to the fact my dog was going to terrorize him all day. And it was going to be an endless day, at that.

BRAVE Chapter 6

NOT ONLY WAS I ready to drop from exhaustion as the daylight faded away, I was ready to eat a holiday feast. I had shared the fruit with Aiden earlier, hand feeding the bear as Shadow bounced around, curious as to what we were doing. But as my grumbling abdomen made clear, that was not enough to sustain me. My stomach growled, even as my eyelids dipped. My head bobbed, and I jerked awake.

Shadow lay curled at my feet, and Aiden paced slowly in the cramped space. My bedroom was larger than most in the castle, but it was not big enough to allow for the restless roaming of the bear.

The click of nails was hypnotic, and I struggled to keep my eyes open.

Pressure on my shoulder yanked me awake. I shot up, straight in the chair I had been slumped in, and turned, gasping at the chiseled chest in front of me. I blinked and looked up into Aiden's amused smile.

"I have no idea how you could sleep through that ruckus," he said.

The churning noise in my belly was loud enough to rival Shadow's growls. But my wolf pup had, in fact, slept through the god-awful noise as well. I shrugged, and my gaze dropped to the silken throw blanket Aiden had tied around his waist.

"Any chance you could find me some clothes?" he asked.

"Aye." I yawned and stretched. When I went to stand, my head spun, and I stumbled.

Aiden caught me and sucked air through his teeth. He made sure I was steady, and then his hand went to the raw cuts on his side. At least they weren't oozing. There was something to be said about the healing abilities of transforming into a bear and back.

A soft knock on the door interrupted the moment. I stepped back out of his arms.

"Come in," I said as soon as I was sure my feet would hold me.

Sheri stepped inside with a tray overloaded with food and a bowl of milk for Shadow. My wolf pup stretched and trotted over to Sheri as if he thought all that food was for him. I didn't think I had ever been as grateful as I was at that moment.

"Thank you!" I followed her to the dressing table where she changed out the brimming tray with the empty one. "Think you can find something suitable for Aiden to wear?"

Her cheeks turned red as her gaze flitted to the nearly naked man in my room. "Are you sure?" she whispered in my ear.

I smiled and looked down at the floor before glancing at her sideways. She caught my dimples and suppressed a smile of her own.

"Aye, I'm sure," I whispered after a moment.

"Very well," she said and turned towards the door. Her gaze lingered on Aiden until she was out of sight.

Aiden put his hands on his hips and cocked an eyebrow at me. "You hesitated for a minute too long, my lady." He crossed and glanced at the array of meats and breads on the tray. "After you," he said, waving at the food.

Just his proximity clouded my thoughts. I picked at the food, unable to think of anything else but his hand between my legs last night.

His hands landed on my waist and I jumped.

"Are you just going to pick at that?" he whispered before running his tongue along the edge of my ear. "Because I have something much more interesting for you to eat than a tray full of food." His hands squeezed my hips, and he pressed against my back.

My heart fluttered, and my mouth went dry. I reached for the cup of wine, dousing the dryness in my mouth with the sweet concoction. I didn't dare turn, because the moment I faced the man, whatever logic remained in my mind would flee in favor of his lips.

"I'm undecided as to what to have first," I said and licked my lips, forcing myself to focus on the food instead of the steady pressure of his hands and the pleasant circle of his hips against mine. "Besides, Sheri will be back soon."

He purred in my ear, letting his tongue follow the line of my neck. It tickled and tantalized, and then it was gone, along with his touch. I glanced over my shoulder to catch him crossing to the window.

Aiden MacMahon had to be the sexiest man I had ever laid eyes on. The physical attraction was undeniable. But beyond his desire to bed me and to be free of the curse, I knew nothing about him. I took one of the chicken legs and turned in his direction.

"Tell me about yourself," I said.

Aiden turned, both his eyebrows arched. "Why?"

"Because I'd like to know more about you."

He laughed and looked out the window. "I'm not one of your suitor's, so there is no point in this conversation. Besides, it looks as though they are setting up for a beheading. Any bets on whose head will be on that chopping block?" He pointed to the courtyard.

I dropped the chicken leg on the plate and crossed to stand at his side. My eyes narrowed and my hands clenched. "That is not going to happen."

Shadow rubbed against my leg in a show of solidarity.

The door opened, and my father waltzed in with a couple of guards. Sheri was behind him with an armful of clothing, her face as shocked as mine felt.

"I see our prisoner has woken."

"He is not a prisoner." I stepped in front of Aiden, blocking him behind me. "He saved my life. Both our lives."

"We are not doing this, May," my father said through clenched teeth. "Take him to the gallows."

The guards started towards Aiden.

"No." I stood tall. "You told me to choose a husband. I choose Aiden. If you kill him, I will follow him into the afterlife, and I will take you with me."

No one in the room moved. My father stared at me with his jaw hanging open. Sheri clutched the clothing to her chest with her eyes as wide as I had ever seen them, and the guards stared at me in the same shocked expression everyone else wore.

"Leave my bedroom. Now." The resoluteness in my command was unmistakable.

The guards took a step back, unsure of what to do next. I glared at my father. The gauntlet had been issued, but my heart thundered in my chest at the indecision I saw in his eyes.

He glanced at Aiden and sneered.

My chest tightened, but I kept my face neutral, praying my fear didn't seep through my façade.

My father nodded at the guards.

They stepped forward, grabbing my arm, and pulled me along with Aiden out of the room. The king held up his hand before we passed and stared into my eyes.

"When you issue a threat, you better damn well be willing to follow through with it," he said to me and then pointed at the door.

I didn't speak. I didn't argue, even as they marched both of us to the courtyard where a small crowd had gathered for the beheading festivities. Anger festered inside me, creating a potent cocktail that swirled in my blood.

Aiden hadn't said a word since we were dragged from the room. I glanced at him as we were lined up side by side. My blanket still hung from him, but it had slipped enough for me to make out the sharp outline of his hips.

He glanced at me as they put another wooden block in the space in front of me.

A hush fell on the crowd.

I ripped my arm from the guard's grip and took a step forward, dropping to my knees in front of the chopping block. "If this is a world that persecutes a man just because he carries a name that was outlawed over a hundred years ago, I do not wish to be a part of it." My voice projected over the crowd. I lay my cheek on the wood and looked up at Aiden.

He slowly dropped to his knee and adopted the same position, his eyes locked with mine.

I reached my hand out, and he threaded his fingers through mine.

A disturbance started in the back of the courtyard. The crowd that had been so ripe for a killing turned.

"Why is Princess May up there?" someone in the crowd called out.

Their rumblings grew louder until my father climbed up on the stage.

"She chose a MacMahon." He pointed at Aiden.

"So what?" several of the people in the gathering called out.

"That's a ridiculous law," others chimed in.

"It doesn't warrant death!" still more yelled.

"I would have chosen him, too." A few catcalls echoed from the back.

Aiden blushed, but kept his gaze on me, our hands still intertwined as the masses argued our fates.

"You are the king. You can change the laws of the land."

I broke eye contact with Aiden and looked up, straight into Sheri's upturned face as she repeated verbatim the words I had said the morning after the feast. She still clung to the pile of clothing I had asked her to retrieve.

"You cannot kill your only daughter and strip this land of a future queen full of the kind of grace this nation needs. One with a heart so pure that only she would think of saving a wolf pup from certain destruction. You cannot deprive this land of a ruler who will deliver swift justice as effortlessly as a worthy pardon. Not for a century old grudge that no longer has meaning!" Her impassioned plea riled the crowd further.

She had been there for me time and time again over the years and was my closest and strongest advocate outside of my parents. It humbled me that she would stick her neck out for me in such a public way.

My father stood clenching and unclenching his fists as he scanned the crowd. He crossed to the axe and picked it up, then positioned himself before lining up the blade with Aiden's neck.

I leaned back on my heels, still holding Aiden's hand. He didn't move from his position, nor did his eyes leave me. He squeezed my hand tighter, waiting for the end.

My father raised the blade in the air.

"Do not do this," I said, my voice low with a warning thrum I had never heard.

My father hesitated and moved his focus to me.

His eyes widened the same way the guard who unlocked the dungeon cell for me had.

The crowd gasped and fell silent.

I didn't dare move my gaze from my father's, but Aiden's hand squeezed in a way that defined involuntary shock.

My father slowly lowered the axe and took a shaky step back. The color bled from his face, leaving him pasty under the shadow of the moon.

I glanced at Aiden. He wasn't looking at me, but beyond me with eyes wide with fear. His grip on my hand tightened.

Metal hit wood. My gaze snapped back to my father. The blade of the axe stuck out of the wood deck at his feet. The echo of the bang was enough to snap everyone out of what had bewitched them.

"Bring them to the throne room," my father said, low enough for only the guards to hear, and then he stormed out of the courtyard.

BRAVE Chapter 7

AIDEN AND I WERE dragged into the empty throne room and forced to our knees. A blade was held at each of our throats, keeping us in place.

My father stepped into the room, his normal, calm demeanor gone. His face was as red as I had ever seen it, and his hands were in fists so tight they were almost white. He paced the floor with his lips pressed into a thin line. His eyes bore through me.

Nearly two minutes of silence went by before he spoke. "Put the swords away," he growled.

The blade under my chin disappeared, and I slouched as the stress keeping me upright evaporated. Aiden reached for me.

"Do not touch her," my father snarled, then he turned his brutal glare my way. "What the hell did you do out there?

I blinked at him. "I told you not to kill Aiden."

"You conjured a ghost!" His bellow echoed in the great hall.

"I most certainly did not."

"There was a spirit surrounding you," Aiden said.

"Why would you call that...that thing?"

I stared at my father. "I did not call any spirit." My heart hammered in my chest as I glanced between my father and Aiden. "On my mother's life," I added, raising my hand to make my oath have more impact.

"Do you swear on his life?" My father pointed at Aiden.

"Aye." I didn't dare lose eye contact with him, because the moment I looked away, he would mistake it for a lie.

He stopped pacing and deflated before my eyes. His gaze shifted to Aiden. "If she didn't conjure that ghost, you must have."

Aiden laughed, and the guard closest to him jabbed the blunt end of his sword into Aiden's side. His laugh caught in his throat as he doubled over in pain. His head touched the ground while he wrapped his arms around his midsection.

"Did you curse her?" Father pointed at me, his voice bouncing off the stately rock pillars.

"No." Aiden gasped and pulled himself back onto his knees with narrowed eyes. "Did you?"

My father blinked and slowly took a seat on his throne. Defeat creased his brow, and he ran his hand down his face. The way his gaze traveled between the two of us bloomed hope in my heart.

He glanced at the guards. "Leave us."

The guards left us alone in the room.

"Get dressed," my father ordered Aiden, pointing to the pile of clothing Sheri had left behind.

Aiden climbed to his feet and crossed to the clothing. I tried not to let my gaze wander in his direction, but I couldn't help it. My insides clenched with disappointment as a shirt covered his bare back, and I looked away.

My father was studying me from his perch, and when Aiden crossed and offered me his hand, I took it, despite the tightening of my father's jaw. Aiden helped me to my feet, and then we both turned to my father.

With our hands still clasped, Aiden cocked his head. "Did you curse her?"

"Perhaps I did, but not by intention," he said softly. "Just as your family has been cursed all these years, Marigold's wrath may have wrapped itself around the only female descendant to grace the Stewart line since her death." His sharp stare landed on me. "There is more to the story than just the cursing of the MacMahons."

Aiden squeezed my hand and glanced at me out of the corner of his eyes. Heat rose in my cheeks, and I licked my lips before pressing them together. I shifted my weight and focused on my father.

He leaned forward and rested his elbows on his knees, studying the floor. With a sigh, he looked up. "I did not want to believe the lore." His gaze passed over the two of us and traveled up the columns to the ornate colors painted on the ceiling. "But I should have known better when I saw you at the castle." His eyes locked on Aiden, and he shook his head slowly.

I shifted closer to Aiden, my body trembling under the tension. Nerves bit at my skin, and the longer my father remained quiet, the more demanding the sensation became. Aiden's grip on my hand tightened, calming me.

The fog that clouded my father's eyes cleared, and he stood, his face changing back to that hard resolve that made my stomach sink.

"I will make a deal with you," he said, staring at Aiden. "I will recant the law that makes your name a capital offense, and in return, you will leave this castle and never return."

My stomach dropped.

Aiden's hand squeezed tight, and he glanced at me. The longing in his eyes produced a physical pain in my chest, as if my heart had been ripped from my body. When his grip loosened, letting my hand go, I thought my legs would fail.

"And if I refuse?" Aiden said.

"Then you die today, regardless of what my daughter says."

I balked at my father, my jaw hanging open as my brain stalled. Did he not see what had just happened in the courtyard?

Aiden stared at the ground. The corner of his lip sucked between his teeth as he glanced at me. The fact he was contemplating his choices tightened my throat.

"Accept the deal and go," I whispered. I couldn't imagine living in a world where he wasn't alive.

He nodded. "Fine. I accept your terms." His voice cracked, and his hands curled into fists as if his body did not agree to his promise. "Can I say a proper goodbye?"

My father waved for him to proceed.

Aiden turned to me, his blue eyes reflecting the sadness in his down-turned lips. He closed the distance and wrapped his arms around me, hugging me tight. His lips pressed against the top of my head. "Goodbye, May," he whispered and then stepped away, turning and heading out of the throne room.

When the door opened, the guards blocked his exit.

"Let him go. I am recanting the law that calls for his death," my father announced.

The guards let Aiden pass.

I watched until he disappeared around the corner, waiting for him to glance back, but he never did. I spun, sending a glare at my father. "Why?" was all I could muster.

The doors of the great hall closed, and my father looked down at me. "Because a union between a MacMahon and a Stewart is forbidden." He stood and came down the steps to stand in front of me. He placed his hands gently on my shoulders. "It cannot be."

"Why?" I yelled and knocked his hands away from me. The anger built inside me, making my skin tingle.

"Because it will bring Marigold back from the dead, and she vowed to destroy everything the Stewarts loved." His lips pressed together as he gripped my arms. "Do you love that monster?"

I recoiled, but my father didn't let go. "He isn't a monster." My voice was breathless as the anger transformed into fear.

"Do you love him?"

My gaze darted around the room. I had only known him for a few days, but the squeezing of my heart told me the truth. While I knew little about Aiden MacMahon, I had been ready to join him in the afterlife.

"Why would Marigold destroy everything we love?" I didn't understand where this conversation was going, and I wasn't ready to admit I loved the man. At least, not to my father.

"Because as soon as Marigold gave birth to an heir, my great, great, great grandfather had her burned at the stake for witchcraft. Her dying decree was that she would destroy the house of Stewart as surely as they had destroyed the house of MacMahon. The firstborn female in the house of Stewart would be hers to command, and the two houses would collide, bringing forth ultimate destruction."

It sounded a little too cryptic to me. At least with Aiden's curse, the cure was much clearer than the witch's dying rant.

"You are the first female born to a Stewart since Marigold burned at the stake. And the fact that her ghost appeared out there..." He nodded his chin towards the courtyard and shook his head. "I cannot take the chance of that witch destroying you or your mother."

The mention of my mother made me stiffen.

"All that I love," my father whispered.

I thought of all I truly loved, and my heart squeezed. Aiden was included, alongside my parents and Sheri.

"How do we stop this?" I whispered, afraid that the door allowing Marigold in may have already been opened.

"You are to never see that man again."

BRAVE Chapter 8

I LAY IN BED thinking about all my father had said. The idea of never seeing Aiden, of never feeling his lips on mine or his hands on my body, left me cold.

Doubt laced itself into everything my father had told me. I rolled to my side, staring out the window at the dawn's soft light. My longing for Aiden was greater than my fear that my father's story was real.

After a near sleepless night, I climbed out of bed and made my way to the dining hall for breakfast. The only activity in the room was the servants bringing the food in. I piled my plate with sweet breads and meats before sitting down to graze.

My parents came in just as I had swallowed my last bite.

"I'm going back to bed." I stood as they sat. "I didn't get any sleep last night."

"Arc you fccling all right?" my mothcr asked.

I nodded. "Just exhausted." I headed to my room.

While I was tired, I needed to buy myself some time. With Shadow on my heels, I dressed in my warmest hunting outfit, donning pants instead of a skirt, and put pillows under the covers so if anyone looked into the room, it would look like someone was in the bed.

I tucked my hair up under a woolen hat and slid Shadow into a bag before I took my bow and arrow from the back corner. When I slid out of the room, I kept my head down so no one would recognize me.

A group of men were heading out, and I trailed them. Not one guard paid me any attention. They assumed I was with the group of hunters. As soon as we hit the woods, the men went straight, and I peeled off to the right, keeping my steps as quiet as I could. I tried to remember my hunting track from the other day. I needed to find that field, as well as that barricade that had stopped me.

When I could no longer hear the men I had exited the castle with, I let Shadow out of my bag. He walked alongside me, sometimes bounding ahead, only to stop and look back. I crouched and slipped him a piece of meat I had taken from the hall. He ate it in one bite.

"Find Aiden," I whispered, and his ears perked up. "Find the bear."

His tail wagged, and he turned, putting his nose to the ground like he had understood my request. I followed his zigzag pattern, letting him lead me through the thickening woods.

We came upon the small glen where I had first seen Aiden. Shadow skirted the nest of bushes, finding a small space to make his way through. I dropped to my knees and looked through the opening. Shadow looked back at me from the other side. I sighed and pushed my bow and quiver through and then got down on my stomach.

I wiggled my way through the opening like an inchworm. It took what seemed like forever, but when I got to the opening, Shadow licked my face and moved back, allowing me to crawl to my hands and knees. I kneeled in the small space. The entire alcove was blocked by gnarled bushes. In the far corner, a dark opening caught my attention.

Shadow was already heading that way. My heart pumped raw adrenaline through my veins as I crawled towards the opening of the cave. Shadow stood at the entrance with his nose in the air. He bounded into the darkness. I scrambled after him.

The blackness of the cave was broken only by Aiden's wide blue eyes, that seemed to glow. Shadow's panting and scraping of nails against rock were the only sounds in the space. I blinked, forcing my eyes to adjust to the dark.

A low rumbling in the bear's chest caught me off guard, and then I remembered the hat. I pulled it off, and my hair fell in loose curls. The growl stopped, and a huff filled the space. His blue eyes kept me entranced as they moved closer.

"Hunters in the woods," I whispered.

His gaze jerked towards the entrance.

"They didn't follow me. No one knows I'm here."

Aiden turned and lumbered deeper into the cavern. I hesitated, but Shadow followed as if being near a large grizzly bear was normal. With my vision slowly adjusting, I carefully made my way in the direction I thought they had gone, shuffling my feet so I could navigate around any rocks I came in contact with instead of tripping over something.

Shadow came back to my side and nudged my knee before bounding back into the darkness. As I walked, my eyes seemed to adjust. Either that or the cave was getting lighter. Rushing water filled my ears. I skirted around a boulder, stepping into a larger cave with a small waterfall. It was warm here, like a mid-summer day, and the water glowed, filling the space with blue light.

Aiden stood knee-deep in the water and batted a fish onto the rocky shore near where I stood. The second it hit the ground, Shadow was on it, tearing flesh from bone and eating his fill. Several fish skeletons lay in the far corner with a fire pit that lay barren of wood or ash. A small straw bed sat near the fire, along with clothing drying on the rocks.

This was Aiden's home. I studied the walls and the crystals hanging on the ceiling that seemed to carry their own warm glow. I couldn't imagine the bear fitting into the underbrush clearing that I had crawled through to get inside the cavern, nor could I imagine Aiden doing the same.

"Is that the only way in here?" I pointed to the cavern where we had come in.

Aiden was too focused on the task at hand and dove for another fish. He came up with it in his mouth. It disappeared between his teeth, and he lumbered onto shore, shaking off the water. Warm spray doused me. He crossed to the corner opposite the bed and made himself comfortable.

My gaze turned to the straw mat, and I yawned. "I didn't sleep last night at all. Mind if I lie down?" I pointed to the bedding.

Aiden huffed.

I took that as a yes and crossed to the bed, took off my shoes, and curled up on the soft straw. His scent filled the space, and before I knew it, my eyes closed.

CRACKLING WARMTH PULLED ME from sleep. Aiden, in his human form, kneeled next to a roaring fire with a spit filled with fish cooking over it. His bare back faced me, and I reached out, running my fingers over his skin.

He jerked and looked over his shoulder. "Good morning." He smiled.

"Don't you mean good evening?" I stretched my aching muscles.

Shadow stretched, too, from his perch next to me and then licked my face.

I sat up, pushing my wolf pup away. The cave still glowed with an ethereal light. It reminded me of Aiden's eyes.

"So, this is where you live?" I twirled my finger around.

He pulled a crude plate from a shelf in the wall and dropped the cooked fish on it. He handed me the plate and sat back, leaning against the rock next to the bedding and stretching his leather-clad legs towards the fire.

"Why did you come?" he asked after I started picking at the dinner he had served me.

"I can leave if you want me to." I put the plate down on the bed between us and stood.

"If I wanted you to leave, I wouldn't have cooked you breakfast." He raised an eyebrow at me.

I sat back down and returned my focus on the food. Cooked salmon always tasted delicious, and these were beyond fresh. The fish melted in my mouth and I shared a few morsels with Shadow. When the bones were picked clean, I handed Aiden the plate.

Despite the fish carcasses lying about, the cave didn't stink with the stench of decaying flesh. Instead, it smelled like honey and spring rain. I climbed to my feet, crossed to the water, and crouched down to wash my hands. It was hot, like a newly drawn bath. I glanced over my shoulder.

"It's a hot spring, but the center is deep and cold. That's the channel where the fish swim through."

I cocked an eyebrow and stood, shaking the warm water from my hands before wiping them on my hips. Aiden climbed to his feet and crossed to me.

"Why did you come?" he asked, his voice soft and tender. His fingers brushed my cheek, tucking the stray hairs behind my ear.

"You know why," I said, breathless from his touch. Every cell in my body wanted him. I couldn't deny this strong connection.

He leaned in, and his lips crushed against mine. His arms wrapped around my waist, pulling me against his hard chest. The kiss transcended, making my body vibrate with need. I wanted to feel that same freedom, that same high I felt in my bedroom. I wanted all of Aiden.

He broke the kiss and stared down at me. "I can never set foot in the castle."

"I don't care." My hands trailed down his chest to the clasp of his pants.

He grabbed my wrists, holding them still. The carnal need in his eyes and the tension in his face belied his motion. "I am a bear by day," he said, his voice quivering.

"I don't care."

"My offspring are cursed as well," he said and stepped back. "I do not wish this life on anyone."

I stared at him, measuring the need pumping through my blood and the desire so clearly outlined in the fabric of his pants. My fingers nimbly unbuttoned the shirt I wore. I stripped the fabric from my shoulders and tossed it aside.

Aiden groaned at the sight of my bare breasts. "Please, May," he whispered.

His eyes begged me. For what, I wasn't sure. I peeled off my pants and stood at the edge of the water without a stitch of clothing on.

His pupils dilated, leaving only a thin edge of blue around the black abyss. His fingers fumbled with the clasp on his pants. He closed his eyes and pulled his hands away, clenching them.

I closed the distance, placing my palms on his chest. His heart raced underneath my hands, and his eyes jerked open. His breathing quickened. He stared down at me, trembling under my touch.

"Don't you want me?" I asked in a hushed whisper, laying my vulnerability at his feet.

With a guttural growl, he tore his pants off and then had me in his arms as he walked us into the water. His lips captured mine, walking us backwards until I lost my footing. He continued until the heat vanished and all that wrapped around us was the frigid depths of the water. He pulled away from my lips, his breathing ragged. When I wrapped my legs around his waist, his eyes clamped closed and his lips pressed together.

He pushed beyond the cold, into warmer waters on the inside of the cave lake, near the waterfall. He lifted me onto a rock and kissed me deeper than he had ever done before. I shook with need. When the kiss broke, I whined, but his lips trailed down my cheek to my throat. The sensation of his tongue swiping my skin and his butterfly kisses pulled a moan from deep inside me.

His mouth attacked each breast as if they were his only sustenance, nipping, licking, sucking until I thought I would go insane. Every sensation brought forth a cry from my lips.

With a wicked grin, he moved lower, kissing my belly, and running his tongue in a circle in my belly button. He pushed my legs wider, and I thought my heart would explode when his mouth clamped down on the spot his fingers had manipulated the other night.

His tongue was more magical, more commanding, than his hands had been. I laced my fingers through his hair, keeping him in the spot that produced the most decadent sounds from my mouth. So much so, that Shadow howled from the other side of the lake.

Aiden chuckled, his hot breath making me shiver. He glanced up at me and grinned as he gently nibbled. He pushed his fingers inside my hot path and wiggled them, creating delicious waves through my entire form.

Muscles tightened, and a heat so strong wrapped itself around me. I cried out his name, relishing the way it echoed on the rocks surrounding us as a rush of wetness flowed from between my legs.

Aiden's hands and mouth left my skin, and he stood with my fingers still entangled in his hair. The tip of his hard member brushed my sensitive nub, and then he plunged his hips forward, sending his hardness deep inside me.

I gasped as pain and pleasure collided. My eyes widened, as did his smile. He gripped my hips, pushing himself farther inside me until our bodies touched. Aiden's eyes closed, his head fell back, and his mouth parted in a pleasured sigh.

I yanked his head towards me, crushing his lips to mine, and he twisted, pulling me off the rock and into the warm water. My back slammed against the side of the rock with the force of his thrust. I arched into him, crying out into his mouth. Our frantic rhythm created waves in the pool, and grunts of exertion sounded from both of us.

Our lovemaking was on the verge of violent, but it brought me beyond this realm, filling me with power like I had never experienced before. Intense sensations filled every pore of my body. A grinding twirl of my hips or raking my nails across his back brought forth pleasure as a growl with my name on it.

Intense heat flushed through me, tightening my muscles, and I tilted my head back with a scream of satisfaction as I peaked. His mouth clamped on my throat as he rode me hard through each wave of ecstasy until he plunged deeper than he had before and cried my name to the gods as his hot seed filled me.

Trembling, he held me tight, still coupled, his head resting on my shoulder and his chest heaved in time with mine. I kissed the spot where his neck and shoulder met, and his flesh transitioned into a map of gooseflesh. He lifted his head and captured a gentle kiss, sucking my lower lip between his teeth.

He uncoupled from me, and the sudden emptiness sent an ache through my body. Taking my hand, he led me under the waterfall. The chill in the falling water invigorated me, and I stepped close to his warmth, letting the water soak through every strand of hair.

Aiden tilted his head back under the deluge before rubbing his face. He stepped behind the waterfall into another cozy alcove.

As soon as I stepped behind the wall of water, Shadow howled in discontent from the other shore. I poked my head back through. "Shush. We are right here."

The wolf pup climbed up on the bedding and curled up in a sulk only I could read. His eyes locked on our location.

I crossed into the alcove and ran my hands through my hair, smoothing it away from my face. It was darker in this space without the glow from the pool or the crystals at the top of the cavern.

Aiden leaned against a rock, his legs crossed as well as his arms. He stared at the ground.

I stepped closer, and his gaze flicked up, stopping me in place. It was hard and full of resolve.

My heart recoiled, and I wrapped my arms over my exposed chest.

"We can't..." He closed his eyes and ran his hands through his hair. "Damn it, May," he snarled. "We just can't." He waved towards the waterfall. His jaw tensed as he stared at me.

My chest hurt. I had given him everything in that moment, and he stood here rejecting me. My eyes stung, and I turned away before he could see the tears that I fought back.

"Aw, fuck," he whispered. A moment later, his hands landed on my shoulders. He gripped them tight and pressed a kiss on the top of my head. "My mother died giving birth to me. All the MacMahon women die in childbirth. I just can't..." His chin pressed down on my head, and his arms wrapped around me. "Just like I can't even consider the cure."

I turned in his arms, looking up at him. The hardness in his eyes had been replaced with melancholy.

He nodded towards the waterfall. "That can't happen again. I lost complete control, and it is too dangerous for you."

My insides twisted with disappointment. "And what if I want to take the risk?"

He smoothed my hair back and planted a gentle kiss. "No. You dying is not a risk I'm willing to take. Even though I had a taste of heaven that I'll crave for the rest of my life, I can't."

My heart wanted Aiden.
My body wanted Aiden.
My soul wanted Aiden.

Anger bloomed inside me at the injustice, and power flooded through my veins with it. The surrounding air swirled and before I could utter a sound, it pierced through my back like a lance, filling my form and shutting my voice down. I was trapped in my body.

Aiden stepped back, his eyes wide with horror. "May?"

The cackling laugh coming from my mouth made me shiver. "*Parere me.*" Marigold's ghostly voice flowed from me. The words formed a mystical fog that surrounded Aiden.

He stiffened when it pierced his skin, seeping into him like a fatal disease. His eyes muted gray. I struggled to get loose of Marigold's mental grip. Pain flashed in my head.

"Silly girl, you cannot break my hold. Righteous anger let me in, and now I control your flesh as well as your lover's." My form sauntered to Aiden.

He looked down at me with gray, lifeless eyes. I screamed.

BRAVE Chapter 9

MARIGOLD WAS INSATIABLE. DEMANDING Aiden perform until he finally fell into an exhausted stupor just before sunrise. I was bruised and battered from his voraciousness, and while I was locked inside my mind, I still felt the pain accosting every muscle.

Shadow had fled the area, shaking and soiling himself from the cavern entry as he watched. He sensed the evil and whined every time Marigold spoke. I hoped Aiden could break free once he was in bear form, but the sinking feeling in my stomach told me that was wishful thinking.

The night transitioned to morning, and Aiden transformed. His bear still slept where he had fallen. Marigold strutted around him, her hands rubbing the beast's fur. The softness of it clung to my skin, squeezing my heart further.

"Oh, to be mounted by such a mighty beast," she whispered with such curiosity that I gasped. Her intentions terrified me.

Aiden stirred and swung his massive head in my direction. His eyes reflected that same muted gray. I shivered.

Marigold still wielded power over him, even while in bear form. She crossed to one boulder and draped herself over it. Inviting the bear without words.

He crossed to where Marigold had me draped, and he sniffed at me. He turned, heading towards the water.

Marigold snarled within me. "*Tolle eam.*"

The bear stiffened and turned in such a stilted manner, I thought he would break. As he started towards me, Shadow darted from his hiding place and put himself between the bear and where I lay. My wolf growled with such heinous intent that my heart leaped into my throat.

I couldn't tell him he was a good wolf. I couldn't tell him to get out of the way, either.

Aiden's paw swiped at the little thing.

Shadow buried his teeth in Aiden's paw. Aiden bellowed in pain, trying to shake off the wolf. His eyes flashed blue for a moment, and Shadow released, flying into the lake from the inertia. The wolf surfaced and swam to shore, then shook and slunk back into the dark.

Aiden licked his paw, showing no interest in me. When he glanced over, the blue was gone from his irises and only gray remained. Still, he didn't approach me. He didn't conform to Marigold's command.

"*Tolle eam,*" she yelled, still holding my body against the rock, like a drunk harlot looking for action. She wiggled my butt.

That got his attention. Interest flashed across his bear features. He lumbered over and climbed on my back. The weight of him yanked the air from my lungs, nearly crushing me.

"*Prohibere!*" Marigold squeezed out, stopping Aiden before he started. As the bear retreated, Marigold stood and turned, regarding him with disgust. "We can't have your precious girl being crushed to death before the eclipse. That would ruin my fun."

The eclipse?

"Aye. Today is the day we die trying to break the MacMahon curse." She cackled, and a wave of gooseflesh covered my bare arms. "If you hadn't provided me with the perfect entrance, I would have had to take you by force as you slept."

Aiden's eyes flashed for a moment, and then that obedient gray overshadowed them.

Marigold picked up my discarded clothing, sneering at the pants and shirt. "What kind of clothing is this?"

It's my hunting outfit.

"Well, we will just have to make do." She glanced at Aiden's shirt hanging over the rock and dropped my clothing. The soft fabric caressed my skin with his honey scent as Marigold put the shirt on. It fell to just above my knees. She grabbed his belt and fastened it around my waist. "This will do far better than your hideous hunting outfit." She pulled on my boots to complete the outfit and glanced at Aiden. "It is time to head to Stonehenge. Lead the way, mighty beast."

He lumbered past where I stood, and Marigold followed, forcing my muscles to obey her nefarious order. I already knew what the ritual entailed. The thought of Aiden drinking enough of my blood to leave me on the brink between life and death turned my stomach.

"Child, he will drink every drop. He will not stop until your heart does," Marigold whispered.

My lips spread in a smile that was not my own, and I struggled to break free of Marigold's mental grip.

The path out of the cave was not as hard to navigate as the path I used coming in, although the entrance was hidden behind a large patch of prickly bushes.

We stepped into the thinning woods. The sunshine played between the leaves. Bright rays dotted our path until the woods gave way to an open field. The sight of my father's army surrounding the majestic stones was welcomed. He must have found me gone during the night and sent his men out to stand watch. A piece of me rejoiced. Marigold didn't have a prayer of making it through the crowded field.

Aiden stopped at the edge of the woods, and Marigold stepped beside him, putting her hand on his head. His soft fur tickled my palm.

"*Invisibilia,*" Marigold whispered and then stepped into the open glen.

I kept waiting for someone to see us, but she navigated through the men like we really were invisible.

When we stepped into the great circle, she turned and put her hands up. *"Praesidio!"*

The space around the rocks shimmered with her protection spell, and my heart sank. Shadow ran from the wood line, weaving in and out of the guards as they moved. They nearly tripped on each other as the wolf pup navigated the same path we took. The moment my dog came in contact with the barrier, his little form was thrown back ten feet.

"No!" I cried, but it was only in my head. Marigold's laugh was the only thing flowing from my mouth.

Shadow climbed unsteadily to his feet and let out a heart-wrenching howl. The guard close to him drew his sword, intending to take down my furry friend. I cringed as the blade whistled towards Shadow, but it met the unyielding steel of my father's sword.

He glanced up at me through the shimmering barrier, his expression stoic.

"Let them go, Marigold!" he called, his gaze narrowing.

The witch keeping me captive laughed and turned away, dismissing my father in a way I would never dream of. She propelled my form forward, nearly throwing me onto a flat stone in the middle of the array.

She sat me up like an old rag doll, spreading my legs wide so my calves dangled over the edges of the rock. Leaning back on my palms, she said, "Come here, my beast." She raised my shirt high enough to give Aiden, along with anyone beyond the barrier, quite the view. "Time to hunt for some honey with that tongue of yours," she purred.

I cringed and renewed my mental struggle.

Aiden climbed onto the rock with his front legs and stuck his snout between my thighs, obeying the order. Mortification crept through me, but Marigold kept that hideous smile on my face and glared at my father. Her satisfaction as his face turned red zipped through me.

I growled and forced my body to respond. My hips bucked, and my hands slipped, knocking the witch backwards. Our head connected with the rock, sending a dizzying wave through me.

Aiden's head snapped up, his eyes wide, and blue flashed for a moment. He was struggling to gain control, just like I was.

Marigold screamed in frustration, shooting my right arm over the edge of the rock. The sky above us darkened as shadows began blocking the sun.

"*Indicem minibus apertum carpi ulnaris!*"

Aiden hopped off the rock and crossed to my wrist. His teeth flashed and captured my flesh between them, slicing to the bone.

I screamed, but the sound never left my head.

"*Absorptio!*" Marigold cried.

His mouth clamped down, drinking my blood with such fervor that my head spun. For a moment, the fact the sky was near black didn't register. The pain in my arm was too great. My heart slammed in my chest, each beat weaker with the bear suckling my blood.

The moment the moon blocked the sun in totality, Aiden transitioned to man. His grip on my arm was as feral as the bears had been. He consumed my blood in large pulls, sucking, swallowing.

His gaze moved to mine, and despite Marigold's hold on both of us, I saw the desperation in the gray-blue of his irises. Marigold just laughed as he drained my body.

The world swam. My father's cries from outside the protection spell echoed in the space around us. Shadow's mewing matched that of Aiden's.

When Marigold grabbed Aiden's hand and placed it between my legs, he actually cringed, but that didn't stop his fingers from their slow swirl on the spot that his tongue had played with last night before Marigold had taken over.

The gray in Aiden's eyes faded, replaced by a sheen of tears. Yet he kept pulling blood from my mangled arm, swallowing my life in greedy slurps. He silently pleaded for me to hold on, for me not to die before the moon passed through the sun.

I could see it in his soul. I could feel it in his fingers as they played gently with me, fueling my adrenaline, pumping my heart harder. Killing me faster.

When a tear slid down his cheek, I knew he had no control. This was the curse itself driving him. This was Marigold in her finest hour.

Marigold's laugh continued as my vision faded. Rays of the sun hit Aiden, and he closed his eyes. The strength of his drinking lessened. His teeth dislodged from my flesh, but his lips remained on my skin. His tongue swiped back and forth over my torn flesh as if his motion could bandage the damage.

Tears flowed from his blue eyes as he opened them and stared into mine. Pain etched his face as the sun bathed him in light. He forced his hand from between my legs, the strain of it tightening the muscles in his neck, and he cradled my arm in both of his, sobbing.

The slowing of my heart pounded in my ears.

"Aiden," I forced out between Marigold's cackles.

He pulled his mouth away from my arm, momentarily gaining control, just like I had. "Don't die."

Then Marigold took control again, forcing his mouth to cover the wound once more.

His request was a tall order, especially since darkness had already taken control over the edges of my vision.

Aiden jerked away. "NO!" he cried to the heavens, still cradling my limb. His grip on my upper arm tightened like a noose.

"*Et abiit suppeditat animus cupidine!*" The cry came from outside the protection spell.

With the last of my strength, I turned my head and looked straight into my mother's eyes. My father kneeled before her with a knife to his throat. Tears cascaded down my mother's face.

"*Accipere sacrificium meum,*" my father said.

The knife slid across my father's throat. I gasped. Blood splattered the ground in front of him. Marigold, being the greedy witch she was, favored the king's body over mine. She fled with such force that my body jerked from the rock, yanking a cry of pain from my lips.

Aiden collapsed on the ground, and Shadow darted through the space now that Marigold's protection spell had been broken. My arm ached, and the light around me faded. I heard nothing above the buzzing in my ears.

I stared at the reanimated body of my father and blinked, trying to make sense of what I was seeing. A blade flashed and severed the head from the body, but what rolled on the ground did not look like my father. It looked like the prize pig from our stable.

More words were uttered, and then a flame lowered from a familiar hand between the rocks, lighting the pig's head on fire. My father glanced at me, the torch in his hand, his expression stoic and hard.

A yank at my waist focused my attention behind me. I stared at Aiden as he ripped the belt from around me.

He looked beautiful in the sunlight, his eyes bluer than the sky above.

"Aiden," I whispered, and his gaze found mine.

The brightness at the edges of my vision grew. A jerk on my upper arm pinched. The light filtered over everything, and even Aiden's blue eyes faded into the white.

BRAVE Chapter 10

"IF SHE NEEDS MORE, she can have more!" Aiden's voice penetrated the blackness surrounding me.

"If you continue, you will die."

I didn't recognize that voice, but the words hit hard. "Don't die." I forced the whisper from my lips.

Silence and then feet shuffling about the room. Pain registered in my arm.

"Hold this tight," that strange voice said.

My fingers tingled with the pressure being applied to my arm. I tried to open my eyes, but all I saw were glimpses through my thick lashes before my lids would become uncooperative again.

"Come on, May. I know you're in there," Aiden whispered, pulling me farther out of the black.

My eyelids fluttered again. Aiden's blue eyes came into focus. He looked haggard and pale.

"There's my princess," he said softly.

I glanced at my arm. His thumb pressed down on a bandage over the inside of my elbow. He had the same peculiar bandage on the inside of his arm that he was also applying pressure on. Rough stitches traversed my lower arm and wrist. No wonder my entire arm hurt so much.

Memories flashed before my eyes, and my gaze snapped up to Aiden. "The cure," I whispered, feeling felt like someone stuffed my mouth with wool.

He smiled crookedly, and some color bloomed in his cheeks. "That...well, aye, it seems to have worked."

"And Marigold?"

"Gone."

I lay back on the pillow and closed my eyes, letting sleep yank me down into the dark world I had been floating in since the world had filled with white light.

MY EYES OPENED TO the canopy above my bed. Every muscle in my body felt as if someone had taken a training sword to it. I tried to move and groaned as new pains surfaced.

A chair scraped, and the bed squeaked.

I turned. Aiden sat on the edge of the bed. The dark circles under his eyes made me blink, and I raised my eyebrows.

"You look like hell," I whispered.

He smiled. "Well, at least one of us looks well rested." He glanced at the foot of the bed.

Shadow was curled up at my feet and sound asleep. I glanced back at Aiden. His smile faded.

"You scared the daylights out of me," he said and pushed the hair away from my face.

His touch sparked the same strong desire within me, and I leaned my cheek into his palm. His thumb traced my lips, and that deep longing surfaced in his eyes. He pulled his hand away and stood.

"I, um..." He closed his eyes. "I need to go. I just wanted to make sure you were all right before I left." He turned and started towards the door.

I forced myself into a sitting position. "No." The word came out strong.

His back stiffened and his hand hesitated on the doorknob, yet he didn't turn.

"Did that night mean nothing to you?"

He glanced over his shoulder at me, his eyes sad. "It meant everything to me."

Aiden slipped out the door, leaving me alone with my sleeping wolf pup and a body that felt like I had gone through a war. I climbed to my feet and nearly collapsed under a wave of dizziness. Sheer determination kept me moving, and I opened the door.

Aiden had his hands on the doorjamb and must have been resting his forehead against the wood. His head jerked back, and he stared down at me with wide eyes.

"Get back in bed." He straightened.

I held on to the door for support and shook my head. "Not unless you stay."

"I made a deal with your father, and now that you seem to be on the mend, I have to go."

"No more deals. No more threats. No more running. You are going to marry me."

He laughed, just as full and musical as I remembered. "Your parents will not buy into that, and I'd rather not have my head on the chopping block again."

"We lifted the curse, right?"

Aiden's gaze moved to my window and the bright light filtering in through the room. He nodded.

"So, what is the problem?"

"I damn near killed you." He glanced at my bandaged arm. He reached out to touch me, but he folded his fingers into a loose fist and took a step back.

"You were not in control."

He pressed his lips together in a tight line before sucking his lower lip into his mouth. "I might not have been in control, but I remember everything from the moment that thing took possession of you. And your arm isn't the only area I hurt."

"It wasn't you."

He glanced up at the ceiling. "It was, as much as I hate to admit it. That witch released my darkest desires while we were in the cave." His gaze dropped to mine.

I reached out and grabbed a fist full of his shirt, and his eyes widened when I yanked him in to the room. I stumbled, depleted of all my energy, and my weight slammed the door closed. My legs trembled, but I willed them to hold me in place. When I was sure I wouldn't crumple to the ground, I moved the wave of red hair that fell over my face and stared into his dazzling eyes.

"Please, don't go." I stepped towards him. My legs failed, but before I hit the ground, Aiden's strong arms caught me. He swept me up, carried me to the bed, and tucked me under the covers.

With a heavy sigh, he sat on the edge of the bed and took my hand. He turned it over and started the same slow inspection of my palm that I had done to him. His touch was soft and sensual. When his gaze finally rose to mine, a fire blazed in the blue depths.

"Do you want to be with me?" I whispered.

"I thought we established that pretty clearly in the cave."

"We established you wanted me. That is different."

A dimple appeared in his cheek, and he refocused on his inspection of my palm. The curve of his lips straightened as his fingers followed every line. His silence made my skin flush with uncertainty.

I tried to pull my hand away, but he gripped my wrist tighter, continuing his slow tracing of my palm.

"I can't imagine not being with you," he finally said. "But I am baffled that you still want to be with me with all that transpired." He let out a soft laugh. "Your father nearly beheaded me on the spot." His gaze lifted to mine. "I'm only alive because I had knowledge of blood transfusions."

My eyebrows knit together.

"I've studied at the monastery at night since I was old enough to read." He shrugged.

"Transfusion?" I asked, but my brain circled around the rest of his narrative.

He pointed to the bandage on the inside of my arm. "It saved your life."

I sat up, ignoring the wave of dizziness. "But..." Concern laced my voice as I glanced at the same bandage on the inside of his elbow.

He pressed his fingers to my lips. "The thing about blood... It regenerates over time as long as you don't lose too much. You lost way too much, so the only way to bring you back was to supplement your blood. I volunteered since I was the one who nearly drained you. That's why I look like hell, as you so eloquently put it."

"Oh." I blinked as some memories came rolling back. "I'm not sure what happened out there. I thought my father died, and then I saw him set a pig on fire?" I cocked my head, still fuzzy about what was fact and what had been conjured by my brain right before I had lost consciousness.

Aiden smiled. "Your father wielded a magic spell that fooled all of us, including Marigold. I couldn't believe he offered himself instead of you, and when it turned out to be a pig he was offering..." He chuckled and shook his head. "I didn't have a moment to appreciate that irony until now."

"She was a greedy witch," I said, remembering the intense interest that had sparked when she thought my father had offered himself in exchange for me. I shivered, and Aiden reached for my hand.

"Thank God for that." He squeezed my hand.

I couldn't agree more. "So, will you stay?"

"I made a deal with your father."

"You don't want to stay?" I slid my hand out from under his and crossed my arms. This deal stuff was bringing forth hot irritation, giving me the illusion of strength.

"I never said that." He leaned back, adopting the same posture.

The door opened, interrupting our standoff. My father walked in. Behind him, a servant carried a tray of food. It wasn't my lady-in-waiting, though.

"Where's Sheri?" I asked as the servant put the tray down on the table in the corner.

"I let her go," my father said and stared at Aiden.

Aiden lowered his eyes and gave a nod. He stood.

I grabbed his hand, refusing to let go, and glared at my father. "He is staying," I said, with a bite in my tone. "And I want Sheri back."

Tension layered the room. My father dismissed the servant with a wave. Once the door closed, his hard gaze bore into me.

Shadow lifted his head as if he knew there was another storm brewing.

My father opened his mouth.

"Father, I don't want to be disrespectful, but this is ridiculous. You pardoned the

MacMahon name. The curse is lifted. So there is no reason for you to force Aiden to leave."

"After what he did to you?"

"He did nothing. Marigold made him do every slight you think he served me. And you vanquished her."

"I can speak for myself," Aiden said, glaring at me, squeezing my hand. "I had no control over what happened at Stonehenge. The moment I met your daughter, I knew I would never willingly walk her into a death sentence. When I walked out of the throne room, I had already made peace with the fact I would be the last MacMahon to walk the earth, but your daughter sought me out." He dropped his gaze to mine. "And I made her angry," he finished, looking at my father. "I was the catalyst that let Marigold take possession."

My father's hands fisted, and his eyes flashed cold.

"He made me angry because he refused me." I didn't want to fuel whatever fury had been building in my father by telling him we had slept together and then he had refused me. He would never understand that. But he needed to know exactly why I got angry. Otherwise, his mind would go where it didn't belong.

His hands uncurled, and his brow furrowed. "You... refused her?"

I squeezed Aiden's hand in a silent warning.

"Aye. I love your daughter, and I could not sentence her to a cursed life."

My entire body froze at his admission, and I stared up at Aiden with a slack jaw. A smirk cracked my father's face. He tried to wipe it off before I saw it, but he wasn't fast enough. I snapped my mouth closed.

He studied Aiden with a deep crevice on his brow.

Aiden shifted and dropped his gaze to the floor.

My father slowly crossed his arms. "Let's say I entertained my daughter's insane idea. What do you have to offer in exchange for her hand?"

My skin tingled with shock, and my eyes widened.

"I wouldn't barter for her like she is livestock," Aiden sneered.

"Is that because you have nothing to give?"

"No. It's because she is a beautiful woman who should be treated as an equal. A partner. You don't barter for a heart like it is a thing to be collected or owned." There was just enough distaste in his voice for my father's eyes to narrow.

My heart soared.

"However, if you were to give this union your blessing, I would promise to love her until my dying breath. To make sure her life was filled with joy and to do my best to protect her from the sorrows in this world." He glanced at me and then back at my father.

"And marrying her would give you the throne," he said, his face still pinched with distrust.

"No, Your Majesty. When the time comes, May will rule. And I will follow my queen to the ends of the earth if that is what is required."

My father's eyebrows arched, and his mouth popped open for the briefest of instances. He glanced at our clasped hands and stroked his beard thoughtfully. "I still do not trust your motives, Mr. MacMahon. However, your argument is compelling enough to give you and my daughter some time to court. If, after a fortnight, she still wants to marry you, I will consider it." He turned and started towards the door, but paused before he left the room. "And that does not mean screwing her, you understand?" He glared over his shoulder.

Aiden nodded, and my father strolled out.

I blinked, staring after him, and then my gaze snapped to Aiden's. He stared at the door, dumbstruck, with his jaw hanging open. When his gaze slid to mine, it held something I hadn't ever seen in his eyes. Hope.

BRAVE Chapter 11

AIDEN HELD MY HAND as we walked through the woods. The electricity between the two of us had only grown since my father gave us his permission to court. But this was the first time we'd had the strength to leave the castle grounds. Shadow bounded ahead, pouncing on rustling leaves and generally being a puppy.

I smiled at the wolf's enthusiasm, as well as his need to keep returning to us to make sure we were still nearby.

The past week had been filled with conversation and chess matches, while we both recuperated from Marigold's aftermath. We saw eye to eye on many things, but my father's rule was not one of them. That had been the source of many quiet but spirited debates. He had hardly touched me since my father made our courting rules clear, and it was driving me mad.

Aiden's easy smile warmed my insides, and all I could think about were his arms around me and his mouth on mine.

"Do you want to go to the cave?" I asked, afraid to look at him.

His gait slowed. "Why?" he asked, his voice cautious.

I glanced at him. "I'd like my hunting clothes back," I said, batting my eyelashes.

He chuckled. "Liar."

Heat filled my cheeks, and I suppressed a smile. Instead of dignifying his accurate assessment, I kept walking.

"If we go, will you behave?"

I grinned and looked at the ground, letting my loose hair hide my face. He swept it away and stared at me with a cocked eyebrow.

I rolled my eyes. "Aye, I'll behave."

He kicked at the leaves and sighed. "Sure."

We kept to the woods instead of crossing through Stonehenge, and it took us longer to get to the cave entrance than it would have if we had crossed through the great rocks. Navigating in the darkness proved to be more challenging than either Aiden or I thought it would be. Without the benefit of the bear curse, Aiden was just as blind as I was. Every time he stumbled, foul language tumbled out of his lips and I would giggle. By the time we entered the cavern, his face was red with frustration. I crossed to my crumpled pile of clothes and folded them neatly on the rock.

The splash of water pulled me away from my task, and I turned. Aiden's clothing was piled on the shore, and his bare ass broke the surface as he crossed the expanse beyond the cold current into the hot springs on the other side. He stood in waist-deep water with his back to me and wiped his hair off his face before turning in my direction.

Aiden looked tired, but more refreshed than he had all week.

"What happened to behave?" I asked.

He just grinned. "I'm behaving."

I cocked my eyebrow.

"What? A man can't take a swim?"

I kicked my boots off and stripped. Aiden's gaze traveled from head to toe and back before I dived into the water. When I surfaced, I understood his sudden burst of energy. The water was invigorating until I swam into the cold spot. The river's current pulled at me, and I didn't have the strength to fight it. My eyes widened in fear as I was sucked down under the surface.

Aiden moved fast, grabbing my hand. He yanked me to the surface and into his powerful arms, leading me to the hot springs beyond the frigid underground river. With his arms wrapped around me, I laid my cheek against his chest, trying to catch my breath. His heart beat just as wildly as mine.

"Maybe this wasn't such a good idea," he said once his breathing slowed.

I stayed in place, enjoying being in his grasp. He kissed the top of my head and stroked the hair away from my face. With his palms resting on my cheekbones, and his fingers threaded into my hair, he studied my face with such seriousness, I almost squirmed.

He leaned in and gently captured my lips in the sweetest kiss. Warmth spread from my core all the way to my fingers and toes, rivaling the hot springs surrounding me.

My fingers glided down his chiseled chest to the outline of his hips. I opened my mouth, and our tongues rolled together in a seductive dance. When my hand wrapped around his manhood, he gasped and pulled away from my lips. His body remained in place.

"May, I promised your father."

I gently stroked him and smiled. "You promised you wouldn't screw me. I don't see us screwing, do you?"

He blinked and then closed his eyes, letting out a groan. "No, but if you continue what you're doing, I'll lose any sort of restraint I have," he said, but didn't stop the slow movement of my hands.

His jaw tightened, and the veins in his neck stood out as he looked down at me. Hunger invaded his features, and it thrilled me. This was the same look he had when he'd taken me that first time. His lips crushed mine, and he turned me into the rocks. His mouth was greedy and insistent, and his tongue explored the depths of my mouth.

He still tasted like honey. My knees weakened at the power in the kiss. I stroked faster, and he groaned into my mouth. His hands lay flat on the rock on either side of my head, as if touching me would melt all his resolve. Just our lips and my hands remained in contact.

"Stop," he whispered against my lips. "Please. I won't have enough energy to get us across the river if you don't." He opened his eyes and met my gaze. Raw need blazed in his irises.

As much as I wanted to satisfy the need in both of us, I pulled my hands away, leaving us both frustrated and on edge. It was a sound strategy, especially since we struggled with the river's undercurrent as we headed back to the shore.

The moment we stepped onto the sand, Aiden pulled me into a bear hug. His lips found the spot where my neck and shoulder met, sending gooseflesh across my skin. He held me tight while his hardness pressed into my stomach with nothing to stop him from lifting me in his arms and taking me right there, but he restrained.

He released me and stepped away. His chest rose and fell like he had sprinted to the castle and back, mimicking mine. I stepped close and dropped to my knees. His eyes widened, and the moment my mouth slipped over the tip of his member, a low moan escaped his lips.

His fingers threaded into my hair as he guided me. His grip tightened, and I met his gaze. He stepped back, away from me, his entire body trembling. I stayed on my knees, wiping my mouth with the back of my hand.

His chin dipped to his chest, and his fists clenched as tight as his eyes. He took deep breaths, and when his eyelids flew open, I knew he'd lost the battle.

He pushed me back in the sand, and I wrapped my legs around his waist. This time, he slid inside me with care, his eyes rolling back as he went.

I winced when his entire length filled me, and he stilled, searching my eyes. I was still sore from what Marigold had made him do to me, but I wanted this. I wanted him.

"My god, you are heaven," he whispered, and kissed me again, remaining still until I ground my hips to his. He moved slowly, savoring the burn, and I focused on the tingling pleasure every time our hips met.

This was the opposite of our frantic first time; it was sweet and gentle and made me forget about the aching soreness. By the time he was ready, so was I, and our cadence sped up until we both cried out, our names echoing in the chamber.

He rolled off me and stared at the ceiling. "Your father is going to kill me," he said and covered his face.

I glanced over at him. "It's not like you could have told him we didn't sleep together before this," I said, flashing a smile.

"True." He lowered his arms and took my hand in his, his gaze on the ceiling. "You still want to marry me after a week in my company?"

"Only if you want to still marry me."

He turned his head, and the most glorious smile spread across his lips. "I could spend a hundred lifetimes with you, and it still wouldn't be enough." He climbed to his feet. "We should head back."

Before getting dressed, we washed the sand off each other. Aiden gathered what little belongings he had. It all fit in a satchel he had stowed in the corner, and he slung it over his shoulder.

I hand combed my wet locks and scooped up my hunting clothes before we headed out the way we had come. This time, we were both more surefooted, and we stepped out of the woods to a stunning sunset.

"I don't know about you, but I don't think I have enough energy to go around this time," Aiden said as Shadow danced around our feet.

I stared at Stonehenge. A dark shiver ran down my spine. The shortest route was right through the thing, but I did not want to step inside the rocks. "As long as we go around the rocks to the south, I'm fine."

He nodded, understanding. The north side was where my father had beaten Marigold, and going near where she was killed felt too much like tempting fate.

<hr>

EVERY MUSCLE FELT LIKE putty by the time we got to the castle. Aiden looked every bit as exhausted as I felt. The only one of us that seemed to exude energy was Shadow.

My stomach growled loud enough for Aiden to glance at me.

"I could eat an entire deer right now," he said.

"You and me both."

"Where have you been?"

My mother's voice cut through the courtyard, making me jump.

We both turned towards her.

"We went to pick up my things," Aiden said. "It took us longer than expected. I'm sorry if we worried you, my lady," he said with a sweeping bow. He stood and gave her a crooked smile of apology.

She wrung her hands together, and her gaze bounced between us. "There is still food in the dining hall." She waved towards the great hall. "Your father has been waiting for your return."

I blinked the exhaustion away and handed my clothes to the nearest servant. We followed my mother into the dining hall to get some much-needed food.

My father sat at the center of the table with his arms crossed and only a wineglass in front of him. Most of the food had been removed, but it looked like a meat pie and some fruits remained.

I crossed to the food. Aiden followed me, and we piled our plates high with whatever was left. When we were done serving ourselves, there were only crumbs left on the serving platters.

I nearly fell into the closest seat. Aiden collapsed next to me. I was too tired and hungry to mind my manners, and I stuffed a large piece of meat into my mouth just as my father spoke.

"Where have you been?"

Aiden also had a mouthful, so I put my finger up, asking for another minute before answering.

"They went to get Aiden's belongings," my mother said for me.

I nodded, still chewing.

My father sipped his wine, studying us as we ate. I knew I was eating at a speed that wasn't normal, and when I finished everything on my plate, I leaned back and belched.

"Sorry, but the walk took every ounce of energy from both of us," I said as I wiped my lips.

Aiden showed more restraint, finishing a few minutes after I did, and he sat back in the chair, closing his eyes. "Thank you for the delicious meal," he said, like he had each night he'd joined us for dinner.

"Tomorrow, we hunt," my father said.

Aiden opened his eyes and stared at him. "You want me to hunt with you?"

"Yes. I want to see how good you are with a bow and arrow."

I studied my father, gauging whether this was some sort of trap. "What are you hunting?"

"It seems there has been another bear sighting." My father glared at me for a moment before refocusing on Aiden.

Aiden's smile faded. "An arrow is just going to piss a bear off."

"Then you better have good aim."

"I have impeccable aim, but a bear's hide is thick. The only time an arrow is successful is from close proximity." Aiden shifted in his seat and glanced at me. "I'm not sure I'm in the most optimal health to take on a bear." His cheeks turned red.

"Father," I started, but he raised his hand.

"No arguments. He is going, or he is leaving this province for good," he said.

I balked.

"I would be honored, Your Highness," Aiden said.

Even though Aiden's answer lacked sincerity, my father nodded and raised his glass. "To success."

Aiden and I raised our glasses as well.

"Aiden will stay in my room tonight," I said.

My father spit his wine out. Aiden choked on his wine, coughing and sputtering as he looked at me with wide eyes. My mother's jaw hung open.

"Over my dead body," my father answered and wiped his chin.

"If you insist on bringing him on this fool's errand, I would at least like to know what it feels like to lie in his arms." I tilted my head as if I had just asked for honey in my tea instead of calling my father out on his outrageous idea.

"May," Aiden wheezed. "Please don't make a scene. I will be fine." He tried to take my hand.

I yanked it away from him. "We barely survived today's walk without collapsing. How are you going to be sharp enough to kill a bear?" I glared at him. "The last time you went up against a full-grown grizzly, you were a bear, and you were almost killed. Am I supposed to smile and wave good luck to you when I know you are walking into a death trap?" I spun on my father. "And you, you were almost annihilated by that bear, too. How do you expect to survive with someone so weak at your side?"

My father placed his cup on the table and met my glare.

"I am not weak," Aiden said from behind me, his voice full of steel and fire.

I turned to him and put my hand on top of his clenched fist. "Normally, you are not. But you are still recovering from the transfusion. You were the one who told me it would take a couple of months before either of us was at full strength. And you need to be at full strength to go after a bear."

My father crossed his arms and leaned back in the chair while my mother busied herself by smoothing out the folds of her dress.

I glanced at all three of them. Neither my father nor Aiden budged in their commitment.

"Well, then, if you go, I go," I said.

Both Aiden's and my father's expressions mirrored each other's. The first thing to fade was the anger, and then their eyes widened. Before either of them spoke, their heads shook. As one, they said, "No."

"You will stay in bed and rest," Aiden said. "And I will not be joining you in your room tonight, regardless of what you want. This is your father's house. His roof, his rules."

"Then it is settled," my father said and stood, taking his leave with my mother.

"Aiden." I turned to him.

He pressed his fingers to my lips. "Stop. I promise I will be fine." He leaned close and gave me a light kiss. "I will see you tomorrow when I return from the hunt."

I watched him go with my stomach in knots.

BRAVE Chapter 12

SUNLIGHT STREAMED THROUGH MY window. I blinked, disoriented. I didn't think sleep would ever come, but it had and deep enough for me to miss seeing the hunt off.

The shuffle of fabric made me jump. I snapped my head to my dressing table. My mother sat in the seat watching me with a hint of a smile on her face.

She stood, crossed to the bed, and took a seat on the edge. "Your father will make sure nothing happens to Aiden. He actually has grown fond of him, but needs to test where his loyalties lie."

"By going after a bear?" I said and sat up. A deep ache in my muscles reminded me of our activities yesterday.

"No, by protecting his king."

I cocked my head.

"I don't understand it either. I told him it was foolish, but they won't be the only ones out there. Samuel and Edward are going with them.”

I relaxed a fraction. Both Samuel and Edward were accomplished with a bow and arrow, as well as a sword. They had to be as my father's closest guards. But the gnawing worry persisted in my belly.

I slipped out of bed, wincing at the tightness in my derriere. I limped to my wardrobe and pulled out a proper dress for the day. What I really wanted to do was put my hunting clothing on and go after him, but I knew Aiden would be aggravated with me. Besides, how far would I really get with the state of my body?

After I dressed, my mother brushed my hair, and I closed my eyes, taken back to when I was little and she would spend hours brushing my hair until it had shone in the candlelight. Her soft touch relaxed me. When she set the brush down, I met her gaze.

“Your father sees how happy this man makes you and wants to be sure his motives are pure.”

“Aiden's motives *are* pure.”

Her smile seemed strained, but she nodded and helped me down to the sitting room to wait for the men to arrive home. I paced while she patiently sewed.

Finally, she put her embroidery on the table. “May, sit down. You are making me just as jumpy as you are.”

The sun had passed beyond midday, and while I knew the men wouldn't be back until dusk, I still had an unsettledness that I couldn't calm.

"I can't. Not until Aiden is back safe."

My mother shifted and glanced out the window. The worry lines around her mouth grew deeper, and she shook her head, replacing them with a smile instead. But the glimpse of her unease was enough for me to take a seat and still my restlessness.

Moments later, commotion filled the castle, followed by the shattering of stoneware. My mother and I both stood and ran toward the great hall. I stopped at the door, trying to reconcile what I was seeing. The dishes and candles for the feast had been carelessly swept from the table, and my father lay on the wood plank with his leg drenched with blood.

Aiden's shirt was streaked red.

My heart plummeted.

Aiden turned in my direction. "Get bandages and wine now!"

My feet wouldn't move. The side of his face bled from claw marks, but he didn't seem to notice. My mother disappeared from my side.

Aiden looked at Samuel on the other side of the table. "Go put the blade of your sword in the kitchen kiln until the handle is almost too hot to hold and then bring it back."

Samuel limped away, leaving Aiden alone with Edward and my father.

"You will need to hold him still when Samuel comes back, understand?" Aiden barked at Edward.

Edward nodded.

Aiden tore the splint off my father's leg and tossed it aside. He ripped the wet fabric of my father's pant leg.

I gasped. My father's eyes dulled enough to jumpstart my heart and I raced to his side.

"What happened?" I asked.

"Your betrothed saved my life," my father said, his voice laced with agony.

"I haven't saved you yet," Aiden said, tightening a belt around my father's thigh.

His lower leg looked like the bear had used it as a scratching post. His skin was torn to the bone, and the bone poked out of the skin.

Samuel came back in the room with his sword glowing red, and my mother came in with an armful of bandages.

"Move his good leg," Aiden said and took the sword from Samuel. "And give him something to bite down on."

"What are you doing?" My father's eyes widened, making his features much paler.

Aiden glanced at him. "Your leg or your life. That's the choice."

"Just bandage it up," my father insisted.

Aiden glanced at Edward. "Put your belt in his mouth," he said.

Edward slid his belt off, doubled it, and shoved it between my father's teeth. Then he pulled my father's good leg far enough away to not get hit with the glowing blade in Aiden's hands.

He lined up the blade and looked at my mother.

"Don't you dare," my father growled around the leather.

"He won't make it," Aiden said softly.

My mother nodded. "Take his leg," she ordered.

Without hesitation, Aiden brought the sword down, yelling with the force of it. Skin sizzled. The blade embedded in the wood below my father's leg.

My father screamed despite still clamping down on the belt.

Aiden turned to me. "Get me honey."

I turned and ran into the kitchen. When I came back, Aiden was sewing a patch of skin he had ripped from my father's discarded appendage onto the blunt end of my father's leg while my mother poured wine over the wound. My father had already passed out.

As soon as he was done stitching skin to skin, he dried the leg with the bandage and threw it on the floor. Then he turned to me with his hand out.

"Honey," he said, and this time his voice sounded a little weaker.

I poured it into his hand, and he slathered it on the wound before wrapping my father's leg.

When he finished, he wiped his hands and took a seat. "You can take him up to his bed. We will need to change that daily until it heals," he said to my mother.

She nodded. Edward and Samuel helped carry my father as my mother led the way.

I picked up a clean bandage and doused it with wine. Stepping closer to Aiden, I tilted his chin up so I could see his wounds better.

I dabbed the cuts. He didn't even wince. Instead, he gave me a tired smile.

"I couldn't get to him before the bear did." He brought his hand to his face. When he pulled his fingers away, wine and blood covered them. "But I took that bastard down." He stared at his hand. "How bad is it?"

"Not bad," I said and smoothed a thin layer of honey over the cuts. None of them were deep enough for me to stitch, but they would leave a scar. I glanced at the table and the wood still smoking from the hot sword. "Where did you learn that?"

"Same place I learned about transfusions," he said and wiped his face.

"Come on. Let's get you cleaned up." I helped him to his feet and let him use me for support.

Now that his adrenaline had faded, his steps were unsteady. I took him to the bathing area and stripped him of the soiled clothing, inspecting every inch of him to make sure there weren't any more wounds. After my thorough once-over, I helped him into the iron tub.

"It isn't the hot springs." I handed him a washcloth and poured warm pots of water over him until the water ran clear down his chest.

He scrubbed his hands as I cleaned his hair and shoulders with a second cloth. When he was done, he leaned back in the tub and just stared at me.

"Did your father say betrothed?" he asked, his sleepy eyes searching mine.

"Yes."

Aiden smiled and climbed to his feet, drying off with a towel I handed him. The wardrobe in the bath had a few extra pairs of clothes, and I handed some to him. I didn't think my father would mind.

Aiden pulled on the clothes, and then I led him to my room and made him sit at my vanity while I spread another thin layer of honey on the cuts. Then, I made him lie down under the covers in my bed. Before I finished tucking him in, he had fallen asleep.

Instead of climbing in with him like every fiber of me wanted to, I went to my parents' room and stepped inside. My father lay under the covers and my mother gently swiped his forehead with a cloth. She looked up at me; her smile tense.

"Thank Aiden for me," she said. "If your father pulls through this fever, he won't be happy with the choice I made, but he will adjust." She wiped his forehead again.

"If?" I blinked and stared at my father, looking so meek and sickly in the bed.

My mother raised her gaze and nodded.

I came to her side and reached for my father's hand. "Father, please fight this. I want you to walk me down the aisle. I want you there to celebrate and drink wine until you say something incredibly sappy and sweet. I need you to be there, so please fight this fever and come back to Mother and me." I squeezed his hand and kissed his cheek before I gave my mother a hug. While I wanted to stay and carry on the vigil with her, I knew she wanted this time with my father.

"Let me know if anything changes," I said and headed back to my room. I stripped my clothing and pulled on a nightshirt, climbed under the covers, and snuggled next to Aiden.

He rolled, wrapping his arms around me, and pulled me tight to his chest. The cadence of his breathing smoothed out again.

With his arms around me, he soothed all my worries about what was to come. I didn't know if tonight would change my father's acceptance of Aiden, or if he would default to exiling him out of anger for his own situation.

I could only pray that all would work out. Just before I drifted to sleep, I caught Aiden's soft whisper of my name. Calm settled over me. If there was a fight to be had, we would hit it head-on.

I smiled and let the night pull me into its depths.

BRAVE Chapter 13

TOWN BELLS RANG, AND the doors to the throne room opened. Anyone who was anybody stood within the walls. The place was packed beyond capacity. I marveled at the town's finery on display.

After all, a royal wedding was at hand.

A thin aisle separated the rows of chairs on the main floor, and as the crowd turned to face us, Aiden stepped into view.

My heart stilled, and I sighed at his regal beauty.

He looked magnificent in the formal clothing of the court. His tunic was a deep blue with black leather insets that matched his pants and boots. His crest stood out against the crushed velvet, adding to his outfit. He clasped his hands behind his back and turned fully in my direction. The minute our eyes met, an electrical current passed between us as strong as it had that first night we had met.

Aiden's smile grew into a magnificent grin that brightened my heart. I could see the twinkle in his eyes, even at this distance.

"Are you sure about this man?" my father asked, leaning into me as if what he had said was a big secret.

I glanced at him with his crutch under one arm and his other hooked through mine. "I've never been surer of anything in my life."

With that, we started the slow procession towards a future filled with promise and adventure, not to mention all the steam I could handle.

The End

A FRACTURED FAIRY TALE -BOOK 4 TANGLED

How dark is obsession?

Imprisoned in a tower from the time she was old enough to walk, Danae longs to experience more than just what is within her ornate cage. But her mother insists the world is just too dangerous for a precious light-bringer.

When Danae encounters a disgraced dark-bringer, their combined power lights a fire within her soul, illuminating the tangled web of lies her captor has spun.

Danae learns that while her magic can renew hearts and heal wounds, it cannot erase the ultimate betrayal.

TANGLED Chapter 1

MOUNTAIN RANGES AND VALLEYS peppered the view outside my window. A world I had yet to explore. Its beauty left me breathless whenever the full moon crested the mountaintops, shedding an eerie glow on everything below. Tonight was no different. However, a restlessness that had started two years ago on my eighteenth birthday burned through my blood hotter than when it first ignited.

I yearned for freedom from these castle walls, and yet, I had no means of escape. My only visitor was my captor masquerading as a doting mother who would prefer to see her only child locked up in a tower than let her experience all that life offered.

The books on my shelves were tattered and torn, and the words faded from too many readings. My prison was more adorned than the prisons I read about where men and women starved in squalor. It was fit for a queen, or so my mother told me, but it still was made to keep me contained.

Mother and I had argued endlessly over the past two years. I wanted to leave; she wanted to protect me. I lost every argument, especially when she brought up my father's demise and how she barely got me out of the house before the thing burned to the ground.

She said I was a light-bringer, and if I were let out of this decorative dungeon, my power would be coveted for gain. My life would be slowly drained by those greedy bastards who existed around every corner just waiting for the chance to steal it away.

While she made the world seem frightening, I still wanted to experience it. Reading about adventures was getting old. I wanted to live one. I turned away from the window and doused my bedside candle, then slipped into bed for the night now that the sun's warmth had disappeared.

"DANAE! LET DOWN YOUR hair!"

I rolled over and covered my head with my pillow. I didn't want to deal with my mother today, but I knew she would just keep yelling up to me and spoil the nice quiet of the wilderness surrounding me. Even the birds fled from her grating pitch.

I sighed and climbed out of bed, corralling my hair with me. I dropped the long strands out the window. My mother waited patiently while I wound my hair around the sturdy hook next to the window, like I had done ever since she hid me away in this tower. Once I was done, I waved for Mother to start her ascent. The ends of my hair swirled in the dirt. I sighed. My mother had trimmed my hair just last week, and it looked like at least a foot lay on the ground. Every time she cut it, it seemed to grow back faster than before.

Before she climbed up my hair ladder, she collected the ends and slipped them into the bucket she kept behind the bushes. Sunlight glinted off the scissors she pulled from her backpack. Before she climbed up, she trimmed the ends of my hair, taking off close to a foot above the ground so my hair wouldn't fall into the dirt. As the sheet of locks fell into the bucket, the familiar *tink* of metal against metal reached my ears. Freshly spun gold strands fell into the pail in place of my hair. I had seen it a few times when my mother cut my hair in my quarters instead of at the base of my prison.

She shimmied up my hair and climbed in the window, then pulled her backpack off. My mother had raven hair as dark as the night, and it curled into mini spirals that made me jealous. My hair lay in straight plaits. The only time it held body was after it had been braided for a length of time, but even then, it only offered soft waves. My mother's skin was as different from mine as her hair. She had a dark honey-colored hue, whereas I could rival fresh cream.

I asked her once how she could be my mother. She said I was the spitting image of my father. She had gone to the window and looked out with that faraway look only reserved for when my father came into the conversation, like she needed a moment to regroup before her brain would work properly.

"How are you today?" she asked as she studied me.

"Do you have any new books?" I asked, avoiding the question. I was in no mood for another squabble, even though the aggravation was right there at the edge of my nerves. She had been by with food earlier in the week, but I had asked her to bring something new for me to read the next time she came.

"You already have plenty of books." She waved at my book-lined walls before emptying the contents of her bag on the table.

"Ma, do you even listen to me?"

She stopped unloading her bag and glanced up at me with her eyebrows arched. "Of course I do, but there was nothing new or appropriate at the market."

"Then why didn't you say that?" My hands went to my hips, and I cocked my head at her.

She shrugged and finished emptying the contents on the table. Meats, breads, vegetables and fruits graced my table. The same things she always brought.

I sighed, knowing I should be grateful. If anything happened to her, I would likely starve to death in this remote tower. The thought terrified me, and I opened my mouth to share that fear, but "When can *I* go to the market with you?" tumbled from my lips.

She crossed her arms and stared down her sharp nose at me. "You already know the answer. It is too dangerous out there for you."

"Why?"

"People will be drawn to you, and the closer they get, the weaker you will get until you have no more light within you. You will die." Her eyes were wide and sincere.

I took a breath and let it out slowly before nodding. No one wants death, least of all me. But I wanted more than the life I was relegated to. I just didn't know how to convey that to my mother. Instead of launching into the same old argument, I let it go and focused on the offerings she'd brought with her.

I took them and placed them in the cupboard near my little kitchen. The flame in the oven always burned. My mother had said she hired a sorcerer to tie her lifeblood to that flame. If it ever went out...

I shook the thought out of my head. If that flame ever extinguished, my existence up in the tower would end. Anytime the thought accosted my mind, my skin turned to a bumpy map. If that flame went out, my panic would send me plummeting to my death, because jumping would be much more preferable to starvation.

TANGLED Chapter 2

MY MOTHER DEPARTED SOON after she came, leaving me in the solace of the tower. I sat on the windowsill watching rabbits frolicking in the woods down below. When the rabbits stilled and then scurried away, and a plume of birds fled from the trees, I scanned the woods, looking for the cause.

What kind of animal could make all the wildlife flee?

And then I saw him. My eyes bulged at the man seated on a steed as black as night. The man's hair matched his horse, and his broody expression changed as he caught sight of my tower.

I jumped down from my perch and pressed my back to the wall by the window. My heart pounded in my chest as if seeing the man below had been taboo.

"Hello?"

His voice drifted up the wall, like a snake dipped in honey. It terrified me, and yet his deep tone heated my skin more than the eternal flame in the oven. I bit my tongue, ignoring the need wracking my muscles to step into the window opening so he could see me.

"Go away," I whispered to the ceiling, as if he could hear me from thirty meters below. I swore I could smell his essence. A musky, deep-woods smell like just after a rainstorm, and it caressed my skin on the light breeze.

"I can see a flickering light up there, so I know someone is home."

I closed my eyes and sighed. His musical voice weakened my knees, and I grabbed the edge of the windowsill. All those romantic scenes I had read in the novels my mother brought me flashed in my mind, and my breath caught in my throat. Curiosity scratched across my skin.

When a sigh reached my ears, along with the crunch of leaves, I chanced a peek out the window. My dark-haired man trudged away, disappearing into the woods.

My heart plummeted. I almost broke my silence to call him back just so I could hear his musical voice again. But my mother's warnings kept me silent. I turned away from the window, scanning my home. My gaze landed on the flame in my oven. I shivered despite the warm glow.

Instead of pondering anymore about the stranger, I turned to my bookshelf, letting my gaze drift over each title. Nothing struck my fancy, so I took a seat at my dressing table and ran my brush through my free hair.

I needed a change, so I braided thin strands. It took me long into nightfall to finish braiding my hair. My stomach growled, demanding food, so I stood, picking up my hand mirror to see the results of my efforts. Hundreds of thin braids adorned my head and came together in one long braid that was easier to manage than my mane of free hair.

The braid would make it easier for my mother to climb the next time she came. I put the mirror back on my dressing table, crossed to the cupboard, and made myself a bowl of vegetable soup.

When my stomach was satiated, I cleaned up my dishes and blew out the candles. The light from the oven dimly lit my chambers as I crawled under the warm blankets. Just as my eyes closed, a haunting melody drifted up from the ground below. A deep voice joined along with the plucks of a cittern. I sat up and stared at the open window with my heart thumping against my ribs as if it wanted to be set free to dance. I held my hands to my breast, trying to quell the need driving me to my feet.

I crossed to the window and glanced down. The handsome rider from earlier leaned against the foot of the tower, plucking an instrument and singing. My body swayed to the melody as my hands gripped the sill. The dichotomy of my thundering heart versus the slow sway of my form caught my breath in my throat. It was as if the music had given my body a life of its own without my knowledge.

The music stopped, and so did my swaying. The man stepped away from his perch and looked up. Even in the dark, I could see the flash of his white teeth when he smiled.

"I was sure someone was up there. And it seems I was right," he said.

"Please go away," I whispered.

"And she speaks!" He uttered a light laugh before he bowed. "I am Zacharia Stone, Prince of Zanderfeld." He straightened.

I licked my lips, and my gaze went to the dark forest, unsure if I should stay and listen to that sweet timbre of his voice or turn and climb right back in bed.

"It is customary when someone introduces themselves for you to introduce yourself in return," the prince said when I remained quiet.

I glanced up at the stars twinkling in the sky, debating. Every warning my mother had uttered filled my head, and I couldn't bring myself to speak my name. "While I am honored to meet you, dear prince, I cannot tell you my name."

There was a brief pause, followed by a sigh. "Very well, my lady," he said and returned to plucking the instrument in his hands. His voice accompanied a moment later.

My body swayed with the slow euphony. My eyes became heavy, and it was only then that I realized his music affected me as if it were a magical spell.

"Cease!" I cried, and the music stopped.

"You dislike my playing?" the prince asked from below.

It lulled me, taking hold of my form in a way I never knew was possible. "Please take your leave, now," I said and turned away, crossing to my bed. I couldn't stay at the window all night.

He obeyed my harsh order. I listened and was rewarded with the sound of shuffling feet fading away.

TANGLED Chapter 3

HE CONSUMED MY THOUGHTS all night. I tossed and turned until I finally slipped into a restless sleep. My mother calling to me drew me from the bed, and I stumbled to the window, then wrapped my braid around the hook before dropping the rest of it down to her.

When she came through the window, I pulled my hair back inside. My mother smiled and swung her pack off her shoulders. She tipped it upside down over the table, and two books fell out along with a bushel of golden apples.

"I felt so bad that I couldn't find you something at the market that I went again, and this time, these were brand new." Her gaze went to my hair. "You did well with the braids."

I ran my hand over the back of my hair. "It passed the time." I crossed and picked up the leather-bound books, lifting them to my nose.

I loved the smell of a new manuscript, so I gave my mother a smile. "Thank you."

She studied me. "Are you all right?"

"I didn't sleep well." I flipped through the pages of the book without looking at her. I couldn't bring myself to tell her about the prince. "Nightmares," I muttered and then glanced at her.

Her features softened, and she stepped close to give me a hug. "Well, maybe those books will keep you entertained for the next couple of days while I am away. When I return, I should have some fresh fish for you." She pulled away.

"Will you stay and eat with me when you get back?"

"Of course," she said and led me to the window. "I'm just sorry I can't stay later today. Those apples will make a very sweet pie."

My mouth watered as I glanced at the bushel. I knew exactly what I was spending my day on.

I smiled at my mother as she dropped my braid out the window. "Maybe I'll save you a piece," I said while she started her climb down.

She waved as she disappeared into the woods. Collecting my hair, I turned and crossed to the apples. The choice between baking and reading left me chewing on my lip. I picked up the book and fanned through it, stopping at a page that grabbed my interest.

"Danae, let your hair down," she called again.

I tossed my hair out the window without securing it to the hook. I held the braid in place and leaned against the wall, still enthralled with the story in my hand. The shuffle at the window pulled my attention away from the page.

The book fell from my hand. My eyes widened as I stepped away from the man who hopped to the floor from the windowsill. I pulled air into my lungs and opened my mouth to scream, but he moved across the distance and clamped his hand over my mouth. His eyes were green with silver streaks, and they sparkled as he studied me. His dark hair was shaggy, like he hadn't had it cut in a while. His broad shoulders towered over me, and the same heady scent filled the space between us, tightening the muscles in my stomach.

"Shhh," he whispered and pulled my braid back into the room, looping it in a neat pile. "I will not hurt you. I promise." His gaze darted to the window. "Please don't scream," he added and removed his hand.

The tingle his skin made on contact with mine disappeared. I stared at him, frozen in the spot where I stood.

He glanced around the room and then landed back on me. He shuffled out of the view of the window and then cleared his throat and bowed.

"It is nice to formally meet you, Lady Danae," he said, and straightened.

My gaze narrowed.

"I sang for you last night." He pointed towards the window.

"You tricked me."

He opened his mouth and then shut it. Color bloomed in his cheeks, and his gaze dropped to the floor. "Yes. I'm afraid I did."

"Why?"

He brought his gaze back to mine. "Curiosity," he said with a shrug. "And I can honestly say it was worth it." He grinned. "Plus, I needed a place to hide until the king's army passes through."

My eyebrows rose. "But you're the prince?"

He chuckled and glanced out the window. "That I am." He pressed his lips together and turned away, crossing to my bookshelves.

The tension in the air between us created random sparks when he glanced over his shoulder at me. It was as if having him in the close space charged the air the way a thunderstorm charged the sky. It caressed my skin, leaving me shivering with goosebumps on my exposed flesh.

"You have a lot of books," he said.

I didn't speak. Having him in my space left me uncomfortable and anxious. If my mother came back and found him here...

"You can't stay here," I said as hot panic burned through my veins.

He turned, facing me. His eyebrows drew together. "Please, just until dark?"

The way his eyes pleaded with me, I couldn't send him away, so I nodded. "But just stay where you are and let me do what I need to do, okay?"

He nodded and his shoulders relaxed.

I crossed in front of him and picked up the apples, then headed to the opposite side of the room to fix myself apple pie.

"So, how do you get out of here?" he asked.

I kneaded the ingredients together for the crust. "I don't."

He stepped closer, cocking his head. "You don't? You mean you're imprisoned here?"

"I wouldn't say that." I glanced up at him, although that was exactly what I had felt like lately. "My mother said it's not safe out there," I added in response to his furrowed brow and began slicing the apples into the bottom of the pie crust.

He leaned on the other side of the counter and bit his lower lip as he continued to watch me put together the pie. "There are some dangerous places," he finally said. "But they are far from here. Nothing out this way is dangerous except for maybe the occasional lightning storm."

I turned and slid the pie into the oven and then wiped my hands on a towel, studying him. He was handsome in a rugged way, and his smile warmed me from the inside.

"So why are you afraid of being out there, then?" I asked.

He stepped away from the table and turned his back on me. Just when I thought he was going to ignore the question, he said,

"My father wants me to pay for my treasonous behavior."

"Treason?" I had read enough to know what that word meant.

The prince sat heavily in the chair at the tiny dining table, and I took the seat opposite him.

"I made a mistake," he whispered, as if the world beyond could hear him. "In a moment of anger, I let the darkness out." His gaze found mine, and he shrugged, offering the saddest smile. "What was done could never be undone, and because of that, the chosen heir to the throne no longer exists in this realm."

His eyes turned almost a jade color as he spoke, and the silver veins nearly glowed against the darkening green. He blinked and looked away, and when his gaze returned, his eyes were back to the light green and the silver no longer glowed.

"How long have you been here?" He twirled his finger around.

"For as long as I can remember." I glanced around at my cozy home. It wasn't bad, but not having the freedom to step outside and run in the grass or smell the flowers or swim in the ponds irked me.

"Would you like to go outside?" he asked.

I couldn't help the smile that surfaced. "Someday," I said under my breath.

He reached out and touched my hand, but I pulled mine away. A spark danced between our skin, and we both stared at the mini-lightning bolt. It tingled over my flesh. I forced my gaze away. He still stared at the connection until I pulled my hand under the table. His eyes jumped to mine, widening.

"Are you a... a light bringer?" he asked.

I moved my chair back, trying not to gasp out loud. I shook my head. "Why would you say that?"

He held up his hand, his eyes wide. "The lore we were told all our lives. Whenever a dark bringer and a light bringer come into contact, storms brew between them."

"Nothing happened when you covered my mouth," I said, trying to keep my composure, but that tingle that I had felt came rushing back.

He moved, and I clamored to my feet, but he was faster, taking hold of my shoulders. I put my hands on his chest to push him away, and the contact sent a jolt through me. We stood inside a circle of light, and the power rushed through my veins, quickening my breath. When I glanced back at him, he was still staring at the stormy circle encompassing us. His gaze moved to mine, wide and with awe.

I blinked. "What is a dark bringer?" I whispered.

He stepped away. The connection between us failed, and the room snapped back to normal. Disappointment made my bones ache.

"While light bringers breed life, dark bringers bring the opposite." His cheeks bloomed color, and he slid back in the seat, rubbing his face. He glanced back up at me. "They said the last light bringer had died."

I raised my eyebrows. My mother never told me there weren't any more light bringers.

"And she will rise from the darkness and bring light back to mankind," he whispered, staring up at me.

I rolled my eyes at him and escaped to the other side of the room to check in on the pie.

"We are the last of our kinds."

The pie was golden brown, and my mouth watered. I took it from the oven and set it on the counter before crossing to the window. His words pinged around my head, and I did a small assessment of how I felt. I was not drained. As a matter of fact, this encounter had magnified my strength.

I glanced at all my books. Not one of them talked about light or dark bringers. Nothing on my shelves seemed real.

I met his gaze. "What lore?"

He leaned back in his chair. His long study of me made me shift in place and cross my arms over my chest. He stood, closing the distance between us. He raised his hands, palms first. "Place your hands on mine," he said softly and waited.

I stared at his palms and then placed mine against his. That electric storm that had encompassed us earlier reclaimed the surrounding air. The prince threaded his fingers through mine and stepped closer.

"The lore says the last light bringer is the long-lost princess of Antaries, who was ripped from her home by pure evil. The dark bringer was created to save her, and together they will wipe out the darkness hovering over all the kingdoms in the land."

I pulled my hands away. "And you believe this lore, my prince?"

"Please, call me Zach," he said and sighed. "I didn't until just now."

We stared at each other.

"Can't you feel it?" he whispered, his voice filled with awe.

I took another step away. "I don't know what I feel." I eyed him suspiciously, wondering if this was another spell like the music the prior evening. "For all I know, you could have cast another spell over me."

He cocked his head, and his hands fell to his side. "Another spell?"

I waved towards the window. "Last night."

He straightened, and a crease appeared between his eyes. "I didn't cast a spell."

"You most certainly did. When you sang, my body couldn't help but sway to the song."

"Really."

The slow smile that found his lips sent a thrill through me, and I looked away. When my gaze returned, his had turned towards the cooling apple pie. He licked his lips and glanced my way.

"Any chance I could have a piece?" His hands slipped into his pockets, and his head tilted in a way that was endearing.

"Only if you tell me more about what is out there." Something about what he had said struck bells in the center of my being, and I wanted to hear more.

"I'll tell you anything you want to know."

I cut us both pieces of the pie and brought them to the table. Thankfully, I had two sets of silverware, or otherwise the prince would have had to eat with his hands. Although, the thought of him licking his fingers clean twisted my insides.

He closed his eyes and let out a rumbling noise with his first bite. "This is heavenly," he said and picked the rest, as if he wanted to savor it instead of inhale the food.

"So, what is out there besides the king's army?"

Zach pushed the empty dish away and leaned his elbows on the table. "Thick woods with all manner of woodland animals, quaint towns full of the nicest people I have ever encountered, which is a far cry from the people within the palace walls." He glanced towards the window, and his eyes became distant. "Oceans as vast as the eye can see. It's glorious until you meet up with a pirate or two." He grinned and glanced back at me. "There are dangers, but there are more blessings than darkness, despite what everyone says."

"And what does everyone say?"

His smile faded. "That the end of times is nearing. That the darkness will overtake the land unless the last light bringer can be found." His gaze met mine. "The darkness has its grip on my kingdom, and that is my fault. I let it in, and the only way for me to go back is if I have the light bringer. Otherwise, my head will be on one of the posts outside the castle walls."

"My mother said I would die in the world out there. That humanity would suck the light from my soul."

Zach sighed and glanced at his hands. "So, you are a light bringer?"

I opened my mouth and then clamped it shut, shaking my head. It was easier to avoid voicing a lie than to speak it. Only half the day had passed, and I had another few hours before the sun went down. My heart wanted to trust the prince, but my mind couldn't. Not with all the warnings my mother gave me. Although, I did not feel weakened by Zach's presence. It invigorated me, set a constant tingle on my skin. It was a heady feeling, and I enjoyed it, but I didn't know if that was because he was a dark bringer and I his opposite, or if this was what it would be like with the rest of humanity.

His eyes narrowed as he studied me. "You are a light bringer," he said, this time with more force.

"I am not," I said, but my voice cracked. I picked up the dishes and brought them to the sink, ignoring the knot in my stomach. I cleaned the plates and put them on the shelf with my meager kitchen accessories. When I turned, I slammed right into his chest.

His hands gripped my upper arms, and he leaned in, planting his lips on mine. My mind went blank, and only the softness of his lips remained. My hands cupped his elbows as a flare of want flushed through my skin.

He broke the kiss and stared down at me. The silver streaks in his irises glowed. We stood staring at each other, and then he stepped away, running a hand through his thick hair. His chest rose and fell like he had run miles, and a light sweat broke out on his forehead.

It was just a kiss, but it was my first, and the way it consumed me left me breathless.

"I should go now," he said and headed towards the window.

Conflicting emotions wracked my form. It was still a few hours until sunset, which left him in danger if what he told me was true, but I also felt the heat between us, afraid it would ignite if he stayed. "Was my kiss that bad?"

His laugh filled the space, and he turned towards me. "No. Just the opposite. It was like stepping through the gates of heaven, and if I stay..." He closed his eyes. "I can't stay."

I started towards him, but he put his hand up, stopping me.

"Next time I come, I'll bring some rope, so we can make you a ladder." He gathered up the hair on the ground and tossed it out the window.

I moved closer to the window, and before he could climb out, I touched his arm.

"I will be back," he whispered and then was gone.

The tug on my hair continued until he reached the ground, and then the weight released. I pulled the length of my hair in the window as he walked away from the tower. He glanced back, his gaze meeting mine for a moment before he turned away.

I couldn't wait to see him again.

TANGLED Chapter 4

DARKNESS DESCENDED AND WITH it came the music. I glanced down as he leaned against the wall, playing his instrument and singing. Between his voice and the soulful tune he played on the cittern, I couldn't help the sway of my hips.

"You're doing it again," I called down.

He glanced up but didn't stop playing, although his smile reflected in the moonlight.

"You know I will not sleep again if you continue..."

The music stopped.

"Let down your hair," he said.

I laughed down at him.

"Seriously, I want to see what this does to you." He held his cittern out.

I considered it, but didn't want to seem too eager. "Fine," I said after a moment. I dumped my hair, and he climbed up. As soon as his feet touched the floor, he helped bring my hair back in the room. Included with his instrument was a thick braid of rope. He peeled it off his shoulder and laid it on the floor.

"It isn't nearly long enough," he said. "But it's a start."

I stared at the rope and then up at him. "Where am I supposed to put that?"

He used his foot and shuffled it underneath my bed, fixing the bed skirt as soon as it was out of sight.

I raised an eyebrow. He was quick to find the perfect hiding place, which made my skin burn with questions.

He grinned. "I've had to hide a thing or two before."

I crossed my arms, again wondering at the wisdom of letting him into my little abode.

Instead of addressing my inquiring stare, he pulled his instrument from his other shoulder and started plucking that haunting song. His voice started slow and sultry, like a lullaby, and I couldn't help the sway of my hips. A slow figure eight flowed through me, and I turned, letting myself get lost to his music, his voice.

When his arms wrapped around my waist, I gasped, but he kept the haunting melody, swaying his hips around with mine. The intimacy of our movements stopped my breath. When his lips kissed my neck, the music stopped. He spun me to face him and his hands cradled my face. His eyes burned, the silver veins glowing.

He leaned in and kissed me, but this time, his tongue swiped my lips. I opened my mouth in surprise. His tongue explored my mouth, creating a heat through my entire form. I matched his movement. A low rumble built in his chest as he pulled me closer.

I could kiss him like this forever.

He pulled away from my lips and glanced at the stormy bubble encompassing us. His gaze moved to the bed and then met mine.

I shivered at the intensity in his eyes.

His hands moved from my face down my arms, and his fingers interlocked with mine. "You are too damn innocent to taint," he whispered, seeming to talk more to himself than to me. His hands squeezed mine. "And too trusting." His eyes bore into mine. "What if I was here to do harm?"

I raised an eyebrow. "You would have tried to hurt me earlier if that was your intent."

"And do you drop your hair to anyone who calls for it?" he asked.

I shook my head. "Until you tricked me, I only dropped it for my mother. You have been the only one who ever came upon this tower, besides her."

"Ever?"

I nodded.

He released my hands and crossed to the window, looking out over the dark woods. "People should be able to see this place."

I crossed and stopped next to him. Light peppered the distant hills, like fireflies in the summertime. I smiled at the familiar view.

"If we can see evidence of lanterns, it stands to reason that they should be able to see this tower."

I chewed on my lower lip and turned towards my ever-present flame. If my mother could conjure a flame like that, could she conjure a cloak of invisibility over this tower? I knew she was a strong mage, but no one until Zach had passed near. At least that I was aware of. That nugget seemed awfully strange.

"Tell me more about the lore," I said, staring out the window. "And start at the beginning."

He clasped my hand. "The story starts in Antaris with the queen's announcement that she was pregnant with a child. The queen fell sick, and the king set out to find a cure for her deathly circumstances. It is said he found the last existing flower of light from an elderly woman's garden. The king brought it home, crushed it up, and gave it to the queen in a nightly tonic that restored her from the brink of death, like the fabled light bringers. When she gave birth, it is said the girl glowed with the light of the flower. The lore also said when strands of her hair fell out, they turned to sticks of spun gold." He let out a laugh.

My chest tightened.

"That just seems way too out there for me to get a handle on."

"What happened next?" I asked.

"They say an evil enchantress wanted the golden child for herself, and she stole her away from the king and queen, setting fire to the castle as she escaped." He sighed.

Quiet permeated the space between us.

My gaze turned towards the flame in my oven. "And?" I asked, returning my gaze to the outside world.

"The king and queen died in the fire. People assumed the baby, and the enchantress perished because neither was ever seen again." He glanced at me. "I was born on the day the flames took the king and queen to their deaths. Storms pummeled the landscape, and darkness shadowed the land for many years following their deaths."

I shivered, turning this over in my head. Could my mother be the evil enchantress? Again, my gaze traveled to the flame.

"I would bet my life that child was you."

TANGLED Chapter 5

ZACH TALKED LONG INTO the night before I finally sent him away. I lay in bed, staring at the ceiling. The chill in the air had nothing to do with the night, and everything to do with the story he'd told. If there was any truth to it, I had been bamboozled all my life.

I started dissecting every memory I had with my mother. Every word, every action, every nuance. Especially when she talked about the fire that took my father. Was it all a lie? Were her tears those of a crocodile?

The lights in the distance crawled under my skin. They certainly should be able to see us. That made much more sense than anything else. So, why didn't anyone chance across this tower in all these years?

I had no answers to all the questions accosting my mind. Restlessness kept sleep at bay yet again.

The morning light had long brightened the room, but I rolled away from it, too tired to greet the day like I usually did. I wanted nothing to do with the light as darkness clasped its icy hands around my heart.

"Danae," a familiar voice called.

My heart leaped into my throat. I rolled to my feet, nearly running across the floor, and glanced out the window.

"What are you doing here?" I hissed.

Zach stepped back and pointed at his chest.

"Yes, you. If my mother finds you here..." I glanced over the fields and woodlands. I didn't have the foggiest idea of what she would do. Although if there was any truth to what my instincts were raging, he wouldn't last the day.

"I made sure no one was in the area," he said and held up another roll of rope. "It still isn't long enough, but it gets us closer to getting you out."

I did another scan of the area, then wrapped part of my messy braid around the hook and dropped the rest.

Zach climbed up quickly and placed the rope under the bed with the other roll. "One more roll like that, and we should have enough." He wiped his hands on his thighs and reached for me.

I was stuck in place, with no way to sidestep him until my braid was freed from the hook. He kissed me, pressing me against the wall in a way that made me shiver.

"You need to go," I whispered under his lips.

He pulled away, searching my eyes.

"Let her come."

My eyes widened, and my heart picked up, throbbing in my chest. I shook my head. "No. Please. I have no idea what she is capable of."

"Neither do I, and I really don't like you being at her mercy." He reached out and hauled my hair inside, unhooking it from the clasp before turning to me again. "If the stories are true, you aren't safe."

"My mother would never hurt me," I said, almost as a reflex, but after the words flowed from my tongue, I wondered if that was the truth. If she killed to lock me up in this tower, would she be mad enough to kill her golden goose? The question haunted me.

I crossed to what remained of the pie and offered Zach one of the forks. He dug into the soft, sweet apples with me.

When we finished, he collected the pie plate and the forks and washed them for me. That simple gesture made me smile. In all the years my mother had been coming and eating meals with me, she never once lifted a finger to help, beyond bringing the food with her.

He wiped his hands and turned towards me. "Are you sure?"

"Am I sure about what?" I totally lost track of the conversation with my view of him doing the dishes.

"That she won't hurt you."

I took a breath. My gaze landed on the eternal flame that would burn until the life bled out of her. I finally nodded. "I'm not sure that whole folk lore that you spun was the truth."

He chewed on his lower lip. "Do you still want to escape this tower?"

I nodded. "Yes."

The tension in his face released, and he smiled. "Good, because I have no idea how I'd get you out of here if you refused to leave."

I cocked my head and narrowed my eyes.

"I'm not built to stay locked up in a place like this forever," he said while twirling his finger around. "It's nice and comfortable and all, but I would miss the adventure out there." He pointed out the window. "You are going to love the world."

Longing to be free scraped at my skin. I sighed. "If that story isn't true, my leaving is going to upset my mother."

"If it is true, it's going to drive her into a state of fury," he countered. "Either way, you need to assume she is the most dangerous animal in the woods."

I crossed my arms. "She's not an animal."

"Either she is a heartless enchantress or she's a mother scorned."

His point hit home. "Anger or disappointment. Great." I turned and flopped facedown on the bed. Regardless of what my gut was telling me, the choices of her reaction stank.

The bed dipped, and I turned towards Zach. He settled on the edge and started running his fingers through the front of my hair, stopping as he approached the braided strands before starting the slow stroke again. Each time his fingers touched my skin, that force field would awaken, and it would slip away as his fingers lost contact.

We both seemed mesmerized by the flow of it. When his gaze returned to mine, I sucked in my breath, suddenly not at all relaxed. Not with my entire being tingling with his proximity to me.

He licked his lips, and his fingertips ran down the side of my face to my ear. His light touch tickled as he traced the outside of my ear, and it positively burned as he ran it down the side of my neck.

"I think I need to go," he said, his voice husky and deep.

I lifted onto my elbows, and his gaze dropped from my eyes to the front of my dress.

He stood. "I have to go," he said and crossed towards the window. He climbed onto the sill, but stopped and turned back to me. He looked at the snaking river of my hair and let out a strained laugh. "I need you to get out."

I stood, gathering my locks, and went to him.

His gaze softened as he cupped my cheek. "If I stay, I will do something neither of us is ready for."

As much as I wanted to explore what he was insinuating, I couldn't help the worry that bit at my heels. I tossed my hair out the window.

He descended with ease and waved as he sauntered off into the woods.

I collected my hair and then took a seat at the table, cracking the book that I was reading when Zach had tricked me. I couldn't believe two days had gone by since he first came to my window. I shook thoughts of him out of my mind and focused on the words on the page of the manuscript.

TANGLED Chapter 6

MY MOTHER CALLED UP. I glanced up from the book, folding the corner of the page to keep my place. I was almost finished devouring the new story, and a little irritated that I had to stop reading to assist her climb to my fortress.

"Still reading?" my mother asked as she pointed to the book on the table.

I nodded, trying to figure out what exact question to ask to expose the cracks in her story. "I think it's time you tell me what happened the night my father died."

A crevice appeared between her eyes as she glanced between the half read book and me. "There was a fire," she started and licked her lips. "And you know the rest."

"How did the fire start? And how did you make it out with me?"

She placed her backpack on the table and wiped her hands on her shirt. "I don't know. It all happened so fast. Your father handed you to me and told me to run. I did, thinking he was right behind me." She said all of this in a deadpan tone that told me nothing while staring at the floor. Finally, she raised her eyes to me. "He wasn't, and I had you in my arms. I couldn't go back into that inferno."

"How did you find this place?"

Her eyebrows rose, and she shrugged.

"How did you even get up here?"

She cocked her head. "What's gotten into you?"

"You've never told me anything beyond that my father died in a fire and I'm curious."

Her gaze landed on the book. "What exactly is that story about?"

"It's a romance novel, Mother," I said, rolling my eyes. The lack of her answering scratched my skin like a dozen sharp knives. "And you are avoiding my questions."

She crossed her arms. "I'm not avoiding them. I just don't remember. It just was. Why are you asking all these questions? Did something happen while I was gone?"

I glanced outside. "Why hasn't anyone ever come by besides you? I can see lanterns on the other hills at night, so I don't understand why no one has ever come calling."

Her mouth popped open and her eyes widened. "Someone happened by, didn't they?"

I shook my head.

"Look at me, Danae."

I forced my gaze to hers and kept her stare. I had to force my muscles from fidgeting.

"Did you see someone?"

I bit my lip.

"It's okay, I just want to know what you saw," she said, taking my hands.

"I didn't see anything," I said, but my voice squeaked. I cursed my honest nature, wishing I could spin a lie as good as she could.

Her eyebrow rose. "It's not like you to lie to me."

I closed my eyes and hung my head. "I saw someone in the woods. He seemed to be lost, and when he came upon the tower, he called until I told him to go away."

"Did he?"

"Did he what?"

"Did he go away?"

I nodded and met her gaze. "He went toward the hills." I had told the truth about our first encounter. I just hoped she wouldn't push for more information.

Her features smoothed out. "That's it?"

"Yes, and I got to thinking about why that man was the only one who stumbled upon this tower."

She studied me. "That answers my questions about the lantern lights in the distance, but why do you keep asking about your father?"

I looked beyond her at the window and shrugged, trying to think of something reasonable. All I could think of was the timbre of his voice and the way he kissed. "He sang a song..." I snapped my mouth closed and met her gaze, hoping she would miss my slip-up.

"Does this man have a name?"

I hesitated and then shook my head.

Her eyes narrowed.

I must have hesitated a little too long. "He said he was a prince," I mumbled.

"A prince?" She leaned her head back and laughed. "Princes are known to break hearts, young lady. Or have you learned nothing from your love stories?" She waved at my expansive collection of books.

I glanced over my shoulder at my collection. None of them had prepared me for the intense connection that had hit when Zach touched me. I craved it as much as I craved food.

"What else did this so-called prince tell you?" She crossed her arms.

"He asked if there was a way into this tower. I told him there wasn't and sent him on his way." I turned back to her.

"So why all the questions about your father?" she asked again.

"What happened before the fire?" I asked. "All you have ever told me about is the fire. You have never told me about anything else. What was life like in the palace? What was it like to give birth to me? Was the pregnancy hard, or was it easy?"

Her eyebrows arched. She opened her mouth to speak, but her gaze fell to the book again. "What exactly is in that book?" She marched over, opened to the page I had marked, and scanned the prior pages and a couple after.

The warning bells in my brain started clanging.

She turned back to me, and I cocked my head, waiting.

"Look, it was painful and messy, and I just don't like talking about it," she said.

"What did you and Father like to do before you had me?"

She glanced out the window as if searching for the right words. "We rode a lot and hunted in the woods." She studied my hair. "It looks like your braid could use tightening."

"I will be sure to re-braid my hair later. Right now I want to hear more about Father." I sat down on the edge of the bed, waiting.

She pressed her lips together and ran her hands through her hair. "I would prefer to let the past stay in the past," she said. "It hurts to talk about him."

This was the same song and dance I always got when the subject turned to him. "So, how many other light bringers are out there?" I nodded my head towards the window.

Her eyes narrowed. "Why?"

"Because the song he sang was about the last light bringer." My voice rose, louder than I had intended it.

"My dear, it was just a song," my mother said.

I waited for her to answer.

"Too many, and they are all suffering," she snarled.

The candles flickered as a light breeze swirled through my home.

I cocked my head and drew my brows together.

"Did the prince tell you otherwise?" she asked.

"No."

She blinked and then sighed. "It sounds like you were taken by the prince," she said. "And I'm sure he seemed like a nice man, but I wouldn't rely on him to come back if I were you. He will break your heart."

"I don't expect him to come back," I said, hoping she would buy it. When she nodded, I exhaled. The blood rushed to my head, and I crossed to the backpack on the table, curious for a distraction to curb the growing aggravation burning my skin. The more she talked, the more I believed in the lore and doubted all her good deeds.

The pack contained fish wrapped in paper to keep them fresh, and a dozen fresh fruits to go with the seafood. "Thank you," I said and dumped the contents onto the table.

"I need one of those fish to bargain with at the market tomorrow."

I put one back in the bag and handed it to her.

She slipped it on her back and nodded towards the window. "I should go, but before I do, I need to trim your ends." She picked up the tail end of my braid and held it within the backpack. She cut right below the last band holding the braid together. Heavy metal banged together in the backpack, and then she closed the bag and shouldered it as she waited for me to toss my hair over the windowsill.

I watched her go, waving when she turned. Then, I trudged over to the food and collected it all to prepare the fish to be cooked this evening. Until then, I had a book to finish and a growing hope for Zach to come calling again.

TANGLED Chapter 7

I FINISHED BOTH BOOKS by the next evening between bouts of pacing and staring out the window. Zach hadn't come back. Neither had my mother. I sat at the table picking at the last piece of cooked fish until I finally dumped it out the window, disgusted at my lack of appetite.

I tossed the dish in the sink and crawled into bed. Darkness washed over me in waves of doubt.

Doubt in my mother.

Doubt in Zach.

Doubt raked over my skin, leaving me exposed.

I shivered and wrapped the covers around me tighter.

Questions floated through my mind as if they had a life of their own, sucking my strength from my bones. Days went by before my mother returned with a bag full of food and more books.

But Zach hadn't come back. Darkness threatened to overtake me, keeping my tongue silent and my mood sullen. Even the books did not carry me away from this bitter feeling coating everything around me.

Weeks went by without Zach. I suspected all of his stories and promises were indeed a ruse, as my mother had tried to tell me, and that the only one who truly cared for me was my mother.

"May I braid your hair?" my mother asked, pulling me out of my thoughts.

I nodded.

She undid the frayed braid and brushed my hair until it shined in the darkening room. With delicate hands as light as feathers, she braided my hair into one continuous braid. Layers fell softly over my head and tightened at the nape of my neck. I didn't think I had ever seen her braid my hair this way before.

I smiled at the results as she tied the end of my braid and cut the ends into a blunt line. The hair fell into her bag with the familiar *tink* of metal on metal.

"There, that looks much better," she said. She wrapped her arms around me and kissed my cheek. "I know you have been down, but hopefully, the new books I brought this time will brighten your disposition." She gathered her things. "I must head back to the market, so I won't be here tomorrow. I will try to make it back the day after, but just in case, you have enough food to last the rest of the week."

I pressed my lips together against the disappointment. Her visits had kept the darkness from wrapping itself around my heart. But I understood. She had brought me enough food to last a few days.

I let her down my newly formed braid and hauled it back inside after she trudged off into the woods. I watched until long after she disappeared, then went to turn.

"Danae," a raspy voice whispered.

My heart leaped into my throat. I glanced down. My breath locked in my chest at the sight of the bruised man glancing up at me. His skin was sullen and his clothing ripped and ragged, but I would recognize those green eyes anywhere.

I dropped my hair down, and he started at the long braid, then stooped and put a ring of rope over his head, stumbling under the weight of it. His hand landed on the tower, and he dipped his head to his chest. He stood still for far too long.

"Zach?"

He looked up at me. Tears shone on his cheeks. "I don't know if I have the strength."

I took a deep breath. "Tie the end of my hair around your waist."

His eyebrows rose. "You can't pull me up."

I wrapped my hair around the hook. "We will never know until we try."

He stared up at me and then slowly tied the end of my hair around him.

"Let me try to climb," he said.

When my hands gripped my braid at the top, and his hands held my hair at the bottom, the current between us ignited. That silver flash in his eyes glowed. Energy surged. He ascended my hair until he reached out and took my hand in his. I helped him into the window and pulled my hair back inside.

Zach crashed to the floor.

I turned to him, crouching next to his battered body. His breathing thinned to a raspy whine.

"I didn't think I'd ever see you again," he said, and his eyes fluttered closed and his exhale wheezed. His chest stopped moving.

My heart thundered. I placed my hands on his chest. Nothing happened. No spark of energy between us. Nothing. Hot panic filled my blood. I leaned down and placed my lips on his. He didn't kiss back. He didn't even respond to my touch. The bones under my hands shifted, and I pulled my hands away in horror.

"Zach!" I yelled, and a tear escaped, dropping onto his forehead.

Light bloomed from the tearstain, cascading over his bruises, wiping them away, leaving only unblemished skin. More tears fell as my heart cracked.

When the light traveled to his chest, his eyes flew open. He took a great breath. His body arched with sparks and his hands flew to my cheeks, pulling me to his lips. He kissed me like a drowning man's first gasp for air. The flow of power encompassed me as I chased death from his bones.

He groaned in my mouth as scraping sounds filled his form and all the shattered bones mended. The sensation passed from him to me as my light bringer magic saturated both of us, wiping out any evidence of the darkness within us.

Our memories tangled together, and my eyes widened. I yanked away from him, drawing air into lungs that burned. I slid away, trying to reconcile the visions that pinged around my mind. Visions of what his last couple of weeks encompassed.

The brightness in the room faded into that of just natural daytime light as the power settled. He lay gasping as he stared at the ceiling. He slowly sat up and ran both hands through his tangled hair. His green and silver gaze met mine and then fell to the braid rolled across the floor.

"You brought me back from the dead," he whispered with awe. His hands traveled to his chest and pressed down on his ribs. He peeled the rope over his shoulder and tossed it aside, then climbed to his feet.

I stared at him. His perfectly unmarred skin didn't reconcile with the memories of his beatings. Beatings my mother ordered, along with slow torture. None of his trials were evident on his body, but his eyes shone brightly with them.

He crossed and crouched before me. "I need to tell you what happened."

I shook my head. "I saw." I waved to where I healed him. "When I... I saw everything." My vision blurred under a sheen of tears.

He took my hand, and the storm that encompassed us was different. Less dark than it was before, but no less intense. We both stared at the silver and gold webbing surrounding us as lightning crackled over the surface.

"Then you know who you are."

I looked around my prison and then closed my eyes. The woman who had said she was my mother was anything but. She had killed my parents, set the fire that destroyed the palace, and stored me away in this place where only she could get to me just for her own gain. For a never-ending supply of gold and enough light to keep her youth. My stomach soured.

"She meant to kill me," Zach said, and his gaze traveled to a spot on the floor a few feet away. "She almost succeeded."

I stared at the rope. "Do we have enough?" I pointed, as a hardness I'd never experienced before gripped me. I needed out of this prison. Now.

Zach swiveled on his feet and stood. "I think so. It should at least get us to where we can drop to the ground without injury."

"Good." I climbed to my feet and pulled the other two lengths of rope out from under the bed, then helped him tie it together.

While Zach tied the end to the hook outside the window, I turned towards the kitchen and stared at the knives on the counter.

With a growl of anger, I crossed, took the butcher knife, grabbed my braid, and sawed through the hair at the nape of my neck. The sharp blade sliced through. I dropped both the braid and the knife. The floor shook with the weight of the gold dropping to the floor.

Zach's eyes widened as his gaze followed the solid gold twine that used to be my braid. His gaze jumped to mine and my shoulder-length golden locks.

I ran my fingers through my hair and rolled my head on my shoulders. The freedom that gripped me made me smile.

He went to pick up the gold but could barely budge it.

"Leave it."

He glanced up at me and then the spiral of metal with a slow nod. "The rope won't support the weight, anyway." He held out his hand. "You go first."

I gave one last glance around the room and nodded.

"Wrap your legs around the rope and slide hand over hand down until the rope ends. Then you'll need to drop the last few feet."

I did as he instructed, and the moment my bare feet hit the grass below, I stepped away and curled my toes in the thin, ticklish blades. I glanced up in time to see him scale out the window. The breeze whipped the torn fabric around him, and his descent was as careful as mine had been.

The moment he landed, he grabbed my hand and led me into the woods behind the tower. In the opposite direction of where I had first seen him or that my mother ever went.

"Where are we going?"

"As far away as we can get. The minute your mother…"

"She is not my mother. Never refer to that witch as my mother." I yanked my hand from his grip. Anger engulfed me, and my hands clenched.

Zach stepped closer and took my hands in his, slowly unclenching them before threading his fingers through mine. "The minute she finds I am gone, she is going to return. I promised her I would find you again. That I would tell you exactly who she was." He closed his eyes and swallowed.

My heart went cold as his memory seeped into my brain. She had her henchman beat him into unconsciousness and left him to die.

"I clung to the light. It was the only thing that got me to my knees after they left me bloody and beaten on that dungeon floor." His gaze met mine. "The door never clasped when they left. Perhaps she figured I was already dead after being starved and then beaten to such an extent. Or her thugs thought that way and had intentions of coming back and finishing the job after she left. Either way, I knew if I remained, the next meeting would send me to the other side." He unclasped one hand and turned, pulling me deeper into the woods. "I crawled out, keeping to the shadows. I saw her ride off before I crawled into the stables and found my horse. No one saw us slip away, and I am not sure if that was because I wished to be invisible, or that they just were that feebleminded to not notice a black horse dash away."

We made our way around a great rock, and then Zach stopped. His breath sucked in and his hand squeezed mine tighter. I peered over his shoulder at the king's guards surrounding the black horse.

Zach pushed me back to the other side of the large rock. With his back pressed against the surface, he closed his eyes. When he finally opened them, he stared at the sky, shaking his head.

"We can't go back," he whispered. "Which means I have to…" His hand squeezed mine harder.

"No, you don't." I unclasped my hand. "What is your horse's name?"

"Midnight. Why?"

"Never mind why, just stay here."

"Danae…" he started.

I splayed my fingers at him. "Trust me." I walked around the rock and ran my fingers through my hair, unsure of what I was going to do. I knew Zach was in danger, but my only experience with the outside world was limited to him.

Even the books I'd read heralded men as dangers to be wary of, and while I knew I should approach with caution, I took a different route.

I skipped through the woods, calling, "Midnight!"

When I stepped into the clearing, all the men stared with their mouths hanging open.

I forced my eyes wide and rushed forward. "Thank god you found him," I gasped and took the reins from one of the men.

He stared at me as if I had two heads.

"I have been looking for him for hours," I added and smiled at the group.

"This is your horse," the largest of the men said with narrowed eyes.

"Yes. A nice young man traded him for one of my father's prize pigs," I said, trying to recall some of the bartering I'd read in my books. "He seemed desperate." I ran my hand down the stallion's nose and he nudged me. "And I really took a liking to him." I nuzzled him back.

"When did you see this young man?"

I cocked my head and looked up at the sky. "I think it was more than a fortnight ago." I met his gaze and shrugged.

"Where is your farm?"

I pointed to my left, away from the rocks, but also away from where Zach seemed to want us to go.

"Would you like me to help you onto your horse?" the largest soldier asked.

"Oh, no. I haven't gotten the courage to ride him again since that first day. He threw me, and I got a pretty nasty bruise on my backside." I rubbed my butt and winced. "I'll just walk with him for now."

"We can escort you."

I reached out and touched his arm. "I will be just fine. You don't need to escort me home." I wished for the guard to heed my words and leave me and the horse behind. "Besides, you three must have more pressing matters to attend to."

They looked at each other, shrugging.

"We need to report back to the king," the biggest guard said.

"Give him my regards." I smiled as they turned and wandered off.

I remained in place, holding Midnight's reins and petting him gently. I turned the horse in the direction I had indicated our farm was and started into the woods. A quick glance back told me it was the right thing to do. They had stopped at the far side of the clearing and watched as I walked the horse out of sight.

I kept going, keeping the rock formation to my left as I went until I could no longer see the clearing. If I couldn't see them, they couldn't see us. I tied Midnight to a tree and slowly made my way back into the clearing.

Zach stood with a sword to his throat. But it wasn't the king's guards that held him in place. My hands clenched, and I narrowed my eyes at the woman who had held me captive for twenty years.

"Let him go, enchantress," I snarled.

The witch stared at me. The blade lowered as the shock of seeing me without the long flowing locks morphed her features from initial surprise to madness. Her gaze shot back to Zack's, and the blade returned to his throat, nicking his skin. A thin line of blood trailed down to his shirt.

"You nearly killed him. Just to keep up your facade. Just to keep the golden goose prisoner." With each word, I stepped closer, praying she wouldn't cut his throat open. I didn't know if I could fix that like I had fixed him earlier.

"He ruined everything!" she cried out.

"No. *You* ruined everything." I couldn't help the fury that welled up from the bowels of my soul. It was black as night and had only one use.

Her face scrunched in anger, and she readied herself to behead Zach. The blade whistled through the air.

"I bring the light!" Power surged, and I reached for Zach with my mind, wrapping him in a protective bubble.

The moment the sword hit my shield, the sharp metal shattered into dust. It swirled, reforming the sword in Zach's grip.

"And I bring the dark," he said. The low menacing timbre of his voice spread goose bumps all over my skin.

"Don't!" I yelled as he prepared to strike.

They both looked at me with the same slack-jawed expression.

"I do not want her blood on our hands." I met his gaze, and his posture relaxed. I moved my sharp glare in her direction. "But I will not let you imprison me ever again. If you choose to use your spells to coerce me or to kill Zach, I will have no choice but to let him unleash his darkness. However, if you promise to leave us alone for all eternity, I will gladly tell you where the golden braid is." I glanced between the two of them. "That is the deal—your life or your promise to leave us be."

Her lips thinned in frustration.

"What's it going to be?" I asked when she didn't respond.

"Tell me where the gold is," she said in almost a purr.

I crossed my arms as the magic infused in her words tried to penetrate the wall I had built between us and her. Anger flared inside me, clenching my muscles.

"You have one more chance, enchantress." When she didn't speak, I glanced at Zach and gave him a nod. "Then I will gladly bring your head to the king."

She swallowed, and her gaze jumped between us. "Wait!" She gasped as Zach raised his sword. "Fine. Have it your way," she snarled at me.

"My way includes a spell you cannot break, safeguarding Zacharia and me from your insidiousness." I pointed at her. "And I will know if you try to alter the spell for your own bidding."

Her lips peeled back from her teeth. "Fine."

She whispered ancient words that I was unfamiliar with, and the air shifted around us. I closed my eyes, allowing my light to seek her magic, to test it for underlying weaknesses and any harmful intent. When I was satisfied it would protect us from her, I let the shield down. Her spell settled over us.

I inhaled and opened my eyes.

"Greed comes with a price," Zach said to the enchantress. He held his hand out for me. The moment our fingers intertwined, the light shined around us. "You might not like the cost," he added and turned me towards the woods where I had Midnight tied up.

I glanced at him as he sheathed his sword, then raised an eyebrow.

He gave me a wry smile. "If she tries to remove the gold with that rope, it won't support the weight. I'm not sure if it will even support her weight if she tries to climb up." He shrugged. "Besides, I knew your mo—" He clamped his lips closed on the forbidden word. "I knew the enchantress was greedy. I knew she wouldn't pass on that gold, so not only is the rope compromised, but I put a little bit of my darkness into that golden braid. The only person who could ever get it away from that tower is you. Only a light bringer can nullify the darkness that will poison anyone who touches it."

"Why would you do something like that?" I stopped and tore my hand from his.

"Because if she got that thing out of the tower, she would become the richest woman in the kingdom. Maybe even richer than my father." He stared me down.

I shrugged. "So what?"

"She could buy her way into the palace and end up as the queen," he said, his voice a soft hiss. "And where would that leave you?"

I blinked and stepped back. All manner of horrible possibilities flashed through my head.

"She had no issues imprisoning you before. What makes you think she wouldn't do it again if she had that kind of power?"

A dark shiver ran through my form. As much as I wanted Gwendolyn out of my life, I couldn't condemn her to wasting away in the tower. "As soon as you are safe, I need to go back." I started walking again, but he didn't follow. When I turned, he had his hands on his hips and a deep crease between his eyes.

"Where you go, I go," he said. "And we are not going back that way."

I rolled my eyes. "Please, Zach. I cannot condone that kind of death. The thought of wasting away in that tower terrified me daily." I pointed in the direction that we came from. "It was my worst fear, and I don't wish that upon anyone. Not even the enchantress."

He looked at the ground, then turned his back to me and glanced at the sky, muttering under his breath. When he turned back, his stare was hard enough to chill my bones. "Fine," he said through gritted teeth. "But let's at least get my horse first."

I nodded, and he stormed past me. Lightning burst between us as his shoulder rubbed mine. As soon as we reached Midnight, he hauled me up on the stallion's back and hopped on behind me. With one arm gripping me around my waist and the other holding the horse's reins, he shot through the woods like an expert, leaving me breathless from more than the chilly wind on my face.

We came in from the north side of the tower. The setting sun painted the tower in its bright light, and even from this distance, I could see the frayed rope swaying from the handle.

My heart jumped in my throat as we neared. Zach slowed Midnight to a walk. Ugly rants fell from the window. We weren't within view of it, but the screeching was nothing like I had ever heard. On the ground, chunks of broken gold dusted over the dirt. The largest piece still had the rope latched around it.

"I told her she wouldn't like the price of her greed," Zach said and stopped a few feet away from the tower.

"Help!"

I stepped around the smashed gold and looked up. The enchantress leaned out the window, her black hair streaming in the wind. She straightened, glaring down at us.

"You came to gloat?" she hissed.

"No. I came to stop you from this..." I waved at the broken gold and most of the twine lying at my feet. "While I wished you gone from my life, I did not wish this kind of horror on you." I glanced at the gold and then at Zach.

He stared at me with a cool gaze. "Don't ask me to apologize after what she did to me." He crossed his arms. "She was willing to kill me to protect her magical fountain of youth and unlimited supply of gold."

I could see his point, but it hadn't been all bad for me. There were many years where we would play hide-and-seek and other games. She had read to me many times until I was almost too sleepy to let down my hair for her. She fed me and brushed my hair whenever she came. She taught me to cook and to read. I stared up at the woman who imprisoned me my whole life, and a deep pain filled my core. She did all the things my parents would have done had they not been cut down in their prime.

Tears leaked from the corners of my eyes, but I wasn't sure who I was crying for.

Darkness radiated from within each broken bit of gold.

I glanced at Zach, wiping the tears away like they were gnats. "You certainly cursed this thing pretty good."

He gave me a crooked smile and shrugged.

"We can't just leave it lying around like this."

"Only you can touch it."

"I get that, but what will happen if someone else happens by?"

His smile faded, and he scanned the broken pieces. "They will die." He glanced up. "The enchantress should have died from touching it."

My gaze landed on the witch's gloved hands.

"How do I break the curse?" I asked, focusing back on the more detrimental problem before us.

"All you have to do is touch each piece."

I reached out to the one encircled by the tied rope, and the minute my fingers grazed the cool metal, the chunk of gold shifted. Reeds of golden hair fell to the ground where gold had once sat. My gaze shot to Zach's, and his raised eyebrows relayed the same surprise, sending shockwaves through my form. I raced around, touching the shiny metal. In all cases, golden hair fell where the rock had been before. When I finished, I turned back to Zach.

"And here I thought perhaps we had a way for me to buy my way back into my kingdom." He let out a light laugh and shook his head. "But then again, I don't think even that amount of gold would wipe my slate clean."

I glanced back up at the enchantress. "I will try to send help."

Her hard gaze softened, and she closed her eyes. "Child, there is no way out of this tower. I made certain of that when I locked you up here. Your hair was the only ladder." She plucked the remaining fray of rope in disgust. "This is a cruel twist of fate, but it isn't your doing."

She turned from the window, leaving only the empty space gaping back at me. Zach put his arm around my waist and led me away from the tower and away from the woman who was now imprisoned in a nightmare of her own making.

TANGLED Chapter 8

DARKNESS DESCENDED AS WE stepped into the woods across from the tower. I glanced over my shoulder just before we were out of view. The small light still shined from the tower. I sighed, wondering how many times the enchantress had made this same trek away from my prison, only to look back to make sure that light was still burning.

My throat tightened. Sorrow for what had been and what could have been bit at my skin, making me tremble. Zach's arm tightened around me, and his gentle lips found the curve of my neck. Lightning sizzled between us.

He jerked away, pulling on Midnight's reins. I turned forward and gasped at the semi-circle of king's guards wielding weapons.

"Looks like my time is up, too," Zach whispered in my ear as his grip on me tightened.

Hands grabbed us, yanking us both to the ground. Zach scrambled to get up, but a fist drove him back to the ground. When the guard pointed his sword at Zach's throat, I found my voice.

"Please don't," I said, pulling the guard's glare from Zach. "He saved me from being imprisoned in a tower for the rest of my life."

The guard's gaze narrowed even more. "What was in it for him?"

"Nothing," I answered.

He looked me up and down. "I'd say you're a far cry from nothing."

"Don't you dare touch her," Zach said.

The guard pressed the tip of the blade into Zach's throat. "We will do what we damn well please with your little harlot," he said. "And maybe we will let you watch."

Anger radiated from Zach in waves, bristling the hair on my skin.

When two other guards grabbed me and dragged me away from Zach, panic filled me, creating a dangerous brew. I tried to fight them off, but they just laughed at my struggles and ripped at my clothing. I clawed at one of them, and he backhanded me across my cheek. I stumbled and was yanked back between the two men.

"I bring the dark." Zach's dangerous hiss filled the clearing.

Everyone halted, turning in his direction. He held the severed head of the guard who had had him at sword point when I was dragged away. Zach's blade dripped with blood. Midnight whinnied and reared up behind him, creating the perfect backdrop for the lightning whirling around Zach.

He tossed the head in our direction. "If you don't want to end up in the same state as your compadre, I suggest you unhand her."

His eyes glowed with those silver streaks, and this time the streaks bled into his skin, snaking through it in a frightening, unearthly pattern fueled by his rage.

Hands released me, and I crumpled to the ground, staring at the man who had not only freed me from my prison, but had just saved my honor.

The guards backed away.

Zach advanced, his intent clear in his predatory motion.

I scrambled to my feet, putting myself between him and his prey. His eyes narrowed.

"Move, Danae," he said in a growling rumble that seemed to quake the earth under our feet.

I tensed. "No."

"They hurt you."

I brushed my cheek where the pain flared from the guard's backhand. "But that doesn't call for a death sentence."

"Their intent was to do irreparable harm. To break me, so that I would allow them to bring me home to face the gallows." His gaze flitted away from mine. "They underestimated the strength of my wrath, just like my brother did."

"You murdered the king's son," one guard sneered.

"I delivered justice," Zach bellowed.

The darkness had overtaken him. Lightning singed the lower branches of the surrounding trees, and the ground trembled.

Zach's transformation frightened me, but I stayed put, blocking him from the guards.

"I bring the light," I whispered so only Zach could hear.

His gaze snapped to mine. "I swallow the light," he said through gritted teeth and stepped closer.

His hand darted out and grabbed my hair, yanking me forward until his nose nearly touched mine. The madness I saw there made me swallow hard.

"I bring the light," I said calmly and forced my palm to his silver-lined cheek. The connection of our skin sent a shockwave through the clearing, bowing over humans and trees alike.

I stared up at the clear sky. The stars winked back at me as I slowly sat up. Zach lay motionless a few feet away. I scrambled to his side. His eyes were open, focused on the heavens above. No trace of the silver remained in his skin, but those familiar silver veins remained in his green irises.

Finally, he shifted his gaze to me and blinked. "What happened?"

I glanced around. Every guard was down, but none moved. I didn't know if they were alive or not.

I shrugged. "I guess our powers clashed?"

He sat up slowly, holding his head like he had the worst headache known to man. He took a breath and surveyed the damage. Midnight whinnied, still standing tall. The horse was the only thing left upright within a hundred-meter radius.

A low chuckle emitted from Zach's lips. "That's an understatement," he said and climbed to his feet. He retrieved his bloody sword and sheathed it before heading towards Midnight.

I stood. "What are you doing?" I asked as he mounted Midnight. "We need to make sure they aren't hurt."

He guided Midnight to where I stood and extended his hand. "They were going to defile you in every way. I don't care whether they are alive or dead. But I do care about you. So please, let us get out of here before something worse happens."

I stared at his hand and then back into his sincere eyes.

"If they are alive and they wake to find us here..." He sighed. "Please, Danae, please don't make me fall into the darkness again."

I reached for his hand, and he pulled me onto Midnight. As we passed one of the guards, he moaned and rolled to his side. Relief swept through me. The blast hadn't killed them. Before I caught my breath, we tore out of the clearing, heading in the same direction as we were when the guards ambushed us.

"Where are we going?" I asked when I was sure my voice wouldn't shake.

"I have been running long enough. It is time this charade of my father's ends."

I glanced over my shoulder at his grim determination. The blaze in his eyes burned with every silver flare of darkness.

"You killed your brother?" I asked.

His grip on me tightened. "Yes."

The night weighed down on me, and I shivered.

"I always took the blame for his..." Zach sighed. "His fixations. He was twisted in ways no child should be. It started with animal mutilations that he blamed on me, and my father believed every word that twisted freak said. The fact I carry the darkness inside me didn't help my cause." He pulled me closer. "They do not understand what the darkness is. My father feared it, thinking it caused the strange deaths in the kingdom." He shook his head and kissed my shoulder. "The darkness craves justice, not mayhem."

The cadence of Midnight's hoofs lulled my tired mind. I closed my eyes and leaned back into Zach's chest, relishing the silence that had fallen between us. His broken explanation left too many blanks, and I was too tired to fill them.

"What happened?" I finally said when it was clear that he wasn't willing to go on.

"I fell in love." He sighed.

I glanced over my shoulder at him, drawing my eyebrows together.

"Sorry. You aren't my first," he said with a sad smile.

The words made my head spin away from his past to this moment. My mouth popped open at his admission.

His tight features softened, and he kissed my cheek. "But I hope you are my last," he whispered. "I confided in my brother that I was going to the market to find a suitable wedding band. When I arrived back home hours later, I entered my bedchambers as he finished sawing through her spine. He propped her head on my pillow and had the audacity to grin at me like what he had done was a grand gesture. A gift. Pieces of the woman I wanted to spend the rest of my life with were strewn about the room like discarded, soiled clothing." His voice cracked, and his forehead dropped to my shoulder. "The darkness demanded justice, and for the first time in my life, I let it override all that had held it at bay. And the darkness delivered. When I was done, I stood at the entrance of my father's throne room holding my brother's severed head by the hair. I tossed it down the aisle, glaring at my father before I walked out of the castle, mounted my horse, and rode away from the kingdom."

I trembled at the vision he'd painted. Zach wrapped his arms tight around me.

"I've been hunted ever since, and as each year passes, the belief that I was the one maiming animals and torturing and killing peasants becomes a more solid conclusion in the eyes of the kingdom."

"And your mother? What does she believe?"

He was quiet for the longest time. "I never knew my mother. She died giving birth to me."

My heart squeezed, and I wrapped my arms around him, holding him as tight as he was holding me.

"I can't continue running. Not if I have half a chance at a life with you. But I'm afraid that even your light magic can't fix what I did in my father's eyes. He only sees what he wants to see. And my father wants to see my head on a post."

TANGLED Chapter 9

AS WE APPROACHED THE kingdom, a brigade of the king's soldiers surrounded us. Zach held me tight as swords were unsheathed.

"Let us pass, and I promise no harm will come to you," Zach said as Midnight halted.

"What is the bounty on his head now?" the guard with all the medals pinned on his coat said.

"I think it has raised to a hundred gold coins," another guard said.

"I..." I started, intending to protect Zach.

"Shh. Not now," Zach whispered in my ear, stopping me from announcing that I'd brought the light.

I glanced back at him, and his eyes sent a warning I heeded.

"Please let us pass," I said, taking Zach's lead and turning my attention back to the guards. "I need assistance."

There were enough men here to figure out a way to help the enchantress.

Zach gave me a sideways look.

"This man saved me from a misguided enchantress. However, she is now stuck in the tower she had kept me prisoner in. And while I was not happy to be imprisoned, I do not wish her to waste away in that tower."

Swords lowered, heads cocked, and gazes moved from me to Zach and back.

"What is this garbage?" the lead guard snarled, his glare hard enough to make me swallow and reach inside for my magic.

A small group of guards came out of the gate that I recognized. My stomach dropped as the lead guard stared at me with narrowed eyes. He was the one I'd convinced that Midnight was mine in the clearing.

"She is a witch," he announced, pointing at me.

All the swords rose, pointing at us.

Zach tightened his grip on me. "Do you really want me to unleash my darkness?"

The guards stared back warily.

"Let us pass." This time it was delivered as a growling command.

I didn't dare glance back at him. The silver glow at the corner of my eye told me enough. I had seen what happened to Zach when he allowed the darkness to overtake him. While I knew he wouldn't hurt me, I couldn't guarantee he wouldn't wipe these men out.

The head of the guard paled and backed his horse out of the way, allowing us to move through the gates of his father's kingdom. People stopped in the streets and just stared at us, scrambling out of the way as we passed. Crowds parted until we came to the palace.

The king stood on the top step with his sword drawn and his free hand clenched in a fist. The muscles in his jaw jumped. His green eyes glared at his only remaining son. "Take him to the gallows!" he bellowed.

They dragged Zach from the horse, but didn't touch me.

"I will deal with you after." He pointed the sword at me and turned, following the crowd.

I jumped off Midnight and forced my way through the crowd. By the time I cleared most people, I got a clear view of Zach with his head clamped in the gallows. The blade at the top shined even through the streaks of rust.

His father climbed the steps and reached for the handle that would release the blade.

"I should have killed you the moment your mother pushed you out into this world." His voice bellowed in anger and disgust.

Zach's gaze scanned the crowd until he found mine. My magic sizzled the moment his father pulled the cord.

"I bring the light!" My call filled the air along with the streak of magical protection that raced towards Zach. I wasn't sure it would get there in time as gravity pulled the blade fast towards his throat.

My feet pushed forward in a dead run as panic pulsed through my veins. Heads turned in my direction. Zach's eyes widened.

The blade collided with my power and it, along with the entire gallows holding Zach, turned to dust.

Zach stood, dusting off his clothing before turning to his stunned father. "Light bringers don't save the damned," he said. "And dark bringers don't murder on a whim." He turned to me and started in my direction.

I was almost to the stage when pain pierced through me.

Zach's face altered, and he charged, screaming words that failed to register. My gaze moved to the other side of the stage where his father had been standing. The king lowered the bow with a satisfied glare. I looked down at the arrow piercing my chest and then up just in time for Zach to catch me.

"Danae!"

His bellow jarred me, as did the snap of wood. Zach flung the two pieces of the arrow away and pressed his hands on the wounds on my back and on my chest.

He leaned close. "You are the light," he said as tears tumbled from his eyes. "Banish the darkness," he added and pressed his lips to mine.

Confusion clouded my mind along with a fading light. My heartbeat slowed, and I had trouble drawing a breath. Zach's tongue swiped mine, creating a dark tingle in my soul. His last words made no sense. Then I felt the burn of dark poison filling the hole the arrow had made. I screamed under his lips, arching against the pain. White light filled the air, clearing a path right through me.

Air filled my lungs and feeling tingled back through me as my body infused with renewed strength. When the light faded, I stood over a pale-looking man with fading green eyes. He smiled up at me, and it took me a moment to recognize Zach. I blinked, and my heart roared in my chest as the world buzzed around me.

"No, no, no." I dropped to my knees. Tears blurred my eyes and splashed on his cheeks.

"I owe you a debt, witch," his father said from on stage.

Zach's memories swarmed, showing me exactly what had happened throughout the years. The manipulations of his brother, the damnation from his father.

I turned, sending every memory at his father in a blast of angry light. The surge lit up the king, lifting him into the air. His eyes rolled back, and when the last of Zach's memory faded, I closed my fist, releasing the king. He slammed down on the wood and fell to his knees.

"You were too blind to see," I snarled and turned back to Zach.

Zach's eyes were closed, but his cheeks weren't as pale as they had been. Another one of my tears landed on his forehead. Light flared, sparkling over his skin. I reached out to cup his cheek, and the moment our skin met, he pulled in a great breath and his eyes shot open.

That familiar green and silver intertwined in his irises, and he covered my hand with his own.

People backed away at the spectacle of lightning bursts that surrounded us. Some fell to their knees.

I stroked his cheek. "I bring the light," I whispered and smiled through a sheen of tears.

"I bring the dark," he said and sat up, capturing my mouth in a kiss that left me breathless. When he pulled away, he stared deep into my eyes. "Together, we rule the land."

I cocked an eyebrow at him, and he grinned, shrugging.

"Or we can just roam from place to place. Whatever you please, Princess."

I looked around at the fear carved into the surrounding faces, and then my gaze landed on the king. He was on the podium with his face in his hands, sobs filtering out between his fingers.

I turned back to Zach. "I think you need to have a conversation with your father."

He glanced up at where his father sat crying. "What did you do to him?"

"I gave him your memories," I said.

His gaze snapped to mine, and his mouth popped open.

"I helped the blind see the truth." I pressed my lips to Zach's, and then we stood. My protections still sparked around us because I did not trust the crowd at our backs. Nor did I trust the man sobbing on the stage.

Zach cleared his throat. "Father?"

The king startled and looked up from his hands. He blinked and his composure came roaring back, along with a glare. "What did you do to me, witch?"

"She is a light bringer. The last light bringer. And you almost killed her," Zach said, his voice going hard. "She is the one I was created to save."

"That's impossible. The last light bringer died in the Courtland castle fire twenty years ago."

"Her name is Danae," Zach said, staring down at his father.

He blinked and brought his gaze to me as if seeing me for the first time. His eyes grew into large saucers. He jumped to his feet and turned towards a cowering squire near the platform. "Get me the last painting of the Antaries royal family!" When the squire didn't move, he bellowed, "Now!"

The crowd swarmed closer, and the king glanced at Zach with a wary eye.

"I gave you his memories. Are you still so blinded by your faith in your eldest son not to believe what I allowed to be shared?" I asked.

The king looked at me and then out into the crowd. "After Zacharia left, the killings stopped," he said, still denying the truth I'd shared with him.

I gritted my teeth and squeezed Zach's hand tighter. The lightning surrounding us flared with my agitation. "In all the years since he left, had there ever been rumors of the same mutilations occurring wherever he had been seen?"

His father's gaze slowly lifted to mine, and the color bled from his cheeks. He slowly shook his head.

"As a matter of fact, all the rumors that made their way back to you proved the exact opposite. Didn't they?" I couldn't help the contempt in my voice.

His gaze dropped to the ground.

Before he could answer, the squire ran onto the platform with a large frame in his hand and turned it towards the king. There, in a full-color painting, was a woman who could have been my twin, holding a swaddled infant as a stately man stood behind them with his hand on her shoulder.

I stared at my likeness, and an icy shiver gripped me. These were my parents. I glanced at Zach, who unthreaded his fingers from mine and wrapped his arm around my shoulder, pulling me close.

His father turned back to us and cleared his throat. His hands wrestled together nervously, and he looked out over the people of his kingdom. He cleared his throat. "It seems I have made a grave mistake," he started and glanced down at Zach. "I have blamed the wrong son for the horrors that befell our land, and my youngest son is not the monster I painted him out to be." He rubbed his face. "It seems he may have saved the kingdom from a darkness far greater than I could ever perceive, and I hope someday he will find it in his heart to forgive me."

Zach pulled me tighter to his side and planted a kiss on my forehead.

"Oh, and Princess Danae of Antaries did not pass in that fire after all." He waved towards me. "I give you the last light bringer."

We turned towards the crowd, and the murmurs fell silent. Slowly, the entire population dropped to their knee, bowing.

I glanced at Zach and back at his father, who had adopted the same pose. The king was bowing to me. I blinked.

Zach chuckled. "Welcome to the real world, Princess Danae."

TANGLED Chapter 10

THE KING SAT AT the feast table, and Zach and I took the seats opposite him. A bounty of food graced the tabletop, but I wasn't hungry. I had more pressing issues now that it seemed we were accepted into the fold.

"Your Highness, I need to try to save the enchantress." I picked at the food Zach put in front of me. "I cannot let her languish in that tower."

"But you would have her waste away in a dungeon?" he asked around a chicken leg.

I sighed and glanced at Zach.

"We can't just let her go. She murdered your parents, and hid you away for twenty years," he said.

"I do not want her blood on my hands."

"What would you have us do with such a criminal?" the king asked.

I leaned back in the chair and shrugged. "I don't know. What she did was horrible and unforgiving. But she did not treat me harshly.

She taught me to read, to cook, to sing. She made me laugh and feel safe whenever she was present. It wasn't a terrible life, just limited. And yes, I realize she used me for her own gain, but..." I shook my head. "I suppose if I remembered anything about my parents, I might feel differently."

They both ate in silence, weighing my words.

"You need to eat," Zach said, pointing to the plate in front of me.

"I need to keep my word," I said. "I told her I would try to find a way, and sitting here eating this feast while she starves to death is not... palatable to me." I pushed the chair back and walked out of the room. Frustration itched at my skin. I stepped outside onto the balcony, breathing in the cool air.

Zach's hands landed on my shoulders. "Are you sure about this?" he asked. "She is a powerful enchantress, and while you and I are now immune to her spells, none of these people are." He waved his hand over the town below. "People could get hurt." He wrapped his arms around me and held me to his chest. "She is dangerous, Danae."

"So, we let her die in the tower? That doesn't feel right."

He sighed in my ear. "No, it doesn't. But neither does unleashing her wrath on our kingdom."

"Perhaps we can save more than just her physical being," I said. "Maybe the simple act of trying to save her after all she put us through would break through her evil core."

"You are an optimist, Princess." He kissed my temple. "I will gather some men and head out in the morning."

"I'm coming with you." I turned in his arms.

He shook his head.

"I *am* the light."

He rolled his eyes. "Yes, you are. And I would prefer..."

"To keep me safe? To keep me locked up in this castle?" I challenged him, raising my eyebrow to punctuate my words. "I don't think so."

His lips thinned, and his brow furrowed. "Damn it, Danae," he muttered. "That's not fair. I'm in love with you, so yes, I want to keep you safe from harm. I don't want to keep you locked up just for myself." He cocked his head. "Well, maybe I do, but not for the reasons that witch did." He smiled at me, and the warmth radiating from him seeped into my skin, heating my soul.

"But you can't keep me buffered from the world. I need to experience it, and I want to be by your side while I do. We are more powerful together than we are apart."

He sighed and glanced out over the kingdom. "Fine. You can ride with us."

I hugged him tight and then peeled away from his arms. My stomach growled. It was time to eat to prepare for our journey in the morning. Back inside, Zach held my chair for me and pushed it to the table when I sat.

"She is going with us tomorrow," Zach said and took the seat next to me.

His father wiped his mouth and leaned back in his chair, studying me. "Light bringer, you are truly an enigma."

I smiled.

"You remind me of your mother," he said. "She was full of spirit, and there was no other heart so full of love for her people than Queen Evelyn."

"And what of my father?"

"King James was a fine man. He did not need to rule with a heavy hand. His people would have laid down their lives for him like *that*." He snapped his fingers. "As much as I'd like to think I am a fitting king, I could never measure up to him as either a ruler or a father." Red bloomed in his cheeks. "I obviously lack the skills to ferret out where a problem truly lies." He waved towards Zach, and his gaze dropped to the table.

"I forgive you," Zach said.

His father rose from his seat. "But I don't forgive myself. I have a lot of making up to do." He traded glances with Zach and gave a nod before he left us alone in the dining hall.

"Thank you," Zach said after his father left the room.

"Huh?" I mumbled around a bite of warm chicken pie.

"For making him see the truth," he said, still looking at the empty doorway.

"Considering you somehow saved my life, and I almost took yours in the process, I think we are even." I dabbed the corners of my mouth with a cloth.

He caressed my cheek with the back of his knuckles.

"You're really in love with me?" I cocked one eyebrow at him.

"I have been since the moment I first kissed you."

I smiled and focused on my food. I had yet to declare my feelings. Being near him was like being forever bathed in sunlight. Warmth flooded every cell, making my skin tingle. When I thought I'd lost him, my heart felt like it exploded in my chest and all that was left was an empty husk. When he touched me, my soul burned for him.

He shifted in the seat next to me. "You don't feel the same?" he asked, his voice timid and almost shy.

I put down my food and turned towards him. "Words aren't enough to describe how I feel." I took his hands in mine and opened the gates to the sensations he brought forth inside me. I let him see what was in my soul. The slow smile that spread on his lips made my heart skip a beat.

I pulled my hands away from his. I had not had my fill of food yet and focused on quieting the beast growling in my abdomen.

When I finally finished, Zach led me to my bedchambers. He opened the door to a room that rivaled the size of my tower and a bed that was double what I'd had for the last twenty years. "You can stay here tonight. I'll send a servant to wake you in the morning."

I turned. "Can you drum up some clean clothing?" I asked, waving at my soiled and torn dress. "This dress has seen better days and I would appreciate something clean to wear that didn't have my dried blood on it."

He glanced at my dress, and then down at his equally soiled clothing. Neither one of us had changed from our trials out by the hanging posts.

"I'll make sure you have clean clothes for the ride." He turned to leave.

"You're not staying?"

He paused in the doorway and glanced over his shoulder at me. "Your virtue would be in danger if I slept in the same room with you." He closed the door on any further conversation.

I sighed, peeled off the bloody dress, and crawled under the crisp sheets, shifting until I found a comfortable position. Exhaustion weighed my muscles and my eyes closed. Sleep dragged me away to a land of laughter and love.

TANGLED Chapter 11

THE KNOCK ON MY door startled me from sleep. I sat up, disoriented in the darkened room. The door creaked open, and a spry little girl came inside, carrying clothing for me.

"The prince asked me to bring you some proper riding attire," she said and put them on the chair by the dressing table. "He said to be ready within the hour." She bowed and left the room.

I climbed out of bed, found the chamber pot, and did my business before dressing in the leather riding pants and button-down shirt. I pulled the straps over my shoulders, tucking in the shirt's tail. Thick socks and boots that came to my knees were next. I crossed to the curtains and threw them open to a still dark sky. The sun hadn't even come up.

I grabbed the riding coat and put it on as I headed out of the room. The girl that delivered my clothes waited to escort me to the dining hall. I stepped inside, looking identical to everyone in the room.

Zach looked up from his seat and smiled, then stood and crossed to me. "You even look lovely in a guard's uniform."

"I was thinking you would find me a proper riding dress," I whispered and looked around him at the twenty men stuffing their faces with sweetbreads.

"I have asked that the staff find you some proper dresses for when we get back," he said. "But I think you'll find you are warmer and end up with fewer saddle sores with this than with a dress." He reached back and patted my butt. "Now go grab some food. There's no telling when we will have another decent meal."

I did as he asked, and he followed me into the heart of the room. No one paid me any notice, but Zach stayed close. When I looked across the table, the man on the other side was staring at me through a black eye. His jaw hung open.

He was the thug who had grabbed me in the clearing when Zach and I were ambushed. Fear bloomed, creating a hot flush through my form. I reached back and yanked on Zach's arm.

He turned, and I pointed a shaky finger at the man.

"I'm aware," Zach said. "They missed yesterday's festivities, but my father has brought thcm up to speed. And we have already had a little chat." He rubbed his knuckles. "Haven't we, Timothy?"

His mouth popped closed and his gaze dropped to the table. "Please accept my apology, my lady," he muttered and got up from the table, leaving Zach and me staring after him.

I turned back to Zach. "Can you trust these men?" I whispered.

"They are loyal to the king," he said and nodded. "To a fault, as we found out."

"Yes, but are they loyal to you?"

"Now they are, considering I am the rightful heir to the throne."

"What did your father tell them?" I asked, scanning the room.

"That we are going after the enchantress that killed your parents and she should be brought back alive to stand trial for her misdeeds." He glanced at me. "When we get there, I will be the one that goes up the ladder to retrieve her."

I bit my lip.

"No. Don't even ask," he said, reading into whatever facial expression I had been conveying. "You are not going up there. Period. And I'm not having any of these men go, either. She could cast one of her spells."

I studied my hands and nodded. While I didn't like the idea of him risking his life, at least I knew she could do him no harm.

When we got outside, the horses were lined up, and Zach took me to Midnight. "You're taking my girl, so you behave. We have a good day's ride ahead of us before we get to the tower," he said to the horse.

Midnight whinnied like he understood, and Zach helped me into the saddle, handing me the reins before he mounted the gray speckled stallion in front of us.

We cantered out of the kingdom with Zach leading the way. As soon as we hit the open fields, he sped to a gallop. I held on to the reins and the edge of the saddle until I got the cadence of movement, so every hoof beat didn't result in a jarring of my spine. Once I got the motion, the gallop exhilarated me.

Midnight moved alongside Zach and he smiled over at me. Both of them had been the only creatures to successfully find the tower on multiple occasions, and while I was sure Zach knew the way, I was skeptical of Midnight as he pulled into the lead. Zach coaxed his horse parallel to us.

"Let me lead," he said. "Otherwise, you'll make these other horses drop."

Midnight slowed a fraction, letting Zach take the lead.

"I swear this horse understands you," I said.

Zach just grinned and shrugged. "He does," he said and slowed as we approached the woods.

Midnight relinquished control and let Zach take the lead as we rode single file on the slim path.

We stopped at a stream to let the horses rest and drink. Zach pulled out a couple of wrapped sweetbreads and handed them to me before dipping in his bag for more. The rest of the crew were doing the same.

It didn't take long before Zach gave the order to remount the horses. By the time we crested the last hill, twilight had descended. In the distance, I thought I could make out a shape, but my eyes deceived me, showing me nothing. Zach halted, and Midnight did the same next to him. The crew followed suit.

He squinted at the dark valley below. "We should make camp here and finish the journey in the morning."

I scanned the horizon again and saw nothing but mountains. No tall tower. No beacon of light shining high above the trees. Nothing. Unease filled me, and I shifted, torn between getting off this horse for a few hours and bolting ahead and letting Midnight lead the way. My sore bottom made the call, though, and I slid off the saddle, right into Zach's waiting arms.

The rest of the soldiers tied the horses up. They cleared off the grass and set up a rock perimeter where those who had disappeared into the woods came back and dumped wood into the center. Before long, they had a roaring fire and their bed mats laid out around the warmth.

I stood, scanning the valley.

"Can you see anything?" Zach asked from behind me.

"No." I shook my head, but something pulled at my center. It was like I knew we were close enough to see the structure, but my eyes just wouldn't quite make it out.

He stepped to my side and met my gaze. His brow creased. "I swear this is the valley."

I scanned the landscape. "I believe the tower is here. I can feel the familiar vibrations of it, but I just can't see it."

He took my hand in his. "Let's get some sleep. Maybe the daylight will illuminate the lost tower."

He led me back to the campfire, laid out a mat, and waved at it. "For you."

"What about you?"

Silence fell over the group as all eyes locked on us.

"I'm used to the dirt," he said and took a seat near me.

Talk picked up again, and Zach undid his saddlebag and handed me another wrapped morsel to eat along with his canteen. He tossed logs into the fire throughout the night as the crew slept.

I couldn't sleep. I just stared at the fire, gaining comfort from its warmth as well as having Zach nearby. He finally scooted even closer, and I laid my head on his thigh as he leaned on the saddlebag for support. His soft snore made me turn my head. Zach's chin rested on his chest and his arms crossed over his stomach. He looked just as angelic asleep as he did when he was staring into my eyes.

I smiled and turned my attention back on the dying fire. I tossed the nearest log onto the embers, and flames licked hungrily at the wood. One of the close soldiers stirred and glanced over at me.

"I can keep watch for the rest of the night," he said with a voice filled with sleep.

I smiled and gave him a nod of thanks.

"Zach," I whispered, and his eyes popped open. "Why don't you lie down with me to keep warm?"

He received a nod from the soldier who offered to take watch, and then he stretched out behind me, wrapping me in his arms. "Night, princess," he whispered, and then he started snoring again.

I tried to suppress a grin and met the now awake soldier's gaze. He gave me a smile and focused back on the fire. He hadn't been among the ones in the clearing. He had been in the courtyard when Zach and I nearly died. He'd witnessed the miracle we created with our powers, and that was the only reason I closed my eyes and allowed myself to drift off to sleep in Zach's arms.

"PRINCESS?" ZACH'S WHISPER TICKLED my ear.

I waved at the sensation. My hand smacked his cheek, and I opened my eyes. The group was packing their stuff already. I rolled and glanced at him.

"It's time to go," he said and brushed my hair away from my face.

Groggy and sore from yesterday's ride, I climbed to my feet and stretched, then stepped off the mat. Before I could reach down and grab it, Zach had it all rolled and tied to the back of his saddle.

He handed me the canteen and led me to the hill. We stood gawking at the empty valley. I blinked and went to look away, but something out of the corner of my eye caught my attention. I squinted, and my eyes widened.

I was on Midnight in a flash, riding ahead of all the others, straight towards where the tower had once stood. I slowed Midnight as I approached the smoldering rubble. The ground around the base shimmered with melted gold where the strands of my hair had been. Zach stopped next to me, and we both sighed.

"No wonder we couldn't see the tower," he said.

"I need to know if she was in there." I met his gaze as I dismounted.

He hopped to the ground, as did the others.

"It's still hot," I said, pushing a burned stone aside with my toe.

"Is this gold?" one soldier asked, dipping his sword into the soft melted metal.

Zach and I exchanged a glance. "Yes," I said after a moment. "But it is cursed, so be wary of letting it touch your skin."

All the men took a step away from the golden puddle, making their way as far from it as possible.

"Why don't you stay over there," Zach said, pointing towards an unsinged tree trunk a few feet away. "That way, if this rubble shifts, there is no chance of you getting hurt."

I didn't argue. I took Midnight by the reins, led him to the spot Zach had indicated, and took a seat on the stump.

The men poked with their swords and shifted rubble with their boots, cautious of the still smoldering piles. Zach pulled something out with his sword. Half charred and half gold.

I gasped at the skull as it slid the length of his sword. He turned my way and unceremoniously dumped it between us. We both stared at what was left of the enchantress. The gold preserved half her face, but the skull side was just charred bone. I stared at the horrified half scream forever encased in gold and shivered, turning away.

Whatever ailments I had wished on Gwendolyn for what she had done to me and my family, this was not the way I wished her life to end. In flames and partially preserved by the melted gold that had once been the braid she'd used to climb up the tower.

"We are done here," Zach said to the men and then turned to me, pointing at the congealing gold. "We can't just leave this here."

I bit my lip and turned, looking at all the horses. My gaze landed on the rolled bed mats. I didn't know if it would work or not, but we had to try. I wasn't sure if the curse Zach placed on the gold was truly gone. The only thing we could do was cover it and hope no one attempted to dig up the rubble.

"The bed mats." I pointed.

His eyebrows arched, and then he glanced at the puddle. "We need to cover the gold with our mats and then try to cover it with dirt, so no one removes any of it and carries the curse with them."

Without question, they collected their field bedding and arranged it so none of the gold bled through. Then they kicked dirt, rocks, and ash on the liners. They used one of the rope ladders to topple the remaining portion of a standing wall down onto the mats. By the time the men finished, they had eliminated any visuals of the gold and made it look natural as opposed to someone trying to cover up a hidden treasure.

I was impressed. My gaze landed on the skull a few feet away from me. An icy shiver returned.

Zach approached me, taking a knee in front of me. "What would you like me to do about..." He nodded towards the skull.

"Bury it."

He stood and turned. Finding a soft spot in the soil, he dug, but the guards took over until it was deep enough that a scavenger wouldn't dig it up. They used their boots to roll the skull into the hole and then covered it neatly.

They stepped back, allowing me to come forward for a moment. It was as if they knew I was conflicted about this woman. My chest hurt, and my eyes misted with tears. I mourned a woman most would have spit on, but the only thing that kept coming to mind was the means by which she cared for me and not how she used me for her gain.

Zach wrapped an arm around my shoulder. "Come on," he whispered in my ear. "We have a long ride back."

I glanced up at him and then at the group of soldiers. "Thank you," I said and received silent nods as they dispersed and readied their horses.

"Looks like we are all sleeping in the dirt tonight," Zach said and led the filthy entourage back toward the castle.

TANGLED Chapter 12

I SAT IN FRONT of a dressing table in a slip that someone had retrieved for me. My skin was dry and clean after a much-needed bath. I combed my short hair away from my face, working the miniscule knots out with care. It was nothing like brushing my multi-yard mane I'd had, but it still soothed me.

Since we'd returned from the destroyed tower, Zach had been sequestered by his father and the brigade we traveled with. The trip drained me both physically and mentally, and I didn't have the energy to even speak to the servants who'd drawn my bath.

I had stayed in the water until the warmth had long since fled the tub and every speck of grime had disappeared from my skin. Even wet, my hair remained as golden as it had ever been. Out of curiosity, I plucked a stray hair. The thin filament solidified into a gold strand between my fingers. I placed it gently on the center of the dressing table with a sigh.

I set the brush down and turned, crossing to the fine dress laid out on the bed, but all I really wanted to do was crawl under the covers and let sleep take me into tomorrow.

The creak of the door spun me around. Zach stepped inside, closing the door behind him. He slowed as his gaze landed on me in just a silk slip. He stopped a few feet from me. His mouth moved, but nothing came out.

He cleared his throat. "I should have knocked." Color bloomed in his cheeks. "I can come back," he said and hooked his thumb over his shoulder.

His presence gave me a surge of energy. I didn't want him to leave and have the utter exhaustion return.

I stepped closer, and sparks surged between us. "I am glad to see you," I said, closing the distance.

He let out a laugh and took a step back. "Maybe you should put some clothes on." His voice came out low and husky, and his breath quickened.

I looked down at the silk covering me. "I do have clothes on."

His green eyes shimmered with silver streaks as he stared at me, and then he moved, crossing the distance with purpose. His lips crushed mine, sweeping me backwards until we crashed into the bed. His hands traveled over the silk as warmth ignited in my core.

Zach pulled away and stepped back with his hands out to his sides. The muscles in his jaw jumped, and he closed his eyes. His nostrils flared as he inhaled through his nose. When his eyes opened, silver streaks of lightning lit up his irises. "I keep forgetting how innocent you are."

I reached out and grabbed a handful of his shirt, pulling him back against me. "Maybe I'm not as innocent as you think." I needed him near me for more than just the energy burst. The last two nights sleeping in his arms had been the highlight of the trip. It dulled the pain from a loss that shouldn't be affecting me this way.

He laughed and wrapped his arm around me. "I'm the only man you've ever kissed."

"True."

"And you are aware that I want to do a whole lot more than just kiss you," he said, raising his eyebrows.

Heat filled my cheeks. I was acutely aware of the longing in his gaze. It matched the raw need pulsing in my own veins. I nodded slowly.

The smile that played on his lips heated my skin and made my heart beat harder in my chest. The hunger that gripped me had nothing to do with food, and I licked my lips.

"Danae," he whispered.

"Zacharia," I whispered back.

"I'm trying to be good."

"Why?"

He stared at me for so long that I didn't think he would answer.

"Because I want our wedding night to be your first time." He stepped back, fumbled in his pocket, and dropped to his knee. He opened his hand, revealing a beautiful ring. "This isn't quite what I had planned, but will you marry me, Danae?"

I stared at the ring and shot my gaze to his. My stomach fluttered, and my heart expanded in my chest. My vision clouded behind a sudden sheen of tears. I suddenly understood what genuine joy was. My hands covered my mouth, and I blinked. Hot paths tickled my cheeks.

He cocked his head, and his smile faded.

I realized I had never spoken. I never acknowledged his question. "Yes." I gasped through my fingers. His shining smile flashed at me, and his eyes sparkled.

He stood and slipped the ring on my finger. The diamond was surrounded by slivers of jade that matched his eyes. "This was my mother's ring."

My heart squeezed at the sentiment. It wasn't a ring picked out at the marketplace. It was something with a deeper meaning.

I pressed my lips together as more hot tears cut paths down my cheeks. "It's beautiful," I whispered.

"*You* are beautiful." He leaned in, capturing my lips in a tender, sweet kiss that had no intention of anything more.

But I ran my hands into his hair, holding his mouth to mine as our tongues played in languid circles, igniting the heat that seared through my soul.

When he pulled away, I groaned, thinking he was going to leave me with this shaking need that I had no idea how to satiate.

Instead, he slid the straps of my slip off my shoulders, and the silk fell to the floor. His gaze fell with the fabric, and when it returned to mine, it burned through me.

"I don't think I can wait," he said, his voice full of the shaky heat flushing my form.

I reached for the buttons on his shirt, undoing each one as quickly as my hands would allow. The fabric covering his chest shed to the floor, and my fingertips slid down his defined muscles. Need closed the distance between us, and his lips found mine again. The dress laid out on the bed was flung to the floor, and he picked me up and set me down in its place.

His hands and mouth trailed down my body, creating tingles that shot right to my core. Every motion, every lick of his tongue sent heated lightning through me, and the air surrounding us echoed with it. By the time he returned to my lips, I was ready, but he just stretched out between my legs with his pants still on. The slow grind of his hips against mine pulled a moan from my lips.

He smiled down at me, his breathing labored, and he closed his eyes, stilling his body.

I gasped. "Zach." I did not want this heaven to end.

He clenched his teeth together and slowly opened his eyes. With a strained smile, he pulled away. "As much as I want to take you right now…"

I leaned my head back and groaned. My heart raced with adrenaline and disappointment. The duality of both did nothing to quell the heat gripping me.

"When are we getting married?" I asked, my voice raspy with the need racking my form.

"Whenever you would like," he said.

I shot my gaze to his. "Right now."

He winked at me. "Royal weddings take time," he teased and licked my throat. "But I could be convinced to sneak away to the chapel and have the priest marry us right now if you'd like." He settled on me again and circled his hips, slowly grinding his hardness against me.

"Yes!" I said breathlessly and yanked his mouth to mine. Not only did the frantic kiss broadcast my feelings on the matter, but his low groan only heightened the throbbing need inside me.

He laid his forehead on my shoulder, blowing air out between his lips. I circled my hips in response, and he tilted his head, giving me a sideways glance.

"Fuck it," he growled.

I didn't think it was humanly possible to take off a pair of pants in the millisecond he did, but before I could catch my breath, his member was as deep inside me as possible. My eyes widened with the bloom of pain, overriding the pleasure.

Zach closed his eyes as a soft smile spread across his lips. "You are heaven." His eyes opened and met mine. The slow cadence of his motion soothed all the initial pain. He didn't rush but took his time, and each time I peaked, he would slow back down to start the build-up again.

Sweat broke out on his brow, matching the glistening on my skin.

"I could hear you call my name forever," he said, his voice deep and rough, reflecting the wild silver dance in his irises.

This time, when the wave rushed over me, tingling right down to my toes, his body tightened, and his eyes clamped shut.

"Danae," he groaned in such ecstasy, my body responded in kind.

I pulled him to my lips, kissing him as both our bodies relaxed into languid puddles of flesh.

He rolled off me. "We should probably go to the chapel now."

"I can't move." Every muscle quivered with pleasure. "I may never move again," I said with a sigh and a smile.

"Well, here's the thing. People are waiting for us."

I lifted my head. "Who?"

He pressed his lips together in a smile of apology. "My father, the priest, the king's guard. I think perhaps the town may have gotten word as well."

"Of what?"

He reached for his pants and pulled them on before glancing at me. His cheeks bloomed red. "The wedding."

I stared at him and blinked.

He picked up the dress that had been laid out for me. "You were supposed to be in this when I came in." He bit his lip.

I slowly sat up, inspecting the dress he held. It was fancier than what the enchantress left me to wear, and I hadn't noted the intricate beading or the lace bodice, or the fact it was ivory.

"It was my mother's, too."

"You're serious?" I jumped up and swiped the slip off the ground, throwing it on in haste. My heart hammered in my chest, and I stepped in front of the mirror. My cheeks had red splotches and my hair was a mess that I didn't think a brush could fix.

Zach came up behind me and put his hands on my shoulders. "Relax. You look beautiful."

Of all the wedding fantasies I'd dreamed up over the years, this wasn't one of them, but just the look in his jovial eyes calmed me. I ran my hands through my hair and then the brush until I was satisfied that no more knots existed. When I turned, he was in his fine clothes and had the dress ready for me to step in. His fingers against my back sent tingles through me, already reviving that ceaseless hunger I had experienced earlier today. I glanced over my shoulder at him as he finished buttoning my dress. It fit almost as if it had been made for me.

He smiled, glancing at me in the mirror. "Are you ready for this?"

I stared into his sincere gaze. "Yes."

He grinned and held his arm out. Interlocking mine in his, we waltzed out of the bedchamber as if walking on the clouds themselves.

The End

Will the ice queen keep her royal station, or will the fight for the throne end in a bloody battle?

Elsa must marry before midnight of her twenty-fifth year or lose her kingdom. The only problem is that no man in Bryggen can be near her without getting frostbite.

Kyle Bryggen, the founder of the kingdom Elsa rules, has been in hibernation for two hundred years, and now he is awake and wants his kingdom back.

They could be a match carved in ice, except every time they meet, they want to kill each other.

When a diabolical senator manipulates the law to his own purpose, Elsa must choose between the lesser of two nightmares.

One will lead to the ruin of her kingdom, and the other will lead to her death.

FROZEN Chapter 1

I STOOD ON THE balcony of my castle overlooking Bryggen and the ocean beyond, my heart heavy with my responsibility. The fall air, chilly and refreshing, did nothing for my mood. I sighed. This was the year I had to find my soulmate, or otherwise, my kingdom would be lost.

My sister, Anna, found her true love many years ago, and she and Kris had been together ever since. They even had a horde of children running around the castle, making it a lively place to be. While I got to play the doting aunt, it also served as a reminder that the clock was ticking away.

If I didn't find someone soon, my ability to produce an heir to the throne would be nullified, and with it, our family's reign would end. While Anna was my sister, and her children my kin, the senate had made it clear that the offspring of a woodsman were not to be named king.

It was such a silly rule, but one I had no power to overturn. Because the senate was so divided on the issue, they'd put it to a public vote. While this lovely kingdom of Bryggen professed their love of my sister any chance they got, they revealed their true prejudices.

I almost froze the entire kingdom on the spot when the senate announced the results, but Anna assured me she did not want her children to take the throne. I still didn't know if she truly felt that way, or if she'd said what she had to quell my fury.

Either way, the bitter pill I'd had to swallow still tainted the back of my throat.

So, the burden of a successor lay with me, or otherwise the head of the senate, Aaron Brax, would take the throne. He was neither just nor compassionate, and I would hate to see him become the ruler over Bryggen.

The senate gave me five years to find a man suitable to be the father of the kingdom's heir. They expected me to step down either way and to be *"attentive to womanly responsibilities,"* as Senator Brax had put it so eloquently when they'd announced the directive.

Since my parents passed, and I took the throne, Brax had been volleying for my demise.

This was the last year I had to choose a king. If I was not betrothed by the last toll of the bell on New Year's Eve, Senator Brax would become king.

"What are you thinking about?" Anna's singsong voice pierced my thoughts as she stepped beside me.

I glanced at my sister with her dark hair and bright green eyes, a polar opposite to my light locks and blue eyes. Happiness radiated from her the way the cold emitted from me. Having her so near tempered the darkness in my soul.

"I was thinking this year would be the year I find someone able to bear with me." I smiled, softening the words so my aggravation didn't bleed into them.

Anna slung her arms around me and gave me a tight hug, along with a peck on my cheek. "That would be divine!"

I chuckled and turned away from the town below. "I think the fresh air of the mountains is just the thing I need today." I headed inside with the purpose of escaping my thoughts, and this town for a little while.

"I'll go with you." Anna trailed behind me.

"I need some alone time." I glanced back at her. "I have to figure out what to do in the event I can't find someone to put up with me."

Her smile faltered, but she nodded, halting in the hallway as I headed for the back door. She knew where I was headed.

My ice castle still sat at the top of the snowcapped mountain. The freezing temperatures offered me solace and comfort when I couldn't find inner peace in the kingdom below. My escape beckoned.

FROZEN Chapter 2

THE GLISTENING ICE WELCOMED me, and I sighed, climbing the clear steps cascading over a deep chasm. My footing didn't falter on the slick stairs, but I knew well enough that the abyss below had claimed many careless trespassers. Only those familiar with the ice dance seemed to scale the hazard without issue.

The door to my sanctuary stood ajar. I blinked at the breach, and a shiver captured me as if a spirit had walked across my grave. I pushed the door all the way open and paused. I strained to hear anything that would give me an indication of who the intruder was. No sounds drifted my way, so I slipped inside as quietly as possible, ready to blast anything that moved. Fortunately, there was no motion. Not in the grand foyer that shimmered with silver icicles. The simple beauty always took my breath away.

On light feet, I crossed to the heart of the castle, where I used to spend most of my time standing in front of an ice fire of my making. The hearth sat barren, but the white fur ball in the far corner made my heart skip. I gasped at the sight of the enormous polar bear.

His massive head lifted, and blue eyes peered at me from across the room. They widened, and then the beast was on his feet, rearing up to ten feet tall with a roar.

"Don't be growling at me. This is my home. You're the squatter," I yelled with my fingers splayed at the ready, cocking my head to make my point.

The beast dropped to all fours with a grunt and circled around me.

The closer he came, the more nervous I got, but he had done nothing to raise my hackles enough to blast him with ice. Yet.

As he passed behind me, I turned my head to catch him rounding again, but he wasn't there. A low chuckle came from right behind me. I spun, almost letting ice fly. At the last second, I curled my hands into fists, stopping whatever damage I was about to inflict on the handsome man standing where the bear should have been.

His hair was as white as the polar bear's fur, and the same blue eyes peered down at me through wayward bangs as he towered over my tall frame. He was just as formidable in human form as he had been as a bear.

"So, this is your place?" He waved at the ice surrounding us.

I stared at him, still stunned by the transformation. I had heard stories of the man-beasts when I was young, but never had the pleasure of meeting one. The fables of old said they were terrifying, dangerous killers who were to be avoided at all costs. A thrilling chill tickled my spine.

"Yes," I said after my full inspection of him.

"And you are?"

I laughed at him, and when he raised a single eyebrow, I said, "I am the queen of Bryggen."

Both his eyebrows rose in response. "I am king of the Hanseatic League."

I cocked my head. There was only one man who had ever declared himself king of the Hanseatic League, and Bryggen was named after him. But he had perished centuries ago. Kyle Bryggen was said to be ruthless in his quest for power, handsome as the devil, and he ruled the trade routes with an iron hand until the day he'd disappeared.

"There is no such thing," I said, narrowing my eyes at him. I relaxed my hands just in case I needed my icy will.

He smiled at me. "There used to be," he said and continued his circular study of me. "You enjoy the cold, queen of Bryggen?"

I kept quiet, watching him, wondering if he knew anything about me or my powers.

"Hmm?" He stopped pacing and leaned forward a little, his gaze piercing and inquisitive at the same time.

"What is your name?" I demanded, straightening my back.

"I think you already know what my name is. Just like I know exactly who you are. Elsa Glasere."

His voice dripped with vitriol as he said my name, like I had done something that warranted such dislike.

I took a step back, and a chill built in my palms. "Kyle?" I swallowed. "Kyle Bryggen?"

He nodded. "You woke me from my long slumber, young lady." He stepped closer, crowding me as a growl crept into his voice.

His dagger-like eyes pierced right through my soul and I moved back, right into the wall. He placed his hands on either side of my head. His sharp nails dug into the ice as he leaned close to my face. "I don't like being woken up."

I placed my palms on his chest and pushed with more than my physical strength. I blasted him across the room with an arctic wind. "I don't enjoy being cornered." I flipped a strand of hair out of my face and lifted my chin.

He hopped to his feet. His cocky anger was now replaced with wariness.

"I am the queen of Bryggen. And you will show me some respect."

"And if I don't?"

"I will put you in a deep freeze that will last another two hundred years."

His head tilted to the side like a lost puppy.

"If you know who I am, you must know what I can do."

"You melted the ice that blanketed this area. *That* is what woke me from the dead and left me ravenous enough to attack anything that happened my way. It has taken me years to find restraint again."

I didn't have the heart to tell him it was my sister's love that had cracked through the ice and let me reign in the frozen tundra. I had been surprised my ice castle remained, especially with the green hills and flower-filled valleys surrounding it. This haven, this snowy landscape, only encompassed the highest peak in the region. Halfway down the mountain face, the snowy landscape ceased.

Frustration clouded his gaze, and he took a step towards me.

I closed my eyes and concentrated. The same powerful storm that pushed him across the room brewed under my skin. I let it seep from my palms, controlling the gale into a graceful swirl of a breeze. When the first frigid flake touched my cheek, I opened my eyes. Snow gently fell in the space between us, and he stared at it with his mouth ajar.

"I brought the ice to Bryggen. I only meant to pull back what I had created." I closed my hands, and the snow stopped.

"Why did you pull back any of it?"

"Because, while you and I seem to be unbothered by the cold, the people within Bryggen don't have the same resilience." I studied his creased brow as he stared at the snow on the floor. "I am the ice queen."

His gaze snapped up to mine, and he crossed the distance between us in a less predatory manner, then stopped with enough distance to not encroach on my space.

"I made this palace you have decided to... invade." I waved at our glistening surroundings.

"You should learn to lock your doors."

I laughed. "The steps are deterrent enough."

For the first time since I'd laid eyes on him, dimples appeared and the briefest of smiles flashed. He gave me what I thought was a nod before he glanced up at the structure.

"Such attention to detail," he said, and this time his voice was not full of mockery or malice. "I think I'll keep it." His full smile appeared, but his eyes held the challenge his voice didn't carry.

I scoffed at him. "The hell you will."

"Who are you to stop me?" His hands found his hips.

His cocked eyebrow fueled my growing frustration. I raised my hands to show him, and within a blink, his oversized bear paws slammed against my palms, pinning me to the wall, blocking whatever assault I was about to launch. He had shifted so quickly I didn't have time to process the transformation.

He growled in my face, his sharp teeth close enough to tear out my throat. Instead of the fear any rightful person would feel, fury welled up, and I kneed the bastard with everything I had.

His eyes widened, and he grunted, dropping to his knees. The transition to human form was as immediate as his shift to bear had been. Pain webbed through his features as he cradled his balls.

I leaned close. "I expect you to be gone when I return." I stormed out and down the stairs, marching back to town with anger pounding in my veins.

Each audacious act of his flashed pure venom through me, and by the time I got back to my room in the palace proper, I could feel the ice radiating off my skin, matching my malignant rage.

FROZEN Chapter 3

A TENTATIVE KNOCK INTERRUPTED my agitated pacing. There was only one person who would ever dare to approach me when I was in this kind of mood. I closed my eyes and sighed when the door cracked open.

Anna's worried gaze peered around the door, reminding me of when she was a child. Her wide eyes diffused whatever leftover anger still pulsed at my temples. "The footman said you were on a tear."

The last time I was on a so-called tear, I had frozen the land. I laughed at the terminology and shook my head. "I just met someone that infuriated me. He basically has taken over my ice castle."

Her eyebrows rose, and her mouth popped open. She was probably the only one in this kingdom who knew what my ice castle meant to me.

"Someone is living there?"

Someone, something. I didn't quite know how to categorize Kyle Bryggen. Especially since he, by all rights, should be a pile of bones in a grave.

"Yes. And I told him he needs to be gone when I come back."

She blinked. "He?"

I rolled my eyes. "Yes. He." A broad smile broke out on Anna's face, and my eye-roll turned to a glare. "Don't even suggest it. He is way too..." I snapped my lips closed, trying to find the right word. "Infuriating."

Anna chuckled. "What does he look like?"

"A polar bear," I said. Shock registered on my sister's face, and it was my turn to laugh. "Yes, he is one of those things."

She gasped. "A man-beast?"

"Yes. And a royal pain in my ass," I mumbled as I turned away from her. I had to admit, in human form, he was quite pleasing to the eyes, and the white hair didn't detract from his rugged good looks. In fact, he looked only about ten years my senior at best. Being a man-beast certainly hadn't aged him, and he looked damn good for someone close to two hundred years old.

"If he was a bear, how do you know he was a man-beast?"

"Because he shifted." Sometimes Anna's brain didn't quite catch up, and I had to be patient while she connected the dots.

She chewed on her bottom lip. "So, what did he look like as a man?"

"Hair as white as a polar bear, eyes blue and icy, and the type of body that rivaled his polar bear form." Just describing him out loud sparked irritation. For as hot as the man was, he was an epic jerk. "But he had no manners."

"What did he do?"

"He decided that the ice castle was his for the taking."

She raised her eyebrows.

"He's lucky I didn't turn him into a giant ice cube."

"Did he try to take anything else?" Dread filled both her voice and her eyes.

I laughed and shook my head. "If he had, he would be an icicle." I stared out the window at the mountain. "I will go back tomorrow to make sure he heeded my orders."

"You can't go alone," Anna said.

I turned back to her. "Have you met me?"

Anna crossed her arms, and the glare she leveled made my skin prickle.

"He is too dangerous to bring anyone up there with me."

"All the more reason for you to take a dozen guards with you."

"The guards will slip off those stairs. You've seen it before. Besides, I can handle him." We both had witnessed the perils of those ice steps. I didn't want to be responsible for sending anyone to their death, either by falling into that endless chasm, or at the hands of Kyle Bryggen. I had no doubt that the heathen would kill on sight.

"Then I will go with you."

"Oh, hell no." There was no way I was letting her near the ice palace again. The last time she had been there, she almost died.

"Not after the last time you went. Besides, Kris would never forgive me if anything happened to you."

She pressed her lips into a thin line.

"If you make a big deal of this, I'll just give the man the palace."

Her arms slowly fell to her side and her eyes widened. She knew how much that place meant to me. I'd created it out of thin air, so the idea of giving it up to protect my little sister wasn't taken lightly.

"You aren't just saying that to make me back off, are you?" she asked once she seemed to recover from the shock.

"No. I can handle myself where the man-beast is concerned. But I can't handle him while I'm trying to protect someone else. We both know how bad I am at multitasking like that."

My gentle reminder set all her fight on pause. She gave me a nod and turned to leave. "Just promise you will be careful," she said from the doorway.

"I will." As soon as the door closed, I collapsed on the couch. I needed to go through the papers the senate had delivered this morning, but I wasn't in the mood to get more aggravated.

I closed my eyes. His face appeared on the back of my eyelids, and I growled, shooting to my feet. I needed to shake this fixation. I stomped over to my desk, took a seat, and started shuffling through the mundane paperwork.

The senate wanted to restrict where people emptied their chamber pots. I scribbled my name on that new law without delving into the pages of facts that accompanied the cover page. I could get on board with cleaning up the streets. It might be a pain to dig a hole for the waste, but it certainly was better than the free-flowing rivers of sludge that carved canals on each side of the road.

The next one perplexed me. They wanted to put a law in place that stated that the males of Bryggen starting at sixteen must go out and pillage nearby countries every five years. That one I read at least three times before I tore the paper in two. I would not condone that sort of act under my rule.

The last rule actually pulled a snorting laugh from my nose. They wanted me to sign a law that if a man challenges another to a fist fight to the death, he must accept or pay a penalty of four deer to the challenger. I sighed and closed my eyes. This was what men came up with when closed in a room for twelve hours at a clip. But at least this one gave the person challenged a way out of a fight to the death. I scrawled my name on the paper and set that aside.

The rest of the papers were updates on population statistics, tax collection values, and kingdom budget shortfalls and excesses. I scoured over each one. When I leaned back and rubbed my eyes, I felt more focused than when I'd started.

Unfortunately, *he* was still there, gnawing at the back of my mind.

My gaze pulled to the window and the snowy peak beyond.

"Damn it," I muttered and finished my daily sovereign duties.

FROZEN Chapter 4

THE NEXT MORNING, I woke before the sun rose and snuck from the palace. If I had waited until the sun broke the horizon, Anna would have been tailing me despite our conversation yesterday. I quickly slipped from the kingdom without notice of the dozing guards.

My journey to the mountain peak was quicker than it had been the other day, my purpose two-fold. I climbed the steps, but instead of entering the ice palace, I turned and stared over the valley just as the sun poked from the horizon, dousing the land in its honey-colored hue. With the beauty of the sunrise tempering my aggravation, I turned and marched into my ice castle.

The white fur in the corner set off another tirade of irritation.

"I thought I told you to be gone by the time I returned." My voice echoed, vibrating on the ice.

The bear gave me a cursory glance before turning away with a huff.

I took a step towards him.

"Don't."

The voice came from the stairwell, not the direction of the bear. I stopped short and turned. Kyle stood with bloody bandages in his hands. My eyes widened, and I scanned his form for the source of the wound.

"A hunter shot him," he said, nodding toward the bear in the corner.

A million questions fluttered in my head, and I blinked, turning back toward the bear. Was he one of them? Had he been here yesterday? Was he as good-looking as Kyle? The last question riled my feathers. I glanced back at the man who put the sizzle in my blood.

"Before you get that pretty little mind of yours in a tizzy at someone else squatting in your castle, he is injured and confused and will likely take off your head if you get any closer."

"Is he one of you?" I nearly spat out the words.

Kyle laughed. "No. I'm the only one left like me. No others survived." Bitterness crept into his voice. He turned and continued up the stairs with the bloodied bandages.

I stared at the bear and then scurried up the steps to find Kyle in my bedroom, where he stepped out onto the balcony and dropped the bloodied rags into the ravine. He turned, and his eyes narrowed at me.

"Are you here to make another sad attempt to kick me out?" He crossed his arms, smearing blood on his shirt.

I tore my eyes away from those crimson swaths and met his gaze. "I told you to be gone by the time I returned." I adopted the same stance as him, jutting my chin out with authority.

He crossed the distance and glared down his nose at me.

When he cocked his eyebrow, I opened my palms, intending to blast him into the ravine. Before I let my power loose, he had my wrists plastered to the wall far enough away from me that nothing I conjured would hit him. His body pressed against mine in a way that didn't allow me to use my knee like I had yesterday.

He stared down at me, and the corner of his lip turned up. Fire blazed in his gaze.

"I see you have not come to terms with the arrangement." His voice was soft, and yet it held an edge that sent a shiver down my spine.

"I built this palace," I snarled up at him.

"You are quite the engineer. But it is mine now."

I let out a guttural roar and tried to break his grip on me. He pressed his full weight against me.

"Are you trying to summon the bear?" A growl crept into his voice.

I continued struggling against his iron grip.

He leaned close to my ear. "I would heed my warning. The bear is hungry, and once he comes forth, I will not be able to stop him from ripping out your tender throat."

I stilled, wondering whether he was just saying that to get me to calm down or if he really was straining to hold the beast inside him.

He pulled away from my ear, meeting my gaze. His eyes were on the verge of wild and his jaw clenched as he held me in place. The pressure of his chest on mine increased with each deep breath of his.

His form molded to mine in a way that brought heat to my cheeks, as well as other places. I tried to shift under his weight to still the pounding in my chest. My heartbeat had traveled into the frenzied zone, and I wasn't sure if it was just from the anger biting at my skin.

I shook my head to get rid of the unwanted thoughts, and dimples appeared in his cheeks, despite the clench of his jaw.

"Have you gotten control over the mangy beast yet?" I asked.

His eyes narrowed and his dimples disappeared. "What if I said I just like being this close to you?"

He had the audacity to press his hips closer, making me hyperaware of his body. The hardness of it felt divine against me and made me wonder what it would be like to have him inside me instcad of trapping me against a wall.

I clenched my teeth and forced my wrists to bend far enough to send a blast of ice towards his head. I missed, but just the action made his face turn red and his lips press into a line that made them nonexistent.

His chest rumbled with a growl, and before my eyes, he shifted. The polar bear's weight pressed the air from my lungs, and his paws nearly crushed my wrists. I couldn't air the scream trapped in my lungs until he leaned back enough to aim his fanged mouth at my throat.

The bear bellowed and spun away from me. I crumpled to the ground, gasping for breath, and stared at the arrow sticking out from the creature's backside as he charged towards the bedroom door.

A glimpse of a figure with long brown hair dodging him set my heart back into overdrive. Without thinking, I shot my palms at the bear and captured him in a wall of ice.

Anna stood just beyond him with a bow, trying to thread the arrow into it with hands that shook too much. If I hadn't made Kyle into an icicle, she would be dead. She ran to me, dropping the bow and arrow on the floor before throwing her arms around my neck.

The crack of ice caused me to push Anna behind me. Kyle shattered the cube and roared at us.

I aimed my palms at him again. "I will knock you clear into the ravine if you so much as take a step in this direction." With Anna here, my voice sounded just as fierce as the bear's roar had.

He must have seen my intent reflected in my eyes because he huffed and shifted back into a man.

"That wench shot me," he snarled and reached behind him, grasping at the arrow embedded in his ass.

"She is most certainly not a wench," I growled back.

His face contorted into a grimace as he tried to pull the arrow out. He didn't have the dexterity to do it without causing more harm. It was like watching a puppy chase his own tail.

"Oh, for heaven's sake," I said, curling my hands into tight fists. I marched behind him, slapped his hand away, and yanked the arrow out.

He howled and spun on me.

I cocked an eyebrow at him. "Perhaps if you hadn't acted like such an ass, you wouldn't have been shot in your backside." I turned away and nodded for Anna to join me at the door.

I glanced over my shoulder in time to see Kyle rip his shirt off and press it into the bloody wound on his well-formed butt cheek.

I blinked at the sight of his marred skin, slowing to a stop. His body had whip marks traversed across his back and arms as if someone had taken a belt to him and hadn't stopped until he was within inches of his life.

My stomach plummeted at the thought.

Anna tugged my arm. "Elsa," she whispered.

I turned away from Kyle, conflicted.

I stepped onto the landing and glanced down the stairs at the fur ball in the corner. The steady rise and fall of its back told me what I needed. The bear on the first floor was asleep.

"Don't wake the bear downstairs on your way out," I whispered.

She balked and waved her hand in Kyle's direction.

"I promise I will be okay," I said. "I will be along as soon as I help him tend to his wound."

She pressed her lips together, and I shooed her away.

As soon as she was out the front door, I turned back to Kyle. His back was to me, and he held the shirt in place with his head dipped low. I studied the patterns on his back, and they tugged at my heartstrings. This was a man who knew nothing about mercy or kindness.

"Let me help," I said when Anna was at a safe distance from the palace.

He stiffened and glanced over his shoulder. "I thought you and that wench had left."

I crossed my arms. "You knew I was still here."

His lips pressed together in a smirk, and he shrugged. "You know, if she was aiming for my heart, she's a terrible shot," he muttered and turned towards me.

"She wasn't aiming to kill. Anna doesn't have that in her." I crossed and took the shirt from him, studying the amount of blood on the fabric before folding it over. I pressed it back in place.

"But you do." He eyed me warily.

I nodded. "Just as you do," I replied, meeting his stare. I pulled the fabric away a second time. There was a new patch of fresh blood soaking into the fabric. "I think you may need me to stitch you up."

"I'm fine," he said. "With the arrow out, I can just shift, and the bear will take care of the healing."

"Then why don't you?"

He was quiet as he glanced down at me with a crooked smile. "It's been a while since a woman held my ass."

"Oh, for the love of..." I threw his shirt at him and stormed out of the room, leaving him to deal with his wound himself.

FROZEN Chapter 5

BY THE TIME I got back to the castle, I was ready to give Anna a piece of my mind. Her running up there was just too dangerous, especially since she had two children to tend to.

I stepped into my chambers to find Anna sitting on my couch, waiting for me to come back.

"What were you thinking?" I snarled.

"I was thinking about saving you. That bear was ready to tear your head off."

"He is all roar," I said, but even I heard the absence of truth in my statement.

She leveled a look at me that always made me fidget. It was the same one I had given her in the past and gotten the same results. It was the *'you are so full of bullshit and you know it'* gaze.

"He wouldn't have killed me," I said. Maimed me for sure, but I'd like to think he would have stopped short of draining my life away, especially with that mischievous grin he'd given me just before I left.

"Who are you trying to fool? That bear was seconds away from attacking, and you know it." Anna's anger filled the room and echoed in her voice.

Heat filled my cheeks, and I glanced away. I hadn't heeded his words of warning. I poked the bear and nearly lost my head. Anna was right. I wasn't trying to convince her. I was trying to convince myself.

I crossed to the window and glanced up at the snowy peak. The ice glinted in the sun, and my mind clouded over with the feel of him pressing against me. If only he wasn't such a genuine ass. I sighed and turned back to Anna.

Her eyes narrowed. "You have a thing for that heathen." She waved towards the window.

I opened my mouth to disagree.

"Don't even try to deny it. I can see it in the color of your cheeks and that dreamy look you get whenever you look in that direction."

My eyebrows rose. "What dreamy look?"

She rolled her eyes. "It's the same look you've given me grief over when Kris is working in the yard and I'm watching him. I caught a glance in the mirror once and you were right. It is the goofiest expression."

I pressed my lips against the smile. "Maybe I'm just dreaming of having my ice castle back," I said to defer the conversation. But she had struck a hidden nerve. It was as if I was compelled to look his way, and that bloomed the heat of aggravation under the surface of my skin.

My stomach growled, reminding me I hadn't had anything to eat. Anna's features softened at the grumbling.

"You haven't eaten anything, either?" she asked.

"No. And I better eat soon, or otherwise, my trip to the senate will be a different mess." I crossed to my desk and stuffed the papers I'd signed yesterday into my satchel, resigned to an afternoon of boredom within the senate today.

But not before Anna and I raided the kitchen. The castle cook, Buster to all who wandered these dark hallways, was more than willing to serve us up scrumptious delights. He glowed as radiant as his white chef hat when we raved about the delectable selections he offered.

Neither Anna nor I had cornered him in the kitchen since our parents died, so this was a rare occasion for all of us. We reminisced about our younger years with Buster, laughing as he continued to recount our fearless feats.

It was well past the time of the opening of the senate floor by the time I took my leave, but I had signed bills to deliver and a warning to issue regarding the plunder law they'd thrown together. As I walked through the door, I heard voices arguing from the senate floor. I stopped to listen to the lively conversation on poaching. It wasn't until a smooth baritone voice rose above the others that a chill ran down my spine.

I threw the door open and stepped inside before the knight guards could announce that the queen had arrived. From across the floor, our eyes met.

A blaze of anger flushed through me, and I clenched my fists.

He broke my gaze first. "Ah, the voice of reason has arrived." He waved towards where I stood, silencing the senate. Then he turned and took a knee in a bow so formal that I nearly laughed.

Kyle Bryggen was quite the actor. If the senate knew he was one of the bear shifters of old, they would quake in their boots.

"And what is it I am deemed so reasonable about?" I said, projecting my voice as I made my way down the steps to the floor. Keeping my distance, I crossed the floor and handed the secretary the papers I'd signed yesterday. When I finally returned my attention to Kyle, he was back on his feet with his hands clasped behind his back.

"Poaching," he said. "Shooting bears for their fur."

I crossed my arms. "A bear hide is especially warm when winter falls, Mr...." I rolled my hand to make him finish my sentence.

"Bergeron." His eyes blazed.

I narrowed my gaze. He used an alias in the senate house, and I wondered why, especially since he had been so full of piss and vinegar up in the ice castle.

"Well, Mr. Bergeron. What is your beef with Bryggen's hunters?"

"I think it is a sick practice and should be stopped immediately. Especially since I was walking in the woods and was nearly clipped in the ass with an arrow."

I cocked my eyebrow. So that's what he was going with. "Well, sir, you were probably somewhere where you shouldn't be."

His face reddened.

I turned towards Arron Brax. "Senator Brax, what do you think of Mr. Bergeron's proposal?"

Senator Brax was studying the dynamics between Kyle and me with a sharp eye. "I'm not so sure I'm against this man's proposal. He is talking about hunting for sport as opposed to hunting for survival."

I actually laughed. "And you sanctioned a law that directs our young men to go out and plunder nearby countries?"

Kyle raised an eyebrow.

"That was the only law that passed my desk that I ripped to shreds. I agree that hunting or plundering for sport is wrong." I leveled my best challenging stare at the good senator.

He shifted in his seat.

I turned towards Kyle. "I will see to it that this is voted on today, sir."

The edge of his lip curved up, and he gave me another deep bow. "Thank you, My Queen."

I waited until he left the floor and the chamber closed for deliberation before I turned to Senator Brax. "It seems we are in agreement for once." I glanced around. "And the lands have not frozen over." I grinned at him and then turned my attention to the house. "If you so choose to write up a law protecting wild animals from being hunted for sport, I will sign it on the spot as long as the language used is specific to hunting for sport. We all know that having an unclear bill signed into law has unintended consequences, so be careful with the message."

I let my gaze pass over each of the men, and they nodded. We had had something similar happen with a poorly worded bill about abolishing drinking. After my father signed it into law, the senate realized they had abolished all forms of drinking, even having a glass of wine with dinner, which was the farthest thing from their original intent of cleaning up the drunks in the street. The law was recanted and refined to abolish drunken and disorderly acts in public places. Many of those senators remained as acting law makers in this audience.

"I will expect the new bills on my desk by nightfall," I said and bid my leave. It was time to chase down Mr. Kyle Bryggen and find out just what he was up to.

FROZEN Chapter 6

THE WARM SUNSHINE MADE my eyes squint as I stepped outside. I didn't get more than two paces away from the senate building when a shadow stepped to my side. I glanced at Kyle as he kept pace with me, his hands still clasped behind his back and his eyes roaming the kingdom with curiosity.

I took a moment to take a closer look at him as he walked beside me. He had donned a blue tunic with gold trim that brought out the color of his eyes, and his boots shined like new. He looked freshly bathed and smelled like a clean breeze through a pine forest.

I narrowed my gaze. "Did you steal those clothes?"

"No."

He didn't seem bothered by the accusation in my voice or by the skeptical eye I gave him. He continued to scan our surroundings, and the corners of his lips tilted in a smile that would have melted my heart had he not tried to kill me earlier that morning.

"I'm not sure whether I like your ice castle or this place better."

Any thoughts of how handsome he was evaporated with this statement. I spun towards him. "Bryggen is my kingdom. Not yours." I poked my finger into his chest.

"And yet it carries my name." He cocked an eyebrow at me in that silent challenge that made my blood boil.

"It most certainly does not, Mr. Bergeron." His alias spat from my lips, and I glared up at his impossibly handsome face. "Do I need to put another arrow in that ass of yours?"

"You did not put the first one in my ass."

"I'm a much better shot than my sister. I wouldn't just leave you with a flesh wound."

"You certainly are a feisty one." His eyes sparkled in the sunshine.

"I am the queen and you should show some respect." I turned and marched off.

Or so I thought.

When I got to the castle gate, he reached beyond me and opened the door for me. "Like this?" he asked, almost too quietly for me to hear over my pounding heart.

I glared up at his dancing blue eyes. The memory of the beast ready to tear my head off kept me from swooning at his natural charisma. I gave him a curt nod and entered.

He stepped inside with me.

"I did not invite you into my home."

He just grinned at me and looked at the grand entry. "It lacks your special touch," he said after his inspection.

I huffed. "And yet, you are still standing here."

"It would seem so." He slid his hands into his pockets and stared down at me.

"What do you want?" I shifted under his intense stare.

His nose flared, and he glanced around again. When his gaze landed back on me, a shiver slid up my spine.

"What do I want?" He stepped closer and his voice carried a dangerous growl. "I want everything I lost."

I blinked at him, not understanding what his point was.

He crowded me against the nearest wall. "I thought I just wanted your ice castle tucked away from civilization. But being here, eating my fill at the local pub, and seeing what my city has become, I decided I want it back."

"You can not have it back." I straightened my spine, glaring up at him.

His finger hooked under my chin, jerking it upwards. "You are the only thing standing in my way."

His mouth crushed down on mine. My brain stalled for a moment, despite the unwanted kiss. It was demanding and took my breath away. I placed my palms on his chest, and before I could relish the sensation of his warm lips, I blasted him with the frustration filling me, sending him crashing into the opposite wall.

The fury of his advances and his words mixed into a dangerous cocktail filling my veins. I advanced on him before he could scramble to his feet.

His blue eyes were wide, and for a moment, I drank in his fear.

"You have the audacity to think you can just take what you want?" My hands tingled as my voice echoed in the great hall. Ice glazed the floor around me, spiraling out with the release of my anger.

"You were the unwise one that woke me from centuries of sleep." His face transformed into an angry mask. "And I have every right to take back what was once mine."

"Leave now and do not return, or otherwise I will make you an icicle." The walls surrounding us had already coated in frost.

"And how did that work for you the last time you tried to do that?" He crossed, towering over me again. "I am not afraid of a little ice." He growled down at me, and his teeth elongated. "But you should be deathly afraid of an angry bear."

"Get out!" I pointed at the door as the first threads of fear weaved through the anger.

He laughed and stepped back. With a sweeping bow, he turned and sauntered out of the castle, leaving me stewing. And through all this shaking rage, the feel of his lips on mine sparked a heat deep within me.

I let out a guttural roar and stomped to my room, leaving a trail of ice in my wake.

FROZEN Chapter 7

IT TOOK HOURS FOR the pounding in my temple to abate. Every time I thought I had control over the spell of rage, I would glance out the window and see him sitting at the pub across the way, having a grand time in my kingdom. That shifty bastard.

The senate secretary came by with the stack of papers for me to review and sign, but every time I tried to read a paragraph, the feel of his lips on mine interrupted my focus. In a matter of a few days, that man had gotten under my skin in a way no other had.

I glanced up at my ice castle. Even if I wanted to retreat to the cool calmness I always found there, I would never get past him without notice. And the animal would probably follow me.

That thought brought on a surprising thrill, and I blinked, startled by the urge to tempt destruction. Kyle Bryggen was not a man to trifle with. Neither was his alter ego, and yet, I was truly entertaining the idea.

With papers strewn about my desk and none holding any of my attention, I stood, stretching. It was time to occupy my mind. I cut through the castle and across the inner ward to the modest home I'd had built for Anna. I needed the diversion that only children could bring.

I knocked on the door, because as much as my sister chided, I did not want to just waltz in as if I owned the place. She deserved the same respect she had always shown me. She opened the door with my nephew on her hip, flour smudges on her cheeks, and her hair out of place. The instant her eyes fell on me, that harried look on her face transformed into a smile.

Without a word, she handed me Dennis and waved me in as she scurried back to her kitchen where her other two children sat patiently waiting for their mother to finish baking. The sweet smell of cookies hung on the air, and I smiled at the dough rolled out on the table with painstakingly carved shapes molded into the confection awaiting the next cookie tray.

Reindeer, bears, trees, and even snowmen graced the table, all decorated with sugars and fruits. My mouth watered just looking at it.

Anna pulled a tray from the oven and set it in the only spot not littered with waiting cutouts. When Sara reached for them, Anna knocked her hand away.

"It's too hot," she said to her daughter.

Sara turned to me and raised an eyebrow.

"Oh no," Anna said when I started laughing.

"The last time I cooled down your mother's cookies, I broke her cookie sheet, remember?" Even though I was turning down her silent question, I eyed the confections, tempted. I remained patient, though, and once the rest of the dough carvings were placed on the sheet and put in the oven, I leaned over and blew a small, cool stream over the hot cookies, cooling them down enough for all of us to sample.

I reached out and plucked one from the mix, handing it to Dennis before I took one for myself. Both Sara and Kristoff grabbed a cookie as well before Anna even turned from closing the oven.

"Elsa," she sighed and glanced at the cookie carnage occurring as the four of us devoured the snacks we held in hand before reaching for seconds. She joined the foray and closed her eyes after she took her first bite.

I took a bite, and the sweet confection melted in my mouth with a burst of nuts and cinnamon. "You always make these just like Mom's," I said as I put Dennis on the ground to finish his cookie.

A blush filled Anna's cheeks. "You have the recipe, too."

I laughed. I had tried my hand at cooking, but I couldn't seem to get the batter right. Either it was too doughy or too hard. It never melted in my mouth the way Anna's did.

"You are a much better cook than I could ever hope to be."

Anna wiped her hands on a cloth, and after shooing the children away from the kitchen to go play, she started piling the cookies into her cookie box. I helped her stack them gently between pieces of parchment paper.

By the time we were finished and had the counter cleaned up, the second batch was ready. Once the hot cookies were laid out on the shelf and Anna's coveted cookie sheet out of range, I cooled the sweet treats down, and we continued packing them away.

"What brings you by in the middle of the day?" Anna asked.

I pressed my lips together and sighed. "He came down from the mountain."

Anna's jaw tightened, and her eyes narrowed. "What did he want?"

"Bryggen," I said. I hadn't told Anna exactly who the beast-man was and for some reason, it stuck in my mouth. "He doesn't want to destroy Bryggen. He wants to rule it," I clarified, but my words didn't alleviate the growing fear in Anna's widening eyes.

"He can't possibly..."

I held up my hand. "No, he can't. At least not right now."

She cocked her head.

"I have until the end of the year to find a suitable husband." My voice carried my distaste just as clearly as Anna's frown displayed hers.

"I really hope you find someone." Anna sighed. "Because I don't know who would be worse, that beast or Senator Brax."

I huffed a laugh. Senator Brax would be much worse, at least for anyone of the female persuasion. He would like to see all of us relegated back to a man's property. Although I wasn't sure exactly what Kyle's thoughts were. He just seemed to want to conquer as opposed to rule.

Neither choice was good, so I just had to find Mr. Right in a sea of wrongs. It wasn't like I hadn't dated since I'd thawed the land, but none of the men who attempted to woo me could stand being near me for long. The chill I apparently emitted was just too much for them.

And the only kiss I ever had where a man didn't wince was with Kyle.

I blinked and returned my attention to Anna now that her head was cocked, studying me. I shifted self-consciously and tried on a smile. I succeeded, as Anna's head straightened and her lips curved into that cheery disposition I was accustomed to.

"Don't worry. I will find someone suitable." I wasn't so sure with the meager pickings in Bryggen, but the words seemed to help both of us shake off whatever dark cloud had rolled into the room. "I better get back and finish going through the papers that were delivered earlier. I just needed a pleasant distraction."

Anna smiled, and as we crossed to the door, she handed me a box of the cookies we had packed. "I know you have a sweet tooth, and instead of bothering Buster at odd hours tonight, you can have these."

"Thanks, sis." I gave her a hug and left.

The sun had dipped to the horizon during the time I'd spent with Anna and the kids, and my heart felt lighter.

FROZEN Chapter 8

THE MOMENT I STEPPED into my office, my lightheartedness disappeared.

Senator Brax stood at the window with his back to me, studying the town below. I cleared my throat, and he turned. His face pinched in irritation.

"I was beginning to think you would never attend to your duties." He waved at my paper-laden desk.

"To what do I owe the pleasure?" I asked, ignoring his dig. I was in no mood for his games.

"The senate had some qualms about your behavior today." He glared at me. If it were up to this asshat, women would be slaves to the community, bending over backwards based on any man's whim. After all, he condoned a law that would celebrate rape and pillaging.

I crossed my arms. "I have every right to speak my peace. I am the queen of Bryggen."

He stepped to my desk and picked up the papers on the top, shoving them in my direction. "Not for long."

I kept my face neutral and yanked the papers from him. Even the name of the unanimous decree left my skin colder than normal. Modified Marriage Decree. My heart pounded with each word I read, dropping lower until it cramped my stomach and made me flash a glare at the senator.

I turned my back to read the rest. I did not want this criminal to see my reaction. I swallowed the bile in my throat.

"This is insane," I said, waving the papers. "What you and the senate are demanding is ludicrous."

He stepped close, crowding me against the desk. His sharp stare made my skin crawl. "Regardless. It was a unanimous decision. We don't feel you are fit to continue to rule over Bryggen."

"I am far more fit than you are."

His hand shot out and clasped my throat, pulling me even closer to the vile stench drifting from his mouth.

I clenched my hands. Senator Brax made sure there was a clause protecting him in the decree. If anything unnatural befell him, I would hang for treason. It was spelled out ad nauseam in the decree. The only out I had was finding a suitable man to rule by my side. Otherwise, I would be forced to marry the senator, and he would take the throne.

"I am willing to forgo frostbite to produce a royal heir. How many men can say that?" he purred in my face.

I tore myself from his grip. "I still have until the passing of the next full moon." My voice cracked as I shook the papers at him. The proclamation was not one I could just rip up like an ordinary bill. It was a unanimous decision by the senate.

Senator Brax laughed. "There isn't a man in town who would take a stand against me."

He was right. No one in this kingdom would stand against the senate, and Senator Brax was the senate.

I pressed my lips together in disgust, and he crowded me again. This time his salacious grin nearly made me gag.

He reached out and wiped the corner of my lip. "Besides, the senate has to approve your chosen suitor in a unanimous vote."

I stared at him, dumbfounded.

"I can count at least one dissenting vote."

"You bastard."

His fingers ran down my arm. "I gave you enough time to get used to the idea. If you choose to disobey, I can always start harming those closest to you."

The thought of him touching me closed my throat, but the thought of him harming Anna or her children left me sick to my stomach. My gaze dropped to the papers and then moved back to his salacious grin.

"Get out of my office," I hissed once my brain jumpstarted again.

He smiled and stepped closer. "Get used to the idea, or be willing to see your sister pay the price." He turned and left me gripping the edge of the desk with the sweet confections roiling in my stomach, threatening to spill onto the wood floor.

FROZEN Chapter 9

AS THE LAST OF the light bled from the sky, I stared out over the mountain with the papers still clutched in my hand. I still couldn't fathom what had driven the senate to make such a choice. They were sentencing this kingdom to doom.

My mind stalled at the sight of Kyle weaving his way up the hillside, carrying a satchel over his shoulder. To my surprise, he stumbled, but caught himself before carrying on towards my ice castle.

I actually laughed out loud at his drunken meanderings, but my laughter was short-lived. A shadow trailed behind him. I followed its movement, wondering if it was man or beast. Soon the shadow doubled, and as they darted from one tree to the next, at least two men were following Kyle.

Could Senator Brax have caught wind that the stranger from the senate floor had escorted me back to the castle?

I stared at the papers as things started adding up. It wasn't my behavior on the senate floor that caused this debacle. It was something either the senator saw or heard that led him to force this on the kingdom. If he were that heinous, perhaps he would try to take out what he perceived as a threat.

I growled under my breath. Anger heated my skin, creating a dangerous sizzle in the air. I shoved the papers into my pocket and grabbed the cookie box on my way out.

I had to warn Kyle.

I slid on one of the staff's hooded coats and slipped out the gate unnoticed, then scurried as fast and silently as I could to catch up to the shadows following Kyle. I flanked the woods on the right opposite from where I had seen the men. My coat blended with the woods almost as fully as theirs did.

Kyle was singing as he weaved towards home. His voice carried on the wind, deep and rich, and it twisted my gut in a way that I didn't understand. For all the asinine things he had done, I couldn't fathom why I was trying to save his ass.

I stared at the said body part and sighed. He was wondrous to look at, but in his condition, I wasn't sure whether the shadows following him or the icy steps to the palace would prove to be the thing that killed him.

This vile and very drunk creature might be my only hope.

I nearly choked on a laugh, pressing my lips together at the wild card I had suddenly pinned my freedom on.

Before I could fully digest what my mind had conjured, movement across the open field caught my attention. Two men stepped out of the woods. One with a bow and arrow and the second with his sword at the ready. When the archer strung his bow, my gaze shot to Kyle, cluelessly drunk and still weaving a path up the mountainside.

If he had any idea that an attack was underway, the polar bear would come out, and these men would be torn in two. At least that was what I hoped for, but as the shot was lined up, I knew this would end with Kyle's murder if I didn't stop it.

I clenched my hands into fists, and when the archer let the arrow fly, I shot an icicle at the weapon, knocking it off course. It whizzed by Kyle.

Kyle stopped, staring after it before he turned. The tense set of his body told me enough. He was going to shift, and I couldn't have that this close to the kingdom. That would get him hunted like a rabid dog.

Before the archer could get another arrow threaded, I blasted both him and the man with the sword, killing them almost as surely as Kyle would have. My stomach roiled at the sudden knowledge that I had taken human lives. This wasn't self-defense like in the past; this was a calculated move to save another being. I nearly choked on the bile lining my throat.

I swallowed, shaking the sudden wave of nausea away. I would have a hell of a lot to explain in the morning when the hunters found them, but I would deal with that then. I would rather face a firing squad than be married to Senator Brax.

Kyle's head whipped in my direction, and his jaw fell open. I crossed the distance until I was within earshot.

"You can't shift within sight of the kingdom." I picked up the bag he'd dropped. "And you can't climb those stairs alone." I trudged in front of him, then stopped when I realized he wasn't following.

I turned, and he still stood staring at the icicles I had made of the men.

"Kyle," I snapped, and he spun toward me. "Chop, chop." This time, I didn't wait for him. I continued until I got to the ice stairs.

The snow crunched behind me, and I glanced over my shoulder at him. He still listed back and forth, but it wasn't as pronounced as when I first saw him leave the kingdom.

"Do you need help so you don't fall off the stairs?"

He came close to me and stared down into my upturned face with a crease between his eyes. "Why?"

I sighed. "I saw them following you."

He looked up at the ice castle, far removed from the kingdom below. "I am a threat to your reign. Why would you save my life?"

I didn't want to get into the lesser of two evils with him. Instead, I offered him my arm and nodded toward the stairs.

He kicked off his boots and trudged up the steps with his bare feet without my help.

When he got to the landing, he glanced over his shoulder. "Are you coming in or not?"

I hesitated and shoved my hands in my pockets. The paper sliced my finger. I yanked my hand out and pressed the cut to my lips. I stared up at him.

"I won't bite. I promise," he said, and his face remained stoic. Not even a hint of a smile appeared.

I picked up his discarded boots and climbed the stairs, wondering if I was trading one unpleasant situation for a worse one. As I passed him holding the door open for me, I decided this might just be the easier pill to swallow.

When I dropped his boots in the castle, he put his finger to his lips and pointed towards the bear in the corner. "I'll be up in a moment," he whispered and took the sack from my hand.

I climbed the stairs to the bedchamber and stopped to watch him below.

Kyle laid out food for the sleeping polar bear with such care that my heart warmed. His gaze turned up and met mine. He paused and wiped his hands on his pants as he straightened. An intensity burned in his eyes, and my breath locked in my throat.

He climbed the stairs, and when he passed me, my skin tingled. The moment I stepped into the bedroom, he closed the door behind me. Before I could blink, he had me against the wall, his mouth on mine.

I opened my mouth to protest, and his tongue slipped between my lips, teasing in a way that made my knees weak. Despite the dizzying bliss he created, I pushed on his chest, breaking the kiss, but this time without blasting him across the room.

He pulled away, and his gaze dropped to my hands splayed on his chest. "Why do you deny the desire I see in your eyes?"

"Whatever you see in my eyes does not give you the right to just take what you want."

"I'm not."

I raised my eyebrow. "What do you call kissing me without permission?"

He stepped away and narrowed his eyes. "If you are not here to follow through on this...this thing between us, then why did you come? Why did you save me from those men?"

"There is nothing between us." The words twisted my stomach. The kiss had been divine, and I could see myself falling into his arms and getting lost in his touch. But I didn't have the luxury of finding out if he truly was the one for me or if he was just playing me for the position I held.

He pressed his lips together. "I disagree. There is enough hostility breeding between us to cause an explosion."

"Hostility?"

His lips formed a smile and his cheeks reddened before he shrugged one shoulder. "What would you call it?"

Heat filled my cheeks, and I glanced at the floor before meeting his gaze. We could discuss this burning sensation caressing my skin, or I could divert the conversation to the more critical issue at hand. I leaned on the cool ice behind me and sighed, reaching into my pocket. I brought the senate's decree from my pocket and held it out to him.

Kyle pulled the papers from my hand, but instead of glancing at them, he focused on my finger, studying the blood running from my cut. He brought my finger to his mouth and covered the cut with his lips, his eyes locked on mine.

My heart thundered, and my mouth suddenly went dry.

He smiled against my skin. "Now I understand why the bear wants to eat you. You taste like honey."

He let go of my hand and turned, crossing to the lamp next to the bed. After lighting it, he took a seat and studied the papers. He took so long reading each page that I thought maybe he wasn't educated enough to read.

But then he glanced at me. "You're betrothed to that ancient senator?"

"Hell no." I shook my head.

He waved the papers in the air. "According to these papers, it seems unless you have a proper approved-of suitor, then you are betrothed."

I glanced out the window at the kingdom and shuddered. "God help Bryggen. Senator Brax will ruin this kingdom."

He stood and crossed to stand before me. "Why did you bring this to me?"

"I need a proper suitor. One with royal blood." I stared into his blue eyes.

Kyle pointed at his chest. "You think I have royal blood running through these veins?" He laughed. "Besides, who's to say I won't ruin Bryggen?"

I bit my lower lip. "You are the king of the Hanseatic League."

"Just because I ruled the trade routes doesn't make me of royal blood." He stepped closer. "Besides, according to these, the senate has to unanimously approve your choice." He rolled his eyes. "And without revealing my true lineage, there is no way that group of men will cast their votes for someone who seemed to care for wildlife more than their precious trophies."

"Still..." I whispered. "I have to try."

He cocked his head. "Again, why me?"

"Because you are the only man I have ever met that doesn't flinch when he touches me. Despite this open hostility between us, I would rather spend my time with someone who can be in the same room without turning blue or shivering so much they chip a tooth. Even if you are a supreme ass."

Color clouded his features. "I want to rule."

"You want to conquer."

He inhaled, making his nostrils flare. "A beast by nature conquers." He stared at me and blinked, as if the conversation had just settled in his mind. "You would be my... wife?"

"That is what I am proposing. But I will not be relegated to the background. I will serve no man."

"But you expect that of me?"

I licked my lips. I didn't know what I expected.

The papers dropped from his hand, and he closed the distance, towering over me. His gaze sharpened. "I will not be ruled," he growled.

"Then be my equal." The words tumbled out unbidden.

"Prove that you are my equal."

I reached out and grabbed his shirt, pulling him to me, then snaked my hand into his hair and yanked him to my lips. His eyes widened before they closed, and our mouths parted. Tongues intertwined in a slow dance that left me breathless. His hands threaded through my hair, holding me in place as the kiss deepened.

Hostility.

He had used that word more than once, but it was more like a fiery sexual tension between us. One that when he pulled me against his body made me shiver in his grasp. His warmth surrounded me, nearly suffocating both of us.

He was the first to break the kiss. That cocky smile surfaced.

I pushed away from him. The balcony beckoned, and I ignored his salacious grin, crossing and stepping out into the chill of the evening. Kyle's hands descended on my shoulders moments later.

"Do you honestly believe the senate will deem me fit to be a suitable candidate for king?"

I snorted a laugh. "Senator Brax already sees you as a threat."

Kyle stepped into my view with his head cocked.

"The papers. The attempt on your life. Somehow, your interaction with me got back to the senator, and he acted in his own best interest."

The slow smile that spread on his lips thrilled me. "The good senator could be attacked by a vicious bear."

"And then I would be executed."

Kyle shrugged. "Then I wouldn't have to share the throne with anyone."

"You really are an opportunistic bastard."

"I never pretended to be otherwise." He reached out and pulled me against him. "Besides, you have not yet accepted your fate." His gaze drifted inside to the bed and then back to me. "You have not proven yourself to me."

"And you think me fucking you will do that?"

"Such a dirty mouth," he whispered and traced my lips with his fingers. "But fucking me isn't the point. Now, fucking the bear and surviving..." He cocked an eyebrow.

"I will do no such thing." I went to step away.

His arm wrapped around my waist, yanking me against his hard body. His other hand drifted from my lips, down my throat, to the V between my breasts. He traced the line of my gown, and my skin turned into a relief map of bumps. "I cannot imagine that

Senator Brax will be quite as..." He stared into my eyes. "Exciting to bed than I would be."

His touch nearly boiled my blood. Hostility flashed into desire, and each sweep of his fingers brought heat to the surface until steam rose from my skin. Damn him. I wanted everything he was insinuating, and it burned as badly as his hands did.

He unbuttoned my dress slowly. With each button freed, his gaze became hungrier, his hand more demanding. He moved me back into the bedroom, steering me with purpose. "If you are to be my queen, you must make this sacrifice," he whispered.

I grabbed his wrist, stopping him in place. Doubt peppered my mind. His intensity overwhelmed me, and his intent scared me more than the bear ever had. But I was the queen, and he needed to bow to my whims.

"If you are to be my king..."

His mouth crushed mine, and the tearing of fabric followed. I didn't know who was more violent—me tearing his shirt in two or him slicing through my dress. But the moment ended with me pinned under him on the soft bedding.

His hands explored, as did his mouth. He drank me in like I never imagined a man could. Biting, nipping, licking his way down my body. Steam rose where his palms met my flesh, sizzling and drawing a wanton growl from both our lips.

When his mouth clamped down between my legs, I thought my world would explode.

The expertise in his tongue pulled a howl of pleasure from me. He continued until I thought I would lose my mind. I arched into him, wanting more than just his tongue. More than just his playful fingers. I wanted him to take me, to own me, to make me his.

Instead of obeying my pleas, he pulled away, leaving me gasping and desperate. When he straddled me, his manhood stood at attention in full view.

He smiled. "Quid pro quo, My Queen."

I blinked up at him and then looked at his hard shaft, the object I wanted inside me despite its ample length and girth. He took my hand and guided it along his length, purring as I stroked him in my loose grip.

"Get that mouth dirty," he whispered in a commanding tone as he stared down at me. The challenge of his statement reflected in his eyes. "Only then will I give you what you were begging for."

"Or I could freeze it and break it off and satisfy myself." I smiled and squeezed a fraction tighter.

He burst into laughter, full and engaging, like I hadn't just threatened his manhood. His fingers found the sensitive nub between my legs. He slowly circled, bringing the fire back low in my belly. His playful smile remained.

"That wouldn't be quite as fun," he said as we continued to stroke each other.

I lifted onto my elbow with my brain in a fog. The manipulation by his fingers was as delicious as his tongue had been. His free hand threaded into my hair, and he guided me towards him. Nerves bit at the back of my mind. I had never done any of this. Before today, the most I ever indulged in was a kiss.

"It will come naturally," he said.

I glanced up at his soft, reassuring smile. "And if I bite?"

"Then you will need to deal with the bear."

A thrilling fear filled me, and his smile faltered.

"Please don't bite." His thumb caressed my cheek. Need like I never thought possible flashed across his eyes. He closed them, drowning in the moment's intensity.

I opened my mouth and slid it over his hard tip. The rumble that filled his chest satiated the curiosity of what would happen if I chose to bite. This was so much more satisfying. I watched the dominance in him melt as if he were made of one of my sister's cookies.

I went as far down his shaft as my mouth would allow, but when I slid back, his grip on my hair tightened and his hips pushed his length farther into my throat. His fingers increased their manipulation of my bud, and I moaned around him.

He groaned and slid deeper, tilting my head farther back. His veins pulsed against my tongue, and the ecstasy etched into his face thrilled me. I had him under my control. I pushed forward, swallowing more of him despite the gag in the back of my throat. His hips met my mouth, and he groaned, tilting his head back.

Unable to contain the heat between my thighs, I cried out with the strength of my release, but it was muted by his length. He groaned, his grip tightened, and I could no longer draw a breath. I bucked, and he released the hold he had on me. I pulled away enough to draw air into my burning lungs, concentrating on sucking his tip until I caught my breath.

His eyes opened, filled with want as they took me in. He continued playing with me while I slid my mouth from his tip to stern and back, relishing the glaze over his eyes and the rumble of contentment in his chest.

His breath quickened, and the glaze over his eyes sparked into a fiery frenzy, matching that of the faster thrust of his hips. Each one drilled deeper into my mouth while his fingers continued their frenzied pitch on my bud. Veins stood out on his temples, and his jaw clenched right before he plunged into the back of my throat with a groan that bowed his body. Salty seed filled my throat, bubbling into my mouth with the force. I swallowed, taking more of him in than I'd thought possible.

I arched with the strength of my release. A rush of hot liquid coated the inside of my thighs, and his fingers slowed, dipping inside the warm wetness as he pulled from my mouth.

"Elsa," he whispered and pulled away, falling on his back next to me.

I swallowed again, gasping for breath and trying to get my bearings. I wiped my face. As out of breath as I was, I was not ready for this bliss to end. I rolled on top of him, straddling him with my hips to his, his member trapped beneath me.

He stared up at me, his eyebrows arching.

"We are not finished here."

His lips twitched into a smile, and he clasped his hands behind his head. "At your service, My Queen," he said in a sinuous tone that flushed my skin.

I twirled my hips slowly, circling and staring down into his bright blue eyes. Mischief and lust danced in his irises.

"Does this mean we are betrothed?" he asked.

"I have yet to make up my mind." I twirled my hips, and he jumped back to life beneath me.

"Liar," he whispered with a grin.

I smiled down at him. I adored this game he played. The dominant and submissive all in the same breath. It was as paramount as the fight between the man and the beast within. "You have yet to prove yourself."

His eyebrow cocked, and he grabbed my waist, picking me up and slamming me down the length of him.

I gasped, my eyes widening at the sudden girth filling me. The sudden pain of my innocence shattering was immediately replaced by a tingle that started at the tip of my head and spread to my toes.

He stilled beneath me, his eyes as wide as mine, but not with lust. No, his gaze was painted with alarm. His fingernails dug into my flesh, creating webs of agony through me.

I slowly circled my hips, hoping that it would change his expression.

He closed his eyes and tilted his head back. "Virgin blood," he whispered, and his breath quickened. "Jesus, why didn't you tell me?" His voice shook. With need, with something else. I couldn't tell, but his body responded, swiveling with me in a lover's dance.

Neither of us stopped our languid motions. His eyes snapped open and the fire within his blue irises blazed inside me. His teeth elongated, and his gaze fell on my throat. His hands tightened.

I cried out and grabbed his wrists, trying to dislodge his grip.

His hands grabbed mine, and he flipped us, pinning me under him. His wild eyes were on mine, both horror and lust fighting on his features. His hips drove into mine faster, like it was a race against time.

I met each thrust with a force of my own; the pleasure radiated from my belly all the way to my fingers and toes. He nuzzled my neck, growling as his teeth scratched my skin. I knew I should be afraid, but a morbid curiosity gripped me, along with the ethereal bliss his body was creating inside me.

His teeth sank into my shoulder, and I cried out. Pain overshadowed the pleasure. I wrapped my legs around his hips, arching into the tornado of sensations.

I took a handful of hair and yanked his head back. He hadn't transitioned, hadn't shifted yet. I pulled him to my mouth, tasting my blood on his tongue. I sucked his bottom lip between my teeth and bit. His blood flowed, comingling with mine, and he yelped before he smashed our lips harder together.

His tongue danced with mine in a fervor that matched our hips. Both our grips tightened, and we both let out a growling groan I was sure echoed across the lands.

My body shuddered beneath his, adding to the tremors filling his form. He rolled off me, his chest rising and falling at an alarming rate.

"Run," he whispered. "Now."

I was in no condition to run, but as the shift took hold of him, he bellowed, losing himself to the beast. I rolled off the bed and grabbed my torn dress, heading for the door.

The bear slid in front of my path, blocking my escape route. I put my hands out, the dress in one and my other splayed as I backed up. My shoulder ached where he had bitten through the skin.

The bear's gaze was wild, like just the smell of me was pushing him over the edge. Kyle was nowhere in that gaze. There was no humanity left. The growling fury radiating from the beast clued me in on his intent. If I didn't think fast, the beast would kill me.

My gaze landed on the dress and snapped back to him as I brought it close, patting it down until I found the pocket I was looking for. I didn't know if it would work, but I pulled the box of cookies out of my pocket and opened it. Then I pulled one out just as my back hit the wall. With a shaking hand, I offered the cookie to the bear, hoping to stop whatever single-minded obsession was going through his head.

He roared at me.

"It's the best cookie you will ever taste," I said, forcing my voice to remain steady and calm, even though I was so far removed from those emotions. Calm was in another stratosphere.

The bear looked at the offering and then at me. He sniffed my sister's confection, and then he stepped forward, sniffing me. Down there. I wanted to push his snout away, but something inside warned me not to move, to remain still and continue offering the sugary confection.

I didn't dare breathe.

His nose moved to the blood running down my arm. He licked it off. Still, I didn't move. I sucked my lower lip between my teeth, and the iron taste of drying blood filled my mouth. I would rather have my sister's cookie right now. I hoped the bear felt the same.

His snout moved back to the cookie, and he took it between his teeth, narrowly missing my fingers. His gaze softened, and he turned away and sat on his haunches. The shift back to man happened quickly, and Kyle dropped to his knees. He looked at his hands, turning them over twice before he looked around the room.

His reaction was so odd that I remained still against the wall.

"What are you looking for?" I asked.

He jerked and spun to his feet. His eyes widened as he stared at me. He wiped his mouth and stared at the crumbs littered on his hand, along with blood from his lip.

"What the..."

"I gave the bear a cookie," I said, holding the box.

He blinked and stared at my shoulder. "What happened after I said virgin blood?" he bellowed. His entire form shook, and a shadow passed over his face.

I narrowed my gaze and reached down, swiping the discarded dress off the floor. "You don't have to look so horrified." I covered my chest. "You were the one who bit me first." I nodded towards my shoulder.

He closed his eyes and took a deep inhalation, then slowly exhaled before he opened his eyes again. Kyle reached for his pants and slipped them on, then focused on me. "Did we finish what you started?"

I glared at him. "What kind of game are you playing here?"

"Just answer the damn question," he growled.

"Yes. And then you told me to run, but apparently, I didn't run fast enough, so I offered the angry bear a damn cookie."

He stumbled back against the bed with his jaw askew. His stare penetrated right through me, and his gaze was so far from the arrogance he so comfortably wore that my breath locked in my chest.

His mouth snapped closed, and he sucked in his lower lip, dropping his gaze to the floor. A crease appeared between his eyes. "You... you should be dead."

"Why?"

"Because the bear kills those who lose their virginity to me. It never fails. At least it never did until today. The moment I break their innocence, the bear wakes and takes over completely. I come to with the walls painted with their blood and their bones picked clean and no memory of what happened. Just the sinking feeling that I killed for the fun of it and not out of necessity." He crossed to the balcony and leaned on the doorjamb with his back to me. "My father warned me, but I didn't listen." He became silent again. "After the first time, we had to run. Once we found a safe province to settle in, he beat the holy hell out of me." His hand rubbed the scars on the back of his shoulder.

I stared at the rest of the scars on his back. Knowing where they came from and why didn't lessen the ache in my chest.

He chuckled in a cold way that sent a shiver down my back.

"But once the beast gets the taste for blood, it is always on the prowl. Hunters learned this, and they tracked their virgins closely. My next transgression cost my father his life." He sighed. "It seems my alter ego's favorite delicacy is broken virginity."

"I guess my sister's cookies are now his favorite."

He turned towards me. I shifted, still holding the torn dress up over my chest and privates, uncomfortable with his candid stare. When his gaze dropped to the box in my hand, he crossed the distance and plucked it from my hand.

He took one out and sampled it. "As good as this is, I doubt it was the cookie that saved you." He smiled. "You fucked the bear and survived. That, My Queen, is uniquely yours, and yours alone."

<hr>

KYLE FOUND ME A shirt that I could wear since my dress was a total loss. I used one of his belts to fasten a waistline, and then I stepped back into the bedroom. Kyle sat at the small table in the bedroom corner, studying Senator Brax's vile decree.

He glanced up when I entered, and his gaze lingered on my shoulder. Blood had already seeped through the fabric.

He dropped the papers and stood. "I need to patch your wounds." He crossed, grabbed my good arm, and nearly dragged me into the dressing room.

"I am fine," I said as he started unbuttoning the shirt. When I knocked his hands away, he grabbed mine.

"You are bleeding," he said, staring me down.

I couldn't argue with him, because he was right. The fabric on my shoulder was already tacky. He sat me in the chair and then turned, rummaging through the shelves and grabbing gauze and other items before dumping them next to me. After he took a seat across from me, he raised his eyebrows.

"I can't very well patch you up through the shirt."

I rolled my eyes and carefully pulled my arm out of the sleeve, trying to poke my shoulder out of the shirt opening.

"Just take it off," he said, exasperated.

I was more self-conscious now than when we were ripping each other's clothing off. I unbuttoned the shirt the rest of the way and slid it off my injured shoulder. Heat filled my cheeks, and I glanced at the floor.

"Elsa," he said softly.

I forced myself to meet his gaze.

"You are beautiful with or without clothes. Even blood smeared as you are, you are beautiful," he said. The softness in his voice reflected in his eyes for a brief instant. He shook his head as if to clear his own mind and then focused on my wounds.

When he poured alcohol on my shoulder, I bit my lip to keep from wincing. His cleaning of the cuts was gentle enough for me to wonder why I thought he was such an ass. When my shoulder was bandaged properly, he handed me a fresh shirt and left me to get myself put together.

"Did you read the fine print?" he asked when I came in, the question clipped. His lips pressed thin, and the fire had returned to his gaze.

"What fine print?"

With a laugh, he looked at the paper again. "Senator Brax has this written so that his vote counts when approving a suitor. That old shit certainly covered all his tracks. Basically, he made sure you would have to marry him. There isn't even an option for you to concede the throne to him as a more palatable choice." He dropped the paper onto the table and reached for the box of cookies. He tossed the empty box back on the table, his face a mask of disgust.

"You ate all the cookies?" I asked, staring at the empty box.

"Is that really what you should focus on?"

His tone reminded me exactly why I thought he was a jerk, and I glared at him. "My sister made those for me."

He pointed at me. "You are going to need to learn to share."

I huffed and waved at our surroundings. "What do you call this?"

His lips twitched into a smile. "You didn't share this castle willingly."

I crossed my arms.

He laughed and turned the chair towards me. "If you're hungry, I have something you can eat." His eyebrow rose suggestively, and he pointed to his lap.

"You really are an ass." I headed for the door.

"Thank you for the cookies," he called after me as I descended the stairs.

When I reached the snow at the bottom of the outside steps, I glanced back at the glistening castle.

He leaned on the balcony, smiling down at me. "When is the wedding?"

I stopped and stared up at him. "Tomorrow at dusk."

"I'll be there."

I turned away. "You better be," I muttered under my breath.

FROZEN Chapter 10

IT WAS WELL PAST midnight by the time I caught sight of the town. It almost looked like daylight in the town square. I racked my brain, trying to figure out what event I was missing, but my mind came up empty. I hurried towards the gates, which now had guards that were awake and on alert.

They eyed my strange attire, but remained quiet as they opened the gates for me.

The moment I stepped across the threshold to my kingdom, I was seized. My hands were covered quicker than I could react and then bound behind my back with a harsh yank.

"Unhand me. I am the queen!"

"Murderess," one guard snarled as they dragged me to the town square.

Almost every citizen of Bryggen was present, holding a torch, which explained the lights. Even Anna and Kris were in the crowd, but instead of the angry masks the rest of the crowd wore, their faces reflected horror.

The crowd parted for the guards dragging me, and in the center of the town square stood the frozen bodies of the men I had killed with my ice blast.

"Queen Elsa, please tell us you have a valid explanation for the murder of these innocent men," Senator Brax bellowed over the din from his perch on the gallows.

I straightened my back. "They were far from innocent. They attempted to kill the man I have chosen to stand by me as my husband." I stared the senator down as a hush fell over the kingdom.

The senator's eyes narrowed. The flush grew in his cheeks. The bastard didn't expect my response. He studied me, his gaze lingering on my clothing, and his head cocked to the side.

"Where is this man?" he asked, looking around at the crowd and then back at me, challenging my station.

"He is not here."

"Does he have a name?" he asked.

"Kyle."

"Kyle, from what house?"

"From the house of Bryggen."

Silence fell over the kingdom. Shocked stares fell on me. I wasn't the only one who studied the kingdom's heritage. It was taught in every home and in every school across the land. Murmurs started in the crowd, like a hissing whisper that grew.

"Are we supposed to believe the long-dead king of the Hanseatic League is your betrothed?" He laughed and opened the pillory next to him on the podium. "Until you impart the truth, you will remain in the stocks, and if you haven't confessed your sins by the time the sun breaks the horizon, the people will decide your fate."

The guards dragged me on stage and forced my neck into the space just before the top of the pillory came down with a bang, locking my head between the wood. My hands were still covered and bound behind me, leaving me helpless.

I blinked, wondering what the hell had just happened.

"Let me out!" I snarled, and cloth was shoved between my teeth, gagging me.

Senator Brax crouched in front of me. "You should have accepted your fate," he whispered, and then looked behind me at the gallows. "Because now you are facing death instead of a comfortable existence by my side."

I glared at him as he walked away, leaving me bent over with my hands bound behind my back. "You bastard," I muttered into the rag.

He produced a knife, and my heart jumped into my throat. The last person relegated to the stocks had been stripped and humiliated before his sentence was passed. It seemed the good senator was going to follow the stockade rule book, despite the fact I was still reigning queen.

I struggled to free my hands as the belt I was wearing was yanked from my waist. The fabric of my shirt fell next, leaving me in boots and the gauze covering my shoulder. My only companions were the dead, propped close enough in proximity for the stench of decay to fill my nostrils.

Senator Brax grabbed my shoulder, squeezing the wounds Kyle had stitched up. Pain radiated down my arm, but I refused to cry out. I would not give the senator the satisfaction, no matter what he had in mind.

I looked beyond the dead to meet my sister's horrified gaze at the back of the crowd.

She struggled in Kris's arms, her cries drowned by the hostile crowd's vile cat calls. I slowly shook my head at her. I didn't want her to become collateral damage of Senator Brax's grand plan. She needed to calm down. Hell, she needed to go get my one and only chance for survival.

I flicked my gaze towards the hills where my ice castle hid and then back to her. Her struggles slowed as I willed her to understand my meaning.

I needed the man-beast. I needed Kyle to stand witness for me, and I needed the bear to tear Senator Brax's head clean off.

Senator Brax stepped into my sight again and waved a metal pear for all the crowd to see. I cringed at the thought of where he intended to put that thing. The crowd went wild. Their blood-lust was as palpable as the senator's.

Anna stilled, and her eyes widened before she turned into Kris's chest. Even from this distance, I could see her shoulders shaking.

Her husband held her with his lips pressed into a thin line. I didn't think I had ever seen a look of pure murder on my brother-in-law before, but it was there now, as clear as the hatred brewing in my heart.

Kris tilted his head so his ear was closer to Anna. He blinked and glanced down at her before returning his gaze to mine. He turned with her, escorting her back towards the castle and their quarters beyond the interior gates. So she did not have to witness my torture.

"Maybe this will draw a confession out of you." The Senator smirked and disappeared behind me.

I hoped Anna got my message, because if word didn't get to Kyle, I wouldn't survive to see tomorrow's sunset.

"She is still the queen," someone behind me snarled.

"Step aside or you will be exiled once she has been sentenced for her crimes," Senator Brax said.

"My family will gladly leave this kingdom far behind if you dare to harm my sister. Until judgement has been rendered, she is still the queen, and you will treat her as such. Torture is reserved for common criminals and spies, not royalty. The humiliation of being locked in the stocks until morning is enough until her trial commences." Kris's voice boomed.

Kris had somehow got onto the podium before that bastard skewed me with that torture contraption. And in doing so, created the perfect diversion that would allow my sister to slip out of the kingdom.

"She is not your sister," Senator Brax hissed.

"She is family, and you are treading on dangerous ground," Kris spat back.

Kris was a large man and was usually as docile as a puppy. But the edge in his voice must have matched that of his stance, because the senator paused.

"This isn't over," the senator said, then stomped off to the edge of the platform and sent a searing glare my way.

I presumed Kris blocked access to me as no one else attempted to dole out their own justice, as so many had in past situations like this. I was so thankful someone stood up for what was left of my honor, because if the senator had his way, I would be as close to dead as possible when they slipped the rope over my head to steal my last breath.

I glanced towards the mountains and prayed Kyle wouldn't hurt Anna. I prayed they would return to Bryggen before the sun crested the horizon.

Otherwise, my betrothed would find me dangling from a hangman's noose.

FROZEN Chapter 11

MY ENTIRE FORM ACHED from being in this position for the last three hours. I couldn't put pressure on my neck without squeezing my windpipe and if my legs gave out, I would surely break my neck. Senator Brax had taken a seat and leaned against one of the posts, his eyelids dipping closed every so often.

A rumble began as a pounding in the ground as if dozens of horses were storming the gates. At first, I wrote it off as exhaustion, but when those that remained keeping vigil started exchanging glances, I knew it wasn't just my imagination. Panic filled their faces as the whispers of an earthquake found my ears.

It had been years since the earth shook in Bryggen, but the memory of that was as strong and horrifying as my freezing the kingdom. At first, all eyes fell on me in that accusatory way I was used to, until the gates crashed open and white fur flew towards the center of the courtyard.

It took me a second to focus on what I was seeing. Kyle and Anna rode on the back of the massive polar bear that had been relegated to the corner of the first floor of the ice castle.

The rest of the crowd froze in place at the spectacle. Kyle hopped off the bear and helped Anna down before turning to me. The bear hovered over them in a protective stance, his massive claws ready to strike at anyone who threatened Kyle.

But that was the least of the shock waves permeating the kingdom.

Kyle wore his coat of arms.

The Bryggen coat of arms.

The white polar bear behind the black and gray boat was one we all studied in school. It was the crest that the king of the Hanseatic League wore over two hundred years before. It was said when he donned his family crest; he was out for blood.

The glare in his eyes confirmed that legend.

Senator Brax's mouth hung open, just like everyone else's.

He hopped up on the platform and ripped the pillory in two, freeing me. The top that had held me in place flew at least ten feet and then clattered onto the wood. Kyle cut the ropes holding my hands together, freeing me from my painful binds. I took a shaky step towards him and collapsed.

Kyle caught me, sweeping me into his arms. He said nothing as he carried me from the podium.

When he whistled, the bear followed. Both Anna and Kris fell in step as well. Kyle marched us into the castle, and no one dared to stop the bizarre procession.

Kyle set me down. As he secured the gate, Anna threw her cape around me, and the bear curled up in the corner and promptly fell asleep. The transformation from angry guardian to docile house pet was disconcerting.

When Kyle turned back to us, his blue eyes pierced mine. Fiery anger filled them, and he crossed to stand in front of me.

"Did he harm you?" he asked, his voice a growl that carried his possessiveness.

My hand traveled to the bandage on my shoulder, but I shook my head. Squeezing a wound and what he'd been about to do to me were different, and I didn't want to send Kyle into a murder spree of his own.

"Kris wouldn't allow him to." I waved to my brother-in-law by my side.

His hard gaze moved to Kris, and he gave him a nod before looking at me. "I don't know whether your sister is brave or just foolish. Rushing into a bear's den is usually a death sentence." His gaze flicked to her. "But I am glad I didn't immediately snap her neck. She also promised me cookies if I saved you." His eyebrows rose expectantly at her.

I pulled the cape tighter around my body as Anna scurried off to get him his reward.

Kris stood guard over me, his expression unreadable as he sized up the stranger in our midst.

"Go take care of Anna and the children," I said.

He glanced at me. "I'm not sure which is more dangerous—the senator, or this man," he said and crossed his arms.

I inhaled and glanced between the man trying to save my honor and the one who had already taken it. "Kyle is much more dangerous than the senator, so it is a good thing he seems to be on our side."

"I will not harm my betrothed." Kyle stood tall, but hostility still radiated from him the way the cold radiated from me. "But I will exact inexplicable harm on those that falsely accused her of murder." His eyes narrowed in a way that sent a shiver up my back.

Kris's arms relaxed and fell by his side as Anna came running back into the castle from her quarters, carrying one of the large boxes of cookies.

"Thank you for taking the time to listen to me, and for saving my sister from that twisted bastard," she said breathlessly and rubbed her throat. A bruise in the shape of a handprint stood out against her pale neck.

Kris noticed it too, and his hands clenched into fists. He glared, his nostrils flared, and his face reddened.

Both Anna and I stepped in between Kris and Kyle.

I faced Kris with my hands splayed in front of me. "Don't."

Anna echoed my words, her hands pressed against her husband's chest. "I shot him with an arrow the last time I saw him, so he had a right to be... skeptical of my intentions."

"He hurt you," Kris snapped.

Anna glanced over her shoulder and shrugged. "He scared me," she admitted. "But he came through in the end."

"I don't like him," Kris said, and Anna laughed.

"Join the club," she said. "Let's go make sure the children are okay." She yanked on his arm.

Kris followed her but glared over his shoulder several times before they disappeared out of sight.

I turned to Kyle. He already had a cookie from the box and was nibbling on it.

"When they come to their senses, they will storm this castle." I waved to the bolted gate.

"Don't you command the armed forces?" he asked around the cookie.

I stripped my gloves, then stretched my fingers and rubbed my wrists. "I share that with the senate. Ever since I froze the land, they wanted some sort of balance. A unanimous vote to oust me from the throne would require the army to be at the senate's direction."

I took a moment to appreciate him in full uniform. He was formidable, and the crest created a certain thrill of fear. His stark blue eyes regarded me, and hunger lay beyond the blue. He smiled.

"I need clothing." I turned and headed to my quarters. It wasn't until the door closed behind me I realized Kyle had followed.

"Your sister mentioned the senator had threatened the pear."

I glanced back at him and let the cloak fall to the floor. "Was it truly my honor that you came back to save, or just your station as the future king?" I turned towards him, giving him a full view of my naked self.

He put the box of cookies on the table and licked his fingers as he slowly crossed the distance. "I can't have my queen mutilated and her chances of bearing my children ruined because of some selfish, self-serving senator." He stopped in front of me. "Had I smelled fresh blood when I approached you, I would have torn his head off on the spot."

"You or the bear?"

He smiled and reached out, then turned my head to the side. "Your bandages need changing."

I yanked my head out of his grip. "Is that all you are interested in? Me as a harvester of your offspring?" I crossed my arms, covering my chest.

He raised an eyebrow. "I am fully aware of you, Elsa. And in case you hadn't noticed, I have formally announced my lineage to this kingdom. That wasn't something I had intended to do. At least not until I was in a position of power."

"Your power was threatened, and that's why you came out of the shadows."

"No. *You* were threatened. That is why I came out." His lips formed a smile. "Well, that and cookies." He hooked his thumb over his shoulder towards the box of sweet confections on the table.

I slapped his chest, and he caught my hand, holding it in place.

"The bear in me wanted to paint that square with the blood of those celebrating your torture." His gaze turned serious. "I'm not so sure I like whatever this is. It makes me reckless." He stared down at my hand splayed on the fabric of his tunic and pulled me closer to him. "But it also makes me feel alive." He met my gaze and dipped down, taking the opportunity to press the softest of kisses on my lips.

My skin tingled in anticipation. He pulled away, leaving me wanting more.

"Now get dressed in finery suited for court."

I tilted my head.

"Summon the priest. We are getting married now, and then I am taking the throne back. The senate is compromised, and we will deal with them as a single unified force of nature."

His sureness in our victory gave me pause. If the senate had taken over the army, innocents would die in the exchange. Besides, if Senator Brax was to meet his fate, I would be tried for treason.

"Did you read that document?"

He smiled and unfurled it from his pocket. "This is the senate's downfall." He tucked it away. "Now go get some clothes on before I do something inappropriate again."

I was not used to being ordered around, and I didn't agree on disbanding the senate, but he had a point. If they unanimously voted to put Senator Brax in as king, they were not doing what was best for this kingdom. And if he snowed them into the vote, well then, he was far more nefarious than I gave him credit for.

FROZEN Chapter 12

I STEPPED OUT OF the dressing room in a fine silk dress that was as blue as Kyle's eyes. The silver flares of snowflakes embroidered into the fabric sparkled as I crossed the room. I opened the cabinet that contained my diamonds and decorated my neck with them before I set my ornate crown on my head.

With all the grace that a queen should encompass, I climbed down the stairs into the entry, where Kyle stood, waiting. The crown perched on his head made my eyes widen. The last man to wear the crown of Bryggen had been my father, so to see anyone else wear it with the same command stalled my heart.

He held his arm out to me.

"You can't possibly marry him."

I turned to see Anna at the far side of the room near the castle courtyard. Behind her in the yard, her three children played with sticks, pretending to sword fight.

on the other, evidence that he had been pulled from bed. He hadn't been in the town square when Senator Brax had accused me of murder or humiliated me. He hadn't been in the square when Kyle made his grand entrance, either.

"Father Kelly, this is Kyle Bryggen. My betrothed," I said, and his eyes went wider. "Please proceed with the marriage."

He blinked and licked his lips, looking around for any sort of diversion that would help him come to terms with my orders. We waited patiently while he wiped his face.

"I apologize. I must not be awake." He glanced at the two of us. "Did you say Kyle Bryggen, as in the founder of Bryggen?"

Kyle smiled. "Yes, Father, she did. And as impossible as it seems, I am indeed real and standing here waiting for you to bless this union."

Father Kelly's mouth opened and closed twice. He smoothed out his hair and positioned himself in front of us. He cleared his throat and looked at Kyle, expectantly.

Kyle turned to me and took a deep breath before his words echoed in the small chamber. "You cannot possess me, for I belong to myself, just as you belong to yourself. But while we both wish it, I give you that which is mine to give. You cannot command me, for I am a free man. But I shall serve you in those ways you require. I pledge to you that yours will be the only name I cry aloud in the night. The first bite of my meat and the first drink from my cup belongs to you. I pledge to you my living and my dying, each equally in your care. I shall be a shield for your back and you for mine. I shall honor you above all others. This is a marriage of equals. This is my wedding vow to you."

I stared up into his intense eyes, captivated by his voice and his choice of words. Their meaning left me breathless. When the priest cleared his throat, I sucked my lower lip in between my teeth before I recited my vows, taking his as my guide. "While we both wish it, I give you that which is mine to give. You cannot command nor possess me, for I am a free woman. But I shall serve you in the ways you require. I pledge to you that yours will be the only name I cry aloud in the night. The first bite of my meat and the first drink from my cup belongs to you. I pledge to you my living and my dying, each equally in your care. I shall be a shield for your back and you for mine. I shall honor you above all others. This is indeed a marriage of equals. This is my wedding vow to you."

"Show me the palms of the hands closest to me," the priest said.

I offered my right hand to the priest, and Kyle put his left out. Our eyes never left each other, even when the sharp pain of the blade sliced into my skin. The priest pressed our bloodied palms together, and Kyle intertwined his fingers through mine.

As our blood mingled, my palm stung, sending varying waves of hot and cold through my veins. His eyes flashed, and his hand squeezed mine tighter. His lips formed a small smile, as if he felt the same wild sensations that flowed through my form.

"With the passing of blood, and the pledging of vows, you are now one in the eyes of God." The priest wrapped a sash around our hands, binding them together. "May God be with you and bless you. May you see your children's children. May you be poor in misfortune and rich in blessings. May you know nothing but happiness from this day forward." He made the sign of the cross. "In the name of the father, the son, and the holy spirit."

"Amen," both Kyle and I said.

"You may kiss your bride," the priest said.

Kyle glanced at him. "Ring the wedding bells," he ordered, and then pulled me to his lips.

An animalistic fervor took hold of me, as if his kiss ignited the part of me that had lain dormant for all these years. Even our wild lovemaking earlier did not compare to the fire lighting my soul at this moment.

Clapping from the chapel entrance pulled us out of the trance, and we both glanced towards my niece and nephews, who were clapping wildly. Anna leaned against the doorframe with her arms crossed, but there was a smirk on her lips, like perhaps she could tolerate Kyle in the end.

Heat filled my cheeks, and the chapel bells chimed just as a ruckus breached the courtyard.

We turned with our hands still clasped. Beyond Anna, I could see a bear charging.

"Get inside!" I cried out and pointed to the side of the chapel that was fortified with stone.

Anna corralled the kids into the corner with her. The army flooded into the courtyard, hurling arrows at Kyle's bear. With our hands still clasped, the burn of his anger mingled in my blood. The beast roared as another arrow pierced his hide. Kyle squeezed my hand and then loosened his grip. Before he could unclasp his palm from mine, I raised my left hand, willing a wall between the bear and those who wanted to harm him.

A shroud of ice formed between the center of the courtyard and the chapel, safeguarding the bear and those of us in the sanctuary. The giant polar bear stumbled and fell short of the opening. A dozen arrows peppered his back, and blood seeped from his mouth.

Kyle let go of my hand and charged to the beast. He placed his bloodied hand on the bear's head in a sign of solidarity. The polar bear's gaze lifted to him, and then his last breath wheezed out. The massive beast's chest slowed and then stopped.

Kyle glared through the glass-like ice, his gaze as hard as the barrier itself. That low growl that signified the start of his shift permeated the space.

"Kyle," I snapped, and he shot a glare in my direction. "My King," I added, softening my voice.

He stared at me, his fists tight enough for blood to drip out of his left hand where the priest had cut him. The other was completely white. I imagined the welts on his palms and took a step closer.

Movement on the other side of the ice caught my attention. I gasped.

Senator Brax stood next to a guard who had a knife to Kris's throat.

"Daddy!"

The cry came from behind me, and I walled Anna and the children into the chapel and out of any sort of danger that may come forth. I stepped close to Kyle and took his hand in mine. He slowly unclenched and wrapped his hand around mine.

I swiped my hand in the air, and the ice evaporated. All the arrows that had embedded in my wall fell to the ground in gentle whispers.

"Let my brother-in-law go," I said and stood at the ready, my hand splayed toward the danger.

"You violated the law," Senator Brax said. "And you must face the repercussions."

"She was protecting me from the assassins you sent," Kyle said. "Arrest him." He pointed at the senator. When no one moved, Kyle continued. "Do you understand what those bells signify? Your queen has married. Which makes me king. And if I recall Bryggen law correctly, as king, the guard works for me. Not you, Senator Brax." He pulled the papers out of his pocket. "You who had the most to lose if this moment came to fruition." He let the wind take the papers.

The guard holding Kris pulled the knife away.

"The law states the senate must approve her choice of suitor prior to marriage. She has broken yet another law. Besides, any man who would dare don the house of Bryggen crest is not stable enough to become royalty."

"Stability has never been my strong suit," Kyle said. "But I assure you, I am of royal blood. I am the house of Bryggen. And I am ruler of this kingdom." He pulled his hand out of mine. "And if you do not unhand my brother-in-law, I will take your head off." He stepped around the bear and stood tall, staring the guard down.

No one moved.

"If you move that knife away from his throat, you will join them on the hanging block," Senator Brax threatened the soldier holding the knife to Kris's neck. "Surrender or he dies."

The number of arrows pointed at us chilled my soul. I could tell Kyle wanted to jump into battle, but the collateral damage was too great.

I slowly closed my hand. "Stand down," I whispered low enough for just Kyle to hear me.

Kyle glared at me, the fury visible in his gaze and the muscles taut across his back. I shook my head and dropped my arms to my side.

"Seize them and take them to the dungeons while the senate decides their fate."

For the second time in less than twelve hours, my hands were covered and bound behind my back.

"Let him go," I said as the guards dragged me past Kris.

"He will stand trial for his treasonous acts as well."

"You bastard!" I kicked out, catching nothing but air.

Anna and the kids cried out from behind the ice as the three of us were led to the dungeon cages for sentencing. Whatever the senator had planned for us, it would not be pretty.

The moment the arrows and knives were not threatening those I loved, then all hell would break loose.

FROZEN Chapter 13

WE WERE ALL SEPARATED in the dungeon. Guards marched me into a room that had a nasty-looking iron hook dangling from the ceiling. It was thicker than a man's fist, and the point glistened with deadly intent. Three equally sharp barbs cascaded down the inside of the hook. It looked like the type of tool used to catch a whale, but I knew better.

It wasn't used for fishing. It was used for killing in the most heinous of ways.

Three guards surrounded me while doors closed and keys jangled in the hallway. It wasn't until the other cells were secure that Senator Brax stepped into the room, holding the king's crown in his hand. He swung the door behind him, but it never latched. The guards moved back, giving him some room.

He set the bedazzled circle on his head. While Kyle looked regal with the crown adorning his white hair, the senator looked like a child trying on a paper crown. He looked ridiculous. He walked over to the iron hook and took it in his grip, studying it before glancing at me.

"This will do much better than the pear." He caressed the sharp point. He crossed to stand in front of me.

He nodded towards the guards, and one grabbed me around the waist. The other two tore a slit in my dress and each grabbed a leg.

I slammed my head back into the face of the guard who held me, smashing his nose. He stumbled back, but his grip, as well as the two holding my legs didn't loosen. I screamed as the senator lined up the hook. The minute the metal touched me, I froze in place at his frightening intent.

He was going to make sure I'd never conceive. The size of that hook would more than likely kill me. I couldn't catch my breath.

"Or you could just agree to marry me and attend to my needs," he said.

I blinked at him. The only way that would ever happen is if he had Kyle and my entire family killed, because Anna and Kris would never stand by and let this nutcase make me his slave. I licked my lips and opened my mouth to speak. When nothing came out, he leaned closer.

I slammed my forehead into his face. A satisfying crack filled the room, and I bellowed, "Never!"

He stumbled and fell. The hook caught on the fabric of my dress, dangling in place as the senator cried out in pain from the floor. His nose gushed blood and his face turned a shade of red I had never seen.

One guard holding a leg reached for the hook.

"That is mine to fuck her with," Senator Brax snarled through the flow of blood.

The guard pulled his hand back as if a snake had bitten it.

Wiping his bloody hands on his pants, Senator Brax climbed to his feet. He stepped towards me, reaching for the metal when the ground rumbled, and the loudest snarl echoed through the dungeon.

The door was nearly yanked off its hinges, and the feral bear charged.

Senator Brax never knew what hit him. One minute, his mouth was hanging open, and the next, a headless body crumpled to the ground. The crown that had been on his head spun through the air and landed on the bear.

The guards dropped me, scrambling for their swords, but none of them were fast enough. The three men met the same fate as the senator.

Blood painted the walls, and the crowned bear lumbered over to where I sat, stunned by the violent justice he'd delivered. He nuzzled me with his nose, and I stared into his deep blue eyes. My gaze went to the crown on his head and I smiled.

"I wasn't sure you would make an appearance or not."

He transitioned, squatting between my outstretched legs. "I will always have your back. It just took a little longer to pick the lock than I thought it would." He glanced up at the dangling hook, and a dark shadow crossed his face. "Almost too long, it would seem." Kyle glanced over his shoulder at the dismembered head of the senator, stood, and kicked it into the corner. "Sick bastard," he mumbled under his breath.

When he turned back to me, he offered one of his gore-ridden hands. I stared at it for a moment. My hands were still bound behind me and I leaned forward, holding them high enough for him to see. He shook most of the flesh off before a sharp claw extended and sliced through the binds holding my wrists together. He offered his hand again, and I accepted his help, despite the roil of disgust that clenched my stomach. As soon as I was on my feet, he reached behind me and picked up my crown. It must have tumbled off with one of my head butts.

He grabbed the keys off one of the bodies and led me out of the room. He unlocked the cell next to mine and swung the door open. He stepped back into the cell we had vacated and picked up the senator's head while Kris stepped into the empty hallway.

"What happened?" Kris asked, his gaze dropping to Kyle's bloody quarry.

"They were going to irreparably harm my wife." He waved towards the cell I had been captive in, but Kris's gaze jumped from the twisted door hanging on the room I had been in, to the bloodbath inside, and then the senator's head in Kyle's grip.

"I thought..." he started.

"Kyle is a man-beast," I said.

Kris's eyes widened, and he paled. "The new king is a... shifter?" His voice cracked.

"I like that description much better than man-beast," Kyle said and led us out of the dungeon.

We stepped into the bright morning sunshine, and Kyle crossed to the castle proper, toward the town square.

Anna and the kids were held in cages, and the Bryggen army had assembled around them. On the platform, the guillotine has been rolled out. I guessed the good senator had already passed judgement without input from the rest of the senate or the townspeople.

Kyle led me up the stairs quietly as Kris crossed towards Anna. Guards stopped him.

"Let him pass," Kyle said, his voice booming.

Faces turned towards us and eyes widened.

"My wife, your queen, has been accused of murdering those men." He pointed at the dead men still propped up at the corner of the podium. "They shot an arrow at my back. That is the act of a coward." His gaze pierced the crowd, traveling over the guards and the gathering townspeople.

"Where is Senator Brax?" one of the guards asked. He looked as if he were going to vomit.

Kyle tossed the senator's head in the middle of the townspeople. They parted as the head came to a stop. A gasp fell over the crowd, and a different guard unsheathed his sword.

"Would you like the same fate?" Kyle asked, his voice feral enough for the guard to pause. "Since Elsa is now my wife, I am your king. I expect you to kneel and show some respect."

No one moved.

"Now!"

Even I jumped at the volume of his command.

Kris was the first to drop to a knee and bow his head in respect. I never insisted the kingdom kneel before me. It was a strange feeling to see the slow progression of familiar faces dropping.

When everyone was on their knees, Kyle continued. "It seems the senate has been compromised by greed and power. Therefore, they are immediately relieved of duty."

Shocked faces shot up to stare at the new king with open mouths.

"Elsa and I will discuss how to go about replacing the value the senate provided, but in its current form, it was only interested in serving itself and not this kingdom, as evidenced by the last decree that called for a ruse that would have made Senator Brax king."

Silence descended on the square as people exchanged confused glances. Even some of the former senators looked stunned by Kyle's announcement.

"This kingdom has made poor choices with the senate at the helm. It will not continue."

"Why should we accept you as king?" one man yelled out. He had been a Brax loyalist, fighting every forward step I tried to make for the people of Bryggen.

"Because he is my choice to stand by my side. And he is worthy of the station," I said.

"Why should we accept a stranger as king?" a man in the audience yelled out, crossing his arms.

"I am not a stranger to Bryggen. This kingdom wouldn't exist if I hadn't created it and oversaw the trade routes in and around this isolated cove." He waved at his soiled tunic. "Do you not recognize this crest?"

The man looked at Kyle's shirt and dropped his gaze. "Impossible," he challenged.

"It is just as impossible as someone freezing the region in a fit of anger," I said, and more heads jerked up. Before I lost my cool and laid frozen waste to this kingdom, no one believed this power pounding through my veins existed. I was impossible incarnate.

"Did he force you to marry him?" a woman in the back asked.

"No. This was my choice." Heat filled my cheeks, and I glanced up at him. I did not voice that this was expedited because of Senator Brax's latest decree. "He can be a bit of an ass at times, though."

Eyes widened. I smirked up at him and raised an eyebrow. His lips toyed with a smile, and then he wiped it away, ignoring my public dig. But now almost every woman in the crowd, as well as a handful of the men, suppressed a smirk.

Kyle rolled his eyes and focused on the soldiers. "Let my sister-in-law and her children out of those cages."

They traded panicked glances with each other. Anna met my gaze and then turned her body so I could see what was behind her in an adjoining cage. Three hungry cougars paced in the tight space.

My heart plummeted. The complete annihilation of my family had been planned. And no one in the crowd looked as if they would have stopped it. A burn rose, heating my skin. I clenched my jaw as the fury of what could have been raced through me.

Murmurs began in the crowd, and Kyle squeezed my hand.

The podium we stood on, blistered with frost. Waves of cold air seeped from my skin.

"You would have allowed this?" I hissed, waving at the plans put in place by the man whose head lay in the dirt.

Gazes dropped to the ground, and faces reddened with shame.

"This will never happen under my reign." Kyle released my hand and hopped down to the ground.

The crowd parted, giving him a wide berth.

"Help my family," Kris said, still on his knees and looking up at Kyle with both fear and sadness reflected in his face.

Kyle crossed to the cage. The snarl that came from his lips made the wild cats cower as equally as it did Anna and the kids. Those surrounding him flinched back, their features traced with fear.

Kyle reached his hand through the bar and ruffled Sara's hair. "Do not worry, little one. That growl was not meant for you."

"That is the only way out," Anna said, pointing at the gate separating the two cages. It was intended to be opened during the senator's killing spree.

Kyle chuckled. "No, sweet sister-in-law. That is not the only way out of this cage." He wrapped his hands around two of the four bars in front of her. Metal groaned as he reshaped the straight rods into bows as easily as she shaped cookie dough. The two center bars were next, and when they were as wide as the outer bows, he stopped.

He reached in and plucked Sara out of the cage, setting her on the ground next to her father. Kristoff was next, followed by Dennis. And then he offered Anna his hand. He helped her out, then reshaped the bars and growled at the cats once more.

When he turned and met my gaze, I thought my knees would give out. His display of raw strength affected me as much as his touch had, and all I wanted to do was consummate our marriage.

His stride was sure when he returned and helped me down from the stage. "Now, if you will excuse me, I have a wife to satisfy." With his arm around my waist, he led me back to the castle.

FROZEN Chapter 14

"A BIT OF AN ass?" he asked as the door closed behind us. "I should punish you for that comment." He towered over me with a cross of displeasure and lust written in his gaze.

"Yes, you can be a supreme ass."

He grabbed my waist and yanked me against his hard body.

I glanced down at our blood-streaked skin. "As much as I want to explore the hostility sparking in the room, I think we need to rid ourselves of that bastard's blood first."

"The bear doesn't mind the blood," he said and pressed his lips to mine.

I pushed away. "But I do. I do not want any part of that insidious evil spawn to be involved in the consummation of my marriage."

Kyle blinked as if my words were a physical slap, recoiling from me. The idea I'd planted raked disgust over his features and he nodded.

I grabbed his hand and led him to a small room that overlooked the sea. Robes hung from posts on the walls, and the inner room was brightly lit with the sun's rays. I removed my clothes, and Kyle followed suit, folding his tunic and placing it on a clear bench. I led him to a spot in the center of the room.

"Where is the tub?" he asked, his brow creased in confusion.

I smiled and moved him a few paces to the right. "Just stand here."

I crossed to a lever and turned it. A circle in the ceiling opened, cascading water warmed by the sun over Kyle. He tilted his head into the fine spray and sighed.

I paused, watching the man who I had struck a marriage deal with, and I realized there was something deeper there. Something that moved me and indeed made me feel alive. He wasn't what he pretended to be. He wasn't a self-serving bastard who just took what he wanted. He had heart and passion and was one of the handsomest men I had ever laid eyes on.

He glanced at me and smiled, cranking his finger towards him in that come hither silent command. I cranked the knob as far as it would go and obeyed his request. As I passed the shelf full of soaps and oils, I grabbed a bar of one of my favorite sweet scents and joined my husband under the waterfall.

"What is this?" He pointed to the ceiling.

"A shower." I handed him the soap. "I designed and helped build it."

"It is a slice of heaven," he said and laughed, taking the soap from my outstretched hand. "Just like you are, my little engineer." He tapped my nose and focused on scrubbing the senator's blood off his skin.

When he finished, he turned his focus on me. He peeled away the bandage on my shoulder and washed me from head to toe with a gentleness that belied his glistening muscles. The care he took flushed my skin more than the water did, and when he stood before me, meeting my gaze, the hunger reflected in his eyes as bright as the sun.

The soap dropped from his hands, and he picked me up in his arms, planting a kiss that made every inch of my skin burn. Before I knew it, he had me against the marble wall, pressing into me. His intensity pulled a gasp from me, and I wrapped my legs around him, pulling him closer. His hardness entered me with such force, I cried out, arching into him with the same frantic need reflected in his ravenous kisses.

We clung to each other, riding a wave of fury and lust and everything in between. His power and possessiveness brought forth my appetite, and by the time we finished, my back ached. We both panted, trying to regain our breath. I was sure if the wall wasn't holding us in place, we would have collapsed onto the floor from sheer satisfaction.

On shaking legs, Kyle carried me back under the water, still coupled and kissing. The cool stream slowed our breath and chilled the steam rising between us. He pulled away and tilted his face into the water, looking every bit like a god.

I wasn't sure this electric bliss between us would continue, or how we would be at ruling this kingdom together, but for a moment, being in Kyle's arms felt like all I would ever need in this world.

His blue gaze dropped to take me in, and he smiled. "Happy isn't so bad," he whispered, and captured my mouth in another kiss.

The End

Dark magic has a price.

While the kingdom's witches and warlocks were slaughtered to fulfill the queen's insidious plans, Maggie White, the last pureblood sorceress, escapes with the help of her best friend and seven dwarves.

Maggie enchants a forest with a blood spell to keep them hidden from the evil queen. But the queen's army of the dead are immune to the enchantment and bypass Maggie's protections.

Even though Maggie has been battle-ready since the day she went into hiding, she is not prepared for the army of the dead or their tainted blades.

If Maggie loses her fight, not only will she watch those she loves die, but her life force will be sucked from her bones, and her magic will give the queen the ultimate power to enslave the world.

SNOW Chapter 1

I WANDERED THROUGH THE thick woods, shooting small pulses of magic from my fingertips. The forest wrapped its pine scent around me while the chipmunks dodged my spells in our daily contest of hide and seek. Today, the rest of the animals that normally joined the game were scarce. I listened for danger.

Nothing broke the silence.

I reached the stream and dropped my buckets into the water. My reflection rippled. My red bow morphed into a morbid wave of dripping blood. I took a shaky breath and dragged the full buckets through my distorted reflection.

It had been years since the queen tried to penetrate the enchanted forest. My protection spell was bound by blood, and none of my bloodline remained. No counter spell would unlock this enchanted territory, and yet any time the forest animals didn't behave normally. My nerves raged.

My illusion of safety didn't stop my nightmares.

It didn't stop my paranoia.

It didn't stop my fears.

After all these years, I still wasn't strong enough to face the queen. My magic was too pure to handle such evil.

Shaking the dark thoughts from my head, I turned back towards the cottage on the other side of the forest.

Henry, my best friend and beloved, leaned against a thick oak tree with a blade of grass between his full lips. His shirt hung open, and the ripples of his well-defined muscles distracted me. His chestnut hair ruffled in the breeze, and he smiled, flashing teeth as white as newly fallen snow.

My skin warmed more from his grin than from the afternoon sunshine. I couldn't help but smile back.

"I didn't hear you following me today." My gaze drifted over his bare chest and back to his gray-green eyes. "I should have known you were there. The other animals weren't playing, just the chipmunks, and we all know they are not the brightest in the bunch."

He pulled the reed from his lips and crossed to me, stretching his hand out for one of the pails.

I raised an eyebrow. I was perfectly capable of hauling water back to the cottage.

"I'm just offering a hand, Maggie," he said in that deep timbre that made me shiver.

I understood why some referred to him as Prince Charming, but he was fierce and protective and sometimes not charming at all. This was *not* one of those times. Right now, he represented his nickname in all its sappy glory.

With a resigned sigh, I handed him a bucket.

We crossed the open glade into the thick forest. The chipmunks stayed hidden. His hand drifted to the small of my back, and the brush of his fingers on my dress created such a delicious heat.

We walked, and only the sloshing water interrupted my thoughts. His smile faded. He scanned the forest, sucking his lower lip between his teeth like he did when he was in problem-solving mode, or when he had news he knew I wouldn't like.

I hoped it was the former. I let him stew on whatever was on his mind until we came into a large clearing. Our cottage sat a few yards away from the woods, with a small plume of white smoke filtering from the chimney.

"What's bothering you?" I asked and opened the door.

Inside, seven dwarves sat around our table with papers strewn about, pulling my attention away from Henry. We stepped inside, and their chatter ended abruptly. Every set of eyes moved from me to Henry and back.

Whatever Henry was brooding over had to do with the concerned looks on every dwarf's face. I set the fresh water on the counter, turned to Henry, and crossed my arms.

He blew a stream of air from his lips before turning to the counter. His shoulders pulled taut, and he put his bucket down next to mine. The stress displayed in every one of his tight muscles set my body on high alert. Henry didn't tense up to just anything. He was my rock, my steady hand, my level head.

When he picked up the flyer on the table and handed it to me, I saw nothing that would cause the alarm sizzling in the air in the small cottage.

My picture stared back along with the queen's bounty on me. According to the advertisement, I was worth one hundred gold pieces, but I had to be brought in alive.

"She upped her price," I said and handed the flyer back to Henry with a shrug. She had been upping the ante for my head for years. This wasn't new, but their faces said there was more than just another rate hike in the bounty.

"These were posted *inside* the edge of the enchanted forest. We caught one of her lackeys at the boundary," Simon, the dwarf with the flaming red hair, said.

His words produced a darkness behind my eyes. The hunters were insanely brave or insanely stupid to breach the enchanted forest.

I glanced at Simon. He was just as protective of me as Henry, and his lips were set in a stern line.

Now that he had my attention, he continued, "He said the queen has hired a powerful mage to locate you."

"Really?" My eyebrows rose.

According to our sources, the queen had wiped the land of all who even remotely carried enchantments in their bones. She ingested the magic, leaving husks behind. I remembered the horrors she inflicted on my kind before the dwarves had whisked me away to the center of the forest for my protection. Besides the queen, I was the only living soul to still contain pure magic, but mine was nowhere near as strong as the queen's dark magic.

At least not yet.

"There are no mages left," Henry said.

Simon shrugged. "He said they know the forest is protecting the lost princess, Snow White. He said they know we are here." He pounded his finger on the table.

I rolled my eyes, feigning a certainty I did not feel.

"He said they know how to nullify the forest's magic," Bernard, the second in charge behind Simon, said. His white hair seemed to drift on an imaginary wind every time he spoke, as if the weight of his words moved the air around him.

That got my attention. I traded a glance with Henry.

"That's impossible," Henry scoffed.

It was utterly impossible, unless the queen had the blood of my ancestors. Only the spilling of their blood, or mine, could undo the protection spell I'd cast. Considering my mother was long buried and my father burned in a funeral pyre, I did not see how they could reverse my magic. But then again, I also thought all the mages in the land had been decimated.

An icy chill rode up my spine, and I stiffened my shoulders so it wouldn't settle in the back of my neck. I was not ready for a confrontation with the queen. I was not ready to have my heart pulled from my chest, not when I had found a home for it with Henry.

I turned, trudged into the back bedroom, and sat on the edge of the oversized bed. Henry followed and closed the door. His eyes held the same dread as I felt settling in my bones. He slid into the spot next to me and draped his arm over my shoulder, pulling me into him.

"We'll figure this out, too," he said.

I glanced at him with an expression that I was sure screamed doubt. "I'm not strong enough yet."

"Yes, you are." There wasn't an ounce of uncertainty in his voice or his face. "You are much stronger than you realize."

"Playing games with the wildlife is nothing. It won't keep me alive against Queen Odette. I have no defense against her dark magic." I stared him down.

"And yet you created this place. You enchanted the forest to keep you safe. You've been able to keep the queen's army out of these woods, and I don't see that changing."

For as much as I loved Henry, he sometimes could think foolish thoughts.

"If what Bernard says is true, then this is no longer a safe haven." I waved towards the door. "Which means we have to run."

Henry stiffened next to me and slowly shook his head. "There is nowhere to run to, Maggie."

He should know. He and the dwarves were the only ones allowed to pass through the invisible gates of the enchanted forest. He had been beyond our sanctuary many times over the years.

I hadn't left these woods since I fled the kingdom and escaped certain death at the hands of the queen.

My chest tightened. I had to come to grips with the reality of engaging in a final battle with evil.

SNOW Chapter 2

WHEN THE FIRST SIGN of light peeked through the curtains, I'd finally had enough of a night full of terrorizing visions of the dead. I was ready for the day and for the distraction of my morning chores. I crawled out of Henry's grasp, trading the warmth of his arms for the coolness of the floor.

I crossed to the window in a sleep-deprived stupor, feeling like I was still dreaming. I half expected a rotting hand to reach through the window. Cautiously, I brushed the curtains aside. Dark clouds swirled overhead, bringing with them an ominous feeling.

The chill settled on the air like a layer of newly fallen snow. I shivered and rubbed my arms, turning away from the grayness attacking the day.

I pulled my boots and jacket on and stepped out of our bedroom, careful not to disturb Henry. He wouldn't be happy with me sneaking out without him, but I wasn't a child. I could do my daily chores without a protection detail.

The central room was full of seven cots where the dwarves kept watch. Their sentry, Domino, sat next to the door with a steaming mug between his hands and a scruff of yellow hair haphazardly sticking out from the top of his head. He nodded toward the last of the warm cider bubbling over the fire and smiled.

I bit my lip, considering detouring from my chores to indulge in a cup of my own. Apple cider, apple pie, just about anything to do with apples was my weakness. I loved the fruit probably more than I should. I also knew if I didn't partake before my morning trek, the rest of the dwarves would polish it off long before I returned.

I veered towards the pot with a thought of only taking a smidgen. Of course, the mug I chose wasn't suited for just a smidgen; it was more like a beer stein. The ladleful I scooped nearly filled my glass. I considered dumping some back, but I needed to heat the chill from my bones.

Besides, this was hot apple cider.

I pulled a chair out from the table and raised my glass to Domino. He did the same, and we drank in silence as the rest of the clan snored.

Simon had a snore like a soft scrape. Bernard's was a little more like a saw cutting wood. Ruse's snore reminded me of a roaring fire, which was a good match to his flaming red hair. Klen's sounded like a rush of air and then a clicking, like his tongue was trying to remove itself from the roof of his mouth. Wally's was a high-pitched whistle that sometimes hit a nerve, making me twitch. And last, but not least, Blackie, whose nickname represented the color of his thick hair and beard, slept in silence as deep as night.

The symphony of sounds soothed me with each sip of cider.

By the time I finished the drink, Henry's shuffling came from our bedroom. My escape into the quiet woods would no longer just be me with nature. Henry didn't want me out of his sight now that we knew the queen was circling the forest. As much as I liked my quiet magic games with the wildlife, I had to admit, having Henry by my side to witness the antics made it more real.

I smiled and stood as he stepped into the room. Our eyes met, and my heart melted at the warmth in his gaze. It was almost as endearing as the heat of his arms. I set my cup on the counter and met him at the door. We nodded to Domino and slipped outside without waking the rest of the clan.

The cool air wrapped around us, tightening my chest. It didn't feel right, and I traded a glance with Henry.

He was already scanning the horizon with his hand clasped around the hilt of his sword. "No magic today," he whispered. "Not until this passes."

I grabbed the empty buckets by the door and headed off towards the river. Instead of hanging back like he usually did, Henry walked next to me, his gaze moving from side to side, assessing the quiet filling the forest. It wasn't until we got to the water that we both halted.

Guards surrounded both sides of the stream, coming out from behind us to close off our passage back to the house.

The forest had forsaken my magic.

I dropped the pails at the same time Henry pulled his sword. I focused on the magic within me, stretching the light out in a protective barrier around the two of us, and wished for a sword of my own. Funny thing about magic—sometimes when you wished for something while employing a protection spell, the universe obliged.

A heavy sword like nothing I had ever seen before materialized between my hands. The metal glowed with deadly intent, and I stared wide-eyed out at the dozen guards facing me. Henry had an equal amount of guards on his side of the semi-circle.

On closer inspection, the guards were not as they seemed. Their eyes held an ethereal glow, and their skin was too sallow to support life.

The blood in my veins chilled, and I shivered.

This was the army of the dead, which meant they were not susceptible to the same bounds of earthly magic that I employed in this forest.

I glanced over my shoulder at Henry. He met my gaze with worry lines etched on his brow. The queen had somehow commanded the dead. My throat tightened. My mother had been in a grave within the castle walls. Fear as bright as the light surrounding my sword burned inside me.

My grip tightened on the hilt of my weapon, and I pressed my back against Henry's as my mind raced for a spell to kill that which was already dead. Only a phrase came to mind.

Gravis ad vos.

Back to the grave you go.

It was as if the fates had left me to fail on my own.

As the soldiers closed the distance, I steeled my nerves and stepped forward, meeting the closest one with a swing of my sword. It cut clean through the middle of his body. A second later, the top half teetered to the ground. There was no blood, no scream of anguish, nothing.

"*Gravis ad vos*," I whispered. At the words, the dismembered form exploded into a dust ball. I jumped, knocking into a warm back.

I spun, my heart clanging in my chest.

Henry's sword caught mine before I could do any damage. His eyes were as wide as I imagined mine were.

"Duck," he snapped.

I dropped, and his sword whistled over my head.

He whirled around, meeting the threat behind him once again.

I took his cue and turned towards the remaining flood of soldiers on my side. I had barely enough time to raise the sword and block an attack. The whistle of Henry's sword gave me strength as he cut down those on his side. I parried and twirled, cutting down two in a row. Each time the dead fell, I whispered the same incantation.

Dust swirled on the air, choking me. My arms ached from the weight of the metal in my hands. My next parry wasn't fast enough, and the soldier's sword tore through the fabric across my back, scraping across my skin.

I arched away from the burn, letting out a roar of pain. I spun, bringing my sword around in a wild arc. I caught the guard at the crook of his neck, tearing through bone and sinew.

My back ignited as if someone had doused it in oil and set it on fire. My knees buckled and I stumbled. Henry caught me, peeled the sword from my grip, and laid me on the ground. Black spots filled my vision.

Henry stood over me, fighting the remaining guards with a grace and speed I lacked. Each parry brought with it a clang of metal that made me flinch. And when the whistle of his blade didn't meet metal, it sliced another guard down. He defended me with such brutality that my breath caught in my throat from more than just my crippling pain.

When the last guard fell, I whispered the magical spell that would send the dead back to their graves, and they puffed into dust.

Then my world went dark.

SNOW Chapter 3

VOICES FADED IN AND out while I remained on the floor, locked between blackness and agony. The burn on my back kept my chest tense, and I barely drew enough air to remain conscious.

"There has to be something you can do!"

Henry's sharp tone cut through the haze keeping me under, and I opened my eyes to a dark, tight space. We were no longer in the clearing by the river. And this definitely wasn't the cottage. I had no idea where I was or why the air surrounding me was so stale.

An icy chill gripped me, even with my back's fiery inferno.

I tried to move, but a hand pushed me back down.

"Stay still," a voice whispered.

It took me a moment to recognize the voice. Ruse was holding my shoulder. The sting in my back roared back to life, like an entire wasp nest had fallen on me. I pressed my lips together against the tortured wail that wanted to escape.

It was only then that I noticed the swaying. I focused on the rough surface under my fingertips and cheek. A familiar squeak caught my attention, and I closed my eyes. I was in the back of the wagon Henry used to get supplies when we needed them.

A yank at my skin pulled the air from my lungs and I groaned.

"Shhh," Ruse whispered. "You need to be quiet and still in case we cross the queen's guards."

If they crossed the army of the dead, we were totally screwed, but I would not argue. I wasn't in any condition to fight. I closed my eyes, letting the darkness drag me back under.

Time melted into shocks of pain from whatever the dwarves were doing. Jolts of agony yanked me from a semi-conscious state, only to fall into the bliss of blackness moments later.

When the cart finally stopped and the tarp that hid us was stripped from the back, a chilly breeze caressed my skin, waking me from the stupor I had been in. I inhaled, the cleanness of the air filled my lungs, and wiped the stale taste of death from my mouth.

My head cleared, and I pushed myself onto my hands and knees. Discomfort raked my back like a witch's claw and I winced. Tensing increased the pain. Clamping my eyes shut, I counted to ten, forcing myself to relax.

Henry was at my side when my eyes opened.

"No matter how I do this, it is going to hurt," he said and ducked his head under one of my arms.

When he stood and pulled me up with him, my chest locked, and every muscle seized. Before my lungs allowed a breath, Henry scooped me into both of his arms. Just the brush of his skin against my back brought forth the black spots in front of my eyes.

"Breathe," he said and hopped off the end of the cart.

A strangled cry escaped from my lips. The breath that had been locked in my chest squeezed out in short bursts with every single one of Henry's steps. The narrow path he carried me down wound through the woods for longer than I could stand. Tears burned my eyes, leaking out of the corners.

He slowed to a stop in a small, covered glen, and the dwarves rushed past him, laying out blankets on the ground.

Henry met my gaze. The creases around his eyes and lips echoed the same worry I saw in his irises. He gently put me down on my side, and he winced more than I did.

He lay down next to me and stared at the thick canopy over our heads. His hand raked down his face, and he turned his head, meeting my gaze.

Domino crept behind me with a tin in his hand. A moment later, coolness drizzled down the length of my back, and the sweet scent of honey drifted around us.

I closed my eyes. The cut on my back must have been bad for Domino to part with his prized honey. He went to great lengths to find excuses not to share his healing salve with anyone unless the situation was dire.

"We will keep watch," he said and handed Henry the tin. "Keep this, just in case."

I stared at the tin in Henry's hand and then turned to watch Domino disappear down the winding path.

"Where are we?" My voice was hoarse and filled with the discomfort racking my body.

"One of my hiding places south of the enchanted forest."

"South?"

"I can't exactly take you north." He raised an eyebrow.

"I could hide in plain sight." I winked at him and attempted a smile.

The worry lines around his eyes smoothed out, and he smiled, but it was fleeting, fading away the second his hand cupped my cheek. "I thought I had lost you." He fell onto his back and pressed his palms to his eyes.

That was when I noticed the bandage around his hand. Three fingers and his thumb poked out. I couldn't tell if his pinkie was wrapped under the bloody gauze or not. He followed my gaze and sighed.

"I lost my little finger to whatever poison their blades carried. Domino cut it off before the toxins spread."

"Poison?" I choked on the word. Fear as feral as the dead soldiers gripped me. My entire back had been sliced by one of their swords.

His solemn eyes met mine. "You need to rest. You have lost a great deal of blood."

I stared at his bandaged hand and swallowed with a spitless mouth. It felt as if I'd swallowed a mouse whole. "I was struck by one of their swords."

Henry nodded and rubbed his face. Those worry creases around his lips were back.

"Am I going to die?"

"I don't think so. They used up every one of their leeches on your back." He shivered visibly and met my gaze. "They think they got all the poison."

The dwarves had a swamp full of leeches for just this type of purpose. They'd had run-ins with the evil queen a time or two, and those leeches had saved their lives.

I had seen the fleshy creatures greedily drink their blood. I had seen them absorb the poison and turn gray. I had seen them writhe on the ground until they shriveled up and died.

The image of the sheer number of blood suckers drinking from that open wound made my stomach roll. I closed my eyes and breathed through my nose, trying to quell the turmoil in my belly.

Henry's warm palm on my cheek brought my gaze to his. "You were out cold for it all." He didn't add the 'thank the heavens' that reflected in his eyes. "It wasn't until Domino stitched you up that you stirred."

I didn't want to ruin his perception that I was oblivious to the pain. I had been in and out the entire time they worked on me. It explained the sensations of tearing flesh and the excruciating agony when they ripped those poison-filled vessels off.

I trembled, and my teeth chattered. The cold ate away at my skin and filled my bones.

Henry sat up and grabbed a blanket, then covered me with the soft fabric. He moved close enough for me to feel his heat. His lips covered mine in the softest of kisses.

"Rest. We have another long ride tomorrow."

SNOW Chapter 4

TOMORROW CAME FASTER THAN I imagined it would. One moment, I was staring into Henry's eyes, studying the flecks of green speckling the gray background of his irises as the light faded from the sky. And the next, the bright sunlight pierced through the hidden glen where we'd slept while birds chirped their morning songs above.

Henry lay curled up next to me, still wrapped in slumber. His dark lashes rested on his high cheekbones. Whatever tension had filled him last night, keeping his jaw tight, was not present in sleep. I sighed at the beauty of my handsome prince.

I moved to get up, but the debilitating agony gripping my back froze me in place. The hiss from between my lips snapped Henry's eyes open. His entire body tensed. He sat up next to me, and his gaze darted all around us.

"It's just me," I said through clenched teeth. I pushed myself up on my hands and knees.

He hopped to his feet before I was able to get to mine, and he gripped my elbow, helping me to stand.

The chill in the air caressed my skin, leaving gooseflesh in its wake. I shivered and glanced at my clothing for the first time. I only had a thin undergarment on. One that I reserved for those hot summer nights when I needed something light. It was one of Henry's favorites, with an open back and a low neckline.

Henry stared at my back. His eyebrows drew together, creating a wave of worry lines around his eyes before his gaze traveled to mine.

"What is it?"

Henry swallowed, and his brow smoothed out. He shook his head. "Nothing." He smiled, but it was one of those placating grins I knew so well.

He opened his mouth to speak again, but before he spoke, I tilted my head, giving him a sideways glare. I didn't even have to say a thing. My stare told him he better not tell me another lie.

His lips pressed together, and his cheeks bloomed red like I had caught him eating the last piece of apple pie. He swiveled his gaze to the surrounding area, looking at just about everything but me.

"Henry."

He glanced at me. "I don't think they got rid of all the poison." His voice cracked with the dread reflected in his gray-green eyes.

I turned my head, but I couldn't see the wound blazing on my back. I closed my eyes, clenched my fists, and reached for my magic. I centered myself, feeling the growing orb in the middle of my body. I sent pulses directly toward the pain, but my magic recoiled like it had encountered a viper.

I gasped. Whatever poisoned me was seeded with magic so dark that my pure enchantments couldn't combat it.

My eyelids flew open, and I met Henry's gaze. Hot tears stung the corner of my eyes. "I can't stop it."

His brow furrowed. "You tried magic?"

I nodded.

He went into action, grabbing everything on the ground in one arm, and with the other, he grabbed my hand. "The queen can track magic."

His words scraped across my skin, leaving an itchy residue that made me want to scratch myself raw. I had just put all of us in danger.

"We need to move. Fast," Henry barked at the dwarves guarding the exit path. He threw the blankets and honey salve into the back of the cart and helped me up and into the tight space between the hay bales.

I was nearly shoved to the floor by the dwarves as they got into the cart and covered me back up. We lurched forward, and one of the little men fell onto my legs.

"Sorry, Maggie." Blackie's deep voice pierced the dark surrounding us.

Another blanket was folded under my head to keep me from banging it on the wooden planks. The ride was rougher today, and several times the cart hit bumps that lifted us all in the air.

"Where are we going?" I asked loud enough that I hoped Henry could hear.

"Hobgoblin Caverns," Henry answered.

I clenched. Hobgoblin Caverns. Where the trolls ruled. Witches were a delicacy to them, and no magical being in their right mind would enter their dwellings. Even the queen wouldn't dare enter their home.

"They will kill us!"

"The troll king owes me a favor," Blackie said, placing his hand on my arm. "They will not kill the only mage left that can destroy the queen."

I let out a high-pitched laugh. "I cannot even beat her new army of the dead. How in the world do you expect me to beat the queen?"

"It is your destiny," Blackie said.

I nearly choked, and it wasn't from the stale scent of morning breath clustered under the blanket. My destiny. I didn't believe in destiny. I just knew if I faced her before my back healed, I would fall, and the world would be forever cloaked in darkness.

SNOW Chapter 5

"I NEED YOU UP here with me, Blackie," Henry said as the cart slowed.

"Fold the tarp and make sure you surround Maggie," Blackie said and climbed out from under the blanket, sealing us in the dark.

The dwarves made quick work of folding the cover and surrounding me. A blanket covered my back, allowing my head and shoulders to be exposed. They each stood on a piece of the blanket, stretching the fabric over my back in an uncomfortable cocoon. Each stood with their arms crossed, facing forward in a protective stance.

I couldn't see the entrance to the Hobgoblin Caverns, but as we got closer, the cart was engulfed in the horrible stench of decay and terror.

We slowed to a stop, and the ground shook beneath us. A shadow fell over the entire cart, and I gulped my fear, forcing it into my stomach where it festered like an infection.

"What do we have here?" A voice barreled over us, creating a wind that nearly knocked over the dwarves surrounding me.

"The king owes me a favor, and I am here to collect," Blackie announced.

The troll chuckled. "I smell magic among your clan. It has been too long since I've tasted magical blood."

All the dwarves drew their swords, crisscrossing them over me. I could just see part of their defense, but I didn't think their meager weapons would hold against this giant beast.

"You cannot touch my princess!" Blackie said. "Not unless you want the full force of your king's fury."

A growl rippled the air. "And who are you to stop me?"

"Blackie Sunhaven."

Silence fell over us like a sweeping cloud.

The shadow decreased by half.

"I apologize for my rudeness, Sir Sunhaven," the troll said. His voice had softened, and his tone echoed genuine remorse. "You may pass."

"Sir Sunhaven?" Henry whispered as the cart started forward.

"It's a long story," Blackie mumbled.

I caught sight of the troll guarding the entrance as we plodded along under him. He was massive, larger than the castle walls surrounding the queen's kingdom. The sharp claws at his fingertips made that festering fear inside me bubble like the surface of an erupting volcano.

If these creatures were this large and foreboding, why hadn't they joined the war against the queen years ago?

I wasn't sure I would ever get an answer to that silent question. I only caught a fraction of the trolls' stares as we navigated the cavern streets, but the ones I caught screamed hostility. We were strangers in their domain, and I was their main dessert.

My nerves jumbled into a crescendo of shocks that rocked my body with every clop of the horse's hooves. When we stopped in front of a castle so tall I could barely see the top poking through a layer of clouds above, every one of my cells shook. I doubted my ability to stand, but when the dwarves pulled the blanket off, I pushed myself up to my feet, clenching my jaw against my muscles' rebellion.

With careful steps, I moved to the back of the cart. Henry waited for me. His eyes were somber when he reached out to help me down from the back. He kept eye contact long after he placed me on the ground. Even without words, I could see the depths of his love in his unease.

I prayed that coming here wasn't a mistake.

Henry clasped his arm around my waist, and we followed Blackie into the castle with the other six dwarves following us, keeping a healthy distance between us and the trolls that had gathered to see the spectacle.

Guards within the castle surrounded us, leading us into the massive throne room decorated with gemstones and gold. It sparkled, mesmerizing me, making me forget my fear. It wasn't until my gaze fell to the throne in front of us that the hot scratches of anxiety returned.

The king of Hobgoblin Caverns sat in a straight-backed chair. He was larger and more fierce-looking than any of the other trolls I'd had the distinct horror of seeing. His gaze narrowed at me and his nostrils flared as he tilted his head back to take a whiff. He licked his thick lips and smiled, revealing layers of the sharpest teeth I had ever seen.

"You brought me a gift, Sir Sunhaven."

"No. I brought my princess to your caverns for her safety," Blackie said from his post in front of us. "She is the last pureblood in the kingdom and the only one that can defeat the queen."

The king leaned forward, scowling at Blackie. "I do not care about the kingdom outside these cavern walls. This is my domain, and the evil queen is of no consequence to me. But a fine delicacy of pureblood magic... That is quite the prize."

"Then you will have to go through me," Henry said, his tone fiery just like his eyes.

Blackie turned, leveling a glare that shut Henry up. He turned back to the troll king. "Unfortunately, you will have to go through us all," he said. "And that would be a stain to your good name. No one would deal with you if they knew you were not true to your word."

A rumbling growl filled the room, and the king slammed his hand down on the arm of the chair.

My knees shook, and Henry's grip on me tightened. We were at the mercy of these beasts, and unless the king honored his agreements more than his stomach, we were in trouble.

"I will let you leave the city." The king pointed at Blackie.

Blackie shook his head and took another step forward, unsheathing his sword and pointing it at the king. "You owe me your life. I am calling in that favor right now." He pointed his sword in my direction. "She must survive, or otherwise darkness will come to your caverns and you will be as helpless to stop it as we were. The queen left the lush hills of Dwarfland as a desolate scar."

The king laughed. "You compare a land of midgets to this land of giants?"

Blackie raised an eyebrow, and the king's laughter subsided. "I alone defeated your best warrior." He cocked his head. "Imagine how invincible a city of us were. The queen still slaughtered our families, our friends."

I stared at the little man in front of us, startled at his words.

"The seven of us had a task, one that required us to be away. Otherwise, we would have fallen to her evil, too. Do you know what that task was, King Trenton?" Blackie asked and waited.

The king leaned forward. "What could possibly take all seven of you away from home during a war?"

Blackie pointed his sword at me. "Snow White."

Gasps echoed in the chamber, but the king sent a silencing glare to his guards.

"It's actually Maggie White," I muttered under my breath. I hated my formal name. It was redundant, and irritated me, making me sound like a docile little girl instead of a strong princess warrior.

Blackie glanced back at me, his gaze transmitting a warning. I heeded, dropping my gaze to the floor.

"Snow White was the figment of a senile old man," the troll king said.

"My father was not senile!" I snapped before I had the good sense to tie my tongue. I straightened, ignoring the flare of ripping pain across the length of my back. "I warn you not to speak ill of the former king."

Blackie stared at me with his mouth open and eyes wide with shock.

The king sent a deadly glare at me. "Witch, I will speak ill of anyone I choose."

I pulled on my magic, conjuring the fiery sword I'd fought the dead with. "I have battled against the army of the dead. You don't scare me." I held the sword at the ready, tapping into my power to keep my body upright and fierce.

"Maggie," Henry said from behind me. When he placed his hand on my shoulder, he winced and withdrew it like I had burned him.

I ignored Henry and his damned reasonable tone. My blood simmered. I was tired. I was in pain. And I was hungry. Ravenous, as if I hadn't eaten for days. I was hungrier than I could ever remember being.

I gripped the sword tighter as my temper escalated.

"You sit here in this cavern, hiding from the world, when you could help us save it from the horrors the queen will ultimately deliver. You say this is none of your concern, but it is, because if you do not help us, the army of the dead will march through here and decimate your lands, leaving no one alive."

The troll king sat back, blinking his eyelash-less lids. His dark gaze locked on me. "The army of the dead?" he asked with a frown.

I lowered the blade and pressed the tip to the floor to steady myself. "Yes. The queen has command over an army of the dead."

His hand swiped out and grabbed me. The sword fell to the ground with a clang as he pulled me close to his face, two stories above the ground. "What kind of fool do you think I am, witch?" he bellowed in my face.

I recoiled and pushed on his tight fist with my hands, trying to break his grip. Terror washed over me as completely as his sour breath.

"She was struck by one," Blackie called from below. "Look at her back!"

The troll king turned his hand so he could see what was exposed of my back. His eyes widened, and then he opened his fist as if I were diseased.

I fell through the air, gasping. I reached for my magic to slow my descent, but the fall was faster than the spell. I hit the floor hard.

Hard enough to rip a yelp from my chest.

Hard enough to rattle my bones.

Hard enough to shoot pains through every muscle, and I collapsed into a heap.

The king stood and picked his foot up as if he were going to stomp me out of existence.

Blackie stepped next to me, raising his sword. "I would not do that if I were you."

The king hesitated, his face a grim mask of frustration. He slammed his foot down next to the throne, shaking the ground with the impact. "You would give your life for this infected witch?"

"Yes." There was no hesitation in his answer.

Henry stepped forward and collected me in his arms, then moved us out of the king's immediate reach. I trembled in his grasp. Every muscle still shook from the collision with the floor.

"I believe the myth," Blackie said.

"I do not." The king spat his words like a viper spits venom.

"And yet you dropped her as if you were holding hot iron." Blackie's head cocked to the side.

The king wiped his hand on the side of his pants with a grimace before meeting Blackie's gaze. "I will let you and the other six dwarves stay in my kingdom, but the human and the witch must leave."

Blackie shook his head. "No. That will not fulfill your debt."

"My debt owed to you is not enough to keep that witch within these walls."

"Whatever you require, I will pay."

"You do not have what I would require to allow her to stay here...alive."

"What is it you require?" Blackie asked.

"Her magic."

I blinked, staring up at the massive troll. Without my magic, I would have no hope of surviving against the army of the dead, never mind if I had to face the queen.

Blackie glanced at me and then at the floor. He shifted his weight, and then, after one last glance at me, he looked up at the troll king.

God help us all.

Blackie nodded. "But not all of it."

"But..."

Blackie raised his hand, stopping me with both the motion and a glare that would silence just about anyone. "Trust," he mumbled and turned back to the king. "And you have to heal her."

The troll crossed his arms and narrowed his eyes. "Healing her is not possible. Anyone with eyes can see the poison has already started to eat away at her." The king waved at me. "By the rise of the next full moon, she will become one of the undead."

I gasped, and I glanced at Henry. He was studying the floor, his lips pressed together tight. As if sensing my stare, he looked up at me. The agony of the king's words seared right through his green-eyed gaze.

"Is there any way to free her of this curse?" Henry asked.

The king sneered at him. "According to the myth your dwarf friend believes, she must kill the spell master before the next full moon."

"And if she fails?" Henry asked.

"Then she becomes the master's minion."

SNOW Chapter 6

I PACED THE SMALL camp we made outside of the Hobgoblin caverns. The king's words still rang in my ears, sending throbs of shock to every nerve ending. Every time I glanced at the night sky, I shivered. According to the troll king, I had less than a week before I became one of those ghastly things.

"Maggie, sit down," Henry said, and patted the log next to him.

"You lied to me," I hissed.

He ran a hand down his face and closed his eyes. "Blackie got us exactly what we needed without having to sacrifice your magic."

"That doesn't matter. You told me you thought they got all the poison."

Henry opened his mouth and then closed it. His gaze dropped to the ground. He nodded. "What else was I supposed to do?"

"Tell me the truth. We are together, no matter what. Isn't that what you have always told me? That despite what life has thrown at us, we would survive?"

He climbed to his feet and crossed to where I stood. "We will survive this."

Even though he sounded sure, his eyes betrayed him. Loss lived in his irises. Even with Blackie and the rest of the dwarves still pleading our case for some other solution, I knew just as well as Henry that I was doomed.

Doomed to play right into Queen Odette's evil plan and lose everyone I loved.

He pulled me into his arms and brushed his lips against mine. "Somehow, we will survive."

I wished I could believe him, but my heart told me a different story. If I stayed, I would probably be the one who killed my love. I couldn't stand the thought of Henry's blood on my hands. But he would never let me leave without him. My only hope was to sneak out while he slept. And there was only one thing that made him sleep sounder than if I used magic.

With my mind made up, I kissed him with all the urgency pooling in my belly. I wanted him to understand just how much he meant to me. And words didn't seem powerful enough. As my hands unclasped from around his neck and slid down his muscular chest, the kiss deepened. When I slid my hand around to cup his ass, he pulled away from my lips.

His eyes searched mine. "You're injured."

I lifted a single shoulder. "Not enough to stop me from making love to you once more before I'm too far gone."

He cupped my cheek with his hand. "Maggie," he whispered with such love that my heart squeezed. His thumb caressed my lips and his eyes shifted from gray to green, the way they always did when the mood struck. "Are you sure?"

I smiled and closed the distance, covering his mouth with mine. Our tongues intertwined in a slow dance of need. He pulled me beyond the fire and onto the blankets that littered the floor. Once within our little private enclosure, Henry dropped to his knees and pushed the hem of my nightgown up, ducking underneath the fabric, surprising me with gentle foreplay.

His ministrations with his fingers and tongue left me breathless. He erased any sense of pain with a longing so deep I nearly moaned. When he pulled away and stretched out on his back, unclasping his trousers, I lowered on top of him.

His length filled me, and his hands slid up my thighs to rest on my hips. Each slow stroke created an intricate web of pleasure through my body. Languid motion like the slow roll of the ocean captured us. Bliss coursed through my veins in warm pulses.

I stared into Henry's eyes, memorizing his captivating gaze and the small smile playing on his lips. A thin sheen of sweat covered his forehead as we kept the slow pace despite the need bringing me to the brink. I wanted this slow ecstasy to last long enough to sear it to my deepest memories.

His eyes closed, and he tilted his chin back, the muscles in his jaw and neck tensed. His hands gripped my hips tighter, his fingers digging into my flesh. The wave hit me and I cried out, lifting my gaze towards the heavens. He followed me into our momentary paradise.

I trembled with my release and with every aftershock until I fell forward, draping myself over Henry. He kissed my cheek.

"Are you okay?" he whispered in his all-too-husky, after-sex voice.

"Yes," I pushed myself back onto my knees and uncoupled from him, then shifted so I lay down next to him.

Henry buttoned his pants and rolled towards me. He took my hand in his and brought it to his lips. "I love you."

"I love you, too." I yawned. The physical exertion took more than I'd expected, and my eyelids slid closed. The soft caress of his thumb on the back of my hand lulled me. When his thumb stopped moving, I forced my eyes open.

Despite how exhausted I was, I needed to leave when I knew Henry wouldn't immediately wake. His breathing evened out, and I slid my hand out of his. He shifted, his hands closed into loose fists, and he tucked one under his cheek.

I studied his sleep-relaxed face and sighed. I clenched my teeth against the sudden sheen of tears that ballooned out of nowhere.

When his eyes started moving under his closed lids, I knew it was time to sneak out of our little camp. I pressed my lips together, refusing to let any sound of discomfort from moving slip out. Getting up was much more difficult now that my muscles had stiffened.

I finally got to my feet and took an unsteady step towards his horse. Thankfully, Henry had untied Rio from the cart earlier, and all I had to do was unravel the rope from a tree limb and lead him away from the camp before I mounted his bare back.

Rio waited patiently for me to climb up on him. It took me a few failing tries out in the open. Then I spotted a fallen tree and led the horse to the space next to the biggest of the limbs. This time, I mounted the beautiful stallion.

I clicked my tongue and grabbed two fistfuls of his mane, steering him away from the camp. I glanced over my shoulder and prayed Henry would forgive me when he woke, but I doubted it was that simple.

Prince Charming would likely become the Prince of Darkness, raining hell on anyone who crossed his path when he realized I was gone.

SNOW Chapter 7

NO LIGHT PENETRATED THE trees as Rio navigated through the brush. My eyes kept closing, but I refused to succumb to sleep until we had gone far enough that Henry could not catch up on foot. Besides, if I fell off the horse now, I doubted I would ever get back on.

So, I held on like my life depended upon it, or the lives of my love and my friends, to be more precise.

The wind stripped the heat from my bare back, and I shivered. Each pound of Rio's hooves echoed in my bones, rattling my teeth. I needed to get to the cottage and get some proper clothes before I headed into the heart of the queen's kingdom.

Rio ran faster now that he wasn't saddled with the weight of the cart. I prayed we would make it home before the next sunset. Even then, I wasn't sure I would last that long.

By the time the sun lightened the sky, my stomach rumbled, folding in on itself at the pure emptiness. I couldn't stop to satiate my hunger, especially since I was sure Henry was already awake and panicking at my absence.

So, we rode.

Relentlessly.

I held fast, despite the exhaustion and pain pummeling each muscle. All I could envision was how good my bed would feel once I got home. But that was as much of a fallacy as dreaming about a proper wedding.

Henry had always told me that as soon as we beat the queen and claimed the kingdom back, we would get married in such a grand royal wedding that the entire countryside would talk about it for years. I closed my eyes, envisioning the pearlescent gown I would wear. Henry stood before me in the royal colors of his family, blues and reds so deep they nearly blended together. A gold embroidered lion stood out on the front of his tunic in a proud display of his family crest.

Heat rippled through me, and I blinked my eyes open. Rio entered an open field, and I could see the enchanted forest in the distance, shimmering like a beacon. The late afternoon sun beat down on my back, and I slowly sat up.

I'd lost half the day, but at least I had clung to Rio, even as sleep pulled me into its grip. A deep longing cramped my stomach. It was stronger than hunger pangs. It was the agony of having that dream ripped from my future.

Tears blurred my vision, running hot trails down my cheeks. The swell of sadness mixed with anxiety in my blood, leaving me quivering. I swiped the tears away, focusing on the tree line. The open glen left me exposed.

"Please don't let them be here," I whispered to the wind.

Midway through the field, a rumbling from the north yanked my attention away from my destination. An entire army galloped towards me. My heart pounded as loud as the hoof beats tracking us.

I gripped Rio tighter, crying, "Go!"

The horse either understood my command or the panic in my voice. His burst of speed nearly threw me from his back. I clamped my thighs against his sides, ignoring the burn flushing the inside of my legs as his muscles worked under my grip.

We crossed the distance and fled through the icy wall of my magic. It had changed since I had gone, leaving me hollow inside instead of giving me a calm sense of peace. I glanced over my shoulder, expecting to see the legion following us, but all I saw were the trees and the shimmer of the shield beyond.

I laid my head against Rio's neck, wrapping my arms around him as he slowed to a canter. My breath came in ragged gasps that matched the horse's. It didn't take us long to reach the cottage. Rio went straight to the drinking trough, and I slid off his back, collapsing on the ground, drained.

I pulled myself up the side of the wood and dunked my head in the trough. The cold water was like a slap, and I flung my head back, whipping my soaking hair with it. My hair thwapped against my skin like a wet flog.

The chill went straight to my bones, so I climbed to my feet, heading inside. I could not fight the queen in a flimsy nightgown. I needed something warmer, along with something that wouldn't expose my injury. If Queen Odette knew I had been struck by one of her dead soldiers, she would likely just wait until I was hers to command.

I ran my hands over my face and into my wet hair, fighting with the tangles. The smell of apple cider clung to the air. My eyes adjusted to the darkness, and every cot was in a state of disarray. Blankets half draped, pillows askew, slippers half tucked under the beds. They didn't even take the time to pack their most precious belongings.

Blackie's whittled wood collection still sat on the shelf next to his bed. Domino's pipes still sat on the table next to his bed, along with his rich tobacco. Simon's cards remained half shuffled. As I glanced around, a lump formed in my throat. They'd dropped everything for me yet again, and what had I done to repay them? I'd left them at the mercy of the trolls.

I forced myself to move and crossed into our bedroom. Henry's natural cologne filled the air, and I inhaled, relishing the smell of honey and sawdust just as much as the smell of the cold apple cider.

I shook my head and crossed to my dresser. One look in the mirror and I cringed. My hair was a mess of wet knots and my body streaked with dirt. My once white nightgown looked like someone had poured mud over it and mixed it with blood. As much as I would have liked a bath to wash the sludge from my skin, I didn't have time to indulge.

I pulled my nightgown off and discarded it on the floor. My cream-colored sparring shirt lay on top of the pile of clothing in the second drawer down. I pulled it over my head with a wince and clasped the red leather around my wrists with pins that doubled as picks in case I came across a lock my magic wouldn't penetrate.

The matching skirt with red leather trim came next, then I pulled the red leather corset over my shoulders and laced it up the front. The red leather would hide any hint of blood seeping from the cut on my back, although it was a bear to tighten.

Each yank of the cords pulled a hiss from my mouth and caused a slow spin of dizziness. When I finished, I closed my eyes and leaned on the bureau. I had to count to ten to make sure I wouldn't pass out. After the initial bout of vertigo, the room stopped spinning, and the pain subsided.

I dragged my brush through the knots, wincing just as much as I had when I'd tied my corset. But at least straightening the tangles didn't bring waves of dizziness. When I finished, I tied a red ribbon in my hair and stared at my reflection. Besides the dark circles under my eyes and the layer of dirt marring my skin, I didn't look as bad as I thought I would, but I still looked more battle weary than battle ready.

I crossed to the far wall where our weapons hung. I stared at my mother's broadsword, studying the royal designs inscribed in the steel. I still remembered the lessons she gave me whenever my father allowed her to leave the court. She was fierce and brave and just, and my heart still contracted with her loss.

I ran my fingers over the cold steel before I slid my hand into the basket hilt, pulling the blade from the wall. With my mother's blade in my hand, I turned and walked out of the bedroom with a new sense of confidence. Before I left, I grabbed a half-eaten loaf of bread and tore a sizeable piece off with my teeth.

When I stepped outside, I glanced at the trough where I had left Rio. The horse wasn't drinking water anymore. I closed the door and glanced around the clearing. He wasn't in the clearing. I whistled and waited.

Rio didn't come. I leaned against the closed door. With one last look in the direction we'd come from, I turned the opposite way, towards the north. Towards my likely demise.

SNOW Chapter 8

INSTEAD OF FOLLOWING THE walking path, I made my way through the woods. The trees and bushes offered more protection than the open road. I didn't know if anything had breached our haven since we were attacked by the small group of dead soldiers, and I didn't want to find out.

I hadn't ventured this way since we'd settled in the cottage, and now I understood why. The woods were thick with prickers and undergrowth. My progress was slower than the road would have been, especially since I had to hack my way through the thicker brush.

I burned through the bread I had eaten, and now my stomach was making noises like an angry hog. If there had been any forest animals in the vicinity, the grumbling in my belly would have sent them scampering away in horror.

My arm ached in a way that made it feel as if I were carrying ten gallons of water instead of a broadsword. Each swing became less and less effective until I had to strike multiple times to clear even the smallest vine.

My senses were playing tricks on me as well. Exhaustion had a way of doing that to me. It messed with my perception. Too many times I spun to sounds behind me. Too many times, I confused the rumbling in my belly with the ground groaning underneath me. Too many times, I jerked my head at something at the edge of my field of vision.

I didn't know which I needed more—food or a nap.

When the space beyond my hacking sword opened up, I rubbed my eyes to make sure what I was seeing wasn't a mirage. I stepped through the last of the underbrush into a wide-open glade full of trees.

Apple trees.

My mouth watered, and I stumbled forward on legs that felt more like stiff planks than flesh and blood. By the time I reached the nearest tree, my stomach cramped in anticipation, and it took me three tries to cut an apple from the branch.

I caught the red delight and heartily bit into it. Sweet tang filled my mouth, and I closed my eyes, relishing the taste. When only the core was left, I plucked another one from the tree. And another, and another, until a dozen cores littered the surrounding grass.

With a satisfied stomach, I crossed the orchard. Just before the woods, I caught a golden flash in the closest apple tree. I turned, taking in the sea of red apples framing a bright golden apple. This one was larger than its red cousins, and curiosity filled me.

I couldn't recall having an apple of this color, and wondered if it would be just as sweet and crisp. My mouth watered, despite already having my fill. I pierced the golden orb with my sword and inspected it. I gripped it and pulled it from my blade, testing the consistency and weight of the apple.

The firm fruit smelled like honey and apple and cinnamon, all mixed in a delicious brew that I hadn't encountered before. I tore a big enough chunk to get a full taste of the fruit. While it was crisp, it was also more than sweet. I swallowed the bite and took another to confirm whether I liked it or not.

Sourness wrapped around my mouth, turning the sweet into a puckering tang. I swallowed and stared at the apple in my hand. A shiver spread through my body. I sniffed the apple just to make sure one side hadn't turned overripe, but it still smelled as good as the apple cider had the other morning.

I took another bite, this time with more caution. The same sweet blast of juice caressed my tongue, but then it turned vile. This time, I spit the remnants on the ground. It didn't seem to staunch the terrible taste that tightened my throat.

I dropped the apple and took a few steps before the world tilted. I stabbed the ground with my sword to steady myself, but it didn't help. I coughed and wheezed, clawing at my neck as whatever was in that apple closed down my airway.

My knees gave out, and hitting the hard ground pushed the last of the air from my lungs. I sounded like a boiling teakettle taken off a stove. My arms fell to my sides, and I fell forward, thwacking the ground with my full weight.

The surrounding woods started moving, but my eyelids refused to stay open. The last thing I heard was a dry chuckle that reminded me of brittle leaves.

SNOW Chapter 9

COLD WETNESS FLOWED OVER my face. I shook my head and wet hair stuck to my cheek. I blinked and tried to step away from the stream of chilling water, but I could not. It drenched my clothes, and I shivered.

"Close it." The sharp voice rang in my water-logged ears.

The waterfall slowed to a stop. I shook as my vision righted. My wrists were encircled by iron manacles. My boots had been stripped, and frigid metal bit into my ankles. There was no range of motion for either my hands or feet and no access to magic with the iron holding me in place.

I shook my head, clearing my wet hair out of my eyes.

The room that came into view clenched my bladder. This room was Queen Odette's death room, and I was in the honored spot. Rivets carved the floor, leading into the deep red, shimmering pool that wreaked of iron. I swallowed, and my gaze darted to my right.

Perched on an unadorned throne at the top of the steps was the queen. Her blonde hair fell in soft curls down her shoulders, and her light blue eyes pierced into mine like an eagle targeting her prey. Her petal-pink lips twitched into a smile.

Her outward beauty hid the vile evil residing within her alabaster skin. Hatred rolled off her like a malignant disease.

The frigid air wrapped around me, leaving my teeth chattering as violently as the iron chains.

Queen Odette stood and crossed the distance. The white dress she wore drifted behind her as if it was made of smoke. Languid and deadly, she approached me, inspecting me like a treasured pet.

I pressed against the rough wall, shrinking away from her.

"I was pleased that the apple my mage placed in the orchard caught your attention," she said. Her voice dripped like honey, sweet and soothing, and she reached out and traced a line from my throat to right above my heart, where she dug her sharp nail into my flesh.

I sucked air between my teeth at the sudden flare of pain.

"I cannot seem to take the magic nestled inside you." Her gaze slid to mine, and she tilted her head. "It seems I need your permission."

A bark of a laugh escaped from my tight chest.

I had witnessed her stealing the powers of others. Not once did she need their permission to take what she wanted. Every time, the bodies were left as dead husks, drained of magic, drained of blood. Blood used to fill her infernal pool.

And with each death, Queen Odette had glowed with the infusion of life.

I had no idea why she couldn't gain access to my magic. She never had that issue before, at least not that I had been aware of. But I thanked the gods for that small gift, or otherwise, I wouldn't be breathing right now.

"Give it to me," she hissed as her eyes blazed.

"No." The growl in my voice sent her back a step.

She pulled her fingernail from my skin and pointed the dripping digit at me. "I promise you, you will regret refusing me."

I narrowed my eyes at her, conjuring up a glare that matched hers. I lifted my chin in defiance. "You will never possess my magic."

The way she smiled at me sent burning fear through my blood. Fear that stripped me of a retort and left me trembling.

She turned and stomped across the room, then disappeared into the hallway. When the door slammed closed, and I was sure I was alone, I slumped against the wall, blinking the sting from my eyes. My heart clanged in my chest, powered by the adrenaline rush fading in my veins. The cold seeped in deeper, right down to the marrow.

I clenched my jaw, forcing my teeth to remain still despite my constant shiver. I focused on my wrist and the cuff links I'd specifically attached to help if I found myself in a situation like this.

I twisted and turned my wrists until the hem of my sleeves reached each of my palms. The concentration needed for such a slow task took my mind off the hideous cold that penetrated the room. With my fingers, I slid the fabric along from one side to the opposite side, feeling for the lock picks I'd hid.

Nothing.

I closed my eyes, convinced I wasn't trying hard enough.

I repeated moving each sleeve until it covered most of my hands. My inspection became frantic as I searched, my blood pulsing in my temples.

The cuff links were gone.

Despair wrapped its frigid hand around my soul and squeezed until I thought I would burst.

I yanked at the iron, letting out a scream containing every ounce of my frustration.

SNOW Chapter 10

THE ECHO OF MY scream bounced around the room like a mountain yodel that carried for miles.

The door creaked open and Queen Odette entered. She crossed and stopped in front of me, opening her hand. "Looking for these?"

My lock picks sat in her palm. She turned her hand over, and they dropped to the ground, along with the last vestige of hope I had.

I snarled and lunged for her as red fury filled me, roaring like an unchecked forest fire.

Queen Odette recoiled, stepping back, her face falling into a mask of shock for a brief instant. She brushed her dress, reset her face, and then turned towards the door, snapping her finger.

A figure wrapped in a dark cape crossed to her. My mother's sword peeked out from under the fabric.

"That's my sword," I snapped, glaring at the figure.

A skeletal hand came up and pushed the hood back.

I stared in horror at the empty sockets and the thin gray mask of skin covering the skeleton that stared in my direction. When it raised the sword, turning it one way and then the other as if inspecting it, I thought I would vomit.

"I believe that is yours, correct, Margaret?"

"Yes, my grace," the skeleton said in a gravel-laden voice.

It had been almost fifteen years since I'd heard that voice, and although it sounded like she was speaking through a layer of dirt, I still recognized it. My knees nearly gave out. Even though I had guessed that Queen Odette had given my mother's dead body reanimation, it still shook me to the core. This thing, this monster, was my mother, risen from the grave to serve this... this vile, evil bitch.

My brain couldn't grasp it.

Flashes of my mother brushing my hair, tucking me in bed, kissing my forehead, singing me lullabies, hugging me until her sweet floral scent wrapped around me as tightly as her arms... So many vivid memories. And every one of them overlaid this skeletal thing with my mother's real features.

"I would like to see how sharp it is," Queen Odette said.

The skeleton of my mother raised the sword, pointing it at me. She paused and tilted her head. Even though she didn't have eyes, I could almost envision her bright blue irises peering at me in her silent and questioning gaze.

Queen Odette studied me. "Shoulder."

Even before she finished saying the word, the tip of the sword sliced through my shoulder, scratching over bone and slicing tendon before the metal scraped the wall behind me.

My breath locked in my chest as the pain flared, hot and wild.

When the blade retracted, I cried out.

The skeleton showed the bloody sword to the queen.

"That will be all for now, Margaret," Queen Odette said, dismissing the dead mage.

Hot liquid dripped down my side, staining my shirt. I watched the thing that was once my mother scuttle out of the room like an insect. My mind screamed, but I wouldn't allow another sound to escape from my tightly closed lips.

I focused on the queen.

An amused smile played on her lips, and all I wanted to do was wipe it off.

She reached out and poked the wound in my shoulder, digging her finger between the broken folds of skin.

My eyes bulged with the pressure of my agony. I grunted, clenching my teeth. Tears burned as they filled my eyes, but I couldn't give in. I didn't care if she cleaved off my arms, gouged out my eyes, cut my tongue out. She would not get me to agree to give her my magic.

That would be the world's death sentence.

She wiggled her finger, scraping her nail on my already raw skin. "I have a feeling physical anguish will not be the thing that breaks you."

Her whisper left me cold. I stared at her and reached deep inside myself, mentally stroking my writhing magic, trying to calm the panic gripping every cell.

With a vicious yank, she dislodged her finger and wiped her hand on a clean section of my shirt. She tapped my nose. "I'm sure I can find something to break that resolve of yours."

She turned dismissively and marched out of the room.

Air rasped into my lungs as my chest tightened. My shoulder throbbed and my back ached. I glanced at the windows and the darkening skies. Dread laced its icy fingers through mine and squeezed in a painful grip.

I prayed.

I prayed for my mother.

I prayed for my friends.

But more than anything else, I prayed for a miracle.

SNOW Chapter 11

THE NIGHT CAME IN all its freezing glory. Wind whipped through the windows, swirling around me in a mini twister. My breath created frost on the air and my teeth chattered relentlessly.

I had no idea how many hours passed while I shivered in the dark. My fingers numbed about the same time as my toes, and since then I had just stared out the window wondering what horrors the queen would bring with her the next time she entered the room.

By the time the sun rose, I could hardly keep my eyes open. My fingers had gone numb and my knees had long since given out. I kneeled on the cold floor with my arms spread wide by the chains.

I closed my eyes, letting my mind drift to Henry. Pain shot through the center of my being, right to the core of my soul. I wanted to tell him I loved him one more time. I wanted to see his smile and hear his laugh. I wanted to feel his tender touch lighting my skin on fire. My mind shuffled through random memories, sustaining me, reliving them through every breath I took.

The warmth of the sun heated me and made the hideous death room almost bearable. Bright rays danced on the blood pool, making the walls shimmer red.

My stomach growled, but I ignored it, concentrating on the magic inside me. While the iron shackles kept me from tapping my magic to impact anything around me, like undo these god-awful restraints, I still had mastery over it inside my skin. I wielded it against the death that crept through my blood, slowing down my demise.

With each second, I could feel the light inside me decaying. I had no idea how I would beat the queen at her morbid game, but I needed to live. I needed to survive long enough to plunge a blade into her dark heart and banish the dead.

The squeak of the door pulled my eyes open, and I glanced at the procession of lifeless soldiers. They took spots as sentries around the room.

It wasn't until two soldiers dragged in a violently moving sack that dread sucked the air from my lungs. Curses as dark as the queen herself flew from inside the burlap, and when it was cut open, Domino fell onto the floor on his hands and knees in front of me.

I gasped.

His gaze lifted to mine. His eyes widened, and he stilled. All the fight left him, and the horror reflected in his eyes tore at my insides.

"You must not give in," he whispered. "No matter the cost."

I swallowed the bile that burned the back of my throat. The queen's kill room was only meant for death. Those that entered never left. My chest squeezed as I stared at Domino's deep, soulful eyes.

I opened my mouth to ask where the others were, but Queen Odette stepped into the room before I had a chance. My mother trailed behind the queen, still holding my sword. Sunlight glinted off the metal, screaming its harmful intent.

If they had Domino...

My skin broke out in a sweat, and any chill still set in my bones disappeared with the flash of hot fear. Blood flowed like lava in my veins, pumping hard enough for me to hear the dull thunder. My throat dried out. Swallowing felt like someone had shoved a handful of rough sand in my mouth.

Queen Odette stepped behind Domino and grabbed his hair, pulling his head back far enough for me to see the tendons press against his skin. His Adam's apple bobbed. She pulled a blade from her belt and held it to his throat. "Give me your magic and I'll spare him."

Domino stared at me. Fear flashed in his eyes as he whispered, "Don't."

The queen yanked on his hair and whispered a dark incantation that stripped him of his voice. He shook his head, defying her without words.

I clenched my jaw as tears blurred my vision. "No." I forced the word between my teeth despite every fiber of my being screaming to save my friend. The decision tore me apart just as effectively as the blade slicing through Domino's throat.

Blood splattered over the front of me.

I shuddered, blinking as the horror of the moment sank in. I tilted my head back and screamed my sorrow, my fear, my oath. I couldn't reconcile the goodness I professed with the refusal to do the one thing that would have saved him.

The queen waited until Domino no longer twitched with any hint of life. His eyes glazed over as the last of his blood trailed into the pool. She dropped him to the ground and stepped over him, approaching me. She wiped the knife with the hem of my skirt and slipped it back into the sheath before crouching in front of me.

She studied my face. "You killed your friend."

"You murdered him."

"You could have saved him," she said and stretched to her feet. "You had the power to change his fate, and yet you let him die."

I glared up at her. "You enjoyed killing him," I said, but her words had crawled under my skin like a scarab beetle.

Her slow smile chilled me. "*Ex mortuis resurrexerit credent,*" she said as she raised her hand in the air. Black smoke flew from her fingertips and wrapped around Domino, seeping into his mouth.

His eyes flew open and his vacant stare choked a hiss from my tight chest. His reanimated form climbed to its feet and crossed to stand in one of the empty sentry spots.

The chains holding me rattled with the force of my shakes. My gaze traveled over the rest of the room. There were six vacant sentry posts. My gaze shot back to the queen.

"Perhaps a painful death will change your mind." She snapped her fingers.

Another sack was dragged in. Simon came out fighting, his red hair matching the hue of his face. He got a couple of blows in before he was subdued. Struggling, he was dragged in front of me.

My throat tightened when he stilled at the sight of me. His eyes widened at my blood-covered clothing. Fury filled his eyes and his struggles resumed.

"You bloody arses! You hurt my princess!" One arm got loose, and he pounded the guard who still held him fast. He didn't realize he couldn't hurt the army of the dead with his fists.

The queen stepped out of the shadows and fisted her hand in the air in front of her.

Simon went rigid, and his eyes bulged. Then he screamed.

It was so high-pitched and full of agony that I winced. I opened my mouth to speak, to beg the queen to stop this madness, but Simon shook his head, despite his continued scream. His gaze was focused on me, even as each blood vessel popped, spreading red over the whites of his eyes.

"Stop!" I yelled, and the queen's hand relaxed.

Simon fell to his knees, gasping for breath. His hoarse whisper of "Do not," and the sharp warning in his gaze closed my throat.

He knew what this room meant. They all knew it because they had seen just as many horrific things as I had within these walls before they stole me away.

"Will you give me your magic?" the queen asked.

Simon shook his head.

I clenched my teeth. Tears blurred my vision and heated my cheeks. "No," I whispered.

When Simon's screams resumed, another piece of my soul died.

By the time Simon passed from this world, I felt like I had been gutted. I hung in the chains, gagging between sobs as the smell of human excrement mingled with the sickly sweet stench of blood.

The queen crossed toward me and put the tipoff her dagger under my chin, forcing me to raise my gaze to hers.

"Are you ready to comply?"

"No."

Ruse, Klen, and Wally were paraded in one by one, with the same horrifying and bloody results. Each more horrific than the last. And every one of them told me not to give in. Not to agree to the queen's ransom.

I wished I had the time to tell them how much I loved them. Instead, I sobbed apology after apology until they all sounded as hollow as I felt.

The queen sheathed her blade and stood in front of me. "You could have prevented their deaths." She pointed at the five new foul-smelling sentries whose bodies continued to purge the last vestiges of their humanity.

Her stomach rumbled, and I glanced up at her with a glare.

"This killing business always makes me ravenous," she said and crossed the room. As she stepped into the doorway, she said, "There are still two more, but I will save those until after I satisfy this hellish hunger."

SNOW Chapter 12

HOURS PASSED, AND MY gaze kept falling on the sentries. The dead remains of my friends had reanimated at the queen's command. Death surrounded me. And I knew there were two more to come before my time ran out.

I forced myself to my feet and blinked the last of my tears away. I prayed my magic would hold off my demise long enough to figure out how to get out of these chains. I unclenched my tight fists and winced at the stiffness. Slowly, I stretched my fingers, biting down on a groan.

I needed my hand to work. If I was to cut down the queen, I needed to be able to hold a weapon, and right now, I had my doubts I would be fit enough to strike a death blow.

I continued the slow motion of stretching my fingers and then tightening my fists until the blood flowed into my tingling fingertips, warming the muscles enough to be loose. Thankfully, my mother had pierced my left shoulder and not my right one. I still had my sword arm if the opportunity presented itself.

My gaze rose to the windows, and the colored streaks of the early stages of sunset painted the sky. I steeled myself for the next onslaught. I would not let my friends die in vain. I would avenge their deaths, and I would release them to move on to whatever lay beyond.

Just when I thought I had myself together, the door opened, and Bernard was dragged in. His exposed skin carried the colors of bruising—green, blue, and deep purple. When he looked up, revealing gouged eye sockets, I gasped. Blood streaked his face, and his normally wispy white hair hung in tangled mats.

He was brought to the center of the room and dropped to the floor. He crawled to his hands and knees and stayed still. His breathing was as labored as mine.

The click of the queen's heels dragged his blind gaze in her direction. Fear filled his features.

I clenched my jaw and blinked the sheen of tears that blurred my vision away.

Queen Odette grinned at me. "Since I had the chance to eat, it is only right that my newly acquired soldiers get to indulge in a feast." She snapped her fingers and waved at Bernard.

The five dwarves descended on Bernard like a pack of jackals.

I dry heaved as his screams echoed against the rock walls. I would never unhear the wet sounds of ripping flesh or the grunts as the undead had their fill. It was the most gruesome of the deaths and the one that nearly undid me.

I dropped to my knees and hung my head. I didn't look up as the queen snapped her fingers. But I did glance at what was left of Bernard. Bones glistened with rusty-red streaks. He looked like something left out in the wild, picked nearly clean from the scavengers. When Queen Odette's spell reanimated the skeleton, I closed my eyes.

"Now that was exciting," Queen Odette said.

I looked up at her. "You vile bitch," I hissed.

Her palm connected with the side of my face, swiveling my head to the side. The sting was immediate and reminded me I was still alive, and I still had my magic. But the raging heat inside my skin didn't feel right. It felt tainted and blackened and evil. As evil as the queen herself.

She glared at me and then turned towards the guards. "Bring the last prisoner in."

A group of four guards marched out of the room.

"The trolls were so cooperative," Queen Odette said as she waited. "Handing over your friends as if it was a bargaining chip. The instant we had them in our possession, I leveled their kingdom. The entire mountain collapsed, and not one of those double-crossing heathens survived." She smiled.

I forced myself to my feet, blinking at her words. Hope flared in my chest. Henry had not been inside the troll's castle. He had not been within their caves. Only the dwarves had been, and while I mourned each of them, it would not be the same as if Henry were dragged in front of me.

I would not survive Henry's death.

Footsteps echoed in the hallway, and I braced myself for the next gory killing.

SNOW Chapter 13

THE DOOR CREAKED AS it opened, and two leading guards stepped inside. The rattle of chains darkened my already morbid disposition.

They yanked on a lead as they crossed into the room with the rest of their squad. The guard handed the queen the rope, and then they all stepped aside.

Henry stood in the center of the clan of guards in shackles. His hands were chained behind his back. His chest was bare and clear of bruises. The only bruise he had encompassed his right eye and crept over his temple into his dark hairline.

I could not draw a breath. Every moment we'd spent together flashed before my eyes. Hope fled as fast as the strength in my legs. I dropped to the ground.

My movement drew his attention, and the hardness in his features softened. His soulful eyes captured me, tearing every last piece of my heart to bits.

The queen sauntered over to him and ran her fingers down his chest. "Such a sexy thing. It's such a shame." She grabbed the front of his britches and squeezed.

His green eyes narrowed at the queen.

She released him and circled around him, running her hand up his chest and pulling his head back, only to lick the side of his throat.

"I'll make you a deal. I'll let you live for another day if you promise me a night I will never forget," she purred.

He cringed and shuffled a step away from her. "No." His voice was as steady as a rock, and his gaze locked with mine.

Anger sparked in his eyes, and I couldn't tell if it was the queen's request or if he was finally coming to terms with the fact that I'd left him after he gave me the exact thing the queen was bargaining for.

She wrapped her arm around him again and rubbed the front of his pants. "Oh, come now. You didn't have a problem with it when you thought I was her." She smiled at me. "He was a wonderful stallion to ride."

His jaw clenched, and his cheeks filled with a red hue.

My stomach roiled at the thought.

She took a handful of his hair and dragged him to the spot where she had killed Domino. She kicked his knee, and he dropped in front of me.

I love you; he mouthed.

Her blade pressed against his throat. "Your magic or his life."

Every piece of my resolve crumbled. Beyond her, the full moon crested above the windowsill.

Tears blurred my vision as a sob escaped my chest. The blade pressed harder into his skin, and a bead of blood slowly rolled down his throat.

"Fine," I screamed. "You can have my magic, but only if you let him live."

"No, Maggie!" he yelled.

"Yes. I cannot do this. I cannot watch you die, too. She can have it all as long as you live."

The guards dragged him away and clasped the chain to the wall.

He didn't know my magic was already tainted with death. I had run out of time. This was my only hope. Perhaps the poison running through my veins that was once pure magic might just be my saving grace.

If I died, she could control my magic through my reanimated form. Either way, she was going to get the magic. This way, I might still have a chance to strike her down.

She crossed and put her hand on my head, closing her eyes. Her nails dug into my scalp, and she hissed and stepped back. The glare she delivered sent a shiver down my spine. She fisted her hand.

Henry screamed.

"Stop!" I cried.

She squeezed tighter, and Henry dropped to his knees.

"The iron." I raised my hands. "I will give you my magic, but I can't with the iron shackles!" Panic made my voice shrill and shaky, but my words seemed to penetrate the queen's anger.

Her hand opened, and Henry dropped to the ground, gasping for breath.

Hot tears poured down my face. "Please don't hurt him anymore," I said. "You can have it all. Please." I hung my head. Sobs ripped from my chest as the last piece of my sanity broke.

She had been right. Physical torture would have never broken me. But Henry had been her ace in the hole. The rest of the dwarves were just a sick primer. Something to feed her greed of stealing life. I was sure of this as she stood back with a smug smile.

Guards unclasped the iron from my wrists and ankles. The remains of my mother grabbed my right arm, and one of the other undead grabbed my left arm. They brought me to where the deepest rivets ran to the pool and forced me to my knees.

I harnessed my magic as best I could and bowed my head, glancing sideways at the sword in my mother's other hand.

My thoughts ceased the moment the queen's hand landed on my head. Burning pain gripped every cell, and instead of trying to hold on to this festering poison, I catapulted it out of me and into Queen Odette.

A wave of dizziness overcame me as the queen stripped every ounce of magic. She took a shaky step back, and I glanced up, smiling at her as my fingers blackened with death.

She pulled the knife out of her sheath with fingers of the same color. The black death my magic had claimed inside me had been passed on to her as well.

I lunged for my mother's sword, my sudden movement shocking enough for neither guard to recover before I gripped the handle, ripping it from my mother's dead hand. I ducked and rolled as the queen's knife sailed where my head had been seconds ago.

I screamed a guttural roar, and with the last ounce of my strength, I thrust the sword up while the queen was still off balance from her attempt to finish me.

The blade pierced through the queen's chest, slicing her evil heart in two. Her piercing scream echoed, and her knife clattered to the ground. She reached for the blade protruding from her chest and stared at her blackened hand. She raised her gaze to mine and stumbled back, tripping on the stairs to her bloody pool. She fell backwards.

I dropped to the floor.

"Gravis ad vos," I whispered.

I tasted dust just before the world faded out.

SNOW Chapter 14

COLD SCRAPED AGAINST MY cheek, and I rolled to wipe it away. Wetness covered my skin. I pulled my hand away, opening my eyes. Tacky rust colored my fingers, and I blinked. The background behind my hand sent a raw chill through my form.

The queen's kill room.

I scrambled to my feet, stumbled backwards, and gasped. The entire place was coated with blood from ceiling to floor, and the pool was nearly empty. My mother's sword stuck straight up from the bottom of the pool. The glistening steel was as pristine as it had been when I took it from the wall at home.

I blinked, and then the slow roll of memories of my last couple of days replayed in my head. My gaze shot to where I'd last seen Henry. A blood-covered lump lay on the ground, but nothing else remained inside the room.

I stumbled to him, dropped to my knees, and touched his shoulder. "Henry?"

He stiffened before lifting his head from the ground. He stared up at me with wide eyes before glancing around the barren room. A crease appeared between his eyes. He sat up and slid back against the wall.

His gaze hardened. "I'm not falling for this again," he growled.

I closed my eyes and hung my head. How could I show him it was me and not the queen pretending to be me? I rose to my feet. The motion stretched the fabric across my back. I winced, and an idea formed.

I slowly undid the buttons on my vest, then the shirt underneath and peeled them off, hissing at the bloom of pain in my shoulder and all down my back as I pulled the fabric away from the raw skin.

Henry's gaze landed on the cut on my left shoulder. His jaw tightened, and he glared at me.

My shoulder injury wasn't enough to convince him. I turned, praying that the cut doled out by the dead still traversed my back.

The chains rattled behind me, and I turned.

Henry was on his feet. His breathing became ragged as a tear slipped from his eye. "I thought I lost you," he whispered and hung his head. Tears cut clean paths through the grime layered on his face.

I closed the distance and wrapped my arms around his neck, holding him as tight as I could. He nuzzled his head in the crook of my neck. We stood like that long enough for me to shiver. I pulled away and put my blood-soaked shirt back on.

"Think you can unchain me?" he asked and turned, holding his hands out expectantly.

I stared at the steel holding him in place.

He looked over his shoulder and raised an eyebrow.

I met his gaze and sighed. "The queen took all of my magic."

He slowly turned towards me, blinking like a million dust mites were attacking his eyes. "But...but I thought when she stole magic, it killed the mage."

I wiped my face. "So did I. But for some reason, she couldn't just steal my magic. She needed my permission to take my magic."

His jaw dropped.

"Apparently, I was far different from any of the others who came before me. As it was, my magic kept death from spreading through me and turning me into one of those vile things the queen commanded. She didn't know I had been struck by one of her dead minions."

I turned and crossed to the area in front of where I had been chained and crouched down, feeling my way through the disgusting layer of blood-soaked ash. My throat tightened on a gag. I could have sworn this was the spot she had dropped my lock picks.

"She didn't know I was fighting a battle even more deadly than she was. So, when I finally agreed to let her take my magic, it was already as tainted as I was. I pushed it out of me as forcefully as she tried to take it. I think the transfer shocked her enough to give me that opportunity to strike her down." I crawled in circles while sifting through the ashes of my friends. Talking seemed to be the only thing stopping me from dry heaving.

"What are you doing?"

"Looking for my picks. The queen found them while I was passed out. She dropped them just out of my reach before she had my mother run the sword through my shoulder."

His silence settled on the room.

I glanced at him and met his gaze. "You weren't the first one brought in here." I pressed my lips together to stop the sudden swell of mental anguish. I needed to focus on getting Henry out of the chains before I could deal with all that had happened in the last twenty-four hours. "My sacrifice paled compared to what our friends sacrificed."

My fingers brushed over a bump on the floor, and I stopped, digging my nails against the rock until a small pin pressed into my finger. I scooped it up and wiped it on the cleanest spot I could find on my shirt. I crossed and kneeled down, undoing his ankle shackles before I released his hands.

The metal clanged on the floor as he pulled me into his arms, holding me as tight as I had held him a few moments before.

"I need to get out of this room," I whispered, and he turned us toward the door. I broke his grip. "Wait." I turned and crossed to the pool, then stepped into the layer of blood and gore coating the stairs. This time I did gag, but that beautiful steel blade had saved my life and I was not going to leave it behind.

With the sword clasped in my hand, and Henry's arm wrapped around my waist, we became the first captives to ever walk out of the queen's kill room.

SNOW Chapter 15

I TOOK A SEAT on the palace steps. Henry sat next to me and took my hand. Even though we were both still covered in gore, just sitting outside made it easier to breathe.

Dust swirled in the air, blocking most of our view. Pounding footsteps echoed off the buildings. I stood, holding the sword at the ready in my right hand, with Henry next to me on the left.

When the royal guard marched out of the dust, they stopped at the sight of us on the stairs. Hell, I would have too. We were downright ghoulish, covered almost entirely in blood and carrying a pristine sword.

I wasn't in any condition to fight the entire royal guard, but if they attacked, I would find the strength.

They glanced up at the castle behind us, and then their gazes dropped back to us. Confusion clouded their faces. They exchanged glances with each other, and the weapons in their hands lowered.

The head guard took a step forward. "Where is the queen?"

"Queen Odette is dead," I said. The snarl in my voice made the guard step back, even though the wave of relief that flowed through the guards could be felt in the air.

A few of them smiled.

"And the army of the dead?" he asked, his voice lilting up with hope.

"Dust." I waved at the smoke still dissipating all around them.

He glanced down at his feet. "And how do I know you aren't deceiving me?"

I lowered my sword and waved towards the building behind me. "Feel free to search the castle, but I'm going to sit down while you do, if you don't mind." I handed Henry the sword and lowered myself to the stairs, trying not to wince.

Henry stood protectively over me. His stance screamed he would give anyone a fight if they approached us.

The head guard picked six of his men and commanded them to search the buildings and report back. A handful of guards climbed the stairs as far away from us as possible.

The head guard turned back towards us. "Who are you?" he barked.

"Maggie White," I said, barely able to keep my eyes open. Exhaustion flowed through me, making my limbs heavy.

He blinked, like he didn't quite believe what I had said. "Snow White?" he whispered with reverence.

Good lord, how I hated that name. When I was little, everyone called me by my middle name, so I wouldn't be confused with my mother, and it had stuck. It wasn't until I was tucked away in the woods with Henry and the dwarves that I insisted on using my real name. I nodded. "Please call me Maggie."

The soldiers came out. "Something exploded in the queen's kill room," one of them said.

"What happened to the queen?" the head guard asked.

"She turned into one of the army of the dead just as I uttered my last spell. The spell that made the dead crumble. She, like the rest of the army, became dust."

"I think the queen exploded," Henry said.

I looked up at him. With all the blood covering the walls and floor, it made sense. Only an explosion could have emptied that pool in such a vile and disgusting way.

The head of the guard shifted his weight. He glanced up at me and stilled. "All hail our new queen, Snow White!" He dropped to his knee and bowed his head.

I nearly laughed until the entire guard dropped to their knee.

"Please..." Henry's hand clamped down on my shoulder, stopping me from telling them not to be ridiculous.

I hissed, and he jerked his hand away. His eyes were wide enough for me to see the apology clearly without him having to speak.

"Please rise," I said, and climbed to my feet. "What's your name?"

The head guard's cheeks turned red. "John, my lady," he said and avoided my gaze.

"John, I have no intention..."

He stared at me with such hope and gratitude that my words died in my throat. Beyond the royal guard, common folk gathered with the same hope etched in their bright eyes. Hope as if the darkness over the kingdom had finally been lifted.

I cleared my throat. "I have no intention of meeting the rest of the kingdom while looking like this," I said softly. "I would think my king would agree." I glanced up at Henry. We would likely scare the bejesus out of the commoners.

He curved his lips into a smile and nodded. "My queen is right." He helped me to my feet, and the guard escorted us back into the castle.

"You can clean up in the queen's private quarters," John said.

I shivered and shook my head. "I would prefer to wash up in the river next to our home in the enchanted forest."

His expression dropped.

"Or anywhere else but the queen's quarters," I added. "But I would appreciate if someone would go to our cottage and fetch our things, so I have something suitable to wear."

"The queen has..."

I put my hand up. "And please take everything of Queen Odette's out to the common area and burn it." I wanted nothing that vile witch had left behind to remain and give her a chance to haunt the castle. "And please have someone clean this place from top to bottom. There will be no kill room in my castle."

John actually smiled. He turned to his men. "You heard the lady!"

The entire guard scurried out, leaving Henry and me alone with John.

"I used to play hopscotch with you in the courtyard when you were little," John said as he turned back to me.

The memory of a guardsman playing with me while my parents were off attending to their duty came flooding back.

His amused gaze took me in and then shifted to Henry. He offered a bow. "You've taken excellent care of her, Sir Henry."

Henry bowed in return. "Not as good as I had hoped."

I glanced between the two men, missing a link on how they knew each other.

Henry straightened and wiped a stray hair from my face. "John made your escape possible," he said. "Without his help, we wouldn't have gotten you out, and all our lives would be drastically different."

"Well, thank you for your help," I said. "And now if you would point us to where we can wash up..."

"This way, my lady," John said and led me to a room that had a large tub full of steamy water.

I headed straight for it.

"I will send some handmaidens to help you," John said.

I turned. "Henry will help me, but you can tell the handmaidens to bring us towels and bathrobes, please."

He stared at me openmouthed with brows forming perfect arches.

"He is my betrothed."

John's shocked expression went back to neutral. "As you wish," he said and bowed before hurrying out of the room.

Henry's silly smirk didn't fit with the bloody smears covering him.

"What?" I peeled the soiled clothing off, looking forward to getting into the hot bath.

He shook his head, took off his pants, and joined me next to the steaming water. He offered his hand, and I took it, allowing him to help me into the water before he climbed in behind me.

His legs straddled my hips, and the water went almost to my shoulders. I held my breath, dunked under the surface, and shook my head before coming up for air. Henry did the same, and then pulled me against his chest, wrapping his arms around me.

We sat in silence as the blood sloughed off our skin, turning the water pink. Despite being warm and safe in his grasp, the shakes started. He kissed my temple as he reached for the scented soap on the table next to the tub and washed my skin with such tender care that the tears that I'd barricaded inside me tumbled out in a torrent.

His way of consoling me was to make sure every speck of blood and gore was gone from my skin. And it was the only thing he could have done to make me feel better about my choices. I let him do the same to himself, and it was only when he pulled me out of the water that he wrapped his arms around me, holding me as the last of the tears purged.

He grabbed a towel that had been delivered while we bathed and wrapped me in it, then draped a second over my wet hair before he dried off.

"They all died," I whispered.

His gaze was locked on my shoulder. "You're still bleeding. You need medical attention." He grabbed the last towel and balled it up, pressing it to my skin. "Handmaiden!" he yelled.

A girl appeared at the door as if she had been standing in the shadows. "Yes, my lord?"

"Can you find me a doctor? Maggie needs someone to look at her shoulder," he said and brought me over to a bench.

I leaned against the wall. Between the trauma of the last few days and the warmth of the water, all my energy had sapped to nothing. I closed my eyes just for a moment.

The world tilted, and I slipped into darkness.

SNOW Chapter 16

A BRIGHT STREAK OF sunlight lit up the room, making me squint. I tried to roll away from it, but Henry's grip around me tightened, keeping me in place.

"Light..." I whispered with a voice so hoarse I thought my throat would rupture.

His lips touched my temple, and he slid his arm from under me. He crossed to the window and pulled the curtain enough so the sun wasn't in my eyes. His gaze met mine as he returned, and the softness in his face felt like a warm blanket.

He sat on the edge of the bed, poured a glass of water, and handed it to me. "How are you feeling?" he asked after I took a sip.

My entire body throbbed, but the water satiated my thirst enough that the dryness in my mouth wouldn't scrape my throat whenever I swallowed. "Like I've battled every soldier in the kingdom."

He smiled and rubbed my cheek with his knuckles. "You were in pretty tough shape for a while."

I cocked my head. As far as I remembered, we had just taken a bath, and I had needed to close my eyes just for a couple of minutes.

"You've been unconscious for days."

I sat up quickly and nearly threw up the water I had drunk. I took a deep breath and grabbed Henry's arm for stability as the room slowly spun. I blinked and glanced around the room. "Where am I?"

"Your old room. They wanted to bring you to the queen's suite, but I said no. So, we settled on this one. It's in a wing of the castle that has been closed for years, so it's not in the best shape, but it was also untouched by Queen Odette." He turned towards the door. "Anne," he called.

A fair-haired handmaiden stepped into the room. Her creased brow smoothed at the sight of me sitting up and she smiled. "I will go get some food for the queen," she said before Henry could even open his mouth.

She scurried away.

He planted a kiss on my forehead. "I have another surprise for you," he said and left the room.

I studied the faded fabric on the bed and the tattered curtains. The shelves had been dusted recently, but the neglect was clear. This room felt as downtrodden as I did. It was suiting considering what I had allowed to happen. The dwarves were dead because of me. If we hadn't visited the trolls, their kingdom wouldn't have been crushed. Even though I'd beat the queen at her own game, the victory was hollow.

The door creaked, and Henry stepped to the side.

Blackie hobbled in on a makeshift crutch. His right foot was missing, and he looked as banged up as I felt. He crossed the room and squeezed me in a tight hug.

"I thought…" Tears choked the rest of my words.

"Aye, same here." He pulled away and briskly wiped his eyes. "But the queen underestimated my survival skills. As she obviously did with you as well."

"Did any of the trolls survive?" I asked, dreading the answer.

Blackie sighed and glanced at Henry. When he returned his gaze to me, I knew the answer, and my chest squeezed tight.

"No. I don't think anything could survive the magnitude of that avalanche. The only reason I am alive is because the king tricked me. He locked me in a cell made of iron as payment for his debt. I didn't understand why being chained in an iron cell was repayment. Even after the caves crumbled and my twisted iron cage sat on top of the rubble, I didn't understand. It was only after I saw the army of the dead carting my brethren away that I understood. We had been doublecrossed."

I bit my lower lip.

"I didn't know if they had you two. I only saw my brothers being marched along in shackles, similar to the one that held me to the iron floor. At least the king only put a single shackle on me, or otherwise…" He shivered and shook his head. "Gruesome process, but I didn't die from it. Visions of vengeance gave me the strength to make it to the castle, but by then, you were already victorious." He smiled and patted my hand.

"Victorious?" I laughed. "I may have killed the queen, but it cost far too much to call this a victory."

"We all knew what victory would cost. We knew we were not destined to see what became of the kingdom after the queen's reign ended," Blackie said, giving me a hard stare. "And we all signed up for the job knowing this." His eyes watered, and he looked up at the ceiling. "We knew, so please do not take the burden of their deaths as yours."

Henry sat on the edge of the bed and took my hands in his. "I wasn't there to fight them off, either. So, you are not alone in feeling responsible."

"They slaughtered the trolls outside the gates. Had you remained, you would have died on the battlefield. Going after Maggie saved your life just as being thrown into that iron cell saved mine," Blackie said. "Survivor's guilt can ruin you if you let it." Blackie's gaze pierced through me as if he could read the grief in my soul.

"I could have given her my magic sooner and spared their lives," I said, voicing the anguish locked inside.

"From what I understand from Henry, you slayed her when the full moon rose into view in her kill room. *That* is what the prophecy demanded. That was the *only* time you could destroy Queen Odette." He sighed. "Besides, if you thought for a second that giving the queen what she wanted earlier than you did would have spared us, you are sorely mistaken. We would have died just for keeping you from her for so long, and it wouldn't have been an honorable death."

I knew he was right, but it still didn't stop the pain. My physical discomfort was tolerable, but now that I was awake and aware, every time I closed my eyes, I saw their blood spill. Their screams still rang in my ears.

"Their deaths were not honorable." Tears filled my eyes and spilled fresh paths down my cheeks.

Anne chose this moment to come back into the room with a tray full of food. All my old favorites, from apple fritters to apple cider.

"I told her apples were your weakness," Henry said.

"She used an apple to poison me," I whispered and stared at the tray. Any appetite I may have had vanished, replaced by a frigid chill. I glanced at Anne. "Is there any way you could find me something else to eat that doesn't have apples as part of the ingredients?"

Her bright smile faded, and she dropped her gaze to the food. She blinked a few times and then curtseyed. "Yes, my queen." She started out of the room.

"I'm sure both Blackie and Henry would like some of those pastries," I said before she got halfway to the door.

She turned. "Would you like me to leave the tray for them?"

I nodded, and her smile returned. As soon as she left, I met Henry's shocked stare. "She ruined apples for me." Heat filled my cheeks. "But you two are more than welcome to have some."

Blackie didn't need to be told twice. He was across the room in record time given his injury, and he nearly polished off the tray while we waited for Anne to bring me something else.

"What now?" I asked Henry.

He squeezed my hand, leaned forward, and planted the softest kiss on my lips. "You rest, and when you are feeling up to it, we can take a walk through the castle proper. They brought back everything from the cottage, so I've been doing some redecorating. I hope you like it."

Walking through the queen's castle didn't appeal to me. However, the idea of Henry decorating scratched at my curiosity. I wondered if every room had swords as decorations. I swung my legs to the side of the bed.

"You need to get better before we explore," he said and plumped up the pillows behind me. He pushed me backwards into the soft pile he had created. "And then once the doctor says you are well enough, we'll have your formal coronation," he added. "And then perhaps a royal wedding."

The way he cocked his eyebrow warmed my soul just as much as his words and that cocky little smirk playing on his lips.

"Perhaps," I agreed with a smile.

SNOW Chapter 17

AFTER ANOTHER WEEK IN bed, the doctor finally declared me healthy enough for my coronation. The handmaidens made such a big deal out of dressing me to the hilt for the ceremony that I didn't have the heart to burst their excitement. I pulled Henry aside as they rushed about.

"Before we let anyone into the castle, I want to see what you have done with it," I said.

He nodded, and as soon as they finished my hair and getting me into the fine silk dress, Henry cleared his throat.

"Don't let the world into the castle just yet. I'd like to show Maggie around first, so she can see what we all have done before we open the doors," Henry said.

"Yes, my lord," the handmaidens said in unison and left the room.

Henry escorted me out of my sick room and into the castle proper, into the chaos of servants running around setting up for the ceremony.

Amusement peppered my skin with warmth as I walked the halls of the newly decorated castle. The dark drapery had been replaced by festive colors. The rooms had brightened without the stifle of black magic. Windows glowed in the sunlight, and it was as if all the darkness shrouding the kingdom had fled with the death of Queen Odette.

Outside, the streets sparkled with activity and laughter. People seemed to flourish in the absence of evil.

The queen's quarters were completely transformed. Henry had replaced everything with the modest furniture we had at the cottage. It was endearing to see all my stuff laid out the way we'd had it. Even my mother's sword was mounted in the exact position it had been back home.

I stood and stared.

"Is something wrong?" he asked, and fidgeted next to me in his royal colors.

I turned to him. "No. Not a thing is wrong with this room. And I have to admit, you have done a fine job with the rest of the castle. But there is one more room I need to see before the coronation."

He paled and shifted his weight. "It's not ready yet."

"Is it clean?"

He nodded.

"Then I want to see it."

"Fine, but Blackie will not be happy."

"Blackie?"

"He's overseeing the remodeling." Henry pushed his hands into his pockets. "He wanted to be the one to show you what he has done to the space after the ceremony."

I knew I should have been patient and waited, but I wanted to see what he had done up there. I wanted to see what he could possibly be doing to erase the horrors that still plagued my nightmares.

We approached the room, and I stopped, staring at the polished wood door. It was stunning compared to the marred door that had once been in its place. I ran my fingers down the soft grain and wondered whether the transformation of the room would do anything to quell the horror it once portrayed.

I pushed the door open. The ominous creak that had been there was no longer. The door swung open in a silent swish of air. I blinked at the brightness inside. Gone were the gray walls and the gullies in the floors, replaced by shining white stone.

Despite the beauty, my heart filled with trepidation as I crossed the threshold. I guessed visiting the place where you'd been meant to die would do that to almost anyone, but I still stepped inside, stubbornly swallowing the bitter taste of fear.

The blood pool had been transformed. Pristine water filled the white basin, sending refracted rainbows throughout the space. The throne remained on the now white pedestal, but it had been embossed with gold and jewels, adding to the brightness already blanketing the room.

Even the grand columns sparkled in white marble. My gaze didn't know where to go. The room was stunningly beautiful. Sentries marked six spots around the room, and I blinked at the five I could see.

They were so detailed that I thought they were real. I gasped, covering my mouth. Motion in front of the sixth spot yanked my attention. Blackie swiveled and nearly dropped the palette in his hand.

"For the love of..." He glared at Henry.

"She insisted," Henry said, putting his hands up in surrender.

I stared at the painting he stood in front of.

Bernard.

Blackie had even painted Bernard's wispy white hair perfectly. I did not know Blackie was so talented with a paintbrush. My gaze drifted back over the rest. Simon, Domino, Ruse, Klen, and Wally were just as flawlessly portrayed as Bernard. And every painting had them at their best moment, with their personalities captured on their painted smiles.

Blackie turned back to the painting and made a few final adjustments before hobbling back.

"I know they died in here," he said with his back to me. "And I know it is hard for you to be within these walls, but I needed a place to honor their sacrifice without reliving the horror of their deaths. I needed to replace those memories with something capturing the beauty of each of their souls. A place to remember them in all their goofy glory." He put his palette and brush on the table next to him and adjusted his crutch to turn towards me. "I thought about painting a waterfall on that wall and streams leading to the pool, but I like the feel of the white walls."

"It feels purified." I didn't know where that word choice came from, but it felt right, purged of the darkness like everything else in the kingdom. "And you captured them at their finest." I waved at the murals, blinking back the heat in my eyes.

I bit my lip and looked at the throne. The mirror behind it caught my attention, and I climbed the steps and crossed to the wall. My chest tightened at the sight. I stepped closer and ran my fingers over the gilded frame.

"Where did you find this?" I asked with a choked voice.

"In the storage area under piles of junk. Why?" Blackie asked.

"It was my mother's mirror," I whispered and stepped in front of it to see if the glass still contained a touch of magic after all these years.

"Mirror, mirror, on the wall..." I whispered before I touched the glass.

The image rippled like a pool of water. Just beyond the reflection of the room sat a bridge surrounded by the most colorful flowers in full bloom. The entire area was bathed in light. All six dwarves stood smiling at the foot of the bridge, and when my parents stepped from the light to welcome them, they all turned towards me and waved before being swallowed by the golden glow.

The image faded. I blinked back tears and laid my palm on the glass, saying my silent goodbyes with a much lighter heart than when I'd walked into this room.

I turned to Blackie and Henry and nodded. "You did a beautiful thing," I said and sniffled.

Henry patted Blackie on the back, then climbed the steps and took me in his arms. He gave me a kiss that made my knees weak.

When the kiss broke, I palmed his cheek and whispered, "Thank you."

He leaned his forehead against mine. "Are you ready to rule this kingdom?"

I stepped back, took a deep breath, and smiled. "I am ready to accept my crown."

The End

Will dragon's blood be enough to save the kingdom?

Long, long ago, a princess was born into the Kingdom of Light. She was said to be the most beautiful baby in all the world, and her tears turned into the morning dew. The king named her Aurora after the goddess of sunrise.

Royals came from far and wide to honor her birth, but one guest was not there to celebrate. When it was her turn to present a gift, the dragon queen offered something much darker. A curse that would claim Aurora on her twentieth birthday with the prick of a spinning wheel. Everyone in the kingdom, except King Henrick, would plummet into eternal darkness. Thus, the king would know the true meaning of loss.

Only three fae were left to bestow their gifts to the princess Aurora, and although they could not erase the dragon queen's curse, they could offer the kingdom a gift of hope.

Darkness would be banished with true love's kiss. King Henrick hid Aurora with the fae in the middle of the kingdom's enchanted woodlands to keep her safe. But dragons are born of magic, too, and Aurora's hiding place was not far from the dragon's lair.

A Sleeping Beauty retelling with a little bite.

SPINDLE Chapter 1

AUTUMN FINALLY LET ME hunt without hunching over me like an overzealous mother bear. She had caught sight of a deer and went after it while I followed a bunny off our normal game trail. The scent of wet leaves itched my nose, but I tried to ignore it as I crept forward with my bow at the ready. The rabbit had to be around here somewhere. It had darted in this direction. I did my best not to make noise as I stepped through the brush, but I hadn't been blessed with the same light-footedness as the fae.

A twig snapped underfoot, sounding louder than normal with my attempt at near silence. And my furry prey hopped out of the brush. I aimed, tracking it while I blew out a stream of air. Then I let my arrow fly and held my breath. The arrow went straight through the rabbit's head. A clean death, if there ever was such a thing.

The sight of the rabbit's death twitch overshadowed my triumph of the hunt. I crossed to my quarry and kneeled, stroking its silky fur as the heat bled out of the body. A lump formed in my throat.

"I'm sorry, little one," I whispered.

"Why apologize?"

I startled, snapping my head toward the voice.

A boy.

I blinked at him as if he were an apparition.

His stance was confident, mature, and proud. He had to be older than me, perhaps even ten or eleven. His dark hair was pulled back in a severe ponytail that made his green eyes stand out. Flecks of gold glinted in his irises, captivating me with their beauty. His eyes seemed to shimmer, even with the canopy of trees shading us.

He tapped his ornate sword against the trunk of the tree as if his hands had different intentions than the rest of him. The tap-tap-tap pulled my gaze away from his face. His clothing was finer than a farm boy's, and the sword he held was ornate, as though it belonged to a knight.

I focused back on his face, completely forgetting what he had asked. "What?"

"Why are you apologizing to the rabbit?" He pointed his sword at the cooling carcass under my palm.

"Because he gave his life so we could survive." I gave him a look that should have told him what I thought of his question. I gripped the rabbit's ears and stood, holding it close to me in case he thought he was going to strip me of my kill. "Who are you?"

"Rory?" a voice called in the distance, and I jerked toward Autumn's call. When I glanced back, the boy was gone. My stomach tightened with disappointment, and I turned in a circle, trying to find evidence he had truly been standing in this little glen with me. My gaze dropped to the tree trunk. Very faint lines where he had been tapping were visible.

He must have been some kind of fae, or maybe even a ghost, because he vanished like a puff of smoke.

A red-haired, fair-skinned fae stepped through the trees into the small thicket. I smiled at her, but she was clearly perturbed with me. She crossed her arms and arched a brow.

I held the rabbit up for her to see. "I got it."

Autumn sighed and allowed a smile. "That will make a nice rabbit stew." She crossed to me and slowed as she sniffed the air. Her gaze became guarded, and she slung her arm around my shoulders, steering me back toward her trodden hunting path.

I glanced over my shoulder one more time before that little area was out of sight. Scanning the woods, I still couldn't find that boy. Nothing moved.

"You shouldn't wander off like that, Rory," Autumn chastised me as we walked back home. "You know better. This is the trail you should stick to on our hunts." She pointed at the wooded path.

I nodded and glanced at the rabbit. Veering from our normal hunting grounds had been well worth the risk. But even at seven, I knew to keep my opinion to myself.

Something deep down in the center of my soul told me I'd see that green-eyed ghost again.

YEAR AFTER YEAR, I sneaked away from the hunting path in search of that boy. He haunted my dreams, in a good way, but with each nighttime fantasy playing on the back of my eyelids, the longing to find him grew, and the doubt that he had only been a figment of my imagination created an unnamed fear in my heart.

Maybe today would be the day he reappeared. I stretched and stepped out the door to get away from the escalating argument inside. The fae were fighting over my lesson plans. Again.

Marabel, the eldest of the three fae sisters, wanted me to read today. Her hands seemed to speak a language of their own as she stressed the importance of storytelling. In the thick of the argument, her glasses had gone cockeyed on her face and strands of hair had fallen out of her gray bouffant as it bobbed with her animation.

Felicity, the dark fae with violet eyes and dark hair that nearly matched her skin, wanted me to cook. She was more regal in her mannerisms than Marabel, but her graceful animation was more fluid as she made her argument.

Then there was Autumn, the red-haired, cream-skinned fae. My favorite by far because she was the one who let me run around in the woods, hunting or making friends with the wildlife instead of keeping me locked up in the cottage like both Marabel and Felicity seemed to demand.

I silently slid my bow and quiver out of the corner. I was going exploring before any of them were the wiser. It had been almost eight years since I saw the green-eyed ghost in the woods, and I hoped this might be the day I'd find that elusive boy.

With the fae preoccupied, I stepped into the midst of the lush, enchanted forest. It was always bright and cheery here. Even the flowers seemed to sway when there wasn't a stitch of a breeze. The illusion of perfection surrounded us and even as I glanced over my shoulder at the three fae bickering about what my lessons were supposed to be, I knew I was blessed.

I took off in the direction I remembered meeting him. I caught sight of another rabbit and notched my arrow, slinking after it as I had been taught. It never even twitched his ears. I blew out a breath and let the arrow fly. I shot true, and the arrow pierced the rabbit's head, just as cleanly as all my kills.

I kneeled next to the rabbit and went through my ritual of feeling the last of the warmth bleed out of its body while I thanked it for its sacrifice. Although I loved the taste of freshly cooked meat, if I had my way, I wouldn't kill until I absolutely had to. This game killing thing was hard on a girl's soul. If I could, I would eat berries for the rest of my life, just to spare the animals. I stood with the rabbit in hand and gasped.

Narrowed green eyes stared at me down the edge of a sword aimed at my neck. He sniffed the air, and then the metal dropped to his side. His hair was shorter now than it had been eight years ago, but those golden-flecked green eyes that I had dreamed of every single night since I was seven were the same. A goofy smile appeared on his face, etching dimples into his cheeks and making his eyes sparkle.

"I did not think I would ever see you again, Rory," he said.

His voice had become deep, and hearing him say my name was like a cool piece of silk flowing over me. My knees buckled in a swoon, but I locked them and shook away the spineless sensation. His teeth flashed white from behind his soft, oh-so-kissable lips. He was even more handsome than I remembered.

He raised an eyebrow, as if he knew my private thoughts.

Heat filled my cheeks, and I cleared my throat. "I am at a disadvantage. You know my name, but I do not know yours."

"Z—" His eyes widened, and his gaze jerked beyond my shoulder. "I have to go. But I will see you again, Rory." He turned, bolting away as if a wolf were chasing him.

One would have thought there would be some sign that he had been real, but even the leaves in the direction he ran hadn't so much as shivered from the breeze he would have created.

"There you are!" Autumn broke through the thicket behind me.

I already knew the lecture that was coming, so I turned with the rabbit in my hand, giving her my best innocent grin.

"I may have to hide your bow and arrows," she grumbled and gripped the back of my neck to steer me back toward our little abode.

I did not understand her fear of these woods. What could be out here that would cause my favorite warrior fae to tremble? In fifteen years of hunting, I still had yet to run into anything as dangerous as the fae professed.

Beasts or no beasts, I would wander off the hunting path again. I just didn't know how long it would be until I could find my way back to my green-eyed ghost.

SPINDLE Chapter 2

"THE BIRTH OF A queen was supposed to be an exciting event. It started off that way, but soon fell into chaos when the Dragon queen showed up and placed a curse on the child. A curse that would plummet our kingdom into eternal darkness." Marabel recounted the story of the dragon queen's curse for the hundredth time. Her hands moved in broadly animated fashion and her gray hair bounced with each nod of her head.

I kept the smile plastered on my face and nodded from time to time, but my mind wasn't on this old fairy tale that she kept telling me. My mind was preoccupied with what I had overheard the fae chattering about earlier that morning. Something about a celebration for the princess, and maybe, just maybe, I would see my green-eyed ghost at the party.

I had never been outside the enchanted woods and was itching to go to the castle. To dress up in something stunning and dance the night away with a real man, ideally my famous woodland stranger. The forest animals didn't make good dance partners, despite their attempts at making me smile at their antics.

Felicity kneaded dough on the table and rolled her violet eyes at me before swiping a strand of her dark hair away from her face. I pressed my lips together at both the eye-roll and the track of flour that remained across her dark skin. She was just as tired as I was with this story.

"Are you listening?" Marabel stopped and stared at the two of us.

"Yes, ma'am," I answered. "You just said the curse on the princess would plunge the entire kingdom into darkness if she were to prick her finger on a spinning wheel."

"Yes, yes." She launched into a tirade about how the darkness would spread to every nook and cranny of the kingdom.

I glanced out the window, wishing for some reprieve so I could go out in the woods, where I was most comfortable. As if she heard my silent wish, Autumn strolled into the house with a freshly plucked duck for cooking held in front of her. Her crooked smile of triumph didn't deter Marabel from continuing to jabber.

Autumn flipped her auburn hair away from her face and leveled a cocked eyebrow at Marabel. "Give it a rest, sister."

Marabel's mouth dropped open at her sister's brazen comment.

Autumn handed Felicity the duck. "You're the only one who can make this taste like a feast," she added and wiped her hands on a cloth as she winked at me.

"No truer words have been spoken," Marabel said. "If I attempted to prepare it, we would get a much tastier meal by chewing on our leather shoes." She wiped her hands on her apron and started tidying up the place as if her sister hadn't just told her to be quiet.

I stifled a laugh and glanced at the fae folk. They were quite the trio, and life with them had been endless fun. Each one had taught me all their secrets, enough so that I could hunt for myself and prepare a feast, while spinning an entertaining tale. I knew how to mend socks and sew and even how to tend to our garden. I was ready to take on the world.

Unfortunately, none of them were ready for me to spread my wings, even after all these years.

The more I wandered, the more agitated they seemed to get. I was turning twenty in a couple of days and I had never seen the palace. Never mind exploring beyond our small cove carved in the woods; even on the hunting trips with Autumn, we stayed within the enchanted forest. I really wanted to experience what was out there. I wanted to explore our entire kingdom and not just this small crop of land.

As usual, they argued over how to prepare the duck. Even though Felicity was the only proper cook, they all had to put in their ideas before the three of them could settle on a direction. I took the opportunity to quietly slip away. I grabbed my favorite bow and the quiver of arrows leaning next to the door. It was my turn to commune with nature and possibly bring in a bounty that would last us a few more days than the meal Autumn had brought home.

I smiled as their continued bickering wafted out the window, filling the small clearing with their voices. As soon as I stepped into the woods, birds singing, chipmunks chattering, and owls hoo-hooing replaced the fae's squabbling. The familiarity calmed me as well as tickled my wanderlust, and I knew the exact direction I wanted to go.

I paused and glanced over my shoulder, half expecting Autumn to step out from behind a tree and reprimand me for wandering from the worn hunting trail. When she didn't, I headed in the direction that she always prevented me from going. She had never given me an actual reason we couldn't go beyond the magical boundaries. It always set my exploration itch into overdrive. My entire body tingled with the need to break the barriers the faeries had laid for me.

With none of the fae in sight, I picked up my pace, trying to be as light on my feet as possible, but I couldn't move silently the way Autumn did. Before I knew it, the forest thickened. I was farther beyond our normal hunting grounds, even farther than I had been when I met my green-eyed ghost. I even thought I felt a tingle of magic dance over my skin as I passed through an opening in a prickly thicket.

The ground became spongey under my feet, leaving a slick slime on the soles of my shoes. I slowed and studied my new surroundings as I tried to find more solid ground. The deep forest-green of the woods had transitioned to bright sunny flowers and brighter greens of swamp grass braided through the blossoms. It was almost as if the color popped much more here than it ever did in the enchanted forest. Not that the fae folk didn't have colorful surroundings, but this seemed much richer in contrast.

The squishy ground seemed to drive me toward a solid line of bushes in my quest for a dry surface to walk on. But I couldn't seem to break through the thick barrier. Just when I was about to give up, I spied a gap in the branches. I wiggled through and over the berm and nearly tumbled into a steaming body of water.

I straightened and scanned the oversized flowers of yellow, red, and blue that lined the pond. Their colorful reflections danced on the surface. Fluttering wings pulled my gaze to the tree limbs reaching out over the water, and my eyes widened at the size of the birds perched on the ancient wood. They were twice the size of the duck Autumn had brought home earlier.

My heart jumped in my chest at the chance to shoot a prize that big. It would feed us for a week. I reached for an arrow, pulling it from my quiver with slow precision, and notched it in my bow. I climbed up on the rocks at the edge of a sheer drop to the water that was at least three times my height.

I took a deep breath and tore my gaze away from the drop, focusing on the birds again. I took aim and shifted to steady my hand.

My darn slippers still had swamp muck on them, and I lost my balance. A yelp ripped out of my mouth as I fell. I dropped the bow and grabbed for the rock, catching a small outcrop. The liquid sizzled when my bow and arrow hit the surface of the swamp. I stared in stunned silence as the wood burst into flames.

What I thought had been water was actually an acid pool. My heart thundered as my grip slipped from the small outcrop. I slid down the facing until I caught another small outcrop. I cried out, and I kicked the wall to find enough purchase on the rocks to get back to safety, but my shoes were too slippery.

I was too close to the surface and my fingers ached. The quiver on my back slipped off and when it hit the surface, a splash of acid doused my ankle. I screamed as pain nearly paralyzed me.

"Help!" I cried. Tears blurred my vision. I couldn't hold on much longer. As if fate was laughing at me, the grip I held tight to crumbled and I slid further toward certain doom. I scrambled for purchase and luck was with me this time. I caught a crevice and, although it bit into my skin, I screamed my triumph until acid engulfed my foot, and then my scream turned into a wail of agony.

Panic turned my breathing into harsh panting as I tried desperately to climb back up the rock high enough not to feel the burn again. If I perished in this acid bath, no one would know what happened to me. Marabel, Felicity, and Autumn would search forever and never find my body.

"Please help me," I whispered through a fresh set of tears as my fingers, now slick with blood, slipped on the small fissure. My life flashed before my eyes. All the hunting trips with Autumn. All the delectable treats I baked with Felicity, and all the stories Marabel and I created. Memories of my green-eyed ghost swarmed along with every dream of our future. All gone in a pouf of pain and fire.

The moment I lost my grip, something grabbed me around the waist and lifted me from my pending death. My foot still throbbed, and from what I could see, it was a bloody, charred mess. But the pain faded with the sudden thrill of flying over the forest. I had a moment to wonder whether I died and then the flap of wings stirred the air around me, making my foot feel as if I had dipped it straight into the fires of hell.

Strong leathery talons held me, and when I glanced to the side, the edges of bright red, orange, and yellow wings filled my vision. The wings reminded me of bonfire flames. Stunning and dangerous all wrapped into a single image and my breath labored in my chest.

We descended into a field of white flowers and moss, and before I knew it, I was face down on the soft ground. The sweet scent of lilies swept over me, and I rolled, looking up at what had saved me.

My eyes widened, and I tried to scramble away, but my foot was too damaged from the swamp. I gasped and fell on my back, grabbing my leg as tears marred my vision. The dragon dipped his magnificent fire-orange head and sniffed me. His sharp green eyes shimmered with golden flecks, giving me such a strong sense of déjà vu. His snout traveled over my bloodied hands and my injured foot.

I couldn't tell whether he was going to finish what the swamp started or not.

When his gaze moved to mine, I think I stopped breathing. He lifted his head and then brought his talon-like claw to his mouth. His sharp teeth ripped his own flesh. I didn't have time to register shock before a drop of his blood the size of one of Felicity's pies splashed down over my injured foot and a second bathed my hands.

I cried out as paralyzing pain gripped my foot. It was far worse than the acid burn had been. My breath caught in my throat and then I started panting because I couldn't draw in enough air. All the while, the dragon watched, as if amused by my pain. I wanted to shoot an arrow right through one of his golden-flecked eyes.

Rolling onto my belly, I curled up with my forehead to the soft ground so the dragon could not witness the tears that bathed my face with warmth. I clasped my hands to my chest and silently prayed the beast would give me a quick death.

The agony faded into a tingle and I glanced at my hands. My fingers were no longer shredded from the rocks. There wasn't even a trace of my blood. I pushed back on my knees in case the tears in my eyes were showing me a trick. I turned them palms up and then palms down to make sure. But even with the sunlight shining down, my hands were pristine.

I uncurled my legs from beneath me, expecting the pain of my ruined foot to flare, but nothing happened. Sunlight warmed the unmarred skin of both feet. What had been a bloody, burned mess when we landed was now fully healed. I reached down and ran my fingers over the skin to validate what my eyes were seeing. The flutter of my fingers tickled, and I let out a surprised laugh.

A huff behind me stiffened my back, and I slowly turned toward the dragon. He still stared down at me, but this time he actually looked as if he smiled.

My gaze jumped to the talon he tore to bathe my wounds in his blood. His bloodstained talon. The gash he created had mended as surely as my hands and foot had.

Awe filled me, and I met his gaze. "Did you just..." I waved at my foot.

He dipped his snout and sniffed me again, but this time he seemed to rub the side of his nose against my cheek. I reached up and cupped his chin, pushing him away with a laugh. This encounter was nothing like the nightmarish stories Marabel had described.

I climbed to my feet and made my way around him, studying his stunningly vibrant colors. The entire time, his magical green eyes followed me.

When I settled back in the spot in front of him, I smiled. "Thank you."

Glancing at my surroundings, I had no idea how far off the path I was. I didn't even know which way home was, and my heart sank. I bit my lip and looked up at the dragon.

"You wouldn't happen to know the way to the fae village?" If I could get to the village, I could find my way back to our cottage.

He pointed his chin behind me, and I turned in the opposite direction of where we had flown from. I glanced back at his unique green eyes. A part of me wanted to stay with this beast, but I knew I had to get home before the three fae sent out a search party.

"Thank you again." I backed away.

Sadness filled his eyes as I moved away from him. I finally turned toward my destination once I had crossed most of the flower field, but turning away from the dragon had yanked at my chest.

I sighed and kept going, ignoring the pull of the beast.

SPINDLE Chapter 3

BEFORE I STEPPED INTO the woods at the far side of the flower field, a shadow hid the sun, and I glanced up at the underside of the dragon. His magnificent wings took him high enough to block out the light and then he veered in the opposite direction, away from where I was headed. A ride would have been more convenient, but I could just see the fairies' faces if we were to land in the small courtyard outside our cottage.

Marabel would fall in a dead faint. Autumn would grab her quiver of arrows and Felicity would start a fire in the oven to cook the dragon. I chuckled at the thought. I no longer had slippers, and I wasn't sure if I lost them to the swamp or to the dragon flight, but one thing was for sure, the forest floor was much less forgiving than the field had been.

The woods were thick, and by the time I reached the next poppy field, I was ready for the soft ground. This field was blue and gold as opposed to white, like the one the dragon left me in. It was stunning and the sweet floral scent blanketed the air, giving me a sense of relaxation and peace that I did not realize existed outside of our little cottage.

The ground felt fabulous on my feet after the forest floor and I took my time crossing, eyeing another set of woods with trepidation. By the time I reached the cottage, my feet were bound to be torn up enough that even slippers would hurt. So much for being comfortable at the party at the palace.

The next set of woods ended in a thick wall of thorn bushes that reached at least ten feet into the air above me. I followed along the bushes, but could not see a way through. When I doubled back, the same barrier held true. Sighing, I bent over and ripped some fabric from the hem of my tunic and wrapped each hand. I did the same to my feet and then stared up at the thorns.

With trepidation building in my chest like a lead weight, I reached up to grab a branch. The moment my fingertips touched the wood, the bush came alive. I yelped and tried to escape, becoming entangled, but it was futile. Before I knew it, vines wrapped around my arms and legs, pulling me into the sharp shards. Prickers pierced my skin in over a dozen places. The more I struggled, the more I bled.

"Let her go!" a deep, barking voice came from behind me.

The vines receded. I stumbled back, right into the powerful arms of the stranger who commanded the thorn bushes. He steadied me and I turned to face my savior.

Green eyes with golden flecks. I blinked at those familiar eyes. It wasn't just a mirror of the dragon's eyes, either. They were the eyes of my green-eyed ghost.

As he studied me, a crop of dark hair fell onto his forehead. He was built like the farm boys I saw tilling the fields on the outskirts of the fae borders, but his nails were as pristine as mine after a good scrubbing. He flashed a smile at me, and my knees nearly gave out. Something regal about him screamed royalty, and I fought the urge to bow.

My gaze fell on the equally familiar sword at his side. "Zee?" I finally squeaked out.

A dimple appeared in his cheek. "It's actually Zachary. I never got to finish telling you my name before your fae friend happened along." He glanced at the thorn vines. "These vines have a mind of their own." He nodded toward the thorny thistles and then glanced down at my exposed arms. "And it seems they have shown you no mercy." He reached for my hand. His touch was soft and tender as he inspected my wounds.

I was too thunderstruck by him to utter a word. My brain was still stuck on the fact his eyes were the same as the dragon's. But each stroke of his finger seemed to dull the pain of my cuts. It was as if he were magically wiping them from my skin. It took me a moment to get my senses back, and I pulled my hand from his grip.

I had the feeling that if he hadn't come around, the vines would have strangled me to death. "Thank you for stopping them."

He licked his lips and shrugged as if it were no big deal. "What are you doing roaming around in the Dragon Realm?" He raised an eyebrow.

I gasped and stepped back, right into the sharp prickers, wincing as I arched away from the shards. "D-Dragon Realm?"

"Yes." He cocked his head. His eyes sparkled with the same interest I remembered him looking at me with before. "Did you know you smell like sunshine and morning dew?"

I wasn't sure how to respond to his sweetness, even with the alarms going off in my head at the fact I was in the Dragon Realm. In every story Marabel had told me of dragons, they were vicious murderers that killed for sport. But considering I had been saved by one, I couldn't reconcile the stories with the real thing. Especially with the golden flecks in his eyes sparkling in the sunshine, just like the dragon's eyes.

"Were you the one who saved me from the acid swamp?" I asked, instead of acknowledging his strange compliment.

His cheeks turned rosy, and he glanced away with a nod.

Holy cow. My green-eyed ghost was a *dragon.* That explained so much. "And you were keeping an eye on me as I crossed through the poppy fields?" I asked, remembering the shadows he created when flying overhead.

He shuffled his feet. "Yes."

"Why?" I blurted. "Why didn't you shift before and tell me who you were? You scared the hell out of me." I swatted his arm.

"My fierce little huntress scared?" he teased with a grin that was swoon-worthy. "Besides, I could always tell when you were close. Your scent is intriguing and very, very unique. I just never imagined you would be on *this* side of the wall." He looked up at the prickers and then down at me. "So, beautiful one, why did you come to *my* kingdom?"

Heat rushed to my cheeks. It was my turn to shuffle my feet. If I could have scrambled over the wall of prickers, I would have just to get away from this overwhelming pull in the center of my stomach. The sudden image of being caught in his arms with his lips on mine was too tempting. I stared at the ground as the rest of his words sunk in. "Your kingdom?"

"I am Prince Zachary of the Dragon Realm." He waved at the surroundings. "So yes, my kingdom. Why, dear Rory, did you breach the wall?"

"I was just following a hunting trail," I said softly, lost in his piercing gaze. "I did not know I crossed into the Dragon Realm."

He hooked his finger under my chin and tilted my head so I would meet his gaze. He stepped closer as if he had the same rampant thoughts I was. His thumb brushed my bottom lip.

"You are forbidden." He breathed the words as he dipped his head down toward mine.

Forbidden? His whispered words smacked sense into me, and I placed my hands on his chest and leaned back to avoid the kiss he was about to deliver. As much as my inner voice screamed at me for putting this moment on pause, everything I had been taught rushed back, and along with it came my sense of self-preservation.

"I need to get home." I sucked my lower lip between my teeth.

His eyes widened with surprise at my rebuff. From the looks of him, no one ever refused the prince. He blinked and then inhaled and stepped back with a nod. "Now that you know who and what I am, will I ever see you again?"

The longing in his eyes sent my heart beating more frantically than it already was. I opened my mouth to say I hoped so, but nothing came out. I wasn't sure what would happen if he got caught crossing into the fae lands. Dragons were not welcomed, and I didn't want to start another war, especially considering it had been the dragon queen who cursed the princess, if Marabel's stories held any truth.

The prince took another step back and his features hardened. "Do you not wish to see me again?"

I sighed. "You are the green-eyed ghost that haunts my dreams. I *always* want to see you," I said, and the hard lines of his jaw softened with a grin. "But if you ever get caught in the fae lands, I'm not sure what would happen to you."

His gaze traveled up the thorn bushes. "I have rarely been beyond this wall. It is just as forbidden as letting you leave." His eyes found mine. "But you would not survive a night here, either." He reached his hand out beyond my head and winced as he laid his palm on the sharp prickers. "Let her pass," he said.

The bushes parted, leaving an opening a little wider than my shoulders. I hesitated at the sight of blood dripping down his wrist. Instead of darting through the hedges, I took his cheeks between my palms and pressed a kiss to his lips.

His free arm wound around my waist, and he pulled me against his well-chiseled body. Our lips parted and our tongues mingled in a slow dance that left me breathless. If I didn't stop right now, I would never leave this bliss.

I pulled away and darted through the bushes before I changed my mind.

"I will see you again, Rory," he said with conviction, and then removed his hand from the bush.

It closed like the slamming of a door, and my heart squeezed. I took a step closer to the thorny wall, and the vines reached toward me in that malignant way that spelled death.

SPINDLE Chapter 4

EACH STEP AWAY FROM the thistle bushes crashed through me as if a boulder were being slammed into my stomach. I kicked at the dirt, wincing at the stub of my bare toe.

I trudged through the green field until I found a road and then headed away from the direction of the Dragon Realm. But all I could think about was Zachary and the way his kiss had made my entire body tingle with desire.

I only knew the horror stories that Marabel, Autumn, and Felicity had recounted. The dragons had once ruled half of the kingdom, but after the dragon king died, war broke out. Villages on both sides were destroyed, and the barrier Zachary let her through had been erected. But the stories said a wall built by fae magic had been erected so the dragons could not leave their lands.

But if the fae had built that wall of thorns and vines, why had a dragon commanded it? Why had dragon blood opened the wall?

My steps faltered. I stopped in the middle of the road, mulling over all I had been fed over the last twenty years.

"There you are!" Felicity's sharp voice carried on the wind.

I looked up to see the three fae rushing down the road toward me, their faces masks of relief. As they neared, that relief changed into concern.

"What in the king's name happened to you?" Marabel asked as she flitted around me.

I glanced down at myself. My arms still had bloody welts. My feet were bare and nearly blackened with dirt. My tunic was ripped, and the swaths tied around my hands were stained with blood from the thorn punctures.

"I was hunting," I said, still staring at my hands.

Autumn pulled something from my hair and waved it at me. "Where did you go?" Her voice thundered in my face.

I licked my lips and scanned each curiously angry face, peering at me. "I... uh." I shuffled my feet, unsure why I wasn't being honest with them. I glanced down at the ground.

Autumn stepped close and sniffed my hair. She nearly stumbled backward. Her mouth popped open, almost as wide as her eyes. "You smell like dragon blood."

I let out a high-pitched laugh. "Funny story," I started, trying to wipe the horror off her face. "Dragons aren't as awful as you three have painted them to be."

It was as if the world had stopped spinning. All three fae stood rigidly, staring at me with eyes like saucers and chins dangling.

"One saved me from an acid swamp," I blurted.

Three sets of eyebrows arched.

"And he healed my wounds and let me go," I added, trying to erase the panic flitting in their eyes. "And then he saved me from the thorn wall. And let me pass through." I rubbed my hands together, peeling off the fabric wraps, so I didn't have to look at the shock on their faces any longer.

"You went through to the Dragon Realm?" Marabel squeaked.

"That is what I am trying to tell you. I have no idea how I got over there. I didn't cross through the thorn bushes to get there." I chewed on the inside of my mouth, trying to remember how I had gotten in if the thistle barrier truly surrounded the land, but all I remembered was following a wildlife trail.

Autumn and Felicity each grabbed an upper arm, and they marched me back to the cottage without a word. Smoke drifted out the windows of our little abode. Felicity squealed, dropped my arm, and flew inside. We all followed.

The duck she had started to cook when I left was now a charred shell. Thankfully, it had not fallen off the spit and started the rest of the cottage on fire, although the amount of smoke still wafting out the windows and doors would seem to indicate that it had come close to demolishing our home.

A dress in the center of the room was covered in soot and a cake on the counter that had partly fallen remained. The horror at the mention of a dragon did not compare to the devastation painted on each of their faces at the condition of their little world.

Marabel burst into tears, covering her face. Autumn fell into the nearest chair as if she had been shot by an arrow, and Felicity stood still in the center of the room, just staring at the overcooked bird.

"Today was supposed to be perfect," Autumn whispered.

A chill skittered down my back. This was my doing, but the guilt making my stomach roll didn't quite wipe out the questions accosting my mind. "Did the fae make that barrier?" I asked, because I could not get that to settle right in my head.

All three fae turned toward me, exchanged glances, and nodded in unison. They looked as if they had secretly eaten the last piece of holiday pie.

I crossed my arms and cocked a skeptical eyebrow.

"Well... technically, the dragons created the wall of thorns, but the fae hold it in place. Otherwise, it would have grown rampant through our kingdom and swallowed every living creature outside of the dragons," Marabel said.

I narrowed my eyes at her. There were so many holes in her version of the truth that it would look like Swiss cheese if I let them continue. "I need to clean up." I headed toward the bath at the back of the house to clean the grime off from my walking and bleeding in the Dragon Realm.

I hand-pumped a bucket of water and poured it into the warmer before getting another bucket. When I returned with the second bucket, the first was just warm enough to not chill me to the bone. I let the warmer drain into the tub before plugging it and pouring the second bucket. Rinse. Repeat. By the time the tub was nearly filled, I was ready for the bath.

It took a fair amount of scrubbing to get the grime off my body and out of my hair. By the time I was done, the water had turned a disgusting cloudy brown from the dirt. I unplugged the tub, waiting until the soiled water drained completely before closing the drain and adding the last bucket from the warmer to finish my soak.

The last batch nearly scalded, but I forced myself to soak in it, and ease any knotted muscles in my legs and back. My mind wandered to the kiss I had shared with Zachary. When the water was nearly cool, I scooped up handfuls and ran it over my shoulders and hair, wiping off any remaining dirt. By the time I stepped out of the tub, I felt cleaner than I had in weeks.

I towel-dried my hair and wrapped a robe around me. The clothing I had been wearing was too soiled to wear again. I scrubbed them clean in the remaining water before I hung them on the line to dry.

When I stepped back into the heart of the house, it was as if dinner had never burned. A magnificent dress hung in place of the one covered in soot. A tall cake sat on the counter, and a duck roast sat on the table, with all the fixings.

It seemed my fairy godmothers had decided that magic was needed to save the day, which was just as rare as me wandering away from the cottage. I reached for the dress.

"Not yet, child. That is for the palace tomorrow night."

I had almost forgotten about the ball. "Do you think the dragon I met will be there?" I asked as I took a seat at the table. As soon as the question fell from my lips, I knew the answer.

"Dragons are not welcome in King Henrick's court," Felicity said with such a cool voice that I glanced up from the feast before me. "I doubt one would be so bold after the last time." She dug into the meal with no more explanation.

When the meal was over, the cake was set on the table before me. Golden letters glistened in the sweet frosting, wishing me a happy birthday. "You are a day early." I glanced at them.

"We will be at the castle tomorrow night for the celebration." Felicity nodded toward the cake. "Go on. Make a wish!"

Twenty candles burned on the top tier and I stood, closed my eyes, and made a wish to see Zachary again, to dance with him until the sun rose. I took a deep breath and blew. Every candle went out.

I grinned. If only it were that easy.

Marabel, Autumn, and Felicity danced around me, still singing "Happy Birthday." They would continue until I devoured a piece of their sweet confection. I cut a small slice and put it in my mouth.

Their singing stopped as they waited for my judgment of their masterpiece.

The cake literally melted into a sweet, tangy mixture of strawberry and vanilla in my mouth. I leaned back, closed my eyes, and took a moment to savor the goodness. I smiled and opened my eyes to their rapt attention.

"You've outdone yourselves with this one."

Felicity grinned as if I had given her a golden four-leaf clover, and both Marabel and Autumn clapped happily. We all tore into the delectable cake as though we didn't have a care in the world.

Thunder clapped outside the window, making all of us jump. It felt like a foreshadowing of doom. If the world was going to end tomorrow with the princess's curse, I was hell-bent on seeing Zachary one last time before the gauntlet dropped on humanity.

SPINDLE Chapter 5

I TOSSED AND TURNED all night, too excited to sleep, so I climbed out of bed before daybreak and slipped out of the cottage. The skies were just lighting up like a rainbow. The clouds that had crowded the sky the previous evening had spilled their wares and left, as if they knew that today of all days needed to let the light shine. A strange sensation tingled in the air, as if it knew the time in the light was ending.

I shivered and rubbed my arms as I made my way back toward the pricker bushes holding the dragons in their territory. The sun broke over the horizon, nearly blinding me. I squinted as I followed the path the sun lit.

In the distance, a form emerged from the rays of light, and I blinked to make sure it wasn't just the blinding dots from the sun playing tricks on my mind. As I got closer, the form of a man came into focus. But with the light framing him, his face hid in shadows.

Caution flags flared in my mind. This couldn't be the prince. Not on this side of the barrier. It was too dangerous for him to be on this side. My heart clanged in my chest at the thought. Encountering strangers on a deserted path was just as harrowing, and I glanced around for any escape route. The trees were closer to the approaching man than they were to me. But if I could get there, the woods would give me cover.

I sprinted toward the trees. Halfway across the field, I caught movement near me to my right. I took my eyes off the wood line at the same moment a body slammed into me, taking me to the ground in a roll. I struck out blindly until hands grabbed my wrists and slammed them on the ground by my head.

"What. The. Hell," a breathless voice above me said.

I tossed my hair out of my eyes and Zachary's bright-green eyes looked down at me with exasperated humor. My mouth popped open as I stilled. My chest heaved with the exertion, and Zachary's grip on my wrists loosened.

"What are you doing here?" I asked when I finally caught my breath.

He grinned. "I told you I would see you again."

With his body still draped over me, I was helpless to fight off the charm in that smile. It made my heart go into the same pitter-patter that the run had, but this time, instead of an adrenaline rush, heat enveloped me.

His gaze dropped to my lips and then he rolled off me, taking a seat in the grass next to me. I didn't move. I just stared at the deep-blue sky above me, waiting for my skin to cool before I sat up. When I did, I hand combed the leaves out of my hair and glanced at him, leaning back on a single elbow with a blade of the long grass between his teeth. Prince Zachary lounging on the grass like a commoner sent my temperature to high.

He studied our surroundings with interest, but it was nothing compared to the way his eyes shined when they landed on me. It was as if he had swallowed the sun, and light naturally found the golden chips in his irises.

"You are taking a risk being here."

He laughed. A full throaty sound that I could get used to, and I was sure I would hear in my dreams for weeks to come.

"I have to say, despite the reaming I will get from my mother when I get home, tackling you in the grass was worth it."

"And yet you moved away from me." I cocked my head and gave him a sly smile.

"Is the lady inviting a kiss?" He rolled onto his hands and knees, crawling toward me like a predator.

I giggled and shuffled back, but he caught me by the ankles and crawled up my body in a way that sucked the breath from my lungs. His touch was light as he ran his fingers up my calves. And then he crawled the rest of the way and settled on top of me. His weight felt good, and we molded in all the right places.

"Why, dear lady, you seem to be a naughty vixen at heart," he purred, and his mouth found mine before I could launch a protest.

The kiss silenced any argument I could come up with in my head to stop where this was leading. The attraction between us was as raging as the fire of a dragon's breath. He took my cheeks gently in his palms and let out a gruff groan as the kiss deepened.

His hands flowed slowly down my neck and if he had stopped there, I would have been content to kiss him until the moon rose. But his exploration did not stop. He ignited me with desire. His lips left mine to trail down my throat and into the vee of my shirt.

A rustling in the bushes pulled us both out of the moment. His nostrils flared as a rabbit hopped out from cover and twitched its nose at us before continuing across the field.

It was enough for me to come to my senses. When the prince leaned in to start again, I gently pressed my hand to his chest.

"I'm sorry. As much as I enjoy...this, I don't really know you."

He covered my hand with his and closed his eyes, taking a deep breath as he rolled onto his back next to me, accepting my not-so-valiant request to stop.

"I want to know you," he said softly, studying the leaves on the trees above us. "But I cannot have you risking your life by sneaking into my territory." He turned his head and met my gaze. He lifted my palm and placed a kiss in the center of my hand.

"And I cannot have you risking your life by sneaking into mine." I rolled on my side and propped myself up on my elbow to look down at him.

He glanced at me and cocked his eyebrow. "I could just ravage you right here, right now, you know."

I smiled. "I think you would already have done that if that was your intention."

"Mmmm. Are you so sure it isn't? I am a dragon, after all." He didn't move a muscle to make good on his thinly veiled threat. "And you are what I covet most."

"Oh. You covet me?" I put my hand to my forehead. "Whatever shall I do?"

He snorted laughter. "You do not strike me as the damsel in distress type, despite your misadventures yesterday."

I chuckled. I certainly was not a damsel in distress. I knew my way around a bow and a sword fairly well. "I am pretty good with a bow. Although my favorite one was eaten by your swamp."

"I shall make you another." He wrapped his arm around me, bringing me closer. "What else do you want?"

"I want my birthday wish," I said.

Sparks danced in his eyes. "And what wish would that be?" He traced a chilling path across my back with his fingers.

"I want to dance with you at the king's ball tonight," I said.

His lighthearted smile faded. "Oh Rory, I am so sorry to have to disappoint you."

"I know. Dragons, even attractive prince dragons, are not welcomed in King Henrick's kingdom." His stomach muscles twitched under my fingertips as I traced lazy circles over his loose shirt.

"I'm not so sure I could stay in human form if I went anyway," he said in a dark tone. "I might be inclined to eat King Henrick."

I blinked and pulled away from Zachary.

"King Henrick killed my father. Took his blood to heal his ailing wife." His tone carried the bitterness of growing up without a father as he stared up at the sky. "If he had just asked, I'm sure my father would have given him some of his blood, but the bastard got greedy. He wanted to slaughter another king for the betterment of his kingdom." He licked his lips and glanced at me. "My mother has never been the same."

I couldn't think of anything worse than losing the one you loved. It must have shown on my face, because Zachary propped himself up and pulled me into another kiss. This one tender and sweet and everything a girl could ever hope for in a kiss.

He pulled back and studied my eyes as though they held the secrets of the world. "I want to learn all your guarded secrets."

"I have no secrets," I said, and closed the distance.

His hand glided down my side, all the way to my knee, and he pulled me on top of him.

His hands drew up around my waist as the kiss deepened. Beneath me, I could feel his hardness form between my straddled legs. He slowly ground against me, moving me in small circles. Those golden flecks in his eyes turned almost as hot as he was making me.

He tightened his jaw and closed his eyes. "You are forbidden," he said, almost as if it were a reminder to himself. "Innocent. Sweet. And oh, so damn edible."

His eyes flashed as he opened them, and I almost saw the dragon forming. I pulled back in alarm.

He chuckled, holding me tightly in place. His hips still circled slowly under me. Enough to bring forth a rush of wetness between my legs. I had never had thoughts of losing my innocence before I met Zachary. And now that was all I could think of.

Zachary stilled beneath me and closed his eyes, pressing his lips together. His eyes opened, and he stared at the sky. "Someday I will show you bliss, but that won't be today." He met my gaze. "My mother is calling and if I don't go..." His eyes filled with instant regret as he moved me off his lap. Zachary cupped my cheek and gave me a soft peck on the lips. "I will see you again, Rory," he vowed. And then he was up and was gone before I could straighten out my clothing and get to my feet.

Disappointment scratched over my heated skin, and I kicked myself for falling so easily into his arms. It was as if fate was forcing us to do things that put us in harm's way. After all, I had ventured out alone this morning with the sole goal of finding Zachary. He apparently had the same impulse.

Damn that sexy prince.

If I didn't watch myself, I'd certainly be eaten by a dragon.

SPINDLE Chapter 6

I TOOK MY TIME on my way back to the cottage. When I entered the glen, the fae were already dashing about, getting ready for tonight's festivities. When Marabel saw me, she grabbed me and ushered me inside with no comment as to my whereabouts. Thankfully, my routine included a morning walk and the timing of my return worked.

Before I spoke, they were already slipping me into the silky dress and tightening the corset until I could barely breathe. The sky-blue satin shimmered, and I smiled at the image in the mirror, even with my blonde hair windblown and knotted from my morning adventure. I could not envision being led around a dance floor by anyone other than Zachary.

A chair slid against the back of my knees, and I fell into the cushion as the three fae flitted around me.

"Should we braid her hair or curl it?" Felicity started brushing the tangles out with an efficiency that made me wince with each yank.

"Braid," said Autumn at the same time Marabel said, "Curls."

Marabel brought out a table with powders and colored chalk and sat right in front of me as if she were going to make me up like the court jester. I put my hand up and shook my head as she brought a powder puff straight toward my face.

"No thank you," I said to her, knowing it would probably hurt her feelings. But I never got the hang of make-up, and I did not want to look strange on my first foray into a royal ball.

"But..." she started.

"She is beautiful without all that fake stuff." Autumn sided with me for a change.

"I agree," Felicity added. "Even with her hair a mess, she would be the most stunning girl at the ball." She yanked at a few strands that framed my face and wrapped them around a tube that she left in place. She did the same with the other side and continued until I looked like a strange version of a porcupine.

She stepped back with a satisfied nod, stepped away for a moment, and when she returned, she had a plate of food that she handed to Marabel.

"Let Marabel feed you so you don't get anything on the dress, okay?"

"Um. Okay." I didn't have much choice in the matter and before I knew it, I was so full that I had to wave off the next pastry Marabel offered. Not a speck fell on the dress, either. If I had been left to eat on my own, I probably would have had at least one stain from a falling bite.

Felicity and Autumn raced about the cottage, dressing in their own clothing suited for court. Felicity returned to me and started pulling the tubes out of my hair. Little ringlets fell, framing my face and falling over my shoulders. She grinned at the effect and then went back to styling my hair.

She finally had Marabel bring a mirror out. She had done a stylish updo that included intricate braids interspersed with corkscrew curls, and the effect made me gasp with delight.

"You will outshine the entire royal court!" Felicity said as she studied me.

Heat filled my cheeks. I only wanted to impress one person, and he would not be there. I wished I could run to the glen where I found him this morning, just to show off this magnificent outfit. Although I was sure by the time I left him, I would be a hot mess.

I smiled at the thought. "Thank you." I glanced at the three fae.

Before they whisked me out of the cottage, I snuck a swipe of frosting from what was left of the cake on the counter. After all, it was my birthday cake and I wouldn't be able to have a piece until well into the evening.

At least, if the curse was a farce. Otherwise, I'd never see that sweet cake again.

I sucked the frosting from my finger as we stepped outside. I drew to a halt at the sight of an ornate golden carriage that reminded me of the flecks in Zachary's eyes. It was far too fancy to be from the modest fae realm we lived in. I had a moment where I thought Zachary would step out and hold the door for me. But that small daydream was ruined when Felicity swung the door open and waved me inside.

A measure of disappointment filled me, but at least my smile didn't falter. I climbed inside, followed by Autumn, Marabel, and Felicity. Their excitement created static in the air around them, sending little sparks of happiness flying around the inside of the carriage.

We lurched forward, and so did my heart. I was headed to the palace. Toward a night with a precarious ending. Tonight, the kingdom would celebrate the princess's twentieth birthday, and it would either end with too much wine, dance, and song, or it would end in ruin as the curse uttered so long ago blanketed the land.

The closer we got, the quieter the fae got. And the louder the ruckus outside the carriage. People shouted blessings as we passed, devotions for the curse to be lifted and the kingdom spared.

"Why do they shout prayers at us?" I asked the fae.

"They shout at all the carriages that are heading to the celebration in the hopes it will somehow lift the curse." Marabel's eyelids fluttered like they had when she told me that the fae had built the barrier between us and the dragons.

Marabel was not being totally honest, and neither Felicity nor Autumn dared to look at me.

"Am I missing something important?"

"No, no, sweetie." Marabel patted my leg and the three fae traded tense glances.

"What is it?" The exasperation in my question brought all three pairs of eyes to mine.

Marabel wrung her hands. "It's just... just that there hasn't been a big event like this since..." She glanced out the window. "Since the princess was cursed. And I'm sure we aren't the only ones who are a little on edge." She gave me a tight smile that I'm sure was supposed to calm me, but it just made this worse.

For the first time, I saw unease in them, and it wasn't from an ill-timed joke like sometimes happened at the cottage. This was true discomfort. I had no idea how nervous they were about this day until that very moment. "Everything will work out," I said, and it was my turn to pat her knee.

"Oh, child, I certainly hope so." She traded a glance with the other fae, who nodded in unison. This time, their smiles were much more natural.

The carriage came to a halt in front of a heavily guarded set of stairs. The door was yanked open by a stern-looking man in chainmail. His other hand stayed on the hilt of his sword. It was a little more than concerning, and I understood the fae's unease on the ride. It wasn't until his gaze landed on me that he seemed to soften. He stepped back with a grand bow.

Trumpets blew on the top of the stairs as Marabel, Autumn, and Felicity stepped out of the carriage. The guard offered his hand to help me out and then bowed again as if I were royalty. The steps were empty except for the men standing guard and the road behind us was absent of anymore carriages.

A chill climbed my spine as I navigated the stairs behind the fae. Guards rushed to open the doors, and we entered the massive castle throne room that was bigger than anything I had ever seen. The crowd milled on the floor and on a pedestal opposite the grand staircase sat King Henrick and Queen Lila.

Both sported severe expressions, as if they had not had a moment of peace in decades. The queen once may have been beautiful, but she looked like nothing more than a dried husk, with mousy-gray hair and lips as thin as lines. King Henrick looked no more impressive than his queen, with a belly that screamed of excess and a graying beard that looked as if someone had attempted to trim it but had failed. His hair was no better, sticking out in random tufts on an otherwise balding head.

The one endearing thing I noticed was that they held hands. It was such a small detail, but one I noticed right away.

The trumpets blared behind us, so loud I nearly tumbled down the stairs. I turned to see who was entering the grand ballroom, but just like in the street below, no one was behind us. When I turned back, all eyes were on the four of us, and both the king and queen were on their feet.

The dullness that had settled over them when I first laid eyes on them seemed to shatter and the king's bright smile lit up the room. The queen covered her mouth as if she were truly overwhelmed.

A hush fell over the crowd as the last of the trumpet blare faded and the sea of people parted, leaving a clear path between us and the king's pedestal. A chair next to the queen's was empty, and I glanced around, trying to guess which face in the crowd was the princess.

"Come." Felicity grabbed my hand. Autumn grabbed the other and Marabel moved behind me and fluffed my dress so it wouldn't catch on the stairs.

Everyone stared at me and I tried on a smile, but it felt so foreign. I did not like this attention. Especially with the king and queen rushing across the floor to meet us. The fae must really have done something sensational to get this type of attention.

When I neared the bottom of the stairs, I scanned the curiosity in every face of the crowd, and my gaze landed on a very familiar face. My heart tripped, and I stumbled right into the king's arms.

A collective gasp filled the air and the heat of embarrassment painted my cheeks. I was sure I was as red as some of the ballgowns. He steadied me back on my feet, and I shot Prince Zachary a quick look. He winked at me with a smirk. I forced my focus back on the king.

"I'm sorry, Your Majesty." I curtsied.

King Henrick smiled down at me in such a warm manner, it was as if he had wrapped a soothing blanket around me. "You are more beautiful than I ever imagined." He stepped back and looked me over from crown to toe and back.

I gawked at him like a damn fool, but that was abruptly interrupted by the queen as she threw her arms around me and pulled me into a tight hug. I glanced at the one responsible for me losing my balance. The smile on Prince Zachary's face faded as his gaze bounced between me, the king, and the queen. The seriousness carved into his features made me want to rush over to him and wrap my arms around him. I wanted that playful smile back, but Zachary seemed just as perplexed as me.

"My dear Aurora, it is so good to finally have you home," the queen whispered in my ear.

I imagined my face sported the same shock as Zachary's. I pulled away, nearly falling on the stairs behind me. "Ex...cuse me?" I stuttered and looked at Marabel, Autumn, and Felicity.

"Welcome home," King Henrick said with a broad grin.

This time, I sat down on the steps and just stared up at the king and queen, dumbfounded by their words. *Home?* My home was in the enchanted forest with Marabel, Autumn, and Felicity. Not in this oversized monument.

Autumn kneeled before me and took my hands. "Child, you *are* Princess Aurora, heir to the Kingdom of Light. King Henrick asked that you be protected from the dragon queen until your twentieth birthday."

"And you couldn't have given me a warning?" The fae's duplicity made my skin feel like a million ants were marching across it.

Autumn traded a glance with Marabel and Felicity and then met my gaze. "We could not. We took a potion that silenced us whenever we felt the need to divulge your true identity. We were not to speak of it until the king and queen welcomed you back into their home." She squeezed my hands, and the sincerity in her eyes quelled my uneasy itch.

I blinked, still numb from their words. *I* was the cursed princess? It took a moment to sink in, and then I looked around at the crowd watching this very spectacle.

I glanced back at the king and queen and cleared my throat. "I don't understand. You are my parents?" I climbed back to my feet, waving away any help from the fairies. I didn't know whether to be grateful or furious.

They had, after all, abandoned me my whole life and put a gag order on my caretakers.

They nodded. "We needed to ensure your safety after these three powerful fae countered the dragon queen's curse. We did not know if she would make good on her threats and neither of us could bear the thought of you being hurt, so we felt you would be safer in their hands." King Henrick waved to Marabel, Autumn, and Felicity.

I considered his words and the sincerity in his deep-brown eyes. "And you and your armies could not protect me in this fortress?" I waved my hand at the palace surrounding us.

He glanced around. "We are not infallible. The day of your christening taught us that," he said. "And while it was a hardship on us, you were safe, which is all that truly matters." He turned around toward the rapt crowd. "Come, it is time for celebration." His voice boomed in the hall. The music started as we made our way toward the pedestal.

Zachary stepped out of the crowd as we passed. "Princess, may I have this dance?" He offered his hand before any of the guards surrounding us could intervene.

I stopped and took his hand. Just the idea of being in his arms was enough to send my heart racing.

"There are other suitors..." the queen started and pointed toward a group of men nearest the thrones.

"I would like to dance with *this* suitor." I smiled and allowed Zachary to lead me to the middle of the dance floor despite the frowns that formed on the king and queen's faces, as well as the confusion reflected on Marabel, Autumn, and Felicity's faces.

"Princess," Zachary said with almost a growl and bowed his head. Then he pulled me against his chest and planted his palm at the small of my back, keeping me in place. He moved with grace as he twirled me around the floor.

My heart thrummed in my chest, and I could not tear my gaze away from his very intense green eyes. This is what I had wished for, but there was a tension in Zachary that hadn't been there earlier. It bordered on hostility.

We moved around the floor in tight circles, weaving in and out of the other people trying to do the type of dancing I was accustomed to in the fae village. This was not the same. This was something both exciting and dangerous.

"You didn't know," he whispered almost accusingly, just above the music.

Whatever spell he had on me broke, and the story about his father flooded back into my head. *I was the daughter of the man who killed his father.* I slowly shook my head. "I didn't know. As far as I am concerned, the enchanted forest is my home, not this monstrous palace." I leaned back, studying the tight set of his lips. "Did you?"

The corner of his lip twerked upward, and his eyes softened. "No. I did not have the slightest clue. Had I, you would have been dead either by the acid pool or by my fire, and I would never know this ache in my chest or the fact you cloud my every thought."

I planted my foot and forced him to stop this maddening spin he'd swept me up in. He pulled me closer, staring down at me. Heat enveloped me as though I had stepped right into the heart of a dragon flame. His eyes shimmered, and he licked his lips as his gaze moved from mine down to my mouth and the memory of our kiss flushed my skin.

A guard's hand came into view and landed on his shoulder.

We both stiffened.

"It's time for the princess to take her rightful seat," the guard said. There was no leeway in his request, or the tight hold he had on Zachary's shoulder.

I gripped Zachary's hand tighter, not willing to let go just yet, especially after his declaration. I tore my eyes away from his and glanced beyond the guard at the king and queen standing in front of their thrones. A chill captured my skin. That man ruthlessly killed Zachary's father for his own gain. I did not want to have any part of a kingdom built on murder.

"I would like to dance a little more," I said to the guard, jutting my chin out as if that would make a difference.

Zachary smirked and looked away.

"I'm sorry, Princess. King's orders."

My prince stepped back, out of the guard's grip, and bowed, kissing my knuckles. "I will see you again, Rory," he said softly, and then disappeared into the crowd.

The guard led me up the steps to where the three thrones sat, and my father stood next to my mother with a frown on his face. Marabel, Autumn, and Felicity cowered behind him. And that vision sent my blood to the boiling point. I was not a child. If they were unhappy with my actions, they had no right to take it out on my family.

"Why is my fae family hiding behind you as if you have reprimanded them?"

The king's bushy eyebrows rose, and his face turned red. He swiped his finger toward the chair. "Sit!" he barked.

The music ground to a halt and, once again, all eyes were on me. The way Marabel, Autumn, and Felicity looked at me was just shy of visual begging. I stared the king down, ignoring their imploring eyes.

I had heard stories about the dragon queen all my life, but no one except Zachary ever told me why the queen went to such extremes. I wanted to hear my father's viewpoint on the murder. "Tell me about the dragon king."

King Henrick blanched, and his eyes widened. "Sit," he hissed.

I crossed my arms and tapped my foot impatiently. Although I was raised to respect my elders, I was not used to being ordered around. I did not like it one bit. I glanced at the queen. She did not wear a mask of anger like the king. In fact, if I had to read her expression, it looked like a barely concealed smirk. She nodded toward the seat. Her silent request was much more welcoming.

"I will sit," I mumbled and crossed to the third throne. It was decorated more for a child with hand painted animals adorning the back, rather than a future queen, but I guess that was to be expected. I settled into the seat as the king waved his hand.

Music filled the ballroom yet again.

The king settled in his seat and snapped his fingers. The suitors formed a line, and the first approached. He had greasy black hair that fell over his dark eyes, a thin, almost nonexistent mustache, and was skinnier than a twig.

"Duke of Dewimeth," a guard announced.

He bowed and then put his hand out in an invitation to dance. The way he eyed me was more as if he were sizing up livestock.

I raised an eyebrow. "No, thank you." I kept my hands folded neatly in my lap.

The queen leaned over. "Aurora, dear, you must dance."

"I was dancing." I stood, but instead of accepting the man's hand, I turned and fled into the vast network of halls. It was as if they were trying to crush my free spirit and shove it into some preconceived idea of who I was supposed to be. I blindly ran, moving as far away from the music as I could. I found a dark and quiet corner and pressed my back to the wall, trying to blend in so I wouldn't be noticed.

Hushed voices drifted in from the balcony, rising over my ragged breath. I slid closer.

"I won't be party to your madness!" a man's voice argued.

"She dies tonight, either by your hand or by the curse. You swore you would follow through. Otherwise, I would not have let you leave the safety of our sanctuary," a woman hissed.

"I will do what is necessary. Now go, before you are caught," the man snapped.

The curtains flared out at a sudden shift of air, and I caught the profile of the man as his gaze raised to the sky.

I blinked and gasped. *Zachary.* A chill skittered down my spine. Zachary's gaze snapped in my direction, and his eyes widened as they met mine.

He had been sent to kill the princess.

To kill *me.*

I spun, intending to flee, but a powerful hand grabbed my arm and pushed me into the wall face first. He covered my mouth. I glanced over my shoulder, but Zachary was not focused on me. His wide gaze was locked on the window, as if trying to shield me from whomever he had been talking to.

I tried to push him away, but he was as solid as a stone wall. I couldn't tell whose heart banged harder as he pressed against me. His heartbeat drummed against my back in a frantic beat that matched his hissing breath. A light sheen of sweat broke out on what I could see of his forehead.

My mind buzzed with questions and the longer he kept me in place, the angrier I got. Who did he think he was, handling me this way?

He cocked his head, and then twisted us around with a grip around me that was stronger than his dance pose. "Shh," he whispered in my ear, his breath hot against my skin. He led me across the room and down the hall until he found a small room with only one door. He pushed me inside, closed the door behind us, and let me go.

I turned to face him. "You were sent here to kill me?"

He mopped his face with his hand and shrugged. "I was sent to kill the princess as payback for my father. But I had no idea—"

I struck out and my open hand slammed into his cheek, silencing him. I didn't want his excuses. "The fact you came here with murder in your heart makes you no different from my father."

His hand covered the reddening skin, and he blinked at me. His mouth formed words, but every time he moved his lips, nothing came forth. He closed his eyes and leaned his back against the door, hanging his head. "Maybe I am no better than he is," he said. "I admit, I had dark intentions, but..." His eyes opened and zeroed in on me. Hunger and frustration echoed in his irises and he moved forward, pinning me to the nearest wall as his lips crushed down on mine.

I opened my mouth to protest, but his tongue darted in so fast that I froze in place at the desperation in his kiss. I shoved him away.

"No!" I pointed my finger at him. "You lost that right. You chose hate, and I cannot..." I pressed my lips together as a sheen of tears blurred my vision. "I cannot be with someone so intent on taking a life."

"I'm a dragon. I take life all the time." His tone hardened as he crossed his arms and stepped back.

His words struck deep inside me, and I recoiled. "You... you kill for sport?"

His gaze moved away from me, and his jaw tightened. He shook his head. "No." He breathed the word as if it were a curse. "*I don't.*"

The chill that captured me thawed when he looked back at me. But I wasn't fooled into melting into his arms.

"So, what does 'I will do what is necessary' mean?" I jutted my chin out in defiance. If he was entertaining trying to kill me, dragon or no dragon, he would have a fight on his hands.

His lips pressed together, and he shook his head, raking both hands through his hair. "I don't know. I didn't want my mother harmed and if the king finds out she is in his territory, he will have her killed. And the last thing in the world I want to do is harm you." He waved at me and turned his back, laying his forehead on the wood. "Which puts your father at the top of my target list. But if I kill him, my mother will never forgive me, and neither will you. I am in a lose-lose situation."

The anguish wrapped around his every word moved my feet and I placed my hand on his back. He didn't move at first, but when he glanced over his shoulder at me, there was a spark in his eye, as if an idea had formed.

"What?" I asked softly.

He inhaled deeply. "Our kingdoms could form an alliance." He turned toward me. "It would certainly beat being married off to one of those fools who the king assembled just for that purpose."

I stepped back and crossed my arms. This wasn't how I ever envisioned being proposed to, but the way Zachary looked at me was exactly the way I wanted to be looked at, with raw desire.

The way the duke had looked at me, along with all the others my father had gathered, was more like someone at a livestock auction. To them, I was just a thing to own. I bit my lip.

Zachary studied my face and a slow smile formed. "Marry me so I can ravage you in the poppy fields like I've dreamed of doing since I first caught your scent."

I cocked an eyebrow. All I seemed to dream about was him as well, but still. He made it sound as though he had been pining for me forever. As a prince, I'm sure he had a line of pretty women throwing themselves at him. He reached for me, and I stepped back.

His eyes sparkled in that thrilling way they had in the field earlier today. Like the predator he was, he stalked forward and took me in his arms.

"Marry me so I can kiss you like this any time I want," he whispered in a husky voice and then pressed his lips to mine, gently coaxing my lips to part.

This time, I melted into him. The kiss brought a soft moan to his lips, as if he could never get enough of this, even if we were together for a thousand years. My entire body tingled with desire, and my arms ensnared him as I deepened the kiss.

He broke away. "Is that a yes?" Hope shined bright in his eyes.

The door banged open.

"Release my daughter at once!" the king growled from behind us.

SPINDLE Chapter 7

TWO BRAWNY-LOOKING GUARDS HELD me in place while other bigger and meaner-looking guards searched Zachary. The tip of my father's sword pressed against his neck as the guards tossed each hidden blade out of reach. Zachary had enough weapons on him to wage a one-man war.

When they finished the search, they forced him to his knees, and my father withdrew his sword, sheathed it, and glared at the two of us. He glanced at the array of sharp cutlery and his nostrils flared. He kicked the knives to the far side of the room with a grumble and started pacing.

No one knew what Zachary was.

No one knew he was more deadly than all those weapons combined.

And if they did, he would not live through the night.

Zachary remained still under the inspection, but I could tell a storm was brewing inside him. He kept his head low, but the muscles in his jaw jumped every so often, as though he were grinding his teeth. His cheeks remained flush, but he refused to look at my father as the man paced the room, muttering under his breath like a crazy lunatic.

The fae were escorted into the room, and King Henrick turned toward them, pointing an accusing finger.

"What have you been teaching her out in those woods?" he bellowed. "I found her with this... this heathen in the pantry."

"Do not yell at my family." I tried to yank out of the guard's grip, but they held fast. If the fae got close enough, they would smell the dragon blood, just as they had when they found me after my adventure in the Dragon Realm.

Zachary glanced at me. His eyes had changed enough for me to fear he was close to losing control. If Zachary shifted, he was likely to be struck down before he could do any damage.

The fae stopped short and sniffed the air. Their eyes widened, and they seemed to huddle together as their gaze shot to Zachary and then to me. It wasn't my father's overbearing growl that shocked them.

"He's a—"

My heart lurched. "My boyfriend," I blurted. "I met him near the fields on the outskirts of the enchanted forest. He's a farm boy."

All three of the fae tilted their heads like lost puppies.

"Farm boys don't dance like he does." My father pointed an accusatory finger at Zachary. "Who are you?"

Time slowed as Zachary looked up. His eyes shimmered, giving away his heritage. I twisted out of the guard's grip as my father's face went ashen. His eyes widened for a fraction of a second and then narrowed with malice. He reached for his sword.

"I'm the son of the king you killed," Zachary declared in a low and menacing voice.

My father's intent was written in the scowl on his face and his roar. All I could envision was my father's sword slicing Zachary's head clean off. I reacted, throwing myself between the two men despite the peril.

My father didn't swing his sword in an arc like I imagined. If he had, he could have easily stopped before the damage was done. No, he lunged as if fencing, and the tip of his sword pierced my chest. Agony seared my entire body, and I screamed before my lungs closed. The blade retracted, and I glanced at the shock on my father's face before I crumpled to the ground.

"No!" Zachary yelled and threw the guards off him with a guttural growl. He pulled me into his arms, cradling me as if I were the most precious thing in the world to him.

My father stepped closer.

"You old fool! Don't you think you've done enough?" he snapped at my father and then focused on me as everyone else in the room started bickering with one another.

All the noise drowned into one high-pitched buzz. I couldn't draw a breath. Hot tears slid from my eyes as I coughed. Red dots splattered on Zachary's tunic.

"Hold on, Rory," he whispered, and then pushed up his sleeve, exposing his arm. He put the soft flesh to his lips and dragon fangs appeared as he ripped his wrist wide open. He held his hand over me, and blood flowed from his torn skin right into my wound. "Please, just hold on," he said as his sharp teeth disappeared again.

His blood mingled with mine and the minute it seeped into the sword wound, I bellowed my pain in a high, gurgling cry. My body wanted away from the scalding dragon blood, but I knew what this burning agony meant. I arched into it and kept eye contact with Zachary.

My father must have known, too, because he called off the guards, ordering them to move away from us. Even the fae were relegated to the far side of the room.

Even knowing that he was healing me, concern reflected in Zachary's eyes. It wrapped around my heart even more than his blissful kiss had. I panted until my body realized the foreign substance mingling with my blood was not harmful. Pain gave way to tingling, as though I were just waking from a long sleep and I sagged in Zachary's arms.

The fae stepped closer to us.

Relief made me dizzy, but as I blinked away the wooziness, the paleness in

Zachary's cheeks gave me a rush of adrenaline.

How much blood had he lost?

My gaze shot to his hand. Blood still flowed from his wound. It wasn't like his dragon form that had healed just as quickly as my wounds had. He was in mortal danger. Marabel was close enough for me to reach out and grab her silk scarf. I wrapped the fabric around his shredded wrist and met his tired gaze.

"Thank you," I said.

His lips twitched into a ghost of a smile, and then he leaned into me. I held his wrist tight as hot panic flushed my skin. He couldn't die. Not now. Not after saving my life.

"I'm okay." I palmed his cheek. "You can heal yourself now."

He smiled weakly. "I need some food and a nap," he whispered and slumped on the ground next to me.

"Throw him in the dungeon," my father barked and swiped his sword from the ground, sheathing it and sending me a hard expression.

The guards reached for Zachary, and I covered him, glaring at them. "Do not touch him," I snarled like a rabid dog. We were both covered in blood, and I glanced at my father. "I swear, I will strike you down if you try to harm him again."

"Put them both in the dungeon," he amended his order.

This time, I didn't struggle in the guard's grip. Instead, I walked close to the men hauling Zachary's nearly unconscious form away. As they carted us out of the room, my father's glare landed on the fae.

SPINDLE Chapter 8

THE GUARDS DRAGGED ZACHARY into the cell and held me in place on the opposite side as they fitted restraints around both wrists, not bothering to remove the scarf I had wrapped around his open wound. He sagged in the shackles as they snapped a metal collar around his neck and attached it to the wall with a thin chain.

"Bastards," I snapped and tried to get loose from their grip. Zachary needed food. He needed water. He needed sleep. Otherwise, he would die in this dank dungeon.

Zachary didn't react. In fact, I wasn't sure he was even breathing. His skin had gone nearly ashen. My heart drummed in my chest as they dragged a cot in for me and set it on the opposite wall. I expected chains as well, but when they pushed me down onto the thin bed and stepped away, my mouth dropped open. At least they hadn't put us in separate cells. That would have been the last straw for me. I would never forgive my father if Zachary died.

"Please, can we have some food and water?" I asked before the iron door could be slammed closed.

The guard hesitated and then gave me a nod. He disappeared, and the door clanged with such finality that I shivered. I stared at our dismal surroundings and rubbed my arms. I stood and stepped toward Zachary, but the echo of footsteps getting closer diverted my attention.

A small door at the floor opened and a metal tray with bread and a tin cup of water sat on it.

"Thank you." I retrieved the food. I headed toward Zachary, and halfway across the room, I hit an invisible barrier. The water cup fell off the tray. Fortunately, I caught the bread between the tray and my body. Unfortunately, the bread was now partly soaked with blood.

I couldn't get to Zachary to feed him or give him a drink. I tilted my head back and let out a scream that echoed throughout the dungeon. Shrill and full of anger, I threw the tray across the room. It banged the wall near Zachary.

Zachary jerked his eyes open and blinked at the surroundings. His gaze fell on his wrists and then his fingers barely brushed against the metal on his neck. "Fuck," he whispered in a hoarsely weak voice and straightened so his weight was on his feet and not supported by the chains. He winced.

Blood still slowly dripped from his fingers. When he finished inspecting his situation, his gaze landed on me and drifted down to the bread in my hand.

"May I have some?" he asked.

I stared at the tray now on his side of the invisible barrier. "Think you can catch?"

He cocked his head, but he did nod and opened his good hand.

I stepped back enough so my tossing arm wouldn't hit the barrier and lobbed the bread. It hit the barrier and bounced back at me. Fury welled up inside me, tainting my vision with a red hue. I threw myself into the invisible wall and pounded on it, intending to break through with sheer force until exhaustion collapsed me on the floor.

The door creaked open. King Henrick stood just outside the entrance with his arms crossed and a scowl framing his lips.

"What have you done to my daughter?" he demanded of Zachary.

Zachary stood tall and flipped his hair back. "I have not *done* a thing to your daughter."

My father's fists clenched.

"Why did you lock us in here like this? He needs food and sleep." I waved toward Zachary.

"He wants you to watch me die," Zachary answered before my father could. His voice sounded much stronger than it had when he woke from his stupor, but his face was still deathly pale and dark circles had formed under his eyes. Blood still dripped from his wrist.

I gasped and snapped my head in my father's direction.

"He came to kill you," my father replied, to my incredulous glare.

"I know. But he didn't know *I* was *your* daughter until tonight. Besides, if he wanted me to die, he would have let me bleed out in your chambers. He didn't have to save me. He could have just as easily shifted and torched the room, too. But he didn't. What does that say about him?" My hands shot to my hips. "To me, that says he is a man of honor, even if every fiber of him wants to kill you for murdering his father." I pointed at my father. "He is a better man than you ever were."

My words seemed to defuse my father's anger.

"Why didn't you just ask my father for his blood?" Zachary blurted.

King Henrick ran his hand down his face and took a deep breath. "It wasn't enough to save them," he answered and looked at me before he crossed his arms and glanced at Zachary.

The slow meaning of his words hit me. "You... asked?"

My father pressed his lips together and nodded. "I did what I had to do."

"My father refused?" Zachary asked, with wide, unbelieving eyes.

The king shook his head. "No. He did not refuse, but it was not enough. When he stopped, I made a choice. A choice that brings us here today on the eve of my daughter's twentieth birthday. The night your mother's curse is set to come true. And here you are, with enough weapons to take down the entire royal family."

Zachary leaned back against the wall and tilted his head. "I will not harm Rory." He met my gaze.

"Her name is Princess Aurora. And I would be a fool to believe you." He glanced at me. "You should heed my warning. Until the sun shines through that window, neither of you are leaving this cell. And if he dies in the meantime, that is not my concern."

"I will never forgive you if he dies," I yelled.

My father scoffed at me and turned back to Zachary. "That is a very special collar. If you attempt to shift, it will break the inner seal and rows of deadly belladonna-coated blades set in the outer collar will pierce your neck. If the blades don't kill you, the poison will."

The cell door slammed, and my heart dropped into despair.

SPINDLE Chapter 9

*H*OW MANY HOURS UNTIL *sunrise?*

My chains rattled as I shivered from more than just blood loss. It was damn cold in this cell. At least the cold seemed to slow my bleeding. Even so, I couldn't do a damn thing in human form. And the deadly collar around my neck kept me from shifting and fixing this entire situation. With no food, and no way to rest chained this way, I didn't have much of a chance of making it through the night.

My brain kept circling around what Rory's father had said. *Them.* He had said my father tried to save them, but it wasn't enough. I glanced at Rory, and a lump formed in my throat at the dichotomy of emotions assaulting my already weak form. Hate for her father for taking away mine, and gratitude at what he had done because my father's death had made Rory possible.

I glanced up at the window, wishing for a miracle.

At least we weren't totally drenched in darkness. Moonlight lit up the cell enough for me to see Rory's frantic agony, and it surpassed my own.

She clawed at the invisible wall until red streaks marred the air from her bloodied fingers. Seeing her near hysteria hurt more than the cramps in my muscles. She collapsed, sobbing, and all I wanted to do was break these chains and hold her until she stopped crying.

"It's okay," I said, even though I knew it wasn't. I would never feel her body against mine or the flutter of her heart as I kissed her. Just thinking about her lips made my cock twitch.

She looked up at me and her eyes held a devastation I didn't know how to fix. She shook her head slowly as tears glistened in the moonlight. "Seeing you suffer will never be okay." Her soft voice cracked.

"I should have..." I closed my eyes and all the opportunities that I had to make her mine passed before my eyes. "I should have just taken you this morning. Damn the consequences." I leaned my head back as far as my collar would allow. I inhaled her scent, letting it wrap around me like a soft caress.

She sniffled. "I wish you had, too."

I opened my eyes and looked at her. Regret was a beast more savage than my dragon side. This was not the last emotion I wanted to experience and yet it layered over every breath, every thought. "At least I got to dance with you." I tried on a smile just for her.

It must have been more natural than I thought because her lips curved into her soft, secret smile, and damned if that expression didn't move something deep within me. I was serious in the closet when I suggested we marry, but it had nothing to do with uniting the kingdoms. It was a purely selfish want. But the odds of that happening now were not in my favor.

Somewhere, church bells started their midnight toll. She glanced out the window, and I followed her gaze, allowing a smidgen of hope to find its way into my soul. It was crushed the moment I looked back at Rory.

Her smile slowly disappeared as her eyes glazed over like someone under a spell. I should know. I had dabbled from time to time in control spells. And she certainly represented the slackening faces of my victims. My heart dropped to the floor.

"Rory?" I asked.

She showed no signs of hearing me. She stood like a marionette and took a stunted step forward. There was nowhere to go, but that did not stop my pulse from racing, creating hot pain in my wrist as the cut reopened from the newly created force of blood.

"Aurora!" I yelled, struggling against the restraints.

No response. She took another step toward the door and, like the magic that had gripped her, the door swung open on its own accord. It had to be that damn curse of my mother's.

"Rory! No!" I bellowed and watched helplessly as she walked out the door.

I yanked the chains holding me in place and let out a cry that I was certain would alert the guards. But no one came. I realized the wall that kept Rory from me also muted my calls for help.

Still, I ranted until my voice failed and I slumped against the wall. "God damn it, Mother. Why?" I knew her reasoning. She had explained the glory of her revenge daily, poisoning my mind against humans since the day my father died.

"Fuck," I muttered, and considered shifting. I didn't have much to live for if Rory died. But if I took that route, there would be zero chance of saving Rory from my mother's grim curse. I banged my head against the wall, inhaling the last of Rory's lingering scent.

The air changed, like the days of the black death, when the wind shifted to bring the stench of rot to the other side of the wall. I had gagged on it then and I gagged on it now, coughing and spitting, so it didn't take me along for the death ride.

But this was worse. It wasn't just a random disease taking life. This was far more evil. It meant Rory was now in the grasp of my mother's curse.

SPINDLE Chapter 10

"WHAT HAVE YOU DONE?" the king's voice bellowed, pulling me from my own near-death stupor.

I rolled my head toward him. "If you hadn't chained me to the wall, I could have stopped her." Even my voice sounded defeated.

He marched across the floor and rattled keys on a round holder, looking for a specific one to unlock the clasps at my wrists. He didn't release the collar. Instead, he unclipped the end of the chain from the wall and dragged me from the room. My muscles seized and I dropped to my knees. But the king didn't show an ounce of sympathy. He just kept dragging me across the floor until I found my footing and stumbled after him like an obedient dog.

When he pulled me into the ballroom, I stopped short at the sight of so many bodies. They looked as if they had dropped in place and they smelled like death. The entire palace seemed to be in the throes of the curse. The king yanked me forward and pointed at his wife.

"Fix this!" he demanded.

I blinked at him, and my eyebrows rose. I had as much power over this as he did.

I scanned the bodies, looking for Rory. I needed to find her. I needed to know whether she was alive or whether my mother had indeed killed her. "Where is Rory?" I turned back to the king.

He pulled out his sword and pointed it at me. "Fix this," he roared.

His eyes were wild enough for me to understand there was no reasoning with him. I opened my mouth to speak, but nothing came out. All I could do was shake my head. "How?" I finally asked.

His entire face turned red. And he lifted his sword, intending to use it. I tried to yank away, but he held the chain fast.

A dragon crashed through the palace doors, sending glass and cinderblocks flying over the unconscious, nearly dead patrons. Her timing was impeccable: the king had his sword at the ready and paused at the sight of my mother in all her fiery glory, flying across the expanse.

But what caused my eyes to widen was the limp body in her talon. I would know that shade of blonde anywhere. The dragon cackled as she tossed the body our way. I lunged to catch her, but the chain holding me in place stopped my progression. Rory's body crashed down on the platform in front of us with enough force to break bones. I turned and yanked the chain right out of the king's hands and fell to my knees by Rory's side.

My mother's talons had done just as much damage as the crashing fall. My hands hovered over her because I was too afraid to touch her and do more harm. At least she was mercifully oblivious of her fragile state, but that didn't stop the sting of my own tears. I did not have enough blood to fix this. At least not while I was in human form. And even in dragon form, I did not know if it would do any good. But I had to try, consequences be damned. Maybe my blood could reverse the damage my mother's curse had done. I would have one shot because as soon as the belladonna tainted my blood, it was no longer a viable option.

"Oh, Rory," I whispered and leaned over, pressing my lips to hers one last time. My tears dripped on her face, baptizing her with what little emotion I had left. Then I glared up at my mother. "I loved her, and your damn curse killed her!" I growled and climbed to my feet, blocking my mother from Rory's body.

My mother stared beyond me, and her face morphed into fury.

A moan yanked my attention behind me. Rory's eyes fluttered open. I could not believe what I was seeing, nor did I understand it. *If my mother cursed her to die, how the hell was she breathing?* She gasped and wheezed, and her contorted and pain-filled face told me with her current condition, she wouldn't be breathing for long.

Others stirred as well, including the queen.

The king glanced around and then back at me. "You? You're true love's kiss?" he growled in disgust.

I didn't have time to answer. My mother's roar demanded all our attention.

"Nooo!" My mother reared back. Her chest glowed with the building blaze.

It made my choice easy. She was going to blast us with her fire. None of us would survive that. I closed my eyes and forced the shift. At the same time, I raked my talons over the inside of my arm, spilling more blood than I intended, right onto Rory. She screamed in response.

I expected excruciating pain. I expected daggers to bore into my flesh. But it never came. I blinked my eyes open and glanced down. The metal collar lay at my feet. The clasp on the back of the collar had been sheared clean. I never heard the metal hit the wood. Not with Rory's cries of agony filling my ears.

I glanced over my shoulder just in time to see the raven-haired fae set up another arrow. She gave me a nod and aimed toward my mother. I spread my wings, blocking the royal family and the fae alike from my mother's wrath.

My arm still dripped blood and spreading my wings wide made me grind my teeth together. I was not healing. Even my mother noticed, and her gaze softened for a moment. But then she looked beyond me again and that insane anger that had darkened her soul returned.

I stood fast. I would protect Rory from my mother's wrath, even if it meant my end.

"Move, boy," she snarled, as smoke curled from her nose.

"No." There was no use in trying to explain to her that her killing Rory was worse than what the king did. The king's actions were born of love and desperation. Hers were born of bitterness and hatred.

"He needs to know what true loss is!" she screeched so loud that people just coming out of their stupors covered their ears.

"Someday he will. But today is not that day. He did not kill Father out of anger or hatred. He made a shitty choice out of desperation. But his reasoning was more noble than yours. You want to kill for spite. He was just trying to save the woman he loved. I don't condone it, but I understand it."

"He has poisoned your mind."

"You are the one who poisoned my mind. My entire childhood was filled with lies," I bellowed at her. She had always told me humans weren't to be trusted. They should be killed on sight. Luckily, very few slipped through the walls built around our land. But I had blood on my hands, too.

"Move or you will perish with them!"

I clenched my jaw. "So be it." I refused to budge. "But know this. When you finally calm down and look around at the needless destruction you caused, it will not relieve you of your hatred. It will not bring Father back. And you will have destroyed the last piece of him you have left." I swallowed hard and steeled myself for her fire.

Rory fell silent behind me, but I couldn't look to see whether the sudden hush was from the healing or whether my blood was not enough and she had perished. I could feel the weight of that on my already taxed heart.

"Please don't hurt him." Her small voice welled up from behind me as she slithered between my wing and my torso. Tears of relief blinded me. My blood had done enough to help her walk, but she still looked as though she had kissed death. She stood in front of me with her arms spread wide as if she could withstand the dragon flames if my mother let loose.

"Rory, get back," I said softly.

She looked up over her shoulder at me with tired eyes and shook her head.

I wrapped my wing around her carefully, trying not to wince from the blood still flowing from my torn flesh. The movement created a spiral of agony through my entire limb and I winced, losing connection with my dragon form. The shift back to human form was immediate, and I sagged under the weight of it, dragging Rory to her knees along with me. The slam into the floor ripped a groan from my chest. I pulled Rory closer so I wouldn't fully collapse on the ground.

My mother stared at us, blinking with her dragon maw hanging open. I don't think she understood the direness of my situation until that moment, and it shocked her motherly instincts back into her. At least for the moment. With her, I never really knew whether it would hold or whether she would turn back into that bitter widow again.

"Zachary?" she asked with a healthy dose of concern. She took a tentative step toward us, careful not to step on any of the humans scrambling out of her way.

I put my hand out to stop her and blood still dripped from my wrist. "She is my heart. Please don't..."

"You're... you're hurt," she gasped.

I bit my tongue on my initial reaction and just nodded. I didn't think she would appreciate sarcasm right now.

"What did they do to you?" Her voice hardened.

"Nothing. It was my choice. Rory jumped in front of a sword meant for me. I couldn't let her die." I glared up at my mother. "But because of your damn curse, we were locked up in a cell where I couldn't get the food or rest I needed to heal." I shook the creeping cobwebs from my head. "This is all because of your damn hatred." The world spun around me, but I grimly held fast.

She crept closer until she was within swatting distance. All around us, swords had been unsheathed and were directed at her. Archers had arrows ready to sail, but the king had his hand up, holding them all from attacking. I didn't think he would attack. Not while Rory was still in my grasp. But my mother had been willing to kill her own son just moments before, so maybe King Henrick would sacrifice his only daughter, too.

My mother raked her sharp teeth over the palm of her talon and hurled a giant blood ball at us.

"Hold!" the king bellowed.

Her aim was impeccable. Her blood hit us with enough force to knock us on our back. It covered us from head to toe, seeping into my mouth and my wounds while stealing my breath from my chest. Rory whined against me. I clenched my fists and clamped my eyes closed as my mother's blood healed me from the outside in, seizing every muscle.

"Damn it, I said hold!" the king yelled above my own panting breaths. The ground quaked with footsteps, but I could not open my eyes.

The wounds in my arm and my wrist stitched up in a symphony of raw agony.

When the pain faded, my heartbeat returned to my normal healthy rate and my muscles relaxed enough for me to draw a big breath. Now I knew exactly how Rory felt when I first doused her acid-burned feet with my blood. I glanced at Rory and was rewarded with a light coat of sweat on her forehead and rosy, healthy cheeks. Even her eyes looked bright, and her lips formed a small smile that shot straight to my soul.

I glanced back toward my mother, expecting to see her concerned look as we finished the painful healing process. Instead, her dragon form lay prone across the ballroom floor with at least a dozen arrows sticking out of her chest. Blood oozed from her mouth and her eyes had already taken on the glossiness of the dead.

I sat up and a wave of dizziness almost dragged me back down. Rory sat up next to me and gasped.

"Oh, Zachary." She placed her hand on my arm.

The warmth of it did nothing to quell the building anguish. Blame formed in my mind, but I squashed it. Rory certainly wasn't to blame for my mother's actions.

My gaze landed on the king as he rushed toward the fallen dragon. Fury encompassed me and I clenched my fists. *If he hadn't killed my father...*

I glanced at Rory.

If he hadn't killed my father, this beautiful woman who stole my heart would not be.

Besides, her father had been shouting "Hold" while we were in the throes of healing. I could not target this unmanageable fury at him. I hung my head and captured the emotions swirling inside me, locking them away so they didn't get loose, and created the kind of devastation I was trying to dissuade my mother from doing. I did not want to end up with a dozen arrows in my heart. Nor did I want to hurt the innocent, which was everyone in this room—save two. King Henrick, who moved toward my mother's dead form, and the queen of dragons, who lay dead on the ballroom floor, were the only tainted souls here.

Rory's hand stroked my back, and her head nestled against my shoulder. I pulled her tighter against me in a quick hug, and then released her and climbed to my feet.

I crossed the room on legs that felt as if they were encased in rocks. The crowd parted, wary of me, but still they bowed in a sign of respect. Whispers of "Dragon King" reached my ears, and I nearly scoffed, but they were right. Now that my mother lay slain on the floor, that left me in charge of the Dragon Realm.

King Henrick stepped aside, giving a solemn nod. I stopped by his side and traded a glance with him.

"I'm sorry about your mother." He even sounded sincere.

"I'm sorry, too." I glanced over my shoulder at Rory. "My mother never should have taken out her anger on a child." I met his gaze and then focused on my mother. Her scales had started the dulling process, bright colors bleeding into monochrome. I laid my hand on her cheek and leaned in close.

"I wish I could remember you before my father died." My voice cracked, and I cleared my throat, reining in the crumbling walls around my emotions. "I know you wanted me to toe the line. To keep your vendetta alive. But I can't. I'm going to unite our kingdoms and hopefully bring peace to the region."

A noise near me pulled my attention away from my mother. A few men with buckets in one hand and swords in the other approached. I stared at them and furrowed my brow.

"Not now," King Henrick whispered.

I turned fully to face the king. Rory approached as well, with the same quizzical look I was sure I sported. The crowd closed in around us.

King Henrick splayed his fingers and motioned his hands in a *calm down* motion. I glanced at the buckets again and it all snapped into place. "Are you planning on harvesting her blood?"

King Henrick opened his mouth to speak and then seemed to think better of it. Instead, he just shrugged. "Dragon blood heals the sick."

"Absolutely not." Rory beat me to the punch and took a position next to me. "There will be no harvesting of dragon blood. Period." She looked right at her father. "Ever. Do you understand?"

"But she's already dead." One of the men with the buckets waved his sword towards the dragon.

"This is the queen of the Dragon Realm. Show a little respect," I snarled.

"Fine." King Henrick waved the poachers away. "What do you propose we do with her?" he asked after the men disappeared into the crowd.

"I will bring her home to our people, and we will hold a proper funeral." I glanced down at my bloody clothing. "But if I go like this, it will start a war."

SPINDLE Chapter 11

I STEPPED CLOSER TO Zachary. He looked so lost and yet so in charge, and the combination of vulnerability and strength pulled at my heartstrings.

I glanced down at my clothing and winced. I looked just as bloodied as Zachary. "We both need to clean up and we need a change of clothes." I met my father's gaze, and he nodded, snapping his fingers in the air.

Like magic, a man and girl skittered to his side.

"Take him to the guest quarters and find him something suitable to wear," King Henrick addressed the man and then waved at the girl. "This is Anna, your lady-in-waiting, and she will take you to your quarters."

Anna bowed. "My lady." She waved toward the hallway beyond the throne.

"One moment." I put up my finger while Marabel, Felicity, and Autumn came to me, doling out hugs. When Autumn wrapped her arms around me, I whispered in her ear, "Please make sure the dragon queen is not touched while we clean up. Okay?"

"No one shall touch a scale. You have my word," she said.

I peeled out of her arms and stepped to follow Anna and the man my father had charged with making sure Zachary was taken care of. The two of them walked side by side, chatting as if they knew each other. Zachary kept in step with me.

We passed by the closet we had been in earlier and the memory ignited a heat inside me that rose to my cheeks. I glanced sideways at Zachary, and his lips formed a sad smile when our eyes met.

At the end of the hallway, his man turned left, and Anna turned right. All the heat in my face faded, and a chill gripped me as I took a few steps in Anna's direction. I did not want to be away from Zachary. My heart jump-started in my chest and I stopped to turn back toward him.

He had stopped as well and turned in my direction. Neither of our guides seemed to notice we had stopped.

"I don't want to be separated from you," he said.

I nearly melted into the floor on the spot. His vulnerable admission matched my exact sentiments. I reached my hand out and nodded my head in the direction Anna went. He didn't hesitate. He crossed the distance and took my hand. Warmth radiated from the spot our skin made contact. His eyes still held a haunted sadness that made me want to wrap my arms around him and hug him until that look went away.

When we reached my room, I nearly stalled in the doorway. It was bigger than the entire cottage in the enchanted forest.

Anna gasped at the sight of Zachary standing with me. "He's not supposed to be here," she said, wide-eyed.

"I won't tell if you won't." I pulled him inside, still gawking at the room. Zachary didn't seem as impressed as I was until we stepped farther inside, and the bathing pool came into view. It was larger than the acid swamp had been, and steam rolled slowly off the water like a silent invitation.

He dropped my hand and headed toward it, ripping his clothes off as he went. As each piece of clothing dropped, more of his golden skin appeared. He was as perfect as a god, and I followed, stripping my clothing off despite Anna's faltering protests.

"Can you get us some clothes?" I asked and then I stepped into the warm pool. Zachary was already submerged under the water, surrounded by a rust-colored haze. I looked down at the water as I walked, leaving the same rust-colored trail as he did. The dried blood dissolved around me, and I dunked under as well, running my fingers through my hair to clean what I could.

I surfaced, and Zachary stared at me.

"The chill that settled into my bones in the dungeon is finally gone." He splashed water on his face, still looking like an Adonis.

I glanced away from him, afraid that I wouldn't be able to control this need to feel him inside me. A pyramid of soaps on the other side of the pool caught my attention, and I used it as a distraction from the building heat. There were several scents, from flowery, to sickly, to refreshingly citrus. I chose the latter, but before I could start scrubbing the rest of the bloodstains from my skin, Zachary snatched the soap from my hand.

I glanced over my shoulder at him as he ran the soap over my back. His touch was light, and his brow knit, as if the soap could erase the horrible memories of the last twelve hours. I closed my eyes and indulged in his gentleness.

Disappointment bloomed when he handed me the soap and moved away. I scrubbed my stomach and breasts, soaped up my hair, and then rinsed off before turning to find him sitting on the steps, looking out the window. I bit my lip at the sadness radiating from him.

His wet skin glistened and his hair dripped unchecked. I crossed and took a seat next to him, reaching out to touch his forearm. He sniffled and glanced at me. His eyes glossed over and he blinked. A single tear slipped out of the corner.

"My mother is dead."

The sorrow strangling his voice shot straight to my heart, and I squeezed his arm.

He blinked again and his lips twitched into the saddest smile I had ever seen. It wasn't until his gaze ripped from mine to scan my form that interest wiped away the devastation. When he looked back into my eyes, the same heat I had been feeling resonated.

I did not resist when he pulled me to him, and his lips crushed against mine with blissful demand. The moment was broken by a small squeak behind us. We pulled away as if touching each other burned. My gaze snapped beyond his shoulder at Anna with an armful of clothing.

I cleared my throat. "Thank you, Anna. You can leave that on the bed. And if you would be so kind as to make sure we are not interrupted again, by anyone, even my father, I would be ever so grateful." I sent her a smile.

"I, um..."

I raised an eyebrow, and Anna stopped fidgeting. Her gaze kept bouncing to Zachary, and I couldn't blame her. He was beautiful to look at when he was dressed, but impossible to tear your gaze from dripping wet.

"Yes, m'lady." She averted her eyes. Blush painted her cheeks, and she dumped the clothing on the bed before scurrying out and closing the door behind her.

Zachary turned toward me and cocked his head. A smile toyed with his lips, and the blaze igniting in his eyes thrilled me. He stood, giving me a full view of his exceptionally chiseled form, and offered me his hand.

I took it, expecting to be taken right there on the pool steps, but he pulled me from the water and handed me the towel from the bench. He took the other towel and started drying off his body. I did the same, towel-drying my hair as I mulled over his reserved actions. It was as if he had a change of heart from earlier. As if all this pain and death had stripped him of being able to be attracted to me.

He wrapped the towel around his waist and turned. I hadn't bothered hiding my form from him and dropped the cloth on the ground, hand-combing the knots out of my hair. His chest rose with a great inhale as he scanned me from tip to toe and back.

"Damn," he whispered and met my gaze.

I stepped forward and licked my lips as I cupped his cheek. My other hand landed lightly on his chest. The pounding of his heart against my palm told me all I needed to know. I slid my hand into his wet hair and pulled him to my lips. This time, the kiss was magical enough to slow time. I stripped him of his towel and was rewarded with a low groan in his throat.

Zachary's hands gripped my cheeks as he deepened the kiss and he maneuvered me to the wall before he broke the kiss. His green eyes flared bright as he stared down into my face, searching my gaze for any doubt. "Are you sure?"

I smiled up at him. I had no doubts about this moment. "I want all of you."

His smile rivaled the heavens above, and his hands slid from my face, down my throat, to my breasts. His touch sent tendrils of heat tingling through my entire form. I reached for him, but he stepped out of range.

"Not yet," he said, and his lips followed his hands.

He gently sucked my nipples until they were so hard, I thought I'd scream. He sent a sly grin up at me as he trailed down my stomach, stopping to delve into my belly button. His hands slid to my hips as he dropped to his knees in front of me.

He drew his knuckles across my sensitive bud, and I gasped at the sensation. Zachary lifted my leg and hooked it over his shoulder, running his fingers from my knee to my core in a tease that left me breathless. When he leaned in and licked me, I ran a hand into his hair, keeping the other against the wall to maintain balance.

When he said he wanted to devour me, I never guessed that I would be so incredibly satisfied. He built me up to the breaking point and then dialed back until I was too crazed to reason with.

"Please, Zach. Please, dear God," I panted.

"Come for me," he whispered, and then went back to his masterful ministrations.

My entire body felt as if it were on fire. And when I finally came, it was a rush that nearly blinded me with its force. All I wanted was him inside me, and he obliged, standing and entering me in one motion as he wrapped my legs around his waist.

I didn't catch my breath at my body's reaction to Zachary. It was like stepping into heaven. We moved in frantic thrusts until his muscles tightened and he groaned, and another wave of heat filled me.

He panted in my ear, with his weight pinning me to the wall. We stayed that way until both of our breaths evened out. When he finally unwrapped his arms from around me and pulled away so I could see his face, the sadness had returned to his eyes.

I swallowed hard and tried on a smile.

He gently kissed me and let go of my legs, uncoupling and letting me slip to my feet. My legs couldn't hold my weight and his grip tightened as he turned and pressed his back against the wall, with me firmly pressed to his chest.

"Dear Lord, you are amazing. I could stay in this room with you forever," he said with his head back and his eyes still closed. By the time he regained normal breathing, that bliss that covered his face faded. He glanced down at me. "But I have to go bury my mother."

His words were like a cold slap of melancholy.

"Will you come back?" I asked, afraid of the answer. He had a kingdom to run now, and I was his enemy's daughter, despite what he had said in the closet before we both almost died.

He smiled and wiped my hair from my face, planting the softest of kisses. "Of course. I plan on marrying you." He gave me another peck and picked up the towel, wiping off the sweat from his chest before he crossed to inspect the clothing.

I used the towel I had discarded to clean up before I stepped next to him, mildly disappointed that he was covering up his god-like form. I pulled the dress over my head and smoothed it over my skin. This was a different gown than what I had been wearing. The midnight-blue satin was sleeker and hugged my form more than the ballgown from earlier.

I turned toward Zachary, and he was staring at me, with his hands paused on the buttons of his shirt.

"What?" I looked down at the dress. "Is this not to your liking?"

He laughed. "Oh, it is very much to my liking." He finished buttoning up his shirt. "As a matter of fact, I don't know how I am going to walk out the door with you looking like that." He pulled me close and delivered a kiss before he slipped on the dinner jacket that was left on the bed. He put on his boots and took one last look at me.

"Can I go with you?"

Zachary bit his lower lip, contemplating, and then shook his head. "It's too dangerous. My people will be angry when I bring my mother's body back."

Danger didn't bother me. Besides, he had stepped into this castle tonight, knowing the dangers. "And you coming here wasn't?"

He looked up at the ceiling and then back at me. "I'm not sure you are really seeing this from our side. Imagine if I had killed your mother and father, and then you brought me here. How would the people of your kingdom react?"

"I didn't kill your mother or your father."

He sighed and pinched the bridge of his nose. "Okay, what if my mother killed your parents, and you brought me, the offspring of the person who killed their king and queen, here?"

It finally sunk in with a cold certainty. I was the child of the people responsible for their kingdom's monarchs' deaths. I did not think the people of the Kingdom of Light would take that lightly if the tables were turned. They would think I was a traitor and string me up along with him. "Your kingdom already hates our kind."

He nodded.

My chest tightened. "I don't want to be separated from you," I whispered and met his shimmering eyes.

Zachary cupped my cheek and gave me the softest peck on the lips. "I don't want to be separated either, but I have a duty to my kingdom and some serious damage control to do before I can think about us. My mother instilled a vicious degree of hatred in every heart in the kingdom. I need to undo that before there is any hope of peace between our kingdoms."

I knew he was right, but that still didn't stop the tightening in my stomach or the tears misting my vision.

"You have work to do here as well."

I blinked and focused on his eyes. "What work?"

"Humans hunt dragons for our blood. That practice has to stop."

I couldn't argue with him. I couldn't see taking the life of a living, breathing animal just for healing properties, but I was a minority in my thoughts. People would still want the magical healing qualities and if it wasn't given, it would be hunted. People were awful that way. My thoughts zeroed in on a solution. "What if your people were willing to donate blood?"

His lips twitched into a smirk. "Out of the kindness of our hearts?" He raised a brow.

"There must be something we have that you need."

He cocked his head and studied my face. "There may be some bartering power there. In certain seasons, food is scarce, so that is a means of trade."

"We have plenty of farms." I smiled.

He laughed. "Honey, we eat meat, not rabbit food."

Heat filled my cheeks. I forgot for a moment that he was a dragon at heart. Still, it was something that our kingdom had an abundance of. However, with the dragons eating all their meat, what would the people of the kingdom live on? It was all giving me a headache, so I stepped close and hugged him tight.

"Come back to me."

"I will always come back to you, Rory." He kissed the top of my head and then peeled out of my grip. "Always." He turned and walked out of the room without so much as a glance back.

SPINDLE Chapter 12

I FOUGHT EVERY URGE to run after Zachary and beg him not to go, but he was right—I had to figure out how to heal my kingdom's hearts and minds before we could be happy together. Instead of heeding my heart, I turned to the window, taking deep breaths so I didn't cave in to my desires. The sky beyond my ornate window had just started its daily waking process. The black of night had already transitioned into that deep morning blue. Distant rays played on the horizon, rising toward the heavens like a celestial stretch. Soon, all the colors of dawn would paint the sky.

With a heavy sigh, I crossed to the mirror and gasped at my image. My hair was a knotted mess. Thankfully, there was a brush on the counter.

"May I get you anything?" Anna stuck her head in the door.

I pulled the last of the knots free and then glanced at her. "No, thank you."

She frowned as though I had robbed her.

I sent her a warm smile to soothe her obvious unease. "I'm sorry, but I have never had a lady-in-waiting. I don't know how this works."

The furrows in her brow smoothed out. "I am here to help with anything you may need."

This was going to take a tremendous effort to get used to. Having a servant was almost as uncomfortable as the grandness of this castle when so many impoverished people were in such proximity.

"Why don't you go enjoy what's left of the food? I will be out in a moment."

"Thank you, m'lady," she said and curtsied before she ran out of the room.

I sighed at my image and set the brush down in its place before I headed back to the ballroom. I didn't want to stay here with all that had happened. I just wanted to be at our cozy cottage, which was closer to Zachary than this cold castle.

Both Zachary and I almost died, and the undertone of doom still hung in the air.

I came around the corner just in time to glimpse Zachary flying out of the palace with the limp corpse of his mother gripped in his talons. He was magnificent in dragon form, and the farther away he flew, the more his coloring blended with the breaking dawn.

My gaze dropped to the dance floor littered with those who had been crushed by the dragon when she fell. My stomach did a slow roll at the carnage, and I swallowed the burn of bile.

Musicians had already packed up and left, along with most of the guests. All that remained were my fae family, the king's guards, and the castle staff. The latter two were attempting to clean up the mess. Neither the king nor the queen was still in the ballroom.

Felicity turned toward me, as if she sensed my presence. She nudged Autumn and Marabel before she sauntered over to me with a solemn expression. As she came closer, she tilted her head and looked me over as if something had changed. Marabel and Autumn came up behind her, wearing the same curious expression as Felicity.

I shifted under their stares, but when they stepped in for a hug, I gladly accepted the warmth of their love. If I couldn't be with Zachary right now, all I wanted was to be back in my warm bedroom in the forest. But I knew that was impossible.

Anna scurried over to my side. "Can I get you anything, m'lady?" she asked while wringing her hands. Her gaze kept going to the dead strewn over the floor.

I pulled out of the hug with the fae. "Is there anything you can do to help?" I waved at the bodies.

"We cannot bring them back to life," Marabel said with a voice so filled with sadness that my throat tightened in response.

"I know. But can you help clean up? Maybe move the bodies to wherever they can be viewed or turn them into dust that the families can save. Or better yet, crystals that could be kept in their homes?"

The three fae looked at one another and then closed their eyes. Magic swelled in the air and a small tornado captured each body, turning it to ash before it reformed in the shape of a beautiful vase of flowers. Each vase was etched with the deceased's name, and different vibrant colors captured their essence.

People gasped and then clapped through their tears as their loved ones became something lovely and bright.

I knew they were strong, but I never guessed how powerful they really were. I should have known when I woke up from the curse. The dragon queen had cursed me to die along with the entire kingdom, and the fae made it so we all just fell asleep in a deathlike state who true love's kiss could undo.

I blinked, and my gaze shot out to the horizon where Zachary went. I knew there was something between us, but it never dawned on me he was the one that the fae had prophesied. I glanced at them. "Did you create the bond between Zachary and me with your magic?"

Their mouths popped open, and their eyes widened. "The dragon prince?" they asked in unison.

I nodded. "Yes. The dragon prince. Was that your doing?" I pointed at them.

They adamantly shook their heads. "No. We just wished for true love's kiss to banish the curse."

I believed them and headed for the throne pedestal. I took a seat on the stairs as the entirety of all that had happened last night pummeled my muscles. The castle staff still rushed around to clean up the rest of the mess, but at least they weren't transporting corpses off the dance floor.

Marabel, Autumn, and Felicity sat next to me on the stairs and we silently watched until most of the activity dwindled to just a few people tidying up the last of the remnants of the ball. The sun was high enough in the sky to highlight the gold and silver accents in the ballroom.

I looked up and the mural on the ceiling captured all of my exhausted attention. I laid back on the steps to get a better view and nearly laughed out loud. It was almost comical to see a mural with humans and dragons living side by side on the ceiling of the castle of the Kingdom of Light. I wondered how many times my father looked up at that ancient mural and cringed. After all, he had been the one to cause the last twenty years of hostilities.

"The dragon prince?" Autumn asked after the last of the staff had left the room, pulling me out of my thoughts.

I shrugged and my cheeks heated as I sat back up. "Yeah." I couldn't meet their inquiring gazes.

"There have been rumors that he is a cruel, cruel prince." Autumn crossed her arms.

I scoffed at her. Of course, the rumors would paint the royal dragon family as horrible, but with the wall, there really wasn't any viable source of information beyond speculation. "Does anyone have proof of that?" I glanced at each of them. They all slowly shook their heads but opened their mouths to speak. I put my hand up to stop whatever further arguments they were about to launch. "He saved my life. End of story."

I let out a heavy sigh and stared at the giant hole the dragon queen had carved in the castle wall.

"Do you think..." I waved to the destruction.

"We need some rest before we do another large spell," Felicity said.

I gave them a tired smile. "Well, if that's the last casualty of the night, we should count our blessings."

SPINDLE Chapter 13

MY HOPEFUL THOUGHTS WENT straight to hell a few minutes later, when a rider on horseback barreled into the castle through the wall. He drew the horse to a stop a few feet away from us. Both he and his steed had wild eyes, as if they had seen the start of a bloody war.

"The barrier is gone, and dragons are burning the fields!" he whispered with a ragged voice and then fell off the horse, landing at my feet. His entire back was singed and bloodied. I glanced at the horse and what I had thought were streaks of mud was actually the young rider's blood. He had ridden all this way to warn us of the chaos at the far side of the kingdom.

I moved to his side, but there was nothing I could do. His injuries, along with the hard ride, had taken everything from him. A lump formed in my throat at the senseless loss, and I glared at the opening. I had to stop them before anyone else was harmed.

I didn't even turn back toward the fae. Instead, I jumped on the horse's back and slammed my heels into his side. He took off as if dragons were chasing him again and I steered him out of the castle doors.

The fae called after me, but I needed to stop any escalation in hostilities before it got to the point my father retaliated.

I drove the horse faster and held tight to the reins. My heart pounded in my chest and my mouth dried of all spit at the plumes of smoke in the distance. It took hours to reach the farmlands, and the sun had not been kind on my exposed skin, but I didn't care. I only had one thought circling in my mind: *protect the innocent souls.*

I drove the poor horse beyond normal limits and the beast complied, seeming to understand the urgency of the situation. When I rode past a huddled group of farmers toward the terror in the skies, they screamed for me to hide, but I ignored them. I passed several dozen people and every one of them oozed fear at the flying flame machines wreaking havoc all around them.

I kept going almost to the line of blackened soil and stopped. I climbed onto my feet on the horse's back and held my hands up, screaming "Stop" like I had the authority to make the dragons cease their warlike behavior.

I did not think this through at all. These were not like the creatures in the enchanted forest that would stop and listen to me and do as I said.

Talons wrapped around my waist and yanked me into the air. I struggled in the grip as the dragon brought me higher into the sky. High enough to see bodies broken in the fields below. This was their game, and I was now at their mercy.

Even knowing that my life could end just like those below, I kicked and screamed, clawing at whatever purchase I could get on the dragon's talon. I would not go quietly, and I certainly was going to draw blood, too, if I could.

The dragon tossed me into the air, laughing as he did so.

"Asshole!" I screamed at him. Another talon snatched me out of the air, jerking me to a stop. I punched at his grip around me.

"None of those fools even thought to fight us." He chuckled ruthlessly. "You are either incredibly brave or incredibly stupid."

"You are an idiot!" I snarled and reached behind me to claw at the talon with my own fingernails. The talon tightened, and I cried out at the pressure.

"She's a pistol." The dragon tossed me to another dragon as if I were nothing more than a toy.

Each impact jerked the air from my lungs. However, they were flying away from the fields and the innocents below. Somehow, I had diverted their attention enough to stop the destruction. Although the volume of land blackened—along with the number of bodies strewn in the fields—made me fear the consequences.

I got a clear view of the Dragon Realm between my jaunts of fighting and being tossed from one dragon to the next. At least their talons hadn't pierced my skin, but I was going to have some serious bruises. My entire body ached, but I still fought. Their lewd comments sent a chill of dread through me. If they got their way, I would be their chained concubine until they tired of me and ended my life. And my death was described in horrifying detail.

My breath caught in my throat as I was tossed yet again. This time, I hit stone and tumbled across a rocky floor until I hit a wall hard enough to make me see stars. Rough hands grabbed me, yanking me to my feet. Two men with the same glittering eyes as the dragons who snatched me off the horse pulled me farther into a large interior cavern filled with people who didn't even give me more than a cursory look before they continued mining rocks from the walls with scrapped and bloody fingers. Each person looked half-starved and their exposed skin sported bruises. Every single person was also branded with a dragon symbol.

The men dragged me toward a fire pit with half a dozen brands glowing red. I renewed my struggle, breaking free from the two thugs. I bolted through the entrance and skidded to a stop when four men turned toward me. Their eyes shimmered with interest.

"Spitfire," one said, and I recognized the voice. My heart dropped just before a body tackled me from behind.

"This one needs to be tamed. Chain her in here," the biggest man said. He was the one I had called an asshole.

I struggled in the man's grip, even after my right wrist disappeared under the bite of a shackle anchored into the right wall. I pulled my left arm against my chest, resisting the guard as he tried to yank it free. The others gathered close and the largest man held another shackle out for my arm. The clasp pinched as they slapped it on and stepped back, huffing just as much as I was.

I snarled and yanked, but it was futile. When the men got within kicking distance, I lashed out, connecting with one of their shins. That earned me a slap across my cheek. Heat bloomed where his hand connected, and I glared at him, blinking away the stinging tears.

"I promise you will pay for this," I said.

They laughed at me and when I kicked out again, one grabbed my leg and put a leg restraint around my ankle. I kicked my free leg and was rewarded with a grunt. I smirked until they forced that leg into a fourth shackle.

I was totally screwed, and fear finally showed itself as trembling. These were not merciful beings. Their minds had been poisoned by their queen, and some war pact seemed to have been started at her death. The barrier between our kingdoms had perished with her, and now her people were hell bent on destroying the Kingdom of Light.

I knew if I revealed I was the lost princess, my chances of survival would diminish. But I also had heard their vile banter in the skies as they carried me here. Their version of taming me into submission aligned with the complete helplessness of my current state. I had no defense against anything they wanted to do to me, and the spark of interest in their eyes made my blood run cold.

Footsteps approached from behind. One man reached a sharp claw out and tore the shoulder hem of my dress, exposing my right breast and my back. Then he grabbed my hair in his fist and pulled my head forward. I struggled against his grip, but there was nothing I could do.

He stood close enough for me to see the outline in his pants. His free hand reached out and pinched my breast. For a moment, nothing registered and then the smell of burning flesh reached my nostrils. My body reacted, arching away from the source of pain burning my shoulder, and I screamed. The man holding my hair pressed against me, and I guess he decided branding me and pinching my breast wasn't enough of a punishment for interrupting their fun in the fields. His clawed fingers dug into my skin and his breath quickened in my ear.

I pulled away from him and the burning brand bit deeper into my shoulder. I gagged on bile and swallowed between cries. The others laughed at my reaction.

Metal banged on the floor behind me. "You are our slave now," the man who scarred me whispered in my ear. His claw raked down my back, shredding the silk dress along with my skin.

I tried to pull away, but that pushed me into the bastard standing in front of me. My hair was released and the man in front of me stepped away, yanking his nails from my skin.

The man behind me sniffed the air around me, and a low growl formed in his throat.

"You smell like dragon blood."

My heart thundered at the accusation filling his voice.

"You killed our queen," he said.

"No," I whispered through the debilitating pain. But it wasn't convincing, not when every muscle in my back was singing with acute agony and the man in front of me was reaching for his pants. His expression had changed from interest to one so full of hatred that I shivered.

The man behind me grabbed a handful of hair and yanked my head back, forcing me to look into his feral face. "I'm sure the prince will want to have a word with you once he is done grieving. Until then, we will see what kind of spitfire you really are."

When he released my hair, I slammed my head back, right into his nose. The connection left me dizzy. "Perhaps you should get your prince before you sign your own death warrant," I said through gritted teeth.

A hand came from behind and gripped my neck so tight I could barely breathe. "If I had my way, I'd mount you and shift just so I could watch as I tore you apart from the inside," he growled.

Someone cleared their throat, and the men stepped back.

"The prince gets first rights," an elderly voice said from behind me. "You know this rule," he added in a chiding manner.

The two men closest to me sneered at me. One pointed. "I will get my turn with you." He turned and took flight out of the cave, along with the rest of his friends.

"Thank you," I said before the shuffle of feet got too far away.

"I wouldn't be thanking me, young lady. They may have been the more humane end, considering you reek of the queen's blood."

SPINDLE Chapter 14

I HAD NO IDEA how long I stood with my legs wide and my arms pulled almost too tightly to the sides. My shoulders ached. My back still felt as though I had been doused in hot coals despite the shivers that the icy wind blowing through the caverns created. The pool of blood below me had all but dried, even though it still felt as if hot trails worked their way down my back and legs. It was maddening, and I more than understood Zachary's pain in the dungeon.

My eyelids felt as though rocks had been tied to them. I fought to keep them open, but I was losing the battle. The jerk of my head falling forward shocked me awake again, and I blinked the sleep from my eyes. But again, the darkness beckoned.

I coughed and tried to draw a breath, or at the very least, swallow, but that was getting difficult.

Coolness met my lower lip, and I jerked away. My eyes widened at the young woman holding out a small tin cup.

"Water." Her voice was as weak as I felt.

"You will be punished for giving her water," a voice hissed from behind me.

The girl scoffed and held the cup to my lips. Cool liquid slid into my mouth, quenching the dryness. I swallowed it and drank the rest, letting it provide me with a small second wind. "Thank you," I said, meeting her gaze.

"I have never seen anyone fight the dragons before," she said with awe. "Usually they are blubbering fools who beg for mercy."

I gave her as much of a shrug as I could muster in my position. Begging wouldn't work with those men. And reasoning wouldn't work either. Dropping Zachary's name would have only done more harm to his crusade.

The woman started to go.

"How long have you been here?" I asked.

She bit her lip and glanced over my shoulder at the woman who I couldn't see. "I don't remember." She met my gaze. "Too long," she said under her breath and stepped away.

"And the prince knows about this?" I asked before she disappeared out of my range.

She pressed her lips together and nodded. "Anyone who falls into the prince's favor dies a horrific death." She scurried away, leaving me with more questions than answers.

Time stalled and the aches in my body gained traction into blinding pain that brought black spots to the edges of my vision. My knees finally gave out, but the shackles around my wrists held me fast. My head lolled forward, and my hair hung over my face.

Wind whipped through the cave. It took my muddled mind a moment to realize it wasn't wind, but the pounding of wings I heard. I wanted to raise my head, but I didn't have the energy.

The scratch of several talons filled the space, and then the sound of footsteps approached.

"This one needs breaking." A man grabbed a handful of hair, pulling my head back enough for me to see shapes before me. "If you do not want the honors, I will gladly take that role."

One figure stopped in the middle of the group of men. Someone held a torch out close enough to illuminate my face and blind me. I turned my head away from the heat.

"Let go of her." Zachary's voice was colder than the wind.

The hand holding me released my hair and my head dropped forward again. A hand cupped my cheek and raised my face. I tried to pull away, but I was too weak. I met Zachary's gaze.

"Unchain her!" His voice barreled through the room and everyone froze in place, and then people shuffled around.

Both my arms released, and I collapsed forward. Zachary caught me and lifted me off my feet. I didn't even realize my ankles had been freed until I was in Zachary's grip.

"You fools," he growled and turned away, carrying me out of the cave.

"Let the slaves go," I whispered.

Zachary looked down at me. "We will discuss that when you are better."

I found the last of my energy reserves and pushed against his chest and nearly tumbled to the ground. "Let them go. We are not at war. You should not keep humans enslaved."

He glared at me. "We will discuss this later," he said through gritted teeth.

Before I could wage another argument, he transformed and gripped me gently in his talons as he took off into the air.

"Damn it, Zach," I whispered.

The beast huffed and glanced down at me with his green eyes blazing.

Soon after his shut-up glare, I faded into the black.

⊰·❦·⊱

WETNESS BATHED MY BACK, followed by acute agony, that knocked me back into the darkness.

I woke with a gasp and sat up in a strange bed, disoriented. A hand landed on my back and I jumped.

"It's okay." Zachary's tired voice came from next to me. "You're safe."

I glanced toward his voice and reached out, cupping his cheeks. "Did you let them go?"

Silence followed, and he pulled from my grip.

"Zachary?" I reached out and only found an empty bed. The curtains across the room pulled back, framing his form in the moonlight. He glanced back at me.

"I had a difficult time pulling the dragons back into our kingdom after the thorn wall disappeared. They wanted revenge for the queen. I finally won that argument. You were another explanation that did not go over well."

He left the curtain open and crossed the room. "You were more of a fight than pulling the troops back was." He ran his hand through his hair and took a seat on the bed with his back to me. "They still don't know you are the princess, but they know you saved my life. They also know my mother saved both of us before she was killed."

"But you are imprisoning innocents," I said.

"Yes. And right now, they are safer where they are. With your disappearance, your father is bringing the fight to us." He glanced over his shoulder. "I need to know if you will stand with me."

I reached out and touched his back, running my fingers over his smooth skin. My heart squeezed. I had more of an alliance with this man than my own blood. I wished it was more of a struggle for me to choose a side, but as long as Zachary was fair and just, I would stand in his court.

"No one else dies."

Zachary met my gaze and held it for a full breath before he nodded.

"And once a peace treaty is signed, you will release those prisoners." I poked his back.

"Once we marry and peace is certain, I will release the humans." He turned my way, pulling me into his arms. When his hand brushed the back of my shoulder, I winced.

"Sorry." He kissed the top of my throbbing shoulder. "The brand didn't heal." He sighed. "I'm told it will take a while."

Fantastic. I was branded as a slave. "What will this mean to your people?" I asked, remembering the degrading way the dragons had treated me. With this brand, I might never be treated as an equal.

"You are mine."

I pulled out of his arms. "I am not something to own," I snapped and turned to get up.

He grabbed my wrist.

I yanked my arm from his grip and got out of the bed. "But I do. That says you are mine in the eyes of the public. It means you will be safe."

"You do not own me," I snarled.

He moved fast, blocking my exit before he took me in his arms. "I've coveted you since that first day I laid eyes on you. I claimed you the day I saved you from the acid pool." His eyes blazed with fire. "And I sealed that claim before I left your castle."

"I am not your slave."

He laughed and looked at the ceiling, as if asking it for some wisdom. "I never said you were, regardless of the branding on your back. When I couldn't erase it from your skin, I embellished it. You have the mark of royal blood. So yes, they will recognize you as belonging to the king."

I still wasn't convinced. Especially after what the kind slave who had given me water had said. "Is that what you did with all your slaves?"

His smile faded, and he stepped back, looking at the floor instead of me. His features held remorse. He shook his head. "Before you wandered into our kingdom, I was as brutal as my mother. I believed her lies. I believed your kingdom rejoiced in my father's death, therefore I acted brutally and without mercy."

"You... killed them for what? Sport?" He had told me he hadn't killed for sport. "Because it was fun to kill the poor human slaves?"

He bit his lip and shook his head. "It wasn't for sport. And it was far from fun. Taking a life never healed the wounds deep in my heart."

"Then why? Why would you so callously take a life?"

"I thought I was avenging my father's death by slaughtering the ones I found... attractive." He wiped his face. "I thought I was betraying my father's memory every time I had a physical reaction. So... I tore them to pieces."

I stepped back, putting distance between us. "And what about those times you saw me in the woods hunting? Why wasn't I included in your search for vengeance?"

He pressed his lips together and stared at me in silence.

"Well?" I snapped when he didn't answer.

"I was going to kill you, and then you apologized to that rabbit and sent my entire world into chaos."

I didn't know how to feel. I blinked and opened my mouth to speak, but I couldn't think of anything that resembled an appropriate response. "Those slaves were innocent."

"I know that now. Why the fuck do you think I haven't been anywhere near the mourning hall? I cannot pay my respects to a woman who made me into such a fucking monster." His voice rose as he stalked toward me.

He grabbed me and planted a violent kiss on my lips.

"You showed me the truth. You allowed me to see the goodness in humankind. You, Rory. You also showed me just how wrong I had been and how unjust I behaved." He looked around the room. "I do not deserve to be the head of a kingdom. But I have no choice, and I need you by me to keep me humble."

I stared up at him, still unsure of what to say. I did not know whether I could be with someone so callous.

"You changed me, Rory. The times I saw you hunting, I did not understand that pure souls exist, but I knew you were different, and I looked forward to getting a hint of your scent. When it didn't come for so long, I thought the same as you. I thought you were a ghost. Something I created in my mind to temper my fury." He drew his hand through his hair. "I can't lose you," he said softly. His eyes held a deep anguish for everything he had done in his past.

If he could find it in his heart to forgive my father for what he had done, and no longer saw humans as the enemy, I had to give him the benefit of the doubt despite the fact my brain could not wrap around everything he just laid on me. "I'm not property," I finally said.

"Then be my partner. Be my queen."

Before I could answer, a knock sounded on the door.

"Come," Zachary said, loud enough to be heard in the hall.

The door creaked open and I could only see the iridescent eyes of a dragon in human form in the hallway. "Sunrise is almost upon us, my lord," he said. "And the general is waiting."

SPINDLE Chapter 15

A KING'S CORONATION WAS supposed to be a celebration of passing the seat from one generation to the next, at least from all the stories Marabel told me. Yet Zachary's step onto the throne and control of the Dragon Realm was anything but. Only a few dragons stood in the throne room when we entered.

"Are you serious?" a few of the dragons standing in the shadows said in unison. They waved at me as though I were an annoying pet.

"Yes. I'm serious," Zachary snapped and looked at the general. "Can we get on with this? I have a war to stop."

The high general of the dragon force stared down at him from his perch on the throne pedestal. His ribbons and medals pinned to his uniform covered his entire right side, and the royal dragon crest covered the left. In his hand, he held the king's crown. His gaze drifted to me and then back. "This is a private affair. One that a human should not be present for." His distaste came through in the word human.

Zachary took a large inhalation. He leveled a glare at the general. "I am the last in the royal bloodline. Are you going to deny me the throne because of an unwarranted prejudice?"

Silence layered on the room, and I glanced at Zachary. He kept eye contact with the general and his calm mannerism seemed to break whatever standoff was occurring between the two.

"No," he said through clenched teeth, and then closed his eyes to gather himself. He shifted the crown to be in both hands and nodded at Zachary.

The general uttered an ancient oration in a language I did not recognize before he set the crown on Zachary's head. The moment he removed his hands, the crown ignited in a ring of flame that matched the markings of his dragon form.

My shoulder flared with pain, but I bit my lower lip, trying not to let the whimper escape. Zachary glanced down at me and then his gaze moved to my back. To the brand on my shoulder. His eyebrow cocked and then he glanced at the general and gave him a subtle nod.

The dragons in the room bent a knee to their new king. I went to do the same, but Zachary shook his head and threaded his fingers through mine.

"There will be no more attacks on the Kingdom of Light," he said.

Heads snapped up and mouths popped open for an instant, and then gazes dropped to our intertwined hands. Hardness replaced the shock on most of their faces.

"But..." the general started before he had the good sense to close his mouth.

"We went through this already when I first arrived with my mother's body. If they attack, then we have a right to defend our kingdom. However, if I *can* broker peace between the realms, then killing humans for food or any other reason beyond self-defense will become a criminal offense."

My eyebrows arched at his statement and this time, I was the one with the mouth hanging open.

"If I of all people can rise above the anger and hatred my mother sowed into me, the same hatred that brings war to our lands and threatens our people, then all those who live in our majestic kingdom should rise to the same challenge. Acting as savage beasts is beneath us. We must set an example and show our true strength. The strength of our minds. If we seek to wage war for the sake of war with the humans, we will never see an end to it. I, for one, do not wish to see that kind of destruction. I will not risk my people when there is a chance for peace standing right here before us." He glanced at me and then back at the general. "If they are unwilling to come to the table, then I will have to rethink my position."

The general sighed. "Yes, my lord." He nodded.

"Thank you. Now, on a different note. Please make sure the elders are present when I return from the border. I will marry the princess of the Kingdom of Light and putting an end to this madness."

Their gazes locked on our intertwined hands. A couple of the guards looked confused, but the others practically had steam rising from their heads. However, no one made a comment. After all, Zachary was now their king.

"Let's go stop your father before he starts a war no one wants," he said to me and transformed, with me gripped in his talon. My stomach dropped as Zachary took to the sky like a speeding arrow.

The dragon force was something to behold from my perch in the sky. Thousands of dragons soared over the land, headed toward the border, and an evident fight. Zachary flew high and then dove at a speed that terrified me. He successfully beat the pack to the border, where my father's army had assembled en masse.

My heart hammered in my chest at the sheer number of arrows pointed in our direction as Zachary landed at the front of the dragon force.

He gently set me on my feet and transformed into human form as the general landed behind him. The general spread his blue and red wings out wide, holding off the rest of the dragons. It was a spectacle to see, and the troops yielded, waiting for their orders from either the general or their king.

I turned toward my father's army, and too many weapons were aimed in Zachary's direction. All I wanted to do was jump in front of him and yell for my people to cease their hostilities.

The dragon force surrounding us could wipe out the entire human army with just one fiery breath, and that could include us if the news Zachary announced in the castle hadn't reached the front lines. I wasn't sure his people had the ability to let go of their hatred so readily.

Zachary took my hand and crossed over the dried husks of the thorn bushes that had been there a couple of days ago. I could almost feel the sting of them as they crunched under my feet. I swallowed hard at the unyielding firing line. Hundreds of arrows were aimed in our direction. The last time arrows were aimed at a dragon, she ended up dead. I did not want to see that pattern repeated today.

"Hold!" the king bellowed and came forward.

Zachary raised his hand and glanced over his shoulder. With only a hand signal, the dragons behind us relaxed and stepped back, giving us the ability to negotiate before they rained havoc on the human force.

"What are you doing with my daughter?" King Henrick growled as he came within hearing distance.

Zachary glanced at me. "Saving her life. She seemed to think she could stop the rest of the dragons in their misguided actions earlier. My apologies for their behavior. They did not have the king's blessing to launch that attack."

King Henrick blinked at Zachary and then looked at me. "Is this true?"

I kept a grip on Zachary's hand and nodded. I wished Zachary had insisted on an outfit that covered my back. I felt uncomfortable in this dress. I would rather be in my hunting pants and soft shirts that I used to wear. Having my shoulders exposed made me feel naked, but I understood it was necessary until my shoulder healed completely. At least the dress looked a bit like the one I had been wearing when I rode out of the castle before all hell broke loose.

"Thank you for keeping her safe and returning her to us." He put his hand out as if he expected me to cross and take it.

Zachary laughed. "I did not keep her safe for you. I kept her safe because before the sun sets tonight, she will be my queen. And we"—he pointed between the king and himself—"are going to sit down and figure out a reasonable peace treaty between our kingdoms. One that benefits both sides."

My father's face turned bright red and his hand went to the hilt of his sword. "Humans and dragons have never wed. I will not allow it," he snarled.

"I'm not asking, Your Highness."

Zachary's hand tightened on mine. I squeezed back to let him know I was with him and would not run away if this all went to hell. The only thing that kept my heart slamming like a galloping horse were the arrows still aimed at Zachary's chest.

"I am inviting you and your royal delegation to the peace table." Zachary layered a warning into his voice. "Or we can keep the hostilities going and wipe each other off the map."

My father's knuckles whitened on the hilt as his lips disappeared, but he did not unsheathe the sword.

"Need I remind you, my parents, the king and queen of *my* kingdom, were killed on your land? One murdered by your hand, the other an unfortunate mistake. I would be well within my rights to strike you down on the spot. But your heinous act made Rory possible." He glanced at me. "And for that, I am inclined to forgive."

His tone held a chill that made me shiver, but he was trying to put a twenty-year grudge behind him.

"Your thugs killed several innocent farmers today," King Henrick said. "That cannot be dismissed."

The dragons behind us rose to their full heights, casting shadows over us. Their aggression seemed to agitate my father's troops.

I tore my hand out of Zachary's grip and stepped between the two kings, splaying my hands to either side. "Stand down!" I shouted. "Both sides, just stand down. Go home. Hug your children and live another day. This is not worthy of more killing. Dragons are not the enemy," I said to the humans gathered, and then turned to the dragons. "And humans are not the enemy." I would not let either side flex their testosterone. "Two decades of high tensions borne of hatred cultivated by your queen does not disappear in an instant. I understand that." I spoke to the dragons. "Your kingdom has not fallen. Just as mine has not. Trust in each other needs to be rebuilt, and I believe it can with time and the right treaty in place between our kingdoms. With the right agreement in place, we can prosper at a level beyond what we have ever seen, as long as our minds are not being poisoned with hatred."

My father stared at me as if I should just shut up and be a humble daughter. But Zachary barely contained his smile. The more I spoke, the more his eyes sparkled with pride. When I finished, Zachary raised a challenging eyebrow at my father and waved the dragons away.

All but the general obeyed, retreating towards the castle. The general stayed with his king, but gave us enough room to negotiate. Even with his showing of true leadership, my father kept that level glare at Zachary.

"Come home, girl," he said to me in a stony voice.

"I am home." I stepped back by Zachary's side. "And if you decide to retaliate instead of taking the peace offering, there will be nothing anyone can do to stop the dragons from annihilating your kingdom."

"Send the fae to settle your mind on what you fear most. They have the power to see the truth. Besides, I am sure Rory would like time with them here. And then, when your fears have been eased, bring your delegation to our castle." He glanced over his shoulder at his general. "If King Henrick sends a delegation, see that they arrive safely."

"Yes, Your Highness," the general said.

Zachary looked back at King Henrick. "I assume you know the way?" His voice lilted up at the end of the sentence as if it were a question.

My father pressed his lips together and glanced at both of us before he gave Zachary a curt nod.

Zachary took my hand and backed up onto dragon property, transforming gracefully. He reached for me with his talon.

I swatted it away and gasps sounded from the Army of Light, as if I had committed an atrocity that was sure to have me turned into cinder in a snap. It made me suppress a smile. "No. I don't want to be carted around in a talon. If you insist on flying, I get to ride."

"As you wish." He bent down so I could climb up his wing.

I crawled up his scaly wings and settled on the back of his neck and tightened my thighs, gripping his horns to steady myself.

When I looked forward, the entire force of guards had their mouths dropped open at the spectacle. Even my father looked shocked. I smiled and waved before getting my grip set.

"I'm good," I said to Zachary. When he launched into the air, I gripped tighter with both my legs and my hands. The wind whipped through my hair and I got one last look at the armies below, all staring up in awe. Zachary arched around and headed toward the castle in the distance.

Flying on his back was much more freeing than being clasped in a talon. The air surged around me as his wings lazily beat in the air. The Dragon Realm was stunning from this height, colorful and lush. It extended as far as the eye could see, or at least until the endless blue took over. I couldn't tell whether it was a body of water or the sky.

"What's that in the distance?" I asked.

"That, my dear, is the ocean," he said. "I will take you there once we get this peace treaty in place." He dove toward the castle, bringing his wings close to his body like he had done before.

Adrenaline made my skin tingle and my breath caught in the rushing air. Tears blew from the corners of my eyes, and I laughed like I did when I was a child running through the woods at top speed. This was far more exciting.

Zachary evened out and drifted on the wind until he landed softly on the ground outside the castle entrance. He bowed so I could slide off and then shifted back into human form with a smile so enchanting that my knees weakened underneath me.

He clasped my hand in his and headed inside the castle into the room that he had been coronated in earlier. Gold glistened in the sunlight, giving the room a soft hue that didn't erase the severity of the onlookers standing on the throne pedestal. A half dozen elders stood waiting for the king, along with a few of the men who had been here earlier.

As we got closer, the oldest one, with white hair and even whiter eyes, stepped forward.

"You are dishonoring your mother and father," he said with a shaky voice of the ancient.

"No. I am not. Do you know the reason my father was killed?"

"It was cold-blooded murder." Another stepped forward, not as old as the first.

"That is exactly what my mother told you, wasn't it?" Zachary asked, but his tone wasn't argumentative, like it had been with my father on the battlefield.

"Yes."

He pressed his lips together and looked down at the ground. "Were humans our enemy before my father died?" He looked up.

They all traded glances.

"Well... no," the eldest said.

"Then why must they be our enemy now?"

"Because they killed your father and mother," he said.

"My father's death was not premeditated. It was not murder in cold blood, as my mother said. Those were the words of a wife in mourning. My father was killed in a moment of desperation because King Henrick needed more blood than my father could give and survive. He killed my father to save his own wife and child." He glanced at me. "And it tore my heart apart when I found out Rory was the benefactor of my father's sacrifice." He scanned each face. "If my father had not given his life, my soulmate would have never been born. So, you see, I can forgive my father's death because of this wonderful gift."

"They killed your mother."

Zachary shook his head. "She was angry that the king's daughter survived the curse. She was angry that I chose Rory over her hatred. She was angry that I forgave my father's death." He wiped his face. "Her death was a mistake brought on by her own actions. One minute she was threatening to kill us all, and the next she healed us." He pointed between us. "She lunged forward, and the king's guards reacted, despite the king telling them to hold."

They stared at the two of us. "Why were you wounded?"

"Rory saved my life by jumping in front of her father's sword. So, I saved her life with dragon blood. You know as well as I do that using our blood while in human form has its limitations."

They exchanged glances again, all nodding at Zachary's statement.

"Rory's father put us in a dungeon. He still thought I had nefarious plans for her, and, well, I didn't fare all that well for half a night in chains. And the curse still befell her and the entire kingdom. And again, I attempted to save her."

"If she fell into your mother's curse, how is she standing here? How is the Kingdom of Light not devastated?" The elder waved a leathery hand in my direction.

He opened his mouth to speak but slowly closed it, and I realized the Dragon Realm did not know about the gift the fae gave me after the dragon queen fled my parents' castle.

"My fae guardians bestowed a last gift after your mother uttered her curse and fled. They made it possible for the darkness to be lifted by true love's kiss." I glanced at Zachary.

His eyebrows rose. He hadn't known about the fae's gift.

"Did you kiss me after the curse took hold?" I asked softly.

His eyes seemed to look through me, as if inspecting his own memories. When he focused again, he nodded. "I did. I thought you were dead. It was my way of saying goodbye." He let a little laugh escape. "Your father mumbled something about that, but I didn't pay any attention to him. I was too concerned with my mother's reaction to everyone waking up."

"Your kiss saved all of us," I whispered and squeezed his hand.

He glanced down at our clasped hands and then focused back on the elders. "I may have broken the curse, but we were far from okay. If my mother hadn't shot a blood bomb at us, we wouldn't be here," he finished and met their solemn gazes.

"You have proved that humans are still a menace." The elder crossed his arms.

"Azdok, you must let go of that notion. They are not a menace," Zachary said in exasperation. "I wish to marry Rory, with or without your blessing," he added.

"You will be stripped of your royal status if you do so."

"That is not how this works." Zachary's voice grew cold as his eyes flashed with flame. "I am the son of King James and Queen Magna. The rightful heir to the throne. I have the same magical element surging through my blood that my mother had. The same power that made you quake in your shoes any time she lost her temper. While I have only used it to breach the thicket wall in the past, do not underestimate *my* power."

The wind in the room picked up and lightning stretched across the ceiling, crackling dangerously. I had never seen anything like it. Nor had I ever experienced the raw power radiating from Zachary. The crown on his head flashed into blue flame.

The elders huddled closer together, staring at the light show Zachary seemed to produce.

I put my hand on his arm and he glanced down at me, looking more like a god than a man. Still, I did not cringe away from him. He covered his hand over mine and looked back at the elders.

"Do we have an understanding?" he asked. As if to punctuate his question, a bolt of lightning crashed down in the space between us and the elders, followed by an ominous crack of thunder.

858

SPINDLE Chapter 16

THE DOORS BLASTED OPEN, and both Rory and I turned. I reined in the magic and it filled my form, threatening to overtake me before I got control of it again. I blinked at the three fae marching inside the throne room. They were the same ones who had counteracted my mother's curse. A rotund, gray-haired fae, a tall, dark fae, and an auburn-haired fae all marching as if I were the enemy. Thankfully, they weren't followed by an army. I wasn't prepared for war with Rory's father, and I prayed it would never come down to that.

I glanced at Rory, and her face lit up with a smile that warmed my soul. She broke free and ran to them, doling out hugs as if they were her dearest relatives. I guess perhaps they were, considering they raised her. And they did a hell of a job. The woman had the heart of a queen and within the hour, she would be *my* queen, despite what these old fools said.

Rory drew the fae closer, but with each step along with the whispered chatter, her smile faded. She glanced at me and then at the fae who raised her.

"He does not have me under a spell," Rory said, loud enough to be heard over the murmurings of both the fae and the elders on opposite sides of the room.

Irritation spurned a rawness in my blood. Another hurdle that almost had me throwing my arms up in defeat. I drew a deep breath and turned my back on the elders, crossing to Rory's side.

If it wasn't for the fiery-haired fae, I would have been killed by the blades in the collar when I shifted. "I owe you a debt of thanks for saving me and then protecting my mother's body while we cleaned up," I said loud enough for the elders to hear. All I needed was for them to declare these fae as the enemy. I bowed my head in respect. Their combined magic radiated from them, and I recognized the ancient power I had been too preoccupied to notice back at King Henrick's castle.

"Prince Zachary, have you put a spell on Aurora?" the dark fae said. Her eyes narrowed as if she looked straight through to my soul.

"Felicity." Rory sighed in annoyance.

The dark fae glanced at her. "I need to be sure this is not some ruse manufactured by the son of the dragon queen." She waved at me.

Rory glanced at me with wide eyes. "He didn't even know who I was," she said, defending me.

"Rory is right. I did not know she was King Henrick's daughter when I saved her from the acid lake," I said. "Her scent caught my attention years ago, and her beauty stole my heart."

The older fae put her hand over her heart, as if I had reached in and touched her with my words. But the one with the flaming hair rolled her eyes. Rory joined her, but at least she had a smirk.

"I opened the thorn wall for her to leave our land," I added, and their smiles faded. "I possess the magic to do as you suggest, but I have never used it to manipulate her mind. That is low, even for me."

The redhead crossed her arms, as did the raven-haired fae. The one with gray hair seemed to be just as enamored with me as Rory, and I shifted, turning my attention back to the skeptics.

"He was ready to forsake the crown to marry me," Rory said.

If I truly walked away from the crown, our lands would fall into anarchy. War would rain death on both our kingdoms. No, I was not willing to forsake my crown for her, as much as that pained my heart. But I was hellbent on having both the crown and Rory. There was no other way to bring peace to the region.

"I'm not willing to walk away from the crown or you," I said, making my intentions clear. "I have asked her to be my queen for more than just the practicality of a union between our kingdoms. She gives me hope and a sense of happiness that I have never felt in my entire life. If anything, she has enchanted me."

The one Rory called Felicity asked, "May I see your hand?"

I reached my hand out to her, and she took it and turned it over. She followed the lines on my palm with her finger, studying it as one would study a flower. Her brow creased, and she tilted her head, jerking her gaze up to mine. Her eyes widened, and she stepped back, exchanging an awed expression with the other two fae.

"Prince Zachary is Rory's fated mate," she gasped.

"It's actually King Zachary now," I corrected and stared at my palm, looking for exactly what Felicity had seen. Only skin with lines etched into it appeared. I dropped my hand and met her gaze. "Fated or not, I want Rory by my side, but I need to convince the elders to let go of the hate my mother poisoned them with."

The three fae exchanged glances and then said something in an unfamiliar language, sending a roll of sparkling magic toward the elders. I watched as it circled around the dragons and then all at once charged into them. Light filled their forms, and they gasped, arching their backs as black smoke bled from their skin, chased out by the light.

It was liberating to see my mother's poison squeezed out of the elders. They all blinked and looked down at their hands and arms, as if seeing themselves for the first time in ages.

"Do you think you could do that for the entire kingdom?" I asked them with a voice that held the awe I felt.

They blushed and shook their head. "We can only do that in small doses or in cases like this, where your mother's evil has such a tight grip that your wisdom can't penetrate."

The elders glanced around the room until their gaze fell on me and they all bent a knee, as if it had been me who released them from the darkness.

Little did they know, it was Rory who truly would release us all from the chains my mother put around us. I knew that with every fiber of my being.

"Azdok, will you please do me the honor of officiating my wedding?" I asked as they rose.

"Yes, Your Majesty," he said, without the nasty tone he had been using before.

Magic bloomed in the air, and I glanced at Rory. Her dress transformed into a beautiful wedding gown. One that was fit for a queen. I looked down to find my threads had changed as well. Rory was a vision in white, and I had my family's royal crest on my chest, along with the traditional marriage tunic of the Dragon Realm. I glanced at the fae with a nod and turned toward the vestibule to the side of the throne pedestal.

Azdok took his place in front of the altar. He picked up the sword from the mantel behind him and faced us.

"Swear you now, on this sacred blade, that there is no reason known to you that this union should not proceed." Azdok held out my father's sword, one hand on the ornate handle and the other holding the blade carefully.

Rory and I ran our index fingers along the edge of the blade, breaking the skin before we pressed our hands together, mingling our blood in a sacred union.

"I do so swear," we said in unison.

"Heavenly Father, creator of all things both in heaven and Earth, we humbly ask thee to bless this union. May these thy servants seek goodness all the days of their lives. May they be strong in defense of what is right, may they be united as one even as thou art with God. May they be numbered amongst thy sheep. We humbly pray in the name of the Father, and the Son, and the Holy Spirit. Amen."

Rory and I and the fae and other elders that gathered around us said, "Amen."

"Do you Zachary, King of the Dragon Realm take unto thyself, Aurora, Princess of the Kingdom of Light, as your lawful wife, and pledge unto her before God and these witnesses to be her protector, defender, and sure resort, to honor and sustain her, in sickness and in health, in fair and in foul, with all thy worldly powers, to cherish and forsaking all others, keep thee only unto her, so long as ye both shall live?"

Rory grinned up at me, and I nearly forgot there were other people in the room. When she lifted her eyebrow, I chuckled and nodded. "I will."

"Do you Aurora, Princess of the Kingdom of Light, take unto thyself King Zachary as your lawful husband and pledge unto him before God and these witnesses to honor and cherish him, to cleave unto him, in sickness and in health, in fair and in foul, be his one true and lasting counselor and solace, and forsaking all others, keep thee only unto him, so long as ye both shall live?"

"I will," Rory said, clear enough for the entire room to hear.

Azdok leaned close. "Do you have rings?"

I reached into my pocket, praying that the fae's magic had not made my parents' rings disappear. I had slid them into my pocket before we were shuttled to the coronation room for my induction to the throne. My fingers closed on them, and I smiled and nodded, handing them over to Azdok.

"Heavenly Father, bless these rings which King Zachary and Princess Aurora have set apart to be visible signs of the inward and spiritual bond which unites their hearts. As they give and receive these rings, may they testify to the world of the covenant made between them."

Azdok gave me my mother's ring, and I faced Rory.

"Rory, wear this ring as a symbol of my trust, my respect, and my love for you." I slid the ornate band on her finger, and to my surprise, it fit.

Azdok handed Rory my father's ring, and I held my left hand out for her.

"Zach, wear this ring as a symbol of my trust, my respect, and my love for you." Rory slid the ring on my finger.

"This circle will now seal the vows of this marriage and will symbolize the purity and endlessness of their love."

He glanced at both of us solemnly. "Thou hast pledged troth of thy own free will and sworn upon the Sword and exchanged rings as symbol of your binding love. May it be granted that what is done before God be not undone by man."

"Before I proclaim you joined, thou must kiss three times on cue."

I was ready for this part, and I pulled Rory against me, grinning down at her sparkling eyes.

"Once for luck."

I pecked her lips.

"Twice for love."

This time, my kiss lasted a little longer.

"Thrice for long life."

I'm not sure what I expected with the third kiss, but Rory held me tight, forcing me to twirl tongues and lose most of my mind in that single moment.

"By the power vested in me by the Dragon Realm, I now pronounce you husband and wife."

We were still kissing when Azdok announced us husband and wife, and the only reason I stopped was the whooping of the fae.

SPINDLE Chapter 17

I PICKED RORY UP, walked out of the throne room, and headed to my chambers. Although I had made love to her back in her quarters in King Henrick's castle, I wanted to seal this marriage in my bed. I wanted to see Rory's face as she peaked and called out my name. I wanted her writhing under me.

But when I closed the door and put her on her feet, I never expected her to push me against the door. She kissed me with such fervor that I forgot to breathe. Before I knew it, my shirt was being ripped from my body.

Her mouth moved from mine, down my chin to my throat. Warmth followed like a trail of lava as she moved lower. My brain stalled as her hands undid my pants and yanked them down far enough to reveal my rock-hard member standing at attention.

Her sexy smile nearly undid me, but when her mouth covered the tip of my cock, I thought I had died and gone to heaven. This couldn't be real. My wife, on her knees in her beautiful wedding dress, looking like the hottest thing on earth.

I couldn't form words as she slowly stroked me with both her hands and her mouth. I threaded my hands in her hair and guided her as I leaned against the door for support, wondering what I did to deserve this.

Heat pooled in my belly, pulling from every cell. If she continued, I wouldn't be able to stop my eruption.

"Rory," I whispered gruffly.

She glanced up at me with worry lines creasing her forehead. "Am I not doing this right?"

I laughed in the face of such innocence. "You are doing it right. I just..."

She didn't let me finish speaking. She went back to sucking my cock. All it took was a few more strokes of her mouth before I lost it and held her head in place as I pushed my length into her mouth and exploded with a groan.

And the beauty at my feet swallowed every drop. When I pulled away, she gasped for breath and stared up at me with wide eyes and drops of my cum still glistening on her lips.

I leaned against the door and kicked off my pants. I scooped her up and carried her to my bed, pushing the fabric of her dress up almost until it reached her chin. Fabric swirled around her as I dove between her legs with only one thing on my mind: making Rory scream my name. And Lord help me, I nearly came again when she did. She writhed under me, and I kept going, bringing her to the brink again and again until her thighs were thick with her own juices. I tore the dress off her as violently as she had undressed me, but she pushed me onto my back and mounted me.

Rory rode me with abandon. Her body glistened with sweat, making the entire room enhanced with her sweet scent. Every muscle contracted with the strength of my next orgasm, and I nearly bucked her off. As soon as my tremors stopped, Rory fell over on top of me with a gasp. She laid with her head on my chest, her breath heaving just as strongly as mine.

I held her tightly to me and glanced over at the floor where our shredded clothing lay.

"I'm sorry about your wedding dress."

"It's just a dress," she said softly, her voice tickling my chest hairs. She rolled and snuggled into my side.

I closed my eyes and sighed. "We need to still face your father, assuming he takes my treaty offer seriously."

She lifted her head. "I really hope he does. It would be best for the citizens, who seem to be the ones first in line to die, like those farmers."

She was right. A peace treaty for both sides would give both kingdoms the type of prosperity that had been missing for twenty years. I could see the future, and it was going to be brighter than anyone ever expected.

A knock on the door interrupted my silent reverie. I covered Rory.

"Enter!" I called.

One of the castle guards pushed the door open and his eyes widened at the path of clothing before his gaze landed on us on the bed.

"Um, King Zachary, um. There seems to be a treaty delegation at the gates."

I smiled at Rory. "Let them in and get them some food. We will be down in a few minutes."

"Yes, Your Majesty."

After the door closed, I jumped out of the bed and rustled up some clothing for me. I glanced at Rory and then at her ruined clothing. "I'll send up the fae," I said. "In the meantime, you may clean up in my pool." I waved to the small tub in the adjoining room. "It's not as grand as the one in your father's castle…"

"It is perfect." She climbed out of bed and crossed to me, stood on her tiptoes, and caught a quick kiss before crossing to the bathtub.

I had to tear my gaze away from her perfect form. She was worthy of being called a goddess, and a worthy partner in ruling this kingdom, not to mention my lover for the rest of my life.

"It's time for peace," I whispered and set out to do just that. For Rory and for me.

The End

There are three rules all genies must obey: No killing. No raising the dead. And above all else, never fall in love.

I have been granting wishes to the most deplorable of humans for thousands of years. So, when Prince Ali releases me back into the world, I'm not prepared for a selfless man who isn't an absolute bastard like all the others before him.

His stepfather is another story. The new sultan carries out his rule with an iron fist. His return to barbarian ways leaves the kingdom cowering with fright, for the new sultan finds joy in screams of fear and pain.

When Ali comes to me with an impossible wish, I must decide whether to follow the rules, or break them and be banished to my lamp forever.

JASMINE Chapter 1

I OPENED MY EYES to the same darkness that had claimed me for centuries, but something was different this time. I was moving, or more accurately, the lamp I have been stuck in, was in motion. The vibrations filled my metallic world, and I jostled on the small bed made of satin and silk.

I held my breath, waiting for the inevitable rub that would free me from this metal trap. It had been so long since I had my last encounter with a human, and for the longest time, I was happy I had been locked in my bottle. My last encounter left a bitter taste in my mouth and even now, as excitement lit every cell on fire, that doubt came rumbling back like rock crumbling down a mountainside, headed straight for a village below.

Near destruction had made me a little less enthusiastic than the last time, and the time before that.

Hell, no one wanted to let a genie go. They wanted their wishes, and that was that. Back into the bottle until the next greedy sucker came around.

A rush of air filled the lamp and then the magic ignited, and I braced myself for squeezing through the opening. The pain and then freedom that came with it sent a jolt through me, and I threw my arms open wide in the desolate cave where my lamp had been buried all those years ago. My dark tresses floated on the air, and I stretched, feeling every bit of freedom as a genie can when released from their lamp. I finally looked down at the person who released me, but he was facedown on a ledge, barely moving.

The fiery pit that traversed below the entry and wrapped around the stalagmites, eating away at the limestones, burped and bubbled as if it had been cheated of its next meal.

My gaze moved to the top of the stalagmite, where the shiny decoy had always been. But it stood barren, which meant this fool on the ledge had somehow retrieved it, and then the world came crashing down on him. Whoever this man was, the sentry did not take too kindly to whatever he had done. It would be another hundred years before the opening he came into the cavern through expanded again, and by that time, he would just be bones.

My magic carpet swirled around me, rubbing against my midriff as it said hello after so long. I gave it a squeeze. I had missed my carpet, and he obviously missed me.

Seeing my old friend gave my soul the boost I needed. It swirled around and brushed along the man's back, fluffing the back of his thick hair in the breeze it created.

Ant-like footprints on the entry path gave me pause. It looked as though there had been more than one person in the cavern. But what caught my eye were the claw marks on the edge of the ledge, like someone tried to climb from the pit, but didn't make it. My gaze shot to the man lying next to my discarded black lamp.

He groaned and moved again. His hip rubbed the lamp with his motion.

I laughed at the irony. He hadn't freed me on purpose. I drifted down and crossed my arms on the edge of the outcrop he laid on, mere inches from him.

"Psst," I whispered to get his attention.

His head turned in my direction, and his eyes fluttered open for the briefest of seconds before his eyelids fell again. But it was enough time for me to see eyes of bright emerald under those dark lids. His profile revealed a beauty that men usually don't carry. He was all high cheekbones and supple lips, with a crop of dark hair that hung over his forehead. His nose was neither too skinny nor too broad. His form was lithe but muscular, with broad shoulders that tapered to a thin waist and an ass right out of heaven's mold.

He was perfection incarnate, and I sighed heavily, rustling his hair with my breath.

His eyes slowly opened and met mine. His eyebrow cocked, and he timidly pushed himself onto his elbows.

"You are on a ledge," I said, in case he rolled to check out his surroundings.

"Are you an angel?" he asked in a groggy voice.

I let out a hearty laugh and raised myself up so I filled up the cavern above. Expanding enough to make his eyes as wide as the cave's entry used to be.

He tracked my movement with something akin to awe filling his features, making his slack-jawed stare that much more amusing.

"I am a genie, and you have freed me from my prison. Therefore, I shall grant you three wishes."

He rolled back, pressing my lamp into the dirt wall.

"Just don't ruin my home, please." I waved behind him.

"But I thought I gave the lamp to my stepfather." His forehead creased in confusion.

I put my hand on a crumbling pillar next to me and used my magic to raise it as high as the one that had once held the decoy. With a wave of my hand, another imitation lamp appeared on the pedestal. "You mean this shiny piece of crap?"

He nodded and felt behind him, finally pulling my real lamp out. It was as black as night and his rubbing of the side revealed my golden seal embedded in the onyx container. He stared at it and slowly pushed himself into a sitting position so he could glance at his predicament. The shelf he sat on was not big enough for him to maneuver much, and it was a straight drop to the fiery pit below.

As if sensing a possible meal, the earth belched a fiery bubble.

He tucked the lamp inside his loose shirt, and then carefully climbed to his feet. The shelf sent a few crumbled pieces of earth tumbling down, and the pit reached for them hungrily. He looked up at me. "What is your name?" He sounded much stronger and clearer than he had a few moments ago.

"Do you *wish* to know my name?" I teased coyly. If I could get my masters to make vain, silly wishes, I could be rid of them quicker. Although I felt trapped in my bottle, there was a sense of safety that I did not carry when I was outside of it. Plus, the company of the lamp holders was rarely ever interesting enough to want to stretch things out.

He rolled his eyes, shook his head, and turned toward the wall. He studied the face of the cavern before him. He reached for a small outcrop, and it disintegrated under the pressure of his hand, sending dirt crumbling down the wall. Defeat crossed his features and rounded his shoulders. He kicked the wall with a growl of frustration.

His sandaled foot stuck in the dirt.

He unwedged his sandal and stared at the small hole he had made. When he looked up at the wall again, his eyes shined bright with hope.

"Why don't you just wish us out of here?" I crossed my arms.

He leaned his head against the wall for a moment. "Because that would be too easy." He glanced over his shoulder at me, and his green eyes carried enough worry for me to shiver. "And because I know in my bones that my kingdom will need those wishes once my stepfather figures out the lamp I gave him is a fake."

He glanced back up toward the jagged ledge at the top with a bitter laugh. "He pushed me off that ledge intending to kill me." He kicked the wall again. But this time, he didn't step out of the hole. He put his weight on that foot, testing the hold he had on the wall. When it didn't falter, he kicked his other foot higher, creating another step. He continued his mad kick, stand, kick routine, scaling the wall.

This man was as resourceful as he was beautiful. I watched in fascination as my magic carpet parked itself parallel to the little outcrop the man started on. I realized the carpet had taken that station without my bidding.

"What's your name?" I asked as he scaled half the wall.

"Ali," he said, his voice heavy with concentration.

I bit my lip as he passed the halfway mark. "I'm Jasmine," I finally said, just as he reached for the edge.

The shelf crumbled in his grip, and he lost his balance. With a yelp, he was falling through the air. My carpet decided on its own, and flew to the rescue, catching Ali and depositing him on the upper ledge.

There was only one other man in the history of genies and magic carpets who the carpet chose to save in their time of need, and that man was true innocence incarnate. My heart jumped as I took in the wonder in Ali's eyes. He ran his hand over the carpet. It wrapped around his arm, and then unwrapped and settled on the ground next to him like a lost puppy who had found a new master.

Ali's green eyes sparkled as he glanced up at my monstrous form. "Jasmine. Are you always so...grand?" He waved at me.

I shrunk myself to human height and willed legs to form out of the smoke representing my lower half. I landed gracefully next to him on top of the rug. The carpet rolled, knocking me back a few steps. I teetered on the edge, and Ali reached out and grabbed my arm, pulling me back to safety.

The moment his hand touched my skin, my breath caught in my throat. I couldn't draw air as a foreign sensation filled my form. My skin tingled where his hand gripped me and heat flowed out from that connection, warming me like the hot summer sun.

He clucked his tongue at the magic carpet and shook his head. "It wouldn't do any good to harm Jasmine."

"He didn't mean to knock me off the ledge." I stepped to the side, breaking his grip on my arm as I avoided the carpet on the ground this time. I also avoided Ali's curious stare.

He turned toward the outcrop of wall in front of us. His eyebrows rose as he studied the little alcove. "I think this is where I entered." He turned back to the interior cave where the pillar stood tall with the new shiny decoy. Ali scratched the side of his head, scanning the cave before he focused back on the alcove.

He tested the walls with his hands, moving from one side to the other, and on the way back to the center, his hand ran over a block that sunk farther into the wall. One moment, Ali was in front of me and the next, the floor opened and swallowed him.

He yelped in surprise, but it faded.

The carpet barreled into me, taking me along with it down the chute Ali had fallen into. Darkness wrapped around me, sending my heart into frantic thumps as Ali got farther and farther away from me with my lamp tucked into his shirt.

I spilled out of the shaft, falling right onto something soft that made an *oof* as I landed. I wished for light so I could see in this blackness, and my magic bloomed, sending the soft glow in all directions.

Ali's wide green eyes stared at me, and I scrambled off him, standing up and looking around at our newest accommodations. Bones of the dead littered the floor and hung from the walls.

"Charming," I muttered.

Ali stood and glanced around as well. He visibly shivered and shook his head, as if to ward off bad thoughts. Then his gaze narrowed as he studied the cavern. The fabric on some of the more upright skeletons seemed to reach for us in periodic waves.

"There's a breeze coming from that direction." He pointed at the far wall.

"And?"

He turned to look at me. "Where there is a breeze, there has got to be a way out."

"Don't you think these poor souls would have found a way out if there was one?" I waved at the dead surrounding us.

"They didn't have the benefit of light." He sent an endearing smile my way. "Thank you for that." He gave me a gracious bow.

I hadn't done that for him. Just like within my lamp, I did not like absolute darkness and always kept that small space lit by some glow. It reminded me too much of the early days of my creation. Darkness always meant danger, and this space was no different. I gave him a nod of acknowledgment because he did not need to know of my uneasiness with the dark. "You're welcome."

Ali picked his way across the floor to the far wall, where the head of a snake poked out of a hole just as he reached for the wall. He pulled his hand back and stared at the serpent hissing at him.

It made sense to me that there was some sort of guard to keep humans inside, but those in the dark would have gotten bit. I glanced around at the bones surrounding us with a sigh. Snake bite or starvation—what an awful demise. If this man would just wish us out of here, he wouldn't need to risk life and limb.

After a few moments, Ali hummed low in his throat and swayed slowly back and forth. The serpent followed him, spreading his hood out. He moved his left arm out, drifting his hand in the same manner as his body. The snake focused on his left hand and when he had it far enough to the side, his right hand shot out faster than the cobra and pinched the back of its hood. With the beast's head stuck between his fingers and subdued from being able to do any damage, he pulled the snake from the hole by backing up slowly.

This thing was long enough to give me pause, even though I wasn't subject to its venom. There had to be other vermin in this cavern to sustain a snake like the one Ali pulled from the wall. My new master was a snake charmer as well as a kind soul. Something in the way he carefully treated the animal warmed my heart. He did not club it to death with a handy bone. Instead, he picked his way through the bones to the farthest corner away from the wall and set it down on the ground, moving away slowly as the thing coiled up into a small circle.

By the time he got back to the wall, more snake heads poked out. It was as if he had just woken a hydra. Ali glanced up, and my eyes followed his to the rectangular hole that seemed to be the source of the air flowing into the cavern. With the snakes impeding his ability to climb the wall, he returned to my side and looked down under his feet, where my magic carpet rested. He took a knee and ran his hand over the carpet under him.

"Do you think you'd like to try flying again?" he asked, coaxing my magic carpet the way he had coaxed the snake.

"Oh, I—" My protest died on my lips as my traitorous carpet rose with him on it. I hopped next to Ali before they left me in this snake-ridden death trap. "Where to?" I asked, even though I already knew. Especially considering Ali stretched out on his stomach and gripped the front edge of the carpet, as if he had any power to steer the thing.

He nodded at the vent and smiled. "Watch your head."

And then we were off like a lightning bolt. The opening was barely big enough for us to fit without scraping our skin off on the rocks above.

I pulled my magic glow along with us, giving my carpet just enough illumination not to slam my master into the walls or slice him on the jagged rocks above us. My breath caught in my throat at the experience. It was invigorating and terrifying, all rolled into one.

Ali let out a whooping laugh as we shot out through a mountainside over a vast expanse of blue ocean below us. I had never been out this way. I had always been relegated to the desert sands, so seeing the green below surrounded by the brown and white sands stretching behind us felt surreal, like perhaps this was a dream of mine and not a new reality that I was living.

JASMINE Chapter 2

"I THINK MY CARPET is almost out of magic," I said as it seemed to dip more toward the blue waters. Outside of the caverns, the magic the carpet possessed was limited, and it needed to be renewed either by the cavern, where there was an abundance of magic, or in my lamp, where some of the cavern's magic remained.

Ali steered us onto a small outcrop of ground where the ocean met the shoreline. Green fields sat beyond the small stretch of beach we stood on, and I waved my hand, pulling the carpet into the lamp so it could recharge for another ride.

"I guess we walk." Ali glanced at me after the last of the transitioning smoke filtered back into the lamp.

"You could wish us where you would like to go." I spread my arms out with a smile.

He bit his lower lip and looked beyond the lush fields at the desert beyond. Finally, he shook his head and met my gaze. "That would be a waste of a wish. I know getting back is important, especially since my stepfather can be a cruel tyrant. But at least my mother is still at the palace. She will keep him tempered." He stepped off the sand, toward the heart of the kingdom. "I hope," he whispered, low enough that I almost did not hear him.

Palace? "Are you a prince?" I could not fathom a man of such warmth growing up in the lap of luxury. Usually, the very wealthy were also the more self-centered ones who did not have a clue of the average man's plight.

"Yes. My father became sultan when I was very young. I was too young to take on the position when he died. So, my mother operated as the head of the kingdom while I was sent to private schools to learn about commerce and business until I became of age to run the kingdom."

"You are of age, yes?"

"Yes. But by the time I returned from my schooling, my mother had already promised her hand to my stepfather." He walked with his hands clasped behind his back and his brow furrowed in thought. "He took the helm from my mother the moment they married."

"Was that why you sought the magical cavern?" I asked, and his footsteps faltered.

Ali laughed. "No. I didn't believe it truly existed, but my stepfather did. He said he had been waiting to find the right person to enter without being snapped in half by the jaws of the tiger." Ali raked his hand through his thick hair. "He said I was perfect for the job, but I really think he gave me that bullshit to get me to do something insanely dangerous just so he could have a genie at his command." He glanced at me as he bit on his lower lip. "And I'm willing to bet he told my mother I died."

"The sentry is usually very strict on who he lets into the caverns. I don't understand why your stepfather was allowed inside, unless—" I stopped speaking. Only the purest of hearts could cloak another man's nefarious greed.

"Unless?" Ali pried.

"Unless your reason for entering the shaft was pure enough to overshadow your stepfather's selfishness."

"He told me he wanted to give my mother a very special present." He sighed. "He said there was a rare gift in the cavern, and if I could get it for him..." He shook his head. "I should have known better." He glanced at me. "How could I have been so naïve?"

"Those with the purest of hearts usually only see the good in others. They never see the evil that exists until it is too late. Sadly, I have been naïve on occasion, believing my master would set me free with their last wish. But alas, that was long before the bite of cynicism claimed my heart."

"Set you free?" He glanced at me with honest interest.

"Yes. I am bound to grant wishes and only allowed out of my lamp when a new master demands it." I showed him the metal encompassing my wrists. "All genies are bound to their lamps. We do not have the freedom to make our own choices or go where the wind blows." I shrugged. "I am a slave to my magic."

Ali looked toward his home and then back at me, as if weighing my words. "And if you were free?"

"I would become mortal and live out my days in peace, without being at the mercy of whoever holds the lamp."

"You do not enjoy granting wishes?" He moved forward again.

I immediately realized my mistake. I had divulged too much already and in response, my need to flee took hold and my legs became smoke as I started to convert myself so I could return to my lamp. "When you are ready to ask for your wish, rub the lamp."

"I did not mean to offend you," Ali said quickly, covering his shirt where he had stuck the lamp. "I will stop asking questions. I just would like some company as I cross the desert."

"Is that a wish?"

His shoulders fell, as did his head. "No. It is not a wish. I was just enjoying your company." He pulled the lamp out. "Do what you must," he said softly.

Half transitioned into my smoke-self, I stared at him, unsure of whether to escape to the lamp or continue on the journey with him. "You...enjoy my company?" None of the others wanted to talk with me; they just wanted their wishes and then for me to be gone. This was new, and I wasn't sure how I felt about it, but it seemed my body had a more concrete decision. My legs formed again.

"Yes." Ali stared at me and slowly tucked the lamp back into his shirt. "Thank you."

"Why?" I started walking in the direction we were headed before I had stopped.

"I find it easy to confide in you, as if we have been friends all our lives." His cheeks reddened. "It is very strange, but it also feels...natural." He laughed. "Maybe I am naïve in thinking that way."

I reached out and touched his arm. "And I may be naïve thinking that you are different than any of my past masters."

He covered my hand with his and gave it a soft pat. "I hope I am different." His cheeks slowly returned to a normal hue as he released my hand.

I was compelled to confide in him as well. "Granting wishes used to be fun, but it has long lost its allure. I am bound to grant them, no matter how ludicrous they are, unless they are forbidden, like killing someone. I cannot do that."

"Were you always a genie?" he asked.

"It's all I remember being. All this grand magic swelling inside me is only for the use of the master who holds my lamp."

"If you were free, would you still have magic?"

I slowed my steps while I gave his question due process of thought. It was something that had entered my mind when I believed my master would set me free, but that was the only time, and the idea was fleeting because it never came to fruition.

"I do not know. The magic may be tied to the lamp, as am I. If that tether breaks?" I shrugged. "I am unsure any of the magic would remain."

Ali nodded as I spoke, his gaze traveling from me to the sea of sand before us. He slid the lamp into his pants pocket and took off his shirt, fashioning it on his head to provide some relief from the blistering sun above. Even though his skin glistened with sweat, he never once complained of the desert heat.

"Enough questions about me. Tell me about you."

"What would you like to know?"

My immediate reaction was *everything*, but I closed my lips on that response and took a breath. "Tell me about your childhood."

He chuckled as he scanned the sand dunes surrounding us. "I wasn't the model prince. At least, that's what our servants used to say. I got into my fair share of trouble and tested my parents' patience more than I care to admit."

I could not see him causing trouble, and I cocked an eyebrow at him.

"My parents tried to shelter me, but I was too much of a wanderer. I used to sneak out onto the streets and visit the market in the center of Agrabah. It was a festive place where all manners of wares were bought and sold, along with any type of food you could desire. The scents of spices and fresh baked goods used to make my mouth water. And the kindness of the vendors peddling their wares was legendary. But visiting the market only entertained my senses for a little while. Then I ventured out of the city, into the wilderness surrounding us."

A smile found his lips and his eyes took on a faraway look. "One time, I found a stray dog in the wild and brought him home. I must have been seven or eight at the time. Well, it turned out to be a hyena. I didn't know any better, and I snuck him into the palace."

"Oh no," I said. Even I knew hyenas could be dangerous.

"Oh, yes." He laughed. "It ate my parents' bed."

I burst out laughing at the unexpected ending.

"They were not happy, but I couldn't just let this poor animal free to be eaten by the other predators out there." He continued to recount his adventures with the hyena in animated fashion, using his hands as he talked. And his laugh rang like a heavenly melody.

I never laughed so hard in my life. His antics were truly endearing, and it warmed my heart.

His laugh faded away. "My father passed soon after I set the hyena free." He sighed.

His sudden melancholy stroked my skin, making me swallow the lump that had formed in my throat. Before I could ask him more questions of his life, his gaze froze on a spot ahead of us. He squinted; then his eyes went wide.

I looked in the direction that had elicited the fear on his face. I cocked my head at the wall of sand rolling over the desert at us.

"You might want to take refuge in your lamp," he said as he turned in a circle, searching the dunes. When I didn't respond to him, he grabbed me and ran toward a raised mound, skidding to a stop behind it. He pushed me to the ground and climbed over me, covering both of us with as much of his shirt as he could.

All I could feel was his bare chest against my back. My body responded in ways I did not understand, but within moments, I was not thinking at all about how his skin felt against me. Wind howled around us, sounding more like a scream than the wind. I covered my ears as Ali's breath tickled the back of my neck. Sand whipped over us, scratching at the skin of my arms in an unpleasant way. Ali hovered over me, protecting me from the bulk of the sandstorm, but what hit me was enough for me to worry about how he was faring with the sand pummeling him directly.

Why didn't this man wish us out of this noisy hell?

What kind of man allows himself to be beaten in such a violent way without taking advantage of the help that is only a wish away?

JASMINE Chapter 3

WHEN THE WORLD QUIETED, Ali rose from the huddled position behind the small dune. I glanced up at him as he stepped away and shook his head, shedding sand in an arc around where he stood. He wiped at his eyes as tears formed in an attempt to clean out what sand may have found its way under his tightly closed lids.

His left cheek got the brunt of the storm and scratches traversed his skin, a couple of them drawing thin lines of blood, just like his arm that had shielded my head. His side and lower back had those same sand divots in his skin.

I stood up, shedding sand as if it were water. One shake of my hair and all the particles fell away, leaving only my hair to contend with, and I swept it over my shoulder.

"Are you okay?" Ali asked after he seemed to clear out the rest of the sand from his eyes.

"Yes, but you look like you need attention." I stepped close to inspect the cuts on his face. Trailing my fingers under them produced a spark inside me, and I quickly stepped back, suddenly wary of the turmoil touching him caused.

"I will be just fine. But thank you for your concern."

We stepped around the dune, and Ali surveyed the calmness in front of us and glanced back at the storm rolling away. When he turned back toward the direction of his kingdom, he cocked his head.

Ali shielded his eyes as he licked his parched lips. "Do you see that, or am I hallucinating?"

I followed his gaze, expecting to see another wall of sand, but instead, light glinted off something. Something traveling over the sand. "I see it."

"We have not walked long enough for that to be my kingdom." He unwrapped the shirt on his head and draped it over my shoulders. "Just in case."

"In case of what?" I tried to shrug the fabric off.

"In case it is a group of men. A woman with barely any clothes on is a target in these savage times. Covering up is the prudent thing to do."

"What will happen to you?" I wave at his half-naked chest. "You have less on than I do."

He blinked at me and then dimples appeared. "You have not been around in a long while," he said. "Mankind has gotten more...entitled to taking what they desire." He met my gaze. "And sometimes that is at the expense of an innocent."

"How do you know this?"

"I may be naïve in some things, but I have sat in court while criminals have been brought forth for some of the most heinous crimes, so I am aware of the evil in the world. Especially this far outside of the kingdom. Out here, it is lawless."

IT TOOK ANOTHER COUPLE of hours to actually make out a band of roughly a half-dozen men pulling a single covered cart in the distance. They seemed to be walking in our direction, closing the gap along with our steady steps.

I tucked my arms into the shirt Ali had put over my shoulders and buttoned it up as the band of men came closer. My senses itched for me to flee into my lamp, but that would give me away and put Ali in danger.

Two men were chained to the front of the cart, struggling with each step as they were forced on by the rest of the group, who held horse whips and were not afraid to use them on the poor souls pulling the load. Sweat poured off their backs, staining their clothing, and I could smell them at a hundred paces away. Their stench, combined with an underlying animal aroma, filled my senses, and I wanted to cover my nose.

Ali stood tall and walked as if he owned the desert, but his welcoming smile belied the caution that flashed my way in his eyes. His gaze landed on the canteens the men driving the cart pullers had over their shoulders. And then he looked at the cart. His steps faltered.

The cart held a cage, and inside was a large, white tiger with the bluest eyes I had ever seen.

Ali stopped and surveyed the scene. The tiger chuffed as its gaze locked with Ali. His head cocked as the men came closer, and then he looked back at the small group.

"Can you spare a drink?" he asked when they were within hearing distance. But no one paid him a bit of attention.

Every one of them were looking at me as if I were their next meal. Now I wished I had taken refuge in the lamp. I cleared my throat and repeated Ali's request. "Can you spare a drink of water?" I asked.

Five of the men on our side of the cart stepped away from their station and offered me their botas. I graciously accepted one and handed it to Ali.

"That isn't for you," the man who offered it to me snarled, and tried to take it from Ali.

"Oh, but it is." I grabbed his arm before he could snatch it away from my master. "I share with him."

Ali took a long drink and then handed it back to me. I followed suit; the cool liquid slid down my throat in a pleasing manner. And then I handed it back with a nod.

"Thank you for your kindness." I gave him a bow of gratitude.

"Where are you taking the tiger?" Ali asked, his attention focused solely on the animal in the cage.

"It will no longer perform for us. So, we must throw it into the Well of Souls and ask for a new beast to entertain the masses."

Ali narrowed his eyes and scanned the men. "How long has he been performing for you?"

"The wild was never tamed out of the thing," a man on the other side said in a tone that rubbed even me wrong.

I could see Ali's jaw tighten. "So, you are killing this beast just because he is not trained for your traveling circus?" he asked.

"What's it to you?" The largest of the men stepped forward, with his free hand clenched into fists and his other one shaking the whip, as if he intended to use it on Ali.

"I say we just feed him to the tiger and take her with us. She would get a nice fee on the slave market." All but the two chained to the front of the cage surrounded us. A few pulled weapons from their waistbands.

Ali put his hands up and stepped in front of me in a protective gesture that was unnecessary. "We have no quarrel with you," he said, eyeing the knives and other weapons now aimed in our direction.

I squeezed his arm, trying to make eye contact. I wanted him to wish us out of this mess. But when someone on the side of him swung and hit him in the temple, Ali swayed and went down. Thankfully, the men did not check his pockets, or my lamp would have easily been found and I would have new masters to serve.

Instead, they dragged him to the back of the cage, and half the men poked the tiger into the far corner so the others could open the cage and drop Ali inside. They secured the door and then the men turned to me. I gulped and self-preservation took over.

I turned to smoke and swirled around, creating a sandstorm to blind the men before I returned to my lamp in Ali's pocket. I could do nothing about the tiger without him wishing it so.

My heart thundered as I paced in the small space of my lamp. I wrapped my arms around my magic carpet and prayed for Ali not to be eaten by the tiger.

JASMINE Chapter 4

THE LAMP TILTED, AND me with it, and then my entire world shook. The sound of panting breaths filled my dark home. It went on forever. I wanted to see what was happening, but the jostling was so severe, all I could do was hold on to my carpet and get bounced around like a rubber ball. Finally, the jostling stopped, but I had a moment where I felt as if I were falling into the pit and then movement stopped.

Magic light danced around me, and I escaped my small prison at the rub of my master. I closed my eyes, terrified at what or who I would see. Finally, the sounds of ragged breathing made me crack an eyelid.

Ali lay prone on his back, staring at the stars above him as the tiger lay across his abdomen. His chest rose and fell as if he had been running forever. His gaze moved to me. "I'm sorry for taking so long."

I let out a near hysterical laugh. He had no idea of the relief that swept through me.

"I woke after you made your exit. They demanded to know where the sorceress went." He put his hand on the tiger's head and scratched behind his ear. The big cat let out what sounded like a purr. "Thankfully, I was in the cage with my friend here. He seemed to understand and would not let them get near me."

I stared down at the beast as my heart pumped another dose of adrenaline through me. Any normal man would have been mauled to death in that cage. My gaze fell back on Ali's tired smile. "You took in another stray?"

Ali chuckled. "I guess so. Let's just hope he doesn't eat the furniture back home."

I offered him my hand, and he took it as he pushed the tiger off him. He stood and wiped as much of the sand as he could off his body. It seemed like a difficult task, but again, Ali did not complain.

"How did you escape?"

"I waited until after dark when all the men were sleeping, and then I figured out how to pick the lock using his nail." He pointed at the tiger, who stepped close to him and rubbed along his leg as if Ali had become his very best friend in the world as opposed to a juicy meal.

"I bet that took a bit of convincing." I put my hand out so the tiger could sniff me. He bared his teeth, but I didn't pull my palm away. I was not afraid of a mortal animal, wild or not. Especially considering I had the power to turn it into a housecat with the snap of my fingers. Of course, that would not please my master, but if the tiger got aggressive with me, it would not matter.

After all, I had the right to defend myself, even without a master's wish.

"Not as much as one would think." He turned around in a circle. The dark desert stretched in every direction, and he chewed on his lower lip before he went back to searching the sky. His gaze locked on a star formation that looked like a giant ladle, and then he traced a line in the sky until he pointed.

"North is that way." He smiled and patted the tiger's head. "And home is to the north." He got a chuff in return.

We headed in the direction that Ali had pointed toward.

A new strap crossed his bare chest, and I pointed at what looked like a full bota laying against his back.

Ali shrugged. "They had them hanging from the cart, so I helped myself to one so we wouldn't collapse from dehydration before we got back to my kingdom." His hand remained on the tiger's head as if the beast needed the connection between them to keep him calm.

We walked for hours until light crested the horizon. We came to a small oasis with a watering hole surrounded by greenery. Ali took a seat on a patch of grass under a large tree and laid back. Tiger tested out the water and lapped until he was satisfied, then he took his place near Ali.

"You are more than welcome to rest with us or, if you feel safer, you can rest in your lamp. I know we should continue on to beat the heat of the day, but my body is weary, and I fear I might lose my way in my exhaustion."

"All you need to do is make a wish," I reminded him as I took a seat next to him.

He raised an eyebrow. "The wishes you grant me must mean something. They must be for the greater good and not just for my mere comfort. I do not have the luxury of thinking of only myself." He sat up and looked at the watering hole. "Since both you and Tiger are here and awake, do you mind if I take a dip to clean up a little?"

I shrugged and glanced at his newest stray. The tiger seemed to do the same thing.

"Do you mind turning away for a moment?" he asked me.

Amused, I turned my head. His pants dropped into a pile next to the tiger. My lamp stuck out of one of his pockets.

"Make sure no one gets to those," he said to the tiger.

The soft padding of feet on sand, followed by the swish of water, made me glance over my shoulder just in time to glimpse his defined backside. My insides clenched with an unusual stirring. One that I had never experienced, and I understood in that moment that I must try to maintain my distance from this man, otherwise I might very well break every rule set forth for genies. I was already fond of my master in an unnatural way. I had never felt compelled to remain solid just for the company.

He dunked under the water and then surfaced a few moments later. Water slid off his skin under the soft twilight sky, mesmerizing me. He turned and caught me looking at him. The smile he flashed sent me into a heated mess. I looked away quickly and caught the tiger looking at me, almost in amusement.

I conjured my magic carpet so I could stretch out on something softer and cleaner than the moss below. And I curled up on my side and closed my eyes so I wouldn't take another peek of the handsome and very naked prince in the water.

JASMINE Chapter 5

ALI DIDN'T SAY MUCH when he returned and stretched out on the carpet next to me, dressed in the loose-fitting pants again. But my memory already had his bare ass imprinted on it and my heart had the desire to touch him.

"Thank you for choosing to keep me company," he whispered and closed his eyes.

"I have never met someone so...selfless," I said. "You intrigue me."

Dimples appeared in his cheeks, and he glanced at me. "You intrigue me as well. It has been a long time since someone chose to be my companion and expected nothing in return. I find it as refreshing as that water hole." He offhandedly waved toward the water. "I enjoy your company." His eyes closed again, but the smile remained.

I had to bite my bottom lip, so I didn't lean over and kiss his supple mouth. Instead, I rolled onto my back next to him and stared at the stars fading into the morning light, wondering how in the world I was going to get over this connection when his wishes were all fulfilled.

I sighed and turned my head toward him. The tiger had his mammoth head resting on Ali's bare stomach, like a protective sentry. His turquoise eyes stared at me, as if warning me not to touch his master. Ali's chest went up and down with the slow cadence of sleep, and that partial smile remained, even though the rest of his features were in the relaxed status of slumber.

Instead of acting on any instinct of mine to kiss the man, I reached out and scratched behind the tiger's ear. "I like him, too," I whispered. The tiger leaned into my hand and his eyes closed as well.

I did not sleep the way they did. Not when my last nap truly lasted close to a thousand years. Being near this small oasis in the desert set me on edge. If those men came back, searching for Ali, they would certainly run a sword through him and who knows what they would do to Tiger. As far as I was concerned, if they found the lamp, I would be bound to them. And based on our last meeting, they might request sexual favors like others had done in the past.

I shivered with revulsion, but considering eminent danger was not at hand, I could not act on my nervous energy. I could not utter a protection spell without a request from my master. Thus, the limitations of my power.

I pulled my hand away from the tiger's head and stared up at the colors of the imminent sunrise. It had not crested yet, so the sky was set alight with the colors of the rainbow. Near the horizon, the bright yellow colored the sand with the same vibrancy; then strips of orange, red, purple, and blue streaked the sky, fading into what was left of the deep night sky. My mind wandered to his questions. *What really would happen to me if I was freed?* I had never truly pondered that. But if anyone were to be selfless in their wishes, it would be Ali.

Would I become an ancient woman, or would I remain youthful, only to age from this point forward like a normal human?

Would I become mortal?

Would I have any magic left?

Where would I live?

My mind swirled restlessly, creating a storm inside me. Although I really would like to be free from the obligation of granting wishes, I was not so sure I wanted to become mortal. There were so many unknowns, and I had been in this station for thousands of years.

How would I survive without this magic in my bones?

I had no answer, just question upon question piling up in my head until I thought I would explode. With panic riding my blood like a hot chili pepper, I almost succumbed and retreated into my lamp. But a star caught my attention as it burned through the last of the night sky, leaving a white streak in its wake before it faded to nothing.

That shooting star dropped the anxiety filling me to a manageable level. I sat up and glanced down at Ali and then at the water, wondering whether it would feel cool against my skin. I stripped and took the same path Ali had taken. The water lapped at my skin as I entered. The coolness refreshed me, and I dunked down until it covered my head. Bubbles drifted from my nose upward, and I followed them, breaking the surface. I did not remember the last time I indulged in this kind of physical satisfaction, and the years of dirt and grime that I had existed in sloughed off me, leaving my skin radiant in the morning light.

I headed back to the carpet, wringing my hair of the excess water.

Ali's eyes were open and staring at me with an interest he hadn't expressed before. He propped himself up on one of his arms as his lips popped open in a way that was inviting and almost as exhilarating as the water. He blinked and then lowered his gaze, as if he remembered his manners.

"I... I'm sorry," he said as I reached down for my clothing.

"Why?"

He looked at my face and then his gaze dropped to my naked form, scanning me all the way to my feet and back. "I should not be looking at you unclothed," he said softly. "But I cannot seem to look away." His gaze found mine. "Why is that?"

I smiled and pulled my clothing on. Truthfully, I liked his attention. If it had been those men around the cage, it would be different, but with Ali, I didn't seem to have reservations about revealing my true self. Deep down, I hoped he would make a wish that would give me just as much pleasure as it would give him.

I sat down next to him, keeping his gaze. As the seconds ticked by, neither of us moved. Ali gave me the once-over and inhaled deeply before falling onto his back again.

I stretched beside him. He turned his head and stared at me, his expression unreadable for the first time since I saw him in the cavern.

"Is that your actual body?" he asked tentatively.

A flush of uncertainty filled me, but I nodded.

His lips twitched into a smile he was trying to hide. "You are beautiful," he said with such reverence that I shifted.

My face heated, despite the cool wetness still clinging to my skin. I did not know how to respond, but my mouth seemed to have other ideas. "So are you," came tumbling from my lips. My heart stammered in my chest as pins and needles traversed my form, leaving small bumps across my exposed skin.

This time, dimples appeared in his cheeks, and he turned his attention back to the morning sky. Another shooting star streaked across the universe of colors.

"Did you make a wish?" he asked.

"Hmm?" I looked at him.

"On the shooting star. You're supposed to make a wish when you see one."

I rolled my eyes. "I grant wishes, remember?"

That serene smile graced his lips, and my muscles tensed to keep me from doing something insanely stupid.

"Not making a wish is a lost opportunity." He focused back on the sky.

"What did *you* wish for?" I couldn't help but pry. Especially considering granting wishes was my job. Plus, I really wanted to know what he wished on a star for, because he hadn't wished for anything from me yet.

He just grinned and kept his eyes on the sky.

JASMINE Chapter 6

ALI AND THE TIGER slept in the shade during the heat of the day. I tried not to watch Ali, but my gaze kept falling on his peaceful features. He truly was handsome, and my heart skipped a beat every time I studied his profile.

As the sun dipped below the horizon, Ali stretched the sleep from his limbs. His hair looked quite disheveled and totally adorable. He wiped his eyes, climbed to his feet, and crossed to the edge of the water, where he squatted and splashed his face with handfuls of water. Then he wet his hair and hand-combed it back in order before returning to where the tiger and I still lounged.

"We should get moving. I believe we have at least another night's walk ahead of us. If we are not diverted, we should reach my kingdom before nightfall tomorrow, if we continue through the heat of the day." He offered his hand to me.

The connection of our fingertips sparked a fire in me I had thought incapable of ever igniting again. He pulled me to my feet, and my carpet yanked out from underneath me, tumbling me right into Ali's arms.

I swear that rag did it on purpose, too.

Ali held me steady, with one hand firmly planted on my back and the other resting on my upper arm in a light grip that seemed tentative. He stared into my eyes and for a moment; I was lost in his green irises, as if I had stepped into a green field of calm. And then my heart decided to work again and work overtime at that.

With his hand pressed against my back, I had nowhere to escape from the onslaught of want that accosted me. His gaze fell to my lips and then back to mine. He hesitantly released me.

"Are you okay now?"

I sighed, wishing for his arms around me again. "I think my carpet did that on purpose." I pulled my gaze away from Ali and sent a stern look at my magic carpet. It tried to skitter away, but its magic reserves had been drained by a full day outside of the lamp, especially this far from the caverns.

"You still need a little more time in the lamp." I pointed to Ali's pocket.

It rose like a snake shaking its tassels.

I rolled my eyes. "You know your magic is limited, and a full day outside of the lamp is enough of a drain on you, my friend." I waved again toward Ali. "Replenish your powers so we can take flight later."

This time, the carpet obeyed, becoming smoke that swirled around us before disappearing into Ali's pocket, where the lamp safely resided.

Ali cocked his head quizzically at me. "Why don't magic carpets have unlimited power just like you?"

"The lamp is connected to me, just like my binds are connected to me." I showed him my cuffs again. "My carpet is not connected to the lamp in the same way, so being this far from the caverns makes him weak after just a few hours outside of his energy source."

Tiger was not impressed. He sauntered down to the watering hole and lapped at the water for a spell. When he had had enough to drink, he walked past us in the direction that Ali had indicated as his home.

We fell into step beside the tiger. The soft padding of our feet on the sand was the only noise between us until the tiger's stomach made a hideous growl. Ali and I traded a glance. Hopefully, the tiger would find a source of food. Otherwise, we would look too good to resist.

"I don't know when the last time he ate was," Ali said quietly as he surveyed the desert. His stomach groaned as well, and he let out a chuckle. "I haven't eaten in a few days either."

I opened my mouth.

"I am not wishing for food for us." He swiped his finger toward me as if I were the bad guy in this little band of ours. His features pinched in irritation for a moment, and then he took a deep breath and the lines in his face smoothed out. "Sorry. I should not snap, especially when you are trying to be helpful."

"I understand."

Shaking his head, he gave me a sideways look. "You should not be so accommodating. My tone was uncalled for. I'm just tired, hungry, and worried. My stepfather would have been home later the day I was locked in the cave. I am unsure how long I was unconscious on that ledge, so it could be two or three days that have passed already. If my mother thinks I am dead...she will be of little use to the people of the kingdom. Without me as an heir to challenge his position, he will remain the sultan."

"Time in the cavern is not like it is out here in the world. Especially when the sentry closes access like he did," I said.

Ali stopped, blinking as if his mind was not understanding my meaning. "How long is a day in the cavern?" he asked with a breathy voice filled with dread.

"A day in the closed cavern is the equivalent of a full rotation of the earth around the sun."

Ali's mouth popped open and his eyes widened, then he turned and sprinted toward the kingdom. Tiger leaped alongside him, thinking this was playtime, but from Ali's reaction, this was anything but a game.

I commanded my legs to smoke and crossed to him within a blink, pulled by my lamp buried in his pocket.

His eyes were as crazed as a caged wild horse and his cheeks bloomed red with his exertion. "A year or two?" His breath wheezed with the words. "Why didn't you tell me this before?" His pace slowed until he fell to his knees in exhaustion. He uncorked the water container and chugged the contents between each ragged breath.

"I assumed you knew this," I said. At least in my heyday, the people knew of the cavern's hazards, especially the warp in the passage of time.

He wiped his face and shook his head. "I did not, and I need to get home quicker than my feet can take me." He glanced at the tiger. "And I doubt Tiger would let me ride on his back."

Carpet materialized from my lamp and spread out on the ground, beckoning Ali. Ali glanced at it and then at me.

"I did not summon him," I said.

He nodded and crawled onto the carpet and glanced at the tiger. "I'm sorry, but I don't think you can ride along without hurting Carpet. But you can run alongside us." He glanced back at me. "Did you want to ride this out in the lamp?"

"No way." I climbed next to Ali, with the tiger on the sand next to me, and gripped the front edge of the carpet.

Ali grabbed the middle of the front carpet edge. "Only go as fast as Tiger, so we don't lose him." He took a deep breath. "Go!"

At his command, both Tiger and the carpet took off. Wind whipped through my hair as my magic carpet skimmed a few feet off the ground, keeping pace with the charging tiger. Despite the nervous energy emitting from Ali, he let out a laugh. Even in the most stressed of times, he seemed to embrace life.

Miles flew by and as we crested a hill, the kingdom came into view.

Ali pulled back on the carpet. "Whoa."

Carpet skidded to a halt and nearly threw us into the sand. Tiger braced his legs, sending a spray of sand in his wake. My carpet fell to the ground as if exhausted, but Tiger seemed to be invigorated by the free run and paced around us, panting.

Ali climbed to his feet and stepped onto the sand as he surveyed the landscape. "It used to shine like a diamond," he said.

The city below looked as if soot had covered every building except the palace. The palace still shined like a pristine child in the middle of a mud puddle.

I waved my carpet toward Ali. This time, it did not cause a fuss; it wound into smoke and found its way to my lamp to recharge.

Ali glanced at Tiger, and took his bota off and cupped his hand, pouring a little bit of water at a time so the cat could lick it up. Once the last drop fell from the bag, he stood and patted the cat's head.

"Are you going to name him?" I stepped beside him and pointed at the tiger.

He tilted his head and pursed his lips as he walked toward the city below. After a few paces, he said, "Raj."

The tiger glanced at him, as if he approved of the name.

"Raj," I repeated. Tiger certainly was the embodiment of power. "It's a good name."

The closer we got to his kingdom, the more his lips turned down. As we entered the streets, his shoulders rounded, and his eyes filled with tears at the squalor around us.

I caught a few curtains fall back as we looked from side to side. Life existed, but no one approached us.

We stepped out of a narrow street into what looked like a town square, but it was as barren as the streets had been.

"This used to be the market." Ali slowly turned in a circle, shaking his head. "It was always filled with vendors of fresh fruit, fresh breads, grains, and all manner of fabrics. My mother saw to it that those who could not pay would be fed. The vendors kept running tabs she would pay each month." He sighed and bowed his head in defeat.

A small form of what looked like stretched skin over bones approached, cautiously staring at the tiger. The being stuck their hand out. "Spare a cent, sir?" The voice was frail and even my heart broke at the sight.

Ali squatted to the child's level. "What happened to the market?" he asked as he studied the fragile human.

"The sultan..." The child swallowed hard. "Declared that all goods belonged to him and confiscated everything. He closed down the market and left us to starve," the child whispered. "He destroyed Agrabah."

Ali hung his head and then looked up at me. "I wish the people of my kingdom shall know no hunger or this horrid poverty as long as I still have breath within me."

"As you wish." My magic swirled, and the child's eyes grew wide. I turned my palms to the sky, and a whirlwind surrounded us, moving wider with each moment as I reinstated the glory of Agrabah and the bounty of the market, as Ali had described. Every person would be provided what they needed—nothing more, nothing less—and the kingdom would thrive once again.

Houses were brushed clean of soot, renewed to their shining prosperity that Ali remembered. The dust layered into the cobblestone streets swept away in the breeze I created, revealing an array of gleaming stones. The opulence and good fortune of the city gleamed when the wind faded.

And the child standing before us filled out her flesh and now looked like a healthy girl instead of the scrawny skeleton we first saw. She stared at me in awe, and then her gaze moved to Ali. "Who are you?"

"Prince Ali." He stood, glancing around and smiling at what I had created with my magic. As his gaze came back to the child, his grin faded.

The child's eyes widened. An adult woman stepped forward out of the shadows and gathered the child in her arms.

"The prince died." She narrowed her eyes at the bare-chested man standing before her.

"What dark magic is this?" she hissed, attempting to hide the child from us.

"My stepfather threw me into the Cavern of Souls." He ran his hand through his hair as the woman's eyes became as large as saucers. "Time is different there, otherwise I would have been here to prevent all this devastation." He glanced around again and then his head snapped back to the woman.

"Why didn't my mother stop him?"

The woman's face stretched to reveal a sadness in her eyes, and her lips quivered. "The sultana was murdered the day the sultan took you in search of the genie's lamp."

Ali stepped back and reached for Raj to steady himself. His eyes glimmered with tears. "What?" His voice shook.

Before the woman could speak, the sound of hoofs on the cobblestone echoed in the streets. She grabbed Ali's hand and, with urgency, hissed, "Hide! Otherwise, the same will befall you." Then she disappeared down the dark alley.

"Ali," I warned, as the air filled with hostility. I grabbed his hand and pulled him into the same alley the woman had fled into. Raj followed as we kept to the shadows.

Ali leaned on the wall and slowly sank to the ground. The tears that had shimmered in his eyes slowly tracked down his cheeks. I kneeled next to him, and when I touched his arm, he drew me into a hug as he cried tears of loss and grief against my shoulder.

Confusion muddled my brain as I tried to reconcile his grief with this feeling of home that captured my every cell. Being in his arms felt right, even though everything about this was forbidden.

When he finally pulled away, dread covered me like a cold, dark drape, and I shivered. Ali licked his lips. His eyes found mine, and he pressed his forehead to mine.

"Jasmine, please. I wish my mother to be alive."

"Ali," I whispered, my voice carrying the heartbreak pummeling my insides. Bringing back the dead was against the rules. "It's not—"

He gripped my hands as the sound of hoofs drew closer. "Please, please, Jasmine, bring my mother back." He searched my eyes through his tears, begging me with his soul and his words.

Each new teardrop that fell broke a piece of me. But it wasn't until he closed the distance and pressed his lips to mine that my resolve crumbled. That kiss changed my entire world.

That kiss damned me just as much as the words that tumbled from my mouth when he pulled away. "As you wish," I whispered, and my magic swelled. This time, it swirled with darkness, as if reaching into the netherworld to pull her soul out from death's grip. Perhaps I should have warned him that what comes back is no longer whole, but I could not abide his devastation.

The sentry's fury raged inside me as my magic broke the hard and fast rules of genie law. Thou shall not kill. Thou shall not bring the dead back to life. And the worst of all three genie sins: Thou shall not fall in love with thy master. At that moment, two of the three laws had been broken, and I would pay dearly for it.

When my magic cloud cleared, I gasped at the view beyond us. We had been found. One of the sultan's soldiers on horseback blocked the alley entry, and his sword was aimed directly at Raj.

His gaze moved to Ali, and it darkened. "You," he growled, and the sword's aim moved to Ali.

"Run," Ali said, and then he was off, with Raj at his heels.

I turned toward the guard and wiggled my fingers at him just as I turned to smoke. This time when I caught up with Ali, I found solace in my lamp instead of trying to run beside him in this cramped alleyway.

I paced despite the jostling as the dual realities hit me. I had raised the dead, and I had fallen in love. Two deadly sins for a genie. This would be my last foray into the world. After Ali had made his third wish, I would be locked in my lamp, and the sentry would call me home to the Cavern of Souls to destroy me.

My heart broke, and I threw myself on the bed as tears of my own heated my face. With two wishes fulfilled, and my heart already wrapped up in Ali, I was lost even if he freed me.

JASMINE Chapter 7

MUFFLED VOICES PENETRATED THE walls of my lamp, and the jostling came to a sudden halt. But then I was in a free fall that ended with a thud that threw me across the lamp. My head swam with a high-pitched buzz, and I shook my head to clear it. I touched the back of my skull, and my hand came away wet.

I stared at the red smear on my hand and glanced at the wall. A red spot marred the fabric lining the interior. Although I've been thrown around in my lamp more than my fair share, I have never been injured. My heart lurched. I closed my eyes and willed myself healed.

The sluggish magic did as I commanded, but it did not penetrate the pounding in my head. My breathing wheezed as my world spun and I fell on top of my carpet, clinging to it while I sent a silent plea for mercy to the sentry.

Just as I thought my life would be snuffed out, the magic swirled around me, pulling me out into the world again. Ali had finally summoned me. Relief swept through me, and my muscles relaxed until I opened my eyes to a packed throne room in the palace and the meaty thug who held my lamp.

His mustache looked like a hairy snake had perched on his upper lip and draped down each side of his mouth to circle around on his chin. His dark eyes held unlimited cruelty within them, and he sneered at me in triumph.

"I control you now," he announced to me. "Do not speak until I call upon you for a wish. Understand?"

I nodded assent as I scanned the crowd, hoping to find Ali among them. Instead, all I saw were wide-eyed, pale faces.

The doors opened and my heart shriveled in my chest as the crowd parted. Ali was dragged into the room in chains. He fought against the guards, but there were too many of them and he could not free himself from the chains they had around his wrists. The guards strapped each chain, binding his arms to a pole opposite each other, stretching Ali until he cried out.

The sultan took a seat on his throne with my lamp in his lap and grinned. Behind Ali, a small cage rolled inside and was pushed into the corner near where the sultan sat. Stuffed inside was Raj. He could not stand tall in the space, and he could not lay down comfortably. His muscles trembled from the strain, and his hiss brought tears to my eyes.

A man with a scar zigzagging across his face stepped into the room with a bullwhip. He squared himself behind Ali and waited.

Ali glanced around the room in horror, especially when his gaze caught the setup to the right of the throne pedestal. A wooden stump sat in the middle of an alcove, and red stains splashed the wall behind it. His gaze shot back to the sultan and jumped from him to me and back as he blinked to understand his predicament.

The sultan glared at Ali. "You will suffer for your duplicity." He gave a curt nod and the crack of the whip echoed through the room, followed by Ali bowing his back as he let out a painful wail.

Blood splattered the floor as the whip holder wound up for another strike.

"This is what happens when you cross the Sultan of Agrabah!" the sultan bellowed at the people stuffed into the throne room, and they cowered in response.

I opened my mouth to beg for mercy, but I could not make a sound. After all, my master had ordered me silent, and I could not interfere unless I was in danger, or my master made a wish. I frantically scanned the room, looking for the only potential savior. But the dead do not move as quickly as the living, and I did not see the dead among the spectators.

Another snap and more blood. Yet Ali still stood tall, even though tears streaked his cheeks. His green eyes locked on me, and a crease appeared between his eyes. I could almost hear him asking why I did not intercede. I glanced down at the lamp in his stepfather's hands.

His gaze followed mine and then he closed his eyes, sagging in the chains as the next snap ripped another gash in his back.

Heat rolled down my cheek and his eyes opened, tracking the tear that fell for him. I would welcome the sentry's punishment of death for violating genie law. It could not be nearly as painful as watching the man I loved being beaten to death. Especially when I had enough power to stop this, but I was helpless to wield it.

Movement caught my eye. The door cracked wide enough for a dark-haired corpse to clear the space. My magic had not completed the regeneration, and what stepped through the door was not fully recognizable as a human. Bones still showed on parts of her face. Same with her body. But her eyes had reformed, and they were the same emerald as Ali's.

She kept to the shadows. Her gaze fell on the bloody back facing her and her face did not register that it was her son suffering. But when they moved past him to the man on the throne, her eyes narrowed with hatred.

Her gaze moved to mine and creases appeared in what had formed of her forehead.

I pointedly looked at Ali and then back at her, trying to silently convey the direness of the situation and that it was her son being beaten.

Ali sagged in the chains, nearly unconscious.

The sultan waved his hand. "This bores me. It is time for this criminal to meet Allah for his sins." He pointed toward the executioner's station in the alcove.

A man in black stepped from the shadows, his back to the crowd. His sword gleamed in the light filtering from outside.

The chains were unhooked from the pillars, and Ali was dragged to the stump in the alcove. Each arm was wrapped around the wood and then the chains attached to his wrists were fastened, so his cheek lay flush with the outer edge of the wood, leaving his neck centered on the wooden pedestal. He faced the throne.

The agony painted on his face made the sultan laugh.

If I had the power, I would have struck the bastard dead at that moment.

"For your sins, I sentence you to death," the sultan ordered.

Raj wasn't the only one who hissed at the sultan's command.

JASMINE Chapter 8

THE FIRST SCREAM RANG out as the former sultana's hood fell back when she reached up and snapped the executioner's neck before he could strike the deadly blow. She grabbed the executioner's sword and stepped into the light. Those closest to her gasped and backed away as far as they could in the thick crowd.

She lifted a bony finger, pointing it at the sultan. "You will not murder my son as you murdered me." Her grave-like voice penetrated the entire court, creating an eerie silence that no one wanted to break.

All heads turned to the creature now holding the executioner's blade. The only one who could not see the sultana was Ali. But the relief visible on his face tugged at my heart.

I was not so sure he would be thankful once he actually saw the state his mother was in.

The former sultana brought the weapon down in a commanding arc, slamming it into the chains that held Ali fast to the execution block. The chains disintegrated under the powerful slice.

Ali fell away from the block and got his first glimpse of his mother. I could not see his face, but the way his entire body froze and his muscles tightened was enough. He saw the monster that I pulled from the grave. He saw what his wish had procured, and it was not his sweet, loving mother.

The sultan's eyes nearly bulged from his face. His jaw hung askew, and his cheeks flamed at the sight of his dead wife now pointing the blade at him.

"I sentence you to death for *my* murder," the sultana hissed. She stepped closer, raising the blade again with the intent of a mortal strike on the sultan. If she had been fully formed, she would have been able to cross the distance faster, but she was still contending with flesh that was not completely restored and, without the muscles fully formed, moved slow.

"I wish her back to the grave that I put her in!" the sultan stammered. His shaking voice rang forth loud enough for Ali to turn in our direction.

"As you wish," I said through clenched teeth.

I hated the horror etched on Ali's face. Even though she was a walking corpse, she was still his mother, and the heartbreak in his eyes tightened my throat.

Sending a living zombie back to the grave was not the same as killing someone, though. My insides did not twinge at the order, but from the devastation painted in Ali's eyes. I did not feel the fury of the sentry as I granted this wish as I had when I granted the one to make this thing rise from the dead. I hoped this would counteract my sin, but deep down, I knew it wasn't that easy to appease the sentry once a rule was broken.

My magic swirled, and Ali's mother slowly decomposed back into the corpse in the grave and then turned to smoke, captured by the mini tornado of magic I had created. She uttered no cry as I tried to make her demise as painless as I could. I sent her back to whatever plane I had yanked her from.

Light filled the room, and I shielded my eyes from it.

When the dust settled, Ali was halfway across the floor on his hands and knees, but he wasn't headed toward the door. He was headed toward the executioner's blade.

"Stop him," the sultan bellowed as he pointed at Ali.

None of the guards moved. Instead, they stared at the sultan as if he had betrayed them.

Ali reached for the blade, but his injuries were too daunting for him to climb to his feet and wield the heavy sword. He turned toward the guards. "Arrest him for my mother's murder." He pointed toward the sultan.

"By whose order?" one of the younger guards asked.

"By the order of Prince Ali." He pushed himself to his feet.

"Arrest him!" the sultan bellowed.

The mood in the space shifted, and I could smell the anger. It matched the expression of most of the people in the room. When the guards started for the throne pedestal, the sultan issued his second wish.

"I wish to be the most powerful sorcerer in the world," he bellowed.

Before anyone could reach him, my magic swelled.

"As you wish."

Thunder clapped and lightning zigzagged over the domed ceiling, creating roiling clouds that seemed to reach down to the sultan, crackling all around the throne until the bolts converged and slammed into the sultan's chest, filling him with the kind of magic that could destroy kingdoms.

My mouth tasted dirty, as if I had unleashed the end of the world.

The guards and people witnessing the storm backed away. They shook and covered their mouths with their hands to stifle screams and pleas to Allah to save their souls while their eyes widened with horror.

When the clouds dispersed, the sultan stood. "Guards, you will obey. Or you will die," he announced. His magic rolled across the floor, attacking every guard in the room, shutting off their ability to think and act for themselves.

He focused on Ali and waved his hand in Ali's direction.

Ali's gaze met mine and pain shot through his features just before he yelped and released the executioner's sword. The blade dropped with a clang, and Ali grabbed his hand. His palm reddened and blistered.

"Bow to your sultan," the sultan said.

The people and the soldiers slowly lowered to their knee, bowing their heads to their master. He had a new herd of slaves now who would do his bidding, and it made me physically ill.

Ali was the only one who had not taken a knee to honor the sultan. He stood, stoic, with eyes filled with righteous anger, glaring at his stepfather.

"Take a knee," the sultan demanded.

"Never." Ali lifted his chin in defiance.

My stomach squeezed tighter than I've ever experienced. I was going to lose Ali to this dark-souled man, and there was not a single thing I could do. Hot tears leaked out of the corners of my eyes as I silently watched my undoing.

JASMINE Chapter 9

"I AM THE MOST powerful being on the planet. Bow before me!" the sultan bellowed.

Ali shook his head.

"On your knees," the sultan commanded and pointed at Ali, sending a wave of magic at him that dropped Ali to his knees.

Ali held his head high with his teeth clenched tight against the magic trying to bow him over. He resisted it and his gaze met mine.

I could see the wheels turning behind his soulful green eyes.

The sultan pointed at the nearest guard. "You, pick up that sword," he commanded, and the soldier complied.

I wanted to beg for Ali's life, but no sound escaped as the sound of metal scraping on stone filled the space.

"Any last words before I have your head delivered to me on this bronze platter?"

A decorative platter appeared a few feet in front of Ali, hovering in the air with the sultan's powers, waiting for Ali's head to be sliced off by the executioner's sword.

The soldier stepped next to Ali and lined up the blade to the back of Ali's neck. He waited for the order from the sultan.

"You are not the most powerful being on the planet. You don't hold a candle to a genie," Ali said.

I blinked at him. A genie was most definitely more powerful than the world's strongest sorcerer, but that power was bound to the lamp and a master. My eyes widened as the sultan turned to look at me.

"Is this true? Are you more powerful than I am?"

"Yes, Master," I said, but I stopped there. I was not under the obligation to give him all the facts. I was only obligated to answer his direct question. I closed my lips tightly, allowing my disdain for him to show through, as if the idea pained me.

Greed echoed in the sultan's gaze. His eyes narrowed, and he put his hand up, holding the execution for a moment as he mulled over Ali's challenge.

Ali waited and avoided making eye contact with me. He had measured his stepfather's quest for power accurately.

"I wish to be the most powerful genie in the universe!" the sultan demanded.

My lips twitched into a smile. "As you wish!"

A black cloud encircled the sultan, and I glanced at Ali as my magic did as the sultan commanded. The sultan grew large and stretched out his arms as the lower half of his body became smoke. A lamp appeared next to mine on the throne. It was a putrid color, reflecting what I thought of his soul and not something that a person would likely pick up to shine.

He bellowed at the heavens as the power filled him.

The moment the wish completed, I felt the pull of my lamp, but resisted. I wanted to see how this all played out. Everyone blinked, as if awaking from a god-awful nightmare. Even the soldier holding the executioner's sword to Ali.

"I'll have his head now!" the sultan commanded.

The last of the sorcerer's magic failed, and the platter fell to the floor.

The soldier looked at the sword in his hand, at Ali, and then at the sultan as he dropped the sword to his side. Defiance and anger etched into the space around his tightly clamped lips. He took a step back just to make it clear he would not follow through with the order.

I smiled, and so did Ali.

"You have no power over us now." Ali struggled to his feet.

The sultan created a huge fireball and reached back to pitch it at Ali. Before he could launch the ball of death, wrist bindings appeared on his arms, locking him in place so he could not annihilate the people in the room as he wanted. The fireball fizzed out.

"What have you done to me?" he bellowed at me.

"I merely granted your third wish," I said with a coy smile. "Although a genie technically is more powerful than the strongest sorcerer, we are bound to our master's wishes. And when we don't have a master, we are locked in the prisons of our lamps. Enjoy yours." I pointed at the putrid lamp on the chair below.

"And you shall enjoy the pit in the Cavern of Souls just as soon as I can drop you into that fiery hell that you tried to throw me into," Ali said. "That is your punishment for murdering my mother, attempting to murder me twice now, as well as what you did to this kingdom under your rule."

Ali's stepfather cried out as his lamp sucked him back inside. He was not experienced enough to fight it, like I was currently fighting the draw of my lamp.

He turned toward the crowd, and they fell to their knees, bowing to their rightful sultan.

"Please. I do not require you to bow to me. On your feet."

"May we tend to your wounds?" someone in the crowd asked.

Ali glanced back at the chair and then into the crowd. "I will be just fine." He waved toward the lamps. "I can make my stepfather heal me."

There was not a person in the crowd who did not grin at the irony.

"Is there anyone here who needs a wish or two?" he asked, looking around.

"Be careful how you word your wishes, Ali," I warned. "A spiteful genie can do more damage than good."

He glanced back at me and nodded. "Thank you for the warning." He gave me a nod and then looked back at the nearest soldier. "While we are waiting for people to think of what wishes are worthy for Agrabah, can you please let Raj out of that cage?" He pointed at the cage in the corner.

The soldier's gaze became guarded as he glanced at the crouched tiger and back at Ali.

"He is mine. Please release him."

"Yes, Your Excellency." He bowed and hurried to the corner where a set of keys hung. He unlocked the door and stepped behind it as he opened it.

Raj slowly backed up and as soon as he was free, he turned toward the soldier, baring his teeth.

"Raj," Ali commanded, pulling the tiger's attention away from the shaking man. He snapped his fingers and the tiger reluctantly crossed to sit next to him. Ali scratched him behind the ear and then turned back to the people.

"What wishes do you need?" he asked again.

Someone in the back raised her hand. "Can we make the kingdom impervious to disease?"

Ali smiled and nodded. "Anything else?"

They looked at one another, and no one seemed to have anything else to wish for. It seemed Ali's wish for prosperity for the kingdom was enough for these people, and I now understood his selfless nature.

A woman with a veil hiding her face stepped forward. "Your Excellency, might I ask for our queen back?"

Ali's head bowed, and he glanced over his shoulder at me. "I don't think a genie can truly bring back the dead. The body of the dead, yes. But their true spirit?" He shook his head. "I think the genie tried to warn me when I made that wish, but I was too distraught and did not heed her message." He turned his gaze back to the woman. "So, no. Although I would love to have my mother back, it is not possible."

She bowed her head and stepped back.

"Why don't you become a sorcerer?" the guard who set Raj free said.

"I do not wish to wield that type of power." He shook his head. "Now, if you wouldn't mind, I will make the wishes without an audience. I do not want to stroke my stepfather's ego any further."

The room cleared, and when the door closed, Ali faltered. Raj stood, allowing him to hold on to his fur to make his way up the stairs to the throne and the two lamps.

"How do I ask for my back to be healed?"

I thought about how he should word it. Although it was a simple request, the hatred in his stepfather would take advantage of any discrepancy in wording. "Ask him to restore

938

your back to the condition it was prior to the first contact of the whip."

He gave me a nod. "And how should I ask for my kingdom to never know disease?"

That was a harder item to wish for. "Ask that the people of Agrabah to be protected against any and all forms of illness." I pursed my lips and shook my head. "No, that could be misconstrued."

"How about asking that mortal illness be stricken from Agrabah?"

I shook my head. "Still not enough. It needs to be something like what you wished for the kingdom. That health and wellness prosper within the city of Agrabah until..." I tilted my head. "You don't want to pin it to your death, either. You want it more permanent, like until the last ounce of oxygen is sucked out of the atmosphere."

Ali smiled.

"My lamp is calling, and I no longer can hold my grip on this world," I said as my form shrank into the lamp. The sucking sound pulled me in until I blinked and was inside my familiar home.

"I will see you again, Jasmine," Ali said to the side of my lamp.

And then the motion hit, and everything became muffled, as if he hid the lamp in his pants pocket like before.

Although my heart rejoiced in the fact he was my master again, I knew it would be only for a moment. Only to grant his final wish, and then my life would be forfeited to the sentry.

JASMINE Chapter 10

STANDING OUTSIDE THE OPEN maw of the cavern where Ali found my lamp brought chills to the surface. This was the gateway to my destruction for disobeying the code all genies are bound to, and the sentry had opened its mouth for my required sacrifice.

Ali unclasped a backpack with water canteens attached and peeled it off his shoulders before setting it in the sand, giving me a view of his unmarred back. The putrid-looking lamp hung off his finger, while my black lamp sat on his palm with my sigil of a winged phoenix shining bright in the sunlight. My magic carpet danced next to him, as if soaking in the magic of being so close to the cavern and the sentry's unique power source.

I blinked, confused, as the horror of the situation sunk in. "What have you done?" I gasped, staring at the cavern with trepidation filling my form.

"My last wish was to be transported here." He smiled and held up the ugly lamp hanging on his finger. "This way, I can see to it that his lamp is destroyed."

Ali did not understand. I would be sacrificed, too. Before I could open my mouth to explain the laws of the genie to Ali, the sentry spoke. His voice rumbled over the desert.

"You have violated the genie's covenant." His stone eyes blazed, landing on me and reflecting the fire burning in the pit inside. The pit Ali wanted to throw his stepfather's lamp in. "You must pay the price."

My lamp drifted out of Ali's hand, and he grabbed it, turning toward me for answers. "What is he saying?"

"I broke the genie's sacred bond. I raised the dead." My gaze dropped to the ground as heat filled my cheeks. "So, my lamp must be tossed into the pit along with your stepfather's." My heart squeezed as I looked at Ali. I leaned forward and gently pried my lamp from his grip.

"That means..."

I nodded as the confusion cleared from his eyes and they widened in response.

"No." He shook his head, but there was nothing he could do.

I started to turn to smoke, trailing into the lamp with my heart breaking into a thousand pieces in my chest.

This time he reached for me, taking my hand in a frantic grip to keep me from disappearing, and words tumbled from his lips in quick succession. "I have one more wish left." He glanced at me and then at the sharp-tooth mouth of the cavern. "I still have one more wish that Jasmine is bound to grant."

I glanced at the sentry's mammoth head. His eyes blazed in a way that made me swallow hard. And it took at least a dozen heartbeats before he answered Ali.

The rock formation nodded. "Finish your obligation," the sentry commanded, but it seemed more like a sneer.

I turned back to Ali as dread filled my soul. This was the last wish I would ever grant, and then I would feel the bite of the fire below. I licked my lips, trying to formulate the words. My chin trembled as I asked Ali, "What is it you wish for?"

His gaze dropped to the lamp and then moved to the wrist bands binding me before coming back to land on my face. He reached out and palmed my cheek. His warm hand fed the burning coals of panic in my stomach, especially when his gaze softened.

"I wish to set you free," he whispered and took a deep breath. He glanced at the sentry. "I wish to set Jasmine free," he said again to the sentry, in case I could not grant the wish.

I was stunned enough not to be able to speak. *Did he just free me?* What I had always wished for actually happened. I was too stunned to move, never mind utter the words to make it so. I blinked at him as his gaze turned back to mine.

"As you wish." The sentry's voice boomed over us as the source of all genies' magic took hold. The ground shook with the power radiating below us, and then it engulfed me.

I fell to my knees with a shriek as the metal emblazoned in my wrists turned as fiery as the pit below. My lamp became so hot, it scorched the skin of my hands. I dropped it onto the sand, where it burst into a spray of sand and smoke, pulling at the binds as it faded. The metal around both wrists followed down the same path, but it left behind a reminder. My phoenix symbol blazed in my skin as if someone took a hot poker and drew it into my flesh.

My carpet tumbled to the ground as if the destruction of my bindings and my lamp had also destroyed its access to magic.

My ears rang, and then my sight swam. Double, then triple vision gripped me as I blinked desperately to wipe it away. Ali was kneeling before me, holding both my hands, and his mouth was moving.

"Jasmine? Jasmine? Are you okay?"

His voice barreled through whatever buzzing had filled my head.

I nodded, but I wasn't so sure, even after he helped me to my feet. "Why did you do that?" I finally gasped when air filled my lungs. I felt like a newborn baby taking a breath for the first time.

"Because I'm in love with you, and I still had one more wish to make."

His smile, as sweet as it was, did not ease the rising panic making my skin hot. The ground continued to rumble, and the sentry roared with eyes blazing hot with hellfire. A sacrifice was still required; otherwise, the ground would split open and swallow us all.

"Ali, you need to throw that lamp into the pit." I pointed at the putrid lamp in his hand with a shaking finger. "Otherwise..." I could not finish the words, but my face transmitted the horror that my voice could not.

Ali stumbled toward the opening, navigating the quaking ground as quickly as he could without falling or dropping his stepfather's lamp.

"Go keep him safe," I whispered to the fabric on the sand, not expecting it to revive. My eyes widened as sparks of magic jumped from my fingers into the carpet, bringing it back to life. It swirled around me once and then took off after Ali.

I would have gone in with him, but I was not welcome in the caverns anymore. If I followed him inside, I would be struck dead, leaving Ali locked in the cave with no light to navigate out of the catacombs like we had escaped before.

My stomach squeezed as the ground continued to rock below my feet. Even his stepfather's lamp might not be enough to pay for my sins. It might require Ali to satisfy its rage. My heart galloped in my chest, squeezing until the pain was so acute, I could no longer stand. I dropped to my knees, bowing to the sun, praying to Allah to spare Ali.

The ground fractured in a line from the open mouth straight out, and I jumped to the side, avoiding the fiery crevasse now cut into the sand. The sentry's mouth descended, but my carpet flew between the jagged teeth, with Ali holding onto the front. Ali's eyes were wide and wild, reflecting the same panic riding my bloodstream.

The sentry's teeth clanged shut.

Ali flew through the air, landing a few feet in front of me, far enough away from the edge of the newly created ravine to not slide to his death.

He scrambled to his feet, shielding his eyes from the hurricane of sand and wind that swirled around us.

Carpet waved from between the sentry's jagged teeth. One minute, he was between those deadly fangs, and the next, the carpet was sucked back inside the cavern.

The sentry became unyielding stone once again and would stay that way until he forged another genie from the ashes and captured them in a lamp for the next generation of wish seekers.

"No!" Ali yelled and ran forward, slamming his fists against the spot where the carpet had been.

A rip of power yanked from my core with the same burning sensation that had gripped me when my wrist binds were torn off. I folded over with the force of it. Ali's stepfather's lamp had not been enough of a sacrifice, but the magic I had infused into my carpet met the sentry's demand. Otherwise,

Ali would have been sucked back into the caverns, leaving me to grieve his loss alone.

I shook away the fog filling my head and forced myself to my feet. Like a toddler, I took my first awkward steps toward him. I lacked steadiness. "Ali!" I teetered and fell backward onto my ass. At least the sand was a little softer than the unforgiving rock.

Prince Ali turned, looking at me with despair so acutely written in every feature. "Carpet sacrificed himself for me," he said now that he was back in control of his emotions.

"It was my magic that was sacrificed. Carpet came back to life at my bidding and that magic seemed to satisfy the sentry. If it hadn't, the sentry would have claimed you next." I waved at the sharp carvings of the sentry's teeth that were bigger than the world's tallest man and a shiver captured me. Magic sparkled on my fingertips, bright enough for Ali to take notice. I closed my fist quickly so the sentry wouldn't see and decide the sacrifices already made were not enough.

Ali lifted an eyebrow.

Heat stroked my cheeks again. "The answer to the question of whether I would still have magic if I became mortal is yes, a tiny bit remains." I shrugged and cast a wary glance at the sentry's mouth.

Ali trudged through the sand to me, ignoring the opening the sentry caused, and igniting my nerves once more. He took my hands and pulled me into his arms. His frame shook, and then he pressed his forehead to mine. "Do you think it hurt?"

I pulled back and glanced at the opening, wondering whether being separated from me hurt my carpet as it had hurt me. My chest squeezed at the thought, and I looked back at Ali's soulful gaze. "I don't know. He was fabric and magic and over the centuries developed a personality, so I'm not sure if he's been destroyed or just imprisoned. But if my carpet hasn't been turned to dust, we will see him again." I smiled to soften the blow. But I wasn't sure whether the glossing over of facts was more for him, or for me. Either way, I chose to believe he still existed in the dark cavern and prayed my magic carpet would find his way to me again.

Ali licked his lips and his gaze dropped to my mouth before it returned to my eyes. He closed the distance and delivered the type of kiss I have only heard about in the fables that old women told around fires in the desert. It made my knees feel like a sleeping snake, and I wobbled. His arms encircled me, pressing me against him. My mind swirled and my entire form heated as his tongue played with mine in a slow dance that stole my breath, drowning me in bliss.

This was not the same chaste kiss he had delivered in that alleyway, either. This showed me all the promises of the future with him.

"You love me?" I asked against his lips when I surfaced for air.

"Yes," he breathed and pulled me in tighter. The chisel of every one of his muscles pressed against me. "Do you feel the same?" He pulled far enough away to see my eyes.

"Yes," I replied breathlessly.

My reward was the brightest smile I had ever seen, along with the words that spilled from his lips.

"Then be my wife. My sultana. Rule my kingdom with me."

Instead of answering, I ran my hand through his silky hair to the back of his head and pulled him to my mouth, devouring him as if he were my only source of air, showing him through my actions that my only desire was to be with him. But the moment I came up for a breath, I let a "Yes" slip through my lips before I surrendered my heart and my very soul to Ali.

The End

Can a cursed shifter find the love needed to be cured?

My name is Belle, and I was looking forward to finding my mate at the annual Shifter's Ball. Unfortunately, my petty side had to strike out at a homely patron who was not dressed for a ball. She looked more like the one hired to pick up after the horses. And I said so, loudly, as my friends snickered at my dark wit.

That's when karma struck.

That homely patron wasn't as she seemed. She was a powerful sorceress who laid a vanity curse on me, which made me partially shift into this monstrosity that pulls screams from grown men and cringes from my family and friends.

If I had just kept my cruel words to myself, I would not be exiled to my grandfather's dilapidated estate, searching for a way to

break this curse without getting killed in the
process.

950

BELLE Chapter 1

I STIL REMEMBER THE evening I was changed into this hideous thing. It was the night of the Shifter's Ball, where I should have met my potential mate. Instead, I was hanging with a group of my friends, making fun of the guests. One in particular was so out of place, she begged to be mocked.

I was the instigator. Snickering loud enough to be heard by this hideous woman. I commented on her drab choice of gown for such an occasion. It was as if she just grabbed any old thing to sling over her shoulders. Her posture didn't help, neither did her unwashed and unkept hair that looked like a rat's nest with stray string hanging out of it in no real order.

It was as if the girl had not bothered to make herself presentable for something as important as the Shifter's Ball.

Little did I know, she was a witch and not a shifter.

And she had a terribly mean streak when it came to bullies.

She spun on me and pointed her gnarled finger, hissing words in a language I did not understand. Guttural sounds fell from her mouth, and her eyes blazed as if her soul were on fire. Black smoke shot from her finger, and when it hit my chest, my entire form bowed backward with the pain.

But no sound escaped my tight throat. Not a scream and not a howl. My defenses kicked into gear, and I shifted. At least, that's what I thought was happening.

My left hand formed into a wolf's paw, my claws extended and sharp. My snout elongated, and my teeth became razor points in my mouth. My skin tingled where patches of fur sprouted. My left ear pulled, forming into a canine ear, itching as it grew. My right leg shortened to a canine leg, tilting me to the side.

And then everything stopped. My shift froze between human and wolf, and the smoke surrounding me settled into my skin.

My friends gasped and shrank away from me.

The crone continued to point, but now she wore a spiteful smile. "Now you are as ugly as your family's spirit." She waved her hands, and a glass box appeared in my arms, with a beautiful rosebush with dozens of roses ready to bloom enclosed inside. "You have until the last petal falls to find someone to love you. If you fail, you will remain as you are for the rest of eternity."

And with a puff of white smoke, she disappeared.

I looked at my human hand and my partially shifted arm in horror and turned, fleeing to the restroom. In the candlelit stall, I stared at the mirror, wondering when I would wake from this horrifying nightmare.

BELLE Chapter 2

INSTEAD OF GOING BACK into the ball in this state, I ran—if you could call it that. It was more of a lumbering jog that looked more monstrous than I felt. I barged through the front door of my home at the time the ball would have been at full steam, with mates dancing with each other. A part of me wanted to howl my pain, but my mouth would not form the right way to bay my sorrow to the full moon above. My parents turned from their reading chairs and gasped, jumping to their feet with horror written on their faces. They recoiled at the sight of me, just as my friends had.

My mother's gaze dropped to my dress and the box of roses in my hand before she searched my face. "Belle?" she gasped.

At least she recognized the parts of me that still existed. I burst into tears. "Mama, I've been cursed." I took a step toward them.

My father's hand splayed out in front of him. "Do not come any closer." He huddled next to my mother, as if my affliction could somehow transmit to him. "We do not want the family curse to fall upon us."

It was my turn to flinch. I retreated to the shadows. My brain was slow to catch on to his words and just as they settled into my brain, I opened my mouth. But my mother's glare at him silenced me.

She peeled herself out of my father's grasp. "What happened?"

"A witch cursed me."

"What did you do to cause that?" Her tone was as harsh as the look she gave me. She always told me to speak with a kind tongue because I could never be certain of the damage I would cause. Tonight, I wished I had heeded her warnings.

My gaze dropped to the ground, and I shifted from foot to foot as heat filled my face. "I was making fun of the way she looked." I wanted to shrink into myself at the admission and the disappointment on my parents' faces.

"And you can't shift one way or the other?" My father's question snapped through the distance like a slap.

I shook my head. "I cannot. She cursed me to remain like this until I find love or the last petal wilts and dies. If I don't find love, I'm stuck like this forever."

"You have got to be kidding me!" My father laughed in his sarcastic way that said so much more than words, and my mother shot him another warning glare, shutting him up.

"I agree with Father," I said. "I don't have a chance at finding love looking like this." I waved my good arm down my form. Before this curse, I could have had anyone I wanted. I had the looks to seduce and manipulate, but now I was a freak that no one could look at without cringing.

"We need to take this to the council and have them force that witch to turn her back!" My mother's voice hit a pitch that hurt my ears, and I whined.

"The witch disappeared," I said, pulling their attention back to where I stood. Although neither of them would look directly at me.

"There has to be a way around this." My mother sounded more desperate than I felt.

My father finally raised his gaze. "You know better than I do just how much our pack detests the abnormal. They will kill Belle," he mumbled as he stared at me. "They will not let something so horrifying live here within our town. I'm surprised they let her leave the ball alive."

I blinked. "Only two of my friends saw me after the witch cursed me. I hid in the bathroom and then snuck out and ran home." My friends had been horrified into silence, and I prayed they'd keep their mouths shut. But I wouldn't bet my life on their silence, not after the spectacle they witnessed.

He huffed and nodded, as if what I said made sense. But I had seen the pack tear a stranger apart for having a stump for a leg. And I had seen them put down the elderly and the sick in the same manner. I shivered.

My father was right. Our pack did not allow for anyone or anything that would weaken their status, so I could not rely on my friends to remain silent for long.

"What do I do?"

My parents traded a look.

"There's always my father's estate," my mother whispered.

"But that place hasn't been occupied for years," my father said. "We don't even know if it's still standing."

"It's far enough away that the pack won't kill her." My mother's lips formed a frown. "Pack a bag. We will take you to the estate before judgment can be made here."

She hurried me along to my room, and I threw clothes and treasures into a suitcase and slid the box of roses into a backpack before returning to the front room. My parents were already outside, perched on the bench of the cart they used whenever they went into town to shop for food. A few sacks of grains sat on the back and my father pointed for me to climb up next to the sacks.

Normally, I sat on the bench with them, but the exile to the back was as pronounced as my friends' faces at the ball. I was no longer an accepted member of the pack.

BELLE Chapter 3

THE RIDE WAS LONG and uncomfortable. As the path through the thick woods narrowed to the point the cart could not pass, my father stopped. He hung his head and then glanced back at me.

"You must make your way from here on foot," he said. "I can't set foot on your grandfather's property." He looked away, as if carrying a heavy burden that I had no knowledge of.

My mother balked. "She cannot carry her luggage and the grains herself."

"You know as well as I do that I can't cross onto the estate." He glared at her. "Besides, we cannot leave the horse unguarded in these woods."

"Why not?" I looked between the two of them.

"Bad blood," he said.

It wasn't much of an explanation, but my mother seemed satisfied. She nodded slowly, her frantic gaze calming as some unspoken truth passed between them. "You can stay with the cart. I will help her."

She climbed down before my father could argue and hauled a bag of grains over her shoulder. "We will come back for the last bag," she said to me and started up the path.

I carried my suitcase and my backpack behind her, limping along, with my canine leg and human leg at odds with each other.

"Why can't Dad come up here?" I asked when we were out of earshot.

"He...witnessed...my father's death." Her words were broken, as if she searched for the right words.

"What happened to my grandfather?" The winding path brought us over a hill, and a field stretched out before us. At the far side of the field stood a massive home looming on the top of another hill. It was dark and held a spooky quality that left me cold. A winding, overgrown brick path cut through part of the field, leading to a black gate that encircled the manor.

My mother shivered in front of me at the view and then plodded along to the gate. "He was killed by the pack."

Of all the things that she could have said, what fell from her lips chilled me. No one in town had ever spoken of my grandfather. No one had ever spoken of his death.

We passed through the ominous gates, and the dark magic of this place pressed down on me with a heaviness that almost brought me to my knees.

"What happened here?" I gasped, stumbling behind her, confused by this entire ordeal.

"Nothing good," she mumbled under her breath as her head dipped and her shoulders hunched forward, as if she were plowing through a heavy burden.

"So, why are you forcing me to stay here?"

She pushed the door open and tossed the grain bag inside. Then she held the door open for me to do the same. Her hard stare met mine. "This is the only chance you have to live any sort of life. Now put your things down so you can come back and get the last grain sack."

I stared into the dark and dusty entrance and then back at my mother. "I will never be able to find anyone to love me out here." My voice shook with the despair racking my bones.

"And you will die if you stay with us." She peeled the suitcase out of my hand and tossed it inside, and then did the same with the backpack slung over my shoulder. "I am doing this to prevent you from being killed." She took my cheeks in her hands and forced herself to look in my eyes. "I love you. Despite what this looks like. This is your best chance at survival. And people do come along this way from time to time, so you may have the opportunity to find that someone who can look past this horrid deformity and see into your heart." She grimaced as she spoke. "But you have to be sure your prejudices don't follow you. Making fun of the superficial is a horrid thing to do. Remember that, and learn from your mistakes."

Hot tears choked me, and I nodded, following her back to the path where my father had turned the cart around in our absence.

"If anyone asks who you are, tell them you are a Denton," my father said and glanced at my mother.

She nodded. "That is my family name. Use it to protect yourself and us." She gave me a quick hug and then climbed up onto the cart beside my father.

"For your own good, stay on Denton property." My father nodded toward the house. "If you set foot outside of it, expect to be killed." He glanced at me with his lips pressed together and gave me a resolute nod before snapping the reins. The horses took off.

Leaving me at the side of the path, next to the bag of grains.

I maneuvered it onto my shoulder and started the long trek back to the house. When I closed the door, the cold inside pressed down on me, and I crumpled to the floor as tears continued to run hot paths down my cheeks. The skitter of nails on the floor hitched my breath, and my eyes darted from one dark corner to another. Until I finally saw the three mice that had come out of a crack in the wall. They were just as cautious and wary as I was, but at least there were living things here.

"Hi." I sniffled.

Their little ears perked up and instead of running, they came closer, their little noses twitching with interest. They exchanged a glance and then stared back at me.

"Are you real?" the middle, chunky mouse said in a high, squeaky voice.

Now I squealed and backed up, frightened by the fact the mouse had spoken. They startled as well, but didn't run away like I expected. Instead, they traded another look between the three of them.

"Welcome to the Denton mansion," they said in unison, and bowed their heads. "It has been forever and a day since we have had a visitor." They looked around at the disrepair surrounding them. "We apologize for the sorry state of the house," they added with a lilt of despair in their voices.

I blinked at the rodents. They knew my grandfather's surname and they could speak in full sentences, and they weren't frightened of my deformed physique.

"Who are you?" I whispered, afraid to scare them off.

"We used to be the servants who kept this house in order, but when our master was cursed by a dark witch, the entire estate was cursed. We turned into what you see here. And the curse did not lift when he passed away like we thought it would." The heavy-set mouse sighed.

My eyebrows rose. I had never met my grandfather. My mother told me he passed away before I was born, but after what my parents said tonight, I was starting to believe being cursed ran in my mom's family. "Why was he cursed?"

"He played with the witch's affections, with no thoughts to her feelings, and then dumped her the moment another beauty came along. You see, after his first wife died, his warmth and affection withered until he became a cruel shell of a man. Thankfully, he sent his daughter away after his wife died. He could not stand the sight of her because she reminded him of his wife. If she had stayed…" The mouse shivered. "He would have poisoned her with his bitterness."

So, mean streaks ran in the family, too. What an unsettling thought.

I ran my hand down my face with a sigh. "I am his granddaughter," I said. "And I am cursed for the same type of nastiness." Although perhaps my grandfather's heartbreak of losing his wife was more of a valid excuse than my sudden and irrational need to lash out. It was as if I had been channeling something darker, something tainted. Something as twisted as my grandfather.

Their eyes widened, and they stepped back, studying me. "A shifter stuck in mid-shift." The female mouse gasped. "Just like our master."

"Could it be the same witch?" The heavy mouse chittered and looked me up and down. The three of them nodded, as if the same magic could have claimed me. "She is young. There is hope yet." He glanced at his mates.

"Hope for what?"

"To break the curse."

I laughed and pulled out the rosebush. "I have to find someone to love me before the last petal falls. Otherwise, I will be stuck in this monstrous form."

They stared open-mouthed at the glass case and the full rosebush inside. "Follow us. Bring the rosebush." They ran into the heart of the home, doubling back to ensure I followed.

I lurched forward, carrying the box as I went.

At the end of the hallway at the far side of the dark house, the mice ran under a door, and I swung the door open a moment later. There, in the center of the room, on a pedestal, sat a box similar to mine, with a bare rosebush. The bottom of the box was littered with blackened and withered petals. I shivered and stared at my box with trepidation.

I slowly crossed, trembling from more than the chill in the air. A couple of curtains billowed inward. I slid my box of new flowers next to the one with the dead ones, and the ground seemed to tremble beneath my feet. It seemed that the witch who cursed me, also cursed him. And if history repeated itself, I was doomed to remain in this form until my last breath.

BELLE Chapter 4

IT TOOK ME A good three weeks to clean the mansion from top to bottom until the floors and walls shined with the opulence this place once held. I would not live in squalor and filth. Not when I could still function.

I dropped the mop in the bucket and stared at the grand entry in all its glory. Herman, Faith, and Chauncey stood to the side, grinning in their mouse way at what I had done.

"You have no idea how long we wanted to clean this place." Faith's beady little eyes sparkled.

"I'm not one for living in dirty quarters. My mother taught me to even wipe my paws before I entered her house." I sighed. I missed my parents, and I thought they would be proud of me at how I made this place look shiny and new inside.

The outside was still overgrown and unwieldy, but I'd have to wait until spring to make that presentable. The dark magic still pressed down all around me, but at least with the dust and dirt gone, it didn't seem as overwhelming as the first day I stepped into this deserted mansion.

The only room which I did not touch in my cleaning frenzy was the rose room. I couldn't bring myself to go in there and see how many petals had fallen to fate. Or to view my grandfather's failures so acutely present in his bare rosebush.

Instead, I washed all the rags in the sink and hung them outside the kitchen door to dry. I loaded the hearth with wood and started a fire to get the chill out of the air. Half my body was cold, and the wolf half had no issue with the winter chill layering over the home. Soon, snow would cover the ground and game would be easy to pick out. Of course, my hunting skills left something to be desired in this horrendous form. But I found a spear, along with a bow and arrow set, that, with practice, I could get good at. But for now, it was all more a matter of luck versus skill, and luck had been in my favor when I needed food.

I was sure if I got hungry enough, my mouse family would look like meals, but I'd rather starve than eat any of the mice. Not when they were my only friends.

I made another porridge from the grains my mother had left me and sat at the kitchen counter, eating without tasting. I had to re-learn eating as well due to the mix of human and canine teeth cluttering my disfigured mouth. It wasn't pretty, but it was necessary.

Once I finished and cleaned up the kitchen, I found myself in the extensive library. Now that the shelves were free of dust, the titles filling them called to me. If I couldn't live in the outside world, I would experience it through the words of the authors in these books. I took the first one from the shelf and sat on the window seat.

Movement outside the window caught my eye, and I focused on the outside of the estate, beyond the gates. A person wrapped in rags approached. They had a limp, and dark liquid trailed behind them. Whoever it was, they were injured. I closed the book and darted to the door, swinging it open as the intruder leaned against the gates.

The minute their gaze took me in, their eyes widened, and a high-pitched yelp peeled from their throat. They stumbled backward and landed on their ass. Their hood disengaged, showing off a gaunt face that had no right to judge me. He scrambled backward like a spider, forgetting about his own injury in his bid to get away from the monster in the mansion.

"I can help!" I yelled, but he turned over onto his hands, pushed himself upright, and took off at a limping run. I watched until the woods swallowed him whole.

I thought about following, but the horror and fear on his face had been enough to make me reconsider. If I went after him and he had a weapon, he would likely use it out of fear, and I didn't want to play with fire.

I closed the door and leaned against it, wondering just how I was going to find someone who remained in my company long enough to care about me, never mind fall in love.

As I headed back to my discarded book in the library, despair wrapped an icy hand around my heart.

BELLE Chapter 5

FIVE YEARS LATER.
I existed with only the woods and the mice to keep me company. Even the grand library lost its interest after I devoured every book on the shelves at least twice. Even the story of the original royal werewolves and their lost kingdom didn't hold my attention anymore. It was hard to count how many times I read that manuscript and meticulously replaced it after devouring the last word. But that story hit too close to home, with a curse that had to be broken before the royals would once again return to glory.

The rest of the books opened up worlds to me between the covers. Love and loss, battle and victory, sorrow and joy were all outlined within the pages, making me long for a life where I could be the damsel in distress instead of the monster.

With each year that passed, my hope dwindled. As did the rose petals clinging to the vines. Or so the mice told me. I still had not stepped into that room. They informed me that only two roses still bloomed, and Faith said one looked as if it could shed its petals at any moment.

Her voice had been full of the same despair that made my bones ache.

I had had no luck with the other souls that crossed paths with this mansion. Each one reacted similar to that first injured visitor so long ago, screaming or flinching or all but passing out at the sight of me. Some shot curses as to what the hell kind of monster was I, but none broke through the dark magic protecting the mansion from anyone with destructive intent.

I had more than a fleeting viewing with one man who had broken his leg when he fell from his hunting perch. He couldn't run, but he stared at me with horror and revulsion until I finished splinting his leg. I broke a branch for him to use as a crutch and helped him to his feet despite the disgusted frown on his face.

Instead of thanking me, he limped away as fast as humanly possible, without as much as a word.

After that, I only hunted near the mansion. Most nights I went hungry because the animals rarely strayed into the perimeter. I guess the black magic protections freaked them out. Which made sense. My three mice friends would have never survived if this were a haven for wild animals.

Instead of letting myself wallow in pity and self-disgust, I kept the house clean and worked on the gardens, weeding, pruning, and watering when needed. Now, when I stood at the gates and scanned the landscape in front of the mansion, a well of pride filled me. The house looked like it had in its heyday. At least Herman said so. He had been just as proud as I when I brought them out to see the improvements I had made.

Despite my drawbacks, I had learned to be a homemaker, a decent cook when there was meat to cook, and a gardener with a hell of a green thumb. I wished my mother could see this place now. I thought she would be proud of me, too.

I sat on the front step with a book, letting the sun warm my face. Leaning on the column next to me was my spear. I kept it near in case someone attacked my homestead. I normally had a bow and arrow, but today, I just didn't feel like venturing out into the real world.

The wind blew my hair back from my face, and I swore I heard snarling. I paused, lifting my nose. I concentrated on my wolf sense and what I picked up had my skin prickling. There were shifters out there, and whatever they were hunting reeked of fear.

A pack was hunting on *my* property.

I snarled. I didn't like it when other packs came near my property, even though there could be a mate among them. I usually hid when their scent came my way, especially with the last warnings my parents told me. The pack would kill me if they ever saw me.

But the fear coming from their victim had me moving. It wasn't a rabbit or a deer. It was something just as broken as me, and I couldn't let someone else die because they didn't live up to the pack's expectations. I had a healthy amount of animosity toward the pack at this point. If they were accepting of different, I would have never been exiled to this mansion and this lonely existence.

My book dropped on the step, and I grabbed the spear, moving toward the smells in the wind. I smelled blood as I approached a small clearing in the woods. Pleas of mercy came from a bloody lump on the ground, but the wolves circling him were too lost to the bloodlust of the hunt.

I slammed my spear against the tree as I stepped into the clearing. Although I wanted to make shish kebab of the pack members, I knew they would turn their anger on me.

I thought I recognized one of them, but I wasn't sure. After all, it had been five years since I dropped off the face of the earth. Five years of isolation and learning to survive with my affliction. My only hope was that they did not recognize me.

They jumped back from the man, as if he had been the one to make the noise. I was still upwind from them, but the minute my snarl voiced from my human-wolf throat, they turned in my direction. Four healthy wolf shifters bared their teeth at me and then their eyes widened, as if they beheld an angry ghost.

Fear bloomed in their gazes, not disgust, and certainly not murder.

I pointed the sharp end of the spear at them. "Leave *my property*, now."

The closest one's haunches tightened, as though he were going to launch at me.

"If you want to die, be my guest, but this is my domain." I had enough alpha blood in my family tree to exude that type of vibe. Plus, if the bastard jumped, I would spear his ass and probably die in battle with the other three.

The man's head on the ground came up a fraction, as if he sensed the mercy he had been begging for being granted. He looked in my direction, but his face never scrunched with fear or disgust. It remained a mask of pain.

"Leave!" I stepped farther into the clearing, brandishing my spear. "Or I will gut every one of you!" I put my most feral tone into the words, and they backed off, growling as they passed the figure on the ground. One even went to bite his arm. "Leave him and go," I clarified, taking another step closer.

They backed away, wary of me and the weapon in my hand. I also had my skinning knife hanging from my belt, but they didn't know I couldn't hold it and the spear at the same time. I waited until their scent barely drifted on the wind before I looked down at the injured man.

He had curled up on his side and was shaking. I crouched, laid my weapon on the ground, and touched his shoulder. He jerked.

"It's okay. I'm not going to hurt you."

He turned his head in my direction and, good lord, his face rivaled that of an angel. His blue eyes stared somewhere over my head, but the cringe I expected never came.

"Who are you?" he whispered in a shaky voice.

"Belle Denton. Who are you?"

"Adam Cannon. From Winslow."

"You're a long way from home, Adam. Why was the Averyton pack attacking you?"

He chuckled bitterly. "They don't take too kindly to any shifters that have... physical limitations." He rolled onto his hand and knees, trying to get up, but ended up putting his head onto the ground with a moan.

"What is your ailment?" He looked perfectly fit to me. Broad shoulders, trim waist, thick, powerful thighs, despite the numerous bites and gouges in his skin. He was much more normal than I was.

"I'm blind," he said softly. "Been blind since birth, but my home was overrun by a rival pack hell-bent on destroying us, and those who survived scattered."

His voice was losing strength. I needed to get him back to the mansion so I could patch him up.

Perhaps all it would take was a blind wolf to lift my curse. It was something that five years ago I would never have considered. As a matter of fact, I would have been part of the hunting party. Shame accosted me at the thought, and I handed him my spear.

"Hold this while I help you up. I need to get you out of here before they decide to bring reinforcements."

He took the weapon, and I reached down and slid my arm under his armpit, lifting him to his feet. He cried out in pain, but used the spear in his other hand to steady himself.

For a moment, I almost reconsidered helping him. It would be difficult to feed the two of us with what scraps I had left. But I pushed that thought away. Blind or not, the man needed help, and I had what was needed to dress his wounds in the mansion.

As we made our way through the woods, I caught scents on the wind. Adam stiffened next to me as well.

"There's more of them," he said, and we both picked up our pace.

I knew them leaving was too good to be true. My grandfather's lands hadn't been marked for years, and the lands they were on were on the boundaries, but it still was considered Denton property.

With the mansion in sight, I nearly picked him up and ran, but I wasn't that strong, even with all the physical workouts of upkeeping the house and garden. But I moved faster; so did he, even with his almost constant hiss of pain.

My mind drifted back to the stories of the monster in the woods that the pack hunted down years before I was born. I gasped as the truth barreled through me harder than the magical barrier. My grandfather had been torn to pieces by the pack. Whether he went there with the intention to die or not, he had been in the badlands, where the property lines blended.

I was certain it had to have happened in the same area they were attacking Adam. I even remember traveling to the forbidden woods with some of my friends on a dare. One of them told the story of the monster in the woods that scared everyone who passed by him until one day the elders of the pack slaughtered him.

I blinked at the memory. These parts were off-limits to the pack. We had been told numerous times to steer clear of this area. Most of the pack listened, but there were people like me and my friends taking dares all the time.

As we crossed the field, another truth hit. *Damn. That ghost story was about my grandfather.* I shivered.

When we hit the magical barrier, Adam choked on it, coughing up blood. I almost dropped him on the ground, but I adjusted my grip and yanked him through despite his cry of pain. Then I swung the gate closed behind us, locking it while he sputtered and coughed, covering me with splatters of blood.

"What the hell?" he whispered through the cough.

"Cursed magic." I didn't have time to say more, but I could tell by his stiffening jerk, it wasn't something he expected. Hell, no one expected cursed magic, and I imagined anyone injured would feel it more acutely. I slowed our pace. "We're coming up to the steps." I led him up the stairs and into the grand foyer, where I gently placed him on the floor and left him to retrieve my book. In the distance, I saw the pack breach the woods. I closed the door on the view and focused back on my guest bleeding on the marble entry.

He aimed the tip of the spear in my general direction, although he was off by a couple of feet. If he launched it, the stick would fly harmlessly into the door. "What type of curse?" he gasped, although his coughing and sputtering had stopped now that he was inside the house.

I let a bitter laugh escape. "I don't know. A curse. But it explains why the boys attacking you went to get reinforcements. It wasn't just to finish you off." I tossed the book onto the hall table, the sound making my guest jump.

"What was that?"

"The book I was reading when I got a whiff of the pack spilling blood on my land."

He lowered the spear and laid his head on the floor. "What's the book?" he asked, even though his breathing was thready.

"*The Adventures of Tom Sawyer*. Maybe I'll read a little to you once I get you patched up." *Assuming there's still daylight.* "I'll be right back. I need to get the medical kit." I left him before he could argue and ran down the hall with my heart in my throat.

A terrifying thought scratched at my skin. *The dark magic would keep the pack at bay, wouldn't it?*

Although that was worrisome, the injured blind man on my foyer floor was more pressing. His injuries were serious enough for me to have my doubts, and it wasn't as if I could contact a healer to help. I was on my own.

I prayed the pack wouldn't breach the dark magic and that the stranger wouldn't die on my watch.

BELLE Chapter 6

ADAM HAD FALLEN UNCONSCIOUS during my run for the mending kits, towels, and clean water. I had to tear most of his clothing off to clean and dress his wounds. He was going to have some nasty scars if he survived the blood loss.

Once he was cleaned and the floor mopped of all traces of blood, I stretched out a warm, dry blanket, dragged his clean form onto it, and then pulled it across the foyer into the living room and deposited him in front of the hearth.

I wrapped the blanket around him like he was an infant and started a fire. As soon as the flames were warm enough, I retrieved a pitcher of water, a pot, and a couple of glasses, along with the vegetables I had left. I poured water into the pot and dumped the vegetables in. A vegetable broth was the best I could do, and Adam would need something to gain strength once he woke.

If he woke.

I swept that thought away as I hung the pot over the fire and took a seat on the couch. When I brought a glass to my lips, that was when I saw the tremble in my hand. I had gone on autopilot the moment I stepped into that clearing and now the entire afternoon had me shaking. I glanced down at my clothing and closed my eyes. I was covered in blood and needed to wash it off before I ended up throwing up the water I just ingested.

I pulled the pot away from the fire. All I needed was to burn the only food in the house while I cleaned up. Then I went and filled the tub upstairs. Plunging into the cold water, I scrubbed my skin and fur clean before I stepped out and found another outfit to put on. The bloody clothing would end up in the fire because they were too soiled to have a prayer of getting the stains out.

I stopped at my grandfather's armoire and opened it. I might need to tailor some of his clothing if mine kept getting ruined. But he had shelves upon shelves of trousers and shirts. They were big enough that I thought they'd fit Adam, and I brought an outfit down for him for when he woke up.

By the time I returned, the pot was steaming. It would boil in no time once I put it back over the fire. I added more water and left it in place, checking on my unconscious guest.

His slack features warmed me more than the fire. I checked his pulse, and it was stronger than it had been earlier. I went into the hallway, retrieved my book, and settled myself on the floor between the fire and Adam, where I'd have more light.

Licking my lips, I cracked open my book and began reading Mark Twain's *Tom Sawyer* out loud, only pausing to add more logs to the fire when the flames died down.

My mice came out from the hole and lined up at Adam's feet.

"Who is this?" they asked in unison.

"Adam. The pack attacked him near our border, so I saved him and brought him here to heal." I found my place in the book again and focused on the words, resuming reading out loud.

"He didn't run when he saw you?" they asked. They were as used to the reaction to me as I was at this point.

"He's blind," I said between words and continued the story.

Their little mouths hung open, but their eyes sparkled with the possibilities. I glared at them over the book and shooed them away with my paw, seeing as my hand was holding the book open.

I had learned to do a lot of things with only one hand over the last five years. I was blissfully self-sufficient, something I did not think possible when I first set foot in this house. The only thing I lacked confidence in was the belief that anyone, blind or not, would find me attractive enough to fall in love with, and I did not want to see the hope rise in the mice eyes staring back at me, as if their curse could somehow be lifted before the last petal fell.

BELLE Chapter 7

THE FOLLOWING AFTERNOON, ADAM still remained unconscious, but at least he wasn't feverish anymore. It had been quite the night, feeding the fire continuously and re-covering him every time he had gone through night sweats, from throwing the blanket away from him to teeth-chattering shivers.

I continued to feed the fire even though the afternoon sun warmed the room through the windows.

During the night, the pack disbanded and I couldn't catch a whiff of them when I stepped out to cool off. I guess with nothing to see and no way to breach the barrier of dark magic; they decided killing us wasn't worth waiting us out.

I picked up my book again and cleared my throat, starting up on a new chapter of *Tom Sawyer*. Every other sentence, my gaze drifted to Adam's bare chest, and then I'd have to find where I left off. The stilted reading was enough to annoy me, but my unconscious guest didn't seem to mind.

It was right about the scene where Tom and his friend Huckleberry were in the cemetery that a noise sounded from below me, and I jumped. My gaze darted to Adam. He had rolled onto his side and propped his head on his folded hands.

"Don't stop," he said in a groggy, shallow voice.

"I have a pot of vegetable broth." I ignored his plea.

"Not yet. I was enjoying your reading." He looked in my general direction. "Your voice is soothing, despite the tension in the scene you're reading."

I laughed a little. *My growling, half-human, half-wolf voice was soothing? It takes all kinds.* I found where I had left off and began again, but now that I had Adam's rapt attention, it was more difficult to concentrate on the book rather than make sure he was comfortable. Although shifters healed quicker than humans, the sheer number of injuries he had sustained wasn't going to be all better overnight.

I finished the chapter, folded the corner of the page, and closed the book. "It's time to eat." I left no leeway in my decree.

And Adam didn't argue. He sat up slowly, wincing a little. The blankets fell around his waist, giving me a full view of him. His fingers inspected a few of the patches on his chest and arms.

I grabbed the empty bowl off the table near me, along with a spoon, and poured him a ladle of the vegetable broth with some vegetables. "It isn't much." I handed him the bowl. "And here's a spoon," I added after he took the bowl from my hand.

"This is more than I've had in a while." He took a spoonful, blew on it, and dipped it into his mouth as if it were the most heavenly thing he'd ever had.

"Funny, you don't look like you're starving," I mumbled at the muscle definition. But then I noticed the outline of his ribs were a little more pronounced on his sides now that he sat up.

He snorted a laugh. "I used to be quite a bit bigger. Enough so assholes like those who attacked me would think twice about it."

"Mmm. I don't think your size would have mattered." I glanced at the front window. "The Averyton pack seeks perfection. Anyone imperfect is a target." I knew that fact all too well. It was what got me in this predicament. Although, being on this side of things had me reconsidering their entire philosophy. "If I had stayed after I was cursed, I would have been ripped to shreds."

He tipped the bowl to his lips, finishing the rest before he put it down on the floor at his side.

"Do you want more?"

He pressed his lips together and felt around for the bowl. "As long as there is enough," he said, as if he were familiar with lean times.

I glanced in the pot. "Well, if we want anything for dinner, we might want to hold off." I sighed. "I haven't been hunting in a few days and that magical barrier I pulled you through kind of discourages animals within the grounds."

"I thought I smelled mice." He sniffed the air.

"We can't have the mice," I replied quickly, and his eyebrows shot up.

"A vegetarian wolf? Is that your curse?"

I laughed in my snorting way. "No. God, no. The mice are my grandfather's servants. When he was cursed, apparently, they were too, in a different manner of speaking. So, no, we will not be eating the mice inside this house. However, if I find field mice out in the woods, that is a very different situation."

His blind eyes went wide, and his mouth dropped open slowly as my words sunk in. "Are you...a mouse?" His voice squeaked as he asked the question.

Oh my, that tickled my funny bone, and I laughed like I hadn't in years. Many more years than just the five relegated to this house. "No," I managed to say, but the thought of it just dropped me into the land of insane giggles.

His lips eventually twitched into a smile, and he put the bowl out in his outstretched hand, a few feet away from where I sat. "Save this for later," he said through his own chuckle. "And I guess that really was a stupid question to ask."

"No, no, it wasn't." My laughter finally sputtered out, but not before my human face was coated with hot tears of mirth. "I have not laughed like that in years." I took his bowl from him, setting it by mine. "Thank you."

"No. It's me who should thank you." He waved at the patch jobs across his chest.

"Speaking of your injuries, I should redress your wounds. Many of those bandages are sweat soaked from your fever." I pulled open the cabinet under the table next to me where I had stowed the medical supplies the prior night and pulled out the bandages and the bowl I had used to clean his wounds. I added water from the pitcher into a bowl so that I could dip a clean cloth in to wash his wounds again.

"I should be fine," Adam said as I set things down next to him.

I snorted a laugh. "Well, I would rather not have to deal with infection, if you don't mind." I moved closer to him and reached for the first bandage, tugging at it.

His hand came up and covered mine, stopping me.

"Really. You don't need to waste your supplies on me."

I studied his face and then moved his hand away. "I have enough medical supplies to patch up an army," I said, stretching the truth. I could replace his patches maybe one more time after this and then my supplies would be exhausted.

The way his lips tilted into a smile caught me off guard, and I took a heavy breath, tugging at the dressing of the one I had started on before. The adhesive pulled at his skin, and he winced. I hesitated and wished I had two hands.

My gaze fell to his. *Duh. I've got three hands at my disposal.*

"I may need your help." I reached for his far hand, placing it on the skin near the edge of the bandage. "Keep your skin stretched a little while I try to get the bandage off, okay?"

He nodded but said nothing, steeling himself as I peeled the patch off again. This time, it came easier with his help.

"Thank you," I said after the first bandage was discarded.

His hand dropped and brushed along my wolf fur. He jolted and his eyebrows rose, but he didn't ask the questions running across his features. I waited for disgust to crawl over the surprised look, but it never came. He just waited patiently for me to continue.

I dipped the cloth into the cool water, squeezing out as much of the water that my fist would allow, and then I blotted the skin around the cut gently.

Adam closed his eyes and laid his head back against the couch. "Tell me about your curse," he whispered with a voice that echoed the grimace on his lips as I continued to clean out his wound.

This gash looked uncomfortable, but at least it didn't have red outlining the cut. It actually looked as if it were healing quite nicely. Still, I covered it once I got all the crusty blood wiped away.

"It's a vanity curse," I said. "I guess so I'd learn a valuable lesson." I huffed and tugged at the next bandage. "Although I'm not sure what the lesson is, especially since my pack wants me dead in this form."

His head popped up and his blind gaze widened.

How could eyes be so damn expressive without sight?

"Your pack?" His hand gripped my wrist, this time with a little more force than before. He pushed me away.

I nodded, and tears sprouted at the hard lines, making his face tragic and beautiful.

"Was that your pack that attacked me?" A dark tone bled into his words.

I realized he hadn't seen me nod. "Yes. That had been my pack before I was cursed."

He shifted farther away from me and ran his fingers over the clean patch. "I don't understand," he finally said. "There wasn't a single redeeming member of that pack."

"Yeah. They are militant in their ways. And if you saw me, you'd probably want me dead, too."

He let out a sharp, angry laugh. "It doesn't matter what you look like. I would never wish you harm for an ailment you are helpless against. It's inhuman."

His venom brought forth a wave of pure shame.

"If you hadn't been cursed, would you have joined them in trying to kill me?"

His question jolted me, and I slid back out of his reach. It wasn't an easy question to answer, and I mulled it over. *Would I have joined in to murder another werewolf just because they were different?*

Sure, I made fun of people who were not in the same circles that I kept, but did that equate to bloodlust?

"Well?" His face reddened at my silence.

"I don't know. Had I not been here learning to be self-sufficient with my own disabilities?" I shook my head, ran a hand down my face, and let out a loud sigh. "Had I been at home with the pack's slanted thought process poisoning my brain the last five years, I probably would have been part of the hunting crew," I finally admitted, even though it burned.

"I shouldn't be here." He started to get up, but his legs, which had taken more bites than his torso, couldn't hold his weight yet. He slumped back down to the ground.

"You can't go just yet. I think the pack has sentries watching the house. I caught wind of them when I went to get some more wood. And I wouldn't put it past them to have the perimeter patrolled, either. They don't take kindly to being bested by a monster."

His brow creased as he looked in my general direction. But I wasn't going to expand on the fact that the same pack killed my grandfather for the same ailments that afflicted me.

"Now, are you going to let me refresh the rest of your bandages?" I asked softly.

He closed his eyes and hung his head. "Fine." Although, with his tone, everything was not fine. It was as if I became his mortal enemy the moment I admitted to being one of the pack that attacked him. I guess if I were in his position, I probably would be in the same frame of mind. I all but admitted if I hadn't been cursed, I would have been a murderer.

I slid the bandages, cloth, and water closer and began removing, cleaning, and replacing all the bandages on his body. After, Adam lay on his stomach on the blanket, with his chin propped in his fists.

I threw all the soiled bandages in the fire. The flames licked at the new energy source, flaring as it greedily devoured the cloth.

"You really would have been party to that?" he asked after a long period of silence.

"I wasn't very nice," I admitted. "I have clothes for you if you'd like," I added at his scowl.

His forehead creased. "You are just full of contradictions." He pushed himself into a sitting position. "You tell me you weren't a nice person. Then you show me just what kind of person you truly are by bandaging me up and offering me clothing to replace the ones ruined by a pack you say you are a part of." He shook his head. "You make no sense."

I sighed. I knew I contradicted all that I had been raised to believe. This curse opened my eyes to the extent of poisonous thoughts I had lived with daily. The quest for perfection in the mirror overrode the pursuit of kindness.

"Would you like some clothes? They were my grandfather's, and I think they'll fit," I said, because he hadn't answered my question.

Adam nodded. "That would be nice. I'm sure it has to be a bit unsettling for you to see a near-naked man lounging on your floor."

"I would think it is more unsettling for you." I stood and retrieved my grandfather's clothes that I had brought down, and handed them to him. "Here. I hope they fit."

"I'm sure they'll be just fine." He pulled on the clothing. The trousers fit him comfortably, but the shirt was just a little too small for him to button. Although it fit the expanse of his shoulders without ripping.

I would have to let out some seams to give him the room he needed in the next pair I offered him. Assuming there would be another pair, given where our conversation had led.

"You don't want that too tight against your cuts. Leave it unbuttoned," I said as he struggled to bring the button to the hole. I can't say I was upset because it wasn't as if he sported a beer belly, like some guys in town. He was extremely easy on the eyes, and I was both relieved that he was mostly covered and a little disappointed because he was so pleasant to look at. My cheeks heated at the thought, and I mentally scolded myself for the inappropriate and shallow response.

That was something I would have thought before the curse.

He gave up. "Think you could give me a hand onto this couch? It might be a little more comfortable than the floor."

"Sure. If you don't mind being touched by a bona fide freak," I said, trying to lighten the mood.

His blind gaze traveled in my direction. "I don't mind if you don't mind."

Oh. He was so not a freak. Those words almost popped out of my mouth, but I clamped my lips tight on them and shuffled over, bending down so my human arm could sling under his shoulder.

"Ready?" I asked, mindful of his leg injuries. The one on his right thigh was still the most tender of the wounds.

"Yes." He tightened his jaw and used his right arm to gain leverage on the couch. "On three."

"One, two, three," I counted and on three, I hauled him up to the couch.

He winced and then shuffled himself back until he seemed comfortable. But a light sheen of sweat formed on his forehead and the smile he sent as a thank-you looked about as strained as they come. The couch itself wouldn't fit his outstretched body, but he could lay on his side with his knees bent.

"Marginally better," he said.

"You're welcome to stretch out on your side if it's more comfortable. There are pillows at each end that you can prop your head on."

"See, you are nicer than you think you are," he said, and this time a more natural smile appeared as he did as I offered. "I promise, I'm not usually as needy as this," he said after he situated himself. "Do you mind reading some more?"

"Not at all." And I launched into the last half of *Tom Sawyer* until the sun went down and the fire nearly sputtered out.

BELLE Chapter 8

DINNER CONSISTED OF THE rest of the soup in the pot. After I finished, I brought the pot and the bowls into the kitchen, and set about scrubbing them clean before putting them away. Then I looked at the pantry to make sure I had missed nothing. The cupboards were bare.

There was no food anywhere. No grains, no vegetables, and certainly no meat. Which meant I'd have to go out hunting. With the sentries posted near my lands. The thought of that made me shiver. They knew I existed and would attack on sight. I didn't have much for defenses either.

Damn. Was this the same choice my grandfather had to make?

I came back into the living room and curled up in my chair, staring at the fire as my nerves piped in and make my skin feel like ants, or worse, spiders, were marching over my body. I shuddered at the thought of going outside.

"Everything okay?" Adam asked.

"No." I sighed. "We just finished the last of what my garden produced, and I need to go hunting."

His brow furrowed with worry. "They are still out there, aren't they?"

I said nothing. I was sure they were there, just waiting for one of us to venture out. It was problematic. If I harmed a pack member, even in defense, they would be relentless.

"Belle?"

"Yes. They are out there. If I don't go, we will starve to death, and you need actual food to heal."

"And what happens if they attack you?" he asked calmly, but the shake in his voice outed his nerves. "I can go a day or two without food," he said, as if that settled the issue.

"And then we still have the same problem, but we'll be desperate enough not to use caution and walk right into an ambush." As much as I did not want to go out, waiting would make it that much more difficult.

He covered his face with his hand. "I feel useless."

"Injured isn't useless." Although it made it difficult. I would prefer someone out there to have my back, but he wasn't in any condition to fight off the pack if they attacked. Neither of us were. I didn't have the luxury of shifting and he couldn't put pressure on his right leg yet.

"You really have lost your grip on reality." He laughed in a way that wasn't all that flattering.

My defenses went up at his tone. "What is that supposed to mean?"

"Injured *is* useless. I can't put weight on my leg. I can't get out of your hair and take my chances out there in this condition. And I can't hunt with you." Adam waved at his leg in disgust.

"You hunt?" It spilled out before I could catch it.

"I'm blind, not incapable." His tone cooled as he turned his head toward me. "Sure, I run into a tree now and then, but what's a little concussion when you get to take down that deer?"

I blinked at him and then my lips formed into a smirk. I didn't want to laugh at the image that played in my mind. When his dimples appeared and he glanced away, I caught his attempt at humor.

"You do not run into trees." I didn't pose it as a question.

"No. Not anymore, but I did a lot as a pup. I learned to smell the difference between the open air and a tree blocking my path. And if I'm running, my pant sounds different when a tree is approaching."

I had never thought of those things. "I hope I get to see that someday."

His eyebrows arched. "You want to see me hit a tree?"

I snorted a laugh. "No, silly. I want to see you hunt someday."

He smiled at my laughter and then it faded into a serious expression that looked almost as if it had crawled into the land of longing. "I hope like hell I will get to hunt again."

I hoped so too. But it would be another few days of healing before he could try to put pressure on it without the fear of it breaking open again. I was amazed that the pack had hit nothing vital in their attack. It was as if they were toying with him for the sheer joy of basking in his fear. The thought set my teeth on edge.

"The chunk they took out of the back of your thigh is going to take time to heal. And you need protein to help with that. You're also going to need your strength for some serious physical therapy to get back to hunting shape. Everything else is superficial in comparison. And you aren't out of the woods yet for infection. That is the one that still needs the dressing changed daily."

He nodded, although he didn't look pleased. "Do you have yarrow growing in the yard?"

"Yes. In the back. Why?"

"Yarrow paste has infection-fighting properties."

"And how does one make yarrow paste?" I didn't know, and although I had been here a good amount of time on my own, I still had a lot to learn about survival.

"The leaves of the flower and a little water in a mortar and grind it into a paste with a pestle." He lifted an eyebrow at me. "Didn't you learn about healing herbs?"

"No. I was taught what was poisonous, though." Even with Herman, Faith, and Chauncey trying to educate me the best that they could on what I could and couldn't eat, they never broached the subject of healing herbs.

"At least you weren't total heathens," he teased. "Go get me some of those flowers and the tools, and I'll teach you how to make the paste. Then we'll discuss hunting again."

Just the way he said it made me think he was going to try to dissuade me from hunting for game. If I had to, I'd go out once he was asleep because the man needed real food, not just vegetable-flavored water.

BELLE Chapter 9

I VENTURED OUT TO the back of the estate with a kitchen bucket and picked what I could of the yarrow between the layers of fallen leaves. At least snow hadn't fallen yet, and it was easy to find the small white flowers that still bloomed. The ground moved ahead of me, and I instinctively pounced, dropping the bucket. For the first time in months, an animal—or reptile, in this case—crossed my property within the magical barrier.

The problem with pouncing on the tail end of a snake was that the head could still strike. I had a hiss as a warning, and I reached my hand out, catching the fangs in the meat of my palm instead of my cheek, where it had aimed. I snapped my teeth on the snake's neck, severing its head from the rest of its body before it could dislodge and slither away. There was no way I was losing this meal.

It took a second for the pain to register, and I grumbled at the head still stuck in my palm as the burn of the venom slowly spread through my hand.

"Damn it," I snarled. I picked up the bucket and the rest of the dead snake and headed inside as fast as I could. I needed the venom out, now. If I lost this hand, I would not survive.

"Adam?" I stumbled into the living room, setting the bucket and the snake on the floor near my chair as I tried not to let the rising panic cloud my mind.

He turned toward my voice, his face a mask of worry. "What's wrong?"

I stared at the snake embedded in my palm and thought of a delicate way to say that I was hurt. He might never let me leave this house at this rate, judging by the fear present in his blind eyes. "I need your help. I seem to have a snake attached to my hand."

He blinked rapidly, as if he were processing my words. "Is it poisonous?"

"It's a copperhead. A pretty good size one, too, so it will make a decent meal or two"—*or a dozen, if we're cautious*—"for us."

His shoulders relaxed. "Did you get the yarrow?"

"Yes." I still stared at the enormous head in my hand and the redness creeping across my palm as the poison spread.

"Okay, then try not to move quickly, but I need you to bring me some soap, some water, and the tools to grind the petals to make the paste, along with a couple of clean rags. If you can do all that by keeping your hand lower than your heart, that would be good. I'll clean your wound and use some of the yarrow paste on it as well."

His calm tone made my pounding heart slow a little and controlled the rising fear. "I won't lose my hand?"

Adam laughed. "No. Belle. It's not like it was a rattlesnake. If that had been the case, I wouldn't be so calm."

This time his laughter didn't trigger my defenses like his earlier cackle had. This was a genuine laugh, one full of mirth and promise, and it warmed my heart. Either that or the poison was affecting me oddly.

I trudged to the kitchen and bathroom, retrieving the items in a dry bucket and one that I filled halfway with water. I pressed the dry bucket of things against my body and carried the water in my swelling hand.

When I returned, I dumped the dry bucket in the center of the table and nested the buckets together to the side of the messy pile of stuff.

"I brought some towels, along with clean rags," I said.

Adam had moved himself into the corner near the table. A light sweat stood out on his forehead, as if the movement had taxed him more than he would ever admit. When I sat beside him, he put both hands out. I placed my hand palm facing the ceiling into his.

"The snake is still...embedded." I winced as he took hold of my hand and traced my palm with the fingers of his free hand.

"I see." He felt the outline and where the teeth still penetrated the meat of my thumb. He cocked his head. "This is a rather large snake." He gripped the sides of the snake's head and yanked upward without warning.

I hissed through my teeth as the pain of it ripping loose surpassed the discomfort of the poison in my hand.

"Soap and a wet cloth, please." He dropped the snake's head on the floor and held his hand out. I went to pull my human hand away, but he gripped it tighter. "Don't move this hand."

"I can't get the soap and a wet cloth with a wolf paw." He might as well understand my limits and my curse. "I am partially shifted. That's what the witch did to me. I don't have two hands like you."

"Fine. Where did you put everything?" His voice was clipped with impatience.

"On the table behind you."

He turned, wincing, and slowly felt along the tabletop. His hand landed on the pile of rags and towels. He pulled one from the pile and felt until he came to the bucket. He dropped the rag in.

"The soap is next to the rags. It may even be under them."

When he found the soap, he pulled the wet rag from the water, squeezed some of the water out, but it still dripped as he turned back toward me. He put the soap on his thigh and gently wiped the cloth from the center of my hand outward.

I watched in fascination as he accurately ran the cloth over the teeth marks, as though he could truly see. He traded the towel for the soap and lathered up my hand before he wiped it clean with the wet cloth. I didn't dare tell him there was still soap near my pinkie when he finished, either. He dropped the wet cloth on the floor, where it landed on the discarded snake head. Then he set the soap on the table and took a clean rag, loosely tying it around my hand.

"Now get me the stuff to make the paste and keep your hand as low as possible." His words were stern, but not harsh.

I retrieved the bucket of yarrow, the mortar, and the pestle, along with the half-full pitcher I used for our drinking and cooking water. It took me longer than normal because I was retrieving things one at a time and handing them to him. When I handed him the water pitcher, he settled that between his legs and got to work.

I sat on the couch, watching Adam pluck the delicate petals off the flowers. When he had a dozen of them in the mortar, he dipped his fingers into the pitcher and let droplets slide into the mortar. He put six drops of water in with the petals and then handed me the pitcher. I put it on the table behind me without turning away. He ground with the pestle, stopping every so often to test the mixture with his fingers.

My hand throbbed just watching him, but he fascinated me enough to almost forget about my injury.

He finally stopped grinding and set the pestle on the table behind him. "Give me your hand."

I put my hand on top of his, and he unwrapped the rag before he smeared yarrow paste all over the heel of my thumb, covering the bites on the first try.

"Did I cover the bites?"

His question brought a smile to my face. "You did. For someone who's blind, you're pretty accurate."

His lips quirked into a hint of a smile at my incredulous tone.

The bites prickled, as if my palm were a little too close to a fire. "Is it supposed to tingle?"

He nodded as he wrapped my hand a little tighter this time. "Yes. That's how you know it's working." He leaned back and handed me the mortar. "I think maybe I'm going to need some of that on my leg, sooner rather than later."

My gaze shot from my hand to his pale face. I'd been so focused on the action of his hands that I didn't catch what his movements were doing to him.

"And I think I may need to lie on the floor for this," he added.

"Let me move the things you threw down here. I'd hate for you to step on the snake by accident." I cleared the space and straightened out the blankets on the floor, giving him a little more padding this time. The rest of the snake I hung near the hearth; I'd skin and cook that as soon as I finished tending to his wound. "There. I tried to make it a little softer this time."

He slid down onto the blankets and unbuckled his pants, stripping and setting them aside as he stretched out on his stomach. I moved the pillow with my foot until he felt it and wrapped his arms around it, settling his cheek on it as he faced the warmth of the fire.

I set the mortar down and concentrated on peeling the largest bandage off the back of his leg. This gouge was the worst of them and right now, the edges were an angry red.

"Put this on the entire cut?" I stared at it. I really should clean it, but I didn't know whether that would compromise the yarrow paste on my palm or not.

"Yes. As thick as you can get it."

I scooped the paste onto my fingers and gently ran them over the length of the cut, covering the wound—along with the reddened skin at the edges—with the yarrow. He hissed between his teeth when I touched the reddest parts.

"It's a wonder they didn't hit anything vital," I marveled as I wiped my fingers on the wet cloth he had discarded. If they had hit an artery, he would have died before I got him through the front gate. "I don't think I should re-bandage it yet."

He looked in my general direction. "Is that just because you like the view?" His lips tilted in a smile.

I snorted a laugh but found my eyes moving to his round butt cheeks. The view was certainly not bad, and I had to clench my hand to stanch the sudden urge to run my fingers over his ass. "No. It's not just because I like the view." Heat filled my face. "What I mean is, I think it will heal better by getting some air rather than being bandaged."

"Mhm." He smiled and put his head down again.

Now I wanted to swat his ass. "Seriously, I think your pants rubbing against the dressing irritated it some."

His smile faded, and he lifted his head to look in my general direction. "How so?"

"It's red around the edges. None of your other injuries have taken on that angry-looking quality." It wasn't to where red veins were coming from the wound. That was the kind of infection I was afraid to discover on him, because it usually was a death sentence without the proper medicine.

"Then it's a damn good thing you have yarrow outside." He laid his cheek back on the pillow. "You might want to throw that snake head in the fire so neither one of us step on it."

I picked up the head and tossed it into the fireplace, where it landed in the crossbars of the wood and immediately ignited.

"That smells good," he mumbled.

He wasn't the only one with a watering mouth. That smelled divine, and I glanced at the rest of the snake. "Give me an hour, and I'll have a plateful of snake meat cooked up for us."

"You really shouldn't be using your hand so much." He glanced in my direction. "Seriously, you should be resting."

"Yeah, well, we both need food, and that flaming snake head is making my stomach thunder like I haven't eaten in months. Besides, we don't want the meat to go bad." It would only take a little while and my stomach rumbled, making my point painfully known.

"Fine. Just don't...just take it easy. Okay?"

I covered most of him with the throw blanket from the back of my chair, leaving his leg with the yarrow paste uncovered, and then I attended to skinning and cooking the snake.

BELLE Chapter 10

ADAM FELL INTO A restless sleep while I prepared the snake. It took me longer because of my hand, but with my wolf appendage, it was easier to gut and clean out. The guts and skin went into the fire, adding to the succulent scent filling the house.

As soon as I put the snake on the spit and placed it over the flames, I took another look at Adam's leg. The yarrow paste seemed to work. The wound wasn't as inflamed as it had been when I put the paste on. I entertained going out and getting more flowers to crush in case he needed more, but I'd probably burn the snake. Besides, exhaustion was taking its toll, making my eyelids heavy.

In the interest of our meal, I stood and tended to it instead of relaxing in my chair, where I'd likely fall asleep and ruin the only meal we were going to get until I was well enough to hunt again. My getting bitten was just par for the course, but scoring the snake had been a true stroke of luck.

Maybe my bad luck streak was finally through with me.

I had gotten used to this form and survived despite what the witch did. I never lamented over how many rose petals were left, and I wasn't sure whether that was my brain's way of buffering me from major disappointment or getting me to accept what I was. I had resigned myself to be in this form until I died.

But with Adam lying on my floor—granted, he was only here because he was injured—I dared to think of the possibilities. Maybe there was a chance for love, despite my hideous form.

I shook the thought right out of my head as Herman, Faith, and Chauncey came out of the wall, sniffing at Adam as they passed him to come near to me.

Faith pointed her little paw toward the fire. "You'll want to turn those soon," she said in her squeaky voice.

Adam's eyes opened and his head lifted. "Did you say something?" He looked in the general direction of where the mice were.

"No." I glanced at the meat. Faith was right, and I turned the spit so the snake wouldn't burn. She nodded her little mouse head at me.

His head turned toward me. "Then who just spoke?"

"Um. One of the mice." I refocused on him.

His eyebrows arched.

"You told him about us?" Herman looked every bit as annoyed as his voice conveyed.

"He wanted to eat you. So, yes. I told him about you and that we do not eat mice that are in the house." A part of me realized how insane this conversation sounded out loud. In the real world, mice didn't talk.

Adam ran a hand through his hair, leaving it in a spiked mess. "You might want to check my thigh, because I'm not sure if I'm hallucinating."

"You're not," I said at the same time as all three mice.

He cupped his chin in his fist as he settled back on the pillow with his eyebrows held low in contemplation. "Talking mice?" he finally asked and cocked his head.

"We aren't really mice. We were afflicted along with this entire manor when Belle's grandfather was cursed. And this is what became of us." Faith sighed. "There was one more of us in the beginning—Joe, the stable master. But he got stuck outside and froze to death."

"You never told me that." I stared at the mice.

"Why was her grandfather cursed?" Adam asked after a moment.

Herman cleared his throat. "After Belle's grandmother passed, Henry never recovered. He had the sense to send his only child away before he poisoned her innocence. Without her to temper him, he became truly vicious, and most of the servants fled from his wrath. One day a pretty young lady happened upon the manor. He took advantage of her and then threw her out the door after he had claimed what he wanted. Unfortunately, he violated a witch, and she cursed him the same way she cursed Belle. I wouldn't doubt that ancient thing was still walking about, pulling the wool over people's eyes. I think she did it on purpose. She sought the nastiest person in the region and then cursed them."

I made a cutting motion across my throat at the mice. I did not want them to tell Adam the rest. I didn't want him to think I had an ulterior motive for saving him.

But Adam was a smart wolf. "To what end?" he asked, his brow creased in concentration. "For a witch to curse someone, they had to have a good reason and a purpose. Otherwise, they are just as bad as those they are cursing."

He had a point and one that I wouldn't have been able to answer a week ago. At least not with the conviction I had now.

"I think she wanted to teach me a lesson. One I have learned many times over since," I replied.

"What point is that?" He glanced in my direction, but was a few feet off.

"That kindness should be our first instinct, not ridicule. Love should be our knee-jerk reaction, not hate." I took a breath and tended to our meal. "My grandfather never learned that." I tested the piece of meat, and it tasted divine.

"Here, try this." I put the other half of the piece I tested near Adam's mouth.

He opened his mouth, and I popped the piece onto his tongue. He chewed it slowly and closed his eyes. "Just as good as fresh venison." He smiled and his eyes opened.

I slid the snake off the spike, put half of the meat on one plate, and set it down in front of Adam. "I hope this is enough," I said as I moved his hand to the dish so he could eat.

I took the rest and headed toward my chair.

"Aren't you going to eat with me?" Adam patted the blanket. "An indoor picnic?"

The mice all looked at one another and scurried off, leaving me to deal with Adam's half-smile that made my knees wobble.

"Sure." I rerouted to the spot next to him on the floor.

He rolled onto his side, facing me, and moved his plate in front of him. He propped himself up on his hand and sighed. "How's your hand?" he asked as his fingers inspected the plate. The crease between his eyes deepened. "Did you take any for yourself?"

"Yes," I said through a mouthful and then swallowed it down. "It was an enormous snake, and that's half of it." My gaze moved to where the blanket just barely covered him. Rolling the way he had exposed enough of his leg and ass to make the room feel ten degrees warmer.

He nodded and, to my disappointment, moved the blanket over himself a little more. "Just making sure because there's a lot here." He dug into the first piece as if it were a finer meal than it really was. "And it is cooked to perfection," he said after he swallowed. He had the good manners not to talk with his mouth full.

I only could eat a few pieces before I pushed the plate aside. I grabbed another pillow off the couch and threw it on the ground near Adam. "I can't finish mine," I mumbled and stretched out with my back to the fire. "And I can't seem to keep my eyes open." I yawned out the words.

My eyes closed.

"Belle?" Concern laced his voice, but I was already falling into the black of night.

BELLE Chapter 11

HANDS SHOOK ME IN the dark. A chill layered over me and my teeth chattered. A voice whispered in my ear like an early spring wind before a storm, warming the chill from my bones. *Belle, you need to wake up.*

Heat wrapped around me like a vise, holding my legs straight and my arms to my side. I tried to struggle against whatever was holding me still.

"Belle, stop struggling. I am not going to hurt you," a voice barreled in my ear.

My eyes shot open to the cold fireplace. Adam had his arm wrapped around me and his uninjured leg thrown over my legs, keeping mine to the floor. He held my wrist tight enough for my hand to tingle and had my hand on the floor.

"What the hell?" I hissed.

"Just be still and take slow breaths until your head clears."

"Why?"

"Snake poison. You did too much after being bitten." His stressed voice told me more than I really wanted to know.

I slowly relaxed into him. "I'm sorry," I whispered.

His low chuckle tickled my ear, and he rested his forehead on the back of my shoulder. "You scared me." He sighed. "I wasn't sure what the hell to do when your breathing turned to labored wheezing."

My gaze landed on the fireplace again. "How long have I been delirious?" That fire had been blazing hot when we sat down to eat, and now it was reduced to ash.

"Hours."

"And you've been holding me like this that whole time?" I glanced over my shoulder at him. He raised his head from my shoulder and laid it back on the couch right behind him. At least he had chosen a place where he had back support.

"Not the entire time, but most of it when your mice friends said to keep you as still as possible until you woke." He licked his lips. "They calmed me a little. They said you were strong and would survive this, but in order to not make it worse, they insisted I hold you in a sitting position with your snake bite lower than your heart." He still held my hand lower than the rest of me.

"You think there still is poison in my hand?"

His hand relaxed around my wrist, but he didn't remove it. "Probably not, but just keep it there for now." He straightened his leg out, placing it by mine, but the movement pulled a wince.

"How are you doing?" Worry laced my voice.

"I'm doing better," he said, but he didn't sound it. Adam shook his leg and moved his toes. "My leg fell asleep."

"That is the worst," I said, as he continued to stretch and flex his bare leg. "But how is the other leg doing?" I clarified.

"It actually feels a lot better, despite not getting much rest. But I ate a lot of the snake pieces you left on your plate." He sounded as if he regretted taking my food.

I still wasn't hungry, but he had left enough to satiate me when my hunger returned.

"That's okay. You need it more than I do."

He lowered his arm that he had across my chest and rested it on my thigh. "I am going to need to get a little rest."

I started to move, and that arm slung across me.

"Don't move until I wake up. Okay?"

"But the fire." I waved my paw toward the fireplace.

"Look, until I'm certain you are okay, you are not moving. And tending to a fire is the last thing you should do right now. What part of stay still for a while did you not understand?" A little bite of irritation slipped into his voice. He took a deep breath. His fingers trailed over my chest as he moved his hand from holding onto me. When his hand ran over my wolf arm, I jerked.

"Don't," I whispered, afraid that if he touched me, he'd understand what an abomination I was.

His hand remained. "I've been holding you long enough to understand your curse," he said softly. "And it is not as horrible as you think. There is a symmetry to it that is fascinating."

I wanted to shrink in on myself.

"You are still beautiful in your own way." He reached up and stroked from my shoulders down to my fingers on my right arm and to my paw on my left. The feel of his fingertips on the underside of my paw was strange and comforting at the same time. "I've never felt anything like you."

"And how many women have you felt?" I snapped. The thought burned my skin, but I did not move.

"None. Not in the way your tone insinuates. You almost sound...jealous."

"I'm not."

"Mhm. If you say so."

I started to get up, and his arms wrapped around me again.

"Stay still."

This time he whispered it in my ear, and his breath tickled me as it flowed over my skin.

"My mother used to let me study her face in both human form and wolf form so I would know her by touch. And I did the same with my brother and sister, although they were a little less willing to sit still." His face transformed from the tilted smile to something more tragic. His lips pulled down in deep sadness. "I miss them."

Quiet settled between us.

"Where do you think they are?"

He laid his head back again. "I have no idea. My mother sent us in different directions and created a diversion for us. I don't think she made it out alive."

I squeezed his hand gently, and he put a little pressure back, but not a true squeeze, as if trying not to jostle my thumb.

He pulled free, and then he held his hands up in front of me. "I see by touch." He wiggled his fingers, trying to get the levity back into his voice, but it failed, so he just dropped his hands into my lap, lacing his own fingers together, encircling me with his arms in case I had any ideas of escaping and tending to the fire. "Being blind puts me at a disadvantage in a very visual world, but I've accepted it and chosen to live life under my terms. Just like you have."

"No. You are far more accepting than I am."

He just smiled and tilted his head up a little. "If you say so." And then his head dropped back again, and his eyes closed. "By the way, did you know you smell like strawberries and cream?"

"Really?"

"Mhm. It reminds me of one of my favorite desserts that my mother used to make."

"Huh." I leaned my head back on his shoulder, wondering whether Adam really was my shot at happiness. I didn't really care whether the curse was lifted, because he was truly special. I placed my hand over his as we drifted off.

BELLE Chapter 12

NOISE LIKE A HERD of buffalo running across a field snapped me from sleep. "Do you hear that?"

He stiffened behind me. "Think you might grab my pants?" he asked, his voice ladened with sleep. He stretched his arms above his head. "How long did we sleep?"

Darkness still shrouded the living room. "I don't know. It's either still dark out or we slept clear through an entire day."

"You slept through the entire day," Faith said from where they were huddled near us.

I reached for Adam's pants with muscles stiff from staying in the same position. If I was stiff, he had to be hurting as well. I put the fabric in his hands and stood up slowly before I stepped out of his way on legs that felt like unstable stilts.

Flame flickered in the distance, and my mouth went dry. Neither one of us were in any condition to outrun a forest fire. I hurried to the window while Adam pulled on the pants, and I blinked at the torch-carrying crowd outside the gate.

Adam stood up next to the couch with his pants on. He took a wincing step toward where I stood. If he kept going, he'd run into my chair. I went to him and took his hand and led him through the maze of furniture, glad he could walk. But a deep fear rose inside me, stronger than what the scene outside manifested.

Now that he was mobile, Adam was going to leave.

I wouldn't stop him, if that was what he truly wished.

All thoughts of Adam disappeared the minute I swung the door open. The town had come to deliver their own version of twisted justice.

My annoyance flared beyond aggravation at the pack congregated just outside the magical barrier. Their interruption of what could have turned out to be a truly tender moment, one that could have saved me, was more than unwelcome. It was downright lethal. Enough to set my teeth on edge.

Their intent was clear from the flaming weapons they carried, and I scanned the faces I had known all my life. It looked as though the entire town had showed up to end us. When my gaze fell on the people I had considered friends, my heart squeezed. But the real impact didn't hit me until my gaze passed and then snapped back to my parents in the back row. They wielded torches, too.

"Dear God," I whispered as my anger morphed into despair.

"What is it?" Adam asked from beside me. He balanced on one leg, his other still tender, but well enough to support his weight after almost twenty hours of solid sleep.

"It looks like the entire town has come to slaughter me. Including my parents."

His face hardened and a low growl came from deep within his chest. "I'm well enough to fight."

I put my hand out against his bare chest, stopping him from stepping out of the safety of the house. "This isn't your fight."

"The hell it isn't. You risked your life to save me from those bastards." His hand covered mine, and he squeezed. "You've entertained me, fed me, nursed me back to health, and made me feel like I have no limitations. I won't let you go out there alone."

"Adam." I sighed.

He threaded his hand through mine and held tight. "You can't shift. I can."

"No. They'll tear you apart."

"And they won't do that to you?"

I eyed the crowd. Their intent was clear in their stances, their rumblings, and their catcalls. *Kill the monster.*

Instead of answering his question, I said, "With everyone up front, the back is clear. You should go. Save yourself." I tried to dislodge his hand, but his grip was solid and unyielding.

"I can't do that." His voice was soft enough to pull my gaze to his sightless one.

"You have to." My chest squeezed at the thought of him getting hurt again, or worse, him dying. But he stubbornly shook his head. "Why won't you even consider it?"

He unclasped his hand and reached for my face, feeling the jagged lines of my partially formed wolf. When his fingers found my human lips, he leaned in and pressed his to them. It was gentle and sweet.

The crowd hushed at the sight and then roared their anger. A few shot flaming arrows at the house, but the magical barrier separating us from them stopped their arrows, dropping them to the ground, where their flames hissed out in the wet grass.

"Despite what they think, and even despite what you think about yourself, you have a good heart and that's what captured mine. I cannot let them slaughter you just because your outside is imperfect. Not when you are gentle and kind and perfect to me."

My heart stopped, and I stared at him, stunned. Before I could get my bearings and insist he leave, magic swirled around us. It was like being in the center of a tornado. And the witch who cursed me appeared on the walkway between us and the angry crowd. She stared at me with satisfied eyes.

Now I was doubly gobsmacked, and my mouth fell open. I quickly recovered and dropped my gaze to the ground with the humility that filled me.

"Sorceress, I am so sorry for my initial judgment of you and my unkind words." My apology came from the heart. The more I thought about how I had reacted to her, the more mortified at my behavior I had become.

The witch inclined her head, turned toward the angry crowd, and raised her arms. "Belle has more heart than I gave her credit for." Her gaze scanned the crowd. "I cursed her just as I cursed her grandfather so many years ago. And you, as a town, did not learn from either experience. You banished both of them, and if you had your way, you would have ripped her from existence, as you had done to her grandfather."

She turned to me and pointed. A bolt of power shot from her fingers, engulfing me.

I screamed as my bones transformed, reversing the shift, settling my body back into human form. The agony of it drew sweat to my skin, even with the cool air brushing me. Behind me, I heard the squeaks and moans of the mice transforming as well.

"Stop! You're hurting her!" Adam cried, his voice full of panic. He couldn't see the transformations or know this pain was temporary, like a wolf's first shift. It righted the wrongs of the past and breathed new life into me. Silently, I vowed not to let the curse of vanity into my soul ever again.

"No, boy. I am lifting my curse. She truly earned your love before the last petal fell from the cursed rosebush. Unlike her grandfather, who remained bitter and angry and sought to destroy anyone who crossed his path, she accepted what she had become. She learned to live with her disabilities, and even, dare I say, thrive with them. And in doing so, found the compassion that had been locked away in the presence of these hideous and thought-poisoning townspeople. Belle, you have restored my faith in your royal bloodline."

By the time she finished her little speech, my vision had blurred and snapped back to normal. I lifted my hands, both human, and then felt the contours of my face with a soft laugh. My gaze snapped to hers. "Royal?"

"Yes. You have the blood of the originals running through your veins. And for the first time in centuries, a royal has transformed to become worthy enough to break the curse. I thought your grandfather would be able to, but he was too lost in his grief to break through."

I blinked and my eyes widened. The leather-bound book in the library. The story I could no longer stomach. It had detailed the story of how the original werewolf bloodline had been lost to time, but that someday it would be restored when a descendant successfully broke the curse. It was the history of my bloodline.

My legs wobbled, but they held fast when her gaze shifted to Adam. I swallowed hard at the intensity of her stare. I did not want anything bad to befall him. Another bolt shot out, encapsuling him before I could protect him.

The witch said, "You see more as a blind man than most with vision. And as a reward for being truly pure of heart, I can offer you a small reprieve from the darkness. Unfortunately, it can only be while you are in your wild form."

Adam bowed back from the power swirling through him, and as soon as it faded, he shifted and glanced up at me. His eyes widened as he took my uncursed form in from head to toe. He had felt my deformities even moments ago and the way his eyes caressed me warmed my soul.

He looked out at the witch and gave her a thankful nod. Then his eyes turned toward the crowd, still holding their weapons and still glaring at us like we deserved death. A low growl sounded, announcing his displeasure.

I put my hand on his head. "They fear what they don't understand."

Both Adam and the witch looked at me with cocked eyebrows, as if I had said something so profound it gave them pause. But it was the basis for the town's nasty ways. Even my mother had fallen to the weight of fear.

Then the witch turned toward the angry crowd and pushed her hands toward them. The magic protecting this place rolled out and over them, dousing the flames, turning their weapons to dust, and bringing them to their knees. "Until you can see with your hearts and not your eyes, you will be bound in darkness. Until compassion is truly your first instinct, you cannot shift."

People wailed and felt around them for others, clinging to their neighbors in the face of the sudden absence of sight.

The only one who still stood with her eyes locked on me was my mother. Tears flowed down her cheeks.

"Go back to your homes," the witch ordered. "This land is off-limits to anyone with ill intent. And if you as a group decide to come back to wreak your revenge on Belle and her beau, the minute you step on Denton property, you will be cursed the same way Belle was. But for you, there will be no second chance."

People trembled in their forced darkness.

The witch pointed at my mother. "You were spared not because you have compassion in your heart, but to lead them out of these lands," the witch said to my mother. "You stood by while they slaughtered your father, and would have done the same today had Belle not been fortunate enough to find love in her cursed state. For that, you get to witness the consequences. And unless your heart is pure, do not set foot on this property. Otherwise, you will befall the same fate as the rest of these vile creatures."

My mother's face paled, and she slowly nodded, taking my father's hand. In silence, the crowd joined hands and started back toward the town, with my mother leading the way.

Adam shifted back to human form and reached out, brushing my hand with his. "I am sorry about your family," he said softly.

"You are sweet," I said, still watching the procession. "I'm sure I'll see them again someday." At least I hoped I would. I didn't go as far to tell them they would love him once they got to know him, because I didn't know whether they could shed their core belief in pursuing perfection.

The witch turned back toward me. "The land is warded in a similar way that this house was. No one with ill intent will pass through."

"Thank you." I nodded. "Not only for the charms, but for helping me see beyond myself."

She smiled brightly, and then she became smoke that dissipated in the wind. I turned around, looking in the foyer at three very emotional servants. Herman wore a butler's coat, and his shoes were so shiny, I could see the reflections of all three of them in the black patent leather. He was thin and tall, but there was nothing noteworthy about him, except for Faith, clinging to his arm as though she couldn't get enough of him. Her red hair flowed wildly underneath her maid's hat. She put her head on his shoulder and blew me a kiss.

Chauncey stood next to the odd pair in his cook whites. He was still marveling over his hands, as if he could not believe his curse had been lifted. Finally, his gaze rose to mine, and he did a sweeping bow.

"My lady," he said with a reverence I did not deserve.

I giggled in response, holding Adam's hand a little tighter than before. "Please continue to call me Belle. 'My lady' is so formal."

He bowed again. "Yes, my la...Belle." He caught himself halfway through and smirked. "I will go see what you have in the kitchen and make a list. I believe we need to go into the nearest town besides Averyton to stock up on food and toiletries, and clothing for you, my...Belle," he said with a broad smile.

Faith unhooked herself from Herman and crossed to me, throwing her arms around me in an unexpected hug. "Thank you," she whispered in my ear.

I hugged her back. "It wasn't my doing." I glanced at Adam.

"Oh, honey, it was you allowing yourself to be you, despite your affliction." She squeezed again and stepped back. "We must be going to help Chauncey put together that list. I imagine we will be gone a couple of days." She smiled at me and looked pointedly at Adam with an eyebrow raised in that suggestive way that made my entire face heat.

I rolled my eyes at her. "We will make do."

"I'm sure you will, my dear." She and Herman gave me a nod and headed toward the kitchen in the back of the mansion.

Adam stepped closer. "Are we alone?"

I swung the door closed and took his hands. "Yes. How's your leg feeling?"

"My leg is fine." He broke my grip and ran his hands up both arms, feeling my human form. "Would it be terrible of me to ask if I can see your wolf?" he asked just before he pulled me close and planted a kiss on my lips. This time, it was not chaste or sweet like it had been when he thought we were going into battle. This time it was hot and insistent, and I gasped in response as his arms pressed me against his chest. His tongue dipped into my mouth, twirling with mine in the most delicious way, making me forget his question.

When he pulled away, I actually whined.

"And then you can show me around this house. Especially the library and the other places you are fond of."

"Adam." I sighed at the questioning tilt of his eyebrows.

"You can also show me where you expect me to sleep." His lips curved in such a way that I couldn't deny him. He had been in this house for a little more than a week and only just got to experience the living room, and this was such a small part of the house.

"Fine," I conceded and stepped back. Nerves bit at my skin. I hadn't shifted in years and an underlying fear coated my skin with heat.

Before I could shift myself, he shifted and his sharp blue eyes stared up at me, scanning me from head to toe before he stepped closer and nudged me.

"I don't know if I can fully shift." I bit my lips, studying his blue eyes and his white, gray, and black markings of a gray wolf. He was stunning, and I ran my palm over his head, scratching lightly behind his ear. He licked my hand and then backed up, still favoring his right leg despite his declaration that he was good.

I closed my eyes and searched deep for the magic that allowed me to shift. It hid in the center of my chest, but I could see shimmers of it in my mind's eye. I grabbed hold of it and threw open the doors shutting it off from me. They flew wide, and magic flowed into every cell. The shift was faster than it had ever been. When I opened my eyes, Adam's mouth hung open a fraction and his eyes danced with deep joy as they beheld me with my calico coat of white, gold, and gray tones.

He stepped close and nudged me tenderly before he circled me, then he stopped, stepping away as he looked at our surroundings.

I shifted back to human form because I wanted to walk and turn and touch with both hands. His massive wolf head turned back to me, and his wolf smile disappeared.

"You can stay in that form while I show you around." I laughed. "I want to walk and talk and twirl and dance. And later, I want to run in the woods and hunt with you. But right now, I am a little giddy having two legs and two arms."

The smile returned, and I led him into the kitchen, interrupting the trio as I showed Adam the layout of the first floor. When we got to the last room, I stood before it and hesitated.

"This is where I kept the cursed rosebush." I pushed the door open and stepped in, crossing slowly to the cases on the table. One was my grandfather's, withered and bare, and in the other, my rosebush still had one perfect rose with all its petals. The rest were shriveled up on the bottom of the box, but the single pink rose nearly sparkled in the case.

I glanced at Adam. "This shouldn't be."

Adam looked at the flower suspended in life and then at me and shifted back to human form. Reaching for my hand, he pulled me to him. "It's the perfect representation of you, full of life and heart and resilience."

This time, when he went to kiss me, I pulled back.

His sweet smile faded.

"Don't you want to see the library?"

He shook his head and brushed his lips on my cheek, moving to discover the curve of my ear with his tongue. His hands slid over my back and down to my ass, stopping. He stepped away, his breath heavy. He licked his lips and brought his hands up to my face, running the pads of his fingers over my cheeks, my jawbone and then finally, my lips.

"I um. I'd like to see..." He swallowed and then laughed. "I'm not very good at this, am I?"

I cupped his cheek and studied his face and the sudden tic in his cheek under his eye. I stepped closer and captured a soft kiss. "Are you trying to seduce me?" I asked, humor lacing my voice.

His face turned crimson, and he went to step away, but I hooked my arms around his waist, pulling him back against me.

"I'm not saying no. I just have never been...seduced."

His tight muscles relaxed at my words, and a dazzling smile graced his face. "Yes, I'm trying in my very awkward way to...to mate with you."

"So...you'd like to see our bedroom?"

He blinked, and his mouth opened and then closed. He cocked his head. "Our?"

"Is that too presumptuous of me?" Now I was the one who was worried about my choice of words.

His answer was a kiss, and this one burned like a wildfire. His hands tore at my clothing, not waiting for the tour to continue. And I responded, ripping at his shirt as well. His hands left me to strip his shirt off and then returned to my body as they studied every patch of exposed skin there was.

He kissed his way down my neck to the curve of my breasts. His hands gently cupped me, his thumbs traveled over my nipples, and he let out a low groan as they hardened with his touch.

"I thought you were beautiful before," he whispered and then took my nipple in his mouth, sucking gently.

His touch set me on fire, and I whispered his name like a prayer. He lowered to his knees in front of me, trailing kisses from my chest to the pants I had on. He tilted his head up, as if questioning me with his fingers paused on the clasp.

The gentleman in him did not wish to presume, but the outline in his pants told me he wanted me just as badly as I wanted him.

I reached for his fingers and helped him undo my pants. "I'm yours, if you'll have me," I whispered, afraid he might choose a different option, even with his desire on display.

He paused and put his head to my stomach, lowering my pants, inch by inch, as if he were questioning his desires. I stepped out of the trousers, and he tossed them away. When his hands returned to my legs, they had a shake in them.

I threaded my hands through his hair and then slowly dropped to my knees in front of him. The cold marble offset the heat radiating from me. I kissed him and pulled him on top of me as I stretched out on the floor.

Another searing kiss followed, and then his mouth and hands traveled down my body. He paused and gently caressed my core. "I can't see your reactions, so you need to tell me if I'm doing something you don't like."

"I will."

He lowered his mouth between my legs, testing me with his tongue until he found the spot that made me gasp. He grinned and continued to coax me with his mouth and his fingers until my satisfaction dripped and my core wanted more of him. All of him.

Adam kicked his pants off and crawled over me, lining himself up with his hand before he pressed into me slowly. He closed his eyes and tilted his head back, looking every bit as sexy as I had imagined during those dark days.

"Belle," he breathed softly as he thrust deep inside, tearing through what was left of my innocence.

A brief blaze of pain registered and then only pleasure as he draped himself over me and found my lips, kissing me as slowly as his hips moved. His languid motion soon sped up, matching the pace of his tongue. He pulled from my mouth, arching into me as he straightened his arms, giving in to the passion. I moved with him, crying out his name as my hands dug into his shoulders. We both peaked at the same moment with a cry that seemed to shake the foundation underneath us.

The roots of the rosebush crashed through the table and into the ground, shattering marble as it took root in the soil beneath, growing and blooming as though it, too, was free of the curse. It devoured my grandfather's box, the table, and nearly overtook the center of the room, flourishing like the fable had said. When the curse lifted, a beautiful rose garden would take root, wiping out the centuries of royal failures.

I stared at it as my chest heaved and tendrils of pleasure still echoed in my form.

Adam lay his head on my shoulder. "Damn, the earth moved," he whispered.

I burst out laughing. "The rosebush took root," I said, since he couldn't see. "But yes, you rocked my world, too."

He grinned sheepishly up at me. "I'm glad you saved me."

I caressed his lips with my fingers, and he kissed them. "We saved each other. Now, let's go finish the house tour, and then I want to see you hunt."

His grin was infectious as he helped me to my feet. I handed him his clothing and put on what was left of mine. I had to rip the shirt out of the growing rosebush and put on the torn fabric, considering the staff were still in the house.

As we stepped out of the rose room, Faith came running toward us.

"Are you two okay?" she asked, focusing on my ripped shirt.

I opened the door wide, and her gaze fell on the rosebush growing in the center of the room.

Her head snapped to me, and her eyebrows arched. "Well then," she replied and smiled, as if all was right with the world now. She bowed and scurried away, leaving us to mull her reaction together.

"I'm not sure I want to hunt tonight." Adam took my hand and sucked on a couple of my fingers. "How about you?"

My mind went fuzzy as I stared at his incorrigible grin. His unseeing eyes sparkled with mischief that I'd always dreamed of.

"I guess hunting can wait," I replied and led him by the hand to the grand bedroom, where I hadn't slept since the day I found him. The bed looked inviting, and I kicked the door closed behind us.

His lips toyed with a smile. "Did you bring me to the library?"

"Nope." I pulled him to the bed and pushed him back onto the soft mattress. "And it is my turn to discover all that you are."

He snorted a laugh and climbed backward into the center of the bed. "You've had a full view of my wares since day one."

I crawled onto the bed on top of him. "True, but I only looked. I didn't touch. Especially not the way I intend to touch you tonight."

Adam clasped his hands behind his head. "By all means, explore to your heart's content."

And I explored Adam until he was panting with need and then made sweet love to him, giving him a glimpse of the promise that lay ahead of us for the rest of our lives.

THE END

Pirate. Villain. Gentleman?

The first time I set eyes on the scruffy rogue Elijah Hook, I wasn't sure what kind of man he truly was. But when he fought to set me free from the gilded cage the lost boys kept me in, I knew he was worthy of my attention.

When those boys found out I was smitten with the good captain, they spread the most heinous of lies. Stories so offending that the people of San Juan went on the hunt for him, intending to take him straight to the gallows.

Now, I have a choice—save Captain Hook and live at the mercy of the lost boys in Neverland for the rest of my days, or watch them kill my true love.

HOOK Chapter 1

I'VE BEEN IN CAPTIVITY for decades. Tormented and used by a bunch of entitled brats who never want to grow up. They abuse my magical abilities to keep themselves young, and to defy gravity and fly every chance they get. In my natural form in this realm, I'm slight in size, maybe four inches tall at best, and I can fit into a gentleman's hand. However, the children who hold me, and my magic, hostage are *not* gentlemen by any means.

It's a heavy burden on my magic. One that nearly drains me. It's a wonder I have survived this long, but if they keep at it, I won't see many more sunrises.

"Lilly, make me fly," Peter insists as he stands outside the cage holding me hostage. His blond hair stands in spikes, and his dark eyes look as crazed as ever.

I swear the magic keeping him under ten years old all these years has made him even more batshit crazy than he was before. They drove me too hard last night, and I just have nothing more in my magical reserves.

"I can't. I need rest."

He picks up the cage and shakes it, throwing me from side to side like a rag doll in a chariot. His prepubescent face scrunches in anger.

"Do you wish to kill me?" I yell as I tumble into the bars hard enough to leave a bruise.

The shaking stops, but his glare is more focused. "Maybe I'll pluck your wings," he snarls.

"Go ahead. Then my magic will surely be gone." I climb to my feet and dust myself off.

Peter is far worse than most of the others. He's their leader, and I guess he feels he has to show his dominance by beating up the poor, innocent fae locked in this golden birdcage.

It's ludicrous. But that's been my life since my sister ran off with another fae, leaving me to fend for myself. That lasted only a few weeks before Peter trapped me, and I've been at the boys' mercy ever since.

Unfortunately for me, not one of them has a merciful bone in their bodies.

He slams my cage on the table, dropping me to the floor with the force. I don't look up until his angry ranting fades, and I am now alone in the room. I sigh as the flood of relief makes my muscles weak. If I hadn't already been sitting on the ground, I would have fallen into a puddle of shaking flesh.

Peter and the lost boys used my magic to fly all over the island earlier, looking for a hidden treasure that doesn't exist. It's their game, one that takes all my concentration and drains me for at least a day. Then they wanted to go in search of a famous pirate who is said to have docked near one of the outer islands.

They will have to wait another day because I don't have it in me to keep them above sea level for the trek out to the desolate island. Even now, as they talk in the far room, their schemes of taking over the boat and sailing the seven seas pillaging and slaughtering entire islands, sickens me.

The pirate they speak of is renowned for both his generosity and his cunning. Even I have heard of Captain Hook. The mighty pirate who owns the high seas and rules them with an iron fist. Those who cross him disappear into the wind.

If that is true and Peter and his derelicts want to start a fight with such a man, who am I to stop them?

HOOK Chapter 2

SUN BLINDS ME AS I'm stirred awake by motion. I don't know whether it's dawn or dusk, and it takes me a moment to acclimate. The blinding sunset masks the scenery, but I think I know where Peter is headed, especially running at this speed. His favorite place to launch into flight from. The cliffs with a drop of close to one hundred feet right onto the deadliest crop of rocks I've ever seen. And I have seen them up close enough to know.

"You better wake up and get that magic flowing," he says and keeps on running.

This is par for the course. No gentle waking and stretching and a moment to tap into my power. No, this is a panic pulse every time, and it's no wonder I am exhausted afterwards. None of them would survive that fall, and I doubt I would either. The jagged rocks below would break my cage as surely as they would break all their bones. Although, I have dreamed about their cries of excitement turning to fear before the wet sound of flesh meets rock at terminal velocity.

I toss all those thoughts away and weave my magic to enable the boys to defy gravity. They swoop down in swan dives with Peter in the lead and my cage extended out in his hand. I would hit first if my magic ever failed, and the little shit always comes close to nailing the jagged rocks with my cage. At the very last second, though, he, corrects his trajectory to skim over the water by mere inches before flowing back up out of reach of the sea predators.

I just concentrate on keeping them airborne while I hope he will not tax me. It's an empty hope because Peter always pushes me beyond my limit. The distance to where they are heading will likely deplete me of every ounce of my fae magic.

He heads straight toward the outer islands. Toward where they were told Captain Hook and his famous pirate ship are moored. I am sure Peter's pet crocodile uses this area as one of his hunting grounds. Somehow, that monster knows when Peter is on the hunt, and I won't be surprised to see his ugly, scarred back surface near the ship.

My grip on the tether hanging from the center of the canopy tightens at the thought of that ugly beast. That little piece of leather is the only thing keeping me from being squashed against the bars from the whipping wind.

The isle of caverns is farther out over the sea than zipping around Neverland looking for treasure. It takes all my concentration to keep the dozen boys airborne. We loop around it once, twice, and it isn't until the third pass that Peter sees a pirate's pennant almost hidden by one of the large rock formations in the sea surrounding the island.

Shadows on the deck give the impression of people, but as we get closer, there is only one man standing at the helm looking out over the waters with his back to us. The rest seem to be below. Their laughing banter filters out windows into the growing darkness.

"Lock everyone below," Peter says as we approach the man's blind side.

The wind blows at us, sending his voice back towards the island. If it had been a land breeze, Peter's words would have warned the pirate.

With the last of my magic, I spell the ship, locking the doors and stairwells leading to the deck, keeping those already below deck in place until Peter says so.

Our landing is a little rougher than usual, since I'm almost tapped out. Twelve feet slam to the deck, and the pirate turns our way. Even in the low light of dusk, his striking eyes capture my breath. I have no more energy, no more magic to keep the boys on the air currents, and I collapse onto the floor of my cage, but I cannot remove my gaze from the pirate. His unkept, shoulder-length hair is as dark as the night itself blows on the breeze, and his firm jaw is lined with a few days' worth of stubble, but not a full beard like I expected.

His lips turn down at the intrusion.

"Hook, I presume," Peter says and makes a hand signal to his little posse.

The boys fan out, searching for others while Peter pulls out his sword, aiming it at the captain.

The captain's gaze flicks from the sword to my cage and then comes to rest on Peter. He gives a single nod.

Peter lifts the cage. "Relieve the captain of his life."

It's the first time in all the years I've been at Peter's mercy that he has ordered me to kill. He's had me disarm his victims before, but not kill. That, he reserves for himself and his merry band or to the town officials for those that stand in his way.

It is against everything I am. Even if I had the magic to strip the captain of his life force, I wouldn't. Besides, something about the captain stirs a deep longing inside me I've never experienced before. I barely lift my head and deny his request with a slow shake.

Captain Hook's eyes narrow as he stares at the cage in Peter's hand. Then they grow decidedly dark as they slash to Peter. He draws his sword from the scabbard but holds it loosely at his side as his gaze moves to keep track of the others.

The boys gather around Peter in a protective stance. I will give them one thing. They are loyal to Peter to a fault. Schafer, his second-in-command and equal in his depravity, steps closer, his pudginess clearing space as he goes.

"All clear," he says, but Peter doesn't appear to be listening.

Peter glares at me and shakes the cage to get a reaction. I look away from the captain, and my chest feels like my heart's been ripped out and stomped on. I meet Peter's angry eyes and just stare at him, sapped of every ounce of energy, enough so I can't even lift my head.

"I suggest you let the lady go," Captain Hook says with a voice meant for the Gods. It has a musical timbre to it that makes my already helpless muscles even weaker.

My cage rattles as Peter stalks toward the captain. "What did you say?" he growls like an insolent child.

"I said let the lady go before you kill her." Captain Hook stands with his sword out, but not in a battle stance. At least not yet.

Peter rattles my cage. "Strike him down!" he commands.

I don't have enough energy to make the boy rise off the ground right now, and he expects me to kill a man? He is truly insane. I barely lift my head.

Captain Hook brings his sword up, pointing it at Peter. "I will only say this once more, and then I will run my sword through you. Let. Her. Go."

Peter is too occupied with shaking my cage to hear the threat. "If you don't do something, I will feed *you* to the crocodile," he screams at me. His rage fills the air like the stench of rotting seaweed.

The other lost boys have their swords pointing at the threat in front of them. The infamous pirate Captain Hook stands before them, not showing an ounce of fear. After all, these boys look like children, but he should be afraid, and I find myself wanting to warn him.

Unfortunately, I am so depleted of power that my body feels hollow and weak. Even so, the captain's gaze locks on mine, and his eyes radiate a fury so lethal that I swallow hard, thanking the Gods it isn't aimed at me.

Captain Hook steps forward.

The lost boys crowd around Peter with their swords pointing at the captain as well, protecting their leader.

"Useless fairy," Peter growls and tosses the cage.

It flips end over end beyond the edge of the boat they are trying to steal from the captain. My last ounce of power was used to lock the crew below deck, and the doors below rattle against their attempts to escape.

The dark water swirls with danger. When we took possession of the boat, Peter's crocodile, the biggest in the region, surfaced, looking for its next meal.

Peter usually delivers when he goes on the attack, and the crocodile is one fat mother because of Peter's brutality. But this time, it's not a bushel of pirates trying to capitalize on Neverland being thrown in as bait. This time, it's me flying through the air in a cage that will sink to the bottom, and I'm helplessly locked inside. I don't know how long it will take, but I'm facing death by drowning.

"What have you done?" Captain Hook's voice follows me as my cage splashes down sideways on the ocean's surface.

The clash of metal reaches my ears before the water does, and my last wish is for the captain to end Peter.

The force of the water pins me, so all I can do is watch as the cage drops under. The crocodile is there with his open smile. He races toward the cage, and my eyes bug out at the sight. My entire form trembles with fear as his mouth opens and teeth like daggers approach.

I'm not sure which death will be more pleasant. Drowning or being shish-kebabbed by those teeth. I just want it to be quick.

But that doesn't seem to be in the cards either.

The metal of the cage sticks in the crocodile's teeth. He whips his head back and forth, trying to either crush or dislodge the cage. It's only a matter of time before the metal gives under the pressure. It's already creaking. Either that, or the water rushing in and out of my ears is messing with my hearing.

A splash nearby snaps the crocodile's head in that direction.

My lungs strain for me to take a breath, and I almost give in, but then the vision of the captain swimming toward me and leaving a trail of blood behind him makes me hold on. I don't know why. His blood will surely bring other predators, ones that are bigger and badder than the old crocodile trying to kill me.

Captain Hook's gaze finds mine, and he swims harder, reaching us as the crocodile swings around to face him. He grabs the cage and flips himself on top of the beast. He then grips the gator's lower jaw, prying it open as he leverages the cage to pull its top jaw up.

He yells in the water at the strain. Bubbles blow out of his mouth, and then, suddenly, the cage springs loose, peeling a crocodile tooth out that lands next to me.

The captain's yell becomes higher pitched, one of pain versus exertion. He slams the cage against the crocodile's head, stunning both the beast and me with the motion. He launches toward shore, using the cage to claw through the water. I grab a bar and hold on, gasping for air anytime I surface.

We reach an outcrop of rock, and he climbs up, setting the cage beside him. The water behind us still has a trail of red, and I'm sure the crocodile will leap up and end us at any second. I think Captain Hook is thinking the same thing because he rips off his belt, affixes it to just above his bleeding wrist, and yanks it tight. Then he hops onto his feet and grabs the cage, jumping from rock to rock until he reaches the shore.

My heart drops at what I can see of his injury. If he doesn't get medical attention quick, he's likely to bleed out. Where his sword hand used to be is just a bloody stump. He lost his hand to the crocodile.

Captain Hook doesn't stop running at the shoreline or the edge of the jungle. He jogs until he stumbles into a small clearing and collapses onto his back with my cage centered on his chest. He holds his injured arm over his eyes as he breathes heavily below me.

If the lost boys pursue him, I don't think he has the strength to outrun them. I glance back toward shore. There are enough men aboard the captain's ship to keep their sadistic tendencies company for quite some time.

I cough water out of my lungs as I assess my own damages. Beyond a few hefty bruises from hitting the sides of the cage, I am not that bad off.

"Thank you," I whisper through my wheezing.

He just nods, but doesn't speak.

I get into a kneeling position and place my hands on the bottom of the cage. It's the closest connection to this rogue savior that I have. I close my eyes and concentrate, pulling out the last drips of magic in my reservoir. I push it out, commanding it to heal the captain.

He hisses through his teeth and uncovers his eyes to look at me. "I'll be fine. Conserve your energy," he whispers.

I've never had someone refuse my healing magic before. I pull my hands away, doing as he asks. His blue-eyed stare compels me in a way I can't explain. It heats me and energizes me. Water drips from his dark hair, and grains of sand slide off the ends back to the ground. He reaches up and pulls on the lock holding the door closed as if his hand can just crush it and free me.

But this metal is forged with dark magic. It cannot be so easily broken.

His head drops back down, and a heavy sigh leaves his body before he moves the cage to the ground beside him. Then the man reaches across his body into his far pants pocket. His face pinches in concentration. Then he frees a folded knife out from the depths of his pants. That little sticker isn't enough to fight off anything, but still, he slips it between his teeth and pulls the blade open.

With a determined set of his jaw, he slowly sits up. His face pales as he lowers his injured arm, and he closes his eyes, breathing long and slow, fighting whatever demons grip him. Color soon returns to his cheeks, but it's blotchy enough for my worry to flare.

When he puts his injured arm on the cage to steady it, I ask, "What are you doing?"

"Trying to get you out of this damn cage," he says through clenched teeth.

He jams the blade of the knife between the lock and the door. The flat blade slides in with a little effort, and then he turns it so the business end of the blade faces outward, putting pressure on the lock. The snap of metal fills the space.

My heart soars for a moment and then falls just as hard to the floor of the cage. The hilt of his knife still in his grip has a jagged and broken edge. He stares at it in disbelief.

"Damn it," he mutters, and then jams the broken blade into the same space where the rest of the knife is still stuck.

The short stub seems more resilient. His muscles flex, nearly ripping his wet shirt.

Another snap echoes, and I expect to see the hilt of his knife in pieces. Instead, Captain Hook flicks open the door and offers me his hand to climb onto.

"You are free to go." His voice sounds as drained as he looks.

His palm is warm as he moves me out from within the cage, but it has been too long since I truly took flight that my wings can't even hold my weight right now. They flutter behind me, useless.

I drop to my knee in his palm and lower my head in respect.

"I'm not a god to be revered, fae." His voice rings out over the clearing, and his eyes narrow in admonishment. "I'm just a man and certainly not one to be honored in such a way." He glances at his handless arm and lifts it for me to see. "A one-handed man at that."

"You have earned my loyalty by saving my life, Captain."

He scoffs and attempts to stand. He gets one knee under him and teeters, losing his balance. Instead of catching himself with his only hand which I occupy, he falls over on his shoulder with a wince of pain.

His cheeks redden as his gaze slices to mine. "Maybe a little healing might not be a bad idea."

"You think?" I ask with my brows raised.

I offer a smile and place my hands on his palm, concentrating. Not only has his hand been decapitated, but his thigh has a nasty slice, probably made by one of the lost boys as he jumped ship. Both wounds need addressing, so the man doesn't bleed out on me. With everything I have left, I push out my healing power, dividing it between the two injuries.

He winces, but remains still.

When the last stitch of magic inside me flows from me to him, I collapse in his palm, breathing as heavily as he is. I can't even lift my head.

"Sweet fae, did you not save anything for yourself?" he whispers as he climbs to his feet, successfully this time.

I just smile up at him. "You deserve it."

His laugh rings out like a musical symphony. "Oh, my sweet, sweet pixie. I most certainly do not deserve to be saved."

That laugh. I could ride on it forever. It's the sweetest melody I have ever heard. My smile remains on my lips, and I close my eyes.

His sigh brushes over me. After a moment, he slips me into his shirt pocket as gently as a mother tending to her child. I snuggle into the wet fabric warmed by his body heat.

Leaning into him, I can hear his strong heartbeat. It soothes me, allowing my magic to regenerate. The lull of his steps, along with the steady beat of his heart, lures me into a deep slumber. One that is blissfully absent of the nightmares that usually haunt my sleep.

HOOK Chapter 3

I WAKE WITH A start in a hot, cramped space and the illusion of moving. I take a minute to get my senses in order, and to figure out just where the hell I am.

Oh yeah. Hook's pocket. I lean my ear to the inner wall of fabric encasing me, and there it is. His strong heartbeat, but I also hear his labored breathing.

Did you know it is not easy climbing fabric?

Even if I stand, I still can't reach the top to pull myself up to see over the edge of his pocket. And Captain Hook is most definitely moving. I push my back to his chest and use my legs to climb up like one would do if they were climbing up in a tight crevice. However, while my legs move up, my back doesn't, and I'm soon folded like a pretzel. I walk my feet back down to the bottom of the pocket and resign myself to being captive.

His stride slows, and the top of the pocket pulls out. "Ah, you're awake," Captain Hook says with a sexy tilt of his lips.

I should not be noticing things like that. I'm ancient compared to him. Even so, I guess being in the presence of boys has left my mind in the gutter when I am introduced to a man like Captain Hook.

"Yes. And if you please, I'd like to get out of your pocket now."

He stretches his finger into the pocket, and I grab on. With slow movements, he pulls me out and then props me on his shoulder.

"Hang on, little lady," he says and then jogs.

"My name is Lilly," I say as I grip his shirt in my fists.

After a few jarring bounces, I sync to his rhythm. His hair occasionally tickles me, but now that I'm not bucking around like some novice rider, I can study his profile a little closer. His cheeks hold the scruff of a few days without shaving; it's not a full beard like the rumors of him announce. The only thing they got right was his raven-colored hair. Oh, and his piercing blue eyes that can either freeze you in your spot or make your knees knock. What those rumors don't explain is that Captain Elijah Hook is so very swoon worthy.

I look forward quickly because just staring at his profile is making my body pliant enough to fall off his shoulder if I'm not careful.

I blink at the break in the trees and the shore beyond. "Where are you going?"

"I need to find that damn crocodile."

"But what if the boys are out there?" Fear coats my voice. I do not want to be caged again.

The captain slows his gait and glances at me. "No harm will come to you, Lilly."

I let out a high-pitched laugh. "You do not know Peter Pan. He will pluck my wings out of spite."

"My boat is no longer anchored on this side of the island." He points to the rocky outcrops and beyond at the sea.

No boats are visible, but that doesn't mean Peter can't be hiding.

"We didn't see your pirate's mast until we were almost upon you. They could easily hide behind those outcrops." I point at the rock towers shooting from the ocean like God's pillars.

"I still need to find that croc."

"Why risk your life?"

"Because that watch it stole is special, and I need it back." He presses his lips together as he studies the horizon. "Besides, I also need to find my damn sword, which is at the bottom of the ocean." He waves his good hand at the water. "I'm useless to you without it."

I close my eyes and let my magic flow through me. When I open my eyes, a watch materializes on his wrist, and an ornate sword similar to the one he had appears in his hand.

He raises an eyebrow. "The watch is…very nice." He lowers his weapon and takes a moment to study his new watch. "Extremely nice," he says with a voice that carries admiration. "And the sword is almost an exact replica, which saves me from having to search the ocean floor." He glances at me and sighs. "I do not mean to seem ungrateful, because I am so very grateful that you would waste your magic on me, but I still need to find that beast and get the watch it swallowed when it bit off my hand."

I roll my eyes at him. "A gift from a lost love?" It's the only thing I can think of to treasure.

His light laugh strikes a chord in me. I could listen to that for eternity.

"No. There is no lost love. No fair maiden waiting for me to come save her." He glances at me with humor crinkling his eyes. "It's just something I need." He doesn't explain further and keeps walking toward the waterline.

As he approaches the ocean lapping the shore, he scans the water, looking for signs of crocodiles, but there's nothing but a smooth surface, as if the mighty ocean is a calm lake.

He sighs. "Any chance you can wish that thing here so I can kill and gut it?"

I balk at him. "I'm not bringing that monster here, so it can do more harm."

Captain Hook twirls the sword around in his hand. "I am just as good with my left hand as I was with my right."

"No." I cannot let that beast near us. The captain doesn't know the thing is infused with magic, so it will attack anyone who has ill intent towards Peter. And I will say that Captain Hook has a potent reason to have ill intent towards that hellish child.

"Okay. Then I guess I'm swimming." He takes me off his shoulder and puts me on the rock before kicking off his boots. Then he unbuttons his shirt with one hand while I gawk at him.

I cannot believe he is going to go looking for trouble.

Then his pants drop.

And I'm the one suddenly in trouble. I am helpless to avoid looking at the hard lines of his muscles. He is exquisitely cut. A life as a sailor requires hearty souls, and he certainly qualifies with his hard abs, wide shoulders, and tapered waist. As he walks to the water, the muscles in his fine ass mock me with their perfection.

He glances over his shoulder as if he can feel my eyes scanning his heavenly form. The smile he flashes nearly has me swooning. But then he dives under the water, disappearing from view. My heart falls at my feet, and it's replaced by the heat of sheer panic.

I flutter my wings, muttering under my breath at the lack of strength in them. They don't even lift me up a fraction of an inch. Flying to where bubbles are surfacing will not work. I glance around me. I'm just as exposed here to predators as he is out in the ocean.

Captain Hook's head pops up out of the water before he stands. His hair drips as he surveys the area, and then he turns and trudges back to shore with a look of utter disgust on his face. He throws the sword on the ground and then pulls on his pants, muttering about not being able to swim and hold the sword at the same time.

He takes a seat next to me and pulls his boots on, but he doesn't put his shirt on, and I can't say I'm disappointed. His defeat stains the air, and he leans his arms on his knees and drops his head into the crook of his elbow.

"Captain?"

He turns his head toward me. "Please call me Elijah."

I lick my lips and try out his name. "Elijah." It feels like silk across my tongue, and a foreign heat grips me. It's as if the captain's warded with some sort of fae elixir.

A smile temporarily replaces his frustration. "I wish you were human-sized and not so tiny. Then I wouldn't be so concerned about leaving you on the beach alone."

Something shuffles behind us. Elijah grabs me and his shirt in one swipe of his hand and launches towards the tree line. He slides behind a bush and tries not to make another sound. He puts me on a branch in front of him and slips on his shirt before collecting me in his hand again.

We peek between the branches as the noise becomes loud enough to warrant the six figures that break out of the jungle on the far side of the beach.

Peter and a couple of the boys step out onto the shore on the other side, along with a half dozen authorities from the mainland. He points out toward the water and then back near where we are hiding.

My gaze falls to the sand and the captain's sword sitting there along with the boot prints leading right to where we are. That's not good. At least they are far enough away to not be able to make them out yet. I need to make both the sword and his footprints disappear.

Closing my eyes, I conjure up a gale-force wind to whip sand from our side of the beach towards the group trudging towards the water. It's strong enough to wipe away the captain's footprints, and with a little extra push, I make the sword disappear and reappear nested into the scabbard on his waist.

Captain Hook glances down at the sudden weight on his hip. His eyebrows rise, and then he glances at me with a nod of thanks. He retrieves me from the branch and slides me into his shirt pocket. Then he is moving once again, but even to my fae ears, it's as silent as a human can possibly be, almost as if he's a ghost floating over the land.

He keeps going until his feet are sloshing.

"Hold your breath, Lilly," he says in a whisper.

And then a moment later, we submerge. I'm plastered to the bottom of his shirt pocket as he moves through the water. Just when I think I can't hold my breath any longer, he takes a great inhalation of air and pulls himself out of the water.

I sputter into the wet fabric as I try to sit up. His hand reaches into the pocket and scoops me out into the damp air. Darkness surrounds us.

"Where are we?"

"In a cave I found when the tide was out. It's not accessible when it's high tide like right now." He shifted on the rock. "I also don't know if there are predators in here."

I wave my hand in an arc, sending fairy lights across the expanse. The cave lights up, and on the far side from where the captain is perched is a dry patch of beach that seems big enough for the captain to stretch out.

"You seem to have recovered your magic." He places me on his shoulder and slides into the water, and then he cuts through the water slowly, almost leisurely.

"It's easy when I'm not using it to keep a group of old men looking as if they are children and making them fly on a daily basis." I give him a push toward shore in the form of a wave just to show him what I am capable of.

When he climbs ashore, he takes his boots off and dumps out the water, and then he sets them aside to dry. He puts me on the sand, takes his shirt off, and hangs it on a nearby rock. He glances around at the shore, studying the sand.

"What are you doing?"

He smiles. "Making sure there are no crocodile markings."

I look around as the heat of fear wraps around me.

"It's clear. This cave doesn't allow for sunbathing, so we have that going for us." He takes a seat on the cool sand next to me. "Thank you for the lights, but you may want to dim them. They might reflect on the other side of the cave."

I pull back some of the magic, lowering the light enough to still see, but not enough to create a glow through the water. "How long was I out?"

He lets out a laugh. "I've been exploring this little patch of land for two days."

I stare at him, my eyes widening. "Two days?"

He nods. "I found a freshwater spring and some mango trees yesterday and had my fill. I checked on you from time to time, and you snore like a sailor." He grins at me. "I didn't figure on anyone coming looking for me. Certainly not that brat."

"Peter doesn't like to leave loose ends." I wrap my arms around myself and shudder, frowning at the thought.

The captain grunts and then stretches out next to me on his back. When he glances my way with those alluring blue eyes, my breath seems to suck from my lungs.

"I still wish you were human-sized like you were in the land of fae," he mutters under his breath.

I blink, and then my eyes widen at him. "You've been to the land of the fae?"

Humans are not allowed in our realm unless they've done something terrible and are brought in to stand trial, or have laid their life on the line for a fae and are being celebrated for their bravery.

Elijah Hook transported to our realm? I bet he saved someone important.

"Yes, I have been to the fae realm."

His tone catches me off guard. It screams criminal versus hero, and my jaw drops.

"I was young, poor, and incredibly foolish. I'm still trying to right those wrongs." He smiles at me and shrugs.

"You were bad?" It shouldn't surprise me the way this news does. After all, he's an infamous pirate, and the rumors of Captain Hook's escapades are spread far and wide. But after spending a small amount of time with him, I cannot see him being a criminal.

"I was naughty." The way his eyes sparkle and his lips tilt into a grin melts my insides.

I only remember a handful of humans paraded through our palace, but it was so long ago that none of them could possibly be the good captain. Besides, I would remember a man like him if he graced the halls of our palace while I was there.

"Were you ever naughty as a child?" he asks with a teasing tone, turning to prop his head on his good hand.

I sigh and meet his gaze. "I ran away from home with my sister."

If that didn't scream naughty, I don't know what would.

His smile fades. "Why did you run away?"

With his full interest focused on me, I find it hard to articulate the reasons I left a life as a princess to explore the realms.

"Because I wanted to discover the magic of the different realms, and my father said both my sister and I were too young for such foolishness." Oh, how I wish I had heeded his warnings. "Once we got to this realm, it was clear we were at a disadvantage being so small. If we had stayed in the forest where the ley lines were, I think we would have been fine, but we wanted to explore more of this beautiful landscape."

"So, you saw the world."

I nod. "I was as bored in that little location as I had been at home, and my sister had found her heart. They didn't want to seek adventure like I did." I chew my bottom lip and shrug. "I wasn't worldly enough to understand just how evil a child who never wanted to grow old could be." I glance at my fidgeting hands. "My adventure ended as abruptly as it began the day Peter trapped me in that cage." I wave at my wings. "I haven't flown in decades. These things don't work right now."

"Well, we'll have to work on that."

I chuckle. "My muscles are so atrophied, I'm not sure I'll ever fly again."

"Come on. It'll be an adventure." His laugh rings out in the cave, echoing against the walls. His voice is full of mirth as he gives me a side-eye.

His laugh is infectious, and I smile at him as my blood warms into a hot mess. I want an adventure with this man, and he wants to see me in a comparable package to his. Who am I to deny him?

I close my eyes, willing my form into human size as opposed to the miniscule fae package that I'm locked into here. Magic swirls around me as I concentrate. It's not as easy to do as I imagined. I haven't had magic in reserve for years, but the two-day rest gives me a reservoir to tap.

My bones and muscle stretch, snapping through the fabric covering me. The sand shifts next to me, almost ruining my focus. When everything settles into place, my eyes open.

The captain gawks at me, blinking like I'm not really in front of him. His gaze rakes over my entire form like a caress. His pupils dilate and his cheeks flush, and then he seems to regain his faculties. He reaches down for his shirt and offers the garment to me.

I stare at the fabric hooked on his index finger, but I ignore it the minute my gaze meets his. Heat fills me, pooling low in my belly at the raw want in his eyes. I step closer.

He makes a noise in his throat, something between a growl and a groan, and then he licks his lips. "I suggest you put on my shirt before I again do something very, very stupid." His voice is gruff, and his eyes plea with me to do as he asks before we cross a line that is forbidden.

I attempt to swing the shirt over my back, but my wings prevent me from putting the shirt on like a normal human.

His lips tilt into a devilish smile, and his eyes glint with mischievous intent as he watches me. After a couple futile attempts and his snort of a laugh, I hand him back the fabric while my body thrums with the same electricity that fills the surrounding air.

"If I didn't know better, I would think you were purposely teasing me." His gaze slowly lowers and then rises back to mine. "But I know fae have no sense of modesty."

He steps forward and holds the shirt to my chest, and the instant his knuckles scrape my skin, my body reacts in the most delicious way. I place my hand on top of his, stopping his movement. I do not want to hide my form from him. Warmth pools inside me when his gaze jumps to mine. I step closer, and his hand trembles.

"Lilly," he says in a soft warning.

I cannot help it. Something about him draws me closer. I want to taste his soft lips.

"Elijah," I answer, ignoring the warning in his voice.

His hand drops the shirt and moves to cup my cheek. "You are still innocent," he whispers, as if convincing himself more than me. But he pulls me closer, wrapping his handless arm around my back, drawing me in.

"And you *are* an adventure."

His lips twitch into a smile, and then a soft and silky laugh escapes him. "Oh, sweet pixie. I have dreamed of you all my life."

Before I can speak, his lips descend on mine. His hand threads through my short locks, holding my head in place as his tongue swipes across my lips.

His kiss weakens my knees, and I gasp at the sensations traveling through my form as his tongue tangles with mine in a sensual dance. The contours of his body mold to me as if we are meant to be.

I sigh with bliss.

Captain Hook pulls away from me as if I am fire incarnate, and he stumbles, falling on his butt on the sand. "I'm sorry," he whispers, as if he committed the worst sin in the universe. "I shouldn't have kissed you." His words rush from his mouth as his gaze finds mine, begging for forgiveness.

I step back, struck by his panic. Blinking, I stutter, "D-did it not please you?"

He goes to wipe his face with his sand-covered hand and stops. He snaps his hand to get the grains off, and then he wipes the remaining sand off on his pants before he meets my gaze. "It's not that it didn't please me." His cheeks redden. "It pleased me to the core. But it is forbidden."

I slowly lower to my knees on the sand. He is right. Fae law prohibits humans and fairies from having relationships. It's the fastest way to be exiled from the fae realm. But I have been gone so long, it's as if I am already exiled.

I look up at Elijah and scoff at the old ways. Desire floods my mind and my judgement. With that kiss, Elijah Hook blew through a door I thought had been locked forever. Need wraps around me like a python, squeezing reason right out of my head.

"But we are not within the fae realm." I tilt my head, allowing a smile to form. "And here in the human realm, those rules don't apply," I purr, and crawl toward him.

"Lilly, you don't understand." He puts his hand out to stop me.

Suddenly, I'm unsure that he feels the same energy between us.

I pause as a horrifying thought fills me. "Do you not want me?"

The way his gaze melts moves me forward. I don't wait for him to deny what his eyes reflect and what sizzles in the air between us.

"Lilly," he groans as I crawl over his lap and wrap my legs around his waist, but he doesn't stop me when I press my lips to his, resuming the sweetness of his mouth mingling with mine.

Our tongues dance in a languid ballet. My wings flutter behind me, stretching as his kiss sends heat all the way to my toes. My toes and wings curl in response.

Elijah groans and grabs my shoulder, pushing me back. His breath heaves like mine. "Stop before I can't." His eyes flash wildly as he focuses on mine.

"What if I don't want to?" I pout.

I enjoy kissing Elijah. It brings such heat to my insides, and it feeds my powers like a dozen nights of deep sleep.

His gaze narrows. "Have you ever been with a man?"

The way he asks is layered with something dangerous, like an adventure I will never recover from. I shiver at the edge in his tone and shake my head.

He moves me closer until I can feel a hard shaft between us. I wiggle against him, and he grips my hip, stilling me.

"If you continue, I will shatter your innocence, and damn my soul forever." He removes his hand from my hip and lightly traces my lips with his fingers. "And as much as a part of me wants to do just that, it would not only shatter your innocence, but shatter your honor as well, and I cannot do that. No matter what *I* want."

His voice is husky and low, filled with a need so deep it must hurt as much as it hurts me. His finger lingers on my lips, and then he meets my gaze with the barest of smiles.

"I don't understand." I search his eyes for answers, but all I see is his desires.

"Someday you will thank me for being a gentleman." He leans forward and captures a chaste kiss before shuffling back a little.

I don't make it easy for him to disengage. Not with my pride hurting so much by his denial.

"You are more than beautiful, Lilly, and I would be a lucky man to capture your heart.

But I will not ruin you, despite my desiring you in every way." He climbs to his feet and puts distance between us. "If..."

He seems unwilling to finish his sentence. He takes a running start and dives into the water, and then he surfaces in the middle of the cavern's pool. He treads water for a few minutes before he makes his way back to shore.

I snap back into my normal form and find solace under his crumpled shirt so I can hide my tears as the despair of his rejection settles in my bones.

HOOK Chapter 4

WE WAIT IN AWKWARD silence. Neither one of us is willing to breach the chasm that is wedged between us. Elijah rests with his eyes closed, but he's not sleeping and neither am I. Tension fills the cavern, and my lights blink in and out as my magical connection rises and falls with my emotions.

When the tide reaches its lowest point, Elijah puts his shirt on and offers me his hand. The silence that has befallen us is thicker than the knots in my stomach. So, his offer to take me with him is surprising.

I stare at the offered palm and then glance up at him. "Why do you want me with you?"

"I am not leaving you to be captured by that little brat again. Come on. It's time to find that crocodile." Even with the conviction in his words, his eyes still hold hesitation as if I might be poison to him. "Besides, we still have to get you flying with those wings so you can get back to that ley line and your home realm." He tilts his lips into a smile.

I ignore his attempt at levity and focus on the more pressing issue. "The crocodile is likely wherever your ship and Peter are."

"Then it's time to get my ship back and free my crew."

My stomach sinks. His crew is likely at the bottom of the ocean or in the creature's stomach. Peter never leaves his captives alive. I step into the captain's palm, and he brings me to eye height.

"What is it?" He searches my gaze.

"Peter isn't one to let those he captures live. Especially when he wants your boat."

He pales as he looks at the opening of the cave and then walks with purpose. He sets me on his shoulder next to his tight jaw, and just before I remove the fairy lights, I see a sheen in his eyes that wets his lashes. But then the lights go out, and I lose sight of his hidden sorrow.

When we step out into the fading daylight, his eyes are filled with resolve. Instead of heading toward the beach, he climbs up the hill to the highest point on the island. I remain quiet as we crest the rocky top above the tree line.

The captain scans the water in the light of the rising moon. He turns in a slow circle, surveying the island and the waters beyond. On the south side, the island of San Juan sits in the distance, and over the chain of islands flowing all the way out to where we stand, a crescent moon poises over the water.

"I need to get back to the mainland." He sighs as we study the scenery. "And I'm not sure I can swim that distance with my sword." He touches the sword I gave him at his left hip, caressing the handle as if it has become his most prized possession.

I laugh because swimming in these predator-infested waters is a lunatic thought. "The water is unsafe."

"I have to try, but I will have to leave the sword and my boots behind. They'll only weigh me down."

He's contemplating a swim in an environment where he is not the apex predator. Elijah is one man as opposed to almost a dozen boys. It should be easier, and I still have the tingle of magical reserves inside me.

"I can bring you."

He plucks me off his shoulder and brings me to eye level as he shakes his head. "I don't think so. I do not wish to tire you to the point of collapse like you were after you flew those boys to my boat."

"You won't tax me to the point of no return like they routinely did."

"Are you telling me that doing a trip like that will not tire you out?" His eyebrow cocks, and his skepticism bleeds through.

I glance at the distance, annoyed at his lack of faith in me. "It will tire me out, but not to the point of collapse. I trust you will let me rest afterwards." I cross my arms and purse my lips.

IIc graccs mc with a soft smilc. "I can swim it."

He starts down the southern slope of the mountain into the trees, but they end abruptly to a sheer-faced cliff that drops off at what looks like a hundred feet or better. If it had been fully dark, Captain Hook may have stepped off the cliff before realizing the dark gap before him was a drop.

"Damn." He sighs and gives me a side-eye.

I gather fists full of his shirt and smile at him. "Step off."

"Not with you on my shoulder. You could easily get thrown off by the wind, and then we'd both fall to our deaths." He takes me from his shoulder and places me in his pocket, but he makes sure the fabric is wrapped around my front and beneath my armpits and my arms are outside of the edge. "You'll have a better grip this way."

I clamp down with my elbows, making the fit tighter. While my feet dangle, I can brace them against his chest if I need to.

Elijah tucks his shirt into his pants and glances down at me. "I'm trusting you to set me down on the ground safely."

He takes a deep breath and steps off the cliff.

Gravity nearly sucks me out of the shirt pocket, and my heart jumps into my throat. If I had been on his shoulder, I would have lost my grip and tumbled with him to the forest floor.

Elijah's hand covers me, holding me in place. After the initial shock of falling, magic swirls around us in the same panicked way it did when Peter jumped off the cliff to fly. I slow our descent and then, just as we reach the treetops, I propel us forward. Even though the captain just wanted to be lowered to the ground, I am not allowing him to swim those channels between islands.

"Lilly, what are you doing?" he asks.

His hand remains over me, making sure I can't slip out. It's gentle yet firm, and for the first time in a very long time, I feel safe.

"We are flying, Captain." I swoop us lower and over the water on the outside line of the islands.

If Peter is keeping watch, going the direct route would put us in view of his spyglass.

"I can see that, my little sprite. But I thought I told you just to bring me to the land below the cliff." His breath falls over me in a warm stream.

"You did. But I thought you might enjoy this experience."

"Ah. Another adventure of yours." This time, his voice sounds lighter, but he doesn't quite agree that he is enjoying himself.

I glance up and catch a dazzling smile as the captain looks out over the ocean as if this is the most natural thing in the world. We dip down lower, and I jerk my gaze forward, readjusting our height. I do not want to be within reach of a shark or crocodile in the dark waters below.

"If this is tiring you, I can swim," he says.

The joy he tries to hide from me is worth tiring me out. I fly us higher in the air, taking him on a merry ride of ups and downs and banks and swirls until he finally, blissfully laughs. It's a full laugh that takes years off his face, making him look familiar in a haunting way.

I refocus my concentration away from the captain and his captivating smile. If I don't, we'll end up hitting the water, and that would kill the adventure in a wet blink.

By the third island, my energy levels fall lower than I expect. It's not like the captain weighs more than a dozen boys, but perhaps it's because I used my magic to light the cave and to grow to human size for a while. I didn't take a nap after I returned to normal; instead, I stewed on the captain's rebuff of my advance.

I can't fault him. Especially since he's trying to preserve my honor, and from my sister's experiences, I understand just how important a woman's honor is. But rejection still burns.

I force out the magic needed to make it to the mainland, and when we finally reach a remote beach as far away from Neverland as possible, I drop us down in the sand. The landing isn't smooth. The captain takes a couple of abrupt steps and somersaults, and then he jumps up on his feet as if he is trained in bobbled landings.

My body drains of energy, and I slide into his pocket, exhausted.

Captain Hook scoops me out of his pocket, and his sigh ruffles my hair. "This is why I did not want you to waste your magic on me. Those dark circles are back under your eyes, and you need rest." He glances around and then looks at me. "You rest while I try to find out information about my ship."

"It's either moored at the town dock or at Neverland." I struggle to push out the words as I lie in his palm.

"And where are we in relation to the town dock?" He raises an eyebrow at me.

I frown and look away.

"You do not need to protect me from those boys."

I roll my eyes at him. "As if you received that leg wound on your own."

He chuckles and turns a different shade of red than I've ever seen him. "Actually..." He winces. "Not my finest moment, but I was in a hurry to get to you. So, technically, it was self-inflicted, and the very reason I dropped the damned sword."

His suaveness drops a peg or two in my head, but that only endears him to me more. I smile up at him.

"If I had stayed aboard my ship, my crew would be alive, and Peter and his band of terrorists would be fish bait. But I would have lost you."

The melancholy in his voice squeezes my heart, but he underestimates the lost boys. I cannot let him walk into a bloodbath without warning him of their prowess.

"They are vicious things and talented with swords. I think you are not seeing them for what they are. Men trapped in boys' bodies with decades of fighting experience."

He gives me a knowing smile. "I've bested twenty very skilled men who set out to kill me." He nods to his right arm. "And all I received was a minor scratch on my shoulder. I am very adept at sword fighting, my dear. With or without my right hand." He wiggles the fingers of the hand holding me.

"But you cannot defend from both sides anymore."

He lifts his arm, staring at the space where his hand once was. "Well, then, I shall weaponize this arm to even out the odds." He gives me a cheeky grin. "Now, if you would be so kind as to point me in the right direction, I can settle you into my pocket so you can get some rest."

I don't want to direct him, but I have no choice. I point to our right and allow him to get me settled in his pocket before he sets out on his way to get his ship back.

The lull of his steps pulls me into an exhausted stupor, but I'm wired enough not to fall into the black of sleep. I'm somewhere in between when a clamor of many people talking brings me around.

The scent of spirits and drunkenness filters through the captain's pocket, and his motion ceases. A chair scrapes against wood, and then his weight shifts.

"What can I get you?" a harsh voice snaps from the space in front of us.

"Information." The captain's voice has an edge to it I haven't heard before. It carries enough danger to make me quiver.

"Information costs."

The captain moves his arm, and a moment later, something jingles onto the counter.

Did he just bargain the watch I gave him for information?

"That should be more than enough."

The rattle of metal being picked up follows. "Hmm. What is it you want to know?"

"I'm looking for my ship. The *Joli Rouge*."

"And who might you be?" the voice asked, seemingly closer than before.

"The captain of said ship." There is a smile in the captain's voice, but it still has that edge that hints if this person isn't careful, the captain will end up cutting him.

"Why aren't ya' on it, then?"

A thump on the counter makes me jump.

"I had a bit of an accident with a crocodile when I went for a swim, and I seemed to have lost sight of the boat."

A whistle follows, but no words come. Instead, a plunk of weighted glass on wood rings out. "It's on the house, Captain." Glass slides across the bar. "And I believe I heard a new ship was moored in town."

His voice carries a smile, but he doesn't tell the captain anything we don't already know.

"Thank you," Elijah says and then takes a swig of the offered spirits.

He drains the glass in one long pull. Then he slams the glass down on the bar and wipes his mouth with his shirt sleeve, still staring at the bartender. I have enough of a view to see the captain's face go slack.

"You son of a..."

That's all he gets out before his eyes roll back in his head and he collapses forward onto the bar, pinning me in place against his chest.

I use the last of my magic to push him to his side and give me some breathing room. Otherwise, his weight will crush me.

Someone lifts the captain's body and moves him to a room where no noise from the bar penetrates.

"You'll bring me a pretty penny, Captain." The bartender snickers, and chains rattle. Before the door closes, he tells someone to go get the authorities, and then all sound subsides.

My magic is tapped out. I need at least a day's rest to rejuvenate, and I curse my need to show off for Elijah. If I just let him swim, I wouldn't be this useless waif hidden in his pocket.

An hour later, the creak of a door filters around me, and the noise from the bar follows.

"You've done well."

I freeze at that voice and shake against the captain's unconscious form. Peter has found me, and I am helpless against his wrath.

HOOK Chapter 5

A SMALL HAND SLIDES into the pocket and encloses around me. The burn of the iron ring makes me gasp, and then I am free from the pocket and staring into the angry eyes of the leader of the lost boys: Peter Pan.

Two burly men stand behind Peter wearing officer uniforms. Peter has a dagger pressed to the captain's chest, and he gives me such a dark look that my mouth dries in fear.

"You don't have to speak. I'm sure it's been an awful experience being the captain's captive," Peter says to me.

His eyes are full of malice, and the warning is clear. If I deny what he says, whether or not the authorities are here, he will kill the captain.

I nod helplessly as the stench of my burning flesh surrounds me. The little shit wore that ring with the purpose of hurting me.

Peter steps away from Elijah, pocketing the knife before turning to the authorities. "Take him away."

The men each take one of the captain's arms and lift his unconscious form from the chair. His legs have mean-looking shackles that rattle as they drag him away.

The door closes, and now it's just Peter and me.

"Please don't hurt him," I beg.

His eyes narrow. "It's not up to me. He'll be tried for his crimes."

"He has done nothing!" But as soon as the words fall from my lips, I know it doesn't matter. Peter has spun his lies once again.

"Oh, is that so?" He stares me down. "According to some very reliable sources, the captain abused a lot of boys in the most heinous of ways and then stole their fae to keep as his own captive. He's killed, maimed, murdered, all in the name of piracy." Peter grins. "Your good captain should be sentenced before the sun sets."

My chest squeezes hard enough for me to choke. He must see my pain because he laughs.

"Please, I'll do anything if you set him free." My desperation bleeds through with every word.

His laugh fades, and he stares at me, rubbing his jaw as my words sink in. "Anything?"

I nod. I know what they do with criminals in this land. They hang until they are no longer alive or are flayed to death at a post for the entire community to watch. Peter has sent too many people to their deaths with his lies, and he glories in the brutality of the punishments. I swear, if he had a choice, he would be the one swinging the whip. I don't want to see Elijah killed for saving me.

Peter reaches into a bag on the floor by the door and pulls out another cage. This one is smaller and has chains hanging from the top and on the floor. "Promise me you will always serve the lost boys." He caresses my wings in a way that makes my stomach roll.

"Only if you promise to set Elijah free."

His eyebrow rises, and he seems to consider my request. Just when I think he is going to ignore my plea, he nods. "He will be set free if you agree to my terms."

I slowly nod.

He clucks his tongue. "Say the words."

"As long as you set Elijah free, I will serve the lost boys until the day the Gods come and take me away," I say, binding myself to this sniveling man-child.

He sets the cage on the table and dumps me next to it. "Enter, and put the chains on."

I balk at him even though I know damn well I have no choice. My reserves are tapped, and with his damn iron ring, he's stunned my magic enough so I cannot reach it to save myself from this savage.

"Then I guess it's death for the good captain." He crosses his arms.

I growl and march into the cage, and then I clasp my feet first and a single arm. "There. Are you satisfied?" I snap.

He reaches in and clasps my other wrist before he closes the door on me with a smile. "Fully."

"Now follow through on your promise."

"Just as soon as I have you tucked away in Neverland. It would be quicker if you made me fly."

My eyes water. "I don't have enough magic right now." My chin trembles as tears tumble down my cheeks in hot paths, dripping onto the cage's floor where they sizzle. I gasp at the iron coin on the floor. "And you have iron in here. You know iron saps my magic."

He grins evilly. "So, we are walking." He strolls out of the door and out a back hallway into the morning light.

If I had caught some sleep, I may have been able to make him fly part of the way, but now it will take hours while the captain's fate is left to chance.

⊷ ❥ ⊶

THE SUN IS LOW on the horizon as Peter waltzes into the Neverland manor. My heart runs on overdrive as my muscles cramp from being in this position. At least I can fan my wings, working on strengthening those muscles.

His crew lounges in the great room, but the minute he crosses toward the kitchen, they are up and following with interest. They don't look like prepubescent brats any longer. Now they look more like they are hitting puberty. Schafer looks as if he may have the beginnings of fine hairs growing on his upper lip. Bo seems to have shot up almost as tall as Peter, and his dark complexion is now riddled with pimples. Quinn looks uncomfortable in his too-small clothing. The others behind them look like they suffer from the same type of peculiarities.

When Peter places me on the kitchen table, I get a good look at him, bathed in sunlight. He's transitioned to a young teenager as well. His eyes darken as they take me in.

Before anyone can speak, he holds up his hand. Quiet reigns over the room.

He points at me. "You need to reverse whatever this is." He waves at himself.

I bite my lip and stare at him before I open and close my mouth. My magic has not regenerated yet.

"I need a night of rest before I have the magic to do that." I stare him down. "But you need to follow through on your end of the bargain."

I raise an eyebrow. I'm not using any magic for him and these brats until Elijah is free.

"What bargain?" Schafer demands.

Peter spins around to face them, turning his back on me. "We need to head to town to ensure they set the captain free."

"What?" Bo and Quinn say at the same time.

The shock on their faces makes me shift my weight, especially when Peter raises his hand, demanding their attention.

"I promised Lilly," he says. "And in return, she bound herself to me until her last breath."

His smugness rubs me wrong, as do the grins that form on the boys' faces as they look at Peter and then turn their leers on me.

"Let's go set the good captain free," Peter says and heads toward the door.

The clan parts, letting him lead, and then falls into place behind Peter.

I stare after them as uneasiness layers over me. Alone, I question my judgement and wonder if I've just made another colossal mistake.

<hr>

DARKNESS SWALLOWS ME AS I wait for the boys to return. The chains keep me from resting, and no matter how hard I try to break free, all it does is chafe my wrists and ankles. The longer they are gone, the more my chest feels like it's being squeezed in a vise.

The door opens, and lanterns lead the way through to the kitchen where I wait. The boys head into the great room and throw themselves onto the couches, laughing at their prowess. But they aren't talking loud enough for me to pick up their conversation.

Peter crosses to the kitchen. "The captain is free."

He brings me to the window and points to a shadow crossing the harbor, heading to the open waters of the Caribbean. It's too dark to see the mast and Elijah's colors, but the size of the boat seems right.

I sag with relief and give Peter a nod.

His wicked gaze turns to me. "Now reverse our age back to what it was a few days ago."

I huff at his demand. "I need rest."

"We gave you some time to rest." His eyes narrow. "Are you going back on your bargain?"

"No, Peter. I need sleep, and I can't very well sleep chained like this." I rattle the binds holding me in place. "Unchain me so I can lie down."

He lets out a harsh laugh. "Not while he's still within reach." He nods toward the window as he brings me back to the table. "You better figure out a way to gather enough power to reverse this, or you'll be in that room with us tomorrow evening and every evening until you turn the clock back." He points to the great room as a knock on the door sounds. "Power up while we let off some of these crazy teenage hormones."

He sets me back down, but before he closes the kitchen door, I glimpse a couple of prostitutes entering the great room. The boys snicker at them before Peter sends me a knowing smile. He shuts the door, but the carnal noises that filter through are enough to leave me dreading the morning.

HOOK Chapter 6

PETER YANKS THE CAGE forward, jerking me as he walks. "Rise and shine, fae!"

The cuffs binding me tugs on my wrists and ankles, bringing me to a painful waking state. I'm surprised I finally fell asleep in this position, but apparently, I did. Even with the blanket covering the cage, the sunshine seeps through as he walks, swinging me by his side. The damned iron coin is still glued to the bottom of the cage, sapping my strength.

My brain isn't all that fast this morning as everything that happened yesterday seeps slowly back. I agreed to Peter's terms, and he made good on his promise, binding me to him until my very last breath. A part of me withers and dies at the thought that Elijah set sail without me. But his freedom is worth every ounce of pain I shall endure for the rest of my life serving Peter.

The blanket keeping me blind rips away, and my heart drops at the sight of the executioner standing on a platform with his mighty blade. The rest of the platform is empty, save for the square stump bloodied by prior beheadings.

A crowd gathers around us as Peter takes the spot right in front of the stump.

My stomach cramps. The platform will not be empty for long. Peter holds my cage up so I have a clear view, which weakens my knees.

He's never brought me to a public execution. He has always left me to see the damage from a distance, afraid that I might intervene and ruin his fun. The way the boys gush over the gruesomeness of it always makes me physically ill.

Today is different. Peter has me here for a reason. Dread creeps in like a wet fog, and I quake under the weight of it. My mind is not allowing the truth to sink in. But it's shoved right at me the moment the doors to the right of the platform open.

Everything inside of me grows cold. Elijah Hook is paraded out onto the stage half naked, with his arms bound behind him in such a way to hold them in place even without his hand. His lip bleeds, and the bruises on his face and torso look fresh enough for me to understand exactly what happened when the boys came to town last night.

Peter brings my cage up, even with his face. "Like my work?" He smiles. "We were given some time with your friend last night."

I cannot take my eyes away from Elijah. I cannot breathe. But I say, "You lied."

The kicker is I should have known better.

"Maybe now you will understand the price for crossing me."

I turn to him and narrow my eyes. Anger blooms in my chest, spiraling through me like a tornado, wiping out an entire village. Tricking the fae comes at a hefty price, and iron or not, he will soon know the depths of my wrath.

"Besides, technically, he will be free. Just not the type of free you were expecting."

Hatred flares, mixing with the already dangerous fury building in my slight form. I let it grow unchecked.

The guards force Elijah to his knees and push his head down on the stump.

A small man who reminds me of an underhanded tax man with a top hat steps out from behind the guards and lifts a scroll. "For your crimes against the children of Neverland." He waves toward the lost boys and then reads from the scroll again. "And for those crimes committed on the high seas, Captain Elijah Hook, we sentence you to death by beheading."

"What crimes?" a gruff voice shouts from the back, and Elijah searches the crowd for the source.

"Heinous crimes," the little balding man says with a frown, but he doesn't expand on them. He looks at Peter as if looking for confirmation, though.

Elijah's gaze finds me in front of the crowd and locks on mine. His lips press into a thin line as he glares at Peter and then returns his gaze to me. His anger is replaced with a sadness so deep it fuels my rage. Iron or no iron, my magic will not be contained by this imp reveling in the captain's pain.

The executioner steps up to the stump and raises the blade. It glimmers in the sunlight. I close my eyes and wish to be human size again. The binds holding my wrists and ankles tear like they are made of paper, and my body snaps into adult size in a blink, annihilating the cage with a bang that diverts everyone's attention to me.

The whistle of the blade cutting the air stops.

Hushed whispers follow. I stand naked in the town square with my wings fluttering with the wrath I can hardly contain. Magic blasts outward, claiming all that I have given to these terrorists over the years.

The blade lingering over the captain's throat evaporates like it's made of smoke, and so do the binds holding Elijah in place.

"Elijah Hook has done no harm to these villains!" I wave towards Peter and the rest of the lost boys gathered behind him. "They have terrorized for decades and shifted the blame to others. They have caged me, demanding that I keep them young. Well, that ends today. I will not be a victim of their cruelty any longer, and I will not allow Captain Hook to be murdered for their sins."

I spin on Peter and point my finger at him, feeling vindicated as my magic flows back into my form, filling me with even more power. The bastard and his friends age from young teenagers to old men in a manner of seconds.

"Peter Pan is the one whose head should be on that chopping block. Not Elijah Hook. Peter has been the one who has stolen from all of you." My voice echoes over the silent crowd. "He is the trickster who has terrorized Neverland for as long as you can remember."

My wings spread, and the crowd moves back.

Peter growls at me, but I am no longer afraid. Not with decades of power funneling back to its source. It's almost too much magic, but I breathe it in as if it is my life's blood.

Peter steps closer and brings his right fist back, and then he launches it towards my face. Before I can bring my arm up to deflect his punch, a hand darts into my view, stopping Peter's fist from connecting. I look to my side and see Elijah with Peter's fist in his, his face contorted with a deadly fury. He shoves with all his strength.

Peter stumbles backwards and trips over his own aged feet. He lands with an exhale of air and swivels his glare back on us.

"You will not lay a finger on her. You understand?" The growl in Elijah's voice echoes over the crowd as the lost boys surround us.

"She stole my youth!" Peter points at me, and then his eyes widen. He yells, "No!"

A swish of air behind me captures my attention, and then pain explodes in my back, sending me to my knees. The magic-charged air surrounding me crackles as both of my wings fall to the ground.

"I stopped her from aging us anymore!" Schafer shouts in triumph and raises his bloody sword.

"You stupid idiot!" Peter snarls as he climbs to his feet. "Now we can't make her keep us young!"

His admission creates a rumble of gasps in the crowd.

Elijah kicks Schafer in the stomach, sailing him into the platform. His sword flies free from his hand and embeds into the side of the stump like some invisible force has taken over.

Elijah kneels by my side. "Lilly?" he asks as he gently pulls me into his grasp.

"The captain must still pay for his crimes on the high seas!" the greasy bald man on the platform yells over the rumbling crowd, trying to continue this bogus execution.

Elijah looks up at him. "And what crimes are those? Searching the world for hidden treasures with my crew?" He points his stub of an arm at Peter. "The crew that that little shit murdered for his twisted enjoyment?"

The little man's brow creases at Peter. "You told me he pillaged and raped and wiped entire cities off the map." His voice cracks.

The crowd murmurs around us. People look at each other with uncertainty and then at the men who were only children just moments ago.

"Peter is a liar," I say from Elijah's arms and look up at the man who could still steal

Elijah from me. "He has abused me for years, and he threw me to the crocodiles when I refused to use my magic to kill. Elijah saved me, and it cost him his hand."

Talking takes all my energy, and I slump into the captain's arms.

Captain Hook glances down at me and then back at Peter. "She's the only reason I didn't meet the same demise as my crew. He threw a caged fae into the ocean knowing if the crocodile didn't kill her, the water would."

"Is this true?" the man asks Peter.

Peter shakes his head, but he can't quite bring his eyes up to meet the man's gaze.

"Yes!" a hooded figure in the back calls out and moves slowly through the crowd, limping with a crutch. Wood bumps on the ground. It's the same voice that questioned the captain's crimes. He throws his hood back. A stocky gray-haired man who looks strikingly like the captain stands tall, despite his peg leg and crutch. He glares at the crowd surrounding us and points his crutch at the boys, singling each of them out. "These are the boys who murdered the crew aboard the *Joli Rouge.*"

Elijah stares at the man with his mouth hanging open.

"Sorry I didn't get here sooner, Captain." He motions to his leg.

"Who are you?" the little man demands.

"I am Quartermaster Isaiah Hook. The captain's brother." His face reddens as he scans the boys who are now aged men. "I thought I was the lone survivor until I heard rumors that the captain had been sentenced to die today." He wags his pointer finger at Elijah. "This man has not pillaged a village. As a matter of fact, he has revived dying sea towns with the gold and silver we have unearthed."

The little man on the stage sneers at Elijah's brother and crosses his arms. "So, he has never run a sword through a man?"

Isaiah glances at Elijah.

"My sword has made a swift end to rapists and murderers and thieves," Elijah says as he stares at Peter. "I do not profess to be an innocent the way she is." He juts his chin at me. "One who they terrorized daily and left near death probably more times than any of us can count." His grip on me tightens. "Look at them. Cutting off her wings stopped their aging process. What you see is a reasonably accurate representation of just how long they've locked up a fae. And those bastards made her keep them young enough to be overlooked by the law."

"She cursed them," the little man on stage says, unwilling to see the truth.

Then it occurs to me that the little man has been bought and paid by the lost boys. He does their bidding, just as I have bent to their will all these years.

"I did not curse them. All I did was take my magic back, and they maimed me because they wanted to be forever young." I wave at the bloody wings on the ground beside me. "They cut off my wings and nullified my magic. This is what they promised—no, threatened me with—daily."

"And you expect this town to believe a fae and two pirates over a group of upstanding citizens of Neverland whom you have turned into old men?" He scoffs at us and turns to the guards. "Grab him."

Before they can even take a step, a clap of thunder rumbles in the clear sky above us. Then a lightning bolt hits the ground in front of Elijah and me, creating a wall of smoke that surrounds us like a protective barrier.

The king of the fae decked out in his armor and adornments rises in all his glory, towering over the square in a form that is larger than life. He points to the small man on the stage, singling him out.

"You have the audacity to question the honesty of a fae?" His voice rumbles like the thunder above. Wind whips around the square with the power of a hurricane making landfall.

The little man's pants darken, and his cheeks turn ruddy with fear. He moves his head back and forth quickly. "I...I didn't mean to." He puts his hands out to placate the fae king. "I-I'm sorry," he squeals and runs for the safety of the building they dragged Elijah out of.

The entire square cowers as the fae king turns his back on the platform. His gaze moves to Captain Hook and drops to his decapitated limb. He reaches into his pocket and pulls out the captain's severed hand with the watch he's been searching for, still attached just below where it's severed.

"Imagine my surprise when I found *this* inside that hideous beast." He tosses the hand to Captain Hook.

Elijah catches his hand and magic blasts into him from the severed appendage, connecting it back where it belongs. He stares at his regenerated hand as it turns from gray to the color of his flesh, and then he wiggles his fingers, letting out a laugh of disbelief.

My gaze jumps between his healed hand and my father. Fae royalty doesn't just dole out magical favors on a whim. Nor do they look at humans as if they are family, like the way he is looking at Elijah.

The captain's watch shimmers with a fae beacon. Things snap into place, and I meet my father's warm gaze. It soothes my severed soul as much as Elijah's arms do.

My father sent Captain Hook to find his lost treasure.

The king's gaze drops to my severed wings, and the warm moment turns frigid with his fury. The storm gathers around us as he turns to the boys now encased in bodies of old men.

"These are the heathens who imprisoned my daughter?" he asks the captain.

"Yes, my lord," Elijah says and bows his head in respect as if he has been in my father's employment all his life.

My mind drifts to his conversation about being in the fae realm, and again, I wonder what he did.

The king snaps his fingers, bringing Peter's pet crocodile into the square. The crowd gasps, pushing backwards to a safe distance.

Peter points at us as if ordering the beast to attack, but the crocodile smiles in a way that sends a fiery trail of fear up my back. He is no longer Peter's to order around. That much is clear, but it does not seem to register with Peter yet.

I shift and wince at the pain in my back. Elijah's grip on me tightens.

More crocodiles appear, surrounding the boys, herding them into a tight circle. It's only now that Peter realizes he is facing his death and that he no longer has fae magic in his pocket to get him out of it. His eyes widen, knowing that whatever comes next, it will be incredibly painful.

The king looks out at the crowd. "Witness true justice, and understand that crossing a fae comes with swift and often violent ramifications."

Before he can unleash the crocodiles, I blurt out, "Let them live, Father."

He spins toward me with his eyebrows arching. "This is fae justice for stealing you from our sight. For enslaving you and severing your magic." He waves at my bloody wings.

I glance at the pitiful gathering in the square's center. Twelve old men cling to each other with shaking legs and terror in their ancient eyes.

"Death is an end to their punishment."

My words seem to sink in beyond my father's fury, and he tilts his head and nods for me to continue.

"They do not have their youth or my magic to hide behind any longer. Do you not see? Their lives are brief already, and stealing their misery and replacing it with a swift death isn't punishment enough!"

He takes a deep breath and then blows it out through his nose, sending shockwaves through the square, knocking a few of the boys to their knees. My father's gaze narrows, and an evil glint flashes in his eyes.

"Where do they reside?" His voice is filled with malicious intent.

The crocodiles vanish, and I point to the hill above the town square and the only sprawling house gracing the bluff.

The biggest lightning bolt I have ever seen slams into it, turning it to dust.

"You asshole!" Peter cries and turns to the crowd. "You're going to let them get away with this?"

"You are no longer welcome in Neverland!" someone yells back, and the rumblings agree with the lone cry.

Peter's expression darkens, and he turns his angry eyes on me. Pointing, he growls, "This isn't over."

I climb to my feet and stand tall despite the debilitating pain in my back. I stare him down. "It is over, old man. If you ever dare to come within ten feet of me or the captain, I will have you run through like the pig you are." I lift my chin in defiance.

"I should have killed you instead of chopping your wings off," Schafer growls from behind Peter.

It seems the dimwit forgot who is standing by my side.

A lightning bolt turns him to ash.

"I suggest you leave," my father says through teeth that grind with the wrath filling him. "Before I decide that the rest of you deserve the same fate despite my daughter's logical plea."

The boys' heads jerk up from staring at the ash pile where their friend had been standing.

"D-daughter?" Bo asks with a hitch in his voice.

"Yes. You imprisoned the fae king's daughter," Elijah growls at him. "And if I had any say in your sentence, I would strike you down myself."

Peter is the only one that lingers longer than a blink. The rest scurry away as fast as their old legs will take them, which isn't fast at all. Watching the geriatrics leave satisfies my deep-seated anger. Even as Peter storms away, it's in slow motion, and I almost laugh at the irony.

My father turns to us, and his sad eyes take in my mutilated form that I am now locked in, thanks to Schafer's sword. "I cannot bring you home without your magic."

My gaze drops to the ground, and I nod. Without magic, I will not survive the transition to my world. The ley line would identify me as a fallen fae and strike me down for trying to enter the fae realm. It's a protection that was set by the ancients to keep the dark ones from destroying our realm. All fae have a magical signature, or in my case, a magical echo, and without wings, I won't live through the barrier's attack. A human doesn't have any magical signature and will pass through on the will of a fae.

My father tilts my chin up and he gently kisses my cheek. His magic floods through me straight to my injuries, healing what ails me.

"As long as you are with the captain, I will be able to find you." He eyes Elijah. "You are to take care of my daughter as if she is your most prized possession."

Elijah smirks and glances at me. "With pleasure, my lord." He bows.

My father's eyes narrow as he looks between us, and then he decides not to test us further. "Your debt is now paid. You are no longer on my payroll," he adds and then disappears into a cloud of smoke, followed by a clap of thunder that rumbles the ground beneath our feet.

I touch Elijah's hand and the fae watch around his reattached wrist. "So that's why you were adamant about finding that damn crocodile?"

He nods and gives me a half-hearted shrug. "I couldn't notify your father that I found you without it. But it seems something in the crocodile's belly triggered it, anyway."

That thought makes my skin break out in bumps, and I shiver with the chill his words produce. Elijah puts his arm around me and pulls me to his side as he looks around at the people still crowding the edges of the area. He heads to the town docks and his boat that sits waiting for him and his crew.

"You were bound by your debts to find me?" I ask as the crowd parts for us as if we are royalty. I guess in their eyes we are. I smile and nod my thanks for their support as we walk past.

Elijah inhales and nods before glancing at me. "Yes."

"Why?"

"Because I was once young and stupid and attempted to steal the fae king's crown." His cheeks turn crimson as he avoids my gaze.

I blink like I can't believe it, and then my memory rushes back to when I was younger and there was a commotion at the palace. Word came through that a human boy tried to steal my father's crown. My eyes widen at the memory. My father dragged the boy across realms, and I remember clearly the terror in that child's eyes as they met mine.

At that moment, he stole my breath away. The fear in his eyes turned to something else. Something like hope, and he sent me an impish grin that haunted my dreams for decades. It was the only time I saw the human boy.

I stare into Elijah's eyes, the same eyes that left me breathless that first encounter and every encounter thereafter. "That was *you*?"

The tilt of his lips warms me. "I have been searching for you since that day in the fae court."

I ignore his heartwarming words and wave at his form. He should be older than the lost boys at this point.

His brother approaches us slowly, looking more like what I envision Elijah should be like.

Elijah focuses on his brother, stepping away from me to give him a hug. When he pulls away, he turns to me. "Lilly, this is my younger brother, Isaiah."

He bows. "Your grace," he says, keeping his gaze on the ground. He takes off the cloak he wears and offers it to me.

"Thank you." I take the cape and swing it around to wrap around me before looking at Elijah again. "How?" I demand.

I'm not in the mood to be handed over to another trickster.

"I served my sentence in the prisons below the palace and then became your father's gopher. By then, you and your sister had run away, and eventually he started confiding in me." He laughs. "It's the damnedest thing. Your father and I became friends. He trained me in sword fighting and other hand-to-hand combat, and then when I reached the age you see me at now, he made me a deal. He offered me immortality if I would come to this realm and find you." He taps my nose. "*You.* The princess I dreamed of every night since I first saw your beautiful face. It wasn't hard to agree to that deal."

My knees weaken with his words, but he wraps his arm around my waist, keeping me steady, and looks out at the crowd who has not yet dispersed. They seem to enjoy the show.

Elijah clears his throat. "It seems I'm in need of a few crew members. So, anyone who would like to sail with us, come to the dock before sunset." He glances at his brother. "Lead the way, Isaiah."

"Isn't it bad luck to have a woman aboard?" Isaiah asks as he looks between the two of us.

Elijah laughs at his brother. "Not if said lady is my wife."

"You're married?" Isaiah asks with such disbelief that Elijah laughs even harder at his brother.

"Not yet. But we will be before we set sail this evening."

"Oh, you think so?" I say to him as I plant my hands on my hips.

"Yes. And then we can start our own adventure." Elijah pulls me against him and winces. "But that may need to wait until I heal," he adds as he looks down at his bruised chest.

It's my turn to laugh. "I think I'd like to start my adventure right away." I press against him, and he groans in the back of his throat, but he doesn't pull away.

I swipe my lips across his.

Sailing into the sunset every night is going to be an adventure of a lifetime, especially with Captain Elijah Hook at my side.

The End

If you enjoyed A FRACTURED FAIRY TALE: BOOKS 1-10, please consider leaving a review!

Find more books by J.E. Taylor on her website: http://books.jetaylor75.com/

About J.E. Taylor

J.E. Taylor is a USA Today bestselling author, a publisher, an editor, a manuscript formatter, a mother, a wife, a business analyst, and a Supernatural fangirl. Not necessarily in that order. She first sat down to seriously write in February of 2007 after her daughter asked:

"Mom, if you could do anything, what would you do?"
From that moment on, she hasn't looked back.

Besides being co-owner of Novel Concept Publishing, Ms. Taylor also moonlights as a Senior Editor of Allegory (www.allegoryezine.com), an online venue for Science Fiction, Fantasy and Horror. J.E. Taylor is also one of the co-hosts of the popular podcast Spilling Ink.

She lives in New Hampshire with her husband and two children and during the summer months enjoys her weekends on the shore in southern Maine.

Visit her at www.books.jetaylor75.com and sign up for her newsletter for early previews of her upcoming books, release announcements, and special opportunities for free swag!